MARTUTENE

MARTUTENE

RAMON SAIZARBITORIA

*Translated from the Basque by
Aritz Branton*

Edited by Cecilia Ross

Hispabooks
Publishing

Hispabooks Publishing, S. L.
Madrid, Spain
www.hispabooks.com

Originally published in Spain as *Martutene* by Erein, 2012
First published in English by Hispabooks, 2016
English translation copyright © by Aritz Branton
Revision and copy-editing by Cecilia Ross
Design © simonpates - www.patesy.com

ISBN 978-84-944262-7-8 (trade paperback)
ISBN 978-84-944262-8-5 (ebook)
Legal Deposit: M-28335-2016

Printed in Great Britain by Clays Ltd, St Ives plc

The translation of this work was supported by a grant from the Instituto Vasco Etxepare.

MARTUTENE

A NEIGHBORHOOD IN DONOSTIA, between Loiola and Astigarraga, on the southern banks of the Urumea, whose name comes from a half-timbered *baserri* farmstead where the El Estanco bar is now. A group of businessmen originally set it up as a luxury residential area and leisure park. The first small mansions were built in 1906, and little by little, important families from the city and exiled French royalists went to live there. Armenouille is one of the few houses remaining from that period. The bullring was opened in 1908— the first covered one in Spain—and the Berlin Philharmonic played the opening concert. Basically it was a multipurpose area, a glass-roofed "plaza for public festivities," not very successful, and it was destroyed in 1923. The amusement park—American Park, also called Kursaal—was opened in 1910 and had excellent facilities, for instance its roller coaster, although its most famous attraction was the 985-foot-long cave. However, even though the developer, Celestino de Batioil, organized a fake "appearance" by the Virgin Mary, which increased the number of visits in the short term, the park was not as successful as it needed to be and was closed down in 1912 for financial reasons. Because it was easy to get to by tram, it continued to be a place for regular people to spend the day or celebrate special occasions, and in 1929 the gardens, named Campos Elíseos after the Champs-Élysées, were opened, though the name does not reflect the transformation the neighborhood was to undergo; this is undoubtedly much better represented by Martutene Prison, which opened in 1948. Nowadays, the neighborhood is highly industrial—the well-known Industrial Park 27 is there, home to numerous small- and medium-sized companies—and it is also a residential area, with apartment blocks and villas that have survived from that period, and several *baserris* and cider houses. Large-scale infrastructure projects will soon reach the neighborhood to start off the twenty-first century: the Urumea highway, high-speed train lines, and the third Donostia beltway, among others.

PREAMBLE

JULIA REMEMBERS THE DAY SHE MET MARTIN. She remembers the first day she spoke with him, rather; they'd known each other by sight since forever. They met during that first conference on literary translation; Martin was one of the translated writers who'd been invited to participate. Although she hadn't signed up for the conference, Harri also turned up and managed to get into Martin's session. Martin started by saying that he found it difficult talking in public but that he'd had no choice but to accept the invitation—the director, whom he'd long been friends with, had really insisted. And he apologized—bearing in mind how little talent he had for public speaking, he was going to read a text, even though he knew that would be boring for everybody.

His text, as well as not having much to do with the subject, was also too tightly packed to be easily listened to; but it was by no means boring. Often—too often, he would say—you start with the description of a scene that comes to mind: a young woman without a face, wearing nothing but a pale-salmon-colored petticoat—it was shiny, perhaps made of silk—was sitting on the edge of a high, old-fashioned bed, and next to her, standing up, there was a man—his face, too, was not clearly visible—wearing a stiff, dark suit, with one hand on the young woman's shoulder. He knows, because of the woman's youth, soft neck, and healthy body, that her face, which is invisible in the half-light for some unknown reason, is beautiful.

However, the man's face is invisible because he's hiding it behind a mask of a black bowler hat and a green apple, like in Magritte's famous painting; but his constitution and formal clothing give the impression that he's old.

Without knowing why, what you see there—and in fact that's all there is to see—is a strange picture, it creates enormous anxiety, and then a bell starts ringing louder and louder and closer and closer, it's deafening, and he breaks into a sweat, seemingly terrified.

So the picture is deliberate delirium. It comes back to him so often that when he wakes up in the morning looking a wreck, nobody ever asks if he's slept well but, without beating around the bush, whether he's had his nightmare again.

On the day Julia met him, he gave a basic description of that nightmare, without going into details, to demonstrate that any starting point can be used to get to the bottom of something, and then he talked about the habit they'd had of following people around for fun when he was a child. Apparently, they would choose someone walking along the street, just like that, by chance, or because they looked mysterious, mean, wicked, or evil to them, and then walk behind them in the hope that they might lead them to some secret meeting, perhaps a secret date, or maybe somewhere where something dramatic would happen. Sometimes they would lose the trail, when their subject took a taxi, for instance, or they'd get bored and give up, like you give up reading a boring book, but normally they had fun doing it, at least it was more fun than wandering aimlessly around wondering how to spend the long hours of those wearisome childhood afternoons.

Then he started a long, complicated explanation that was quite difficult to listen to, it had to do with the psychological factors behind some people's tendency to write and tell stories about themselves or about others. He appeared to be more bored by his reading than his listeners were by listening to it. His voice was monotonous, flattened, his mouth sounded dry (it made Julia feel anxious), but even so, he didn't touch his water (as she found out later, it was because he didn't want anyone to see that his hands were shaking), and all of a sudden, he started to read really fast, as if he wanted to get to the end, but because the text was very long, it still took him a while.

She felt sorry for him. After reading his sheets of paper, he quickly folded them and put them in his jacket pocket and thanked the listeners for their patience, in a broken voice, although they hadn't been all that patient, moving around in their seats and coughing a lot. He looked really depressed (Julia heard him say *"nevermore"* [1] as Harri dragged him away from the table), and she felt more like hugging him than congratulating him (the latter being what the circumstances demanded), like consoling a child who's forgotten his poem at his school's end-of-the-year performance. Alberdi, on the other hand, spoke as if he were with a group of children eager to hear some stories. He talked in a deliberate, measured way and looked around at people with a smile of pride, in control of his own ability to seduce others, and there was something perverse in that smile. She found him revolting, as revolting as Martin was attractive to her, standing there by her side as if he weren't there at all, calm now that his trial was over. And she was even more indignant during the debate, when Alberdi, in a pedagogical, amused tone, added nuances—that was the word he had used—to many of Martin's explanations and also denied that some of them were right.

His friendly, soft, and humble manners did not hide what he thought of himself. When he said he had a new parable to explain the idea better, people moved around in their seats to get more comfortable, and in the silence that followed, in which you could have heard a pin drop, he started to talk about the railway cattle cars that had transported Jews to Auschwitz, Dachau, and Büchenwald, trucks in which, because there was no extra space on the floors to leave bodies, the living had traveled side by side with the dead as they crossed Europe.

Martin was to say later, when the two of them were alone, that it wasn't a new use of the example, he knew that Azúa had used it in his Dictionary of the Arts, but for Julia, as for the rest of the listeners, it was a previously unknown resource and an appropriate contribution.

It is true that Azúa talks about it is his Dictionary—the captives in each car chose a person and lifted him or her eight feet up off

---

1   Translator's note: In English in the original. The considerable number of expressions and sentences written in English in the original are marked in italics from here onward.

9

the floor to the ventilation holes in the roof, in order for them to relay what they could see from there. Those chosen, having spent days and even weeks locked up, had to get used to the blinding light and boiling heat, and the others had to give those they raised up with such effort some time to get used to their new conditions. However, they didn't all manage to acclimate, and not all of those who did were able to complete their task well—some of them were too precise and got lost in small details; others, on the contrary, talked about what they were seeing in a disjointed way, without establishing connections, making neither head nor tail of anything; others looked at things too personally, linking everything to their own experiences—and so they only lifted up those who were capable of making them feel what was essential for them, those who could make them feel like part of the world of the living and like they belonged to that world, at least for a few seconds.

Martin mentioned Azúa's parable about cattle cars full of Jews on their way to Auschwitz and Dachau again when they went to a bar to have a beer after the round table debate finished.

She remembers him with a serious face (she still has her doubts about how serious he was), describing himself as if he were the watchman the other travelers are lifting up to the ventilation slit, knowing they can't hold him up there for long. He tells them what he sees, sights that stop him from sleeping, there's cool wind on his face and hot, blinding sun in the clear sky, he looks at fields of wheat he'll probably never see again. He was that frustrated observer who, even after being brought down from the ventilation slit and exchanged for someone who did the job better, carried on telling his inevitably detail-filled story, surrounded by the few unfortunate listeners around him.

Narrating the cause of the trauma. Freud and the narcissistic injury. It led to a long conversation. Alberdi having left—saying that he had to get up early the next morning and that, contrary to what many people think, writers are condemned to lead an ascetic lifestyle—there was no longer a single conversational focus to pay particular attention to, and everybody felt free to talk.

Martin talked about people's tendency to tell stories that are of no interest to anyone else, stories told by the person involved, often helped by drink loosening up any emotional control: experiences at boarding school; things that happened during military service and, of course, during the war; what took place in the birthing room—especially before epidural techniques were used. He talked about how people can reach a state of disinhibition in which even the most withdrawn will fling open their shirt or blouse, which they would never do, under any circumstances, if it weren't to show off some irremovable scar there.

Julia herself got up the courage to say that every year, she used to walk from Errenteria to Lezo with her mother to see the Holy Christ Chapel full of ex-votos, walking sticks, and, more than anything else, crutches, and there were always beggars seated all along the way, moaning and making mocking gestures, with deformed torsos, paralyzed, ulcer-ridden, displaying their revolting stumps. Her mother, apparently, had been devoted to the Holy Christ, but Julia hated him, because of the terrible moments he put her through.

At gatherings like that, sometimes the conversations multiply, and although you would rather listen to someone else or even say something yourself, you feel forced to remain engaged with a particular person, as if he or she were in the water and about to drown, holding a flailing hand upward to demand your attention.

There's always someone next to Julia to bore her to death, someone she doesn't want to listen to, who looks at her to ask her to turn her attention to them, and she normally does listen to those tedious kidnappers—not because she feels sorry for them, but because she lacks courage. That's what she thought of when she realized she was only talking to Martin, and when she apologized—"I'm boring you to tears"—he reassured her politely. Her memories were very interesting, he said, and they were just right for illustrating the attitude of certain writers, such as himself, being able to offer shy people who sometimes come up to you, like dogs smelling the garbage and then indifferently going on their way once more, stories that may be made up or are perhaps taken from here and there, somewhat seasoned to meet the demands of convention, but which always come from within oneself, from deep within, a treatment of our own pain which we then serve up.

"All bad writers are pathetic, but even more pathetic are those belonging to the group I myself form part of," he said. Even so, he'd rather have this role than that of some Scheherazade trying to keep an old Persian man content. She's heard him say that quite often since then. On that first occasion, she would have liked to have

11

told him that she really enjoyed reading his stories, but she didn't dare, partly because she didn't want him to think she was being obsequious, but above all because she didn't know what she would answer if he asked why she liked them, and because she was afraid of not being up to talking about his work.

They spoke alone for a long time, protected by the imaginary circle that people leave around a couple getting to know each other. The others looked happy speaking ill of Alberdi; it seemed as if all those who hadn't left with him hated him. They talked about his false modesty, that cloying sweetness of his, his bland, easy literature that delighted undemanding readers. Martin didn't want to get involved in the character assassination. All of a sudden, he said, "What do you like?" And she answered that she liked novels about writers and films about the cinema. She tried to explain what she meant, the famous Ricardou quote came to mind, and although it was the only thing she knew about Ricardou, she couldn't resist using it. "*Le récit n'est plus l'écriture d'une aventure, mais l'aventure d'une écriture.*" And she even gave into the temptation of saying it in French, or was daring enough to do so, depending on how you look at it, and it was obvious that the writer was affected, in some way, by the quote spoken in his beloved Flaubert's language.

"How true that is," he agreed, and he regretted not being able to remember the quote by Miguel de Unamuno, which Julia herself now knows, about how the truly novel thing is how a novel is written—"*Lo verdaderamente novelesco es cómo se hace una novela.*" She's since learned how frustrating it is for Martin to have a quote that would help to define an idea on the tip of his tongue and not be able to recall it.

In any case, although he didn't say that memory is the fool's intelligence, he did say a couple of things in praise of poor memory, or taking the shine off good memory, and it was then that Julia first heard about Beckett's essay on Proust, which she now likes so much that she always has a bilingual edition near at hand. "Only those without memory can recall."

She loved that sentence. Then she felt obliged to ask him what he was writing, without knowing how much he hated being asked that. Harri did know, and said to her, "Hey, you can't ask him that," without caring that saying so made it obvious that she'd been sitting right next to them and listening in the whole time. She remembers that he said "a novel" after a long silence that made her think he wasn't going to answer at all, making her regret having asked the question. "In any case, a novel," he confirmed. It was going to be his first one. She could tell how frustrated he was by not having been able to write a real novel until then, to be no more than a writer of short stories. To his annoyance, Professor Lourdes Arregi had defined him as a "writer of short stories and novellas" in her book titled *Euskal idazleak plazara*, or *Published Basque Writers*.

"A novel in which nothing happens."

At the time, Julia didn't know the real meaning of Flaubert's statement and took it to be a witticism used to avoid talking about the plot of the novel he was writing. "You don't have to tell me anything," she said, regretting her indiscretion. But Martin did tell her some things about his hypothetical novel, even though she couldn't pay much attention to them, due to her nervousness. And now Julia doesn't know if what Harri says, happily and laughing aloud, is true—she says he mentioned the story of a couple whose lives come together when they meet at an airport terminal.

It's true, Harri says, he mentioned his intention to start the novel with a chance meeting at an airport. Although that chance encounter was, inevitably, of no great depth, it was to prove decisive for the couple. Julia doesn't believe it. But what she does remember is that he said "any excuse to show off the scars" while opening his jacket and holding his arms out theatrically, and that, after laughing (she thought he wanted to show that he was joking), he took care of the bill for all the unpaid food and drink—including Alberdi's and that of the people who had left with him—and that she wanted to know what that sarcastic and very attractive man's secret was.

PART ONE

1

Harri Gabilondo took great pleasure in describing where it happened and believed that what she was telling them was astonishing. She always believes that when she tells them about something—it's something amazing and incredible. "You won't believe what happened to me," she'll say, for instance, but everything that comes after that passionate announcement seems dispensable to Julia and, usually, far too long. For Julia—unable to avoid Harri's gray eyes—the pauses she makes when telling her stories are too long, and the gestures she uses to show how amazed and surprised she is are too much, especially compared with the listener's lack of excitement about the stories.

Julia knows that when she finishes the first version of her story, she'll go back to some part she thinks particularly significant in order to underline it and, with her eyes wide open, say "what do you make of that?" Then, without stopping, she'll ask the same thing in Spanish—"*¿Qué te parece?*"—and even though this "what do you think of that?" is no more than conversational filler in her story, Julia thinks that when Harri says it, she's asking Martin, leaving her out of it.

"*¿Qué te parece?*"

Harri's greatest desire is to inspire Martin to write a story in which she features as a character. But she's unable to keep his

17

attention for long. His eyes suddenly dart toward the pages of a book, or he turns the television on very obviously, and when that happens, Julia listens even harder, so that Harri won't get angry. But her efforts are in vain, because what matters to Harri is having Martin listen, and she always gets angry enough to stop being polite. "You two aren't paying attention to what I'm saying," she says, in the plural.

In fact, when that happens, Julia feels for her.

This time, she tells them that she's in love, that it was "*un flechazo*," love at first sight, and she makes even more exaggerated gestures than usual, a hand on her chest, her eyes closed. "You aren't going to believe it."

She doesn't bother to take off her new camel-hair coat—an "incredibly expensive" coat, and no, she won't tell them how much it cost, it's a disgrace how much she paid for it in London—but Julia knows that she'll end up telling them the price even if they don't ask her. It's a beautiful soft coat—though it does make her look very much like a *señora*—and she wants it to break it in as soon as possible so that it'll start looking the way only good cloth can after it's been well used. She was interested in the man as soon as she saw him at the airport; she'd dropped her daughter off at a boarding school in Surrey, where she'd taken her to distance her from "the conflict." She says she doesn't know why, because he looked like your typical Basque man: bearded, checked shirt and corduroy pants, about her age, maybe forty-five, intellectual looking, probably a university lecturer, from the Humanities and Social Sciences Department perhaps, which his two plastic bags full of books, as well as his backpack, seemed to confirm. A man who looked like any other, but with something special, too, something she could see, a spark in his eyes, a warmth. They were sitting across from each other. The man was reading a book whose title she couldn't see, because glasses don't look good on her, but she glanced up from time to time, and then, unlike at first, she looked straight at him, with no embarrassment. Unluckily, the seats to either side of her were taken; she's sure he would have come and sat next to her otherwise. She's sure of that, she repeats. There was a free seat next to the man, and now she regrets not having dared to sit there. She also regrets not wearing the black silk blouse and pantsuit that look so good on her, but which she was afraid of creasing on the journey, instead of jeans.

Harri's habit of drawing stories out, her insistence on giving details that are almost always irrelevant, finally drives Julia crazy. Probably because she herself tends to do the opposite. Martin accuses her of being too direct, but what he really means is too hurried, and he's not wrong there—when she starts talking about something in front of two or three people, she gets frightened she's going to bore them and begins speaking very fast, avoiding all details, maybe skipping over things that would really add to what she wants to say. But, then, we all have our limits, and she'd much rather have her own sort. So she asks Harri to get on with it, to come to the point once and for all, without mentioning that she has work to get back to. She even tells Harri that she's dying to hear about it, and just this once, although he's always complained that Harri is tedious and dull, Martin stands up for her, just for the pleasure of attacking Julia.

"God is in the details," he says, using someone else's words, although Julia almost says that it's the devil who's in them. She knows a lot of quotes in praise of details: "Reality is just a detail"— Márai; "The holiness of minute particulars"—Blake; that famous quote from Nabokov she's forgotten. She holds her tongue so as not to cause a fuss and so that Harri can start her story again as soon as possible. As if Harri didn't have enough of her own to say, Martin's words have given her an excuse to carry on talking slowly, savoring the moment, her gray eyes looking from one of them to the other, as though she herself were amazed by the sharpness of the question she's now asking them: Why are left-leaning and culturally-minded people more cold-natured than executive types? It seems like a fair question. The first wear thick sweaters, warm tops, and big boots, while the latter seem just fine in a shirt, jacket, tie, and thin goatskin shoes. The secret's in the tie, which is the most differentiating garment. And all of that was just to lead into the fact that the man had been wearing not only a checked shirt, a wool sweater, and green corduroy pants but also a blue duffel coat, and finally Martin, who regrets having just spoken out in favor of details, says that she's rambling and tells her to come to the point. Harri goes on to say that she got very nervous when she was thinking about whether or not it was up to her to go and sit in the free seat to the left of the man and that when she, growing increasingly nervous, was just about to decide, the executive in the light flannel suit to her own right got up, and so then she decided to wait, being sure that the man was going to come and sit down in the free seat next to her.

Just in case, she closed the book she had open in front of her and was careful to put it into her bag, because it might have seemed like inappropriate reading to the man—it was Jon Juaristi's *El bucle melancólico*, a history of Basque nationalism. She had been planning to boycott the writer, among other things because he said that he wasn't going to use the murderers' language any more, but apparently Julia had made her read it—the book was very well written and the writer was a great polemicist, and she argued that great polemicists' attacks on attitudes help us to understand those attitudes.

"It's your fault," she blurts out, as if Julia's recommendation of *El bucle* had put her introduction to the man at the airport at risk. She read somewhere about someone who chose books to travel with as if they were clothes: chic books; ones that gives you a serious touch; books for going out for a stroll; ones that make you look young; ones that give you an air of spirituality. You have to decide where to open them. Julia remembers something and giggles. Harri points a finger at her angrily—"You made me, do you remember?" Julia remembers that she'd explained at the time that it was a sentence based on Gorz's famous "I'll never speak German." A wholly inappropriate sentence, obviously, but one that shouldn't be taken literally; it was pure rhetoric, designed to provoke. What's more, it wasn't Jauristi who said it, though that's got nothing to do with what they're talking about. So in the end, did the man sit next to you or not? "He couldn't." She shakes her head in regret. What happened was that as soon as he stood up, the boarding call went out, and he didn't have time to go up to her, everybody started rushing toward the gate, and she, too, had to get up.

"*¿Qué te parece?*"

The telephone rings, and Martin rushes over to the shelves between the living room and the work area to pick it up. "*The penthouse girl,*" he says, looking lively. The two women keep quiet and listen to him speaking in English. Martin speaks fluently but with a terrible accent, he doesn't make the slightest attempt to follow phonetic rules. Apparently, given that it's impossible for him to pronounce really well, he thinks it's useless to try, and that in fact, and most especially, making any effort reflects a complete lack of style. He is very good at sublimating his inability.

"*I was waiting for your call.*" They have no trouble deducing that he's talking with the woman he's offered to rent out the top floor rooms to, because he's explaining where the small Belle Époque mansion is, next to the river (he doesn't say that it's actually closer to the railroad than it is to the river), that it has a large garden with many beautiful trees in it, among them a particularly fine Magnolia grandiflora that gives the place some privacy from the rest of the neighborhood, which is a little rundown but has good transport connections for getting downtown.

He says that they have excellent land, sea, and air connections and laughs at his own joke. Julia is angered by his excessive enthusiasm as he speaks, and when Harri asks who Martin is speaking with, she says she doesn't have a clue, not wanting to hide the fact that she's angry; until that very morning, he hadn't told her that he wanted to rent the apartment out. It's his house, and he has the right to do whatever he wants to with it, but he's always full of doubts, asks her opinion about any trifle, and she's hurt by him being so independent and unforthcoming about such important things.

What's more, she suspects he intends to let the woman have the apartment at no charge, or almost free, and that he only said otherwise because he didn't want her to accuse him of going around playing at being generous (some friends have given him the honorary title *marquis of Martutene* to tease him) only to later complain that people take advantage of him and are ungrateful. They don't take advantage of his generosity; it's his idiotic vanity they take advantage of.

And so Julia doesn't listen to the conversation Martin is having with the woman he wants to rent the apartment to (the train's the easiest way to get there, it's quick and runs on time, she can come by whenever she wants, he's always holed up at home) and instead asks after Harri's daughter. "How's Harritxu?" She's sent her—exiled her, she says—to an elite school for her final year, in order to get her away from the radical environment. A difficult decision, inspired by Martin, to a large extent, and opposed by her husband and by her daughter herself; however, although she's thought of little else over the last few months, she isn't interested in the subject today. Harri looks toward the bookcases, as if to judge whether Martin will be able to hear her, and speaks in a low voice as if to hide what she's going to say, although Julia knows only too well that what she is now going to tell her in secret she will later repeat in greater detail

21

when she has Martin there to listen to her as well; she tells her, so that she can see just how worked up she was at the airport, that right then, right when she heard the boarding call, she absolutely hated Martxelo, knowing that he would be waiting for her at Loiu Airport with that dumb look on his face and that she'd have to go back home with him, tell him stupid things about London, listen to the bad things that happened to him at work at the hospital, and then make dinner. She wanted something to happen to stop him from going to pick her up, an accident, anything, and then perhaps the unknown man would go up to her and, if nobody was waiting for her in Bilbao, suggest that she could go with him.

After hanging up, Martin tells them about the possible tenant, whom he's just spoken with: she's a young American woman, she's very interesting, and he thinks she's a sociologist. He says she won't get in their way, because there's a separate spiral staircase to go up to the top floor. Then, to stop Harri from worrying when she asks if he has to rent the apartment out because of money problems, he says he just felt like having a *penthouse* girl, and after coming out with the pleasantry, and afraid she might not get it, he explains that *penthouse* means a luxurious top-floor dwelling in English. As far as Julia knows, that dwelling has to be crowning an apartment complex as well as being luxurious if it's to be called a penthouse. She nearly says that a *chambre de bonne* would be a better term for the apartment and that she'd like to know what title would better fit the tenant, but she keeps quiet, among other things because he'd react horribly, and also because Harri, who seems to be genuinely worried, stops saying silly things and asks Martin to tell the truth about his money situation. He says once more, trying to be convincing, that there aren't any problems, not making any use of that part of the house just makes him feel guilty, that's why he's renting it out. After saying that, and obviously wanting to change the subject, he asks Harri to tell him what he hadn't been able to hear while he was on the phone, but although she's dying to tell him, she makes a sign as if to say "that's our business" or "it's women's stuff."

It's ridiculous, among other things because she has a closer relationship with Martin than with Julia—the two of them have known each other since they were teenagers, since they went to the French lyceum together. Julia's only recently arrived on the scene, she's a *parvenue*, as Harri usually reminds her when Julia complains about the cloying complicity between her and Martin. There aren't many secrets between them, in some sense they're incredibly similar (twin souls, as Harri would say), they have that awful, revolting habit of whispering things to each other, and Julia's sure Harri knows about intimate things in her relationship with Martin.

So it would be out of character for her to resist telling him about the hate and disdain she felt for her husband, "as awful as that might sound," and sure enough, after complaining, in that affected tone she normally uses to cover up the fact that she's being serious, about Martin being insensitive (she, an honest wife, who is faithful to her husband, is confessing that she's crazy about some unknown man and is prepared to do anything for him; meanwhile, Martin's sitting there talking about *playboy* girls and renting out apartments over the phone), she starts her story again where she left off, in other words, in the boarding lounge, at the moment when the seat to her right became free and the man got up holding his backpack and plastic bags full of books. He took two steps toward her, and her heart started beating like a frightened mare in her chest, but just then, the boarding call went out, and she had no choice but to stand up, as well, although she would have happily stayed sitting there and let the plane take off if the man had made some sign that he intended to stay.

She thinks that he would have stayed, too, if she had dared to remain sitting there and held his look. She has no doubt about it. Now she regrets not having taken that risk, even knowing just how cowardly men are. And, she says, she wouldn't have minded having to remain alone in the boarding lounge and watch the plane take off with the man in it. She would have had the consolation of having tried. Now she dreams about having been brave enough— the man sitting down next to her, the two of them keeping silent while the last call for travelers to Bilbao comes out over the speakers, repeating their names, and watching the plane as it goes up into the air without them.

"Can you imagine it?" she says to Martin, as if to say "doesn't that inspire you?" A gesture of sorrow. She wasn't brave enough, and now, she thinks, she would be, more than enough. Unfortunately, good sense got the better of her and she got into line, although she did pray—something she hadn't done for a long time—that they'd be sitting together. But luck isn't on their side. She sits down first, the man stops at the door, or he's been stopped by the flight attendants, she's not sure why, probably because of something to do with his bags, and when she sees him coming down the aisle, walking sideways, carrying one bag in front of him and the other behind because it wouldn't all fit otherwise, their eyes meet, the man gives her a long, agreeable smile, he even lifts his chin a little to greet her, and she also smiles, in what she hopes is an unaffected way, though she's a little ashamed of her daring, and when he's almost up to where she is, two or three rows in front of her, one of the bags, the one he's carrying on his front hip, bursts, as was to be expected, and ten or twelve books or more fall to the floor.

He crouches down and tries to pick them up, holding them between his thighs and his chest, but they fall down again. *"Joder,"* he swears in Spanish, which proves he's from here, and he lets the stress fall on the *o*, a form of enunciation that makes it seem like he's not really all that put out about it, or over-worried or nervous at blocking the way, even though there are people waiting behind him who are getting visibly impatient, though not enough to prompt any of them to help him.

Harri, however, resolutely gets up without thinking twice, takes her two Harrods bags out of the hand luggage compartment, puts the contents of one of them into the other, and offers him the empty one. The man smiles again, grateful now, and she helps him to pick the books up from all over the floor. They're both crouching down, face to face, he doesn't care about holding up the people behind him, and she's waiting for something to happen, wishing for something to happen, her heart beating fast, when the man and she both reach out to grab the last book, and their hands touch.

There's a beach on the cover of the book, a beach with two empty hammocks on it and a lighthouse in the distance. The man opens the book and reads, *"This book was written in good faith,"* very slowly, with complete calm, as if it were just the two of them on the plane and they weren't holding up any other travelers, as they are, and he offers her the book in English, as well. *"It's a present for you."* But she, fool that she is, doesn't take it, she's incapable of doing anything but looking at the picture on the cover, or rather, she's incapable of doing anything but wondering if it's a beach in the north, with those clumps of grass, the long shadows of the two empty deckchairs, a headland in the distance where there's a lighthouse with a red stripe halfway up it.

She says she remembers it all very well, and even though the man offered her the book again—"*It's for you*"—she paid no attention and stood back up again when a flight attendant—who seemed more like an English nanny—curtly asked them to take their seats. She tells the man she can't accept the book (a dumb thing to say), and when he holds the book out to offer it to her again, she says that she doesn't read English (another dumb thing to say—he could take her confession as a sign of ignorance, and really, who doesn't read English nowadays if they're reasonably well educated, and in fact she does read English, even if not novels, because almost all the papers she reads at work are written in it). But that's what she tells him, before going back to her seat, pushed on by the line of impatient passengers.

They didn't speak any more after that. She heard his voice from a few rows behind her before they took off, and she thought she heard him changing places to let a couple that was split up sit together. He asked for a whisky during the flight, and the flight attendant laughed when he said something, and he often laughed, too, the happy, relaxed laughter of a healthy, sensual man, in no way over the top or vulgar, instead open and frank, and it made her want to be by his side and share his cheerfulness even more. "*¿Qué te parece?*"

Apparently, there by herself, flying over the clouds, she realized that she didn't laugh very much. She didn't want to arrive, she was dying to smell the man again—she closes her eyes to remember: pipe tobacco and perhaps a touch of mint, wool, and the scent of his own skin—and she decided that when they landed, she would stand next to him at the baggage carousel, if only for that purpose, to be able to smell him again, and to give him the chance to ask if anyone was waiting for her, just in case he wanted to suggest sharing a taxi to Bilbao, or to anywhere else in the world. She fantasized about that possibility, and while she did so, she really hated Martxelo, because he was going to be there. She wished again for something to happen to him, even an accident, as long as it gave her the remote chance of getting next to the unknown man. "Nothing like that's ever happened to me before, not even with you"—she pointed at Martin with her chin—"such a violent attraction, so physical. Don't you believe me?" She lifted her chin up again. "I swear to you, I hated my boring husband, I hated my stuck-up daughter, I'd have freed myself of all previous affection, I'd have freed myself from all ties and gone off with the man if he just made me a sign."

This time she doesn't finish off with her usual *¿qué te parece?* She gets up as if she's going to leave but then remains standing in the middle of the room, with her back to the windows that look out onto the garden, and Julia can't see her face, which is turned toward Martin, who's also standing up, at one corner of the bookshelves. With her arms hanging down and slightly outward from her body, she holds her hands open for a moment in a way that reminds Julia of the some miraculous virgin, and after a silence she doesn't dare to interrupt, while Martin for once keeps quiet, Harri says again, "If he made just a single gesture, I'd have gone off with him." There's another long silence after that, long enough to hear a freight train going by, and then she speaks again. "I can't think about anything else," she says defeatedly, with one of her characteristic gestures to emphasize her despair, as if she were shaking her hair dry after coming out of the water, and she reproaches them for not believing her. "It's not true, we do believe you," Julia says, encouraging her to go on, and after having them beg her awhile, she starts again, without having lost an ounce of her enthusiasm for the story, saying that at the passport control desk at the airport, there wasn't any way for her to go up to the man, because he was accosted by an elderly couple who'd ridden next to him on the plane and wanted to ask him their tourists' questions. Apparently she did manage to get parallel to him, because there were two lines, but, unluckily, he was stopped at the control desk, and she had no choice but to continue on to the baggage carousel and hope to see him there, but she waited for him in vain, even as her single large suitcase, the only one left, went around several times, and then she saw her husband, with that dumb face of his, drawing a circle in the air with one finger, trying to tell her that she was missing it as it went by again. She saw the man again in the arrivals hall. There was a peroxide blonde waiting for him. She wasn't very attractive, in fact she was pretty ugly, and despite having dyed hair, she was as pale as milk, almost an albino; she doesn't remember what she was wearing. They greeted each other without much enthusiasm, and almost the first thing the woman asked him was why he was carrying so many books. She and Martxelo weren't particularly affectionate toward each other, either. She cares a great deal for him, she says as an aside, as if she were trying to excuse herself, "he's a good person," but her blood was already boiling, because he started straight in on her,

26

saying how she was so absent-minded that she'd let the suitcase go around three times right under her nose and hadn't even recognized it and that he wanted to get out of there as soon as possible because he'd parked the car illegally so as not to have to pay in the lot, the stingy bastard. (Doctors tend to be stingy, because they get used to having their labs pay for everything.) Even at that moment, she felt sorry for the man who'd traveled with her, because his wife seemed so ugly, so disagreeable, and so un-feminine. She saw them as they were leaving, and she and Martxelo were, too, a few steps behind them, surrounded by people greeting and hugging each other, many young people returning home from English courses abroad and their whole families coming to welcome them, and then suddenly the man and his partner turned around, came face-to-face with them, and Harri couldn't stop herself from saying hello to him. She would have liked to have told him that she wanted to see him again, that you never run out of chances in life—too many things to say in a single look, she admits to Julia, who is moved by her wide smile—but apparently the man pretended not to realize, perhaps afraid of how the peroxide blonde might react if he paid any attention to her. Harri, on the other hand, felt that she was being penetrated by the woman's frightening, curiosity-powered glance. Who was she to say goodbye to her man, she was obviously thinking, and Harri didn't try again, decided to walk on without looking back, sure that the blonde would be asking the poor, unfortunate man where he knew her from, but in the end, she couldn't help herself, and her eyes met his—he, too, had looked back over his shoulder. She can't explain exactly what he wanted to say, but he lifted one hand up, holding the tips of his fingers together. It seemed to be a sign of his shame, suffering, and decline. This wasn't the happy, contented, pleasant man she'd seen at Heathrow, and she was sorry about that, just as sorry as she was angry about her husband, who started pulling her leg as he massaged her shoulders as he usually did to be affectionate or sweet—"Well, well, well, I see you've made a friend on the trip," and other such stupid comments—and then impressed upon her that they really should go and find the car, until finally she said she'd wait for him there with her suitcase and her bags. And so she was standing there waiting when the couple turned up again, the woman first and the man two or three paces behind her, pushing a heavily loaded trolley. The man stops next to the first taxi and lets the woman continue walking toward the parking lot, but then she realizes that she's walking alone, and she stops. She turns around and says—or, to be more precise, shouts—at the man, "What are you doing?" He's standing at the open door of a taxi and has already put his things inside it. "I'm sick of you," he replies in a quiet, calm voice, and while the woman shouts awful words at him, he gets into the taxi, and as he reaches his arm out to close the door, their eyes, "his and mine," meet again. She would have had time, she says, to get in and sit next to him, but she didn't do it, of course. She slaps her thigh as a sign of regret. Now, she'd do it. "I'm going with you," she'd say to him, without batting an eye, but at the time, once more, her courage failed her, or perhaps the thought of doing so never even seriously crossed her mind because she was no longer in London, she was in Loiu. And then Martxelo pulled up in his newly cleaned car. He told her that he'd cleaned it in her honor, and as he turned on the ignition, he asked if she'd met that man in London or if they'd known each other from before, with a jokey tone that didn't hide his jealous nature, to such an extent that she had to tell him that he was annoying her. And yet in London she had really missed him, so much so that she had decided to come clean with him when she returned and, in general, try to be more open and affectionate with him.

Leaning down over the coffee table, playing with the packet of cigarettes, Harri takes one out and holds it between two fingers, as if she were going to light it, even though she doesn't smoke. She holds it beneath her nose and smells it. She'll never forget the voice, and the smell, of the man she's fallen in love with. She says she's sure she changed his fate completely, which is why she now feels connected to him. This is what she says to Martin and Julia, looking from one to the other with a disconcerting smile on her lips that is halfway between happiness and regret.

Finally the sun breaks through the clouds and shines brightly. And with that, the neglected garden regains some of the remains of its fertile beauty after the pleasant rain, although the only things invading it are the tenacious calla lilies. A couple of hydrangeas have appeared; once bright-blue, they are now a dubious pink and could stand a little fertilizer and pruning. The pansies that Martin planted along the path leading down to the river haven't flowered—the fault, he says, of the birds, which he hates. Paying no mind to the couple of alley cats that have taken over the lawn, the sparrows and a few thrushes—which are as big as pigeons—peck at the grass.

There are no curtains on the wide windows. Julia took them down long ago—they were very dirty and she wanted to clean them, which she did, but she hasn't yet found time to iron them. Because of that, light now pours into the room, cheering it up, even though it already has a lot of light thanks to the functional, Scandinavian-style furniture, in contrast to all the other rooms, where there is still furniture from Martin's grandfather's time— heavy, dark, rustic stuff Julia finds oppressive despite the fact that, apparently, it's all very valuable, especially the formal library space itself—an enormous old-fashioned book room housing a sort of alcove, with a divan, that Martin locks himself in, saying he's got writer's block. In general Julia likes the house, because it's comfortable, because the garden—which she wishes were better looked after than it is—provides her with a nice view while she works, and especially because there's a Petrof grand piano there; she likes it so much that she's even thought at times that it's the last thing attaching her to Martin, apart from the remains of their past love, and that it's precisely because their relationship has no future that she's trying to break her connections with the house. That's why she's stopped taking care of the garden, which she used to tend to with such enthusiasm, which she had fixed up so beautifully back when she used to make use of little breaks from work to water plants and pull up weeds. Harri brought it to her attention some time ago, before she realized it for herself, telling her that she was sorry to see the garden so neglected and adding, "it doesn't look like the woman of the house is very in love," which she said as if it were a joke, though she was actually speaking seriously. And Julia had remained silent. She was a little embarrassed, and certainly astonished, to learn that her sentimental situation was so clear for all to see.

And now, as is so often the case, Julia once again doesn't know what to say. Harri turns toward her and complains again. "You two don't take me seriously," she says, in a normal, unexaggerated voice this time, and she doesn't know what to say in reply. What could she possibly say to her? That she finds her sudden rush of love believable, that what she reveals about her relationship with Martxelo is sad, that her idea of suggesting a story to a writer with writer's block is pathetic? "Of course we believe you," Martin says, using the plural.

And then, getting up from his armchair, "a very promising start of a story," meaning that she has already inspired him plenty. He, too, has fair hair, but not much of it, and what little there is stands on end. He's wearing a yellow and black striped robe, he still buys them at the same *college* he was sent to as an adolescent like Harri's daughter, and he's got on his old Church's shoes, without socks. He looks unkempt, as he tends to recently. The tenant could appear at any moment, and it wouldn't be a good idea for her to find him like that, he says, straightening his robe before going up the stairs. Harri, too, is going to have to leave soon, because they've brought forward the round table talk on biostatistics she's attending. Harri has brought some of the traditional *pantxineta* cakes Martin likes so much and which she tends to bring for her afternoon visits, and they're sitting on the coffee table. Julia decides to make tea, which is what they usually drink with them.

THE KITCHEN, TOO, IS QUITE OLD, although it is not the house's original one. It's large, like an old-fashioned kitchen, has a long wooden table in the middle, a storage stove and cooker with a large oven, and a modern glass-ceramic hob, which they use every day, on what used to be a sideboard. She boils the water in the kettle; the teapot, which is stained brown in many places, especially the spout, she finds revolting. She would very much like to get a new one, but Martin, who particularly likes old things—and who also has a puritan, bourgeois guardian's tendency to make things last—would not approve of her doing so. She follows the established norms for making tea. She pours boiling water into the teapot and swirls it around to warm it, she scoops in the tea—a spoonful for each of them and one for the pot—and waits five minutes exactly, making use of the time to wash the dishes Martin's got piled up in the sink. With the faucet off, she can hear voices from the living room, just a murmur, as if they were whispering in the covered-up way they do whenever her back's turned. It used to drive her crazy, but it doesn't anymore.

When she goes back to the living room, the writer's looking extremely elegant. A beige polo shirt and flannel pants of the same color, buckled dress shoes that are as shiny as a mirror, and a raw silk Loewe jacket with leather details on the lapels, cuffs, and pockets. Almost all being worn for the first time. The jacket is beautiful, although it's at least a size too big for him. Julia told him that the day he bought it, but apparently he couldn't exchange it, because he was already wearing it. Harri thinks the same thing, it's beautiful, she says, but she can't understand how he could buy such a loose-fitting jacket, to which he, unbuttoning it to hide the bagginess, replies that it's a habit he got from his mother, buying things large in order not to grow out of them.

When they served the tea, a controversy that was not new came up: Do you add the milk to the tea, or put it in the cups before the tea? Harri brought it up, not knowing that the week before, Martin had emptied the teapot into the sink in anger over that very same question. Julia was sure that she had read that the milk is added to the tea, although she didn't remember why, while Martin thought it was the other way around. The outcome was an argument about the matter, and in order to find out who was right, first Martin and then Julia looked for *Five O'Clock Tea*, but neither could find it, and Martin accused Julia of not putting books back on the shelves and hiding them, an accusation she couldn't accept, not after spending so many hours cataloguing the books, and she really got angry. Because they are still taking stock of the damage caused by that quarrel, Julia curtly says that she doesn't know. Harri's theory—Harri's always all science—is that, by simple logic, the tea has to be put in first, being the indispensable, main ingredient, to which the additional ingredient —milk—is added, she says, and what's more, it's also the easiest way to control the mix and make sure you don't put in too much milk. She also mentions an aesthetic reason: the wonderful braid of clouds that the cold milk forms in the hot tea. Martin, always the aesthete, had used the same dumb argument for arguing that the tea should go in first. But this time, in a completely shameless way, he says that it's the other way around, although he doesn't remember why. In other words, first the milk and then the tea. "That's right, isn't it?" He looks at Julia, as if wondering whether there isn't much difference after all between the two options and one could live with putting either the tea or the milk in first. Martin the peacemaker. They talk about doing it both ways to choose which one they like best, and Julia's furious, because Martin, who finds it so difficult to give way on anything, is now so flexible and ready to reach an agreement, and all because the *penthouse* girl is about to turn up and he doesn't want her to walk into a bad, sulky atmosphere. It made her want to tell

31

Harri all the details of their quarrel—even more than Martin's angry, childish character, what she really hates about him is his ability to pretend that he can control himself when there are other people around.

Martin, who's so mean when it comes to expressing affection, rests a hand on Julia as he says, with a smile, that they can live with the doubt about what comes first, the milk or the tea, and Harri joins him by saying that it would be a different matter if it were the chicken and the egg, at which they both laugh. Probably a way of them saying that she's being hysterical about the whole thing. Julia decides to leave, even though she usually sleeps there on Thursdays and has done so for some time now. She says her mother's gone to Otzeta and she doesn't want to leave Zigor alone. She doesn't know why she thought of saying something that's not just a lie but also an implausible excuse, because not having her mother at home's never been a reason for not staying—her sister lives next door and her son spends almost all day there with his cousins. She thinks that Martin's glad she's decided to go, that he'd rather be alone to be able to receive his tenant properly. Harri reads his mind—"We'll leave you alone with your *playboy* girl"—and she stands up and grabs her green leather briefcase. It's getting late, and apparently the students in her grad course tend to be demanding.

Julia catches Harri lifting her hand up to her left armpit. It isn't the first time she's seen her doing that, and Martin points it out to her now. Why does she touch it so much? It seems she has a ganglion cyst the size of an apple, and nobody pays her any attention about it. She grabs Martin's hand for him to feel it, but he doesn't want to, because it gives him the creeps, he says, and it's she, Julia, who stretches her finger out to touch a lump the size of a chickpea. She's already shown Martxelo, she supposes. She has shown him, yes, but it was pointless, he says it's nothing, he thinks she's a hypochondriac. "So if your husband doesn't think it's anything," Martin argues, "and he's a doctor, after all, you should quit worrying and stop touching it all the time." But he's a pediatrician, she points out, and not one of the best. She puts her green case down on the floor and tries again to get Martin to touch her lump by taking one of his hands, which he's hidden behind his back, hugging him as she does so.

Julia, who's gone to the kitchen on the excuse of having to clean the tea service, hears the commotion—Martin's laughing and asking

Harri not to tickle him, she's complaining that he's too rough and he's hurting her. Julia doesn't like their excessive familiarity and waits awhile in the kitchen, and when she goes back to the living room, she sees them sitting there docilely like two young children at the sudden appearance of their evil stepmother. "He doesn't want to touch my cancer," Harri complains, pretending she's about to start crying. At times like that—although admittedly much less frequently now—Julia wonders if they've ever gone to bed together. She's asked them, too, always in such a way that they could take it as a joke, but never one-to-one. "I'm sure you two have done it," she says as a joke, seeing them playing around. They've always denied it, saying it would be like incest, that they are the living proof that good-looking, healthy, and clever men and women can have a good relationship without there being any carnal side to it; but Julia thinks they've done it at some point. To be more precise, she's sure they did it once.

IN THE GARDEN, HARRI ASKS JULIA, "How's our boy doing, is he writing?" The question itself is a tautology, because he's only ever doing well when he's writing. The main feature of the affliction of writers is that creative work is the only way they can find to be happy. Sándor Márai said something like that very recently. That's why she prefers him to be writing, it makes it easier to be with him, at least he feels alive, it's the only time he thinks he's on the right track. That's the only reason she wants him to write. She thinks that Harri, on the other hand, would like to share some of his fame as a writer. She's often said that it's a pity to let talent go to waste, and she's always on the lookout to see what he's writing, to see if his famous novel is getting anywhere, asking when he's going to finish it. Martin, however, usually gives her evasive answers, if not outright lies, like a bad writer who wants to make her believe that he's made more progress than he has.

Julia knows for sure that he can't stand having to satisfy the expectations of the people around him, whom he fears disappointing if he's unable to write a successful novel. He's even said as much to her, and even if he hadn't, she's convinced that he believes people admire him for his ability to write and, at the same time, that he isn't sure whether he has enough talent to write anything that deserves to be called a novel. Julia thinks he does have that talent, and more than enough of it to write a decent novel, but she'd be happy if he took up watercolors if that made him happy.

She says she's bored of "our boy" but doesn't give any details. In fact, she never really gives her any explanations, although she's more than once been tempted to reveal some secret side of him in order to put Harri's devotion to him to the test. Later on she's glad not to have tried that, it wouldn't have made her feel any better, and if she spoke ill of him, all she would achieve is that Harri would hate her. In any case, Harri puts any negative sides that Martin may have down to the dark part of his genius. And at the end of the day, although Harri's idealized version of Martin drives her up the wall, she wouldn't want to tarnish it. She decides to say that she thinks he's making progress with his novel and that she sees him working on it every day, not mentioning that he spends the days in his ugly robe, sitting down and standing up in front of his computer, up and down, like a punished student incapable of working hard and, after studying, incapable of doing anything else; he hardly goes out, reads very little, wastes the hours away watching trash on television, and drinks a good deal.

She doesn't say that from what she's read of, she's not sure you could say if what he's writing is a novel or not. She has to keep that quiet, among other things because she looked at his computer in secret.

"I think he's making some progress."

Harri looks at her in an inquisitive way, Julia thinks she's trying to see to what extent she's given her an evasive answer, and deciding to be more truthful, she says that she thinks he may have been a little stuck recently. Because of his perfectionism, she adds, so that she doesn't think she's doubting his talent, rather just the opposite.

"If one could only help."

"He's alone in his work."

"I'd do anything."

Turning toward the writer's home, moving her head from one side to the other in order to confirm how much she means it when she says "anything," so much so that it's almost comical, as if saying to Julia that she has no idea just how serious she is.

Julia knows she's truthful and, perhaps because of that, cannot help being sarcastic. "You'd do anything, apart from putting up with him every day." She says that in spite of herself, not much liking letting everyone know that she's the unhappy companion of a genius, but it's too late now to take it back. That's what Harri thinks: Martin is a real genius whose talent should not be wasted, and the duty of all of those around him is to help him bring his work to the world. Julia's the one whose good or bad fortune it is to be the writer's main support. Everyone—Harri, Martin's mother, sisters, and friends— tells her that he seems to be better with her, more balanced, more at peace, and that she must need a lot of patience because, as they all know, it's no bargain living with an artist.

There's an enormous, tank-like machine moving around in front of Harri's car, blocking the way out. So she has to wait. Every single day, they can see the lengthening of the channel that's being cut into one side of the bottom of the valley to open the way for the high-speed train. Another hara-kiri, says Harri, looking gloomy. They've talked about that before, about how the house is going to end up right in the middle of a huge transport tangle, about the contradiction between wanting to protect your surroundings and wanting to have Paris at your doorstep. The two women are brought together by their nostalgia for the landscape. They never knew the surroundings at their finest, but they had known them when there were still *baserris*, large apple orchards, rich kitchen gardens that were fertilized using waste material brought from the tobacco factory—which had a smell they still haven't forgotten—and elegant Belle Époque mansions with beautiful gardens.

Now you hardly see a real piece of green land until you get to Antondegi hill. "Sagastizabal does not exist," Harri says. The Sagastizabal *baserri* had been on the other side of the road, where the Elektra factory is now, and Julia had lived there until she was seven, until most of their land, which went all the way down to the river, got expropriated; her father had no choice but to sell the rest of it. He didn't get much money for it, on the one hand because the land was only reclassified later on and the fixed price was nothing like the market value and, on the other, and most of all, because he had decided that whatever he got through this rejection of his primogeniture would be shared among all members of the family, because the obligation that came with being the firstborn was to keep the house going, which he had been unable to do.

Julia has always been proud of his decision, which then led him to become a coastal fisherman—he had always loved the sea, and

35

the sea was his destiny—but regretfully, when he finally made his dream of owning a boat come true, at the age when other people usually retire, he had to start working in a foundry, because her mother could no longer bear the recurring nightmare in which her husband was found drowned. With inevitable irony, while working at the foundry, he bought a small boat for fishing baby squid after work and on the weekends, and then one Sunday morning, with fine weather and a calm sea, he went out, and the boat was found off Ziburu, empty. Julia remembers her father to have been an honest man. He was proud of having divided up the money from the sale of Sagastizabal among the family, and she had thought her mother was proud of that as well, although she had recently heard a few bitter comments about what he'd done, for instance about how they'd had to pay the price for his fine behavior and things along those lines, and seeing her mother's frustration made Julia extremely sad.

"Sagastizabal doesn't exist." Harri sounds moved when she says that, as if she's guessed Julia's feelings, and she puts her hand on her shoulder, which moves her in turn, because they aren't usually very affectionate toward one another. The expression has become almost an aphorism for them, an aphorism about how to accept one's inability to do anything. Something between the French *c'est la vie*—that's life—and the Spanish *se acabó lo que se daba*—all things come to an end. "*Gureak egin du*, this is it for us. Sagastizabal doesn't exist."

The small stone buildings that were once the stable, barn, and storeroom, as well as the apple orchard that gave the *baserri* its name, are still there; they don't know who they belong to now. "There's still something left," she says, for the sake of saying something, and Harri slowly shakes her head. "Not much." Once, Julia had even been jealous of her straw-colored hair. Now she wears it very short, in layers, which makes the disproportion between her head and body even more pronounced, because she does have a small head, and she moves it all the time to underline her words, in short movements, like a bird Martin often says. But she sees herself as a typical Basque woman, like the ones Arteta used to paint, thin from the waist up and strong from the waist down. Julia thinks she's beautiful. After a certain age, and also because it's more comfortable, she thinks it's better to have short hair, because having long hair shows a pathetic desire to seduce, but she always puts off cutting her own hair, which is curly, black, and has a few gray hairs, mostly at the front, that she doesn't want to dye.

Julia doesn't know whether to mention it or not when she sees Harri making a hidden movement to touch the lump on her armpit, under her coat. She thinks it would be better for her to find a specialist to remove it, but she doesn't want to add to her worries, and at the end of the day, Harri isn't a child. She takes ahold of her hand to pull it out of her coat. She says it's probably best if she stops touching it so often and suggests she should get an appointment with Abaitua, "although if your husband thinks it's nothing, there's no reason for you to think otherwise." She doesn't answer immediately. "My poor husband"—she sounds tired and resigned—"he's a master at not seeing what he doesn't want to. He wouldn't even notice if a tomato grew on my nose." After another pause, she admits that lately, the more affectionate he is with her, the less she desires him.

If Harri's sincerity is not only obscene but also a little uncomfortable for Julia, it's because, above all, she's asking for something in return. Julia doesn't want her to talk about her relationship with her husband, because she, Julia, would then have to tell her about her relationship with Martin, and she doesn't want to. "But I'm not sad," Harri says, with a smile that shows quite the opposite. "Now I've got something to be excited about." Julia doesn't know what she's talking about. "That's great. What is it, may I ask?" Another smile comes with the answer, and Julia really doesn't know if she's joking or not. "The man I met at the airport, of course!"

"You don't believe me, either, just like that idiot," and she points toward the house. "Because he doesn't believe me, does he?" In spite of what the question might suggest, Julia's incredulity doesn't hurt her as much as Martin's; she doesn't care about hers. "I don't know," she says to avoid the issue. The enormous caterpillar tractor has turned around and is throwing up a thick burst of black smoke from its vertical exhaust pipes, and now Harri can move her car. "It really is late now," she says as she opens the door, but she doesn't get in, as if she were looking for the right words to say goodbye with. They're at the top of the stairs that lead down to the road. Julia hasn't used them for some time, even though it's the shortest way to get to the house. For some time, there'd been a chalk outline of a human body a couple of steps away from where she is now. She doesn't remember if more than one person died in that attack, which wounded several. At least the one worker from Elektra, of course, on his way to work at the factory. It had been an enormous explosion. The roar that shook the house had been terrible, but the silence that followed it had seemed even crueler to her, and then screams, and later on police sirens, and ambulances and fire engines. She imagines she must have followed the daily reports at the time on how the wounded were doing, but now she only has a vague memory of it, like the residues of a nightmare.

A scruffy looking woman kicks up a fuss, because they're in the way. She shouts loudly in Spanish about the damn cars—"¡*Coches de mierda!*"—and that's the most polite thing she shouts, but they pay no attention to her. Harri, before getting into the car, whispers in her confidential way, "People get bitter and demanding because life's not going well for them." Julia thinks that maybe she's got Martin in mind when she says that, as well. In any case, she mentions him before setting off. "Take care of him." "And you take care, too."

HER MOTHER IS ALONE AT HOME. They've just come back from Otzeta, and Zigor's at her sister's house. "I wasn't expecting you." Julia doesn't think she sounds annoyed, but it is obvious that she isn't glad to see her. She doesn't like her mother making it so obvious that she would rather she start living with Martin once and for all. She understands her but thinks her opinion is offensive, because it has nothing to do with having evaluated any of Martin's actual qualities—which, by the way, she doesn't think she has a high opinion of; at best she seems to find him strange—and everything to do with the fact that Martin comes from a good family. The best family of all those she knows. Respectable people, moneyed, your classic nationalists. It makes her angry, or rather it disappoints her that her mother thinks that Martin's mother—a conceited, embittered old woman—has "a lot of class" and that whenever she comes up in conversation, she calls her "Doña Sagrario," like most people from the neighborhood do.

She's annoyed to find the refrigerator almost empty, and she realizes it's a very masculine reaction. She decides to make an onion omelet, and while she beats the egg, it occurs to her that not so long ago, it would have been unthinkable not to find enough there to be able to get a decent dinner together. As unthinkable as living with a

38

man without marrying him. As a child, the refrigerator had always been full of leftovers. Some stew, cod with tomato, or a bit of potato omelet. She's hungry. As she watches the egg congeal around the onion, she remembers that Martin bought some Russula field mushrooms, and she feels a little sad. Now she regrets, or, more precisely, she's frustrated that she wasn't able to stop getting angry about seeing Martin so happy as he waited for his American tenant to arrive. Because that's what she felt angriest about. She wonders what he's doing, whether he dared to invite her out for dinner. She supposes not, his seduction techniques are more slow-moving than that.

She can see the house from her kitchen window, there on the low hill, standing out against the cobalt, almost black, sky. There are still no lights on in any of the windows, but the one over the door that looks out onto the garden has already been turned on. She notices that she misses the house when she leaves it. She particularly misses the piano when she's in her own ugly house; even if she had one, she wouldn't be able to play it without irritating the neighbors, not with those paper-thin walls. The same question pops into her mind for the second time recently: To what extent has Martin's status stopped her from breaking up with him once and for all? At her age, she's no longer a passionate defender of romantic love, but she is worried that she may have ulterior motives. She's sure that she read in Beauvoir's *La vieillesse* that a person's money is as intrinsic to them as their nose or the color of their eyes, it's consubstantial, in fact, and there's no reason why being attracted by a man's status and the security, material well-being, and other things that come with it should be less dignified that falling in love with his physical attractiveness; however, after spending more than half an hour looking, she isn't able to find the exact text. But she has come across a curious word—*gribouillisme: fait d'aller au devant des ennuis qu'on cherche à éviter*. It means preempting troubles one would seek to avoid, which is one of Martin's tricks when he deliberately puts himself across as an old man.

She puts the plate with the omelet on the ugly piece of oilcloth that's laid out over the table.

The original white, red, and green squares—there's always been a weakness in the house for those colors, the Basque national colors, especially in the kitchen—are worn away from having been scrubbed so often. She's always told her mother that she hates that tablecloth, and oilcloth in general; she's fed up of buying tablecloths of all colors and types and her mother always using that one. Although she keeps things clean and tidy, she isn't interested in decoration, she doesn't think it's necessary, and of course that's what she takes changing tablecloths to be. It's fine in other people homes, at Martin's, for instance. But not at her house.

The pale-yellow tablecloth reminds her of the kitchen at Sagastizabal—the lower half of the walls painted green, white cupboards and storerooms with handles covered in a thick coat of red paint (and a circle in the same color around them, traced with a glass). A design scheme very similar, in fact, to that found on coastal fishing boats. After dinner, while her mother washed the dishes, her father used to sit with his back against the wall, his feet resting on the firewood basket, and sing improvised rhyming *bertsos* with great enthusiasm and little harmony; he enjoyed singing as much as he liked being out of tune. His endless strings of *bertsos* were usually sad. *"Markesaren alaba"*—meaning "The Marquis's Daughter"—and *"Limosnatxo bat"*—"A Handout"—were his favorites, always the same monotonous tunes. He was happy, because he wasn't hungry and because he was giving his daughters the education that he himself hadn't received. It was a type of well-being based on the modesty of his aspirations, taking the form of the quiet desperation of the age. As a child she had hated those songs and now thinks they're beautiful. She regrets not having sat by his side to sing them, she would give a lot to be able to do that now.

Etxezar. The name of her mother's *baserri*. Her mother never lived there, but her family rented it out from the Marquis of Villafuerte for generations, the latter selling it to her grandfather, Julia's great-grandfather. Julia's grandfather put up what was, at the time, a lot of money toward the purchase—seven thousand pesetas; his boss at the *baserri* where he had been a servant since he was a boy had kept it aside for him. A good man, apparently. But the *baserri* was inherited by the grandfather's brother, and now his grandson is the owner, the son of one of Julia's mother's cousins, an alcoholic bachelor who makes a living without working by selling bits of land from time to time at a bad price to an unscrupulous neighbor. Her mother periodically follows the progress of her ancestors' home's destruction with despair and sorrow, and her heart breaks each time she hears about more land being lost. Today, when she arrived back from Otzeta, her sister told her that he had sold the pine grove behind the hermitage the previous Friday, and on Saturday an employee from town had found him lying on the ground, covered in vomit and surrounded by scattered bills that the dogs were already chewing at.

That's why she looked unhappy and upset. Her dream is to recover the family seat where her ancestors were born and died, and which cost her father who knows how many years of hard work, and she has sometimes said—although never in so many words—that she might ask one of the rich friends her husband had, colleagues of his from the Amaika social club, for a loan to help her buy Etxezar. "If I asked any of them, they'd give it to me," she says, and Julia doesn't know to what extent she's serious, because her relationship with her father's friends doesn't go beyond a short greeting whenever they happen to pass on the street, and she's sure that her father would be terribly embarrassed there in his eternal rest at the bottom of the sea if he found out that his wife wanted to do something that he himself would never have considered even in the most difficult of situations: asking friends for money. Julia suspects that she's hinting for her to ask Martin for the money, and just in case, she once told her mother that if she ever did have enough money to "save" that gloomy pine grove beside Etxezar, she'd rather use it to buy a little house with a garden in Les Landes.

Zigor's walked in. He looks at her first, then at his grandmother, who is still washing the dishes, and then back at Julia. There's a question in his eyes. Julia knows that he's examining everyone's moods and wants to know if she's said something to their grandmother that's saddened her. He's in a serious mood. It seems to her that he's suddenly become a man, and that he's aware of that. He says he hasn't finished his vacation homework yet, and he goes back to his room. Running away from the gloomy atmosphere.

Mother and son do not hug each other as much as they used to, and when they do, it's not the same as before. She feels rigid now, and the thought that he might feel revolted by coming into contact with her terrifies her. The same thing happened to her with her mother; they long ago stopped giving each other kisses, she doesn't know when, though she often dreams that her father's calling her, and she runs toward him, and they embrace. Her mother, who is so affectionate with little children—all those "I could just eat you ups" as she kisses tummies and tiny hands—becomes very physically distant with them when they reach a certain age she can't quite calculate. That's how she behaved with her and her sister, and with her grandchildren, as well. She can remember her sitting with naked babies on her lap, literally kneading them all over with her hands (according to her, it was a grandmother's duty to knead babies in front of a warm fire, and she even has a saying for it: basking the baby), but after a certain point, all physical contact with her disappears. Nowadays, when cultural shifts have made giving a kiss on the cheek such a common form of greeting—even men and women of a certain age in Otzeta have taken on the habit—it's not strange to see her receiving kisses from others, or even leaning forward and offering a cheek herself, and she finds it strange to see her mother hugging or kissing people of her daughter's age, and when they're together in a group, she often feels embarrassed, because it's so obvious that she and her are the only two who don't kiss.

She feels obliged to watch the television with her mother for a while. She withdraws into herself and thinks about things that have nothing to do with what's on the screen: Harri's fantasies, her harsh words about her husband. She doesn't think her mother is paying much attention to what's on the screen, either. In Martin's words—in fact, they're a copy of Faustino Iturberena's—old people watch television as they once used to watch a fire in a chimney: without leaving their own thoughts.

"What's 'solipsism?'" Zigor asks from his room.

Although she knows the answer, she masters her desire to answer the question and, like always, shouts that he should look it up in the dictionary. Martin long ago told him—and Zigor greatly respects him, because he's a writer—that the best way to acquire knowledge is by looking up unknown words in the dictionary. As well as sharing his opinion, the difficulty she was often met with when answering seemingly simple questions of his also influenced her in her decision to instill that beneficial habit; she would be embarrassed whenever her excessive lack of knowledge became too apparent, putting off her answer by using any excuse she could, saying she had something on the stove, or that the washing machine was leaking—as it often does—in order to be able to secretly look at the dictionary herself. Sometimes the problem was not so much the gaps in her knowledge as the enthusiasm to teach she often feels, a mother's need to explain things in all their complexity, to give all the details, to go into related ideas, to look at the causes of things, forgetting that what the boy wanted was to find the easiest, quickest answer; her reasoning usually confused him and made him nervous rather than helping him. "Forget it, I'll figure it out myself," he would finally say, sorry he had asked the question. So now the boy usually sorts things out by himself, often with the help of IT tools, and that's why Julia is amazed when he asks what "solipsism" is. Could it be a way of trying to get her to follow him into the other room, she wonders.

She sits on the edge of his bed after he's gotten in and they talk for a while. It's always been one of Julia's happiest moments. They tell each other what's happened during the day, speak together as if he were a grown man; she wouldn't like to lose the habit, she wants it to always be the same, for them to carry on getting together when he's twenty, whether at his place or hers, or somewhere else—"*chez toi, ou bien chez moi ou sur à une terrasse*," as Reggiani puts it in the song—but she's started to think that won't be easy. Now she's the one who finds it hard to open her heart, she's bitter, and she thinks the boy realizes that. To a different degree, of course, but whatever dark thing it was that separated her from her mother is also moving her son away from her. She thinks that all generations of parents believe that they will have an open, trusting relationship with their children, better than the one they had with their own parents. Julia is sure that it will be like that in her case, but she also knows that it will only be a partial improvement, less than what she hoped for when the boy was a small child.

She wouldn't want him to be too devoted to her, either, to have that excessive love that some men have for their mothers—the love Albert Cohen portrays in his book, for instance—and which comes with a hatred for other women, in her opinion. Unexpectedly, it comes to her that she once carried this well-behaved being, who already has a trace of a blond moustache, in her belly, and the thought makes her stand up all of a sudden. She sits in front of her son's desk. It's too small for him. She says they'll have to buy a new one, and he says it's not worth it. He's very careful about what he asks for, and she's grateful to him for that.

"Hey, *ama*," he says, sitting up in bed. Julia pays attention, instinctively sure that he's going to ask her one of those questions that will put her to the test, rather than a dictionary question. "Why do they stop us from deciding if we want to be independent?" Suddenly she feels very tired, despondent, and doesn't know what to answer. Whenever he comes back from Otzeta, his hands are swollen from playing *pilota*—Basque pelota—and his heart is full of that patriotic *abertzale* spirit. "What do you want me to say?" She realizes they all must have talked about that after lunch at Torrekua and now he wants to have a heart-to-heart with her about it. The boy's obviously nervous. "I don't mean the right to be independent, I mean the right to decide if we want to be independent." Julia gets furious with her sister, her brother-in-law, everybody at Torrekua, because they fill him with ideology; she's angry with herself, too, because she leaves him with them for too long, because it's easier for her that way. The boy's waiting for her answer, his lips pressed tight together, arms folded, and Julia's sure he can read what's going on in her mind. The people at Torrekua really are Basques through and through, and no doubt about it. What is she going to say?

"Things are more complicated than they seem," she comes out with, and she regrets it as soon as she says it. Why does she always need so many words, nuances, and details to explain different points of view? "Everything's very complicated for you, but in fact, things are very simple." Zigor said that, Zigor senior, in 1977, when amnesty had just been declared and he told her he'd decided to go back to leading a clandestine life and she tried to convince him not to: "Things are more complicated that they seem." They got to talking about politics. He said that when Franco died, the apparatus of the state was never purged and everything remained just the same. As simple as that. For her, too, things were simple; she loved him more than anything and anyone else, and she dreamed about having dinner with him and sleeping in the same bed with him, and she couldn't stand living in fear that she would one day hear on the news that he'd been shot dead somewhere. As simple as that. But those were not words that a person who was prepared to give his life for his ideals could hear without contempt.

Now, too, she doesn't know whether to express her feelings or not, she's afraid her son may think she isn't loyal to her own people, and perhaps thinking that will prevent him from ever coming to her. She isn't even absolutely sure that independence is the best strategy for preserving their language and culture, and even if it

44

is, it wouldn't be legal, and according to the elections, most people don't want it to be, either. So why make such a fuss about it? The way forward would be to make good use of the autonomy they've already won in order to convince those who are still on the fence, and whatever any case, violence isn't the way. "Do you understand that?" He's identical to his father when he looks her in the eyes. He nods at her in silence and, with a gesture of boredom, lies down on the bed and faces the wall. Julia is about to ask him for a kiss when her mother calls up from the kitchen to let him go to sleep, it's late and he must be tired out.

When she walks past the bathroom, she sees her mother brushing her hair, which goes all the way down her back. She has gray hair, with an almost even number of white and black strands, like Julia's, and it's curly, as well, but only from the neck down, because she wears it in a tight bun during the day. Julia finds it disturbing when she sees such long hair. Perhaps it reminds her of the iconography of witchcraft—such a clearly feminine feature in such an old mother. She swears that even though she gets so many compliments about it, she's going to get her own hair cut before long.

2

ABAITUA IS BRUSHING HIS TEETH when his wife comes into his bathroom. They've been sharing it for a few days now, ever since Pilar decided to do hers up. She thought that renovating it and opening a door straight onto her bedroom was a very good idea from a practical point of view, but it's one that also means the decision to sleep in separate bedrooms is not going to be a temporary measure.

Abaitua does not go into the bathroom when Pilar's in it, even if the door is open. But she does go in, unless he takes the precaution of closing the door completely, that is. He isn't sure how to take it, though one thing is clear: Pilar isn't embarrassed about her body and sleeping in separate beds doesn't seem to have changed the way she walks around in front of him. Abaitua, however, finds her more distant and unfamiliar by the day and, to that extent, is reluctant to be in intimate situations with her.

He doesn't know how long they've been sleeping in different rooms. At least two months. The current situation started after their last quarrel, and it was Abaitua himself who opened the door to it. "It'll be best if we sleep separately," he said to her that night when she reproached him for his insistence on going to sleep with the radio on; so she picked up two or three pots of lotions, the alarm clock, her robe, and her book from the bedside table and moved into the room next door. He could have stopped her when, at the door, holding her lotions, the alarm clock, and all the other things in her arms pressed up against her chest, she said to him, in that unusual way of hers, that sleeping in separate beds was pushing them apart. "We're separating by moving apart," was what she said. Pilar is a woman of few words. That's why he's thought so much about that sentence, which seemed strange to him. Of course, what she wanted to say was that by deciding to sleep separately, they were closing the door forever on the chance of getting back together; in fact, most of their previous makeups had come about thanks to their physical relationship, which was made possible by sharing a bed and not thanks to talking.

But he didn't care anymore. He was more tired than angry; each quarrel, whatever caused it—they were normally about petty things—opened up a deep wound inside him, brought him deep regret, and he found it more and more difficult to go back to where they were before. He was convinced that even though they managed to make up, they'd end up tripping on the very same stone once again. In a sense, he felt that you could only be sorry about things so much, that there was a limited stock of regret for putting the relationship back on track, and his stock, and probably Pilar's, as well, was running out.

At first, their quarrels and distancings led to the joy of rediscovering each other, realizing that they had to get to know each other again, and in that sense, many of his most tender, exciting memories are from their peace-making. Moving apart to come back together again. The last time was on the beachfront promenade, the Kontxa Pasealekua. He remembers it well. That time it was he who left; he moved into the apartment that previously housed his private practice and which his son is living in now. In that new situation, separated and living alone, he didn't feel like going out with his friends and he soon grew tired of the restrictions the lifestyle forced on him—he had taken only a suitcase full of books and a few changes of clothes with him, and in the office storeroom, which had been set up as a kitchen, the microwave oven was the only thing working—and tired, in fact, of living like a refugee, and almost without realizing it, he started walking around the places where he might bump into Pilar, without knowing to what extent his desire to go back to her was conditioned by his lack of supplies, his inability to manage by himself, or some sort of psychological dependence or possessive

47

desire, or whether, on the contrary, he really did love her. He still hasn't resolved that worrying doubt. On the one hand, he had to admit that during their periods of separation, he hadn't wanted to see his friends and lost his interest in women, even those who offered him their company—they seemed too motherly to him, and he ended up avoiding them—and he missed Pilar terribly. But sometimes he didn't trust that feeling, thinking there was some pathological dependence at the bottom of it and that what he had to do was resist the desire to see her, learn how to be free, and it was laughable, if not pathetic, for him to waste his time like some silly adolescent, hoping to run into her. It was just such a day when they came across one another. She was walking along the roughcast sidewalk, which was later replaced with a terrazzo one as ugly as it is practical, on the far side of the Pasealekua, beneath the tamarinds, as if she wanted to hide, with that curious walk of hers—half aloof and half languid, with her arms hanging loosely at her sides—which now seemed pitiful to him. They'd been separated for more than a month, and all they had to do was say hello—then they held hands and went back home together. Before, their separating had been a way to feel the desire to come together again, building up the strength to find each other once more. He thinks it was that way for Pilar, as well, but recently he suspects that this separation is for the sake of separation itself and not to pick up speed, and he's decided to do nothing to get back together again, leaving things to happen as they will rather than participating in them, with the curiosity of a mere witness interested in seeing how things will turn out.

Pilar has a yellow towel wrapped around her head—it makes her look like Nefertiti, with her long neck, proud chin, and narrow black eyes—and she has another towel of the same color tied around her waist. Her soft skin is covered in pearl-like drops of water, and she's drying one foot, which she's propped against the bathtub, taking particular care with the skin between her toes, to avoid getting athlete's foot. Before, whenever they met up in the bathroom, she would ask him to dry her back and put lotion on it. He liked stroking her soft, cool skin. Few women have such soft skin as Pilar, and he can say that, because the first thing he looks at when he sees a woman in his office is her skin. It's still firm. Her back is muscular, her waist well defined in spite of the structural changes of age. He would rub her back until she told him it was enough. That's enough, *ederra*. Which means "handsome." Or that's enough, *maitxia*, she'd tell him. *Maitxia*—darling—is one of the few Basque words he remembers from his childhood, and Abaitua finds it especially endearing when it's she who says it.

Today, of course, she doesn't ask him to dry her back or put lotion on her. She just says to him in the mirror—in her clumsy Basque, which is a clear sign that she's in a good mood—that she's not going to the clinic that morning and it would be good if he could drop her on the *hiribidea*—the avenue—because her father's called to ask her to meet him at the notary's office again. The old man's trying to tie things down, so as not to leave any loose ends, so that the clinic can remain open and under the family's ownership. You know, "inheritance troubles."

He could also take the fact that she uses the word "troubles" when talking about family matters as a sign of good will, of mutual understanding, unless it's simply that because of her difficulty with the language, she's using it as a way to describe the inevitable bureaucratic chaos. Because she doesn't usually say anything negative even in the worst struggles with her family— apparently in order not to open the way for him to say anything hurtful, because she thinks he hates her relatives—and he's convinced she'd rather renounce her inheritance than discuss money with her siblings and their spouses and make any lack of harmony among them all public. Abaitua would say that, in general, he treats Pilar's family with the respect it deserves; he doesn't ever interfere and seldom criticizes them. The very night before, when she told him that they would have to close the clinic when her father died, he encouraged her by saying that there was no reason to think that should happen—taking care not to say what he was really thinking, which was that her family members and the other partners made sure there wasn't any risk of that happening by always sending patients from the public health service over to their clinic.

Something which Abaitua himself has never done. He's always tried to keep himself separate from Pilar's family's medical business, exaggeratedly so, even, because he has always held himself to be a passionate, honorable defender of the public health system and he wouldn't like to put that image at risk, but above all, even though so many years have gone by since they married, because of a stupid wish to show that Pilar's social status—her father being the owner of a clinic—has nothing to do with their relationship. He's well aware of this impulse of his.

The first time she told him that her father had called her to a meeting to talk about the future of the clinic, she asked him to go with her. She didn't make any specific request. "You'll come?" she asked him, as if it weren't really a question. In other words, she made the suggestion and, at the same time, accepted the possibility that he might not. He answered that he would feel out of place. "I'd just be sitting there" were his exact words, hoping for a more direct request, for her to say "please come," instead of that ambiguous "you'll come?" So that it would be perfectly clear that he had no desire whatsoever to stick his nose in her family businesses and, come to that, so that he could show her that he thought she was quite capable of managing by herself. But it was clear that he really should go with her, it would have been the most normal thing to do, not only because of his profession but also because there was no doubt that her sister would be bringing her husband and that, furthermore, the man would crow louder than anyone else. What's more, if Abaitua didn't go with her, he would have to explain his absence, so that her father wouldn't take it amiss. So why doesn't he go with her? And why doesn't she ask him openly to? He's clearer about the answer to the first question than he is about the answer to the second—he doesn't trust himself to behave properly in the meeting, he's worried that if he goes there against his will, he might get silent and gloomy and, finally, everyone there will get angry and he'll end up saying something inappropriate. It has been known to happen. So when she said "you'll come?" what she was really asking was whether he would behave well; she was asking him to go to the meeting, but only if he was going to be respectful and pleasant, otherwise she'd rather he didn't go.

Pilar, as in so many other areas, is too mistrustful about this. He doesn't find the family he has married into as unbearable as she thinks (she's wrong about what he thinks of his father-in-law, he actually likes the old man), and the way he behaves with them, bearing in mind the natural limits to their relationships and except for the occasional quarrel at Christmas, seems quite appropriate to him. Sometimes he thinks that beyond the matter of his temperament, she believes him to be more upright and uncompromising than he actually is and that, because of that, she's under the impression that he thinks being involved in medicine as a business is despicable and, consequently, he can't stand having anything to do with her family. But he doesn't think of himself as being that upright and intransigent, particularly not upright. To be sure, Abaitua himself has tried to groom his reputation for uprightness through particular types of behavior—turning down the opportunities offered him by his father-in-law, for instance, taking part in organizations in favor of public health, leaving his private practice, which was going so well, when he was given the chance to work full-time at the hospital. Be that as it may, what Abaitua really finds difficult to stand is her thinking him to be incredibly virtuous; nor does he understand her not admiring more what she takes to be such a virtuous, honorable, and selfless way of being. She seems to think it's just the way Abaitua is, that he's chosen this path rather than the path of riches that the butchers at the clinic have chosen, which is one that she tolerates at best. She doesn't know just how high the price for Abaitua's honor is, just how much anger is building up inside him. And her not knowing this makes Abaitua feel like an impostor whenever there's occasion for him to see that she believes that if he's not the head of the Obstetrics and Gynecology Department, or even the director of the hospital, it's his own doing because he doesn't want to be, because he's too upright, too unambitious, unwilling to bargain, and, above all, because he loves his profession too much. Pilar thinks that he's a good doctor, the best gynecologist for miles around. He's heard her say that with pride, and he isn't ashamed, because, to an extent, he believes it to be true.

When he was flossing, he thought perhaps what she had said was "are you going to come with me?"

Now it seems to him that whatever the exact question was, it must have been difficult for her to ask, and that if she hadn't wanted him to go, she wouldn't have mentioned it to him at all. Still, it doesn't escape his attention that what she really wants is a conscientious and agreeable companion, someone who's ready to lie down in the middle of that shoal of sharks, prepared to listen to their exaggerations and stupidities—especially those of her brother-in-law—without getting angry, so that they'd all, her father particularly, be able to see him and see that they were still a couple that got on well together. Answering that he would be out of place was as much a result of wanting to hear her say that he wouldn't be and would he please go with her as it was of pointing out that her foul brother-in-law was allowed, in the interest of family peace, to make all the decisions.

He told her in Spanish that he would feel out of place—"No pinto nada"—to which she replied, "Lo mismo que otros," meaning he'd be no more out of place than anyone else, referring to her brother-in-law, obviously, and while her words demonstrated good will on her part (she could have said something a lot harsher than "no more than anyone else"), she then turned her back on him, which spoiled the effect and seemed to be a way of saying that the conversation was over. Confronted with that doubt, Abaitua decided not to add anything else, and that's how the conversation ended. Later on, he looked for a good moment to say that he would go with her if she wanted him to, but that moment never came, because she didn't look him in the eye for the rest of the day. And now, when she said that seeing as how Loyola's got her car, it would be good if he could drop her on the hiribidea, he misses another good opportunity to offer to go with her. He has to admit that he feels less and less like reaching out to her, and the metaphor works, because when he's with her, it's as if he loses all his strength, as if his muscles were weakened.

It's Pilar who's brushing her teeth in his sink now, although she could perfectly well do so in her own bathroom. Her teeth are perfect, large, completely white. She takes water from the faucet with a young person's movements, and when she leans over, she holds her breasts with her forearm so that they don't hang down. She has never been proud of her breasts. When she was young, they were small and conical—goat's tits, she used to complain—and even though they got larger as she grew older, they were still small, reminiscent of those on the allegorical statues of public monuments, those fine female morphological structures. She loves her flat stomach, wide shoulders, and strong back, her backbone furrowing a deep groove as it goes down to her slim waist. Abaitua's never been interested in the size of women's breasts, and he's told Pilar hundreds of times that he likes her young girl's breasts with their slightly swollen nipples. The first time he saw her in a bathing suit—he remembers well that it was at Ondarreta beach, and that it had green and black diamond shapes on it—he looked down the neckline and saw that her breasts didn't fill the cups, and he moved a finger to spread the elastic edge out a little bit and told her, jokingly, that she was cheating. Pilar reproaches him every time she remembers that, and not completely jokingly, saying that he's been loathsome and vile from the very first day. She has a bad memory of the exchange, unlike him, apparently getting very embarrassed by her small breasts, something he would never have guessed would be the case and in fact, he took her embarrassment to be arrogance at first, because Pilar was very beautiful. And she still is. (Related thought: unless she's done it without him knowing, and he doesn't think that's the case, she hasn't gone for a mammogram for more than two years. She's afraid to go, precisely, because there have been some bad cases in her family, but he doesn't think it's the best moment to remind her.)

She looks at him in the mirror with curiosity, as if she's guessed that he's thinking about her, and that look still makes him nervous. He wonders what sort of expression she would make if he told her he didn't have to go to the operating theater that day after all and could go with her to the notary's office. Although some people do so on the slightest pretext, he can't do things like that, can't not go to work without giving prior notice.

She takes the towel off her head and brushes her hair. That's how she does her hair, just letting it down, and she hardly ever uses a hair dryer. She looks at him with her eyes wide open now, astonished to hear the radio announce that it's eight o'clock. They're running late. He goes into his room, and Pilar follows him. She looks around the room, which is quite untidy, she locates and then, with a brusque movement, picks up the underwear and pajamas he dropped there earlier, and leaves the room again, having made a bundle of the two yellow towels and the underwear and the pajamas, which she'll take to the laundry room. He doesn't know how to interpret what her taking care of him like that—picking up his clothes and even his underwear without making any signs of revulsion—might mean. He thinks it could be a matter of habit, something mechanical, something to do with some resigned, subconscious submission to her role as a woman. He's about to say that he was going to pick them up himself—he really does try to take care of his own things—but, in the end, he keeps quiet.

They're both in the main bathroom again, Abaitua is fully dressed apart from his jacket, he puts some eau de cologne on his hands and then a few drops on his neck, and his wife, still naked, pulls at the clean towel on the hanger to get it straight. That perfectionism irritates him, and he says "I'm very late" without bothering to hide his annoyance. "I'm coming," says Pilar, but she continues to apply lotion from a jar the size of a thimble onto her eyelids. "I'm coming." And he'll wait for her in the car. He normally waits for her in the car when they leave together.

IN THE ENTRYWAY, AFTER WALKING DOWN THE STAIRS as always, he waits at the threshold and looks out at the street from left to right, slowly, trying to see if there's anything unusual. He had long ago given up the routine, but the fact that the trial over what happened down by the river was due to start soon and that his son was back from the United States had reawakened the old fear in him and reminded him of the safety measures he'd seen Jaime Zabaleta take. Zabaleta worked at the time in the Spanish central government delegation. Zabaleta is a deserter from the world of medicine who, like many others in the field, left his original calling to take part in professional politics. Abaitua owes him a big favor. He knows he used his influence to stop the *Ertzaintza*—the Basque police—from making any objections to the explanations he and his son gave of the incident, namely, that the boy didn't know about his friends' criminal activities and told his father as soon as he found out that they were hiding bombs on his grandfather's mastless old yacht, and that father and son wasted no time calling the *Ertzaintza*; although their version was essentially true, a few points could have been questioned. It was also thanks to Zabaleta that he found out that there were no signs of threats, which, reassured him to an extent, and indeed, they'd received none—unless his son had and hadn't told him. But sometimes, depending on his mood, Abaitua does get scared that he might become a victim of some sort of revenge attack for having reported them.

On the sidewalk on the other side of the street, just across from him, there is a young man leaning against a car. He thinks he's seen him around a few times with a neighborhood girl, but he's not sure, and he decides to stay where he is, because he could be standing there waiting for him, waiting to give a signal to some hidden wrongdoer who's ready to attack him as soon as he leaves. He instinctively thinks of taking a step back, but he puts his feet on the threshold again and, ashamed that fear has taken ahold of him so easily, stands up straight, staring at the young man, who, having realized he's there, looks back at him. Apart from the shivering and murmuring of the leaves the south wind is blowing around, everything is still and silent; he wonders if it wouldn't be easier for him to go out into a noisy street full of people, but then he remembers what happened on San Martin Kalea, the same street where his old office, in which his son Loyola now lives, is located, and being on one of Donostia's busiest and noisiest streets hadn't stopped Fernando Múgica from getting killed with two shots to the back of the neck as he left his place of work. His autonomic nervous system gives him an immediate response to that memory, a reaction that, despite the situation, he finds rather fascinating. A flash of light. A drop in blood pressure and then a short fainting sensation, absolute darkness that lasts a second or two. The young man leaning against the car comes out of the mist again and, another two or three seconds later, his vision of him becomes more precise. He has to unfasten the top button of his shirt to breathe properly. He inhales deeply, his arms held out slightly from his body for the sweat to run off, and after regaining his biochemical balance, he wonders if he might not be addicted to epinephrine. He promises himself it's the last time he'll let himself be taken in by that macabre game of suggestion.

Without thinking about it any further, he steps down into the street, and the young man lifts up his chin to greet him. Of course, it could be a signal. But now his tendency to fall into morbid ways of thinking makes him smile, and as he replies to the young man's greeting by raising his own head, he also lifts up a hand, convincing himself that a greeting is the only reasonable hypothesis. Then he checks that there is nobody else on the short street, which is a private access road for the four villas now converted into apartments that are located on it and overlook the bay.

The car's parked outside, not in the garage. Pilar used it the night before. She never parks inside the garage, however often he reminds her that there's a lot of saltpeter in the air and it isn't good for the metalwork. The tires are Dunlops. He gives them a few insignificant kicks and leans down to look beneath the car, as if he were checking to make sure no oil is leaking out. He used to take those same precautions, although he knows, of course, that they're probably no use—there are most likely plenty of ways a bomb can be stuck on in such a way that anyone who isn't an expert won't notice it. But that didn't stop him from looking. It was a matter of dignity, and he worried that some neighbor might realize it was a ritual he went through every morning and think him paranoid, or even that his painstaking safety measures might attract someone's attention or give them ideas.

He hasn't told anyone about his fears. For one thing, because he wants to believe that there's no basis for them. In other words, other people, including the police, didn't see any reason to be worried, and he didn't dare to bring it up with them, in case of what they might say—there were certainly people with more serious reasons to be worried—and he also didn't want to worry his family unnecessarily. He thought they could figure it out together when he explained his idea for their son to go and study in the United States, but Pilar thought it was an excellent idea from the very beginning and didn't mention any suspicions she might have had, and against all expectations, the boy also liked the idea, so Abaitua didn't have to use personal security as an argument to convince them. Of course, the boy could have been worried, as well, could have had dark thoughts in his mind and, like him, be keeping them quiet.

It isn't Pilar's steps he hears in the hall, it's a neighbor's maid and the two children she's taking to school. She says they're late and have to be quick. Abaitua looks at his watch—he really is late. Pilar's delays make him angry; more exactly, what makes him angry is knowing that he's waiting for her because she can't leave the house without putting on some lotion from a little jar the size of a thimble. Thinking that gets him sweating again. He steps into the car and decides to turn the air conditioning on, just as the girl who the young man is waiting for appears. He pushes the seat back for his legs to fit in comfortably and adjusts the mirror. He turns on the ignition. That precise moment, when you turn the engine on, seems the most dangerous to him, probably because it's a sequence that appears in so many films—the car getting blown to smithereens as the victim turns the key.

He's often wondered if bomb victims hear the explosion, and he's also talked about it with a coworker. He once asked a female Civil Guard officer he operated on after she'd been caught in a bomb explosion. Apparently she hadn't heard it, or, at least, she didn't remember it. If it came down to it, it was a consolation to think that hypovolemia is sweet and that receptors, when affected by extreme pain, shut down. These are morbid thoughts that fly around his head like butterflies trying to decide where to land. He won't let them. But he still finds it hard not to go through with his obsessive ritual: first he rubs his hands together, then rubs his knees before putting the ignition key in and remaining still, with his hand on the key, while he counts to three, closing his eyes as he turns the key. Even Pilar's realized. Eventually she comes running out with her bag and a small case. He adjusts the rearview mirror better. His symptoms of anxiety have disappeared, but he needs to take deep breaths and dry his hands on his knees. Then, after waiting for a group of satchel-carrying children on their way to school to pass, he starts the engine at the exact moment in which Pilar opens the back door and throws her bag and small case in. She sits next to him as she does up the buttons on her blouse. She usually finishes getting dressed in the car. She's had to go back up again to turn something off or close a window, which is how she justifies being so late.

He slows down almost to a stop as they approach the newly in-stalled speed bump and goes over it in first gear, very slowly, and he realizes that Pilar is looking at him; she's amazed that he's been in such a hurry and then drives so cautiously. The reason is that it's occurred to him there's no reason for limpet bombs to go off when you turn on the ignition, the way it happens in movies. He's read somewhere that it's more usual for the explosion to take place after several miles, after breaking, on a bend, or just like now, because of the shaking and movement produced by going over a speed bump; there's normally a small vial of mercury that acts as a tilt fuze and completes the circuit.

He knows that the politician Eduardo Madina went more than five miles before the bomb that was stuck under his car went off, and if the explosion only hit his legs, it was because he had long legs and so, like him, he had the seat pushed way back. The traffic is moving slowly, and it's not because there are many vehicles. Pilar usually complains that drivers in small cities are over-cautious and clumsy. She thinks that of her husband. Someone honks at him, and it's obvious that Pilar is nervous; she pulls up the neck of her blouse, takes off her earrings, and puts them in her closed fists as if she were getting ready for a fight. But when she whispers "you're lost again," her voice suggests tiredness rather than anger.

They realize too late that the one-way Arrasate Kalea is now one-way in the other direction, so they have to take the parallel street and go around once again. This new mistake is too much for Pilar, and she asks him to drop her off anywhere, the notary's office is close-by, but he ignores her, accelerates, and—daring and obstinate—takes the wrong way out of De Euskadi Plaza, crosses the new bridge, determined to take her right to the door. But it's not a very good decision, because the neighborhood of Gros is like a rattrap. The first turnoff is a no-entry, and the traffic stops him from getting into the lane to take the second turnoff. He smacks the steering wheel, which makes the horn go off, and continues, fast, up Mirakruz Kalea, getting further and further away from their destination, while Pilar keeps silent, and the only sign that she is frightened or disapproves is that she holds onto the handle above her door. Abaitua doesn't know where he's going, and at this point, he couldn't care less. After speeding past several street openings, he thinks that he wouldn't mind having a bomb stuck under his seat that was going to explode and blow him to smithereens, and he keeps his speed up until he has no choice but to stop, because a crane is maneuvering in front of a huge beveled building that cleaves the road in two like the bow of a large ship. On the top floor, where the sandstone façade is covered with cheerful green tiles, lives a neurosurgeon who Pilar works with and who used to be her lover for a time, Abaitua doesn't know how long. He didn't ask her. He has to bend down to be able to see the long balcony through the windshield, and he makes his rubbernecking obvious. He wants Pilar to know that he's looking at her lover's home; unlike him, she's seen the bedroom, the bathroom, and the living room, because she used to spend whole afternoons there, and at least one night. *La notte.*

Pilar turns toward the window on her side in order to show that the building is like any other for her, and Abaitua is absolutely sure that both of them know what the other is thinking. "They've opened a new bar," she says, without turning her head. As if it were the most natural thing in the world.

He's going slowly now, and the flow of traffic forces him to turn left toward one end of the Gran Vía. He is relaxed, feels quite good; after all the excitement, his adrenaline is back to normal, and that makes him feel at peace. He doesn't know how to control himself, and when something goes wrong, he cannot help wanting everything to go to pieces, and that attitude has even put him in danger of having serious problems in the operating theatre (he cannot forget, among other things, the time when he was doing a hysterectomy using what was, at the time, an innovative technique—laparoscopy—and even though he was having serious problems getting pieces out, he carried on regardless, wrong though he was, and was about to throw the morcellator away. The head nurse's eyes stopped him from doing it, with an expressivity that she would never have been able to put into words, letting him know that he was acting like an ill-behaved child. Since then, remembering that look and breathing deeply while counting to ten has helped him to calm down, but not always, not when outside the nurse's jurisdiction, outside the hospital.)

"Don't go over the bridge again." A calm but firm voice. She has her jacket and bag in her lap and her small case in her left hand, with her right hand holding onto the door handle. Her face is rather pale, and on her left eyelid there is a small bit of white lotion from the little jar. He doesn't tell her. They go back along the Gran Vía toward the place they were a quarter of an hour earlier, and he stops in front of the monument to Iztueta, in obedience to Pilar. She just says "see you later," and he goes toward Frantzia Pasealekua. She'll have to walk across the bridge and almost all the way along the *hiribidea*. At least ten minutes to be added to the previous delay.

ABAITUA GOES UP THE STEPS to the hospital two by two. There are people finishing their cigarettes in groups and alone. Some of them are wearing white coats. A young man wearing a nightgown, his thin legs showing, is sitting in a wheelchair, connected to a tube, and with a melancholy air, he, too, is smoking. The hallway is done in green-streaked black marble, with decorations and inscriptions in the corners reminiscent of a mausoleum, an example of institutional bad taste, resources used on superficial things instead of matters of urgency, all in order to look like a rich country. He moves faster toward the inside staircase, almost starts running to avoid the visitors who are waiting to catch him as he goes past the gift shop. The Spanish and Basque words for "chapel"—CAPILLA-KAPERA—at the top of the two wooden doors are bigger than the names on the signs at the entrances of some of the public hospital's wards. A woman wearing a white coat crosses herself as she steps out. He thinks she's a cardiologist. It looks like she's just consulted God about some difficult case.

By the time he reaches the surgery area, he's wearing his own white coat; without realizing it, he is walking very upright, which could look arrogant, but it's no more than a defensive gesture. There are many patients waiting for him, he's afraid of looks that may be reproaching him for his late arrival, and he stares at the door. You can tell by the atmosphere that there are people thinking *our taxes pay your wages* and looking at their watches. At one time, that would have been unthinkable; attitudes toward doctors have changed a lot. Although Abaitua is in favor of relationships between doctors and patients becoming more equal, he regrets his role becoming so proletariat. He thinks the resident doctor he has to do his appointments with looks aged, although he's still very young. That could be because he's overweight, or because he's quite bald, and perhaps because the glasses he wears look old-fashioned to him. His watch, too, makes him look old, with its thick gold—or gold-colored—chain, and Abaitua sees him check it, too, after greeting him. He doesn't like him, and he doesn't apologize for making him wait. And he asks him in Basque if he's used the time to go over today's cases and, following the nod he receives as a reply, whether he's found anything particularly interesting. *"No especialmente"*—not particularly. He understands a bit of Basque but never speaks it, not a single word, not even *agur* to say goodbye. Abaitua, in a manner out of keeping with his usual self, takes a radical approach with him and speaks to him in Basque as much as possible. They've argued—not too often, of course, they are not on the same professional level—because the young doctor thinks that Basque is taken into account too much when it comes to awarding jobs in the public health system. Abaitua doesn't know to what extent it should be taken into account, or if the extent to which it is taken into account at present is appropriate, but he doesn't come across many doctors who speak Basque well—it's above all those doctors that don't speak the language well who think that Basque-speaking candidates who pass the public health service entrance exams pass them specifically because they're Basque speakers even though they have little training in other areas, and that non-Basque speakers who fail, in spite of knowing a lot about medicine, fail because they don't know Basque—and in the end, people prefer a non-Basque-speaking doctor to take care of them. What he finds more offensive is that a knowledge of Basque being part of the selection process is the only aspect of the entire system that gets into the newspapers, the only thing that is fiercely debated; nothing much is explained about the way requirements and duties of the positions on offer are apparently altered, or how exam papers are leaked to friends or fellow party or union members. Even so, he has to admit that he sometimes uses Basque as a sort of punishment with that aged-looking fat young man. And it's specifically because he's fat. He isn't proud of the feeling of distaste he has for people with disagreeable physical appearances—he finds watching fat people eat to be repulsive, for instance—he knows there's a bit of intolerance in it, but he can't suppress it, as much as he'd like to.

This time, when the other doctor explains that he prefers operating on patients to seeing them in the consultation room, he replies in Spanish—"*No te gusta la medicina, entonces*"—saying that if that's the case, he must not like medicine very much. He says he finds it more exciting—"*más excitante.*" Abaitua isn't surprised; he probably preferred operating, as well, when he was young. It's where a doctor can feel like God, the giver and taker of life. But in fact, there are few things he hates more than the mythical status and glowing admiration granted to surgeons. Whether they admit it or not, there are doctors who use the pleasure of surgery to hide the fact that they don't have the courage to face patients without putting them to sleep first. Some surgeons have always run from the risk of identifying with pain and, because of that, don't want to look outside the area bordered by the green cloth; red flesh, bloodied and depersonalized, is all they want to see. He's read that idea expressed much better somewhere or other and so, in order not to do a disservice to whoever the writer was, doesn't mention it. He admits he isn't much of a teacher. That's led to problems for him, and not just with the aged young man; he's also had them with his son, especially before. He doesn't know how to summarize something without turning it into a caricature, and he thinks it's because of this tendency of his that his points of view often throw people off—they think he's being ostentatious—and that, in general, he has trouble being taken seriously. On the other hand, the fact that fatty yawns so much (in a completely open, natural way, quite unimpeded by any social customs or norms), makes him exhibit more self-control than usual when speaking to him. He's cynical and sarcastic with him, which he isn't with other people; he'd rather be extravagant and eccentric than a bore. Pilar has sometimes told him that he's a real drag. It's because of his obsessive nature, of course, and when they're not angry with each other, he likes to bring up things that he's not very sure about, in order to try out his ideas on her, like someone learning to play the piano and trying out the same passage over and over. He's sorry he's done that. At the same time, he admits that recently, almost everything makes him think of some other story or quote he feels to be relevant. Just like with his father. Every time he used to say "and speaking of that . . . " they'd shield their heads with their hands, as if protecting themselves from being stoned to death. Now he's really sorry that he didn't listen to him more often and with greater attention. Too late, he realizes with sorrow. Now he only knows the headlines of those stories, gists as short as the taglines on movie posters: Uncle Joxe, his father's brother, who was shipwrecked on a frigate in the Buenos Aires estuary; the adventures of his brother Imanol "The Tiger" Ibarluzea on the *pilota* courts of Cairo, Shanghai, and Chicago.

He doesn't mind the nurse saying "one day you'll lose your head as well" when she gives him one of the many pairs of glasses he forgets around the ward as she hands him the day's medical records, but he does mind fatso, who's slumped down in his chair mumbling "*estragos de la edad*," putting his forgetfulness down to the ravages of age. Unfortunately, it was he who opened the door to that lack of respect by mocking himself too often. He supposes that nowadays, not keeping up an image of feigned wisdom—which seems ridiculous to him—brings with it the risk of not being taken seriously. Nowadays young people interpret gestures and words literally. He—probably due to some sort of complex—is incapable of not putting up a wall of modesty that rather than covering up his own shortcomings actually increases them, and likewise incapable of not downplaying his gifts, but they aren't capable of distinguishing false humility.

The young doctor, almost lying down in his chair, has a file in front of him and remarks that this one hasn't got a chance—*"Esta lo tiene crudo."*

Another cultural difference he sees compared with how things were in his day is people's attitude toward those who hesitate before making decisions. Doubts used to be held in higher esteem. Young girls liked young men who had lots of doubts, who talked about the uncertainty of their faith, their existential problems, anxieties, and insecurities. That really has changed. Doubt has become a synonym for weakness and lost its value. It doesn't go down well in the age of monthly gym memberships. Nowadays women prefer strong, muscular, secure, daring men with clear objectives. Surgeons whose hands don't tremble. And many poor young girls confuse psychopathy and perversion with security and daring. And he ruminates: *"Fantasías de la época"*—these are the fantasies of the times. This last musing reminds him how the young doctor didn't know that Pío Baroja, author of *Fantasías vascas*, had been a doctor, and that he still has to put together that list that he's been wanting to compile of doctors who gave up medicine for writing in search of a better world.

The nurse calls the first patient. He's told her several times that shouting out patients' names isn't a good thing to do, and he doesn't want to tell her every day. It's clear that she thinks it's the normal thing to do and that she doesn't understand why he doesn't approve. It's the patient's first visit. He still gets a bit nervous when he sees a new patient—what is the person whose first and last names he's just heard going to be like, what will he or she be asking for? He's proud that he can tell women's ages to within a few months. He figures that the fat woman on the other side of the desk from him—whose bulging eyes could be a sign of hypothyroidism—is forty-two, and she tells him she's thirty-seven. In fact, someone less skilled would have said she was over fifty. She complains. Stomach distension the week before her period. General bloating. Intense mammary swelling. Occasional hyperesthesia and pain. Emotional tension and nervousness. Insomnia and irritability as a consequence. Problems with her husband and children in turn. At work, too. She doesn't know when it started. She's always had it, she says in Spanish—*"de toda la vida."* Her physical examination is normal. Her uterus is swollen, but its shape and texture are normal. He sees that the elastic in her panties has left deep red, almost purple marks on her. He tells her to get dressed. When he asks if she puts on weight after her period, she says she does, more than a dozen pounds, and seems to think that information may help him to arrive at a correct diagnosis. Nobody believes her when she says she doesn't put on weight from eating too much. Apparently her husband tells her that people who don't eat don't put on weight. It is obvious she's sad that people don't believe she's sick. Her husband doesn't—he thinks it's all in her head—and nor do the doctors she's seen.

When she sits down at the desk once more, Abaitua—knowing that acronyms tend to impress people—tells her she has PMS, and she relaxes, happy that her illness has a name. Premenstrual syndrome is the cyclical reappearance of a combination of psychogenic, physiological, and behavioral changes in the luteal phase of menstruation. Until recently, and taking into account the female condition, even the syndrome's worst symptoms were accepted with resignation; today, many women of fertile age, if not the majority of them, are usually treated for it as if they were sick. Without thinking about the side effects or, of course, the pharmaceutical companies' profits. This woman, on the other hand, has clinically significant symptoms. He orders general tests and recommends that she bring her husband to the next appointment if she can.

The next patient is a young, thin woman, born in May of '68—this time Abaitua gets it absolutely right. She has soft brown hair and white, drab-looking skin. She's wearing a casual flowery dress that goes down to her ankles, a thick, loose black sweater, and sandals, as if she were a hippy from her mother's times. Her mother, though, could hardly have been a hippy; she looks conventional, one of those people who see themselves as a typical Donostian—discreet, stiff-necked, and with a trace of bitterness on her lips. The daughter is extremely nervous, she keeps wringing her hands, and it's obvious she bites her nails. When he asks her what the problem is, she takes her sweater off, determinedly holding it by each side until her arms cross, as if it were a sudden decision to do something she had wanted to do long ago but not been able to until now. There are traces of dampness on her dress, the size of two-euro coins, at her nipples. "It's milk," she says. She says it's been happening for a couple of months. She kept it quiet at first, because she was afraid it might have something to do with having engaged in intimate relations, although not complete sexual consummation, until her mother—one of those mothers who might examine her own forty-year-old daughter's closet—found out. They're worried, because a doctor—a well-known psychiatrist who's a family friend, the mother says with obvious pride—has told them that galactorrhea could be the result of a brain tumor.

The old woman says it with a sad voice, but the ever-moving eyes in her aloof face show no sorrow. Abaitua is increasingly sure that there are often psychological alterations behind the symptoms that his patients bring to him, and he finds it hard to ignore them and stick to his specialty. Now, when he turns toward his computer to open the file, he almost says to the woman—who seems to him very old even though she isn't much older than he is—that, in itself, there's no reason why a hypophyseal tumor should be any worse than a mother from whom one has to hide their galactorrhea. He thinks perhaps he should ask her to leave and speak with the daughter alone. He's not sure. He feels less and less sure when he comes into contact with certain patients, not knowing how to give them information or how to interpret the data they give him. Over time, he's confirmed that intuition is overrated and that experience, as well as being an over-tiring way of collecting knowledge, is not always valid. Experience itself has taught him that. He moves around in his chair in order to avoid the mother and look the daughter straight in the eye. He tells her that it is true that around a quarter of the cases of galactorrhea are due to hypophyseal tumors, but most of those are benign. There's no reason for her to worry.

He mentions other possible causes of galactorrhea, more for the resident doctor's benefit than for that of the patient, although the man doesn't seem to be paying much attention and he isn't taking notes. Others do take notes, particularly women, but although Abaitua likes to see that they're interested in what he has to say, he doesn't care if the fat guy's interested or not. He makes a mental note to give him something to read: a case of galactorrhea without hyperprolactinemia caused by a pathological relationship with the mother. Although he himself is critical of all the *psy*- fields, he finds the young man's wholly unholistic point of view insulting—the man's supposedly scientific mindset classifies everything that isn't biochemistry as almost esoteric.

He's used the computer to write up his cases for a long time now, although he's not sure whether it's the best way to do it—the noise of the keys, him looking away at the screen—in terms of the patient feeling comfortable and well looked-after. But he does type fast. He asks her for her medical history; it isn't particularly interesting, but when the old woman says that the girl was treated for depression six or seven months ago, he can't hide his excitement. He thinks— taking the development of psychopharmacological medications over recent years into account—that they might have prescribed her a first generation tricyclic antidepressant, and if that's the case, amitriptyline could be the cause of her galactorrhea. Stranger things have happened. He asks them if they remember the name of the medicine—Tryptizol, Anafranil, or Dogmatil, for instance— hoping it'll be one of those. It's Tryptizol. The psychiatrist who's apparently a close family friend, the same one who terrified them with hypophyseal tumors, prescribed it. He knows him by name, he's quite well known, but he thought he'd be retired by now.

"That's the key to it." He's aware that linking up the increase in prolactin and galactorrhea with Tryptizol isn't particularly difficult, but even so, after putting forward this hypothesis of cause and effect, he expects to see some sign of admiration from the resident doctor. But there's none. Nevertheless, he explains the biochemical mechanism that the medicine produces and gives a short explanation, which he tries to make understandable, to the two women. He thinks that if she needs antidepressants, she should start using ones with selective inhibitors, but that's something for a psychiatrist to say. He says that he will telephone her and that she needs to have some tests done to be on the safe side, and, specifically, so that he can see her again, just in case he has to convince her that she should go to a psychiatrist who isn't on such intimate terms with the family.

He increasingly prefers treating outpatients to the rest of his work in the hospital. To such an extent that he's been toying with the idea of retraining and going to work in a health center, in a small town if possible, and starting to work as a family doctor. It seems to him, although it could be no more than a fantasy, that the relationship between patients and their surroundings in such a setting would allow illnesses to be treated in a more contextualized manner, and that it would make it easier to recover the profession's humanist spirit, which hospital doctors have lost. Because as things are, he has the sensation that he's working in a large factory, with workers rather than doctors—they're all alienated, working on a production line.

Doctors are no more than that, himself included. The main reason his colleagues are discontent is that they don't want to resign themselves to being mere technicians toiling away on the pyelonephritis in Room 312 or the lupus erythematosus in Room 42; they want to be treated in all their complexity as suffering human beings. That's why they have an insatiable appetite for money. Alienated as they are, what they crave is golf, powerful cars, long yachts, or landscaped houses in the south of Spain, and they become envious of their colleagues, and cruel toward them, as well. They are no more than poor devils, at the end of the day, though those who are forced along their production lines are even less fortunate. He likes throwing the young ones into confusion—especially the ones who want a Rolex on their wrists—by bringing out all the anger he has inside.

"MARÍA AMOR." This time, the nurse does not need to sing out the last name. María Amor, Mariamor, Mary Love—an unbeatable name for a prostitute. She's a mulatto from the Dominican Republic. When she comes through the door, Abaitua thinks he sees a tray full of pineapples, bananas, oranges, and lemons on her head. She's the very model of a tropical woman, although he's convinced that she tries to play her splendor down, dressing discreetly and not wearing any makeup. When she comes to the hospital, at least; he's never seen her outside. To greet him, she holds out a hand with over-long fingers, showing the back of her wrist and lifting it up toward her head as if she were going to kiss it, and Abaitua takes hold of it, though not wanting to be overly affectionate.

The cry she lets out when he tells her that the results of her AIDS tests are negative is so high and long that it must have been heard everywhere on the floor. She lifts her arms up toward the roof, her hands pressed together. "*Gracias, Virgencita de las Mercedes.*" She explains that Our Dear Lady of Mercy is the protector of the Dominican Republic. With her hands on the table, she leans toward him until she's almost touching his nose and asks what she can do to thank him.

It's tempting for doctors to claim nature's decisions as their own achievements, they often do, and to an extent, it's to be expected, and when it comes down to it, the opposite happens, as well, doctors being blamed for nature's losses. But he doesn't think it's right. So he says that all he did was order a few tests, she's the one who's healthy and strong. "*¿Sana y fuerte?*" With her arms akimbo, her eyes wide open and almost rolling back into her head, her accent becomes almost a parody as she asks what the doctor is trying to insinuate by calling her healthy and strong—"*¿Qué me quiere decir el doctor con sana y fuerte?*"—and now Abaitua sees her with a colorful polka-dotted kerchief tied around her head—"*¿que estoy gorda?*"— you think I'm fat? And her effusive laughter shakes her whole fine body.

WAR STORIES. The woman's pimp—who died the month before of septic shock—was a small-time drug dealer; they knew him at the hospital, because he had AIDS. The guy himself used to tell the story—without any embarrassment, and proud of his own malice—about how, at a time when ETA was targeting drug pushers, he felt suspicious one day when he got a call from a stranger to do some business. He had a twin brother who looked a lot like him, and who was a sympathizer of the so-called "*abertzale* left"—the left-leaning Basque nationalist movement—and he decided to ask him to go and meet the guy in his place, at the same place and time as the meeting had been arranged for. Apparently, at the time of the meeting— it was set to take place in Irun, in a plaza with arches around it— he was there, hiding behind a column and watching; he saw a couple of guys go up to his brother from behind and shoot him dead. He would laugh as he told the story.

María Amor always said that he was a hyena, but she was completely dominated by him. He wanted intercourse without protection, and she, against her will, gave way on "special days": when they made up after a fight, or when he would come back after days or weeks away and—in her words—cling to her like a child, crying and begging for forgiveness. He would beat her, clearly. Occasionally he threatened Abaitua, as well, saying that he was taking advantage of his position of power, interfering in their private life, and trying to convince the woman to leave him. He also accused him of wanting to take his place. There was one especially aggressive moment when he refused to let them join the assisted reproduction program for serodiscordant couples. The guy knew that there was a way of cleaning sperm and demanded the treatment, but Abaitua knew that the girl only wanted a child of his on "special days" and explained to him that they didn't meet the required conditions for proving they could guarantee a child's welfare that the program stipulated. He was furious and threatened to report him for discrimination. They said all sorts of things to each other. The pimp said that everyone at the hospital knew that he was in love with María Amor and that he wanted her for himself; Abaitua said that the guy's sperm was the cleanest thing about him. The hustler held him by his neck and raised his fist at him but unfortunately went no further, so Abaitua wasn't able to give him a good punch. He was human garbage. He drew a disability pension and, at the current stage of his illness, was costing the public health system twenty thousand euros a year for his retroviral treatment, a lot more than many honest workers make. The infections specialist and he had often said that they'd be doing society a favor if they gave him a continuous perfusion of Midazolam. There was something more than a joke in what they said, but neither of them was daring enough to do anything about it. Abaitua's often thought about it, though, without reflecting very deeply, just playing around with the idea. Given that the valor normally required to murder someone would not be required, and that there would be almost no risk of getting caught, it was the famous dilemma: If you could kill someone by pressing a button, being completely sure that nobody would ever know, would you do it? Of course, he would need a more enticing motive than saving the community a few thousand euros. That beautiful and agreeable woman, who seemed to be such a good person, would be more of a motivation for him—it would be freeing her from that human trash.

It was a family doctor's job to give that healthy woman, whose only problem was the risk involved in her job, her routine checkups, or the area gynecologist could do it; Abaitua was keeping her on without any possible justification. He doesn't know exactly why, and he doesn't want to think about it. At the end of each appointment, he feels he doesn't want to send her to another doctor, he wouldn't want her to think that he's getting rid of her, or force her to explain her situation to another person; he knows she doesn't like that. He has to admit he'd be sorry not to see her there, and he has fun scandalizing the nurses; he knows they know he's in no hurry to get her off his patient roster.

Now María Amor smiles at him in a pitiful way. Few women are comfortable on the gynecologist's table. He decides to let the resident doctor examine her while he goes to look for the old psychiatrist and talk with him about the galactorrhea case. Does he do that because he wants to make it clear to the gossiping nurse that he has no interest in touching the woman? Probably. As he draws the screen to the examination room closed, he spots the resident doctor holding the speculum in his hand, a hand which seems fatter and hairier to him than ever. "Gloves!" he shouts out, and he startles fatty, who, in his shock, drops the speculum on the floor. A ridiculous situation.

THE DOOR TO ORTHOPEDICS ROOM 417 is ajar. He sees mother and son through the gap. The young man is slouched almost horizontally in the chair, reading a book. The old lady's sitting up in bed and staring at something on the wall in front of her. Abaitua is pleased to see that the people in charge at orthopedics have heeded his request and put her in a room of her own, even though there are two beds in it. Kepa greets him without getting up—"*¡Hombre, doctor Abaitua!*"—and pushes aside a lock of black curly hair from his forehead. He's growing a beard, which is also black and curly. Abaitua goes up to the woman and jokes to her in Spanish that they won't be able to recognize her son pretty soon, he's gotten so much hair—"*A su hijo un día no le vamos a conocer con tanto pelo.*" The old lady looks at him carefully, examines his face with no inhibition whatsoever, trying to find out who he is. She looks at things the way disorientated people who've lost their minds do. He takes her thin, wrinkled hand, and when he asks her how she is, she lifts her head up, looks at him, and says in a tired voice, with her thick Andalusian accent, that he shouldn't have bothered coming—"*¿Para qué te has molestado en venir, Juan?*" Apparently, Kepa doesn't know what Juan she's taking him for, either. She had problems knowing where she was before she was hospitalized, but now she's completely lost and confused. He thinks it's partly because she isn't in her usual daily place, but they also give old people Haloperidol and other such psychopharmacological medications, almost systematically, in order to stop them from getting too nervous, and it usually

70

does them harm. Abaitua concedes the son has a legitimate cause for complaint. When his mother fell over and hit herself on the head and lost consciousness, she was hospitalized. They took her to Neurosurgery and found she had a large subdural hematoma, which reabsorbed quite quickly in spite her age and without any need for surgery. But she didn't want to walk. According to her son, even though she's not at all the complaining sort, she started screaming when the nurses made her take walks along the hallways. He told the doctors that these walking sessions were torture and his mother really was suffering, but they didn't pay any attention to him, taking him to be a strange, problematic person, because they had seen him reading, or so he believes. They told him it was their job to know what was good for the patient, getting her out of bed in the morning and in the afternoon, telling her she was lazy and a complainer, even though she couldn't stand up and made signs that she was in a lot of pain. Her son, too, made her get up and walk, because they had told him that if she didn't, she would become disabled, and he dragged her up and down the hallways like a whimpering rag doll. Abaitua didn't hear about it until he got back from his vacation in Italy, and as soon as he saw her, he guessed that she had a broken hip at least. It was obvious just from her posture, and ninety-five percent of old people who fall over break their hips. A simple X-ray confirmed the diagnosis. That's why she's in the orthopedics ward with an artificial hip. And now she's lost her mind and confuses Abaitua with someone else.

When Kepa said he was thinking of reporting the neurosurgery department, Abaitua told him to go ahead, encouraged him to do it. He certainly complained enough about it, insulting and threatening everyone there, but no more than that. He asked what the point of reporting it was, and it was too late now, anyway. What he's really worried about is the possibility of them reporting him for the fuss he kicked up, grabbing the department head by the chest and shoving him. He regrets that now, and consoles himself by saying that he'd rather get to say what he said in front of everyone than receive a small indemnity from public funds. Abaitua would have preferred the opposite option; what happened was worth reporting, and he couldn't stand the department head—his brother-in-law, in fact, Pilar's sister's husband, who also happened to be the director of his father's clinic. Someone knocks on the door and opens it before there's time to answer. Two auxiliaries wearing pink scrubs come in briskly and purposefully. They greet the woman, whose name is written on a small board over the bed—"¿Qué tal estamos hoy, Eugenia?"—and one of them opens the half-closed roller shutter, letting in a ray of light that hurts their eyes. It's clear they're in a hurry, they have to get through a large number of rooms in a certain amount of time, but they treat the woman affectionately, with familiarity, speaking to her with the informal tú form of address, although speaking too loudly for the size of the room, with a forced type of cheerfulness. They ask the men to leave. They're in a rush. Kepa puts on his blue duffel coat and suggests they go for a coffee. It seems Kepa's got something important to tell him; his head hangs low, his hands are in his coat pockets, and although his voice is firm, his "I have to tell you something" is like a little boy's. Abaitua, thinking it's going to be something to do with money, is on his guard.

They decide to have their coffee in a café outside the hospital, Kepa saying that the hospital cafeteria is usually packed, but Abaitua knows it's because he wants to smoke. He doesn't like the cafeteria, either, it's like a canteen in a bus or train station. It creates a bad impression, one even worse than that of the medicine that's practiced there, a more anachronical image. Mass-produced pastries, potato omelets, and greasy fried squid on the bar, and in front of it, workers in white coats with glasses of wine in their hands. That's what he remembers, at least; he hasn't gone there for a long time. He makes Kepa take the stairs with him. In the main vestibule, there's a group of pharmaceutical sales representatives standing in a circle. Perhaps they aren't the same ones he saw when he came in, but they look just the same. As they walk by, several turn toward Kepa and show their disdain for him, to which he replies in a low voice, "Bunch of vultures!" But bearing in mind the strength of his voice, Abaitua isn't sure whether they've heard him or not, and taking his arm, as if he had impaired sight, he leads him straight out to the street.

It isn't easy to choose a bar. Kepa suggests the first one on the right, down the hill, so they can eat some fairly decent fried eggs with fries and chorizo, but Abaitua doesn't allow himself such things at that time of day, or at any other time of day, come to that. He thinks that Kepa should take better care of himself but doesn't say so; he long ago decided not to give more advice like that, he's aware that he seems more and more like a nagging mother. In any case, the smell of fried chorizo makes him want to throw up. "We said we'd have a coffee." They have to run between cars to cross the road. He doesn't care where they go, the coffee's bad everywhere. He hasn't been out hiking in the hills for several weeks now and feels he's moving slowly. He also has the sensation that drivers go faster when they see pedestrians crossing the road where they shouldn't. It's probably a false impression, something to do with the feeling of danger—it's a two-way road, and there's a lot of traffic on it, cars going fast. He asks Kepa if he, too, thinks that they've become the drivers' target, but the other man is two steps ahead and doesn't hear him. It's very noisy, and he's often said he's half deaf as the result of an explosion, which must be true. Abaitua hears him saying that they're a bunch of vultures. He catches up with him. He says he's talking about the pharmaceutical sales representatives when Abaitua asks him. He doesn't know what Kepa's talking about, as he, Kepa, also used to be a pharmaceutical rep. Abaitua found him a job at Schering, although he didn't last much more than a year there. Everyone said he had a veritable vade mecum in his head—he could tell you about the results of clinical tests, about the interactions and counter-indications of all the pharmacopeian products, and he made sales like nobody. Kepa himself tells jokes about it: even the first aid kits in convents were full of the Schering three-phase hormonal contraceptives he sold them.

Problems were soon to arise. Six or seven months after he started work, Abaitua began to hear some other doctors talking. What they didn't like was that when he visited them, it wasn't so much to give them information as to accuse them of having sold themselves to the laboratories. Abaitua knew that he had problems, but he took it all to an extreme at the closing ceremony of a conference financed by the laboratory. The room was full of people drinking cocktails and looking forward to the dinner about to follow, and the director of the conference and the director of the laboratory in Spain were speaking a final few closing words. Kepa appeared just as the act was about to finish, wearing a white coat covered with BAYER, CINFA, MERCK, EUROPHARMA, LIBERMAN, and IBYS laboratory stickers, something like a Formula 1 racing driver, and, from up on the platform, he asked for silence. He was applauded, everyone was happy, and they thought it was going to be some kind of joke. In fact, over the last several years, it had become fashionable for comedians to perform parodies at the endings of conferences. When Kepa started talking, saying that medications had come to occupy the witch doctor's place of honor—"*El medicamento ha sustituido al médico en el sitial del hechicero*"—people laughed, but not for long. There was soon a frozen silence. He said that the amount of public money being spent on drugs was incredible and unsustainable, and that the amount of money spent on developing new products was outstripped twofold by that spent on marketing. The murmur of indignation rose like a wave when he mentioned what had happened in Italy: a class action suit had been filed accusing thousands of pharmaceutical sales representatives, hundreds of travel agents, and thousands of doctors of corruption, of accepting gifts worth double a typical wage earner's yearly income. Then Alzola—people call him Orl, the Spanish abbreviation for ENT specialist, believing him to be the best ear, nose, and throat specialist the world has ever seen—went up to him and told him, in his high-pitched laugh, that he had said enough, and when Kepa paid him no attention, grabbed him by the sleeve, which only made things worse; up until then, Kepa had spoken calmly, but now he started shouting at him to go to hell and that he was sick and tired of organizing trips for him to the fjords of Norway and the brothels of the Caribbean every year, which is when the security guards took him away. And they fired him, naturally.

Abaitua had reproached him for that suicidal outburst, and Kepa had listened to him with his head hanging, like a little boy being told off for being naughty. Pilar, on the other hand, thinks it was daring of him to do that, and fun, as well, and it doesn't stop her from getting on well with him, even though Orl is the brother of Yago Alzola—her brother-in-law and boss. There's no doubt she lets Kepa get away with things she'd never allow him—her husband—to do. They'd had a quarrel about that, as well. What really made him angry was that Kepa's foolhardiness—which Pilar thought of as a heroic act—was something he himself would have had to pay for; he'd gotten the job for him, it had made him look bad, and even worse, now he'd been left without any source of income, and he knew he'd come to him for help finding something again soon enough. And that's just what happened. Kepa had two dreams. The first was to open a small restaurant with just a few tables in it, where he would offer only a few dishes depending on what was available in the market each day. Abaitua had to admit he was a good cook. His second dream was a bookstore where there would be a space to have a tea or a coffee and read quietly, without the latest bestsellers, so to speak, works of the highest quality, and at low prices, chosen according to his own, personal criteria. Pilar said he should help him. The bookstore seemed the more sensible of the two projects to him, or, more accurately, the least dangerous; he didn't think that Kepa, knowing how generous he was, and in the jazz- and blues-warmed atmosphere he wanted to create, would be up to actually bringing his regular customers the check when the time came or be able to stop buying drinks for everyone around him, as he always did whenever he went into a bar. That didn't mean he didn't see any risks in the bookstore business—he did see them, and they were similar to those in the other business— but they decided in favor of culture, because they found a small storefront near the Ibaeta University campus and, particularly, because Edurne, Kepa's wife, had the same fear as Abaitua and didn't think that having to follow a restaurant schedule was going to be helpful in terms of leading an orderly lifestyle. It was a disappointment for Pilar.

They would never know what might have been of the small restaurant; the bookstore, for its part, was not a success. Being next to the campus was not such a strategic place as he had thought. It turns out that the students who go to the university go to attend classes there, and to play cards in the bar, but don't do anything else there, and they buy their books, and probably everything else, as well, downtown. What's more, as well as choosing the books according to his own criteria for taste and quality, he refused to sell textbooks, saying he hadn't left the world of laboratories just to take part in a bunch of unscrupulous professors' dirty deals, making students buy appalling texts that had been copied and pasted together from who knows where and then sold for their weight in gold. He said pushing cocaine would be nobler. Abaitua's blood boils every time he hears him say that. Kepa being so righteous makes him furious—in the end it's he who will have to pick up the tab for his dignity. He lost a lot of money with that bookstore. And at the same time, he can't help feeling guilty about feeling so bad about losing money that he doesn't really need, knowing, as he does, that Kepa wouldn't hesitate to give him everything he had if he needed it.

But he doesn't have anything. In fact, Kepa and his business ideas make him feel guilty and give him mixed feelings. He thinks that the rant he's on right now about doctors and corruption is a way of putting off asking for money, and he decides to wait until they reach the bar before asking what he wants to talk about. *"Tarugueo"*—a Spanish word for "bribery" not found in the dictionary. Even the most honest doctors find it hard to remain a hundred percent free from the pharmaceutical companies—they finance everything. Even though he agrees, and even though Abaitua knows that if he's talking to him about that revolting practice, it's because he's one of the few who agrees with him, he finds it awkward after a certain point, because he thinks he should do something about it and feels quite incapable of doing anything, and then he inevitably has to defend his profession. Not all doctors let themselves be bought, and at worst, while many try not to prescribe generic drugs—they might prescribe Clamoxyl instead of amoxicillin, for instance—he doesn't think many doctors are corrupt enough to prescribe things that will actually harm their patients' health.

Kepa says he's an innocent abroad. He points at him with his finger. They're still in the bar. All the varnished wood tables are either taken or already laid for lunch. They remain at the bar, sitting on tall stools. Does he think there are many other doctors like him, ready to pass up on gifts? Abaitua finds it even worse being put on the altar of incorruptiblity. He doesn't like Kepa considering him to be so upright. He asks him if he knows anyone else who would say no to a case of 1970 Vega Sicilia Unico. He keeps on bringing that up, and Abaitua regrets having told him and knows he tells everybody about it whether it's relevant to the conversation or not. He decided years ago not to accept gifts. He talked with Pilar, and she agreed, although she also probably thought he was exaggerating. She always says he exaggerates about everything. But he got the impression that the concierge—a passionate socialist from a village in the province of Valladolid—understood what was behind his decision when he told him that he wouldn't be accepting any gifts that Christmas. He said it to him when his son was there, intentionally, so that the boy could see that his father took things seriously when it came to corruption. And then, one morning, the concierge knocked on his door with some urgency and said there was a package for him, a registered delivery of a case of 1970 Vega Sicilia Unico, and he wanted to check if he was going to accept it or not. He confirmed that his refusal was for any and all types of gifts, and with that, he won the concierge's respect forever—he was a man who knew the price of the wine, which was from the same area he grew up in, and he went around telling everyone in the neighborhood how honest Dr. Abaitua was. In fact, it was a profitable decision in terms of feeding his narcissism, but he feels like an impostor whenever Kepa reminds him of it with such admiration. He regrets not having given the case of Vega Sicilia to the concierge, who recently passed away, instead of refusing it. That's almost certainly what Kepa would have done.

The coffee's undrinkable. How can it be that when using practically the same coffee—usually it's Colombian—and the same machines—they're usually Italian—the result is so different from what they serve in Italy, he wonders. He thinks it's the human factor. In bars here, they fill the coffee machine up, press the button for the water, and leave it to look after itself. He pushes his cup of coffee—still full—toward the inside edge of the bar, and Kepa, apparently taking that as a sign, says he's left home.

In order to signal that he wants to pay for the coffees, as usual, he taps the bar with his hand and holds up a bill between his second and third fingers, and Abaitua—very surprised, and quite critical—asks him, rather loudly, why he's left home. He wouldn't have been all that surprised to hear that he'd been kicked out. He's always thought him to be incomprehensibly in love with his wife, an affected woman who describes herself as a "psychopedagogue," has badly dyed blonde hair, talks about French and French television whenever she can, and treats her husband with arrogant disdain. Whenever the two couples have gone out for dinner together, she's always complaining about their lifestyle, probably with good reason, but Abaitua thinks she treats Kepa cruelly, especially that way of hers of interrupting him when he gets affectionate—"Don't try to butter me up with your Andalusian charm"—and reproaching him for his faults in front of whoever they're with at the time. Kepa, on the other hand, always takes great care of her, he loves her, admires her supposedly "good" family, her fine manners, and her perfect French. He's proud of her and, like many husbands in love, of everything around her. He's proud of her family's *baserri*, the oldest in the entire region of Goierri, according to him, and even of her parents—her father is a sharp-minded constructor who's made a bundle off his work, and her mother is a witch whose main claim to fame is making the best garlic and codfish *zurrukutuna* soup in the world. But Abaitua's always thought they take him to be a lazy Andalusian, a carpetbagger who showed up there in the Basque Country and married their daughter for ulterior motives. He's often seen in Kepa's beaten-dog eyes that he's aware of his wife's disdain, but, then, it can't be easy to live with him, and his wife does, in fact, put some order into his life.

Abaitua feels forced to say that everyone has problems, wanting to believe that his leaving home has been no more than a quarrel and that they'll sort it out. Obviously, his 65 mph drive along Mirakruz comes to mind, with Pilar about to open the door and jump out without him stopping. "We all have problems," he says, thinking he'd rather leave the matter at that. Having to listen to personal problems makes him feel dejected, but he has to admit it's a relief to see that going for coffee hasn't had anything to do with getting asked for money.

"I couldn't take any more, it's over."

By looking at him, you'd think he was confirming a piece of news that wasn't particularly agreeable, but his voice reveals another emotion. After saying "it's over" for the second and third times, however, he puts his elbows on the bar and holds his head in his hands, showing deep despair and a lack of energy. Abaitua looks around them, afraid that someone might see that gesture, which he finds so over the top; because they're so close to the hospital, someone might think he's been diagnosed with a deadly illness. He doesn't know whether to put a hand on his shoulder or not. He lifts a hand up, but then decides he's overdoing it as well and decides to move a step away. They both remain silent for a while there by the bar, which now has people all along it, until the barman asks if they want another coffee (he seems to think removing the cups while still full is the most normal thing in the world, as if they'd ordered them simply to savor the bouquet). A way of asking them to leave their spaces free for others. Abaitua takes another step away from the bar. He should have something to say to a friend who's left his wife. What he thinks of saying is that he's done the right thing, that she's ugly and affected. But he doesn't know if he'll take that well and, not having anything else to say, sticks to what he said before: "All of us couples have problems." Which puts him in danger of having to say what he and Pilar's problems are if Kepa asks him. He doesn't ask him; it doesn't look like he's realized what's just been said to him. "It's over, it's over," he repeats who knows how many times, shaking his head, and now Abaitua, afraid he might even start crying, suggests they go outside.

Feeling the sun on their faces after two weeks of nonstop clouds and rain is pleasant, and he suspects that there, in the outdoor seating area where they've just sat down, even with the loud noise of the traffic going by, he'd fall asleep if he closed his eyes, and he rubs his eyelids to keep himself awake, a gesture that could be taken to express grief. "You'll have to think about it carefully." He's sometimes thought he's incapable of having disinterested feelings, of being disinterested—to the extent to which the suffering you feel on account of other people's suffering, or the joy you feel on account of other people's joy, can be considered disinterested—and even, in fact, that he's incapable of really loving.

After a time, things will get better, but he doesn't say what he's really thinking, that he's done the right thing in leaving that ugly, bitter woman once and for all—her hands come to mind, white, fat, pudgy hands, with dimples on the fingers; they'd look like a nun's if it weren't for her long nails exposing her pathetic wish to look like a femme fatale—and that he'll soon see the silver lining and be amazed at having put up with her for so many years.

No, says Kepa, there's no going back. That strong, dark-bearded man with traces of dampness beneath the curly hair that goes down to his eyebrows, his noble stare fixed somewhere above the hill in front of them as he says he's always loved her a great deal, still loves her, but they were unable to live together and he had no alternative but to leave. As someone once said, sometimes when the stronger of the two can't do it, it's the weaker one who has to take the leap and make the decision to walk away.

Apparently, they've begun separation procedures. He's given up his rights to the apartment—he doesn't want to keep anything—and found another in Morlans, where he'll live with his mother until he finds a place for her in a home, because he thinks the time for that's come. He says his old mother living with them had conditioned the relationship, but he doesn't think that's why they've broken up. "What do you think?" Abaitua says once again that he shouldn't make his decisions too quickly. To start with, he doesn't trust the elegant, generous attitude of some men when they give their wives the house when they leave; he thinks it's a consequence of feeling guilty, a way of getting away more quickly and easily. He might regret it later. He's sure that if he's had problems fulfilling all his financial duties before, from now on it won't be any easier for him to run a household, look after his mother, and somehow or another lead an orderly life.

For the moment, at least, Iñaki Abaitua feels more relaxed, because the man who's left home hasn't collapsed, but Kepa doesn't seem to be too happy with the help he's getting, so he decides to invite him to have lunch at Arbelaitz in Miramon to make himself feel less guilty, although, in fact, he'd rather go home to see Pilar. When they quarrel, he feels more acutely the need to be with her, because he thinks that the more time they spend together, the more possible it is that the miracle they need to solve their situation will occur, that one of them will say the saving words or make the saving gesture. It occurs to him, although he doesn't like the idea of using his friend's misfortune, that telling her that Kepa's split up with his wife—"Have you heard Kepa's left home?"—could open the way for them to talk about their own situation. Mentally, he tries out different ways of giving the news: with sorrow; in a neutral register; perhaps playfully—"You know what? Kepa's told the old mule to get lost!"—since Pilar doesn't like her much, either. But he can't imagine her reply, or, more exactly, the options he imagines aren't very encouraging—"Oh, really?" raising her eyes from her Sudoku, or without raising them; "It was about time"; or, even worse, "Why don't you leave, as well?"—and he decides to ask Kepa to lunch. He gladly accepts. Apparently, woodcock season's come earlier than usual this year, and they cook woodcock exceptionally well at Arbelaitz. He seems more cheerful in the car, even though he's still talking about his wife. He says she's been very disagreeable recently, embittered. She has money problems, problems with her mother, other problems with their daughter, who's getting bad grades at school, but, then, who doesn't have problems. Apparently, her problems weren't the problem. What he couldn't stand was how jealous she'd gotten recently. She was always watching him, interrogating him, observing him, going through his pockets, and saying any negative thing that came into her mind. Until he got fed up. At the most unexpected moment and in the least appropriate

80

place—"Which is how these things usually happen," he says—he blew up and told her to go to hell. Fortunately, their daughter wasn't there with them.

Now he's talking about the breakup calmly, as if it were quite a far-off thing that had happened to someone else, and meanwhile, Iñaki Abaitua puts all his efforts into driving, because he always gets it wrong at the traffic circle and ends up at the private hospital or the TV station. When they get there, he has to go around twice to make sure he takes the right exit. But Kepa doesn't mind him getting lost, or, at least, not so much; he doesn't get nervous and takes it stride— "Great! We're on another adventure," he usually says—and he agrees with him when he says that there aren't enough street signs and the ones there are are badly positioned. (Unlike Pilar: "I don't believe it, we're lost again!" Et cetera.)

HE'S NOT GOING TO ORDER WOODCOCK. They usually serve it with the head, perhaps so that the customers can be sure that they're being given an authentic specimen of the expensive long-beaked bird, and the practice increases his sensation that they're eating a protected species. He'd rather they left the few remaining birds up in the mountains. And the flavor, supposedly game, is very particular—unequalled, of course—but seems too sweet to him, morbid you might even say, close to the taste that human flesh is said to have. Kepa says it's because they don't take their intestines out when they cook them. The intestines of the lady of the woods— that's apparently what they call them in French, *dame de bois*—are always clean, because they defecate every time they take flight. That's what Kepa says. And he will order it. He's against hunting them, but when it comes down to it, they're dead, and he thinks the flavor that Abaitua finds "morbid" is exquisite. He rubs his hands together with the pleasure of anticipating the food, and his salivary gland is probably producing enough glycoproteins to finish off all the woodcock in the entire Basque Country. He says that their name in Basque—*oilagorra*, literally "deaf rooster"—came about as the result of a misunderstanding: they're thought to be deaf, because they only take flight when their predators are right upon them. But in fact they have very sharp hearing. For the time being, it seems Kepa has forgotten about his emotional problems and is ready to talk about anything, the life of the woodcock or the evil sales strategies of laboratories.

The *maître d'* and the waitresses—there are no waiters—look after them without being over attentive, treating them in an elegant and comfortable way, as is usual in most good Basque restaurants. They're all Basque speakers, and Abaitua is grateful to be able to use Basque to enjoy such a primal activity. What he hates most is having to use Spanish in restaurants and bars—he doesn't like hearing it at church, either—and if he had to choose, he'd rather be guaranteed that he could use Basque in those places rather than in places where he doesn't feel so much at home, in bureaucratic settings, for instance. After choosing the wine and placing their order, Kepa rolls up the sleeves of his thick sweater, crosses his thick, muscular arms on the table, and, moving his head forward, asks if Abaitua wants to know how it all happened.

The story he tells isn't as intimate as he had feared. He had gone to London to look for a first edition of Axular's *Gero*, because a contact of his had told him that there was a copy of the classic Basque book in an old bookstore near the British Museum. It was a lead worth checking out—the last copy sold had gone for thirty million pesetas to the government of Navarre. He could sell it for a tidy sum there in the Basque Country, among other things because the public institutions would compete for it, and he thought he could buy it for much less than what he was going to get for it. He went to the bookstore and had a first look with great discretion, without asking for it directly, because he didn't want the owner to realize, if his information was right, how much what he had was worth. He went there two or three days in a row and bought several interesting books while he was looking for *Gero*, among others an illustrated Escoffier cookbook and a book of poems by Cristina Rossetti with mother-of-pearl covers and gold-edged pages, which was quite expensive, he had to admit, but very beautiful indeed. But he still hadn't found any trace of the book, and one day, when he was having a beer with the owner, with whom he'd become friends, he opened up to him and admitted that he was Basque (until then he had made use of his curly hair and dark skin to claim that he was Greek, so that if he did find *Gero*, he would be able to buy it without showing any special interest and, therefore, at a good price) and that he had been looking for a book written in his old language, with no other aim than that of collecting a piece of his poor heritage. But after treating him to several pints of beer and buying more books off him, he found out that the man knew nothing about *Gero*, Basque literature, or, come to that, Basque itself, and even though he kindly let him look all over the bookstore, there wasn't a trace of Axular's book.

He was disappointed on his way back, although not completely, because the bookseller with whom he'd become good friends and who didn't have a copy of *Gero* could be a good contact in the future for old import-export books (Abaitua was dismayed to hear that they were going to talk more about that later), and after spending two days in the Foyles bookstore, he had managed to find some interesting books for his store.

He slowly nibbles at the woodcock bones without any inhibition, and his fleshy lips look lustful as they shine with oil. Iñaki Abaitua can imagine the story he'd rather not hear. He'd told his wife he was going to London to do a great piece of business, he'd spent a lot of money for nothing, come back empty-handed, and she'd gotten angry. That's more or less what he says, adding some details about Edurne's pathological jealousy. When he arrived back at Loiu airport, she started in on him rather than asking him any questions, mumbling that he hadn't gone there alone and that he was lying when he said once again that the only thing he'd done there had been to see the Tate and the National Gallery and that one evening he'd gone to have a look around Soho, which is more wholesome than even Gipuzkoa Plaza since Thatcher had it cleaned up, and he hadn't spoken with any women except for checkout girls and waitresses.

Edurne is frightening when she gets going, he says. He believes him. Her dyed hair, wrinkled mouth, fat hands, lumpy, dimpled fingers, and long nails . . . She insisted that she wanted to see what he'd bought at Harrods, because he was carrying a bag from there. Some woman had given it to him as soon as he got onto the plane, when the one he was carrying—probably a Foyles bag—burst and all his books fell onto the floor. It was no good. That bag was the proof that he hadn't told her everything about London. Perhaps she felt frustrated when she saw the Harrods bag because she thought he'd brought her a cashmere sweater, but in fact, when he told her that he'd brought her a very special present and showed her the book by

Cristina Rossetti, she almost had a fit. She said that she couldn't buy a decent dress for their daughter and there he was throwing money away on books, completely ignoring the fact that he had gone to London precisely to earn some money, for work. He interrupted his story and held his hands open in front of his shoulders, like a priest at offertory, looked at his woodcock, which was cut open sideways, to see if there was anything left to be nibbled, but all the bones were clean, and then he crossed his arms and admitted that he, too, had been nervous; what with one thing and another, he hadn't had a smoke for more than three hours. He went up to a tobacconist kiosk, because he didn't have a light, Edurne kept on grumbling behind him that her moneyless existence was miserable, that she had to put up with his mother and everything else, a long list of things, and by pure chance, although he didn't realize until Edurne nudged him with her shoulder and said someone had just said hello to them, they walked past the woman who had given him the Harrods bag as he got onto the plane, but by the time he turned around, she was facing the other way and he was looking at a man with bulging eyes who was walking next to her. He knew the woman by her coat, and the man—loaded with suitcases and Harrods bags, his nose and drooping moustache looking as theatrical as his glasses—stared at him.

He says there was no way of convincing her that he'd met the woman on the flight back and that, in fact, he didn't really know her, she'd just given him another bag when his broke, he didn't know her name or where she lived and he'd hardly even heard her voice.

Kepa says he doesn't even dare repeat the things she said to him. As well as being a failure, he was lazy, and a womanizer. You can't imagine the things that came out of her mouth, and everyone at the airport was looking at them. As a simple matter of dignity, and because he couldn't take any more humiliation, he told her he wasn't going back with her, he'd take a taxi by himself, and she, who seemed to be so shaken up because she thought he'd been with another woman in London, said coldly that she thought that was great, he had two days to get his and his mother's things out of the house—after that she'd leave them outside the front door.

So he'd only walked out to a certain extent. It looked like it was the wife who wanted to get rid of him. Perhaps her mother-in-law being hospitalized had given her the chance to see what it would be like to live without dependents. Kepa looks depressed once again, and Abaitua, to cheer him up, thinks about telling him that he's been lucky, that he should be happy to have gotten rid of his miserable wife, that he'll soon remember all the horrible things she said to him, but he's worried about what Kepa's going to do in his current situation and whether, with his disabled mother, he'll be able to organize himself a bit; it looks like a tough way forward.

They both keep quiet. They've had a fair amount to drink, a bottle and a half of 2001 Artadi. *En Euskadi, vino de Euskadi*, as the advertising slogan goes—in the Basque Country, Basque wine. Suddenly Abaitua feels a rush of contentment from his full stomach and the wine. It's because of the realization that Pilar is nothing like Kepa's wife. He wouldn't have been able to put up with a glum, bitter woman like Edurne controlling him for so many years. Obviously, he isn't Kepa. He's often thought that Pilar could do with a more Bohemian man than himself—more open, happier, not so work-obsessed, less dominated by his own superego. She would have been able to get away and travel more with a man like that. As long as there were no money problems, he thought right away. But he's not sure about that, either. Sometimes he thinks he knows Pilar really well, and other times he thinks he doesn't know her at all.

Abaitua isn't going to have dessert.

The customers at many of the tables are speaking to the waitresses in Basque, but then they speak among themselves in Spanish. Like the gentry in times gone by, only speaking in Basque with dogs and country maids. Abaitua would like to know what the waitresses make of that habit; unlike the maids back then, they have a perfect mastery of Spanish, in many cases they speak it much better than Basque, and in lots of restaurants it's the language they speak as soon as they move away from the customers' tables. He draws the conclusion that, at least to an extent, the tendency to move toward Spanish is because there's always someone who doesn't know Basque and, inevitably, that obliges everybody at the table to speak in Spanish, and at the same time, because you only need simple vocabulary to be able to speak with dogs and waitresses. So speaking in Basque in restaurants is something of a ritual, like using Latin at church years ago.

Kepa is going to have dessert—the warm hazelnut cake he ordered at the start and which he likes so much. He himself, though, had trouble fastening his belt in the tightest hole that morning, and he wouldn't be able to stand having to put the prong in the second one. His norms say that belts have to be fastened in the first hole and the loose end has to go through at least two belt loops. Pilar says he's hysterical when he complains that he's putting on weight.

"How's Pilar?"

He asks him suddenly, as if he knew Abaitua was thinking about her. He should tell his friend that they haven't slept together since he got angry when he was driving them back from Biarritz, punched the steering wheel, and they nearly went off the road. Obviously, he realized that day that he was driving her up the wall, but the strangest thing is that he doesn't remember why. It was probably because they were bored stiff in Biarritz. He got angry because when they were going to bed, she complained about his insistence on going to sleep with the radio on, and he said it would be better if they slept apart. He tells him she's fine. She's resigned herself to the fact that they've been shutting her out of work at the clinic, to the fact that Alzola doesn't let her do any operations, and that all the partners are against her because she's her father's favorite.

"You're really lucky."

He doesn't ask him to explain why he's said that. It's obvious—it's because he's got Pilar. He sees him making that typical gesture of his, rolling the sleeves of his sweater up for no reason at all. He lifts his left hand to call the waitress. It seems Kepa's going to celebrate being single again with an armagnac and a Cuban cigar. Abaitua's envious. He doesn't smoke, but he does like good smokers' rituals and the smell of good tobacco and cedar. He takes the opportunity to ask for the check, because, suddenly, he wants to leave. That often happens to him.

Kepa savors the armagnac like an expert, and it looks to Abaitua as if his lips, shiny once more, are made of elastic. When the head waiter appears with the bill, Abaitua says commandingly that it's his treat and he's going to pay. He thinks it's pathetic when people who've eaten together put on a show about wanting to pay the bill—like children in the past who were brought up to refuse extra pocket money or candy until they were offered them three times—and their acting skills go even further and take the scene to its limit, under the waiter's resigned observation, until the latter brings out the classic solution: "I can split the check for you if you like." He's in favor of splitting bills (something

Basques hate very much), because otherwise the richest person, who's also normally the most tight-fisted, comes out winning, and the person who most needs to protect his or her dignity—the poorest person, in other words—has to put on the biggest show of wanting to pay and ends up being the loser. But when Kepa says he wants to pay, he's telling the truth; he likes treating people, he doesn't use credit cards, and he's always quick at pulling money out of the chaos he carries around in his pockets. Abaitua says, "I invited you, and what's more, I've got more money." He's half serious, half joking, and Kepa has to cede to his strong reasoning.

"I like Pilar," he says, putting the end of his cigar under his nose to smell it better, spinning it around between his thumb and forefinger. Pilar says the same thing about him. She likes Kepa. Abaitua remembers the day the three of them got together to sign a bank guarantee for the bookstore. He warned Pilar they might end up losing money, but she didn't mind. Pilar answered exactly what Abaitua was thinking: Kepa would do anything for them. As well as signing the guarantee, Abaitua gave him some cash for him to cover any initial bureaucratic incidentals. It was around midday, and Kepa said that he'd heard about a little bar in the neighborhood of Antigua that had good seafood. He'd booked a table for them to go and celebrate, but Abaitua couldn't make it, he had an operation scheduled to remove a uterine fibroid that afternoon. But in the end it wasn't a long operation. He got home by mid-afternoon, and Pilar still hadn't gotten back. She arrived quite late in the evening, with red cheeks and bright eyes, and seeing her like that, he half-jokingly asked if she'd had a good time, to which she replied so seriously that it was comical. She said, with great conviction, that he'd treated her like a queen. He'd taken her to a very normal looking bar, and they'd been served wonderful oysters and barnacles and an unimaginably good Chablis Grand Cru. Pilar knows how to appreciate good seafood and a good Chablis Grand Cru. One of the things he most liked about her was that she knew how to appreciate products of the land and the sea, and just then, he allowed himself to indulge the not very probable idea that those red cheeks were holding the warmth of a pillow. He's not sure why, but he didn't think she would betray him, and probably because of that he thought it would be completely bearable to him if she'd gone to bed with Kepa, it wouldn't be more significant than the dessert she'd had after the seafood they'd eaten and washed down, as she specifically pointed out, with Chablis Grand Cru. Perhaps the worst thing would be that it was his money that paid for all the fun. Pilar used her toes to take off the high-heeled shoes that she so seldom wears and lay flat out on the sofa with the amused look of bliss that good wine gives you. It didn't occur to him that she might want a bit of fun in bed after the banquet, and in any case, it wasn't part of his routine to make love before dinner. At the time, he didn't know just how alone she felt and how much she needed to be treated as a queen.

"I'M AMAZED BY HOW MUCH INFLUENCE luck has in our lives." They're on their way back now, in the car, at the three-way intersection on the road that runs from the hospitals to Hernani, and Abaitua, wanting to know if he's said that grand-sounding sentence in all seriousness, looks at Kepa. There's no indication that he was speaking with anything other than total seriousness, and he adds, "I find the influence of luck fascinating, I really do." And Abaitua, without having to ask him what he's talking about, knows it's a reference to his breakup with Edurne. The thing is, if that woman hadn't offered him a Harrods bag, perhaps they wouldn't be splitting up. He thinks that's what set the whole thing off. If it had been a bag from another store, or better still, from a bookstore, or just a bag, nothing would have happened. Or if the Foyles bag hadn't burst. Or if he hadn't bought anything. Abaitua makes him keep his window open even though his cigar is out. He finds it hard to keep up his ban on smoking in the car, but he's firm. He knows he has to be strict with Kepa, like with dogs, if he doesn't want him to invade his territory. "Or if you didn't smoke," Abaitua says, and Kepa nods his head. "Or if I didn't smoke," he mumbles.

At the last moment—he's tired, and he wants to be with Pilar—he decides to go straight home without stopping at the hospital. He pulls over across the street from the hospital, without turning the engine off, so that Kepa can get out. But he doesn't seem to want to, even though he's opened the door. He holds his arm out to keep the door open, as if not knowing whether to say something or not, and afraid that he might be about to start talking about money, Abaitua prepares himself. But there's no reason to worry. After a long silence, he says that he's completely convinced that when the woman in the plane conditioned his fate by giving him the Harrods bag, she also determined hers, and Abaitua calms down when he hears that but then feels guilty for having thought ill of his friend. When he asks him why he says that, Kepa replies it's just a hunch. The last time he saw her, she looked full of anxiety. That's what he says, and Abaitua steps on the accelerator a little to encourage him to go. Eventually he gets out. He'll do what he can to arrange for Kepa's mother to remain in the hospital for another week, that way he'll be able to get everything in the house ready for her. He also says the two of them haven't gone out together in ages. There's a long weekend coming up soon, and they agree to talk about getting together.

PILAR IS SITTING ON THE SOFA, leaning down over the newspaper that's laid out on the coffee table, her usual unergonomic position, arms folded and her chest almost resting on her knees. She's doing a Sudoku puzzle, giving it all her attention, she's very, very good at them. If a particular type of intelligence is required to do Sudoku, then Pilar's is very highly developed. Abaitua, on the other hand, doesn't like games involving math, they require a lot of effort and he doesn't find them gratifying, because he's not very quick-minded, he'd say.

Hello. She replies with the same word after looking at him for a moment. She hardly lifts her head from her Sudoku. No more than a look—she could be thinking about something else or be bored—a look that starts at Abaitua's face and goes down, evenly and quickly, to his feet, and then goes up again, quicker, without stopping anywhere, but then it does stop, on his face, for an immeasurably short moment, and although she seems more uninterested that inquisitive, he gets the impression she's seen him on the inside as well as on the outside. He normally keeps still in that type of situation, feeling as though he's being scanned, until she looks back at the newspaper and away from him. Then, when she's no longer looking at him, she tells him he has a little smudge of toothpaste on one side of his mouth that he missed when looking in the mirror, a loose thread on his pants, and his shirt collar is sticking out over his jacket. And she normally tells him about things like that, but he's sure she sees other things that she doesn't tell him about, as well.

So she's staring at her Sudoku puzzle again when she answers hello. It isn't a happy hello or a sad one, just neutral—a little curt, perhaps. He decides to ask her how her day's going. Nothing special. After leaving the notary's office, she helped her father with some papers. He hardly has any operations scheduled. At one time, the clinic had plenty to go on with just maternity cases, but the fall in birth rates from the sixties onward, the ever greater costs required for the new type of care that an increasingly well-informed society demanded, and advances in the public health system put an end to the old man's days of making a living off births, and he had to look for new ways to keep the business afloat. To do that, he relied on his other son-in-law, Yago Alzola the neurosurgeon, and the latter's brother, the ear, nose, and throat specialist. He sent them to the United States, and when they came back, they were able to promote the techniques they had learned there quite successfully, to the point of securing a virtual monopoly on them, which allowed them to stay in business. Kepa says you can't turn your back on Abaitua's brother-in-law without him slicing it open for you. He's operated on each and every slipped disc there's ever been, the operable as well as the inoperable ones, and even ones that didn't exist, and his brother's laryngectomized half of Gipuzkoa; they've really amortized the techniques they learned. But they didn't pass those techniques on, or keep their skills and procedures up to date, and their good run is over. When Pilar tells him that things are going worse and worse, he doesn't point out to her that he had long ago predicted as much himself. In fact, she doesn't give him much chance to say anything about it, and maybe her "and what have you done?"—which she asks without raising her eyes from her Sudoku—is a way of avoiding the subject. He prefers it that way. He says he's had lunch with Kepa, tells her where and what they've eaten—she pays more attention to that, he thinks—and that they're thinking of going up to the mountains on the next long weekend, which is a way of giving her forewarning, if not of asking for her permission, but he doesn't mention the fact that he's split up with his wife. Now it seems too late for him to do that, it was a piece of news to tell at the beginning, when he first came into the living room, saying, "You know what? Kepa's left home." But he remembers his absurd idea—absurd because he doesn't think she would actually ever say it—that she might say "and why don't you leave, too?"

Obviously, he himself could be the one to say, "Kepa's left home, and I'm going to do the same."

He tells her about his day at the hospital, about the psychiatrist who keeps prescribing tricyclic antidepressants, the sixty-year-old woman with breast cancer who's refused to have a mastectomy because she's afraid her husband might reject her. Pilar listens to him while she does her Sudoku, and as if to let him know that she's listening, she says something from time to time. She classifies the woman who doesn't want to lose her breast as an idiot. "Although I guess I'd have to see what her husband's like," she lets slip. He thinks of María Amor and, wanting to inject a bit of humor into things, says she's lost her pimp, but Pilar doesn't remember that story, even though he reminds her about the Dominican prostitute's drug-pushing pimp with AIDS who let his brother get killed. "I would remember that." But Abaitua is sure that he did tell her about them, and also about himself and his friend the infectious disease specialist talking about their theoretical moral dilemma, and above all, he remembers that when he told her about the Dominican woman being dominated and then said that some women have a weakness for psychopaths, Pilar hadn't liked it one bit. He wants to remind her of it, so that she'll say he's right—some women confuse the characteristics of psychopaths with the marks of a person being energetic, daring, and resolute when it comes to decision-making, and that's why they like psychopathic men, because they make them feel secure. "Do you really think us women like psychopaths?" She said exactly the same thing to him last time. He leaves it at that, without taking the trouble to insist that he said "some women" and not all of them. He sees that the skin on her neck has loosened a little, but he still finds her beautiful. Seeing her looking so beautiful, so close, and also so far away, he thinks, as he used to in the past, that he'd like to ask her what she's thinking. "As if I'd tell you!" she used to answer. Sometimes he thinks he can read her mind. He wants to play at that. "I bet you you're thinking about this or about that," and he has the sensation he's got it right, even though she always denies it. "Poor man, you always think I'm thinking about you," she once answered, and he had to admit she was right—all the thoughts he imagined were about him, he never imagined any other possibilities. Now, he could say to her, "You know what? When I was having lunch with Kepa, it occurred to me that you might have slept with him." What would her answer be? She'd probably tell him not to be stupid. And she would have said just that to him—"Don't be stupid"—if he had ever mentioned, back in the day, that he suspected her of having done the same thing with the young neurosurgeon, whom he felt such solidarity for, because he was being shut out at the clinic, too. And yet later on, he found out that he had been right about that all along.

He decides to retire to the studio. Before, when Pilar used to do crosswords instead of Sudokus, and with great skill, as well, at least she used to ask him for help from time to time, mostly when some word about sports came up; it's a subject she doesn't know much about. He, in turn, would ask her for clues, such as how many letters there were in the word, whether she had any of them already, and Pilar would make room for him on the sofa for him to sit next to her, letting him see the crossword. He thinks Pilar liked doing things together—crosswords, at least. Sudoku doesn't give you a chance to lend a hand. It's a more autistic activity, to put it that way.

So he says he's retiring to the studio. He's taken on the responsibility for coordinating a perinatal survey that's going to be carried out by various hospitals. His MD thesis was about something similar, although on a different scale. He tells her a bit about it, and although Pilar does seem to be listening, she doesn't ask him any questions ("What hospitals? Spanish ones? Foreign ones?"), and he deduces from this that she's not very interested in the subject.

THEY CALL THE SMALL ROOM with the glass-doored cherrywood bookcases all around it "the studio." There's a simple table there— a board resting on two trestles that he's used since he was a student. His MD thesis is on the table, leather-bound in two volumes with gold lettering: "Descriptive Study of the Perinatal Area." In the more than one thousand pages of each volume, he tried to describe the then-current situation of care during pregnancy, childbirth, and the immediate postnatal period, a situation so terrible that death rates were two or three times higher than the rates in the rest of Europe. He worked nonstop on it, day and night, throughout 1975 and 1976, with innocent passion, truly believing that his research would be a real wake-up call to people and that, thanks to his influence, essential changes would be implemented to prevent such absurd deaths and grave accidents for newly born children.

He'd been on a work placement several years earlier at Port-Royal Hospital in Paris, and there he had met the neonatologist Alexandre Minkowski. Professor Minkowski was Jewish, the son of a Jewish psychiatrist, and according to his memoires, not a very good Catholic—*Un juif pas très catholique* was the title had had given them. He was highly educated and a decent yachtsman, had white hair, was swarthy, as elegant-looking as an Agnelli, and he had a good figure. He was very smart, and fierce and demanding when it came to denouncing the appalling lack of good care in matters connected with childbirth.

Abaitua will never forget the day he met him. Abaitua was part of a group of foreign resident doctors Minkowski had brought together in order to show them the services he provided. The professor appeared wearing a high-necked, short-sleeved white jacket with buttons up one side. Without saying a word, he took them across a wide, luminous hall to the intensive care ward, where there were dozens of premature babies, some looking like fetuses, with white caps on their heads, connected to wires and tubes. An assistant explained the various devices to them and the jobs of all the people around who looked after them. It was all flawless and transparent white—the hum of the respirators, the beeping of the control panels, the silent caregivers wearing isolation suits—and it looked like something out of a science fiction movie. It was an excellent setup, there was no doubt about that, one of the best ICUs for newborns in the whole of Europe, if not the best. Minkowski, who had not said a word until then, stood in front of the group and pointed at the incubation ward behind him with both thumbs. "Some of the children here are about to die; others will survive and be disabled with incurable brain damage for the rest of their lives. But no more than half of them should even be here connected up to these excellent, expensive machines at all; the other half should have come into the world without having to face any particular risks." Those words were like a revelation for Abaitua, he'll never forget them. He knew, of course, that ignorance about how to care for pregnant women (everyone's ignorance, people's in general and doctors' in particular), negligence (everybody's, once again), and malpractice had consequences in the birthing room, but he had never seen it so clearly, in such a tangible way.

To coin a phrase, he saw the light. If you think about it, not paying attention to a pregnant woman's blood pressure, for instance, is more than just average negligence, it is also a terrible crime, as terrible as watching a child playing on the roof of a ten-story building without doing anything about it. Abaitua learned that from Minkowski. He spent the rest of his time there reading the professor's works and often met up with him. He was a man it was easy to talk and get on with. He used to say that medicine progressed in opposition to common sense and equality and that in the same way that greater priority was given to the Concorde's record times— these were the blissful days of super-aviation—at the expense of the daily public transport that thousands of normal people needed every day, adventurous medical explorers were rewarded while sectors that were of more importance to people's health were ignored.

This was his message: instead of putting your trust in scientific and technical formulas to miraculously cure illnesses, humbler but more efficient measures to prevent those illnesses from occurring should be applied. Minkowski was familiar with the state of pregnancy and birth care all over the world, and he often spoke about China, where rest was prescribed just as seriously and precisely as medicines were—all pregnant women had their blood pressure taken every eight days, and complete rest was ordered if their readings were above 120/80. With that measure alone, which eradicated eclampsia, they reduced their previous mortality rate, which had been similar to nineteenth century Europe's, to the same level as Sweden's, which was the lowest in the world.

He's never in his life been as fanatical about anything else. He dedicated himself heart and soul, making a great effort with his descriptive research of the lamentable situation: there was no system in place to detect problematic pregnancies, women had fewer than half the number of checkups as in other European countries, had a third of all European cesarean births, mortality statistics were suspiciously connected with the time of birth and the particular medical establishment in which it took place, and there seemed to be a strict following in the public sector of the Biblical stricture "in sorrow thou shalt bring forth children," leading to a lucrative market for addressing the resulting problems in the private sector . . .

He received the highest possible marks on his research, but it didn't help to change anything. He hadn't even said anything doctors didn't already know. Of course they knew that only seeing patients five times during their pregnancies—that was the average—meant a higher death rate, and even if they didn't actually know it, they did sense that leaving the simple, easy care that low-risk pregnancies required to midwives and nurses would mean losing a source of income for their private practices. They also knew that many of the children who came into the world drunk on their mothers' sodium thiopental—in cute little maternity rooms in free-standing clinics with pretty gardens planted all around them, without any safety measures for the newly born, induced at whatever moment it was deemed most convenient—would end up being wrapped in aluminum foil and taken by taxi to a hospital to be reanimated, always arriving too late. They knew it, and some of them even denied their patients the chance of turning to a hospital, instead hiding the damage done by their own lack of pediatric assistance in little cots, blue ones for mentally disabled boys and pink ones if they were girls. He had simply put the tragedy into numbers: if all births took place at the Arantzazu Hospital (although it was nothing overly extraordinary, it was the best supplied service on offer), that would be enough to avoid one death in five and to reduce the sickness rate by sixty percent. Some of his colleagues who congratulated him for his excellent grades suspected that, but they had to amortize their investments. He understood them, but what really got him was that many of the people who accepted the status quo were fierce opponents of abortion, and of contraception, as well, and nevertheless they were condemning so many children to death or to life as vegetables. And not as an unfortunate but sadly necessary evil in the interest of helping their offspring, but in order to happily make their own fortunes.

Things have changed. Inevitably, due to cultural, economic, and demographic developments, and now the measures to stop eclampsia and fetal suffering in China, which Minkowski had so admired, seemed old hat in terms of progress. It's always been like that. We don't realize what healthy diets our grandparents had until we've filled ourselves up with sugars and saturated fat. He would have liked to be able to talk to him about all that, but he never crossed paths with him again.

"GOOD NIGHT," SAYS PILAR, sticking her head around the door. Without any special feeling, as if she were greeting someone in the neighborhood she doesn't know all that well. She's wearing a robe with wide blue and gray stripes on top of her white pajamas. She always wears pajamas, except on very rare occassions. He remembers her standing on top of the bed, lifting up one side of her nightdress, comically imitating a model. But he can't picture the nightdress. It's an isolated image, he doesn't know what larger scene it's from.

Port-Royal isn't far from the Luxembourg Gardens, at least not in terms of Paris distances. He used to take a book and a sandwich and go there at midday, and that's where he met Bárbara, outside the hospital, even though she worked in the laboratory. She was a pharmacist. One day he worked up the courage to sit down on the same bench as her. She spoke Spanish, because she had lived in Chile with her ex-husband, an engineer who'd worked for the Allende government in the copper mines. Apparently, one of Allende's biggest mistakes had been to bring in progressive-thinking, incompetent engineers from France, who then lived in Chile like kings, in order to get rid of the right-wing engineers. She'd also lived in India and Australia. A few days after sharing sandwiches on the bench in the Luxembourg Gardens, Bárbara received him at her home, which was near the gardens in the Place Pablo Picasso, at the intersection of Montparnasse and Raspail. She had blond hair—lots of it—and lively, very shiny blue eyes. The most special thing about her appearance, what he remembers best, is her mouth. Her lips, while not thin, didn't stand out; her upper lip was flat, with no dip in the middle, it didn't form a bow shape, what's called a Cupid's bow in many languages. Her teeth were white and healthy, but her upper canine teeth were longer than her incisors, and their lower edge was straight, as if they'd been filed down. He used to joke to her that she had a perfect mouth for speaking French. He doesn't know why he thought that. He thinks they were happy during the months they spent together, but his memory of them is faint. He remembers one time, having been invited by some friends to La Baule, when they didn't get out of bed all weekend. Spending the previous evening in a wine shop picking out a bottle to bring along as a gift. Going down for dinner late on the second evening and having their friends start telling jokes about that famed Spanish passion, and her not liking it. He remembers that she used to put everything into salads, which she made as tidily as if she had been working in the laboratory, and that although he'd forbidden her to do so, because it embarrassed him, he'd find her washing the underwear he'd hidden away. Not much more than that. Perhaps he wouldn't even remember her face if it weren't for a photograph of her he keeps in a book. It's unlikely anyone will ever find it there. Bárbara gave him the book and dedicated it on the first page "à *mon amour basque*"—to my Basque love. There's no date. Though there is on the back of the photo— "oct. 72," and nothing else. She wrote him a letter or two, which he didn't reply to and hasn't kept. She really is beautiful, or that's what he thinks, at any rate. When his stay there finished, he just said goodbye to her. It was time for him to go home.

Pilar has brushed her teeth, and she's now probably putting on different lotions in front of the mirror. He decides to wait until he hears her close her bedroom door before going into the bathroom himself. He'll take a Noctamid, just in case the journey back to the past that turning over the pages of his research work has sent him on keeps him awake. In fact, he doesn't like it much when he thinks back to his youth. He used to say that the two thick leather-bound volumes he's now put back on the shelf make him feel sorry for himself, feel pity for the young man who wrote that work with such enthusiasm, putting in so much effort and sacrifice, and all for nothing. Even if he had worked on it day and night, there was nothing admirable about that young man's feelings, that arrogant young man's feelings; his dream hadn't been so much to stop newly born babies' lives from being uselessly wasted, it was more about having *his* contributions, *his* work, bring it about.

3

THESE ARE SÁNDOR MÁRAI'S EXACT WORDS: "A woman taught me that the real writer's disease is that which prevents the artist from obtaining satisfaction through anything other than his creative process."

Julia has picked up the Hungarian's book by chance and is mechanically transcribing the lines that Martin has underlined. Many are about writing and about death, and while some of them are not without interest, she's asking herself what the purpose of telling things with such precision is, whether it's the author listing the books he's read or recounting his routine visits to the hospital to see his wife, who he says is fading away "too slowly." What makes him think that anyone's going to be interested in what time he went to bed or what time he turned off the light on whatever day in 1988? What is it that makes his experiences special and worth telling people about? She'd like to ask Martin, but he wouldn't like the question.

Here he is. She doesn't realize he's there until he comes up to the table, and she wonders if he hasn't tiptoed up to her, like a boss trying to catch a lazy worker. He's dressed to go out, wearing his raw silk jacket and everything; it's a fine piece of clothing, but unfortunately it's far too big for him. She asks where he's going and remembers, too late, and because of his look of resignation, that he has an appointment with the doctor. "Do you want me to go with you?" She knows he doesn't; as well as jealously guarding his intimacy, she would get in the way of the need he feels to demonstrate his seductive skills wherever he goes, hospital or morgue, with any type of audience, men, women, old people, and children. But she has to ask him anyway. "I'll go alone," he says with dignified regret, knowing that she won't insist. If she did, picking up her bag and putting on her jacket, he'd stop her in panic, saying it was a waste of her time and, in any case, she always went to her gynecologist by herself, as well.

He tells her he'll go alone, using a voice that means that he'll face up to adversity by himself, and after looking at his watch, he says that the young American's coming to bring over her things—fortunately he doesn't call her *the penthouse girl* this time—so he hopes to be back soon, "unless something's up, of course." To reduce the drama of the situation, she asks him what might be up.

Prostates have become a regular topic of conversation with people around him ever since screening tests became so commonplace, probably because the men he knows are of an age that puts them at risk, and the women he knows have partners who are, as well. They're also moaners and cowards. It's because of that, and because of their instinct to compete, that they mention their PSA levels so much, and, of course, the cruelest attack, having their anuses fingered, really humiliating even if they do talk about it jokingly, and she's often thought of telling them it's their just desserts, if only as payment for the tasteless jokes about women's routine gynecological examinations they're always telling, as if they were the most natural thing in the world.

When she reads Márai's words at the end of the book—"I'm ashamed of writing now"—she regrets what she thought of him a little earlier.

OPENING MARTIN'S COMPUTER SECRETLY makes her feel bad, she notices the tension in the middle of her chest. She thinks robbers must feel something like that when they're opening safes. It's strange that she still has that painful sensation even when she knows there's no risk of being caught red-handed. It's because she feels guilty, of course. It wouldn't occur to Martin that she would do that, among other things because, in theory, there's a password for opening the computer, and also because he doesn't think she looks at other people's things. Most people would think of that as a virtue, not being nosey about other people's things, but he reproaches her for it, says it demonstrates a lack of interest in others, a lack of affection. So, not being afraid of her looking things over, he leaves his index cards covered in notes, as well as the pages he prints from time to time for correcting, lying around just anywhere; she's sure that if the computer has a password, it's only because the IT guy gave it one as a matter of course. Not that he was a very skillful IT guy; although the computer freezes if you put in the wrong password after starting it up, Julia's discovered that clicking Enter is enough to get it going. She finds it hard not to tell Martin what she's discovered, especially when he talks about "his" IT guy, but she renounces that source of satisfaction in exchange for being able to check how he's getting on with his work from time to time. No more than that, just to see what he's working on, to know if he's making progress, rather in the same way she likes to check on her son's grades at school. All she really does is confirm what she already knows; Martin's changes of mood reflect how his work's going with great accuracy. Although she has to admit that there is another reason that encourages her to check up on him: she wants to see if he's written anything about her, if he's made use of anything from their private life. She can't really say she reads anything, it's more of a quick look to see if Flora Ugalde—the wife of Faustino Iturbe, the writer and main character of his latest stories—makes an appearance. She has some of her same physical characteristics—the most noticeable being the mole on her jugular fossa—and some of her same psychological traits in the things she says, as well; she's becoming her twin, so to speak. In any case, what she could swear to is that she never looks at anything apart from what he's currently writing, and of course she never looks at his mail. It wouldn't be a lie if she said it's because of ethical reasons, but she can't deny that she finds looking at his intimate things revolting—that's a very strong word for it, but she can't think of anything more appropriate—and the fear that she might come across something that would disappoint her discourages her from looking even more. She'd rather not know.

The Man in Front of the Mirror. That's the title of what he's working on. The main character, a writer whose name has not appeared in the twenty pages he's written so far, is seriously ill with a deadly disease whose name has likewise not yet been mentioned. He's receiving treatment that will slow the disease but not cure him, and he will continue to receive it for at least as long as it can stop the illness from spreading, and for that reason, the effects of the medication might do him more harm than the disease itself. The doctors have set the length of the treatment at one year (most likely), depending on his ability to withstand its harmful effects, and at most (less likely) two years. The man, due to his pessimistic nature, fears the worst and does not believe he has the strength to face up to his own physical decay; he spends most of the day in front of the bathroom mirror (which is, presumably, where the title comes from), watching and waiting to see when some trace of the decay will show on his face. He pays special attention to his eyes' connective tissue, because he thinks it looks swollen, like his gums, and that worries him, because while he was waiting in the outpatient center, he saw a man of around his age whose lower eyelids had flipped outward, their bright red insides exposed; it occurred to him that that could happen in his own case, which had only just begun, because of connective tissue swelling, and it could be due to the very treatment that he was taking. He has not dared to tell to his doctor about this worry, not wanting to come off as frivolous, there being more serious things to worry about. But the man in front of the mirror worries a lot about the stigmatizing effects of the process, not knowing whether it would be worth his while for his organs' decay to halt temporarily if it means having his lower eyelids flip outward, swollen and red, and then as well as being in a terrible state of health end up looking revolting. In any case, indications of swelling have only just started, nobody has mentioned it to him yet, and besides, he's not sure if he can blame it on the treatment. Another thing that worries him, and it is of no lesser importance, is that his hair loss is more and more noticeable; fortunately, he's losing hair from the forehead back and not on the crown, which he checks every day with a hand mirror he holds up at an angle behind him. In one passage, he talks about a visit he paid to the dermatologist to find out if there was any way to deal with the problem. He didn't mention his nameless disease to the dermatologist, nor the chemical treatment he was taking to counteract it, not wanting those things to be blamed for his problem. The dermatologist, who was as bald as an eagle, told him his hair density was enviable for a man of his age; there were ways of stopping him from losing more hair, but he couldn't recommend them, and he assured him that he would not die bald. The man said he suspected that was true, there probably wouldn't be time for that to happen, and the bald dermatologist, who looked very fit, laughed, taking it to be a witty remark. The word "bald" really bothers the man. (In the few pages he's written, he quotes Rigaut's "*je serai un grand mort*"—I'll make a great corpse—twice).

Apart from that, the man feels well and has no serious discomfort to complain of. Due to his limited life expectancy, he lets the days go by quite freely, although sometimes the idea that the time to begin his melancholy countdown has arrived gets the better of him; to try to avoid such moments, he has taken the calendar in the kitchen down and attempts to live without knowing what day it is. Because he still enjoys eating, he takes time to go to the market and do the shopping, and he pays great attention to all the details of the food he makes. He has no other objectives. From time to time, he thinks about going on a trip, going back to somewhere he knows and visiting somewhere he's never been (Cairo, to be precise, and with a crazy idea in mind: to stand in Giza and shout, "Twenty centuries of history are looking at you!"). But he's never been much of a traveler (Martin often quotes that reflection of Pascal's in which he says that mankind's misfortune is its inability to sit still in a room, and he's also a great admirer of Xavier de Maistre's *A Journey Round My Room*), and if that weren't enough, he's also dissuaded by the worry that if his health were to suddenly deteriorate, he would have no way of getting back.

The man is writing a novel, whose plot is never discussed, and he doesn't feel up to finishing it in such a limited amount of time; in addition to that, he's not very happy with what he has written. The reader supposes that he'd almost completely abandoned the project even prior to his illness being diagnosed, and that he sees himself as a failed writer. He writes all sorts of things from time to time, in a chaotic fashion and with no particular objective: memories, mostly unimportant events from daily life, his thoughts ("*ses pensées*," in other words), and above all, "he tries on stories in the same way that some other people try on suits." Julia suspects that the bit about trying on stories isn't his, that he's read it somewhere, even though it does reflect Martin himself very well. His characters, mostly men and women in relationships waiting for a story, their own story, to begin, find themselves materializing on pieces of paper, and shortly afterward, usually after four or five pages, the story ends. He has lots of beginnings of abandoned stories.

The most positive influence the illness has had on the man's life is a newfound interest in watercolors. He's using Hazel Harrison's book *The Encyclopedia of Watercolor Techniques* to learn, and he likes painting out in the yard; since the last time Julia used the computer, exactly a week ago now, Martin has written a couple of pages about how run-down the yard is.

"THERE IS NO LOVE IN A HOUSE WITHOUT FLOWERS." Julia thinks Harri said something like that about the terrible state the yard's in, she doesn't remember it exactly.

The damaged pale-pink hydrangeas that tell of the gardener's lack of interest, the wrinkled violets, the drooping irises that survive anywhere. As if that weren't enough, the rows of bottles buried upright in the grass with their necks showing, which Martin said were to frighten off the moles, do not make the lawn any prettier. He stuck a few dozen of them into the ground (being tired, he buried them increasingly haphazardly as he went on). He'd been told that the sound of air going into the bottles would frighten the vermin and scare them away. The method does not seem to be particularly effective, or he hasn't executed it properly, because there are molehills everywhere; Julia is glad about that, because she supports the moles that Martin is at war with, because they're animals she likes.

The cats' bowls are empty. As she knows, Martin often empties them because the feed is said to attract rats. Martin hates cats—all animals in general, and cats more than any others. "Almost as much as people," he often says. Julia doesn't much like them, either, admitting that they seek protection self-interestedly. She thinks they're a mother and her kitten, and the pair only tolerate the presence of one of the other cats that would like to have the yard to live in, a young male, and only at meal times. The mother is white, and her probable kitten is, as well, with black spots, while the visitor is striped. The latter is the most beautiful and the most affectionate. Julia would like the mother and kitten, which have taken the yard

103

as their own, to accept the other cat for good, but she doesn't know what to do to help that come about.

A taxi has stopped in front of the iron gate, and she sees a woman getting out and removing several things from it. Being shortsighted, she can't make anything out very well, but she does see Martin running toward the taxi. After exchanging the customary two kisses, he and the woman go toward the house along the gravel path, Martin in front, carrying two suitcases with some difficulty, and the girl behind, bags in each hand and a large backpack on her back. Julia wonders whether she should go out to help them, because they've left more things at the gate. In the end, she decides to go into the house and sit down in front of the computer. By the time Martin opens the door, she looks as if she's deep at work there. "It's her," he tells her in a whisper, his head sticking through the half-open door and looking around at everything in the living room as if wanting to make sure that it's in a fit state to welcome their lodger. Disappointed, perhaps, because Julia hasn't tidied up the mess the place is always in while he was out? He invites the girl in by opening the door completely, making a gesture with his hand and bowing.

THE PENTHOUSE GIRL. Julia wants to slap Martin when he uses the expression again. Doesn't he realize it's like calling her "the porn girl"? But the girl doesn't hear, or pretends not to. She isn't the type of girl to get put on a magazine cover, beautiful though she is. She has nice hair, halfway between mahogany and red, coiled up into a bun, in the style of her time; she's around five foot nine, thin, but in the way today's girls are, with large breasts and a fine behind. What the French call a *fausse maigre*, a deceptively thin woman. She doesn't look much over thirty. She seems nice. She's wearing blue jeans and a white T-shirt, black penny loafers, and a blue leather jacket, very much like one Julia herself has had for many years. Her style is very much the same as her own, which is as faithful to the seventies as possible. The girl's weakest point is her wan, freckled skin. Her name is Lynn, and she's from New York.

She works in the sociomedical sciences department at Columbia University and is on sabbatical for the year. She confesses that she came here to take part in the San Fermín festival when they ask her what brought her to this part of the world. "*It's a joke*," she adds

104

immediately. Apparently, she's used to answering that question, and it's a pre-prepared joke. *"A joke,"* she says, laughing from ear to ear. She has a large mouth, one of those mouths where the lips don't fully cover the opening, so it looks as if it has cracks at the sides. It turns out not to be a complete lie that she came for San Fermín. She made the trip with a friend who used to be a teacher of hers and who's taking part in two international anthropology research projects, one about large popular festivities and their contexts, of which San Fermín is one, and the other about violent conflicts, which includes the Basque Country, unfortunately. Her friend has had to go back for a time due to a family problem, and she's been left on her own. On her own and homeless. As soon as her friend went, the owner of the house she was in asked her to leave—apparently he needed the room for his son.

After shrugging her shoulders, she makes a gesture of regret that puts wrinkles on her face and says, *"If life gives you lemons, make lemonade."* It seems he did her a favor, because she's going to end up better off. She's really happy when she says that she thinks the house is wonderful, praising its light and splendid trees, and that gives Martin his cue to talk about the district's golden age, the bullring with its glass roof, the Kursaal amusement park, and the grandly named Campos Elíseos gardens. At the beginning of the previous century, there were only *baserris* here, surrounded by fertile vegetable gardens, and little mansions with beautiful gardens like this one. The house was built in 1910, and they call it "the witch house" around here—because of the conical slate roof on the circular tower there was on one side of the building, of course— despite the fact that no evil stepmothers or sisters have ever lived in it. That's what Martin calls an English sense of humor. He tells her in Spanish that the house used to be surrounded by farmland— *"Antes los terrenos llegaban hasta allí."* He always tells people that, as well as the thing about the witches, and when he does, he never forgets to point out the San Luis Clinic on the other side of the river and say that the old building and the land it sits on were stolen from his grandfather.

Putting ideas together when he mentions the clinic, Julia remembers that she has to ask him about his test results; seeing him so lively, it is obvious they're good. So she says to him, "Speaking of that, have you gotten your test results?" Perhaps at the wrong moment, judging by the look he gives her. Instead of answering, he talks ironically about health checkups—as if the business of illness weren't enough, doctors have added on preventive care to increase their profits. That's Martin's point of view, and the American woman agrees with him—do the deaths that all these prevention programs seek to avoid, she asks, make up for the tiredness and nervousness that they force healthy people to go through for nothing? Probably trying to be nice, she also agrees with her own position that people just get accustomed to going for routine checkups. She seems very diplomatic. If the two of them were alone, without their American lodger, she would tell him, as would most of the women in his circle, that she thinks of going to checkups once in a while as something normal; at least she doesn't get as hysterical as he does every time he has to go to the doctor. Although she'd decided to keep quiet, she thinks of Harri, of that gesture of hers, touching her armpit, and says the worrying thing is a person's symptoms, not the checkups themselves. Then the American girl turns to Martin and says in formal Spanish that she hopes he himself has no cause to be concerned—"*Pero usted no tiene ningún motivo de inquietud, espero.*" "*Of course not,*" he answers in English. And he asks the girl not to speak to him so stiff and politely, because he's not so old as all that.

"TEA OR COFFEE?" After asking the question, while he's making space on the coffee table, Martin knocks over the nut bowl and a glass that he only just avoids breaking. He says they're computerizing their library, "*we are,*" he says, in the first person plural; he seems to be embarrassed by the mess, by having piles of books all over the place. After classifying and registering the books as they had agreed to, Martin was going to be the one to put them back in their places; because she wasn't prepared to continually take on all the work caused by his neglect, Julia has decided not to give in and do it herself this time, even if the books did invade the whole house. "Our yard's in quite a state," he says, still speaking in the plural, and the American girl offers to do some gardening. She would be happy to take charge of it, and Julia can't help smiling, thinking that perhaps love might make the house's devastated yard flourish once more.

Martin asks her what's so funny—"*¿Qué es lo que te hace gracia?*"

The striped cat's exile. Seeing it stepping through the iron gate and calmly walking off up the street after being escorted down the gravel path by the other two.

The American girl reminds Martin that he told her he likes cats—"*Me dijiste que te gustan los gatos.*"

And of course, he quickly says yes, he loves them, the yard's full of stray cats and they always make sure to feed them, and Julia gets the impression that the look in his eyes is asking her not to deny what he's saying. What he most admires about those elegant, lithe animals is their independence, they're nothing like dogs; dogs, as Baroja once said, are the most foolish of animals, because they serve the stupidest ones. He praises cats' incredible senses, which not even the best dogs can improve on, and also their whiskers, which can perceive even the smallest movement in the air, and Julia finds it impossible to sit through this demonstration of feline knowledge, which the girl is listening to with pleasure, without interjecting a cutting remark to the effect that she had no idea he was so well-informed about cats. "*No sabía que estuvieras tan puesto en gatos,*" she hurls at him, and the girl, joining in what she takes to be her admiration, says, "*Yes, you're an expert on cats.*" Julia hates women who seduce men by pretending that they're interested in what they're saying even more than she hates women who show off their breasts. But she doesn't want to be too hard on her because of that; the poor girl could hardly act otherwise in her situation as a lodger in a bargain house. The American girl's very glad to hear that Martin loves cats and is sure that they'll like Max, and Martin says they will, they're sure to like him. It's at this point that Julia finds out that Lynn is the owner of a cat called Max. A striped miniature Danish, beautiful but bad at making friends; she speaks about him with enthusiasm and love. She says she can't live without him, even though he sometimes causes her serious problems. Even so, she says with a sense of humor, she hopes that they don't believe that widely held idea that women who live alone with cats are quite witch-like, and Martin laughs as he assures her that if that's the case, she's in the perfect setting—"*Oh, en ese caso estarías en el marco perfecto*"—but the joke goes flat on him, because he has to remind her that some people call their place "the witch house."

Julia puts the china teapot and the ugly cups and saucers on the table. It's a set that apparently belonged to Martin's grandmother or great-grandmother—"*Made in England by Wood & Sons; genuine hand engraving*"—and it's completely cracked (if only they'd break once and for all, she does put them in the dishwasher, after all), and as she gets ready to pour, Martin puts one hand on the teapot and the other on the milk jug and suddenly orders rather than asks her to stop. Would she do them the honor of serving? The girl looks astonished, a little scared by his abruptness, but picks the teapot up with her right hand and the milk jug up with the other, while they both watch her attentively. She must think they're out of their minds, of course. She has quite small hands and very fine fingers. First she pours into the cup that Julia holds out to her, measuring the milk with a precise movement of her hand. And then the tea. "Why do you do it like that?" Martin asks, and in case she doesn't understand what he's talking about, he goes on to enquire if she has some special reason for pouring the milk before the tea, whether she always does it like that. She says it's something they do at home, her mother does it like that. She's read somewhere or other that people recommend pouring the milk in first for dietary reasons, because otherwise the proteins can lose their properties, and that way the tannin in the tea doesn't damage them, or something like that; but her mother's reasoning, apparently, was that it's better for the cups, because the milk stops the hot tea from cracking the fine china, or, as was their case with no fine china to look after, it stops the bottoms of the cups from going yellow. After giving her explanation, she smiles from ear to ear once again, as if she were a smart student in class, happy to know that she's been able to answer the question.

Martin could barely stop himself from clapping. "You see?" he says, as happy as the American girl. Who would believe he's forgotten that just the day before, he defended the opposite point of view to Harri? And his theory about the aesthetics of the cloud of milk? Julia isn't worried by his dumb behavior, and she's glad she isn't worried by it. What's more, Martin's shamelessness allows her to say that she should get back to work as soon as they finish their tea. "*Oh, les estoy molestando,*" the young American says immediately in Spanish, apparently genuinely concerned that she's being a bother, but Martin quickly says that she isn't. Julia does work like registering books, which is not very demanding, when she doesn't feel like translating or when she needs a break after struggling with an over-long sentence. Sometimes it's quite a mechanical task, although deciding what materials to include or not can be quite a job for her obsessive nature. This morning, at least, it's not. She starts clearing the table after finishing her cup of tea, not giving the other two the choice of having more; she only just manages not to take the cups out of their hands. She realizes she's left the teapot on the tray. She asks them if they want more, and, of course, they say no. The American girl offers to help her, but she doesn't insist when Julia says no, and Julia is glad, finding it irritating when Martin and Harri repeat their false offers to clean up the kitchen after lunch. Especially Harri. She prefers to do the housework by herself, the way she likes it done. She tells her not to worry about it—"*No, deja*"—and the girl sits down again as she's told. It isn't true that Lynn being there will interfere with her work, but she is worried about the fact that from today onward they'll always have her in the house. In the kitchen, she sits with her back against an old coal box that, having been scrubbed with bleach, is so white and soft that it doesn't even look wooden. It used to be in Sagastizabal. Sometimes she still feels the yearning to smoke, even though she gave up long ago. She'd like to sit in the corner without doing anything, but Martin could come in at any moment to find out what she's up to. In fact, in this house, just as much as at her mother's, there's nowhere apart from the restroom where there's no risk of people bothering her. She listens to them talking.

The American girl, in addition to speaking Spanish well, shows the respect that some foreigners have for Basque and uses a few words of it—*eskerrik asko* to say thank you, for instance, and a handful of short sentences, as well. "*Oso ederrak dira*," she says—they're very beautiful—when they bring out the remains of the old tea set. With no inhibition or fear of making mistakes or pronouncing badly, with the impunity that being an outsider gives you. They've often spoken about the subject and have come to the conclusion that apart from some people simply hating the language, one reason many local people, or some, at least, are hesitant to start using what little Basque they know is because it is, at least theoretically, their own language, and they're ashamed of speaking it badly. On the other hand, be that as it may, the embarrassment of speaking a language badly, like most embarrassments, arises when you're with your own people, and less so or not at all in front of outsiders. Martin, however, is not at all displeased at having an opportunity to practice his English. He's like that peculiar type of town weirdo who has no contact with the local people but jumps out to welcome the first stranger who turns up. He has a lot of friends in the English and American expat community in Donostia. That's what allows him to get by with the language, while Julia, for her part, does not. He doesn't make much of an effort to study languages, because he has no difficulty using them, although it is true that by learning them that way, he never understands them in depth. The two of them are talking about books. She thinks the girl must know by now that he's a writer. She'd like to know how he told her. "*I write,*" perhaps? In any case, he won't have said "*I'm a writer*"; never that.

"BEFORE, I READ A LOT OF FICTION, BUT NOT NOW." He doesn't like being corrected, either. At one time he used to read all published literature endlessly, wanting to find something new, but he's stopped doing that in recent years, either because there isn't anything new, or because he isn't capable of finding it. It's striking how many books there are on the shelves that haven't been read completely and that, judging by the evidence—he underlines a lot—were abandoned in the very first chapter. It's obvious that he jumps around when reading, choosing snippets here and there; there are very few books that he reads to the end. Bearing in mind how much gets published, trying to stay up-to-date is an impossible task. He feels inhibited and lowers his voice, knowing that she's listening to him from the kitchen, Julia thinks, but he still keeps on throwing out his favorite lines just the same. One: Apparently Schopenhauer, at the end of his life, said that he only read books that had been published at least fifty years earlier. Another one: The ageing process is noticeable in a person's reading habits; you read less fiction and more history and confessional writing as you get older. Old age is the time to reread things, to go back to the classics. Look at that fancy detail of calling himself old, all to get the American girl to say he doesn't look his age.

Julia decides to go back into the living room, because staying there listening from the kitchen is tiring her out.

"Were you here all this time?"

The young American nods very slowly—a movement that shows serious thought—for the old writer to carry on talking. She doesn't think it's a matter of age. The classics have guaranteed value, and that's why she prefers them, too, she says, once more using her Spanish. She says it in a very straightforward way, as if she were saying that she prefers dark chocolate to white. She looks at Julia, with a *"¿Verdad que sí?"*—meaning "Isn't that right?"—that's intended to bring her into the conversation, worried that she may have left her out. She replies there's no doubt about it—*"No cabe duda."* She could tell her that risks have to be taken, as well, that it would be a pity to miss out on tomorrow's classics. Or that the subject bores her, speaking out like a woman who's fed up. They could talk about that tired old subject of whether or not reading is made too much of, whether the pendulum hasn't swung back since their days, since her and Martin's days, from a time in which reading was dry and difficult, a time when it was respected too much, to now, when not even the slightest hint of difficulty is accepted (*of course*—good things are not necessarily boring, and what's boring isn't necessarily good, and all that). And whether the erosion of the boundaries between literature and subliterature has favored the emergence of a standard of literature that's good but not very demanding, and a type of narrative that flees from experimentation, and all of this, in short, as a result of culture having been made available to all. (And at this point, the composition of his audience making him feel at ease, he risks bringing up the subject of whether there is a connection between the tendency to produce easier things and the reading population being made up mostly of women.) They could also talk about immortality having been the writer's aim ever since Romanticism idealized it, and that aim having come to be represented by social and financial success in what has become a professional entertainment business.

And that's just what they talk about. On the rectangle of grass beneath the magnolia tree, there's a solitary blackbird walking from side to side, as if its back and forth pacing had become an obsessive ritual, and it reminds Julia of Martin's endless walks up and down the gravel path, head down, hands behind his back, when he has writer's block. Harri has her own way of describing that uncomfortable situation: trying to find the right adjective. The blackbird goes quite quickly from the tree to the path beyond it and takes three or four jumps to come back, pausing between each one, pecking away between Martin's half-withered thoughts. It goes back and forth and makes the movements again and again, like a mechanical toy, pecking around the tree and quickly moving away. He looks like quite a happy creature, and she remembers what Harri told her about what happened at the pharmacy. Martin went in to weigh himself, because it seemed to him, for once, that he was losing weight. "That's the good thing about cancer, you get thinner," he said. Apparently the pharmacist, a fat, bald man the same age as him, offered him a little rhyming explanation in Spanish when he stepped up on the scale, with no concern whatsoever: "*Usted como el tordo, la cara delgada y el culo gordo*," which was like saying something along the lines of "you're just like a thrush—a thin face and a fat tush." They laughed about it; that sort of thing could only happen in a pharmacy in this part of the world, and she's amused as she remembers it again. It must show on her face, because Martin looks at her inquisitively. At that moment, they're talking about how "in my day"—he repeats that expression again and again—a good writer aimed to sell five thousand copies at most in the whole of Spain, and today, on the other hand, that's a publisher's minimum just to break even, and their real goal's to sell a hundred thousand. That means that as well as having a product that a hundred thousand people will be able to read, the writer himself becomes a brand image for promotional purposes and a suitable rhythm of production has to be kept up; once a sizeable readership has been gotten together, it has to be fed, so that it doesn't forget about the author. It's like that in all the arts.

Has she realized that even opera prima donnas can't be fat nowadays?

She found it funny the first time she heard him say it.

He should have written a short story called *The Last Fat Diva*, but he hasn't. Writing or singing well isn't enough, you have to have the right image for promoting things, know how to deal with the media, the public has to find you interesting and, if possible, like you as well. He's bored, but he speaks to the interested young American with feigned passion. Julia's heard him say the same thing a thousand times before without him caring about it. He's happy to talk about himself as being disappointed, a loser, and misunderstood. It's as if he's looking at the world from some far-off beach that the foam of vanity and pomp can't reach. Young writers speak about living off their writing and are not prepared, as they used at one time to be, to combine writing with being a librarian, a teacher, or a civil servant, and so they waste their time and talent writing opinion pieces in the newspapers, or commissioned books for the public authorities, or giving lectures and readings, and so in the end it's writing, more than any other job, that separates them from genuinely literary activity. The dream of young writers is no longer to be remembered; they want success, money, and fame, a four-star chef to come and greet them at their table, they want to have a beautiful yard or a mansion on the coast where they can go to be alone and put the finishing touches on their works. In short, they want to be the type of character that's showing up more and more in the wonderful, remote places that appear in movies. That song affects Julia in different ways, depending on her mood. Normally it bothers her. She thinks, and she's told him as much—they've argued about it hundreds of times—that more or less the same things have always happened, there have always been writers of all types, and readers, as well, good ones and bad ones, smart ones and dumb ones, materialists and dreamers, and that in any case, he should do what he himself has to do and not worry about what other people are doing. His case, in terms of income, is closer to Proust's or Flaubert's than to that of a writer struggling to make it to the end of the month. Besides, it makes her sad when he sounds angry like that—his interlocutor might think he's talking that way because of some frustration at not being successful, because he's envious of others' success, but she doesn't think that's true, or at least not entirely. Be that as it may, she knows he wants nothing to do with those sad clubs founded by writers who believe themselves to be talented but aren't successful, clubs they found in order to comfort each other by criticizing success; she thinks he's quite sincere when he says that what hurts him is seeing people with exceptional talent wasting it in the pursuit of success, seeing them getting distracted by that goal and not doing worthwhile work and instead wasting the gifts they have on other work that, because of those great gifts, is too easy for them.

"In my day." He doesn't look like a man about to turn fifty, and there's no doubt any woman would find him interesting. He's losing his hair—a lot of it down the bathtub drain—and he no longer has the body he once did, but he looks full of life as he sits there across from the American girl, a way he hasn't looked for a long time, sure of himself, moving his hands energetically, elegantly crossing his legs back and forth in a sort of galloping motion. His shoes, his oversized jacket, which he's left unbuttoned in order to hide how

113

big it is, and his enormous shirt collar all have a British sheen to them. He'd be excellent in the role of an English writer in a house in Tuscany. Julia wonders if he really is worried about posterity. What would happen if she asked him? She would only ever ask him that as a joke, and he would answer jokingly, as well, so there's no point in doing it. Now he moves his head forward a little to listen to the American girl, encouraging her to speak, and when the girl says she gets the impression that nowadays, if anyone's suspected of liking *Ulysses*, they're expected to apologize for it—"*Well, I'm sorry, I like it*"— Julia is afraid the excitement of it all might give him a cardiovascular attack. Martin sometimes says the same thing about Musil's *The Man Without Qualities*. Nowadays it's usually said that they're very good books but completely unreadable. And it's all right to admit that Joyce and Musil bore you without looking like an idiot. That's fine, but you do have to work at pleasure. A free translation of a Nabokov quote, which is absolutely relevant here: the great artist goes up a slope with no clear path, and when he reaches the windswept summit, what do you think he bumps into? A breathless happy reader. And there, in a spontaneous rush, they embrace each other, and if it's a book that lasts, they're together forever.

In fact, the girl isn't being at all pedantic, and her posture is confident; she's leaning slightly to one side, her left arm hanging behind her chair and the other resting on her lap. It's no bad thing to be able to talk about pleasure, literary pleasure even, on their second meeting. (That's one of literature's important roles, giving rise to interesting conversations.) Julia doesn't have the energy to talk about a subject they've so frequently dealt with, but she wouldn't like the girl to get the wrong idea about her just because she's keeping quiet. She should admit the truth and say that she didn't much enjoy Joyce's *Ulysses*, that she only finished it out of a sense of discipline, and that she couldn't handle the Musil. However she's sure that the blame, if there is any blame, is not the author's, it's hers.

She decides to mention that expression about honey not being made for donkeys' mouths—"*No se hizo la miel para la boca del asno*"— and she doesn't even have to tell the girl what it means, because she already knows the saying. ("But we don't say 'honey isn't made for donkeys' mouths' in English. '*Don't cast pearls before swine*' works better.") She says she likes proverbs a lot, and they exchange a few. *Echar margaritas a los cerdos*—another Spanish way to speak about casting things before swine, but in this instance it's daisies rather than pearls; and a Basque equivalent, *astoari polainak*—saying that something is like putting "spats on donkeys." And for the idea that it's worth forcing yourself up the slope so that you can bump into the writer at the top, two equivalents of "no pain, no gain": *no hay miel sin hiel*, which is a Spanish saying that translates literally to "there's no honey without bile"; and *ez lan ez jan*, the Basque version, which would translate to "no work, no food." And all of this is enough for Martin's eyes to grow angry at his amateur translator's crazy circumlocutions, because it's broken the thread of the interesting conversation they were having, and he says "*I mean, I mean*" two or three times, trying to get the attention of the American girl, who seems to be happy sitting there reciting proverbs, until she finally realizes and then she says "*sorry, sorry,*" also two or three times. Julia thinks about going back to the kitchen on any old excuse. But she doesn't get up, because for some reason or other, she's curious about what Martin wants to say, because it's the first time in a long while that he's looked so enthusiastic. Leaning forward, his forearms resting on his thighs, he rubs his hands together, searching for the right words to say exactly what he means. (When he said "*I mean, I mean*" in English just now, it seemed to her like he was feeling the pangs of some sort of profound pain, "mean" sounding quite similar to the Basque word *min*, meaning "pain.")

She's astonished by a confession she's never heard until now. Sometimes, when a book's really good, he finds it difficult to go on, stops on each page, until finally he has to give up on it, unable to stand it being so good. He asks the American girl if she knows what he means, looking her straight in the eye, and seeing that look, Julia has to stop herself from saying that she, too, knows exactly what he means and it's happened to her, as well, though more often with music, finding herself taken over by an emotion that becomes painful, feeling attacked by it, having to stop listening because she's afraid of going crazy. "Of course she knows what you mean" slips out in almost a whisper—she's moved by sharing that experience—but he doesn't pay her any attention. After saying "give up on it," and without even looking at her, he angrily raises his hand, sick and tired, fed up, as if he were throwing a book up into the

115

air. He cannot read it, because the writer's talent stands in his way, because finding out that he isn't even in the same league as the other writer takes away his own energy to write.

"Because you're a writer!" says the young American, lifting her hands to her face in astonishment, perhaps with admiration. She's read something similar to what Martin's just described somewhere, it happens to many writers. Virginia Woolf almost gave up writing because of Proust. The writer didn't know that.

"A writer, then."

Julia thinks that lifting her hands up to her cheeks is a rather exaggerated gesture, and it's very surprising, with her seeming so smart, that she didn't realize earlier that Martin's a writer; he's done everything possible to let her know that he is, even lighting his pipe, which he never does. He shrugs, lets out a laugh that sounds adolescent and happy at the same time, and says that using the term "a writer" may be going too far; he writes, he tries to write. Someone who writes. A scribbler, at most. He always says the same thing, because he idealizes the figure of the writer and, because of that, thinks it would be vanity to call himself a writer, to put himself in the same category as Flaubert somehow. "Writer" isn't a title you can earn at university. *Un petit écrivain*, perhaps, a little writer. He usually says it in Italian, *un piccolo scrittore*, ever since Julia made him read Natalia Ginzburg's wonderful book *The Little Virtues*—because he doesn't normally read women writers, Virginia Woolf being one of the few exceptions—in which she examines the writing profession with great clarity. Even though he may be a flea or a mosquito among writers, he's gone through the same suffering and worrying as the greatest of them and shouldn't be ashamed to introduce himself as a writer; there are great writers and more modest ones. So he says *"un piccolo scrittore,"* with a gesture of modesty that doesn't hide how proud he feels about it.

She'd like to read something of his.

Martin leans back in his armchair, almost as if wanting to protect himself from her, when she says with great enthusiasm that she'd like to read something of his. But he writes in Basque. His arms are locked on the armchair, he's sitting all the way back in it, he's uncrossed the one leg he had slug over the other and now both feet are on the ground. He wants to run away and take refuge somewhere safe, at the low level that suits him; Basque, too, being a *piccolo* language.

Why doesn't he tell the charming American girl that his work's been translated? Does he want it to be Julia who tells her that some of his writing has even been published in English, so he can make it clear that he himself is not very interested in being read? Or does he prefer to keep it completely quiet, afraid he's not up to snuff because the girl's said she likes Joyce? Julia knows that being aware that the people around him have read his work makes him feel uncomfortable, especially when it's in Spanish; at one time, when his work was only available in Basque and had not yet been translated into Spanish, he could enjoy being considered a writer without having to worry about what people thought of his work, because very few of his acquaintances read, and still fewer of them read in Basque. Many people still use the language as an excuse for not having read anything of his, Julia can confirm that, they really regret not being able to read his stuff, they say when they bump into him that they don't know enough Basque, because they've heard he's about to publish something, and he's fine with that, because he thinks they'd be disappointed if they did read his work. He usually says you don't send a message in a bottle for the people in your own neighborhood to read. Julia is still thinking about whether to mention his translated work or not when the young American insists again in very sincere Spanish that she'd really love to be able to read his work—"*Me gustaría tanto poder leerle*"; she could read him in English, but Julia keeps quiet in the end, she can't be bothered. What's more, there's a train going by.

It's a long freight train, one of those ones that transports cars. They don't see it, but they all keep quiet, waiting for the minute and a half it takes to go past, because it makes a lot of noise. The other trains, the high-speed and the local ones, don't make so much noise. In fact, Julia's used to it by now, and the sound of the trains seldom stops her from doing anything, not even from playing the piano, and she often doesn't even realize anything's gone by. When the last sounds of the train—almost soft as they move away—are finally lost, Martin quickly tells the young American that there's nothing for her to worry about, it only seemed so loud to them because all the windows in the gallery are open, and as she's seen, not many trains go by, and she'll get used to it—like a real estate agent trying to rent out a place down by the tracks. And he looks at Julia to ask her not to betray him, which she doesn't. That's right, she says. What's more, the noise trains make, he doesn't know quite how to put it, it's noble, evocative, much less annoying than road noise. Why aren't ships' sirens irritating? A train passing in the night makes you think about how far it's going, about a meeting, things like that. She thinks Martin is looking peculiar, she looks at his alert eyes to try and find out if he's serious or joking and can't help but laugh. The American girl laughs happily, as well, while Martin remains serious, as if confused.

"DO YOU LIKE BEANS?" Martin invites the young woman to have lunch with them. It's the first Friday of the month, and on the first Friday of every month he always makes Tolosa beans for Harri. Tolosa beans are excellent, really delicious, Martin explains passionately. And they're very pretty beans—black, neither small nor large, just the right size, and shiny. He cooks them without any other ingredients, no pork fat, no chorizo, just some oil. Just a splash of oil. Blood sausage and cabbage on a separate plate. The art involved is knowing how much water is going to be needed, so that you don't have to add any more, and the secret is adding some stewed onion at the end. The most important thing is to stew them very slowly, as our grandmothers used to, he says, although his two grandmothers probably never stepped into a kitchen in their lives. *Do you accept?* The young American hesitates, turns toward Julia, like a child asking for permission, apparently wanting to know whether she's OK with the invitation. Yes, stay, she says, Harri will be excited to meet her, and the young woman accepts. Happily, she says—"*pozik.*"

Martin goes to Donostia to collect the Beasain blood sausages he's ordered and tells them to look after the beans, which he'll leave on the stove with just the right amount of water. Happy, content; he doesn't seem to mind that he's used up the whole morning and probably won't be able to do any work all day. Julia wants to accept the situation with the best possible goodwill—she won't be able to translate her daily quota of pages today, either—but before she knows it, she's sitting down in front of the computer and has taken its cover off. The young American stands up; Julia thinks she doesn't know where to go, that she's not at ease. She tucks her hair behind her ears, which is something that Julia herself does when she has to make a decision. She doesn't want to get in the way. She gives a little laugh. Now that the sun has disappeared behind a cloud, her eyes are darker, and Julia likes the way she looks at things. She's not in the way, she says, as she covers the computer again; she doesn't feel like doing anything.

An occasional translator. That's how she defines herself when the young American asks her if she's a writer. A translator once in a while. She's translating Martin's latest book of short stories, *Historias de náufragos*, the title, which in English means "Shipwreck Stories," being taken from the two longest stories, "Shipwreck Stories I" and "Shipwreck Stories II," and in fact, all the characters seem to be lost at sea, as well. She's translating the second one right now and wants to finish it today. It's about a man who has trouble relating to others—a typical Martin subject—and who's so timid that when he reaches the beach, half-drowned, and with cramps in both legs, he can't bring himself to wave his arms around and shout for help, because he's afraid of looking ridiculous and prefers to hang onto his dignity and poise. Something that could easily happen to Martin himself. He won the Premio Euskadi for the book, it came with a sum of money earmarked for translation, and Martin made her a generous offer in exchange for her doing it, giving her the prize money itself as well as the money just for the translation, so she enjoys the working conditions that translators really need and don't normally have. (Her eyes wander over to the little bronze statue that came with the prize—it's a tree, maybe a yew, with a face at the top, and because it's heavy and has felt stuck to its base, they decided to use it to hold the gallery door open, but she decides to leave it to the prizewinner himself to tell her about that, so that he can enjoy showing her how unimportant he thinks prizes are.) With regard to a question he's often been asked, about why he doesn't translate his work himself, Martin usually says it's impossible, citing as evidence his experience with a couple of short stories. He found the work of translating them tiring and uninteresting, because being the author meant he was free to betray the text continually, and in order to avoid difficulties, or to make improvements, he took it so far away from the original text that the final result was a re-creation of the text, perhaps better than the original version, but it certainly wasn't the original version. He found it impossible, more than anything else, because he had work waiting for him that required greater creativity. That's what he told Julia when he convinced her to accept the job. He's a writer, probably a crappy writer, but a writer, not a translator. It gave Julia the chance to fulfil her dream of asking for unpaid leave for a while from her job at the regional government office working as an administrator in the translation department. Her job there was as an admin worker, not a translator, she wants to make that clear right away. She didn't have the necessary qualifications. Her life story's quite complicated, and for one reason or another, she doesn't have any official qualifications, so her only chance was to apply for admin jobs. Of course, translating work, with a few exceptions, especially when it consists of translating boring administrative texts that nobody will read from Spanish into Basque simply in order to comply with laws about bilingualism, isn't very rewarding in any case.

That's her life. Because she is incapable of translating nonstop for long, she also took on the job of classifying Martin's books and, at the same time, transcribing the sentences that he has underlined in them, filing them away in order to build up a nice "base" for his library, and so it was perhaps fitting that they were kept piled up against the baseboard at the back of the closet. Martin envies writers and speakers who are able to give out appropriate quotes on the spot; having a bad memory, he finds it hard. He'd say that he always reads with a pencil in his hand, like a chicken pecking around in the grass, waiting for clever, precise, special sentences to turn up, to be able to grab them, and that practice of keeping these quotes in the computer, if not in his head, whether or not he ever uses them, serves to console him. Julia doesn't think this "base"-building work is much use, at least she's never seen Martin ever using any of it, but she enjoys transcribing, especially when she doesn't feel like doing anything else. She doesn't follow any particular criteria for choosing the books, sometimes picking them up without even looking at the covers, other times being guided by her tastes or mood: Proust, Rousseau, Beckett . . . They're the authors she has on the table right now. She always finds the underlined parts interesting. Often they're things that Martin himself could have written, normally sentences that express his own ideas, things he might say, or wished he had said, or in some way or other has in fact said. She admits that it's because of this job that often, when she's reading, she finds herself trying to guess which lines he would underline, and she thinks she normally gets it right. And then, sometimes, she's surprised that he hasn't paid attention to certain ideas, reflections, or points of view that she would have chosen, that his eyes have slipped over them and he hasn't used his pencil, and discovering these moments still surprises her.

August 31, 1813. The liberators of Donostia set fire to the city during the Peninsular War. Who needs enemies with friends like that?

September 13, 1936. Navarrese Requetés took Donostia during the Spanish Civil War. People always say that they lost the greatest number of men when they tried to get into the regional government headquarters through the revolving door.

September 27, 1975. The last Franco-era executions, including those of two Basques: Txiki and Otaegi.

Relevant events because she's decided to finish her translation by the end of August; because September 13, as well as being her son Zigor's birthday, is when her unpaid leave from her job with the regional government finishes, so she'll have to decide at that point whether or not she's leaving the job for good, and, if she isn't, the twenty-seventh of September is the day she'd have to go back to work, at eight in the morning, that's when she'd have to clock in.

She doesn't know why she's telling the young American about how Martin's offered to continue paying her to translate another book of short stories, which would allow her to gain more experience in literary translation that she could then make use of to get a professional position in the field but that she doesn't know whether to accept or not because it's difficult to give up her job with the regional government, seeing as it's a permanent position, and seeing as how she's also begun to feel like a kept woman, and especially seeing as how continuing to work in that house would mean maintaining a link with Martin that just prolongs her ambiguous relationship with him. Their professional relationship gets mixed up with their other one, it props it up considerably, and she imagines that if it were to end, she would find it easier to know if she should remove herself from his entire life, as well. Does she understand what she's saying? The young American looks carefully at Julia's lips as she talks, as if she could read them. Why has she dared to bring up this fear that she hasn't told to anyone else? Why tell this foreign girl and not Harri? She's not sure. Perhaps Julia doesn't care what she might think precisely because she's a young foreigner, but she feels tenderness for her when she asks if she understands and the American girl nods her head up and down like a schoolchild.

Another train goes by. Now it's an express, or a high-speed train—she doesn't know the difference, it's one that doesn't stop here, anyway, one going slowly in the direction of Irun, and its slowness means that another express or high-speed train will come the other way in less than a minute. She keeps quiet, listening, against her will, to hear if the train bound for Hernani—bound for Madrid, in other words—really does come, and it becomes clear to her that she hasn't said anything to Harri about her doubts because she knows Harri would advise her to carry on as translator, secretary, maid, or whatever else to Martin, because she thinks it's what's best for the boy, for him to be able to finish his novel, and that's what matters most.

They both keep silent for a while, for quite some time after the train that justified their not speaking goes by. Julia thinks that she's put the young woman in a difficult position by telling her things that are fairly intimate, and thinking that makes her feel ashamed, and she blushes. She'd like to break the silence with conversation leading away from personal matters. But she can't think of anything to say except that she'll soon get used to hearing the high-speed trains go by. A stupid thing to say, and the girl replies to it in a way she finds strange.

"The ability we have to get used to things can be a problem."

Julia is tempted to ask what she means, but she's stopped by the fear of knowing just what she's trying to say. Even so, there isn't any apparent irony when she says it, and her smile now shows the opposite of having any bad intentions. Just to say something, she says she hopes that at least in the case of the noise from the trains, she'll find the ability to get used to things helpful, and the girl nods her agreement. Then she says, "I hope you'll make the best decision for yourself on September thirteenth."

What makes her speak about herself once more when she hears that date?

Why does she feel the desire to tell her about the important decision she has to make before Zigor's birthday? Fifteen years old. A man already. The girl, of course, doesn't know that she has a son. Julia explains that Zigor is a name from the Middle Ages and that in Basque it means "whip" or "punishment." It's true it's a name that sounds nice for men, but right now she doesn't think it appropriate. A name that can mark you. Because it was Zigor's father's nom de guerre. She doesn't know how to explain that and, to keep things short, decides to tell her it's a nickname, when she sees Harri and Martin walking up the garden path toward the house.

"THAT'S SOME HAPPENING he's put together with the bottles," says Harri as she comes in and throws her small green briefcase and a couple of Auzmendi bags on the sofa. She looks lively. In fact, she always looks lively, or at least as if she has something to tell you. "What luck, the doctor says the boy's all right," she says to Julia. She, of course, remembered that he had an appointment. She's brought a bottle of champagne to celebrate, she knew they weren't going to find anything wrong with him, and she doesn't pay any attention when Martin says he's still waiting on some results to come in—the most important thing is that the doctor didn't find anything wrong with him during the checkup. "Did you go with him?" she whispers in Julia's ear as she kisses her hello. A bit of smart aleckiness on her part—she knows he always likes to go by himself—and Julia almost replies that she'd happily accompany *her* if she ever decides to get her lump looked at, but in the end she just says, "He's a grown boy now." Harri gives her a look as if to say "geez, what's with you?" and then she turns toward the American lodger. "So you're our *penthouse* girl." She takes both her hands and sits beside her on the sofa with that warmth of hers that Julia finds so intimidating. She's a torrent.

"What did you say your name was? What do you do? Don't you get bored here? Why have you come to this crazy country?"

She says that her name, Lynn, could be a man's or a woman's, it's a short form of Linnet, Lynnette, Linda, or the ending of names such as Madeleine and Carolyne—Lynn, Lin—or it could come from the German name Lynna, which means waterfall. With regard to why she's in the Basque Country, she mentions the San Fermín festivities and her friend's research again. She works, as Martin and Julia know, as a teacher at the Columbia University School of Public Health. "*How interesting!*" They're almost colleagues, because Harri's an epidemiologist, a civil servant in the Basque government's Department of Health. She adds, with a gesture of regret, that she chose an easy lifestyle, and that she's not sure if she did the right thing.

The beans. Julia doesn't remember the beans until Martin gets up to see how they're doing—*"Let's see those beans!"*—but she beats him to it, throwing out the excuse that she wants to drink some water. It's the beans that need the water—they're dry, as hard as stone, and about to get burned. She adds more than a quart, turns the heat all the way up and then down again when the water starts boiling, all the while listening to the voices from the living room. Now it's the young American who's asking about work—it turns out Harri's organizing a research project about labor and birthing practices, and the American girl keeps on saying *"how interesting."* Even though Julia can't understand what they're saying very well, she's glad they're talking quite loudly, because that way Martin won't realize she's cheating with the beans, mashing up a few in a cup in order to thicken the sauce.

When she goes back to the living room, Martin's clearing the table of its stacks of books, which are laid out in categories, and the other two are still talking about work. Harri can't find anyone to be her temporary assistant for collecting data at the Donostia Hospital registry office, apparently the people who would be good at it all have jobs already and wouldn't be interested in the pittance being offered anyhow. But the Columbia University sociologist is interested. At first Harri thinks she's joking, but she says she's not, she's serious—she doesn't have anything else to do until her friend comes back, and the job would be good for her, a chance to be around other people and see how hospitals here work. She'd be happy to do the work unpaid. Harri says she's delighted and checks two or three times that she's not pulling her leg—it really would be very interesting for her to get the chance to observe her work— and after hugging her several times, Harri tells Martin to open the champagne, they've got a lot to celebrate.

The champagne isn't cold enough yet, and Martin prefers to start with the 2001 Le Pin he's set aside for lunch. They toast the Columbia University lecturer and the fact that Martin's check-up has gone well.

"DO YOU LIKE THE BEANS?" All three of them think they're fantastic. While they eat, Martin talks about the art of getting the amount of water right. It seems he doesn't remember that he told the young

American all the secrets about how to cook the beans already when he first put them on the stove—sometimes Julia finds his repetitions worrying—and of course he hasn't realized that they actually needed more water at the last minute. Julia thinks that although he knows about gastronomy—and he should, he's gone to excellent restaurants often enough—he doesn't have much idea about the basic principles of tasting food, the exact way to evaluate sauces, stews, and the ripeness of fruit that comes from sharing your meals with a father who knows how to distinguish between tomatoes that are local and ones that aren't, who knows where peas and runner beans come from, and who can tell with his eyes closed if what he's eating is a sea bream, a common two-banded sea bream, a common pandora, or a gilt-head bream. Julia's father wouldn't have had any doubt that the beans were going to need more water at the last moment. She has a theory about it, at least to an extent: the children of wealthy families are brought up in more Spartan conditions—with the maids in the kitchen or the friars at a boarding school—than those of working-class families, who are normally brought up by mothers whose only job is to take care of their families, slaves who cover their children with affection. If that's right, then the children of well-off families have more need for affection than families that would be classified as middle class or working class. Remarkably, Martin—who says he didn't sit down to eat with his parents until he was sixteen—agrees with her theory completely.

The young American says she was brought up by her mother, although she doesn't say why. Women who are brought up like that are responsible, but they may distrust men. Julia thinks that, but of course she doesn't say it. Harri starts talking about the problems she's had as a mother. She doesn't know if she's done the right thing in exiling her daughter to England. She doesn't think she ever gets it right with her, starting with giving her her own name, Harritokieta. Apparently, giving children their parents' names limits their development, and that's not even taking into account the heavy burden of the name itself. She has to explain that *harri* is "stone" and *harritokieta* is an "outcropping," so that the American girl can understand the joke, and that makes Julia think of Zigor and of what having been given his father's nom de guerre must mean for him, how he deals with that particular inheritance. Meanwhile, Harri's giving a highly comic version of the trouble that her name, which was handed down to her by her mother, as well, like a condemnation, has given her. People often ask her if the shortened version of her name isn't a man's name, or say it reminds them of Dirty Harry, and it's even worse with her full name, Harritokieta. What a difficult name, they usually say to her, and what does it mean (obviously, barbaric names *must* mean something—Sitting Bull, White Eagle, and so on), and of course, when she tells them what it means, they raise their hands to their heads in astonishment. And this might easily be coming from someone called Pilar, Pilarica, Piluca, or Pilarin, all of which come from the Spanish word for "pillar," and that's a name that receives complete impunity. She's sure it's a very Spanish attitude—how many times has she heard someone being described on the television news as *"de nombre impronunciable"*—having an unpronounceable name—and that never happens to her when she's abroad. In London, nobody makes the excuse that her name's too long or difficult, and they certainly don't make stupid comments. The young American laughs heartily when Harri imitates other people's gestures, and unexpectedly, she has no difficulty saying *Harritokieta*, and she thinks the shortened form that her daughter uses, Harritxu, is very pretty.

They toast Harritxu, unhappily exiled in Surrey, with the second bottle of Le Pin that Martin opens, and while he's uncorking it, he tells the young American about his wine collection. Julia finds his efforts to impress the girl rather moving. Using his best manners, keeping his jacket on, opening two of the best bottles from his collection. They come from a wine cellar that doesn't make many more than five hundred cases, and so that she can appreciate what he means, he says that a winery like Château Lafite-Rothschild produces thirty thousand, as he skillfully removes the cork.

It isn't hard to tell that he's intent on them realizing the value of what they're drinking, and Harri, apparently thinking the same thing, and because she's jealous, or because of the respect that Martin is displaying toward the young foreigner, blurts out that he doesn't have to tell them he's giving them a particularly good wine, they know how to appreciate good wine and deserve no less. What's more, he's getting miserly as he grows older, as the jacket he's wearing goes to show; it may be a Loewe and all that, but it's still two sizes too big for him. Doesn't she agree, she asks the young girl, who doesn't reply right away. It's obvious Harri's put her in a difficult position and she doesn't know how to get out of it. She figures there are two sizes for everyone, some people prefer the larger one and others prefer the slimmer-cut version. *"Maybe a bit too large?"* she replies, forced to by Harri, and then she laughs as if to apologize, knowing somehow that the writer's sensitive about this, and she adds, with great conviction, that it's a very elegant jacket.

"And you're a very diplomatic American," Harri jokes. Martin admits that as far as the size is concerned, back in the days when cloth was made to last forever, he used to buy his clothes with the same criteria as one buys clothing for children, so that it can be grown into, and Harri, on the other hand, buys things a couple of sizes too small, in the hope that she'll lose weight. It is true that she tends to buy tight clothes. She takes a black dress out of the bag she's brought with her and holds it against Julia's body to see what it looks like on her and then complains, saying that it looks better on her, and Julia's sure that with just a word—merely saying that she liked it would be enough—Harri would give it to her. She often gives her clothes that she's hardly ever worn. Harri's decided to change her style and is dressing sexier. *Sexy* isn't a word Julia likes. She finds it slightly laughable, asks her why she wants to look sexy now, and Harri, after shrieking a lot about Julia not knowing, as if it should be obvious, answers it's because she wants to look as attractive as possible to the man from the airport if she bumps into him. Before meeting him, she always hated having to go to the head office of the Osakidetza public health service in Bilbao once a week, but now she regrets having been so determined to bring the biostatistics conference for the health workers back to Donostia; if she hadn't forced the switch, it would have been an excuse to spend another day in Bilbao. Of course, for the young American to be able to understand any of this, Harri will have to tell what she calls the story about the man from the airport again.

REALITY IMITATES ART. But there's no need to force Harri into telling her famous story once more. To start off, she goes back to the roundtable discussion at which Julia met Martin and reminds her that she'd asked him an inappropriate question: whether he could tell her anything about what he was writing at the time. Martin had answered that he was writing a novel that begins with

127

a man and a woman meeting each other at an airport, a chance circumstance that would completely change both their lives. Julia doesn't remember it like that, but she doesn't say anything, and Martin happily nods his head as Harri extolls the gift of foresight that artists such as himself have, as can be seen in the fact that events that he wrote about in his story "Less Avoidable than Death" were later reported as true facts in the newspapers. That's why she says that reality imitates art. She's imagining it: she's lived the start of a story whose script has already been written, and she's sure, given that the story must continue, that they will meet up again sooner or later, somewhere or other, the bearded man and her. "*¿Qué te parece?*" Although she makes gestures to indicate that she's joking—her usual histrionic overacting—Julia begins to doubt whether she doesn't actually believe what she's saying. In any case, the American girl takes her "*¿Qué te parece?*" literally, because she doesn't understand the story she's telling very well, and Harri starts explaining what she calls their "meeting" in full detail, starting at the terminal at Heathrow, how her eyes and those of the bearded man in the duffel coat cross, how she has to hide the book she's reading so that he doesn't get the wrong idea about her—she has to give a short explanation of who Jon Juaristi is so that she can understand—how his bag breaks on the plane and the couple breaks up at Loiu, which is either her fault or a result of her influence—she underlines that—in the sense that if she hadn't taken the same plane as him and come across him, then the woman who was waiting for him wouldn't have said those terrible words to him, to the man she hopes to see soon, the man she hopes will leave that ugly, vulgar woman in order to be with her instead. Julia wants to ask her to stop saying silly things, embarrassed about what the young American might think, but Harri doesn't pay her any attention and after uttering a disdainful "What would you know?" starts to make her storytelling even more dramatic. She was furious about not having gotten to know him, because then she had to go back home with her husband, she wasn't interested in what he was telling her, and she found his affectionate, sentimental behavior revolting. He often gets like that when they've spent a few days apart, and she found it hard not to throw up when he said he was driving fast—literally, word for word—because he was in a hurry to get home after ten days of abstinence. A taxi overtook them at a traffic circle, and there he was. He saw her, as well. A second was enough for her to see the full intensity of his look, and she wanted the two cars to crash into each other so that they would have to stop, so that her husband and the taxi driver would have to sort out the insurance coverage and they, meanwhile, would have a chance to talk. In her dreams now, while her husband and the taxi driver are quarrelling, she and he swap addresses, even have their first kiss. In some of the dreams, the accident is so serious that her husband dies and she and the man are taken away in an ambulance, injured but not seriously.

Julia asks her again not to be silly. She finds her portrait of Martxelo hurtful—he's a sincere, agreeable man. She cares about him. In fact, Harri doesn't seem to be overacting or exaggerating her anger when she replies, with considerable disdain, "What do you mean, stop saying silly things?" Then her disdain seems to become pity—her poor friend seems to think these things only happen in novels. She turns toward the American girl and asks if she believes in *flechazos*. She doesn't really understand her. *Flechazo*: love at first sight. Finally, she says she does, "*definitely*." With that comically serious tone once more, firmly sitting up in her armchair. But she seems then to doubt the tone and how much conviction the conversation requires, saying, "*Of course I believe in it*." Of course I believe, in a very low voice.

Because Harri also believes in it, she can't wait to go to Bilbao, she dreams about meeting him again. Sometimes it's she, Harri, who goes right up to him. She reminds him that they met each other on the plane coming back from London and she had to give him a bag because the one he was carrying full of books broke. Other times it's the man—"Do you remember? I wanted to give you a book." And so on. But most times, they look each other in the eye and fall into each other's arms.

And why does she think it'll happen in Bilbao?

The young American sociologist asks the question completely seriously, in just the same way they were talking about medical examinations shortly before. Harri, too, answers with the seriousness of an epidemiologist—it's a matter of statistics. Although many Gipuzkoans and Donostians particularly use the Loiu airport, especially to fly to London, the population figures mean it's much more probable that he lives in Bilbao somewhere. Intuition tells her the same thing, as well. She thinks the man seemed more open than Gipuzkoans normally do. His way of speaking, the fact that he looked straight in her eyes, the generosity with which he gave her a book, just like that. That's more like a Bilbaoer, she says, looking dreamingly up at the ceiling as she remembers that moment, the man picking up the last book, opening it, and in his manly voice reading, *"This book was written in good faith."* Julia can't take any more. She loses her patience when she hears that the man had a manly voice, not to mention of course those senseless clichés about Bilbaoers and Donostians. She's furious that she has to hear that Bilbaoers are happy and fun-loving and Donostians are dull and boring, but no more so than if she had said that Bilbaoers are crude and Donostians are elegant. It's probably because of her nationalist education that she can't stand these dumb clichés about the two cities, which just create a sort of rivalry between them, and she tells her off. There are all types in all places. It's a stupid phrase, to which, as could be expected, Harri replies, "Sometimes more in some places than in others." They're just about to get stuck in a senseless argument when the young American, raising a finger to ask for permission to speak, asks Harri if she remembers what book the man was going to give her.

It is a strange question, and one that nobody has thought of yet. Harri doesn't know what to say. She says she's tried to remember hundreds of times, but to no avail. Now she regrets not having taken it, because she would have had something of his, it would give her some clue about him, tell her something about him. The only thing she remembers is that there was scenery on the cover. She's very sure about that. And it wasn't a photograph, it was a painting, a watercolor or pastel probably. She can visualize it. She looks mystical again, she holds her hands under her cheeks and looks at the ceiling. It was probably pastel, there was an unspoiled beach, with two empty deckchairs on it, and in the distance, a lighthouse with wide red stripes on it. It was colorful but sad-looking scene, she remembers that. The man probably chose it by chance, simply because it was the last one left on the floor. In any case, before he offered it to her, he opened it and read to her in his serious, manly voice, *"This book was written in good faith."* His English was easy to understand, his accent was the same as ours, proving that her intuition was right and he wasn't English.

"My God, it's Montauk!"

Lynn raises her hands to her face, suddenly excited, as if someone had just turned up by surprise. "It would be amazing if it were *Montauk*," which sounds a little hysterical to Julia, and she doesn't understand why Lynn is so amazed. They admit they don't know what *Montauk* is, they've never heard the name before, and she's thrilled as she explains to them that it's a place on Long Island, Montauk's a hamlet on the eastern end, it has a beach and one of the oldest lighthouses in the States, but it's also the title of a novel by the Swiss writer Max Frisch.

Julia and Martin know Max Frisch very well, he's one of the writers they admire. They've read *I'm Not Stiller*, *Homo Faber*, which has been translated into Basque, *Gantenbein*, *Man in the Holocene*, *Autumn in Peking*, *Difficult Persons*, also called *J'adore ce qui me brûle*; they haven't read his plays but think they've read all his novels, and even so, they've never heard of *Montauk*. The American girl says it's probably his best novel. She explains it's autobiographical, the writer wanted to talk about a weekend he spent in the small hamlet with a young girl, and suddenly she holds her face in her hands again and starts saying *"oh my God"*—incredibly moved—*"oh my God, it's magical!"* She's jumping up and down with the incomprehensible excitement of a hysterical child, and when she pulls herself together, she asks them if they know the name of the girl who spent the weekend on Long Island with Max Frisch. They'll never be able to guess—Lynn. It's magical. *Magical* is another word Julia hates. She hates to break the spell, but she thinks there must be thousands of books around the world with beaches, lighthouses, and deckchairs on their covers. Just as there must be a huge number of books that have a *Julia* as their main character, or even in their titles, thousands of books, and it's no reason to be particularly proud, which the young American seems to be, and all because there's a Lynn in this Frisch novel they've never heard of. She can't understand all the enthusiasm, it irritates her a bit, and that's why she says there must be millions of books with beaches, deckchairs, and lighthouses on their covers. But they don't seem to be listening to her. The book the man offered her could be *Montauk*, says Harri, her face lighting up as if the possibility were extremely important for her. Her two hands together as if she were going to pray, her nose against her forefingers, and her chin resting on her thumbs, she reflects for a moment, and the American girl remains alert. She's almost sure he said, *"This book was written in good faith.*" She's sure about that. Well, in that case, there's no doubt it was *Montauk*, the American concludes, like a doctor telling a patient that a certain medicine will clear up their disease. With a bit of luck, it'll be in the box of hers that Martin helped her carry upstairs that morning. And having said this, she rushes to the spiral staircase leading up to the attic.

The rest of them keep quiet, as if they really were her patient and her two assistants, waiting for the doctor to return and tell them the results of some X-rays. Harri's heard of Frisch but says she hasn't read anything by him. But Julia's sure she gave her the Basque translation of *Homo Faber*, because she'd said hers was getting rusty and she needed to read something in the language. She remembers that Martin once said that *Gantenbein* was Frisch's best work, which she didn't agree with. Harri and Martin wait in silence, while Julia goes over to the bookcase and starts looking for Frisch's books. She finds them quickly, he's one of the authors she's registered. There's *Gantenbein, Homo Faber, I'm Not Stiller*, and the other novels, *Military Service Record, Bluebeard*, some plays—*Andorra*, for instance—a couple of newspapers, his correspondence with Dürrenmatt, but no trace of *Montauk*. She doesn't see it mentioned in the other books, so it must have come out after them. Martin's copy of *Gantenbein* was published by Debate, and hers, which she keeps at home, was published by Barral, an older edition. As she flicks through the pages, she sees that the underlined sentences stop about halfway through, so she thinks it could be one of those books he thinks is a masterpiece but gave up on because, as he confessed, he finds reading them painful. The last underlined paragraph is on page 98—"It always seems to us that a man who feels the absence of a certain ability in a woman doesn't love her enough." Page 96: "Sometimes Lila, like all intellectual women, suffers from depression." Page 75: "Lila cheats on me, to use that dumb expression." Page 73: "He used to think that all the women, all the women he had embraced, felt loved; but all the women he really started to love sooner or later told him that he, like all men, had no idea about love." Page 66: "They had promised not to write each other letters, never, they wanted no future, this was their oath: No repetitions. No stories." Page 65: "Why is it always today?" Page 18: "I'm trying on stories as if they were suits." The first underlined passage, on page 9: "A man has had an experience and is now looking for a story to go with it—apparently, it isn't possible to have an experience that doesn't have a story to go with it—and I worked out that sometimes it's someone else who's got my story."

THE YOUNG AMERICAN APOLOGIZES when she comes back; she's taken so long because her books are still packed away. She goes up to Harri slowly, with the book hidden behind her, and when she's an arm's length away, like a magician who's going to guess the number she's thinking of, she makes a sudden movement and brings forth from the void the object she's made disappear. Julia can only see the reflection of the light coming in from the garden on the cellophane-wrapped cover, but Harri, who's incapable of saying a word, nods her head two or three times and whispers that that's the book, there's no doubt it's the actual book, and Julia's amazed to see her looking quite disconcerted.

She has no doubt about it.

Now she's shaking her head, completely convinced, with a seriousness that's a far cry from the histrionic attitude she had shortly before, and because of that, her verdict seems to be particularly important, and so it is, of course, for the young American girl who's holding it in her hands as if it were something sacred. Harri gently picks it up, looks at it for a moment, and then opens it, turns a few pages as if she were looking for something specific. After reading the words she knows by heart aloud and with great emotion, she holds it against her chest and asks the American girl if she can borrow it. Lynn says yes, and then they both, in their own languages, say that it's magical.

Martin keeps quiet throughout the scene and looks slightly amused, and Julia wonders if he realizes to what extent Harri's putting on a show for him. It's an attractive book cover. Julia almost has to wrench it from Harri's hands to be able to look at it. The beach looks rather desolate, probably because it's empty, and for some reason, she thinks it looks like one of those sad beaches in the northern part of the region that are so often battered by the wind. The sea's blue and calm. In the background there's a promontory with a red-roofed little house on it and a white lighthouse with red stripes. On the beach there are only two empty deckchairs and their shadows. It looks like a Hopper. The title's printed at the top, *Montauk*, with the first *M* and the final *K* set somewhat larger than the other letters and stretching down below them, and in that lower space between them is the writer's name, Max Frisch. The cover's wrapped in cellophane, and the author's on the back cover, in a photo that takes up the entire space, wearing his horn-rimmed spectacles, as always, and with a pipe in his mouth. The sign for Sweet's Restaurant behind him, he's leaning against a trash can, his hands in his raincoat pockets, his right leg in front of his left one, with the tip of his shoe resting on the ground. Frisch wasn't a good-looking man. The sentence on the dedication page is the one Harri remembers—"*This book was written in good faith, reader.*" It's the same observation Montaigne makes at the start of his essays, and Julia would have recognized it had it been in French. "*I am myself the matter of my book.*" A text she's transcribed and knows by heart: "I have set myself no goal but a domestic and private one, I have had no thought of serving either your or my own glory . . . *You would be unreasonable to spend your leisure on so frivolous and vain a subject.*" She opens a page at random and reads: "*Whom is Lynn thinking of?*" Then she looks at the back cover again.

"MONTAUK: *A love story, tender and tenuous, serves to illuminate a lifetime of attachments. Max Frisch, Swiss novelist and playwright, reveals himself as a man, loving, jealous, possessive, and possessed.*" She can't read any more, because Harri snatches it from her hands as if she were afraid she was going to keep it for herself.

Apparently it's time for her to leave for the biostatistics roundtable discussion. The young American's going to leave with her, to go and collect the last of her things and the cat called Max, which are still at the other house. Julia stays there. The American girl seems to think that she, too, is a teacher, and asks if doesn't have a class. It goes to show she didn't actually understand much of what they said before lunch. It's just as well. Harri explains that she's taking part in a course on literary translation, but as a student, and Martin, with a playful laugh, says that she's always attending lectures, courses, workshops, and things like that. He sometimes teases her about what he sees as a compulsive feminine thirst for education, and she knows that, deep down, he thinks it's the result of some complex she has about not having a degree. They're now in the yard. Julia doesn't hear what Martin says to the young American, because she's gone to pick up the cat dishes, and she doesn't pay any attention until she hears Harri say, "These two are like Beauvoir and Sartre." She'd like to know what made her say that. Martin replies, "Obvious differences aside." He hopes, at least, that she won't wreak her vengeance by writing a ceremonial book after he dies. Julia pretends not to hear. The American girl goes up to her to offer to help her with the yard once more, she says she really likes gardening and she's good with flowers. It's remarkable how she knows all the names—the flowers in the pots in front of the house are fragrant violets, and the ones that Martin moved to the flowerbed are a type of pansy, from the old French *pensée*, the Latin *pensare*, a thought, but the current English name is a long way from its origin. Martin is standing next to them. He promises the American girl that he will look after the yard, admitting that it's a little neglected at present. Harri, on the other hand, says that he should stop wasting his time and finish his novel once and for all. Then she looks upward and crosses her hands over her chest, "Let's see if I'm lucky in Bilbao tomorrow." This time Julia can't help telling her that she, too, would be better off if she stopped wasting time and just asked Abaitua for an appointment already. "Ugh, you're such a pill. Can't you see I have other things to think about?"

As soon as they close the iron gate, Martin rushes back to the house, and Julia knows why he's in such a hurry. It's time for Marie Lafôret's segment, and it would be the first time he's missed it since they started broadcasting it. By the time she comes into the living room, Martin's already sitting down in front of the television and Marie Lafôret's talking about the weather, about an anticyclone over the Azores. She really is beautiful, and her signs of ageing suit her, like the good use of beautiful things made of fine materials; those are the words that Martin used to write about a certain television presenter, without mentioning her name. Although Julia agrees— she's a beautiful wordly forty-something woman—she doesn't like *cet air languissant*, that languid French style of hers, which is probably what Martin most likes about her. He calls Marie Lafôret *la fille aux yeux d'or*, the girl with the golden eyes, which is what people called the actress and singer from the sixties who she looks like; and he's not wrong, her "golden eyes, as beautiful as they are sad"—Martin's words again—are indeed very similar to that woman's.

She tries not to make too much noise as she tidies things up in the kitchen, not wanting him to feel he has to offer to help her. She'd rather do it by herself than have to put up with him doing things

135

badly and against his will. But he soon pokes his head through the door and asks how he can help, and because the way she replies that she doesn't need any help comes out a little disagreeably, she tries to make up for it by saying that Harri's out of her mind, an attempt at the type of chitchat a couple that's just said goodbye to their guests might engage in. "You don't understand her" is his answer. With no trace of humor or irony. She turns the faucet off, dries her hands, and hangs the kitchen rag over the oven rail. It's obvious he's challenging her, because he's normally the one to call Harri crazy, and for any reason whatsoever.

"Don't tell me that fantasy of hers about the guy at the airport seems normal to you."

"It seems she's fallen in love."

She knows he's goading her on, and she doesn't say anything, but Martin wants to continue.

"You probably can't understand it."

The calm, natural way in which he says this irritates her. She knows she's going to lose the argument, tries to be as relaxed as he seems to be, as natural as possible, and asks him what he means, does he actually think that she's incapable of understanding someone falling madly in love? She doesn't avoid his eyes. She knows he's serious when he jokingly replies that that's exactly what he means: that she's quite unaware of certain feelings.

"But it's a complete fantasy," she blurts out without wanting to. "The only thing the poor woman wants to do is inspire you, be a model for a heroine in one of your stories."

"There, you see—what some people despise, other people want."

Why doesn't she stick a knife in his belly and stir his innards around a bit? She, too, would enjoy being an inspiration for a real artist to create something fine and beautiful with, or even, if nothing else, being the cockroach in some Kafka piece—that really would be an honor. But giving life to a character in one of his stories is just worthless. But she can't say that, she's not brave enough to attack him on his weakest flank. It's compassion, but also cowardice. Because she doesn't dare to hear what he would probably answer: What could she possibly inspire for him apart from irritation, failure, and misery?

Misery is the only thing he's given Flora Ugalde, misery is what you see in the relationship between Flora Ugalde and Faustino

Iturbe. All he's done is to bring that misery out into the open, her misery, their misery, without anything fine or noble, just misery. Pages and pages spent looking into his memory, "her treason," as he puts it, with the perverse aim of bringing it to life again.

She tries to do something that will let him know that she's not going to stay over that night, but without actually saying it, and she opens the refrigerator. She puts the bits of fresh cod that were going to be their dinner and are currently sitting in a colander into a Tupperware container. He looks at her in silence and makes a show of moving away toward the door and leaving the kitchen. A sign that he has no intention of doing anything to stop her from going.

If he were to ask her why she's angry, she'd admit it's because he was too welcoming to the young American (she could have killed him when he started petting the cat he usually kicked at, just to create a good impression), because he treated her arrogantly and disparaged her work, and because he went out of his way to compare the two of them—obvious differences aside, as he'd said—to Sartre and Beauvoir, leaving open the possibility of occasional lovers and for him to fool around with the young woman. But she supposes he knows all that, and in any event, he doesn't ask her. In the living room, she opens her bag and puts the first two books she comes across into it. "So you're not going to stay over?" he then asks her. She thinks he looks relieved.

THE CIVIL GUARD HAS UNCOVERED half a ton of explosives that two young brothers had stashed in a *zulo*—an underground hideout—in the stables at their *baserri*. They're the type of strong, surly-looking guys you often see in Otzeta, and they're frowning. Their hands are cuffed behind their backs, they're tired and broken. The surrounding woods are being searched; apparently they've confessed that there are more *zulos* than just the one. Julia's mother and Zigor are watching the news on the television. They stare at the images in silence while a voice talks about the damage that the materials the pair were keeping there could have caused. Julia knows that her mother feels sorry for them, and that makes her furious, though not as much as finding out that she, too, pities them. What must have been done to them at the Intxaurrondo barracks to get them to agree to show them where the *zulos* are? And what about the madness the two might have committed? If her mother says "poor boys," as she often has, Julia will say "I'm glad they've been arrested," but she doesn't think she'll say it. She doesn't dare to anymore, because she's told her off about it so often. She's often told her—at the same time as fighting off her own demons—that she shouldn't feel more sorry for people who were only going to bring about destruction and suffering than she does for the victims, who are at times our own kind and, in any case, still people. Her mother would always reject that argument—she does feel sorry for the victims. She'd say that she condemns violence but that the people using it are just unfortunate souls who stand no chance against the police and the army and she's sorry for them. She'd usually take refuge in a sort of resigned silence, above all for Zigor's sake, while those on the television talked about the need to respect the rule of law and said that the suffering caused by violence serves no purpose, and then she'd mumble her disagreement: "The thing is, we're the ones who always end up suffering." It was always something like that, and if Julia didn't stop her, she would start reciting the long rosary of insults and injustices they've been subjected to: they tried to blame the *gudaris*—Basque soldiers—for the bombing of Gernika; they executed her uncle; her nephew's been in prison for twenty-five years; her family's been working hard for generations without being able to get out of poverty; her husband—Julia's father—had to pay a ten thousand peseta fine for speaking in Basque. Until Julia would shout at her, asking what she was talking about, what she was trying to justify, until she'd shut up, but then, after going quiet, she would look at her with a martyr's eyes and say, with deep sadness, "Have I said anything that's untrue?"

Her mother never tells lies. She always uses the same truths in her arguments, and whenever someone tells her they're not relevant, she can't understand how anyone from her family could say that the bombing of Gernika, her uncle's execution, or the centuries of hard work and exhaustion there at Etxezar aren't a problem, however terrible whatever's just happened might be.

When he goes to bed, Julia asks her son how his interviews about the war are going. He's supposed to write a paper over the school vacation, and in order to gather material, he's been going to nursing homes to interview people about the war. It's an initiative designed to promote relationships between the generations and to strengthen historical memory. Julia thinks it's a good idea. Not all kitchens preserve echoes of war stories as the one at her house in Martutene does. In that kitchen, although there have been several remodelings to make it more up-to-date, there's still a small Our Lady of Mount Carmel on display inside a vitrine, a blind goldfinch singing in his tiny cage, a cricket they sometimes try to get drunk by giving it bread soaked in wine, and socks drying on the cauldron chain. It seems amazing to her that there are some kitchens without any memories. How quickly people get used to modern design and halogen lamps. That certainly isn't true of this kitchen.

Apparently, it's not going well, most of the old people only offer him generalizations: the Germans and the Italians helped Franco; war is the worst thing ever; everyone went hungry. In the end, he has more to talk about from the three weeks he spent at summer camp in Urbaso than the old men have from a whole war. What's more, the Donostians don't speak Basque very well, while in Otzeta, on the other hand, they speak it very well, but then it's he who has difficulty understanding what they're saying. What he'd most like to know is whether on the eve of the war, you could sense that it was going to happen.

But he doesn't want to talk about the civil war right now.

WHY WAS HIS *AITA*—HIS FATHER—CALLED ZIGOR? He's lying on the bed with his hands behind his head, looking up at the ceiling. He tends to repeat questions. Julia thinks it's something left over from his childhood, to an extent; he likes hearing stories time and again, and the possibility of comparing different versions of the same story. He was already going by that name—Zigor—when Julia met him. She thinks that when he first joined the organization, someone called Zigor had just been killed in a shootout, and since he needed a secret name, they gave him that one—one Zigor falls, a new Zigor rises. She tells him that she doesn't know, that he had that name when she met him and she doesn't think there's any special reason for it. In any case, he isn't particularly interested in the question itself— he wants to talk about his father. Julia isn't sure what impression she's given the boy of him. It's probably changed over time, just as her perception of the decisions Josean made during his life has changed.

She finds it more and more difficult to talk to him about his father without denying what his grandmother and aunt tell him, and she tries to make what she herself tells him as truthful as possible. Her mother didn't approve of Josean, but since his death, she seems to have decided that it's better for her grandson to see his father as a hero rather than a terrorist or an unlucky adventurer. Her sister has another point of view. She always admired him, and she always does her best to make Zigor feel proud to be a martyr's son. She puts so much effort into it that Julia is afraid her sister's sons may end up hating their own father for continuing to have dinner in the kitchen with them every night rather than giving up his life for the nation. Julia, too, tries to help him think of his father as a generous man, ready to give his life for a noble ideal, because she doesn't think that's a bad thing to believe and thinks it's a fine thing for a son to be proud of his father, and she wouldn't like to spoil his idealized image of him at this stage.

Did he ever kill anyone? His hands are still behind his neck, he's still looking up at the ceiling. This is a new question, something she's often thought about, a question she never dared to ask. She decides to say that she couldn't imagine him killing anyone, and it's the truth. Once, she went across the border to see him, shortly after they killed that businessman Berazadi like a dog. That death had moved her deeply, she'd felt quite close to him, she knew people who'd known him, and she was aware that he was patriotic, that he'd worked to promote the *ikastolas*—the schools where students were taught in Basque—that his employees had looked up to him, and that he'd been a fine man. She was told that he used to make the daily meals for his captors, those children who, when they became frightened that the Civil Guard were onto them, shot him dead. Their fear was greater than their compassion. She'd asked Zigor what a person must feel when they kill someone. It was an indirect question, and the word *must* was purposefully chosen. "Fear, I imagine" he'd replied. Now she regrets not having asked him the question more directly, but at least she can hang onto that "I imagine."

He never killed anyone, she says to her son. She asked him, and he said no.

"But he was killed," says the boy. There's a question behind his words, even though it comes out as a statement. They've always believed that it was an act of sabotage that made his car go off the road and over the cliff as he was driving along the Corniche route from Sokoa to Hendaia. There weren't any witnesses, nobody had heard from him since that midday, and there was nothing to explain his driving along by himself at two o'clock in the morning. What's more, he'd apparently told a lot of those closest to him that he knew someone was after him, and the fact that he'd been wounded in the attack on the Hendayais Bar led them to think it wasn't just an accident. The Gendarmerie, which didn't seem to have investigated very much, decided that he'd fallen asleep at the wheel. Perhaps being assassinated would make his life—in terms of how he'd chosen to lead it and the decisions he'd made—more meaningful than dying in a straightforward accident after falling asleep at the wheel would, but she doesn't want what happened to feed her son's hatred. She doesn't want his father—his death or his life—to determine his existence in any way other than genetically. He looks just like his father—soft, carrot-colored hair, a narrow face, melancholy eyes, a long angular nose, a small mouth, and a weak chin. Considering the life he led, anything could have happened to Zigor, including falling asleep at the wheel. She tells him the police didn't find anything suspicious. The boy wraps himself in his blanket and turns toward the wall, angrily, because it's not what he was hoping to hear. At least he says good night, even if only in a low voice.

ZIGOR IS WRITTEN ON THE RECTANGULAR ENVELOPE, in the black ink of a fountain pen. It's fine English handwriting, perhaps a little affected, the upward strokes thin, the downward ones thicker, the tail of the *Z* underlining the other letters of the name, which gives the impression that the name was written as part of some important rite. It's sealed. There's not much inside it, a couple of sheets, or maybe just one thick sheet. It's the only thing of his she still has. She destroyed everything of Zigor's, in case the police ever came to search the house; that's what she told herself when she got rid of it all, but now she knows it wasn't quite true, she could have kept a few things. He gave her the envelope a couple of months before he died.

"Give it to him on his fifteenth birthday," he said, when the boy was nearly four. He always had the shadow of death over him, and he said those words very seriously, with solemnity, giving the idea that he was in some sort of mortal danger, and she quickly put it in her

141

pocket without taking the time to look at it; it was all she could do. She didn't ask him what it was all about, whether there was any special reason for him to think that his life was in danger. She thought about asking him but didn't; she didn't want to know. She wanted to flee from him, from his world, from danger, from fear. She simply replied that she'd give it to him; she didn't need to swear to it, and he didn't ask her to. "I'll give it to him," and they started talking about something else. What was it about? Why did he seal the envelope? What was in it? Didn't she have a right to know? Why when he was fifteen? Questions that keep her from sleeping many nights but that she never thought of back then. The only thing she was concerned with was not falling into his trap, not letting his tearful, morbid, sentimental ways affect her, not accepting the emotional blackmail of someone positioned so close to death, whether deliberately or not.

She put it away with her invoices and tax returns. She can't say that she ever managed to forget it, but she didn't start worrying about it until Zigor's death made the unknown thing inside it become the sacred last will of someone who'd died, an obligation that had to be fulfilled. From time to time, she took it out of the file and felt it to see how much it weighed, and held it against the light to try to see inside. Even so, she wasn't very curious, she didn't have much doubt about what was inside—a letter written in affected words to justify his life, rejoicing in his choice to dedicate it to an ideal. "I fought for our country so you could be freer." Messages like that, sent from the tomb, could influence her son profoundly and become a terrible burden for him. And now, as her son gets closer to fifteen, she's getting more worried, and her obligation to fulfill Zigor's final wish often keeps her awake at night. Of course, the right for father and son to have a relationship is not broken by death, a father has a right to pass his inheritance onto his son, and the son to receive it, and they both have the right for the privacy of their mutual correspondence to be respected. It is for her, on the other hand, to respect those rights— the father's words, made sacred by death, belong to the son—but at the same time, she has to look after her son's well-being and the greater good (and, to the extent to which his father's words might be a condemnation, to protect him from them). Those are simultaneously her rights and her duties. She's sometimes considered waiting until her son comes of age—which is to say until he's old enough to be able to fully measure the significance of his father's words—and she's also thought of opening the envelope and deciding what to do after seeing the contents. But she hasn't felt able to. Not because it would be a breach of the privacy between father and son, or not only because of that, but mostly because she's afraid of seeing the contents, of hating Zigor forever if, as she believes, he's going to come back from beyond the grave to urge his son to fight and sacrifice himself.

She's sometimes even thought of burning it without opening it. A fantasy, of course. She cries when she imagines how she would feel if she received a letter from her father. A few words for Julia. She lets all her tears come out—she was a fatherless teenager—and feels all her pain. She's still an orphan. She's sure that if he'd ever written a letter, it would have been to tell her that we're in this world to be happy and to help others to be happy—that's what he always used to say. She cries softly, without sobbing or moaning, as she remembers her father's words, and she feels easier. "*Txata fea*," he used to say, poking fun at what he called her ugly little nose, but he would say she was a pretty girl, as well. He could have said that in a letter; although everyone thought her sister was his favorite, in fact it was her. She can't imagine how moved she would have felt if her father had left her an envelope like that. She sets Zigor's to one side, with her tear-soaked hand pulled up inside her sweater sleeve so as not to get it wet.

She hasn't told anyone there's a letter. Partly because she finds it hard to talk about her intimate things, partly because she's afraid people won't understand the ethical doubts that Zigor's instructions have raised for her, or because they'll take them as a lack of respect on her part for the wishes of the dead. It would be useless to look for advice from those closest to her. Her mother and her sister would definitely say that she has to respect Josean's wishes and her son's rights and that she could have refused him when he first gave her the letter. Having doubts at all would seem terrible to them, a serious sin. Harri, on the other hand, would no doubt make her open it at once in order to satisfy her own curiosity. She would think the ethical problem a matter of irrelevance—who knows what that lunatic might have written, she'd say—and while children do require guidance, they also have to be protected from their parents. What's more, if Julia didn't do what Harri told her to, Harri would criticize her and be incapable of keeping it to herself, she'd let

Martin know somehow or another, and Julia doesn't want that to happen. Martin is jealous of her past—she thinks that's why he finds it difficult to get on well with her son—he wouldn't be comfortable with Josean's presence, or presence of a sort, and his opinion on the matter would of course be biased. Whenever Josean's name comes up—and Julia tries to make sure it doesn't—Martin says something unpleasant, even if it's irrelevant. When the American girl went back to the subject of nicknames and pseudonyms at lunch, because she suddenly understood that Zigor was a *"war name"*—and funnily enough, they use the French term, *nom de guerre*, in English—Martin mentioned the *"drôle de guerre,"* the Phoney War, to round out the conversation. "So, she's already told you that she had a relationship with a war hero," Martin said with an insincere smile, and Julia stopped herself from saying what she was thinking, which was that she can't stand people who, out of pure cowardice, never took part in the war and now shamelessly give lessons in morality to those who had.

Even so, those aren't the only reasons for her not talking about Josean's letter, nor are they the main ones. The biggest obstacle is that Martin has asked her to be the executor of his literary will, and she wouldn't like him to doubt her ability to do that because of her doubts about complying with Zigor's instructions.

Martin explained to her in a normal tone, without getting too serious about it, as if he were telling her about some normal, everyday event, that there was nothing in particular to be scared of or to worry about but that he would be more comfortable if he knew that if something *did* happen to him, she would see to destroying his papers, drafts, notes, and his computer. He didn't want anything to be kept. "There's nothing that deserves to be kept, really," he reassured her. "I want to know that you'll throw everything away." It seemed like a genuine request to her, because they once complained together about vultures going through people's trash. He didn't say much more than that, asking only that she go ahead with it regardless of what might happen with their relationship; he hoped she'd keep her word. "You'll do it, won't you?" She said yes and doesn't have any doubts about it. She has sometimes thought about what will happen when the time comes. They haven't talked about it directly again, only indirectly. As she remembers it, Harri once mentioned that she was reading Max

Brod's *Kafka*. She certainly agreed with his decision not to respect Kafka's will and ventured that writers can't really want their unpublished work to be destroyed, that such a wish could be neither true nor credible. Then they discussed whether the world would be different without *The Trial*, *The Castle*, or *Amerika*. Julia thinks not and that another way to describe absurd nightmare situations would have been invented. Then, and with a certain degree of seriousness, but naturalness, as well, Martin said that he didn't have much to leave behind him but he'd rather it wasn't published, and Harri was concerned by that. And that was where they'd left the matter.

Julia knows that Martin trusts her and believes her when she assures him that she'll carry out his will. In general, people do tend to trust her, they think she's sincere. People close to her know that her character wouldn't allow her to break her promises and that she's incapable of revealing a secret. She's not proud of that, because it isn't a virtue, more like an inability, a lack of flexibility, and to an extent, like imagination, it's something connected with an inability to deceive. At the same time, just thinking about doing something unfair makes her feel sick, she has no ability to act wrongly, and she couldn't stand the humiliation if she were ever caught doing so. It's something like the sensation of vertigo when looking over a cliff. The people she knows are aware of her limits in terms of being able to tell lies, in terms of betrayal, and sometimes she imagines that they enjoy sharing things with her that they couldn't trust anyone else with while still maintaining their dignity, sordid things she'd rather not have to hear, she imagines that they're allowing themselves to behave like those who, when faced with a blind person, don't bother to keep their rude gestures and attitudes in check.

She puts the letter back in the file it's sat in for more than ten years. If she had a piano, she'd play something about pain, she'd play Jose Gontzalo Zulaika Agirre's *Oinazez*.

4

Iñaki Abaitua has his jacket on by the time Pilar comes into his room. She's decided to go to the clinic, and can he wait for her a minute. But she's still in her pajamas. She said before that all she had that day was someone coming in with a hyriated disc at the end of the evening and that she was going to stay at home all day and put some documents in order. "Give me a minute and I'll be ready." She's quick and doesn't spend too much time getting made up— very little time at all compared with other women, if some men's complaints are to be believed—but she's going to make him late even if she tries to hurry. He tells her he has a meeting first thing, and could she please get a move on.

He finds arriving late for any appointment embarrassing; he's usually the first to demand punctuality. He can't stand unpunctuality. He doesn't like waiting for any longer than the quarter of an hour required by politeness and doesn't hesitate to tell people who are late that their lack of punctuality is not just a lack of courtesy, it's also an unforgivable lack of respect. He's sometimes asked people— half jokingly, half seriously—who they are to steal even five minutes from his life. And this time it's even more serious, because there are going to be people from outside his immediate group at the meeting, such as Harri Gabilondo, the department's epidemiologist, who is very strict when it comes to manners, and they usually understand each other very well, particular when they're criticizing the general lack of respect and the amount of neglect at the hospital. "And then we say we aren't Spanish!" That's what Gabilondo said once when she wanted to show someone up for their lack of politeness.

"Just a minute," Pilar says once more. She's taken her shower and has a yellow towel wrapped around her head and another one of the same color around her waist. He leans against the side of the bathroom door as he watches her applying lotion around her eyes with her little finger; it's his bathroom, after all, and he wants to make it clear that her being there is making him late. Pilar, looking at him in the mirror, asks him to close the living room blinds, otherwise the sun will get in. She always does the same thing: when she's running late, she asks him to do something or other so that he doesn't feel like he's waiting.

"Here's the expert at last," says Arrese. He's also been known to call him "the learned one" from time to time. That's one of his habits, poking fun at Abaitua for studying too much or wanting to know too much. The one who knows the most, the one who studies the most. *Medicus sapiens.* "My wife's doctor" he also sometimes says. Abaitua thinks he actually means it and that he respects him. The thing is, he likes making a caricature of Abaitua's shortcomings in order to make up for his own, and he mentions Abaitua's lack of practical ability and absentmindedness continually, marking him down as an eccentric scientist at best. He also tends to make a caricature of himself. He often praises his own ordinariness and straightforward character, mentioning his lack of enthusiasm for studying and other shortcomings without any embarrassment, in a provocative way, even. Many colleagues and nurses have told Abaitua—and he doesn't think they do so to flatter him—that it's clear that when he's with Abaitua, it's his own complexes and feelings of guilt that make him speak like that and that the man believes that by rights, Abaitua should be the head of the department, not himself. With regard to that, it's significant to point out that he in fact says department heads do not necessarily have to be the smartest or the wisest individuals in their respective departments. According to him, that characteristic rebelliousness that's deep inside us is rooted in our inability to accept someone less capable than us being put in charge of us, which is a situation that's accepted as normal in more advanced societies, like cars stopping when the traffic lights are red without ever asking why they don't stop when they're green. To be in charge, you only need precisely the amount of intelligence required to be in charge, no more and no less. He's heard him say it hundreds of times.

"The doctor who knows most about perinatal health in all of Europe." He says that to a young redheaded woman; she must be the sociologist Harri Gabilondo told him about. So there's no formal introduction. Gabilondo points at the free seat to her right for him to sit in. The young American sociologist looks to her left, raises her chin, and smiles at him. It's a short, fleeting gesture, a stretching of the lips, a closing of the eyes, and wrinkles appear all over her face. Then she introduces herself in Spanish—"*Mi nombre es Lynn.*" Her pronunciation is clear, but she speaks very low, almost as if she were going to tell him a secret.

The plan is to access all available data over a period of three months relating to subjects' pregnancies and birthings and their infants' first month of life, in order to be able to connect that data with information about mortality and sickness rates as well as the greatest possible number of endogenous and exogenous factors. In addition to that, the Gen laboratories in the United States are doing a related study to look at all the mothers' and babies' mitochondrial DNA. Abaitua is proud that Harri Gabilondo mentions him as a reference in her research. It must have been a lot of work back then, she says. He thinks she's younger than Pilar, though not by much, and there's more contrast between her upper and lower parts— small breasts and wide hips, good for childbirth. Their hairstyles are similar, as well, short with long layers, almost pageboy-style, making them look young and full of life. The color of Harri Gabilondo's hair is very beautiful, straw-blond, and it goes well with her light-colored eyes. People often take her for being Danish or Dutch, but she describes herself as a simple, homegrown Martutene girl.

Abaitua knows that she likes him a lot, and she often shows it. She says that this opportunity to take part in research in conjunction with the best-run hospitals in the world is thanks to him, thanks to the personal efforts of Doctor Abaitua, and that's true. Arrese was hesitant to sign on to the project, because he was afraid his standards wouldn't look very good compared with other people's, although he does normally accept Abaitua's suggestions. Abaitua can't complain in that regard. Arrese accepts his moral leadership and gives him total freedom to organize his work, carry out research, and go to conferences and roundtable discussions; but even so, Abaitua feels relegated to a lower level every time he has to introduce himself as a mere assistant when he meets up with old colleagues from other hospitals or when, as has just happened, Arrese, in his role as head of the department, speaks clumsily, using inappropriate words, even though he knows that people who know them both are aware that his inferior status is a result of his own decision to try to avoid the administrative responsibilities and problems that come with author-ity—and Abaitua himself has encouraged that impression. And Arrese himself often admits, though mostly in a humorous manner, that he's the leader because Abaitua didn't want to be. "Boss by default" is how he describes himself.

In fact, in the past, Abaitua used to head the Maternity-Pediatrics Service when old Olano was having his heart attacks and having to take long periods off afterward; then, when he died, nobody was surprised that Abaitua became the provisional head.

Everyone in their professional environment, including Abaitua, both at the hospital and elsewhere, was convinced that he was going to be made the permanent head, thinking that because of his reputation and professionalism, nobody else would even stand for the job. There was a consensus that the job was his, and although he enjoyed declaring the opposite, he was pleased by that. For mostly aesthetic reasons, he felt obliged to say that he was taking the post against his will and that it was going to be a great sacrifice for him. He complained to those above him and those below him, everywhere, about all the management work he was going to have to do, which would rob him of time to study and to practice medicine, but of course that wasn't the whole truth, because being the head of the department would also bring considerable rewards: as well as pleasing his vanity more than anyone could imagine, he also imagined that the position would enable him to put into practice the improvements he had in mind.

On the very day the position was officially announced, Arrese turned up at his office and said he was applying for it himself. Abaitua remembers the details of the conversation very well, he's relived it hundreds of times. First, as soon as he came into the office, and before saying what his visit was about, before saying what needed to be said, he spoke to him, seemingly offhandedly, about Teresa Hoyos. Apparently, she was being treated by Arrese now. Very few women have ever left Abaitua's care without giving a reason, but Hoyos is one of them. She'd called to cancel an appointment of hers and hadn't returned. It wasn't because she'd forgotten it, or because of any sort of negligence on her part, and in fact, she wasn't that type of person. According to the nurse, she hadn't accepted the alternate appointment date she was offered. Abaitua is sure about that, because he's often asked the nurse to tell him what happened over the phone with the woman, to remember the exact words used, whether she noticed anything in particular while they were talking. He asked her so often that once, overcome by nervousness, she even started crying; Abaitua decided at that point not to mention Teresa Hoyos's name ever again, in order not to make the nurse nervous, and because he thought she might be starting to have strange suspicions on seeing him so affected by losing a patient. But when he heard that she'd started going to Arrese, he lost not only the shred of hope that she might come back one day but also the precarious hypothesis he'd formed about why she'd left. In fact, ETA had just killed her father, who'd been a colonel or a lieutenant colonel of logistics, and Abaitua thought that it was because of that sad event and due to an understandable feeling of rejection toward nationalists and their kind that she wanted to have nothing to do with people in any way connected with them, including himself, even though he was a long way from sharing the ideology of her father's assassins; she would definitely consider him to be a nationalist, and so he was, though not a very fervent one any longer. It wasn't the sort of behavior he would have expected of Teresa Hoyos, but he wanted to hold onto the theory, because it was the best one he could come up with. However, her going over to Arrese completely invalidated it, because the man was a confessed, open, proud nationalist.

He asked, in a straightforward way, how she was, and the answer he gave was that she was as beautiful as ever. He added that he thought her a very sensitive woman. "Sensitive and fragile," he said, and Abaitua, even though he thought the description correct, was astonished. So she was, he agreed. He realized that Arrese's mentioning the woman was motivated by more than just the pleasure of rubbing his nose in the fact that he'd stolen one of his patients, and suddenly he felt all the symptoms of an acute spike in blood pressure—his blood beat fast in his veins, he felt his neck go tense, a thudding in his ears, a tingling sensation in his fingers and toes, saw little lights in his clouded vision. So, it was undeniable that Hoyos had left him, and she'd probably done so because she felt mistreated somehow. He felt lost, defeated. For the first time in his life, he felt lessened in the presence of that clumsy fool. It was also the first time he heard that only a certain amount of intelligence was needed in order to serve as a department head. Less so than to be a doctor, in fact. Then he mentioned bureaucratic inertia, the prevailing lack of professional commitment, politicians' negligence—all the things that Abaitua usually complained about. He understood that for Abaitua—sensitive and delicate as he was, and with such different ambitions than himself—being the head of the department would be a thankless task. That's what he'd come to say, that Abaitua was a research man, a scholar, too demanding and too much of a perfectionist to be able to handle people, while he, on the other hand, had broad shoulders and really enjoyed giving orders and in fact that was all he was actually good for. "I understand why you're not happy, this isn't really for you," he said with great conviction, placing a paternalistic hand on his shoulder. Abaitua felt profoundly demoralized but forced himself to say that he wanted to cure the sick, that that was his vocation and duty, and he had no intention of putting himself forward as department head.

Nobody was surprised by his decision. In fact, he even got the impression that nobody was expecting anything else. Pilar thought it was a coherent decision. "Good for you, let someone else put up with those idiots," she said, adding that she hoped he would have more free time from then on. He doesn't know to what extent his son, who was still a teenager back then, felt disappointed by his lack of ambition, and he tried at least to explain why he didn't want to be a boss. Fortunately, nobody could imagine just how frustrating it was for him to see everyone accept so relaxedly the fact that he'd renounced the position, and to an extent, that relaxed acceptance bothered him, and it still does, their understanding that he turned his nose up at the difficulties, power, and even the money that come with leadership when absolutely everybody else would have killed to rise up in the hierarchy. Apparently, he's "like that." And because he's apparently like that, he's forced to behave accordingly. So he works well beyond his official hours, often does post-operative checkups at night and on public holidays, and that seems perfectly normal to his colleagues, who might easily leave a patient lying open on the operating table for him to deal with so that they can rush off to their own private practices, because that's "their thing," just as golf is some other people's thing, a hobby. Pilar's often said that he's an addict to the practice of medicine. He wonders what she would say if she saw what he's really like—he, as Arrese knows, does everything out of weakness and cowardice, out of guilt.

Every time Arrese looks at him with that mocking half-smile, as he's doing now, Abaitua becomes afraid he's going to say something about Teresa Hoyos. Normally Arrese leaves after giving his peculiar introductions. That's what he always does after greeting everyone, puffing himself up a bit, telling a joke or two, and then quickly, when he gets bored, pointing upward at the ceiling and saying that he has a meeting with "the man upstairs," the director, in other words, and then he leaves Abaitua to lead the meeting. Abaitua figures he's staying on longer today because Harri Gabilondo's there. They have a strange relationship. Harri Gabilondo always speaks poorly of him. She says he has a lack of style and a coarseness that's fairly common among Basque men, but Abaitua thinks she also finds him attractive. Now, while Gabilondo is explaining certain technical considerations, Arrese listens to her with a smile on his face and his hands behind his neck, almost lying down in his chair. He's wearing his usual green scrubs with no coat, although he seldom goes into the operating theatre, because he saves all his strength for operating on whatever they throw at him at Pilar's father's clinic, of which he's a shareholder. He's a strong, healthy man, physically attractive, although also very uncouth, to tell the truth. You can see from his body—muscular arms, a bit of a belly (though not too much of one), supple movements (thanks to exercise; he switched from *pilota* to golf several years ago)—that he both leads an active life and likes to frequent cider houses and grills. Although he's a little younger that Abaitua, he doesn't think he looks it, maybe because his hair's completely white. Harri Gabilondo says he perfumes himself with testosterone. Abaitua finds his blatant masculinity revolting—the mass of hair coming out the wide neck of his scrubs, his habit of taking his feet out of his shoes and massaging them, his shameless scratching of his genitals, which he's exhibiting now, leaning back with his legs stretched all the way out, his arms above his head, showing off his hairy armpits without a care in the world. But many people like him a lot, because he lets people get on with things and because he's a nice man, an uncomplicated man.

EVENLY-SUSPENDED ATTENTION. He likes the term, which psycho-analysts use to describe the technique of listening to things in a mechanical way without paying any special attention to what's being said. Abaitua, however, has another way of listening: as a child, he would have his in the clouds but without leaving the world completely behind, a technique he used for listening to what the friars were saying, and when suddenly one of them would demand "So, Abaitua, what have I been saying?" he'd be able to repeat their last sentence. Nowadays, too, in uselessly extended meetings like this—the type in which some people feel the need to repeat what they've already said and others indulge their belief that time is better spent in meetings than working—he still uses that way of not paying attention to what's being said, listening to just the words and doodling on a piece of paper meanwhile. He's still good at drawing and remembers Guyton's manual on physiology. He keeps himself entertained drawing the figure of a woman seen from the front, marking her arteries, ligaments, muscles, nerves and veins, celiac artery, ureter, uterus, vagina, ovarian artery, lower vasa vasorum, cephalic artery, femoral artery . . . until he realizes that the young American sociologist's looking at him, and they exchange a look of mutual understanding that says that they're fed up, bored. And then a smile. He remembers that when Harri Gabilondo said that she was going to bring an American sociologist with her, Arrese said it wasn't going to be helpful having one of those feminists who believe women should give birth sitting down and that sort of stuff sticking her nose into things. He laughed at his own comment, as well. Her skin is quite white, maybe too white, but she looks healthy.

Two hours to sort out what could have been done in half an hour. A way with words is not a strong point in our country. In general, people approach even the simplest matters in circular movements that close in on the issue little by little, and Abaitua finds it annoying. It seems the young American sociologist doesn't like it, either; she shows her impatience a couple of times when people are unable to define an issue and take their time about it. "*Anyway,*" she says, using both hands to tuck a lock of hair behind each ear, unable to hide her impatience. Then she expresses herself directly and clearly, although also apologizing for her lack of linguistic skill. It seems it isn't a matter of her mastery of the language, more that she knows how to use her linguistic resources well, limiting herself to expressing her ideas in a simple way and without using any rhetoric. She doesn't make many gestures. She rests her forearms on the table and holds her hands together, a little raised up, showing no sign of being irritated. Her fingers are very thin, and when she talks, she looks at the pen she's playing with, but she's also able to look people in the eye. There's no doubt that she's clever, and she uses biochemical terms correctly. She also seems to have that lack of inhibition that Abaitua envies so much in foreigners when it comes to things that affect her personally, when she wants to clarify where she's going to be, and what her specific role is. One of us wouldn't dare to be so open and direct on their first day, and we'd end up letting loose our stored up irritation later on, too late.

She must be under thirty.

The young American sociologist says, "This is probably a stupid question."

But she's having a hard time believing that people are expected to be able to list all the last names, both paternal and maternal, of each of their four grandparents—eight names in total—on official forms in the Basque Country. Her remark causes a stir. All of them compete to recite their own long list of last names, to show the American sociologist that it's quite possible. Arrese, too, says all of his, all of them Basque names, of course. It's a cultural trait of ours, being proud of our roots. They're all saying things like this to explain their attachment to their last names. Abaitua decides to turn off even his evenly-suspended attention in order not to hear things that may irritate him, and he starts reciting to himself all the last names of his own that he can remember. There are exactly eight of them: Abaitua, Segurola, Zubia, Gabilondo, Rezola, Zabaleta, Galarraga, and Aranburu. He knows more—Mekolalde, Juaristi, and Aranguren, for instance—but he doesn't remember what order those ones go in. He remembers a man from Azpeitia, he thinks he was a dentist, who owned a restaurant in Madrid that might have been called Gure Etxea—or "Our House"—and which was advertised as being one hundred percent Basque; the man put twenty last names on his business card, all of them Basque. Being over-proud of having Basque blood was not seen as being at all suspicious in the sixties, and even in Madrid people used to say that any self-respecting person's second last name was Basque. Basques were well thought-of, and their being proud of their family names was considered natural because, among other things, all of them, as everybody knew, had their own family coat of arms and were entitled under the historical charters to noble status. He remembers that when he was a child, he heard his father say that one of his friends, who ran a clothing shop downtown, used to get tearful after he'd had a few drinks and even start sobbing, all because his last name was Calvete—a Spanish name. His father said they used to try to console him by saying that being Basque is something that comes from the soul, but Abaitua could see how pleased his father was with his own situation—he was just a simple worker himself, but at least he didn't have to bear the weight of having a name like Calvete. He was proud of his family names—Abaitua, Zubia, Rezola, and so on—in that they were Basque, and he wouldn't have minded others—Goikoetxea or Perugorria—as long as they, too, were Basque. That was what his father was proud of. Abaitua, as well, though more so previously than now. On the other hand, he doesn't think Pilar cares too much about last names; she wouldn't mind being a Calvete, and their son doesn't care much, either. Young people in general don't worry about these things, not so much, at any rate. They can each project whatever origin they choose to through the way they spell their last names, *Basque-ifying* them, so to speak, if they wish, particularly by using an initial *K* instead of a *C*—he's sure one of his father's friend's grandchildren must be a *Kalbete* by now—and in any case, they tend to display their identity more in their first names than in their last names, or more obviously so.

The fat resident doctor says his extended family name has *Etxebarria* in it twice, "in the Biscayan fashion," he specifies. On his coat pocket, it's embroidered with the Spanish *ch* spelling in the place of the Basque *tx*, which Abaitua thinks might be one of the reasons he doesn't like the man. He scans in search of his fat face at the other end of the table and then realizes that there's sudden, complete silence and that everybody's looking at him expectantly.

"What do you say, Doctor Abaitua?"

155

Maite Leunda, a pediatrician who's about to turn fifty, is addressing him, and it's obvious she's now repeating herself. So he apologizes to her and asks her to repeat the question. She asks him meekly, with that calm voice that many women of firm spirit possess. Her question—and it's something she asks herself, as well—is to what extent there may be a hidden agenda, beyond the project's stated objective, to uncover the genetic blip, the particular polymorphism, that makes the Basques a separate race. She's probably trying to be ironic, and Abaitua realizes that one way to reply would be to express indignation, but he's prevented from doing so by seeing Arrese making a show of looking offended, holding his head in both hands and shaking it from side to side as if he can't believe the stupidity of what he's just heard, and perhaps he genuinely is upset by it. The fact that the young American sociologist is there is another reason for Abaitua to give a measured response. Finally, he decides to ignore Leunda and speak directly to the sociologist, to explain three points. Firstly, and obviously, the objective behind requiring eight Basque surnames is to select subjects with the greatest number of distant ancestors born in the region, in order to run proper differential analyses. And that's necessary because there are some very real distinguishing features: genotypic differences, for example the high instance of the Rh-negative blood type; the increased prevalence of certain unusual genetic diseases, fatal familial insomnia, for one, as well as less unusual ones, such as muscular dystrophy, or Parkinson's disease, which has a Basque variant. From a healthcare point of view, it would be irresponsible not to take all of that into account. And lastly, even knowing that this type of general data about the genetic makeup of populations has the potential to be manipulated politically, he hopes and believes that they're in a more aseptic setting than that here.

Enthusiastic expressions of agreement. Arrese mimes applause, and Gabilondo, sitting next to him, says that nobody could have put it better. Leunda looks at him in silence, like a martyr who's declared her faith and now has nothing left to do but wait for her turn to be thrown to the lions.

After the meeting, Harri Gabilondo takes him by the arm and says, "Hey, you, let's all go grab some coffee and lay into them a bit!" The young American sociologist is standing next to her. She's wearing a rather old blue leather jacket and a white shirt

156

unbuttoned down to the top of her cleavage, the skin covered with freckles. He suggests they get their coffee from the machine and go to his office; at that time of day, the cafeteria will be crowded. Harri Gabilondo agrees that it's like some sort of bus or train station canteen. As she normally does, as soon as they're two steps out of the meeting, she starts giving a comic report on it. She doesn't hold back. What does Abaitua make of Martínez Leunda's outburst? She emphasizes the *Martínez*. It seems she's the daughter of one of those Navarrese *Requetés*, the Carlist militiamen who used to steal furniture and sheets from the houses of those who'd fled Donostia. She kept her *Martínez* well-hidden until a short while ago and has just recently started using it openly, now a proud Spaniard. "*¿Qué te parece?*" She keeps on repeating that question, which, though rhetorical, makes him feel put on the spot and uncomfortable when he has nothing to answer, or when, like now, he's finding it difficult to listen.

Everything's seeming complicated to him at the moment. He remembers his father's friend Calvete and thinks about telling them the story about when he used to get drunk, but he doesn't find it funny right now. He isn't pleased to hear once again that he did very well in the meeting, because he dealt with the problem in just the way Arrese wanted him to; he knows the man's proud that there's a Basque variant of Parkinson's disease, which is why the proteins that control the mutated genes have a Basque name, *dardarin*, from *dardara*—trembling. *This protein, dardarin, whose name is derived from the Basque word* dardara, *meaning tremor.* He's proud that it's special, even though it's a damaging difference. They head straight for the stairs without waiting for the elevator. Gabilondo has to explain to the young American sociologist now, too, as she does every time she uses the stairs with someone new, that it was Abaitua who taught her never to take the elevator and that it's an excellent way to keep fit. Going up six flights of stairs twice a day is the minimum amount of exercise for an adult. It's also a great way to avoid contagious diseases and, above all, bad smells. And people's dirty looks, he adds. The young American laughs.

It seems a lot of people have decided to go down the stairs; the elevators are always full up at that time of day, and it's hard for the three of them to remain walking side by side as they go up. After his usual doubts about protocol—in this case, whether the man should go before the women so that he doesn't see their legs, or go behind them in order to catch them if they should fall—he finally chooses the latter option, in order not to look weak, and what's more, he'd rather not expose his backside to them. Harri Gabilondo has a wide behind—she'd clearly take him all the way down to the ground floor if she fell, carrying him away with her—and her tight skirt forces her to walk up the steps sideways. The sociologist keeps in step with her, though she'd doubtless prefer to go up faster. At one point, she turns around, and Abaitua is embarrassed by the thought that she might think he's checking out her ass. She smiles at him.

She's very glad to be able to take part in this research project, she thinks it's a very interesting piece of work. She seems to be telling the truth. Abaitua says that he's glad she's accepted the job, too. He musters the courage to admit he's forgotten her name. Lynn. *"First name or last?"* Sometimes he can't tell them apart. In her case, it's her first name, but it could be either, she says with a smile. Some people with the last name Lynnsey have shortened it to Lynn, but some people also use it as a boy's name, and some dogs probably get called it, as well. Her *Lynn* might be of Welsh origin. She's taken it to be that, because it's the option she likes best—green, mining Wales.

Gabilondo takes every chance she gets to lay into people. Whenever he's with her, he can't help thinking what bit of him she'll go for as soon as he turns his back. Now she imitates Arrese's ceremony of opening his handkerchief to blow his nose and then inspecting what's come out before finally folding it carefully up again. What can you expect from a doctor who's incapable of using paper tissues? Abaitua can't understand why he uses handkerchiefs, either. The sociologist laughs at Gabilondo's imitations. Being American, and so young, perhaps she's never used handkerchiefs. He uses them and then washes them for reuse, Gabilondo says with a look of revulsion on her face. He tells her not to be mean. He says it without much conviction, not liking to criticize people, even if it is Arrese.

"Me, mean? It's that Martínez de Leunda who's mean!"

He also finds it annoying that half of what she's saying must be difficult to understand for the young American. He asks her if she understands what Harri Gabilondo means when, speaking about Leunda again, she calls her *"esa hija de requeté navarro enchufado en el fielato*"—that daughter of a Navarrese Requeté rubber-stamped into his spot at the municipal impost office. Has she understood? She can't possibly understand what words like *requeté* mean. She moves her hands around expressively and laughs. "*More or less.*" In other words, she hasn't understood a thing. But that doesn't stop Gabilondo from carrying on in the same vein. Although she's quite a bit younger than him, she often says "in our day," in order to create an atmosphere of mutual trust between them. In our day. When being Spanish was seen as pathetic and Basques were the richest, the most anti-Franco, and the most prestigious people in all of Europe. At that time, Martínez Leunda was very happy to be Basque and used only her second surname, Leunda. And now? Now that our best days are behind us, she suddenly realizes she's a Martínez and that she's Spanish. "*¿Qué te parece?*"

Now she seems to be looking at the young American sociologist, as well, waiting for a reply.

He decides to say that she's not wrong about that. He, too, has seen how certain people have turned their backs on the Basque Country now that it has problems, and that fact hurts him. He's also afraid that the rejection of violence will be followed by a rejection of nationalism, and then by an abandonment of everything that is in any way Basque, right down to the emblematic *zortziko* dance. But what's more to blame than nationalism itself?

And why is he hurt by it?

He takes advantage of the fact that Gabilondo's stopped to say hello to someone to change subject. "*What about you?*" She has an impressive résumé for her age. She also studied genetic anthropology at Columbia, which is where she picked up the familiarity she displayed at the meeting with haplogroups, mitochondrial DNA, polymorphism, and other technical ideas. It was only a graduate course, but it was enough for her to realize that science is interested in so-called "traditional" peoples such as the Basques. So it was her anthropological interest in the aboriginal population that brought her to the Basque Country, Abaitua jokes, and she replies that it was, to an extent. She'd read Dos Passos's memoirs, in which he says "*I like the Basques*," and that gave her the idea to come and find out more.

She laughs again when Harri Gabilondo says that she gives a different version each time she's asked what she's doing in the Basque Country. Apparently she's also said she came to see the San Fermín

159

festivities, among other strange reasons. She's started to think she must be with the CIA. The sociologist's laugh is pretty loud, that uninhibited laugh Americans have, her mouth wide open. She's holding a blue file folder, with elastic bands at the corners, pressed against her chest. By the way, don't they think Arrese looks a lot like Hemingway? They never realized, but he does a bit. He'd love it if she told him that. Harri Gabilondo, of course, brings out her testosterone joke, his using it as eau de cologne, and the two women laugh. Now it's the young American who says she's mean, and Abaitua who says she has no idea just how right she is. And then he says what he thought of shortly before—he wonders aloud what she must say about him when his back's turned. Answering more seriously than she intended, Harri Gabilondo swears, "Never anything bad about you." She speaks first in Spanish, then repeats herself in English, "*Es el médico más interesante y honesto que conozco. The most interesting and honest doctor I know. Do you understand?*" The American says she does, and Abaitua tries to hide how embarrassed he is by the flattery. He's about to say she probably says the same to everybody, when the nurse comes in without knocking and looks with curiosity at the three of them, one by one, then goes over to one side of the table and starts organizing prescriptions. There are already people waiting outside. The two women stand up with their plastic cups in their hands. Abaitua takes them from them and throws them into the trash can. He comes out to the vestibule with them. He knows that Gabilondo likes people to be polite to her, and he tries to treat her as she expects to be, even though her gratitude for his courteousness wears on him. "You're a real gentleman, not like some other people." She calls him smart and distinguished in front of the young American sociologist for the second time. They're appropriate compliments to pay an old man, of course, but several women have spoken well of his neatness and pleasant fragrance, as a result of which he deduces that some men don't take much care with their personal hygiene. In any case, he thinks that women aren't very happy with men here in general, often finding them to be clumsy and vulgar. In Harri Gabilondo's case, on the other hand, it's her worry that people won't appreciate her class that leads her to become a little vulgar.

So we'll see each other often, says the young American, and she seems pleased at the prospect. She has lively eyes, unwavering eyes, and he feels shaken up. And angry, too, that a mere child can make him feel like this at his age. When they're in the vestibule and about to say goodbye, he sees Arrese going by with a group of people from his father-in-law's clinic. Orl is among them. "Ah, having a chat, I see?" As if they'd caught them doing something much worse. Of course, what Arrese reproaches him for is not wasting time—that in itself would not be reason enough for reproach—but talking with two women. In order to get over being humiliated and, at the same time, make it very clear that he is capable of talking with two women, he tells Harri Gabilondo, when she says she absolutely must tell him her latest story about "that ridiculous oaf," that he has plenty of time. So after making sure that nobody is going to hear her, moving her head to glance from one side to the other like a bird, she tells them something that happened to a friend of hers when she went to have a consultation with him, something that happened a couple of years ago but which she hasn't dared tell anyone until now. While he was examining her on the gynecological table, apparently he suddenly took his head out from between her legs and said, with a very serious expression on his face, that her discharge smelled terrible. "*¡Joder, cómo te huele!*" Those were his exact words: "Jesus, what a stench!" Her friend, naturally, worried it wasn't a normal smell, wanted to know if it could be cured, but Arrese answered that some discharges just smell more than others, and that boy, hers sure was one of them. Her pap smear was normal, she'd never noticed any smell, nobody had ever complained to her about it, she'd never seen anyone looking at her with revulsion, but from that day on and until recently, until she worked up the courage to go to another doctor, she hadn't let anyone—whatever their intentions, medical or for purposes of pleasure, or for any other reason—get within half a yard of her vagina, protected though it was by tampons, sanitary napkins, and douches. "*¿Qué te parece?*" The women wait to see what he's going to say, Gabilondo's fully away that she's told him something she takes to be very serious, and in fact the behavior— Arrese holding his nose and saying "Jesus, what a stench!"—does seem unacceptable to him. But Abaitua also finds it amusing, above all her face as she tells him the story and the astonishment he sees in her eyes, and instead of expressing anger and dismay, he can't help laughing. The young American, too, finds it amusing, at least she smiles, but his belly laugh is definitely out of place, his reputation as an upright man is at risk, and he apologizes to Gabilondo. He doesn't want her to think that he's making light of the way Arrese insulted her friend. It's just that the story's reminded him of a joke he once heard in the operating theater—that's his excuse. It's his second mistake, because now, as might have been expected, they want him to tell them the joke, but he doesn't want to, because he thinks he's bad at telling jokes. It's a very dirty joke, and that makes him feel ill at ease. The more he refuses, the more they insist. Who on earth can bring up a dirty joke and then not tell it, says Harri Gabilondo. No hinting at it, he has to actually tell them the joke. Seeing no other way out, he uses the good old doctor's excuse that he has a lot of patients waiting for him. He can't tell them now, but he will some other time. The young American sociologist asks whether he'll give them his word as a Basque. "No question—*I promise you*."

WHEN HE GOES BACK INTO HIS OFFICE, the nurse tells him that one of the two women has forgotten a file, showing him a blue folder with elastic bands at the corners. It's too late to catch them, but he leaves again anyway and goes down the stairs. He doesn't find them there. He opens the folder to make sure it's the young American sociologist's, even though he's sure it is. It's photocopies, a novel by one Max Frisch titled *Montauk*.

As he walks along the corridor, he tries to recognize a young couple walking in the opposite direction toward him. The woman's around thirty-five, and although she's familiar to him, he doesn't know from where, or why, as usual. They look so down that he stops to ask them if there's a problem. She gave birth four hours earlier and was told her child had some insignificant problem on his nose, but when she picked him up to breastfeed him, he was suffocating, completely purple. The woman starts telling the story but can't go on, and the man takes over. The child has been taken to the pediatric ICU, and the parents are worried, naturally. From what they tell him, he thinks it must be a posterior nasal aperture atresia. Babies don't have nasal cavities and, when being breastfed, have to breathe through the nose. So they're going to have to perforate his posterior nasal aperture. He tries to calm them down—it's a very easy operation, and the baby's in good hands. It'll all be sorted out. "But we're very, very worried. You do understand that, don't you?" Of course he understands. He takes ahold of the woman's hand and squeezes it with all the warmth he can. She should find that encouraging. But they just stand there in front of him, without moving, and he tells them he has to go, there's an emergency.

THE TELEVISION IS TURNED ON WITH THE VOLUME DOWN. A couple, both of them around fifty years old, is sitting at a sort of school desk that has their names on the front of it. The presenter is standing next to them asking questions, and when they get one right, he makes high-flying gestures with his hands encouraging the audience to applaud them. It's a game show, one he's seen before. Different couples try to demonstrate that they know each other better than the other couples do. One of the partners is asked a question, which can be quite intimate, and the other must guess the answer. The woman, who looks severe and bitter, has gotten a question right and grudgingly allows the man to give her a kiss. The audience applauds. Abaitua would rather the sound were turned up, the pictures interfere with him doing other things anyhow, and he'd like to know what they're asking the man now. Some of the questions they've asked in the past have been so intimate that it's amazing anyone would answer them in public. Pilar doesn't normally watch the show. She only occasionally lifts her head up from her Sudoku, as if glancing to check that the screen is still turned on. Abaitua thinks it's the changes in the intensity of the light that make her raise her head. Sometimes he asks her why she doesn't turn it off, she's not watching it, and often she does switch it off. But mostly she says she's waiting for the news. She loves watching the television news. He's not going to say anything to her today.

He's been waiting awhile for one of them to say something, but he's incapable of saying the first word. He's too lazy to, and afraid, as well, he's not quite sure. He's afraid of what her answers might be and doesn't feel like making decisions. He feels lazy at the prospect of packing his suitcase and afraid of being alone, and he doesn't know which is holding him up more, fear or laziness. But being at an impasse—going neither forward nor backward—is uncomfortable, as well, having to carry on as if nothing were the matter.

He'd like to know what they've just asked the woman on the television.

Abaitua finds it especially irritating how docilely they let his brother-in-law Yago make all the professional decisions, just as long as no problems that might importune her father arise. That hurts him, and he never misses a chance to reproach her for it. Pilar, on the other hand, tries not to give him any such opportunities. She normally answers that he's always looking for excuses to get angry with her family.

Talking about his work at the hospital won't put him in a better mood. He doesn't have anything good to say about it, and Pilar doesn't like having to listen to problems. She gets bored. He knows she thinks he's too demanding, too inflexible when it comes to judging his colleagues, and he has the impression that she doesn't believe him when he tells her about the daily disasters and catastrophes that take place as a result of their negligence and lack of professionalism, although from what she sees at her own job, she shouldn't have any trouble believing him. In her defense, it's because of her own honesty that she finds it difficult to see dishonesty and bad intentions in the actions of others, and however terrible they may be in objective terms, when she's forced to see facts that are objectively horrendous, she always finds excuses and extenuating circumstances. But whenever he shares things with her that are actually worthy of anger and indignation, her understanding attitude toward the offenders irritates him, and she knows that.

When he asks her if she's heard the latest bit of drama, she raises her head from her Sudoku and looks at him with interest. A little interest, at least, he'd say. He tells her he's seen a young woman whose husband became infertile after being treated for testicular cancer and who, because of that, was wavering between whether to adopt a child or to have one by artificial insemination. She had serious reasons for her indecision, because she thought her husband might find it easier to accept an adopted child rather than one that she had with another man's sperm. It's an interesting dilemma. There were psychological and social factors behind the woman's doubts that she was incapable of seeing beyond. She also reasoned that if her husband loved her, he might prefer a child that she had had inside of her and given birth to, but fortunately the whole issue turned out to be theoretical, because men's sperm in these cases is usually frozen before they're given the treatment, in case they later want to have children. So he called the oncology department to make sure, and they told him that they had indeed done that until very recently, but not anymore. When he asked why they'd stopped doing it, they said it was because they were very busy. And no, they hadn't discussed the change with anyone first. All of a sudden, just like that, they'd simply stopped collecting patients' sperm. "*¿Qué te parece?*" "It's absurd." The serious expression on her face says that she means it, but she doesn't say anything else. She doesn't say they should be taken outside and shot, which is what he'd like to hear. "Absurd," and she goes back to staring at her Sudoku.

It must be one of the really tough puzzles.

He asks again, "*¿Qué te parece?*" in the same way Gabilondo usually does, but without it being a rhetorical question, hoping for a reply on the same scale as the anger he felt that morning when he heard they weren't freezing patients' sperm any longer. The reply of a woman who isn't so used to seeing the idiotic things that happen at the hospital. He would have preferred the answer of a furious woman, railing against people with so little sensitivity. But of course, that same woman could also have demanded of him, "Well, and what did you about it? What did you say to them?"

And he himself didn't get as angry as Harri Gabilondo had expected him to when she told him about what Arrese said to her friend. He remembers a joke about a personal ad placed by a woman seeking a man with anosmia for oral sex. It wouldn't be funny if he told it, and although he's tempted to try it out on Pilar, he's suddenly afraid of telling a dirty joke, afraid she might take it the wrong way.

Ten thirty, a good time to go to his bedroom. So he says he's had a bad day and he's tired.

MAX FRISCH, MONTAUK. He's photocopied the novel that the American girl left in his office. "A sign promising a view across the island: *OVERLOOK.* It was he who suggested stopping here." The couple—the man who's suggested stopping there and his friend—is walking along a rough path that's covered with puddles and shrubs. The man's smoking a pipe. The woman's movements are quicker than his, she's a bit younger than him, as well. The scenery reminds the man of other places he's visited on the seaside. But he finds his obsessive memories get in the way. So he's old. The woman's slimmer than him, but not skinny, and her blue jeans are rolled up to her knees—small buttocks in tight trousers. Her reddish hair is tied in a ponytail that sways from side to side as she walks along. Right now they're both astonished to be together.

The man, whose name hasn't been mentioned yet, is a foreign writer on a promotional tour of the States, and his flight back is on Tuesday. He remembers the day when he was answering the press's questions at a hotel and he met this young woman. He helped her put her coat on, and when, out of politeness, he asked her name for the second time, she said *Lynn*, as if her first name were enough. When they all left, the writer realized that the girl had left her lighter behind, a cheap green one that had been lying under the lamp for a couple of weeks.

Lynn. That name wouldn't have meant anything to him if he hadn't met the sociologist who'd forgotten her blue file folder with the novel in it that morning.

The sound of Pilar's steps. She's moving silently but not secretively. She must have seen the light under his door. He hears her going from the living room to the kitchen, probably to check that the gas is off and to drink a glass of milk. Now she opens the cabinet they keep the shampoo, soap, toothpaste, lotions, and other reserve supplies in, because the toothpaste has run out and he hasn't replaced it. He coughs, because he thinks she's standing outside his door, and he doesn't want her to come in thinking that he's fallen asleep without turning the lights out first. Sometimes she goes into the dressing room to take some garment or other from the closet. That situation—Abaitua in bed and Pilar looking through the drawers—is increasingly uncomfortable for him, though she finds it entirely natural. She does whatever it is she has to do and says goodnight. She's never gone beyond that. Perhaps because she's frightened of being rejected, but above all, he thinks, because she doesn't want to give the slightest indication of being vulnerable, of needing him.

That day in the old Renault 12, before they were married, Pilar had held onto his arm in tears and asked him not to leave her. A pathetic image. He doesn't know what the reason had been for threatening to break up the relationship. Sometimes one of the two says, "It would be better if we just broke up," and not always with the best of intentions. The one who believes him or herself to be in the strongest position holding out for the other to show his or her submissiveness, like a dog lying on its back, displaying

166

its belly. The fact is that she held onto his arm, turned toward him in tears, and said, "Don't leave me." He doesn't know what type of wicked satisfaction she must have seen on his face, but there was certainly something—she's never shown him any sign of submission or vulnerability again. But Iñaki Abaitua has never wanted anything else all his life, he only wants her to say she needs him. That she doesn't want him to leave her.

5

THERE IS NOT A CLOUD IN THE SKY, and the sun brings out a metallic shine on the magnolia leaves. The two house cats are lazily cleaning themselves at the ankle of the angel on the old fountain. The statue's right arm, which used to point up toward the sky, is now no more than a stump with a thick iron rod sticking out of it, and it reminds Julia of a cemetery, because she knows it's part of a funerary sculpture that was never put up in the end. Even so, in spite of its somber origins and the fact that the piece of iron in its cut-off arm now points at the bus stop, it has its cheerful days, when its face seems to smile with the play of leafy light and the shadow cast by a streak of moss.

The house is in silence although it's already nine o'clock. There's a heavy atmosphere in the living room, which is particularly untidy. There are two empty yogurt containers on the coffee table, a jar of jam, a carton of milk, and a box of Breton cookies. She gathers that the writer didn't go out to dinner and stayed up late watching television. As he's often done recently, in fact. She has to admit she's a bit disappointed not to find the remains of a dinner shared with the *penthouse* girl. She imagines the linen tablecloth, the old porcelain charger plates, and the ugly four-armed silver candlesticks. That's what he did when he invited her to dinner for the first time; it's funny, but she can no longer remember what he gave her to eat.

She wipes the bit of the table under the glass clean and picks up what she can, just enough to clear the table. The first thing she normally does is make coffee.

The coffee's in the refrigerator. The red mullets that he was supposed to have for dinner no longer look appetizing—their scales are dry, they're white and matte.

MONTAUK. The photocopies of the novel, which they had to order from the National Library because the Spanish edition is out of print, are on Martin's desk. There aren't any pages without underlined passages, so it's clear he was up late reading the novel so enthusiastically recommended by his tenant. *"Absolutely wonderful,"* she'd called it. So he's devoured the whole book in an evening, he who normally has trouble reading a single line, and even more so in the evening. The book cover, which is black and white, is very different from that of the English edition. Underneath the author's name and the title are some large buildings, and a lot of people on the beach next to them. It could be a reproduction of a postcard. At the bottom, in small letters: "Montauk Manor. Montauk Beach. Long Island, N.Y." Montaigne's sentence, the one the man at the airport said to Harri and which was all the American needed to identify the book, is written in Spanish on the dedication page: *"Lector, éste es un libro sincero, y te previene ya desde el comienzo que no le he dado una finalidad que no sea particular y privada . . ."* And then the start of the novel: *Un letrero ofrece una visión panorámica de la isla*: OVERLOOK.

Suddenly she seems to remember that the English version was *"This book was written in good faith."* "In good faith," not "sincere." She can't check the English translation, but she does have the transcription of Montaigne's original to hand. Becuase her classi-fication system works so well, it doesn't take her long to find the Gallimard edition and Montaigne's words. *"C'est icy un livre de bonne foy, lecteur"*—just as she thought. She doesn't know if *speaking in good faith* in sixteenth-century French meant being sincere, but she'd say they're not the same things in today's Spanish and French. When it comes down to it, you can tell lies in good faith, *de bonne foi*, and tell the truth in bad faith, but you can't tell a lie "sincerely." Or can you?

OVERLOOK. It was he who suggested stopping here.

She jumps when she hears Martin's voice next to her. "Enjoying it?" he says. She's astonished she didn't realize he was there until she saw his head over the table, his neck jutting out toward the text she's reading, and she suspects, not for the first time, that he approaches her secretively on purpose, to find out what she's doing. He's wearing jeans for the first time in a long while, a white silk shirt, a lightweight blue V-neck sweater, and he smells of some new cologne. Nothing to do with the scruffy man who usually appears every morning in a tattered robe.

"I haven't started yet. I've had work to do, you know." In fact, she's been very eager to read it, but she hasn't been able to yet, because the American girl took her copy back, but her response is a way of reproaching him for the fact that he, on the other hand, has managed to find the time, and also of throwing in his face the fact that he hasn't written a line in days. And a way of getting over her own feeling of shame caused by him controlling her. So she goes on the attack—"You've changed colognes" (no need to specify that's it's "for the *penthouse* girl")—and the poor man takes a step back so she won't be able to smell him anymore. "My sister gave it to me." Seeing him so low makes her regret having mocked him. In any case, she knows the reason she's in a bad mood is because her work's going badly. She's not making much progress with her translation of *Bihotzean min dut*—a sad title meaning "my heart aches"—but Martin isn't to blame for that. Making an effort to control her bad mood, she asks him if he liked it. A lot. The American girl—he calls her that to show that he's not particularly interested in her—is right. It's Frisch's best book, and it's incomprehensible that it's been out of print for so long in Spanish. She hasn't heard him praise a book with such passion for a long time. He says something surprising: perhaps she won't like it, but she's sure to find it interesting. She'll identify with some passages. He doesn't tell her which passages, even though she asks him to again and again; he wants to see if she'll find them herself when she reads it.

What's more, the *penthouse* girl's come into the yard, and the writer leaves his sentence unfinished to rush out before she gets away. Sheer enthusiasm. He's always like that when he meets new people. At first he's extremely attentive and pays them a lot of attention, until the other person feels the need to show a similar interest in him. Then he tires of them. She's had to put up with him in both phases, and she doesn't know which she finds more irritating.

There's the young girl, who's just taken a shower, wearing a loose-fitting gray Yale University tracksuit and sandals. She has feet to be jealous of—no corns, great toes, perfect nails, and it looks like she's never been tortured by fashionable shoes. And to think she said she practiced ballet until recently! She looks apologetically at Julia as she sits down in the chair that Martin offers her. She doesn't want to interrupt her work. Then, seeing the photocopies of *Montauk*, she asks them if they've enjoyed it, with her eyes very wide open, as if the answer were going to be of great importance to her. Julia's astonished—because Martin very seldom finds nothing to criticize in the books people recommend to them—to hear him give his highest praise. He read it last night without stopping once, that's why he's tired now. When it's her turn to give her opinion, she has to admit that she hasn't even been able to start it. But it's her fault, because she took her copy away.

"How stupid of me."

She slaps her forehead with the palm of the hand. What an awful thing to do. It's as if she's done something really terrible, when in fact all she's done is leave the photocopies of *Montauk* that she made for Julia in Iñaki Abaitua's office by mistake. It's not a problem, she says, she'll read Martin's copy, and the girl looks at her, surprised that she doesn't realize how serious what's happened is. It's very serious, what on earth could she have been thinking? How will she be able to trust someone who's forgotten an important work file? It looks like Martin finds the situation amusing. He says that if she'd read the novel, she'd realize that all Lynns are slippery characters, that they're always leaving things accidentally in older men's rooms to have an excuse to go back and seduce them, and the American girl's cheeks, when she hears this, go as red as tomatoes. It's clear from Julia's expression that she doesn't understand a thing, so they, members of the club of people who've read *Montauk*, explain that Max, an older writer, and Lynn, a young woman, meet in New York in the hotel room where the writer is staying while he's being interviewed by a journalist. Max thinks she's the photographer—there's usually one in such circumstances—but when the journalist finishes his work, Max finds out that she is, in fact, the assistant his editor has assigned him for his stay in New York, and when everyone's gone and the writer's alone, he realizes that the young woman has left her lighter behind.

BIHURRA BIHURTU. In Spanish, *rizar el rizo*. Is that "to gild the lily" in English? So when Doctor Abaitua opens the folder that this

171

young woman called Lynn, who he's just met, has left in his office, he'll find a book about a love story between a man who's getting on in years, like himself, and a young woman called Lynn, and as if that weren't enough, the starting point is that the girl has forgotten something in the room in which they just met. These things particularly amuse Martin, he loves symmetry.

They speak with such enthusiasm about *Montauk* that Julia, who has nothing at all to say, sits down at the table, as if to say it's time for her to start working. She didn't think it was a bad idea when Martin suggested they share a room to work in. They divided up the shelf space, taking their respective heights into account so that they wouldn't get in each other's way and would be able to ask each other things whenever they had any doubts. Martin, of course, could always go to the formal library if he wanted to, but he's worked in worse places.

"*En peores garitas hemos hecho guardia.*" How could you say that? We've had breakfast in more dilapidated sheds. We've warmed our bones in happier inns. We've worked up a sweat in worse coats. We've ploughed worse soil.

The American says, "*Perhaps we're bothering Julia,*" but she replies that they aren't at all and leans back in her seat as if to prove the fact, untrue though it is.

Perhaps the fact that they're whispering, murmuring as if they were in a confessional, disturbs her more than if they were talking normally, and she can't help listening to what they're saying, because Martin's mentioned translation. He says you shouldn't notice the translator in a translation, but he's there all the time in this one. "*El texto chirría.*" He uses the Basque verb *kirrinka egin* a lot. "How would you translate that?" he asks, raising his voice to make it clear the question is for Julia and then sitting back in his seat to wait for her answer. "*To creak?*" The American, when he repeats it, holds her hands to her ears and shows her teeth, to act out hearing an unpleasant sound.

TRADUTTORE TRADITORE.

And then, as if he enjoyed adding to the discomfort that his words have made the American feel, he looks over the pages for examples of the translator's clumsiness. He has the habit of licking his index finger with his lower lip to help turn the pages quicker, something he can't stop doing, even though he knows it's not elegant. Finally, he uses his little finger to point out the words he wants her to read: "*la velluda y blanca chaqueta*"—the hairy white jacket. Of course, she has to read the whole paragraph to see the jacket and its adjective in context: "*De cara a la opinión pública estadounidense, declaro que la vida resulta algo aburrida, y que sólo tengo experiencias mientras escribo. En el fondo no se trata de ningún chiste. Luego, cuando le sostengo la velluda y blanca chaqueta, vuelvo a preguntarle por cortesía cuál es su nombre.*"

Julia agrees that "hairy jacket" doesn't sound very good, but she's amazed it's the paragraph he's most interested in. And of course, they'd have to see how the jacket is described in the original text, apart from being white. The American girl regrets not having the English version to be able to compare the two, she lent it to Harri, but she thinks that what the writer is holding up is a "*shaggy jacket,*" in other words, a jacket with long threads, but all over it, not just on the sleeves and the chest, like an Indian's. Julia finds it fun looking the words up. After searching in a couple of dictionaries, she decides that a jacket made using the type of fabric from the rug in the bathroom that her mother likes so much would indeed be a "shaggy jacket," which is probably *zottelgjacke* in German, but she doesn't know how to say it in Basque. *Peluxezkoa*? Like for a stuffed animal?

The writer thinks that the easiest way to get around the problem would be to say that Max was holding up any type of jacket. Whether leather or knitted—any type of jacket that wouldn't sound wrong. The writer wouldn't care about that, he probably decided to make it a "shaggy" jacket in German because it went with the rhythm of the sentence, nothing more than that. It would only need to be specified if it helped to define the character it belonged to, like a corduroy jacket in Spanish, for instance, which could go to show that a character is a member of the Socialist Party or that he's not dressed formally. Just as long as it's something that doesn't sound wrong. Julia would be in agreement, she said, if it weren't for the fact that even the slightest change she ever suggests to him he decries as betraying his original meaning. The insurmountable distance between a writer and a translator. He keeps insisting on the unimportance of the jacket's material while at the same time making it very clear, with seeming modesty, that he himself is just a *piccolo scrittore*, perhaps even a crappy writer, but a writer nonetheless. The girl's very eager to point out how important translators are, as well.

Julia thinks that she's making an effort to defend her from Martin's slighting, and that moves her, but it also makes her a little angry. It makes her angry that although the American girl has only just met them, it's quite obvious to her that Martin's objective in marking the difference between them is to express disdain for herself. To lend weight to her attempt to defend the nobility of the translator's work, the young woman switches to English, and in order to prove that translation is also an art, she chooses a comparison that she thinks will illustrate the matter better: music and the complementary relationship between composers and players. The poor girl isn't aware that Martin has led her here on purpose and is waiting, amused, to stick in his final argument—Julia can see it on his face. She's seen this show more than once before, he uses the same trick every time a new interlocutor comes along. The other person, just like the young American right now, will say that Bach is great but so is Gould, otherwise we would never get to hear his interpretation of the former's variations, and then Martin will reply, with his humblest voice, that we could all just read the sheet music, the mathematics of music is written down right there, and all the rest is no more than sentimental rubbish.

The American says, *"You're terrible."* That's how the show always ends. Julia is sure that that sentence—"the mathematics of music is written down right there"—and all the rest of it is something he's underlined from somewhere, she's sure he didn't come up with it himself.

SHE CONCENTRATES ON READING the start of her Spanish translation of "*Bihotzean min dut*," afraid something might sound "creaky": "The literature teacher was collecting his pupils' papers when the headmaster came in. His face was pale. He spoke in a low voice— "Ana's father's been hit by a bomb"—but the pupils in the first rows heard him. The teacher wanted to say something and opened his mouth several times, like a fish, but before he could get anything out, the headmaster had already replied to the implicit question. 'He's dead.' The whispering went from row to row and grew to a racket, and you could tell that the pupils were glad that the class had been interrupted." She wonders if it really happened like that.

174

Now there are two swallows sitting on the one-handed angel. One is on the still-complete arm, the other on the head. She once saw a pigeon perched on the tip of a sword in an equestrian statue of Joan of Arc. It was bronze, and it sat in the middle of a square in some French city whose name she's forgotten. She wanted to take a photo of it, but it took off again before she could get her camera out. Each time she remembers that, though she doesn't know why, she regrets not having been able to take the photo, not because she thinks it would have been a good photo but to be able to know what city it was. She doesn't even remember who she was with. Perhaps it was with Martin. It probably was with him, but she doesn't want to ask him, just in case it wasn't, which is a possibility. She finds that gap in her memory incomprehensible—worrying, too.

Could it be, as Martin has sometimes accused reproachingly, that she only holds onto bad memories?

MEMORIES. When the young American asks the writer why he has that big map of Sicily on the wall—it's at least three by four feet—he says he wants to go and live on the island sometime. In Syracuse, in fact. Apparently, that "sometime" is going to be when his parents die, although his saying "when I don't have to take care of them anymore" may lead people who don't know him to think that he's a loving son who changes their diapers and accompanies them on walks. Julia doesn't think he's ever going to carry out that plan of his, and in fact she doesn't care anymore—if she ever did care—that he doesn't include her in it. Because he's never talked about the two of them going away; he never really talks about the two of them, about their future in relation to each other. What really annoys her about his fantasy—and she does believe it to be no more than pure fantasy—isn't him leaving her out of it, it's the need to make it happen in Syracuse. Before she met Martin, three years and seven months ago, Syracuse represented for Julia a feeling of nostalgia for a far-off place, beautiful abundant gardens, the smell of lemon trees, and the taste of honey. It was Henry Salvador's music set to Dimey's poem, and when she listened to it ("J'aimerais tant voir Syracuse / L'île de Pâques et Kérouan / Et les grands oiseaux qui s'amusent / A glisser l'aile sous le vent"—and in what other language could you get away with saying something so corny?), it was like white doves taking flight from her breast—I would so much like to see Syracuse / Easter Island and Cairo /

175

And the large birds who sport / At flying under the wind. Sicily had been her fantasy, and she wanted reality to never spoil it for her. That was why she always ignored the great package deals in the travel agency windows advertising "Sicily: flight, hotel, and car rental," but Martin talked to her about it so much that she finally gave in to the temptation. He was so obstinate about spoiling her dream, about ruining that exact spot, Syracuse, for her. She found everything there irritating—the heat, how Baroque it all was, the tourists in ecstasy ogling at Greek and Roman ruins, the locals believing themselves to be Archimedes, Plato, and Livy. They never got around to what she wanted to do and spent the whole trip looking for a restaurant as good as the excellent Italian restaurant they once found in London, that was all they did. After all the boring walks, on which he was only interested in the menus at the restaurants, he'd complain about having aching legs and about the uncomfortable seats in their rental car—an Opel, she doesn't remember the model. Mosquitos attacked them at night. She told him she'd never go anywhere else with him, and she hasn't. And now Syracuse is the memory of a nightmare. She's never put Henry Salvador's song on again, and whenever she hears it by chance, she cries bitterly.

They're still talking about *Montauk*. The young American has mentioned Frisch's plausibility two or three times. She quotes paragraphs with the devotion of a Jehovah's Witness repeating verses from the Bible, and Martin tries to find them in the Spanish edition, licking his finger to turn each page. Harri, too, usually tells him off about that habit of his—she wouldn't let anyone else get away with it—and about the fact that he bites his nails. Julia doesn't tell him off any more. She feels ridiculous in the role of mother.

A WASTED MORNING. Harri appears on the path in the yard and waves a hand. She sees her bend down, pull out one of the bottles that Martin stuck in the ground to frighten off the moles, and throw it onto a heap of dried grass in front of the shed. She's talking as she comes into the house. "Planting those bottles all around was the last straw for this sad yard." She always says something before saying hello. She's on her way to Bilbao—she waves her hand in the air and moves her hips—and she's popped in to give the sociologist some papers. And to tell her that their meeting with Abaitua's been postponed. And she's brought them some croissants.

The American girl uses a fountain pen. An old Parker with a metal cap. She also uses a notebook, in which she writes down the new appointment with Abaitua; it looks old, its black oilskin edges are worn, and an elastic strip of the same color holds it closed. In the short time Julia's known her, she's realized that the American loves outdated, old-fashioned things, which she, Julia, first experienced when they were just normal things and no longer particularly appreciates. When Harri gives her the chance, the American girl tells her that she forgot her file folder with the photocopies of *Montauk* in Abaitua's office, and this time Julia thinks that the gestures she makes to express how worried she is about it looks real enough. Harri says he must think she did it deliberately, like her namesake in the novel—the same pleasantry Martin said before—and this time Julia understands it without the need for any explanations.

They all start talking about *Montauk* again, and she feels left out once more.

Apparently, what Harri's most interested in is to what extent the description of the weekend the writer called Max spent with the forgetful character Lynn at a place called Montauk is based on his own experience, whether it actually happened to the Swiss writer Max Frisch, which is something that seems completely irrelevant to the writer from Martutene. Who cares about that, it's all fiction, at the end of the day. The argument he usually uses to justify writing about their suffering, his and hers, their joint misery. Then the young American very seriously confirms it, almost in a whisper, seemingly sorrowed at having to remind them of such a well-known phrase: "*Every self, even the self that we live and die, is an invention.*" The writer gestures to show that he quite agrees and, believing that not to be enough, allows himself to affectionately pat her on the back. He looks at Julia with an expression that she can't quite classify—something between insulting and despising— seeming to say, "Have you seen that, you fool? This young charming girl from Yale has perfectly understood something that you can't even grasp."

But Harri is not intimidated, "But did Max Frisch really have a thing with this Lynn?" The response she gets is no more than a charitable silence. "Please excuse me, I studied science," she adds. Apparently, ambiguity offends her rational character and she has to know whether the things she's told are true or false. She takes the English version out of her pocket and spends a while looking through the pages for something. Then she holds it in front of the young woman and points to a passage, which the latter reads aloud: *"I should like to be able to describe this day, just this day, our weekend together, how it came about and how it develops I should like to tell it without inventing anything . . . I want to invent nothing; I want to know what I notice and think when I am not thinking of possible readers."*

Who says that, she asks again, Max Frisch, or the writer who Max Frisch is describing? Are they the same person?

"But who cares about that?" says the writer.

"I do, because I want to know if I'm being told the truth."

"Oh, the truth!" says the American.

ON TRUTH AND LITERATURE. As she listens to them, Julia remembers the dinner parties they used to have, lying around on the floor with their friends, trying harder to convince than to understand, everyone attempting to give the most brilliant quotes. At that time, too, Julia used to listen more than she spoke. Using quotes seems pedantic to her, but she also finds it disagreeable and gets embarrassed when she sees people struggling to express ideas that have already been precisely put forward in books, as if they were the first people to ever debate such difficult matters.

But Harri is no hypocrite, and Julia likes her a bit because of that. After saying she studied science, she dares to ask things that other people wouldn't for fear of looking dumb. Julia holds out her hand to ask her for the book, and Harri's response—she doesn't know how comic it looks—is to hold it protectively against her chest, and Julia has to promise she'll give it back before Harri lets go of it.

Yes, that's what Montaigne says in the English translation: *"This book was written in good faith, reader."*

It doesn't take her long to confirm that *"la blanca y velluda chaqueta"* is "the shaggy white jacket" in English. It's on the sixth page: *"When later I was helping her into her shaggy white jacket."*

TELL ME!

Repite él a menudo, como si alguien pudiera contarse algo a él mismo.

The English version, on the other hand, goes:

TELL ME!

He often says, as if a person could describe himself.

"Describe himself," not, as in the Spanish, "tell himself something."

178

Apparently, it's one of those things that everyone, not just Forster has said. "Fiction is truer than history." But Harri doesn't accept Aristoteles', Forster's, or Faulkner's words (the American girl's added that Faulkner said that fiction is often the best fact), she doesn't accept that you have to go "beyond what's there" or "further than skin-deep." She studied science. Julia often wonders if it wouldn't be ideal, from a pedagogical standpoint, to make sure there was a student like her in every lecture hall, someone who would dare to ask questions and not get overawed by pretty phrases. Harri insists— how can something you make up be truer than what someone who's actually seen it says—but the writer insists as well. "Reality can be stranger than fiction, but fiction's truer." Julia believes him, although she wouldn't be able to define the idea if she had to; the conviction with which he says it is the most convincing argument for her.

Harri has to leave and signals with her hand to ask Julia to give her the book back. It's obvious she finds the subject boring, but before she leaves, she tells them that they haven't convinced her and that she finds it exasperating not knowing whether what she's been told is true or has been made up, and she pays no attention to the American girl's shrugging her shoulders and smiling in despair. It's Lynn who takes the book from Julia and gives it back to Harri. "'*This book was written in good faith,' the man on the plane said. Isn't that true? That's important.*" Her smile shows amusement but not mockery, and that's how Harri takes it, and she says in all seriousness that she's right. And as she puts the book in her green briefcase, she says, "Do you know what I think?" She thinks that while she's reading the sentence, the man from the airport is reading it, as well—that's very important for her—perhaps he's reading it right now, they're sharing those words, they're saying them to each other and listening to each other say them. She opens the book at random and reads, "*Why this weekend in particular?*" And she theatrically closes her eyes. Then says, "I don't know, it's as if I'm hearing his voice."

There's an uncomfortable silence, because the rest don't know if she's being serious. Julia says she's crazy, and she should leave, she's going to be late. She doesn't know why those histrionic expressions of Harri's affect her so much. "Sometimes I think you envy me," she answers, and this time it's clear it's a joke. The other three don't take their eyes off her, and after very carefully putting the book in her bag, she picks up some of the index cards lying on top of the table, pretending she's doing so secretly, and her playing around leads to Martin trying to stop her from picking them up, but Julia gets worried that the American girl may think they're doing it all seriously. She herself is used to it, of course. Harri holds the cards up in the air and as far from Martin as possible, and he pretends to do all he can to take them off her. Let me read them, she shouts in a tearful child's voice. "Pleeease." She wants to know what lies he's writing at the moment. Now she holds the cards behind her back, and the writer has to put both his arms around her. They fall onto the sofa like children. Somehow Martin gets ahold of the cards, he tears them up into tiny pieces and throws them up into the air, which Harri protests about. She sounds convinced as she says, "You're a fool, they could be worth a lot of money one day."

THEY GO WITH HER OUT TO THE CAR. They talk about the zoning and development provisions that are slated to come into effect in the neighborhood. About how the current economic climate might affect those plans. Harri has the most information and seems to know what she's talking about. She also replies very seriously when the American girl mentions something about work to her. Nothing like that silly, girlish routine she often puts on. She seems to guess what they're thinking, because after opening the iron gate and complaining that it's creaking just as bad as always because they haven't put any oil on it, she reproaches them for not asking her about the man at the airport. They don't need to ask her. She says she's decided to take direct action. She smiles enigmatically and refuses to tell them her plans. She says to Martin, "You know what? I'm convinced I'm going to have an experience that's already been written about somewhere." She seems to be talking seriously, and then, to lighten things up a bit, she ruffles his hair and wonders if he's going bald. "As you can see, I tell the truth." She laughs. And then when she says he should go see a dermatologist, Julia—who's been waiting for a good opportunity to ask her if she's set up her mammogram appointment with Abaitua yet—replies that she would be better off tending to her own needs rather than his. She starts teasing again and asks if she's jealous. She jokes about Abaitua, as well, complaining about having to show her breasts to a gentleman in order to see if she's got cancer or not, a gentleman for whom she could easily lose her head. The American girl says she's bad. The three women laugh. They agree that he's an interesting and affable man. But Martin doesn't. He disagrees with them; he's jealous. He thinks Abaitua's quite arrogant. He still has more to say, when the American girl interrupts him sharply, "Well he thinks very highly of you." The seriousness with which she says it would have been comical if her voice hadn't broken a little, and Julia is moved by the firmness she displays in criticizing her landlord. Doctor Abaitua thinks that he's a great writer, and the great writer, afraid that he may have annoyed her, takes a step back. He says he knows that the man reads his work (he looks at Julia for help), he's one of his few readers, and that, too, says nothing good about him. He chuckles. He's known him for ages, and his wife, as well. Perhaps as a way of getting back at them for finding Abaitua interesting, he praises his wife, Pilar Goytisolo. She's a doctor, as well, and she was a great beauty, she still is, he says.

"A great beauty," but still a Goytisolo, and whenever they mention that particular surname in Martin's family—complete with the Spanish *y*—they always have to mention the fact that they were dispossessed by them. The Goytisolos, too, are from Otzeta. All the land around their clinic, on the other side of the railroad, which is surrounded by beautiful hundred-year-old cypresses, used to belong to his family—he makes the usual gestures of despair, scrunching up his shoulders, when he says this—but at the start of the war, when Donostia fell, Abaitua's father-in-law, a young doctor who was a Requeté officer at the time, seized it, taking advantage of the fact that Martin's family, who were Basque nationalists, had had to flee to Hazparne, in southwestern France. After the war, when his grandfather crossed back over the border again to see what the situation was and find out if they would be able to get their property back, he had no choice but to accept a "reasonable" deal for it from Goytisolo, who had just opened a maternity hospital on the land, the first incarnation of the San Luis clinic, in the building in which his own grandfather had planned to open a hotel. He makes the another typical gesture at this point, pointing off into the distance with his arms held wide open, to show the extent of his family's property before the war, a display that always makes Julia think of the devil tempting Christ by showing him "all the kingdoms of the world in all their glory."

"But Doctor Abaitua isn't to blame for that, now is he?" The American girl's voice is softer now, but there is still a bit of a challenge in it, which really surprises Julia. It occurs to her she must be a very loyal woman. Martin looks down again, shaking his head to say that Abaitua isn't at all to blame. The four of them are silent for a moment, until Harri says she's "definitely late" now. The American girl, too, has a lot of work to do and wants to go, and the writer, faced with the prospect of being left alone with Julia, asks Harri to drop him off downtown, he has to go and look something up at the Koldo Mitxelena library.

While they wait for him to go and get a jacket, Harri talks about him. He's not looking very well, he's pale, he should get out more, and do something to lose less hair, there are treatments; Julia feels herself to be responsible for some of the things being brought up. She also wants to know if he's making any progress with his novel. Julia doesn't like the subject and avoids it without bothering to come up with much of an excuse. She points at a thrush, a bird she thinks is a thrush, that's hopping back and forth between the magnolia and the path. "Look at that happy little thrush!" she says, assuming that he must have told her the story about the pharmacist who said he had a "*culo gordo*," but he hasn't. She says the bird is also bound to have some problem or other; everyone does, after all. They try to figure out the motivation behind the bird's ritualistic movements—he goes quickly over to the side of the pebble path and then back again, stopping to peck at the grass after every two or three jumps. Julia has never heard this bird that appears to be a thrush sing, while the pair that usually perches on top of the reed fence hardly ever shuts up. "Chatterbird," she thinks of saying. *Chattering bird, chatterbox,* but not so much as a parrot. *Chatty bird.* Sometimes she thinks the girl doesn't understand a thing. They look like sparrows, but she doesn't think they are, because they're almost completely green. She doesn't know anything about birds, nor does Harri.

The American girl thinks that the Basque word *txori* is not just beautiful, it's also a natural word for "bird," probably because it's an onomatopoeia. She asks them if that's right, if it's an onomatopoeia, but they don't know. *Txio* is how you say "to cheep." They agree that there are words in all languages that seem more appropriate than those in others for the same things. *Txori* seems more appropriate than *bird*, and much more so than the Spanish *pájaro*. *Pájaro* does

182

however seem a better choice for the word's other meaning, describing a wicked, wily sort, than Basque's *birigarroa*.

That reminds Julia of something by the Donostian writer Ramon Zulaika that she read a long time ago. Apparently, he was on a beach in Finland and came across a local person. They couldn't understand each other, because it wasn't so usual for people to know English back then, and they didn't share any other common language. The local wrote something in the sand—unfortunately, Julia can't remember what the word was—and asked the writer to do the same thing. He had to choose a word to respond, and Julia does remember the one that he chose. The Basque word for "butterfly": *pinpilinpauxa*.

The American girl likes the word *pinpilinpauxa*. "Butterfly" is a beautiful word, as well.

To fly—when you say it, it's like your arms are opening wide, Harri says. And she demonstrates.

Martin finds them taking turns expressively repeating words when he comes out. He wants to know what they're up to, but Harri takes him by the hand and leads him to the car; they've already made her wait long enough, too long, in fact. He couldn't find his key, he excuses himself, to which Harri replies that he never remembers where he leaves things. She says it like a mother. And when she takes an eyelash out of his eye, she's absolutely like a mother, telling him to keep still and open his eyes wide, and Julia can't deny she finds it all a bit repulsive.

When they're left alone, Julia asks the American girl if she wants a coffee, and she says "*pozik*," accepting gladly. It isn't the first time she's heard her say the word, which sounds like Russian with her accent. She sits on the coal box as she watches the coffeemaker fill up, her perfect feet dangling down inside her sandals, and she looks younger. "*Tell me*," she says, like in the novel.

"How many of your last names do you know by heart?"

"Six for sure. And another one or two out of order."

"Are they all Basque?"

"Yes, all of them."

"Would it be a problem if they weren't?"

"Not in the slightest."

"Would you mind if your last name were to disappear one day?"

"Not at all. But what is this, an interrogation?"

The girl stirs her coffee, her thin legs swaying a bit as she does. Normally Julia is alone when she has coffee in the kitchen; Martin only goes there to cook, and she finds it strange to be there with someone else. They stir their coffee in silence until the girl says, "*An open question now*," imitating a pollster's voice.

How DO YOU FEEL about being the inspiration for a literary character? That's the question, and Julia doesn't know what expression to put on her face when she hears it. The first thing she thinks of is asking her not to say silly things—"a literary character" seems a bit over the top—but she's also tempted by the chance to get to talk about something she doesn't talk about with anyone else. She doesn't know what to say and plays for time by asking her not to say silly things. She's been told that Flora Ugalde is exactly the same as her physically and "*de mucho carácter*"—a woman with a strong personality. Julia decides to take it as a joke. That description of her character is just a euphemism for saying that she has a temper, and making a carbon copy of her physical characteristics can't be that hard—big lips (she's been lucky in that regard, full lips have become fashionable, but when she was a child she used to bite them whenever she had to have her photograph taken, because people used to call her "Lips"), graying hair that she doesn't want to dye ("jet black with threads of silver" would be one way to describe it), and above all, the mole on her jugular fossa, which makes her neck stand out as singular. She thinks Martin must have enjoyed himself when he created the character; he likes sowing doubts, confusing people. As if it weren't enough that nine out of ten readers think that the narrators of stories told in the first person are the writers themselves (she's read that somewhere, and of course it's reasonable to suppose that the confusion between the narrator and the writer will be complete if the former, too, is a writer), Martin always makes use of real events to lend his stories plausibility, and she also suspects he likes giving critics who enjoy looking for biographical details something to keep them busy. She admits that there are clearly bits of her in Flora Ugalde. Does she mind? Well, not really, in fact, she doesn't mind people deducing that she talks to the electrical appliances in the kitchen, mostly to the washing machine, or that she snores, or that when the hot water in the shower cuts out, she runs down the hallway with her arms crossed to protect her breasts, or that she has no sense of humor. Not nearly as much as she minds when he gives the character faults that she herself doesn't actually have. What most hurts her is when he takes things out of context, twists them, criticizes everything. She's even gotten to imagining him as one of those reptiles that hunts insects with its tongue, on the lookout for words and actions that can be converted into evidence of misery. That's what he does, he hunts for misery. He's a reptile uninterested in colorful butterflies. His insistence on giving bitter, cruel caricatures of her—of both of them, in fact, because he shows no pity to himself, either—and on never showing anything noble, only bringing out the worst, is disappointing. Why does he feel the need to do that? Once, she thought it was a writerly characteristic specifically, but now it's on television, it's something that happens in all parts of society—the need to show misery and vileness. Julia thinks the situation has a lot in common with the type of people who go on television to share their most intimate things with the whole world. The only difference is that Martin uses a format conventionally connected with art and culture.

In fact, he's interested in talk shows, reality TV, and all sorts of trashy programming like that. When the genre was just starting out and that type of show was new in the world of television, his friends used to deny watching them, but he defended them. He used to say—and it was to impress them, to an extent, but also because he really believed it—that they were the seeds of future narratives, sociologists had only to sit back in their chairs and turn on the television to see things they could use for their work. He's fascinated by watching people talking about their sordid lives. He still watches the shows from time to time, but recently he's begun to complain that the format's exhausted, because they always show the same types of people talking about the same things. There's one show where people call others close to them, often people they live with, their partners, parents, brothers, or sisters, to tell them things that are in principle intimate—saying they love them or hate them, they're not willing to put up with some particular attitude or conduct (a lack of care in their personal hygiene, for instance)—but that for some reason or other they'd rather say in front of the entire nation. "*Delante de toda España*"—that's the expression they often use, "*ante toda España*"—instead of saying it in private, and that's led a few people to complain from time to time, saying, "You could have told me that this morning when we were at home." It was something like that for Julia, she would rather have heard directly, for instance, that he found the smell of her shower gel overpowering, rather than having to find out from Faustino Iturbe.

It happens less and less, for one thing because her model, too, has been exhausted, and for another, because Julia has learned to protect herself better. There was a time, however, when they could be sitting there together, each of them going about their own business or talking quietly to one another, and there would suddenly be a special shine in Martin's blue eyes that meant something had attracted his attention (it was like seeing, and almost not seeing, a long agile tongue catching an insect); sometimes it was something obvious and sometimes something that wasn't so obvious, and Julia would ask herself what it was that she had said or done that would be ridiculed next. Of course, Julia knows what attracts his interest, and occasionally she plays at being Flora Ugalde for his benefit, though not often. But in general it's the other way around, she tries hard not to say things that Flora Ugalde will end up saying, and, obviously, she's already stopped doing certain things when he's there. He's described her in the bathroom in full detail— he's portrayed her sitting astride the bidet (why does he describe the towels so meticulously, so exhaustively, in the way his beloved Flaubert describes Madame Bovary's hat?), brushing her teeth, holding her breasts with her free hand, plucking the hairs off her chin with tweezers, and leaning in toward the mirror, her reading glasses on the end of her nose, to measure the mole on her neck. The mole on Flora Ugalde's neck has become a mark of death. It's clear moles are no longer what they used to be. They used to be sung about, along with jet-black hair and strawberry-colored lips, and not so long ago, people used to tell Julia herself that it was pretty, its heart shape standing out so perfectly in the middle of her neck, and her father used to kiss it and call it "my little heart," but now it's completely different, people are obsessed with cancer, and when they see it, what they see is a tumor, or the start of a tumor. The family doctor told her it was a good idea to keep it under observation, and she thought of tracing an outline of it on a piece of transparent plastic with a thin felt-tipped pen, in order to see if it was getting any bigger or not. When she stood in front of the mirror with the bit of plastic in her hand, she realized that responsible action of hers would be stretched into something out of proportion and ridiculously obsessive. And that's what happened. From then on, he hasn't written a single episode in which Flora Ugalde doesn't appear to be obsessed with cancer at all hours of the day—getting up in the middle of the night or leaving in mid-conversation to go to the bathroom "to inspect the silent growth in that little black heart where the illness thrives." He wrote that.

Shortly after meeting him, she discovered the risks of being by his side, but she accepted it as something inevitable if she wanted to live with him. Seeing herself reflected in that painful, pathetic way was a tax she'd have to pay, something she'd have to take or leave. He would find it difficult to renounce something usable, even if it meant hurting the feelings of people he liked or respected, if he thought it might interest a possible reader for a moment, if he saw some way of making it into a sentence. It's his nature, as the scorpion would say. There's nothing higher than making literary use of life, and he has to devote himself to that.

Once, she was weak enough, or daring enough—she's not sure which—to ask him not to use a particular sad incident from her life, one that, unusually, he'd let her read as soon as he'd written it. Against all expectations, he accepted her request, saying that he had only written it for her. Remembering that makes her feels terribly ashamed, because then, to balance out his generosity, she was lowered around him to the level of a dog. She admits she's worried that she may have censored some pages that might have been important for literature by preventing the publication of that narrative (she's never liked widows and widowers who doctor their dead ones' diaries, although she does like Leonard Woolf), but now she's sure that he gave them to her because he saw they were of no value. Otherwise, and with the best of intentions, she's pretended not to notice when she sees herself reflected in his manuscripts, particularly in the pieces about Faustino Iturbe. So he can say explicitly that he takes great care to respect the literary contract, one clause of which—and it's one the critics respect less and less—says that there must be a distinction between the author and the narrator. With regard to that contract, Martin has written that the reader is like a polite gentleman who looks at the dog when a lady has an unexpected moment of flatulence. It isn't much of a consolation, but at one time that's what it was, a consolation. At the end of the day, though, everyone around them respects that hypocritical convention, which doesn't protect her from anything and condemns her to awkward silence. Nobody draws a direct connection between her and Flora Ugalde, though they may suspect one, and so she can't clarify which bits of the character really are hers, which bits are a caricature, and which pure invention (to continue the comparison, she can't allege in her defense that it really is the dog that's flatulent). Sometimes, when someone says they've read something by Martin, she has the feeling they've been looking at her through a keyhole. Once, one of her coworkers kindly said to her that she identified completely with Flora Ugalde in one episode. It seemed to Julia that she was telling her that the miseries that Martin described were fairly universal, that they affected her, as well, and Julia didn't mind her words, they made her more relaxed. But that was an exception. Harri, in fact, who was so insistent about distinguishing between the author and the narrator in *Montauk*, has never said anything about connecting them with Faustino Iturbe and Flora Ugalde. She hasn't even asked her if she was afraid of her mole getting bigger, and that seemed a bit too respectful. Although it could be because Harri doesn't *want* to see the similarities between Flora Ugalde and Julia, because Martin hasn't used her in the same way, as a "literary subject".

Was it Harri who said she was recognizable in Flora Ugalde?

The American says no, it was Iñaki Abaitua. When she told him where and in what circumstances she lived, he said that he's read Martin's work, and as was inevitable, they went to talking about her. He said she seemed like a woman with a strong personality ("*in the good sense*," he'd clarified), very smart and beautiful. She makes that typical gesture of hers, frowning and looking straight at her in order to be taken seriously, and Julia feels embarrassed. She's aware that Iñaki Abaitua knows that Martin suffers no lack of sources for inspiration when it comes to sordid details. Julia used to be his patient—she doesn't like that word, but she likes the one the young American normally uses, "client," even less—quite some time ago. She could say that she had no choice but to stop going to him because of some exclusivity clause when he closed his private practice, but it wouldn't be true. It is true that Abaitua shut down his private practice, but for a while, she and a few others went on seeing him almost free of charge, and that made her feel like part of a special club. She doesn't know why, but she tells her about the time she asked for an appointment because she was experiencing clear symptoms of a vaginal infection. Laboratory tests were ordered, and as expected, it was an infection. He prescribed a treatment to her and said that Martin, too, whether he had symptoms or not, should take the antibiotics, so that they wouldn't pass the disease back and forth to each other in some sort of ping-pong contagion effect.

At that time, Martin often met up with a girl who was writing her dissertation about Basque literature, and Julia was sure that her blood had been infected by bacteria incubated in that girl's vagina. Feeling the shame of a woman who's been cheated on, she didn't dare to ask the question, and Abaitua himself wasn't very explicit; taking her for a well-informed woman, he probably imagined she could draw her own conclusions. Julia wanted to disappear from the face of the earth, she couldn't stand the shame of what he might think about her relationship with Martin. She felt dirtied, too, to put it that way—she had been infected, after all—and in her bewilderment, she started talking about hygiene. She recalled that her mother, although she thought she'd been a good source of information for matters of hygiene and sex generally, once told her and her sister that keeping wet swimsuits on could be harmful and that they had to be careful sand didn't get into their vaginas. She had never understood why she'd told them that so many times, even after they'd grown up, but it occurred to her that she was bringing it up that day because it was summer and she was holding onto the remote hope that the infection might be connected with the beach. Abaitua said that her mother's recommendations were reasonable—warm water makes it easier for bacteria to incubate, and sand, which isn't always clean, can also cause scratches—but that it shouldn't be a problem in terms of indulging in a moment of desire on a beach. She remembers the moment very well, because she wondered if her mother—who had always had a longer perspective on things than she had—had been thinking about sex when she told them about the risks of beaches. Suddenly, perhaps because she's remembering her mother, she thinks it obscene to tell the American girl about her vaginal problems. Not very appropriate, in any case. So she decides to tell her the part about her mole and leave it at that. After leaving his office, she was standing at the top of the stairs—he was always polite and made it a point to see her out—and he asked her if she'd been keeping an eye on it, and then she realized that he knew about Flora Ugalde. She answered that she had and then blurted out a silly, hysterical laugh. Abaitua laughed, as well. He admitted that he was a reader of the *Gaceta Literaria* literary journal, said he thought it was a good idea to keep an outline of it on a piece of transparent plastic, but she'd be better off going to a dermatologist's, it would make her feel safer. And she felt completely ashamed once more, as if he were watching her running down the hallway holding her arms to her breasts, and then Martin cheating on her, and the literature student or whoever it was who was infecting her were the least of her worries.

It did not occur to her that Abaitua might think it was she who'd got infected having an affair, which was impossible, since she knew she was only sleeping with Martin, but the doctor, of course, had no reason to know that. So she didn't think that, she wasn't even capable of thinking it she was so embarrassed. However, she explained the situation to Martin as soon as she got home. She told him she had a vaginal infection, which he had definitely given her, and instead of being shamed into silence, he denied it, with the same conviction as Julia herself, saying it was impossible, arguing that he hadn't had sex with anyone else. He was so firm about it that she ended up being unsure. Probably because she wanted what he was saying to be true. In fact, Abaitua hadn't told her unequivocally that the cause of the infection might not have been sexual, that there could be other possibilities, for instance wearing a wet swimsuit in the sun. Abaitua had in fact said that her mother's advice was reasonable, and she thought, she wanted to think, that she herself was somehow the origin of the infection, the one who might infect Martin if she didn't take her medicine. It would be an exaggeration to say that she ever felt guilty, but there was no doubt that Martin did everything to make her feel so, talking ceaselessly about the dangers of taking antibiotics, the risks of bacteria building up resistance, and the damage caused to the gut flora, which he tried to prevent by eating a lot of yogurt.

Having her doubts about the source of her illness—he was very steadfast, asking how she could possibly imagine him going to bed with that fat literature student—they returned to normality, and once while they were chatting, she had a moment of weakness and told him that Abaitua was one of his readers, and that he liked recognizing parts of Otzeta in his narratives, even if they were given made-up names, like Mendixa, the restaurant where he went every

190

year on Saint Peter's Day with a group of his friends. She knew he was going to like hearing that, and what she wanted to do, to an extent, was to get rid of his stupid prejudices about Abaitua based on the troubles his own family had had seventy years earlier with Abaitua's—although in fact it was his wife's family, his in-laws.

Back then, she still wasn't good at realizing when Martin was questioning her with hidden intentions, until it was too late. It still happens every once in a while, because he uses cunning tricks when he asks her questions—she still falls for that—but above all because she's too reserved, and so, because she feels guilty about that and wants to be more open, she feels she has to give Martin answers without giving it much thought, because her way of suspecting things and distrusting everything gets in the way, and then what she tells him quickly gets used against her. In any event, he asked her what Abaitua was like during the appointment, and she didn't have much to say about it—he'd been polite and friendly and had more of a sense of humor than you might think at first sight, and to have something to say, she told him they'd talked about the risks of sand on the beach, that is, the lack of risks, how it's not a problem if there's a moment of desire on a beach at sunset, and that's also a way for her to attribute herself a certain degree of importance, to let him know that she and the doctor talked about things in confidence. The infection brought changes to their relationship, changes that she thought strange at first and which soon enough began to annoy her. The most obvious effect was an increase in sexual desire and, consequently, their having sex more often; penetration was especially unpleasant for her because of the swelling, but she didn't say anything to him, because he was even more sensitive about sex than he was about other things.

The infection also led to changes other than increased sexual frequency, such as their using condoms. Abaitua hadn't mentioned any need for them, and since they were both on antibiotics, they obviously didn't need to use them if they weren't being promiscuous, which Martin swore time and again he wasn't. She often tried to make him see that there was no point, but he had set his mind to it and said it took no effort and it was always better to use them, without ever giving any real reason why. Until then, neither of them usually ever asked for sex explicitly—Julia did from time to time, but as little as possible, because it was obvious he didn't like it, he felt it invaded his privacy—because it was something that used to seem to happen of its own accord, in a natural, intuitive way, but in the new phase, it became something that was planned. Several nights, when there was going to be copulation, she would hear him opening the box in the bathroom with the condoms in it and then going into the bedroom. He would put the packet on the bedside table, and after getting into bed, the first thing he did was to open it very carefully, as if his fingers were tweezers, and he left the condom on top of the packet for later use.

Sexual duties, so to speak, had been reduced to simple penetration, and she occasionally thought that he might even start using latex gloves, as well. Even so, she thought it must be a consequence of his own neuroses, and sometimes, depending on her mood, she found it amusing. What's more, he was especially happy and congenial those days, they spent a lot of time with friends and a lot of days out and about and often went out to dinner. That's why she wasn't surprised when he said that he'd booked a table at Mendixa, even though he didn't usually like going to Otzeta. Julia did like going, and she associated that decision, too, with the changes brought about by their new phase. They hadn't realized it was Saint Peter's Day until they saw Abaitua in the restaurant, which was packed full. They had an excellent red scorpion fish in green sauce, which you can only get at Mendixa, just like in the old days. They were lucky, because after the meal, all the people around a long table started to sing, and extremely well. They thought they must be members of a choir, that's how good they were, especially the tenor, who sang several solos. While he didn't have a great voice, his taste was exquisite. Julia was easily moved after all the fish and *txakoli* wine, and they almost shed tears as they listened to those old songs they hadn't heard for a long time. It's clear to see that the sediment deep within the heart, formed by the beautiful songs they used to sing with their friends when they were young, is where the seed of patriotism germinates. They were listening to the beating of a collective heart, when Abaitua came up to say goodbye. They talked about singing, saying that it was a custom that was being lost. People used to sing everywhere. There always used to be a few choir folk in every group of friends, mostly from church choirs, two or three people, or people who knew music because they'd spent time at a seminary, and they'd put something together, adding in a few harmonies. That's what Abaitua said. And everybody used to sing at church, services in Otzeta used to be real choral concerts. It was one of the bad consequences of the generalized decline in faith, he said, this loss of musical sensibility. Talking about things like that reminded them of "those days," when, as he described it, "people would put their arms around each other and sing rather than talking about politics." His eyes, too, were shiny, and he told them an anecdote he liked a lot. One night they were in a bar drinking and singing emotionally, and the other customers were listening to them; there was a lot of respect back then for people who sang well. There was a couple at the next table, they looked old and foreign, and they, too, listened as they drank their bottle of wine. They were singing a song called *"Egunsentia"*—or "Daybreak"—that went *"Ixilik dago tantai gañean / lengo txori berritsuba / lumatxo bigun arro tartean / gorderik bere buruba."* They realized that the foreign couple had started singing along with them, timidly at first but then louder and louder: "The songbird is quiet / on the tall tree / its head tucked under / its soft feathers." So they were singing the same song just in a different language, but with the same depth of feeling, and they were astonished that something they thought of as being so typical of their own land could be just as much so for these foreigners. By the time they finished, the old man and woman had tears in their eyes, and they toasted their far-off country and the warm welcome they were receiving in this new one and the fact that the wine was so good. They all raised their glasses together a few times but could hardly say anything to each other; the couple spoke English and had learned only Latin and French at school. They figured they must be Irish, but they couldn't understand them. Julia liked the story a lot, and she told Abaitua so, perhaps with too much enthusiasm, and he told Martin that it was a gift, he could use it if he wanted to. Instead of thanking him or just keeping quiet, Martin muttered something about Lili Marlene and then, quite rudely, said that it wasn't the type of story he liked telling.

There was a full moon out as they drove home. Julia thought that the countryside at the coast, to the north of Otzeta, between Mutriku and Zumaia, was among the most beautiful in Gipuzkoa. Limestone cliffs, soft, light-covered hills. "Sensual hilltops" she'd said on the way there, and Martin teased her—wasn't she being too sentimental? He recalled that she'd talked about sensual hills the first day they'd gone out together, but that time they'd been going from Biriatu to Hondarribia. Martin had said he wasn't sensitive enough to see if a hill was sensual or not. She'd laughed and said that it wasn't that hard to see. They'd played at exchanging sexual references, making use of the countryside. ("Tell me what the sensuality you see there is," he'd said, pointing out the window. "I don't know, *riccordo il diavolo sulle colline, forse*," she replied in Italian, quoting Cesare Pavese's *The Devil in the Hills*. "So it's a matter of roundness." "Yeah, hills turn me on, that's all." "And that's what you art fans call sensuality. When it comes down to it, that's all it is. It's pathetic.")

Since that very first time, they've often talked in that senseless manner, and Julia still feels something special whenever they do. Even that night, on their way back from Otzeta, seeing the smooth hilltops in the moonlight made her forget how rude he'd just been to Abaitua. She was driving at the time, Martin had let her; she was going very slowly because of how much they'd drunk, and as they came into Deba, she remembered something that had happened to her on the beach there. She had no idea what ever happened to the boy. She knew he'd been involved in the war and was planning on going over to the other side. It was very early, and there were very few people on the beach. They were both fully clothed and were lying face up on the beach, perpendicular to one another, forming a T together, the boy's head resting on her belly, and suddenly she saw a pair of black boots a step away from them, and her heart leaped. It was a Civil Guard, and he told them they couldn't remain in that position. "You're bothering those ladies," he said, gesturing toward the promenade. There were some women standing there surrounded by children and looking at them. They picked up their things—a bag and a book or two—and quickly got up, too embarrassed to speak, at least her. Afraid, she couldn't look at the Civil Guard directly, but she got the impression that he, too, was embarrassed about having to tell them off. She'd say that although it wasn't a pleasant situation, it was the first time she'd seen some trace of humanity in a member of the Civil Guard. As they left the beach, they saw the women, who seemed ancient to her, looking on in satisfaction as the two of them walked away without any sign of rebelling against them. They were tame. But she doesn't remember what she did all the rest of the day with that sad, affectionate boy who kept on saying that they wouldn't ever see each other again. She definitely felt guilty—she was going to go home after saying goodbye to this solider who was going to go off to war—and perhaps because of that, she said yes when he asked her to go back to the beach with him. But it was she who suggested they make love. She remembers the cold sand, the dampness, the intense smell of seaweed, and the fact that he didn't penetrate her. "At night, when the moon's in the sky and I hear the murmur of the waves, I'll think of you," he said to her as he did up his fly. It was the first time he said something like that to her, and she felt a lot of affection for him.

She remembered that night as she waited for the traffic light to turn green, and it occurred to her that she'd never make love on a beach again. It was a clear revelation, exact, a flash that surprised her at first and then made her feel even sadder. Martin asked her what she was thinking about. He always did that, and still does when he sees her with her head in the clouds, and normally she replies that she isn't thinking about anything, although that involves the risk of starting a senseless conversation about whether it's possible to not think about anything. Or alternatively, she says that he hasn't earned the right to know what she's thinking, and that puts a stop to it. But she tends more and more to say the first thing that comes to mind—they have to get a new coffeemaker, or clean the curtains— and answers like that disappoint him, apparently because he thinks she should be thinking about something that has to do with him, regardless of whether it's positive or negative. Sometimes, when what she's thinking about is particularly intimate or private, she finds it fun to let him have a glimpse of it for just a split second, letting him see just a scrap of the whole; she enjoys the risk of him guessing what she's really thinking. A variant of this game is to tell the truth, like a magician who shows the cards so clearly that they become invisible. When she does that, he doesn't believe her, or pretends not to, because even though he's always asking her what she's thinking, he's actually scared to know what it is. That night in Deba, while they were waiting at the light for the onramp onto the highway back to Donostia, she decided to tell him she was thinking about part of a song whose title she couldn't recall—"At night, when the moon's in the sky and I hear the murmur of the waves, I'll think of you"— and because he wouldn't believe her and kept on saying that it was no good thinking up something on the spot, she came out with the truth, or almost the truth, and said she was thinking about how she was never going to make love on a beach—opting not to say "never again," because the two of them had never done that together. He kept quiet, as he usually did when she told him the truth or a partial truth. Then, when they started off again, he asked her to stop for a moment, he had to pee, and Julia thought talking about urine just then was vulgar. They were on the boulevard, there were cars around, and she said she'd stop when she saw a gap, but he insisted she stop immediately and, pointing at the Kasino by the beach, told her to wait there for him and jumped out of the car. At the Kasino they served drinks at night and hot chocolate and churros during the day. She'd had breakfast there with the red-headed boy. She sat on the beach to wait for Martin. The sand was dark and heavy. She needed to be hugged—she sometimes feels an unstoppable need to be hugged by someone—and she wouldn't have minded who it was as long as certain minimum conditions were met: strong and soft at the same time, with a pleasant aroma. That indiscriminate need to be hugged worries her sometimes. Martin waved at her from the parapet. "That's better!" he said as he approached the beach, and then something incomprehensible about his prostate gland's incontestable authority. She was only vaguely aware of the existence of that particular gland at the time and knew nothing about how it works, and he hadn't yet made it the center of his very existence. He stretched his arms out as far as he could and said he was very tired. But when they got home, he started writing as if he were possessed. At that time, he still wrote at night. In the morning, he didn't read her what he'd written, and she feared the worst. But later on she forgot about that strange day, and about that night, as well. Until the next edition of the *Gaceta Literaria* came out. There was a new episode of Faustino Iturbe's life that, with a couple of major changes, was a description of their trip to Otzeta. Faustino Iturbe and Flora Ugalde witness the scene at Mendixa. A group of local young people are singing the song about the bird with its head in its feathers, and an old Irish couple add their trembling, emotional voices to theirs. Flora is extremely moved, and on the way back home, she stops the car in Deba, takes Faustino Iturbe's hand, leads him to the beach, and crudely asks him to do her right then and there. An absurd story that ends with Faustino Iturbe starting to feel a horrible burn every time he takes a piss, and with a quote from Goethe defining love as a sickness.

196

They didn't speak for a long time after that, and she never had another appointment with Abaitua again.

The young American, too, thinks the story about the bar is beautiful, the old Irish people joining in with the young Basques. She asks Julia to sing the song. She no longer remembers all the lovely, nostalgic Basque songs she once used to sing so emotionally, but she thinks she can remember this one. She works up her courage, takes the young woman by the hand, and leads her to the piano. She hasn't played for a long time and hasn't sung for even longer. "*Ixilik dago tantai gañean / lengo txori berritsuba / lumatxo bigun arro tartean / gorderik bere buruba*." She can't carry on, because her voice breaks, she just plays the piano part, and after a few moments lets that fade out, as well.

Through the French windows, she can see a gigantic yellow machine, it looks like some military thing, that's throwing spurts of cement down a chute and onto what had been a soft field. She sheds a tear and can do nothing to hide it. Lynn is looking at her, her eyes bright, her chin resting on her arms, which are crossed on top of the piano. "*It's really beautiful,*" she says, putting her hand on the hand Julia has left resting on the piano lid. The girl's hands have very long fingers and short nails. Then she says she thinks they're going to be good friends, and Julia takes her hand away when she sees the writer in the yard.

ZIGOR IS SITTING AT THE KITCHEN TABLE, and his grandmother is behind him, by the window, ironing. Julia had to stand there for a long time before they realized that she was there. They've been deeply immersed in a discussion about the civil war. Perhaps the mother is jealous because her son's had to go to the old people's home to find someone to talk with. Someone, it's clear, has been telling him bad things about the nationalists. They hesitated too much about which side to join during the war, they spent all their time saving right-wing informers, and then they fled as deserters to Asturias, which is something that Julia's mother will not accept at all. She says that the patriots had to fight on two fronts at the same time, against Franco's Nationals in front of them and against the Reds in the rearguard, and the Reds committed all sorts of terrible crimes. They burned down Irun. As far as their surrendering was concerned, they did the right thing—the war in Euskadi had already been lost, because the Republic had stopped sending arms and planes.

She's told her hundreds of time that she shouldn't iron the sheets.

The *gudaris* were great guys, noble and honorable. She says the Reds who were in Otzeta used to wear their caps tilted to one side, they were proud, arrogant, always on the lookout for a fight, and they used to steal cars to go out drinking.

She was employed in a workshop where they made clothes for the soldiers, close to Gernika and a long way from home, when the Nationals took Otzeta. Sometimes, when they talk about that period, she says they were some of the happiest times of her life. Julia and her sister have sometimes wondered whether she might have had a boyfriend back then, but they haven't ever managed to clear that one up. She doesn't mention matters of much importance—what they used to eat, perhaps, or how they organized their work. She saw the bombing, but what she says about it is nothing near as bad as what Julia has seen about it at the cinema. Zigor's generation has seen the giant mushroom cloud over Hiroshima, the flayed Vietnamese girl, and the Gernika bombing has become, objectively, a small-scale tragedy. While she changes clothes in her bedroom, she hears what her mother is saying, almost whispering. She knows she's going to tell him at some point about the woman carrying her child away from the bombing wrapped in a blanket and suddenly realizing that he's dead. She doesn't know if her mother ever actually saw that scene herself, but the image is so well assimilated that she probably feels as if she did. Terrifying. The boy keeps quiet—his grandmother's firsthand story conveys fear, and not even the best cinematic special effects could compete with her.

He must think what his grandfather did during the war was incredible. That's what Julia thought, as well, when her father used to talk about it. Zigor asks her to tell him her version of it when she goes into his room to say goodnight, but as could only be expected, right now he only has ears for what his grandmother has just told him. He was the first person in the neighborhood to volunteer with the nationalists. They were sent to the Loiola basilica for their training, and there were thousands of young men there, all of them cleaning and decorating the church, and as her father used to proudly say, not so much as a single chalice ever went missing. Their first action in the war was to take a hill, whose name he didn't remember. According to her father, they crawled forward, and then, when they were nearly at the top, perhaps growing overconfident and no longer keeping so close to the ground, they were caught by machine gun fire and had to run back down the hill. Many lost their lives, and those who got away were scattered. He was wounded in the ankle and, along with some others, was taken in at a nearby *baserri*. They gave them bread and milk and let them spend the night in the barn, but the next morning, the Falangists woke them up and took them prisoner. The farmer had given them up. The first tricky issue: coming to terms with the fact that a Basque farmer had been the informant, which went against the nobility and loyalty that her father said were characteristic of the Basque race. They should have been executed, but luckily, the battalion or whatever it was that had caught them was led by a colonel from the Erribera area of southern Navarre, a gentleman Falangist, a drinker and a ladies' man, but a good man, who saved their lives and took them with him to Aramendia, withdrawing them from the front to rest. The colonel's name was Munuzabal, and he used to spend the summer in Martutene. He liked Julia's father and arranged for him to be sent to the kitchen as a cook, so he spent the war eating and drinking as much as he wanted. The second difficult question: Being an enthusiastic nationalist volunteer, why didn't he just poison the whole battalion? Julia thinks that's the question the boy is asking himself now, and it's one she would also like to know the answer to, but she never dared to ask her father. In any case, her intuition tells her that the wars you see in movies are nothing like the real ones. The third problem: how to believe the strange, absurd act of bravery that her mother's just told Zigor about. Once, Munuzabal ordered him to come before him. It was after lunch, the colonel had had a lot to drink, and apparently he asked him, "So, Inaxio, if José Antonio Aguirre came here tonight and asked you to hide him, what would you do?" Her father's version was that he said he would have hidden him. It would seem the same thing happened more than once, and apparently her father never changed his answer, he always said the same thing. When the northern campaign finished, he returned to his old neighborhood along with the Falangists, which astonished everybody—they thought he was dead, they'd even held a funeral for him. He said that he'd saved a lot of lives by stealing informant reports from the offices—he literally ate them—and that he'd alleviated a lot of people's hunger by secretly handing out food he snuck back out of the warehouse after it had been confiscated in raids. After the war, Munuzabal wanted to give him a job with the Falange, but he didn't accept it, and he even refused to let the man help him buy a boat as he'd offered to. Munuzabal liked him so much that he turned up the day her parents got married in Otzeta—nobody knew how he found out where and when the wedding was to be held—and, to her father's great embarrassment, gave him a big gift. The last part's definitely true, she's heard her aunts and uncles say so, and they couldn't have made it up. Her sister also remembers, or at least she says she remembers, that the colonel's sisters used to come and visit them when she was very small—the man was still a drunk, a ladies' man, and a bachelor, of course—and that they wanted to take them back with them to their house in southern Navarre, but their father never let them. Later on they lost touch.

Her mother asks her to help fold the sheets. She thinks it's just an excuse; her mother doesn't like her talking alone with the boy about the war. Julia sees her eyes are red. It seems she's just heard that the heir of Etxezar has sold off the last bit of the pine grove for next to nothing.

6

ABAITUA IS EXAMINING HIS TEETH AND GUMS in the mirror. The
necks of some of them are eroded, on some of the incisors in
particular, and he thinks one of the fillings in his wisdom teeth
may be broken. He thinks there's no more significant sign of decay
than losing your teeth, and he's always been frightened by the idea
of it, ever since he had one of his wisdom teeth extracted when he
was still very young. In fact, advances in orthodontic treatments
have been a great relief for him, and at times like now, when he's
looking at his teeth in the mirror, he thinks that the most positive
thing about living in the time period that he does is that when he
eventually has to, he'll be able to make use of those techniques.
Because he has the economic means to do so, of course. He's quite
sure that the cruelest reflection of the difference between social
classes can be seen in people's teeth. In any case, he's less worried
by the slackness of his eyelids, which almost completely cover his
eyes in the morning, than he is by his teeth. Pilar has sometimes
comforted him, without trying to deny the basic evidence, by saying
that the bathroom mirror is particularly cruel. And it's true, perhaps
because the mirror's a high quality one or because of the lighting—
the bathroom lights are powerful—and there are other mirrors that
are more amenable than the one at home, ones that show fewer
details.

"Do you know what?" says Pilar.

The decorator who's redoing the bathroom has told her that there's a clear trend in modern homes toward integrating different things in the same room without any partitions, and apparently restrooms, too, are being left open, without any doors. Abaitua thinks it's an obscene feature of contemporary culture, which values naturalness excessively, but he doesn't answer her.

He spends a quarter of an hour cleaning his teeth. Two minutes with spurts of water; three minutes with dental floss; two minutes with his normal toothbrush; four uses of the electric toothbrush (it restarts automatically every two minutes), two per quadrant, eight minutes total. Pilar says he's going to wear them down. She doesn't use a toothbrush herself, only floss and an electric brush, and her teeth are perfect.

PILAR'S LEFT THE CAR in front of the garage door, she hasn't parked it inside, again. Pilar, who is so careful about most things, is incomprehensibly lazy and careless about a few. She seldom closes screw-top jars completely, she often leaves the refrigerator door open, and she never parks the car in the garage.

There wouldn't be any problem about checking the underside of the car today, there's nobody around, but he's not going to. He's going to be firm about not continuing that senseless ritual.

WHILE HE'S SIGNING PRESCRIPTIONS, the nurse tells him that the night before, when he was in the operating theater, the American girl who left her file folder behind the day before came to collect it but even though she looked everywhere, she couldn't find it, and so she had to leave without it. "But she's sure to come back," she says, as if she were already well acquainted with what the young woman is like. She also tells him that Villar, the traumatologist, is going to marry a younger woman. He himself is a couple of years older than Villar. "As he should," he says, pulling her leg. "If he's going to get married, he's not going to marry someone older than himself!" The nurse is unmarried, around fifty, fat, and she has red veins on her face that give away her intense social life. He thinks she probably hates men, and she often says that men can get fat and go bald without any repercussions while women have to starve themselves and are condemned to doing tai-chi.

Pilar sometimes says to him—and he doesn't know to what extent it's a joke—that he should find himself a young woman so that he can have the daughter he's never had. It would rejuvenate him. What she says about a daughter is true; he's often said, jokingly, that he'd like to have one to look after him when he's old. On the other hand, he isn't one of those mature men who are attracted to younger women, and he finds it revolting when men of his age make jokes and say dirty things about young women who could be their daughters or even granddaughters. In his case, the taboo of incest protects all women who could, in terms of their age, be his daughters, and consequently, he doesn't see them as objects of desire.

He's never linked beauty with youth, and in any case, a woman isn't attractive for him just because she's young. He remembers that when he was a boy and he'd hear people say that no women were ugly at the age of twenty—he'd even heard his father trot out the cliché—it always seemed absurd to him, because there were ugly twenty-year-olds, even very ugly ones, in fact. Of course he does appreciate certain features that are associated with youth, though not exclusively, such as soft skin, bright eyes, fresh lips in particular, but in themselves they're not enough to make a woman attractive for him. In fact, there are even some features of maturity, of decline even, that he doesn't necessarily find disagreeable, that can even be attractive depending on the woman's intelligence and personality: slack breasts, which can suggest generosity and desire; a sensual, broken voice, which can express experience; and tired eyes, which can transmit understanding, knowing, and calmness. There are many women of his own age who seem much more attractive to him than many younger women. The nurse doesn't believe him.

¿LLEGARÉ A COMER EL TURRÓN? On being given a bad diagnosis, some people use that expression—literally an enquiry into their chances of ever getting to taste *turrón*, the ubiquitous Christmas sweet, again in their lifetime—as a way of asking him how long they have left, and they probably aren't the ones who take it the worst. He says yes to the woman who's just asked him, but he doesn't think she'll last more than a year. A lively woman of forty who has a tumor that's spread extensively, a stupid husband, and two adolescent daughters who have no clue what's happening. Abaitua doesn't know if he has the most appropriate face for these occasions; he worries that he may explain things too gravely, coming across as being hieratic and cold.

But even so, he prefers erring on the side of sobriety. He knows that patronizing behavior is an even worse risk. And being the way he is, what most concerns him is accurately reflecting the severity of a given situation. What can a patient in need expect from some anxious, tormented caregiver like Van Gogh's Doctor Gachet? As well as prolonging their remaining time and ensuring the best quality of life possible, someone should teach these people to live out the rest of the time they've been dealt calmly. Without suffering, without hurting themselves. Aided not by volunteers—everyone knows that professionals work for money, but who knows what's motivating volunteers?—but by well-trained, competent healthcare professionals.

There's a bad smell in the room, coming from the carcinoma in the patient's cervix. When Abaitua comes in, the person accompanying the patient, her sister, steps out without greeting him. To get some fresh air. The patient feels no pain, she still enjoys food and, quite significantly, defecates every morning. The problem is the bad smell and the fact that the sick woman is aware that the people who spend time with her are always counting the minutes, waiting to go outside, to escape into the real world. Abaitua stands by her bedside for longer than he really needs to precisely for that reason, so that she doesn't think he also wants to get away from her. It's a useless sacrifice, and because of that, he isn't proud of it.

As he unbuttons her blouse, he remembers the young woman who suddenly opened her sweater and she that said she was lactating. This time it's a mature woman, and in this case she does have a hypophyseal tumor. Operations always involve some risk, but this one's fairly straightforward. It's extracted through the nose. He explains it to her with a sketch. She asks if he's going to do the operation; it seems she trusts him. He says no, it's an operation for a neurosurgeon, and he'll be assisted by an ENT surgeon, but they'll look after her well and there won't be any difficulties.

At the door of the pediatric ICU, Iñaki Echevarría—the fat resident doctor who spells his last name with *ch* and a *v*—asks him what he's up to. He jokes that he's "checking on the results of the havoc we wreak in the world," and he thinks of Minkowski, who used to say that it would be a good thing if obstetricians and midwives visited the incubator ward from time to time so that they could see what the results of their exploits in the birthing room can sometimes turn out to be. Of course, the fat guy hasn't even heard of Minkowski. He tells him how there used to be a time when pediatricians didn't visit the maternity ward until twenty-four hours after a birth, because they thought that newborn babies were as much of an adjunct to their mothers as the placenta was. The first neonatologist to step into this hospital was Rodriguez Alarcón. The head of obstetrics let him come in because he was a nice guy and, more than anything else, because he used to tell great jokes, but he wasn't allowed to touch anything, until one day there was a difficult twin birth in which, as the saying goes, even the father's life was at risk, and it became necessary to put one of the newborn babies into the neonatologist's hands. Once the problem was solved, the head of the service was honest enough to admit that their reanimation techniques had become outdated and that it could be very useful to have a pediatrician specialized in newborns physically present in the birthing room. It's obvious the fat resident doctor isn't impressed by any of this.

At the nurses' office, they tell him that "that American girl" is looking for him, and he thinks they're mocking him a little as they say it. She's in the waiting room. She's wearing a white wool sweater that almost covers her skirt. She does that smile of hers that wrinkles her whole face, and he smiles back at her. He's glad to see her. He's glad, too, that the girl seems pleased to see him.

The young woman's the first to bend down and pick up the books that Abaitua knocks over when he reaches for the blue file folder. "I'm not what I used to be," he says to himself. He congratulates her on her agility and asks her to excuse the mess. He thinks that disorder, like the inability to find one's way, is the result of some psychological problem, some negligence linked to character, although generally people don't frown on it so much when it comes to books and file folders. The young sociologist is now holding several copies of Céline's *Semmelweis* in each hand, and she looks from one to the other, as if astonished they're all the same book. He explains that he gives them out to young doctors when they join the hospital. It's a very good book. The young woman looks at one of the copies, and he tells her to keep it. It's a very interesting episode in the history of medicine. Semmelweis was a Hungarian doctor, a pioneering champion of antiseptic practices. While working at a hospital in Vienna, poor women who were going to give birth used to hide, so that they wouldn't be taken to the hospital. They preferred to give birth anywhere other than the hospital, knowing as they did that they would be sure to die there afterward of puerperal infection. In one ward, the maternal mortality rate reached ninety-six percent, and Semmelweis was convinced that there was a connection between that high rate and the fact that the people in charge of the birthing process always came straight from dissection class. He determined that if they washed their hands with a simple sodium chloride solution, the maternal death rate plummeted. But most of the doctors at the time thought it was not only absurd but also humiliating. What was all this about having to wash your hands? They accused him of manipulating the figures and kicked him out of the birthing room, and then out of Vienna. The poor man went mad, and women went on dying of puerperal fever all over the world, until Pasteur's discoveries finally proved his theory.

He'd say the young American finds what he's telling her interesting, because she doesn't take her eyes off his lips while she listens to him, though he makes himself take into account that it could be because she's listening to a language that she doesn't have a complete mastery of, and that's something he'd understand. She still has the copies of *Semmelweis* in her hands, and he repeats that she should keep one for herself. She thanks him. Then she says, "Poor Semmelweis." And, after a quick smile, "*Hard times.*" He answers that they really were hard times and that even though they're now in the past, there are still some doctors who refuse to wash their hands with the sodium chloride solution. "So to speak," he adds, as if he were explaining a metaphor. He regrets saying it, she might think he doesn't trust her intelligence. As if that weren't enough—"*Of course, of course,*" she says as she nods her head—he suspects that she must be very familiar with Semmelweis's role in the history of medicine. So he apologizes for telling her about things she already knows, and although the girl shrugs her shoulders, it's clear she does know them. The fact that he's been surrounded by people like resident doctor Echevarría with a *ch* and a *v* recently has made him think that everybody's like that. It's also a matter of age. It's started happening to him recently, particularly when he's with young people. Almost everything makes him remember anecdotes, or want to give interpretations of things, prompts in him the need to unravel some memory, thinking that others—and here's the vanity of senility—will surely find it of interest. He tells her this as he's thinking it, rather ashamed, and the girl laughs. His memories, in any case, can't be as old as all that, because if she's not mistaken, poor old Semmelweis must have died toward the middle of the nineteenth century. They both laugh at that. No, he isn't quite that old, but he's old enough for her not to speak to him in Spanish with the more casual *tú* form of address. You only talk to people who are over a hundred with the more formal pronoun.

He has the blue folder in his hands. His idea had been to say that he'd opened it to figure out, by the contents, who it belonged to and that upon seeing that it was a novel—and a novel, what's more, in which one of the characters has her same name—he hadn't been able to resist reading it. He'd also planned on making the joke that people named Lynn seem to be forgetful. But now he decides to keep quiet, he doesn't want her to take him for an old gossip as well as an old bore, or, worse still, a dirty old man, because bringing up the story of the girl leaving her lighter on the bedside table could be understood as the old gynecologist trying to compare himself to the writer in the book. Also, it was very obvious that the file was hers, because she'd kept it hugged to her chest almost the entire time she was with him, and it wouldn't have been possible for someone not to notice that. So she's come to get her file back, and he's wasted her time telling her stories she knows only too well. He apologizes.

The girl's way of protesting that there's nothing for him to say sorry about might be considered excessive—she holds an open hand out to Abaitua and claps the other to her mouth. She says she felt moved by seeing him identify so much with the unlucky Semmelweis and display his indignance about his colleagues' cruelty. That's why she didn't want to tell him that she was already familiar with the book.

The nurse comes in after knocking on the door but, as usual, without waiting for a reply, and Abaitua gives the girl the folder, but too quickly, which he then regrets; it looks as if he's trying to cover up something he's done wrong. *"Here's your carpet,"* he says as he hands it to her. The nurse opens and closes a few drawers in the table and the filing cabinet and, after complaining about the untidiness, finally says, "I'm off." So it's not long before her shift is over. He isn't wearing a watch. He always takes it off for examinations, in line with the regulations, setting it down any old where. He tells the girl that, as well, instead of just asking her the time. It's two o'clock. The girl opens the folder, and when he sees that, Abaitua wonders if he should tell her that he didn't just look at the sheets in it, he also photocopied them, and he decides to admit that he read them. He didn't know that they were hers, of course. But when he saw that there was a character in the novel with her same name, he couldn't hold back his curiosity. But he doesn't tell her he also photocopied them. The girl asks if he liked it.

He doesn't know what he can say to match the degree of curiosity evident in her question. He says he only read bits. He could easily go on to say he likes the naturalness of the relationship between the young woman and the old writer at the beginning—a relationship that the narrator of the novel thinks "has no future" and is "blameless"—but he doesn't think that would be appropriate. So he just says that he liked it a lot—though he does stress the "a lot" —and that he was very surprised to see a character with her name appear in it; when he was reading, he got the impression at times that he was reading about her, because she's the only Lynn he knows. The girl looks at him with amusement, she rests her chin on the folder, which she's holding against her breast. "So now you know the tricks we Lynns use," she says. And Abaitua is extremely disconcerted by the joke that, shortly before, he himself had thought it would be inappropriate for him to say.

He says he's late and looks at his watchless wrist. It only remains for him to hang up his coat and close the window. Keeping the window open for a bit was a necessary hygienic measure after the last patient. The girl waits for him in the corridor, and she makes that gesture of hers, brusquely shaking her head to rearrange her ponytail, the same way as described in the book, and she also tucks her loose hair behind her ear, which he thinks is what she does when she's going to make a decision. He doesn't know what decision she's made. Right now she still has her hand on her ear, holding her hair, and she says that it's nice to have shared reading a good book with someone. And then she laughs.

That short laugh of hers that wrinkles up her whole face.

They've both read two books, the photocopied novel and Céline's *Semmelweis*, but Abaitua feels more secure talking about the latter. If he had to criticize the Budapest doctor for anything, he says, it would be for not knowing that it isn't enough to be right about something if you want a new idea, even if it's a good idea, to take hold. Scientific talent alone isn't enough. A few additional gifts are needed, as well. He feels well placed to talk about this, about how the idea of going straight for an objective is naïve, and he turns to the clichéd example of a whaler—which he says he came across in one of the few books on management techniques he's ever read—explaining that this type of sailor doesn't go straight for what he's aiming at but instead has to zigzag around depending on the wind. He discovered this concept quite late in life, and because of that, he explains it to his son every time he gets the chance to see him. But what leads him to mention it now is pride; he wants to make it clear that if he isn't the head of the department, or even the director of the entire hospital, it isn't because of any intellectual or scientific shortcomings but rather because he didn't meet the wind he was up against with sufficient flexibility. A dumb thing to say, a sign of his need for limitless recognition.

WHEN HE SUGGESTED DRIVING HER HOME, the young sociologist said no, it wasn't worth it, she lived very close by. But he insisted, perhaps with a little too much enthusiasm, and in the end she accepted. Now, as they're arriving at "the witch house," after what would have been around ten minutes on foot, he thinks that perhaps she would have preferred to walk back by herself and he should have accepted her decision, both out of politeness and because he's supervising her research work. He also realizes that he hasn't stopped talking since the moment she came to his office, and he remembers what the writer says at the beginning of the book of Lynn's that he photocopied: whenever he likes a woman, he thinks he becomes a bore all of a sudden. However, he can't say that he's particularly attracted to the girl sitting next to him with the blue file folder on her thighs and her thin fingers resting on top of it. He doesn't even think she's especially beautiful, but he still gets the feeling that he's being a bore. Another thing the writer says: he finds that always remembering something or other gets in the way. He himself has the same problem. Too many images, too many memories that keep piling up around what he wants to say, that he thinks might be meaningful, appropriate, or at least curious but which distract him from the heart of the matter and put him out on a limb all the time. He keeps on repeating the expressions "because of that," "in fact," and "with regard to that" as if they were a chorus. Now he recalls Doctor Cordoba, who they used to call "*caldo de gallina,*" not because of anything having to do with chicken stock, as the phrase might seem to suggest, but because it was also, in somewhat older-fashioned parlance, a nickname for loose-leaf tobacco, which the man smoked—Ideales brand—never removing his hand-rolled cigarette from his lips, even when he was assisting at a birth (which would be unbelievable for the young American), and being hand-rolled, ash and sparks continually fell from these cigarettes of his onto his lips and his now hole-filled shirt, and because of that, he kept on moving one of his hands around as if he were playing the guitar. And that leads him to recall that when he was a child, a man once sent him to buy a packet of "stock" for him—that was what it was like in his neighborhood back then, any grown-up could tell any child to go and do things for them—and then almost slapped him when he came back with a packet of Maggi-brand instant bullion cubes; any adult could also slap any child back then. Recently he's been thinking that telling people his memories is a sign of senility, or pre-senility; he suddenly wonders whether it's an attack of logorrhea and shuts up. But for some reason or other, he's convinced that the young American's interest is more than just politeness. She's paying so much attention to what he says—he's sure now that she isn't looking at his lips because of any difficulty in understanding him—that he feels encouraged to go on talking, and naturally, her happy open laughter when he says anything with a possible double entendre or touch of irony also makes him keep talking. Irony, in fact, is something that Pilar usually finds so confusing—she'll stare at him to work out if he's joking or whether he's being serious—that it often ends up making her angry.

"Why did you become a gynecologist, Doctor Abaitua?" The young sociologist asks direct questions unexpectedly, sometimes in Spanish and sometimes in English. In the novel, the writer, too, thinks that the girl asks questions in a strange way. "As if it were a survey" Abaitua thinks is how he puts it. In this Lynn's case, that would be understandable; when it comes down to it, she is a sociologist, after all. What's more, he reckons it's usual to ask questions when you go abroad. Out of respect, because you want to show that you're interested in the customs, for instance, but she asks other kinds of questions, as well, more personal ones, questions that someone from your own country would never ask you in your own language.

"¿POR QUÉ SE HIZO GINECÓLOGO?"

"YOUR WIFE IS A DOCTOR, TOO, ISN'T SHE?"

"¿CUÁL ES SU ESPECIALIDAD?"

"WHEN DID YOU GET MARRIED?"

He sometimes gives different answers to the question about why he became a gynecologist, depending on the situation and on his mood. "To get to know women better" is something he's often said, but he thinks that too flippant an answer to come out with now. Saying that it was a matter of chance is quite appropriate in many situations, and as such, it fits now, as well. When he was a resident doctor and visiting different services, the head of Gynecology was competent and friendly. They got on well, liked each other, and he let Abaitua do some real work. He thought it was an interesting specialty, among other things because it didn't involve only surgery, and they accepted him into the service. He doesn't know to what extent Pilar's father having an obstetrics practice influenced him— his firm decision not to work with him, the desire to make it very clear that he wasn't going to sell himself out. He knows it was tough on the old man, who loves him and trusts him, probably more than he does his other sons-in-law. So he chose the specialty that should have been Pilar's, and she, probably as an act of rebellion, chose something more prestigious, something that few people did at the time: neurosurgery.

Abaitua has to ask the American girl several times what they were talking about.

In his opinion, and to the contrary of what the young woman and many other people think, neurosurgery is not more difficult than other specialities, but be that as it may, it certainly isn't an appropriate speciality to practice in a small clinic, and Pilar has never made much of an effort to find work elsewhere, either. He's sure she's a good professional, even though she's never been ambitious. She sometimes complains—he thinks rather opportunistically—about the obstacles she's had to face as a woman. That hasn't helped her, of course, and she often accuses him of not being supportive (she had to look after their child and the home by herself). She hasn't had very good luck, either. Her brother-in-law's always kept her in the background, and she found it easy to get used to that subordinate position. He thinks that she's skillful and responsible in her work and that she does what she knows how to do very well. That's what he thinks about Pilar. And he says it without being very sure that the young American will understand him.

He stops right up against the house's iron gate, in order not to hold up traffic. He doesn't know whether to turn the engine off or not, and in the end he doesn't. He just puts on the handbrake and keeps both hands on the steering wheel, pleased that the Volvo has such a quiet engine. The situation is becoming awkward for him, even though it was he who created it. The girl doesn't move, either, or make any sign of opening the door, but finally she breaks the silence. She says he has surgeon's hands. He has surgeon's hands, or at least that's what she thinks surgeon's hands should look like, and when he hears that, Abaitua crosses his arms, which is something he seldom does, and hides his hands in his armpits. They could be the hands of a pianist, of some type of artist in any case. He should be used to being told that he has beautiful hands. Pilar herself has told him. They're strong, with clearly-visible veins and long fingers. He takes good care of them, although he's only ever had a couple of manicures. In hotels. In Rio once. He doesn't feel at ease with his hands hanging over the arm of a hairdresser's chair and a girl at his feet almost kneeling down. He waves the fingers of his right hand in the air. "Don't you believe it—I'm losing my skill in this hand." She doesn't believe him. She hasn't seen him operate, but she's seen that he's good at drawing. She knows that quite well—she sees him drawing in meetings all the time. But only anatomical sketches, he never does artistic drawings during work hours, he jokes. He doesn't deny that he's good at it. He says he has a friend he goes hiking with and that sometimes they take watercolors along with them, to paint. In fact, although they have said they'll do it again, Kepa and he have only done it once, but he doesn't feel any need to correct the fib. He also tells her something he's heard Kepa say: he doesn't really see things until he draws them. The girl turns right around and tucks her legs under her on the seat with a quick movement. "And do you paint portraits?" He paints incredible portraits, he says, carrying on with his joke, and of course, she asks if he'll paint her. Any time. And the girl asks him to promise it, which he does, solemnly, a hand on his heart. *"I promise you."*

Then they fall quiet again, and the gynecologist confronts the silence with his hands on the steering wheel, as if he were driving in the rain. His hands once more. The young American thinks that hands are badly designed—there are too many fingers on them. They'd be much more stylish with one finger fewer. Stick characters in comics only have four fingers. If you're going to take one finger away, which one is it going to be? Abaitua is sure about it. The fourth one, the one next to the longest finger, the one that's only any good for wearing a ring, and for once, the young sociologist disagrees with him. How could a doctor say that? He finds the exaggerated way she shows her surprise comical, her mouth wide open and her hands on her cheeks. The finger that he says is useless, the one called the ring finger in many languages, in Spanish, for instance, is magical: the one on the left hand is connected to the heart via the *vena amoris*. The *s* in *amoris* whistles when she says it. The finger you use for mixing drinks. Apparently, that's why it doesn't have a name in several other languages—Bulgarian, Sanskrit, Turkish. People are afraid of it, because it's magical, because it has powers. And particularly in Eastern cultures, in Japanese, for instance, but in German, as well, and Hungarian, it's called the healing finger, or the medicine or doctor's finger, *digitus medicinalis*. In English it's called the ring finger, and also the leech finger, and because the gynecologist doesn't know the meaning of *"leech,"* the well-educated American sociologist explains it means *sanguijuela* and that it's also *"an archaic word for physicians,"* though she doesn't want to offend him—he's also a doctor.

The well-read doctor didn't know any of that, but he isn't embarrassed by the young American uncovering his cultural ignorance. Quite the contrary—he's pleased to be with a cultured woman who's studied things. What's more, the American sociologist, for her part, doesn't know that this particular finger, which is so overvalued in other languages and is only any good for wearing rings, is called *hatz nagia* in Basque. *Perezoso*, he clarifies in Spanish. *"Lazy,"* if that's the right word. He ventures the theory that in the past, when doctors didn't wash their hands, they used the *digitus magicus* to stir their drinks and, in that way, there was less risk of them then putting it into their mouths or any other inappropriate holes than if they had used more skillful fingers. As far as the young sociologist knows, the term "weak finger" or "lazy finger" isn't used in any other language, and the seriousness with which she says she finds his theory interesting makes him doubt whether she really does.

Digitus nagia gives them a lot to talk about. Speaking of *digitus annularis*, Harri Gabilondo has warned the young woman about men in the Basque Country who wear rings. It seems that Basque men in general do not like superfluous ornaments and look down on wedding rings in particular. Abaitua agrees that's right, and he says that rings were considered ostentatious, more appropriate for Eastern countries and Spanish civil servants, or, more precisely, for secret policemen wearing sunglasses and moustaches. And he tends to agree. What's more, ringless fingers are a sign of noble work; rings not only get in the way but are also dangerous, although that isn't the main reason why Iñaki Abaitua doesn't wear one.

Pilar doesn't wear a wedding ring, either, and they had to use rings lent to them by other people when they got married. That's what they were like at the time. Back then they rejected marriage, because it was a fundamental bourgeois institution; apparently Marx had said it was another way of prostituting yourself, a source of subjugations and boredom. He points at a large white building with a small bell tower on top of a slate roof. That's where they were married, in the chapel at his father-in-law's clinic. It was practically a clandestine wedding, only immediate family attending. Because they got married without conviction, giving way to the circumstances, marrying in order to avoid having to break off from the family, or at least to avoid causing too much of a fuss, because it was the only way for them to live together as a couple. All those old people—widowed old men and women who now live together but remain unmarried in order not to lose the right to continue drawing both their pensions and who boast about how much they enjoy themselves at retired people's dances and on day trips and watching filth on the television—used to be inflexible with young people who wanted to live together without getting married and demanded that they comply strictly with the moral norms in force. He admits he resents it. As far as the young people of the time were concerned, they were obedient when it came down to it, although in order to protect their dignity—and, to an extent, the illusion that they weren't getting married completely—they would insist on getting married in shrines on far-off hilltops and on the officiators being absentminded priests, priests who didn't completely want to be priests and who, later on, became more and more secular, priests who helped them dispense with the paraphernalia that today's young people seem to love. They were able to preserve their informality, so to speak, and they tended to eschew wedding rings, gifts, banquets, and honeymoons, just as Pilar and he had done. They thought they'd be able to escape that way from the institutions they hated and that had made their parents unhappy. But they were wrong about that, as they found out before too long. However, they continued pretending that they believed themselves to be free and, except with themselves, with each other, they compromised on everything else. Protective when it came to their false freedom, they put their commitment to each other to one side, and their false sense of dignity, emotional clumsiness, and supposed authenticity—in other words, taking everything other than vulgarity to be no more than bourgeois hypocrisy—made it impossible for them to do anything that would give meaning to their life together.

He's had the impression for some time now that Pilar blames him for making her challenge her father (among other things, with the type of wedding they had in the clinic's chapel), for distancing her from her old friends because they were right-wing rich kids, and, in the end, for leading a conventional bourgeois lifestyle that wasn't so different from theirs. *"No necesitaban alforjas para ese viaje,"* would be the Spanish way to describe it.

He doubts whether the young American is understanding him clearly now, because he's stopped making an effort to speak slowly or to avoid double meanings and tricky expressions. He doesn't know how to explain the expression *no necesitar alforjas para ese viaje*— literally "not needing saddlebags for the trip," it's a way to explain that someone needn't have expended so much energy on an endeavor, something like saying "for all the good it did"—but at least they have a laugh when he tries to get her to pronounce it properly. He even has trouble explaining what the *alforja*—the saddlebag—is.

And with that, he forgets what they were talking about.

WEDDING RINGS. The young woman reaches out toward the windshield, showing off the back of her hand. She doesn't wear rings, either. In her case, she says, it's in order not to draw attention to her hands. They're too small, she says with resignation. She has very white skin, and her nails are shiny, but he doesn't think she uses nail polish. She has such delicate hands that her joints are highly visible. "They aren't surgeon's hands, are they?" There's no such thing as surgeon's hands, he says, without adding that her hands are pretty. As far as he remembers, he's never seen Pilar with painted nails, either, and her hands aren't the best part of her anatomy. But she does wear rings, though not always. He remembers she has one with a light-violet-colored stone, and another with a green one. And she has a diamond ring, as well, which is a family jewel, and must be worth a lot. But she's never worn a wedding ring. A few years ago, not so long ago, during one of their reconciliatory romantic moments, he decided to buy her the wedding ring he hadn't gotten her back in the day, and he chose one randomly, one that didn't look too big or too small, having gone into a jewelers on impulse without having taken a ring from her jewelry box as a model. He didn't get to see if he picked out the size right or not, because she didn't even try it on. "A bit too late." That was all she said about it. Pilar doesn't trust expressions of affection, just like Abaitua's mother. He's occasionally seen the wedding ring sitting in her open jewelry box.

But he doesn't remember the date of their wedding. Not the day, the month, or the year. It was a winter day, or late fall, because Pilar can be seen in a photo that one of the nuns at the clinic took wearing a coat with a fur collar half hiding her face—a very poor photo. He's often been surprised by Pilar saying "We got married so many years ago today." She gets disappointed about it. He's always thought that she minds too much about him forgetting dates, because she isn't one of those women who are very sensitive about details; in fact, he would say it's easy to overdo things with her, to appear to be overly buttery, but now he knows that she takes not remembering certain dates to be a sign of a lack of respect, and she accuses him of not being interested. And she's right, although he's never seen it that way. His argument is that not remembering the date doesn't mean that he's forgotten the day—he remembers it well. He doesn't know what year his son was born, either, but he remembers very well that it was raining on the day he was born, and nobody could say he doesn't love him, he might even love him too much, in fact. But he has to admit that he does know just a few dates by heart: July 18, 1936; August 31, 1813; April 14, 1931; July 14, 1789; and September

27, 1975. He knows that Pilar's birthday is on the anniversary of the night before the storming of the Bastille, but he has to calculate the year—she's nine years younger than he is. It's true that he hasn't made any effort to remember the date of their wedding, and that could be a sign of negligence, or of something worse still, the desire to forget about it—that's probably what she thinks. In any case, when he admits now that he doesn't know how many years he's been married, he wouldn't like the young American to understand that he, like so many men, is proud of being clumsy and careless, one of those married men who considers himself a bachelor, and so he insists it's because of his bad memory, a shortcoming that may be linked to his poor orientation, but it's obvious he also leaves it open for her to interpret that his forgetting the day of his wedding is because it's a bad memory for him. And yet there is nothing further from his mind than speaking ill of Pilar. And he hates that frequently employed male strategy of attracting women's attention by securing their pity, men explaining their misfortunes to that end.

Where did you meet? At the hospital?

When they were both students. They met at the start of one summer, at the Zaragoza train station, the day before he was going to leave behind the city where he got his degree in medicine forever. He had gone there to check in several suitcases stuffed with his university books, and she'd gone there with a large group of friends to meet someone. He knew her by sight, she was so beautiful it was impossible not to notice her—the best-looking girl in the department—and somebody told him she was the daughter of a Donostian obstetrician who owned a private clinic. They never had any contact in the year they both spent in Zaragoza; she hung out with the rich kids and didn't ever cross paths with him and his friends in the places where they used to go to drink small glasses of wine and sing traditional songs like "Boga Boga." One of those girls you didn't just go up to, and in any case, she was much younger than him. But that day at the station, it was she who left her group and came up to him. He remembers her perfectly. In a short, beltless dress that stuck to her belly a little bit and had long or three-quarter length sleeves, she moved her arms freely, swinging them a little, which almost made her seem a little forward (it was very unusual to see girls not carrying bags back then), almost challenging, marking each pace clearly with her shoulders and hips, and when she stopped a couple of feet from him, she asked him in Spanish if he was going back to Donostia. They didn't even know each other's names. "¿Vas a Sanse?" He hates that abbreviation for San Sebastián, and he hated it even more just then, thinking it a word typical of the group of fools standing behind her in a semicircle and looking on with curiosity and amusement. He said he was going back the next day, and she suggested taking him in their car—they had a free spot. "You can come with us." Later on she admitted that the girls in the group had pointed him out and that she'd gone up to him as a bet; although she looked daring, she'd actually been very embarrassed just then, and even afraid that he might refuse her invitation in front of her friends.

She was known for being very lively, and they called her by the nickname, Piluca. A ridiculous name. He sometimes calls her that, Piluca, when he wants to tease her. He also teases her because she was wearing such a short dress, it stopped several spans above her knees, and Pilar is amazed that he remembers it so well—pistachio green with a square neckline—and she explained that she used to wear either very short skirts or very long ones, almost down to her ankles in order to cover up her knees, which she doesn't like. Perhaps they are quite wide, they're strong, and she has a wrinkle above each kneecap and a soft fold in her skin that looks like something left over from her infancy. He loves that fold, which is a soft as a child's skin.

The young American's legs are quite different from Pilar's. Her knees, in particular, with their small, defined kneecaps, are nowhere near as rounded as Pilar's; they are precise, and he likes that. And her calf muscles are very well developed, her rectus femur above all, and it forms a curve that's visible up to her knees. He likes that distinguishing characteristic, which his grandfather's generation wouldn't have cared for much. On the other hand, they would have liked her skin, because it's completely white, and the golden down that shines on it, also completely white. She says she cycles a lot, that's why she has well-developed calves. She passes her thin-fingered hands over her cyclist's thighs, and Abaitua is afraid she might have seen him looking at them. He would be incredibly hurt if she took him to be one of those dirty old men that sneak surreptitious glances at thighs and necklines. So he tries to seem natural and give his words the air of some technical finding when he says she has well-developed muscles, and she answers, also in a wholly natural way, and leaning back a little so that he can see them better, that perhaps they are over-developed. Too much cycling.

Abaitua prefers hiking. He says that he often goes to the Pyrenees to do stretches of the GR–11 trail with that friend of his. The stretches of the trail that are in the Basque Country, which is the area he likes best. Not out of patriotism, he feels compelled to say, but because the mountains here aren't as high, they're forested and gentler. The real mountains start further east, with their bare rock faces, and he finds them more challenging. They normally stay at a small hotel, there's a nice one in Donibane Garazi, the Arrambide family's Hôtel des Pyrénées, and they spend their days in the hills eating only nuts, dried fruit, and oranges, and in the evening they feast on substantial dinners. Perhaps too substantial. He admits that he sometimes has difficulty dragging Kepa up to the hills, and more than once he's had to set off by himself, leaving his friend sitting at an outdoor café reading a book, because he prefers car trips, visiting unusual places, eating well, and sitting outside reading to hiking. He illustrates his point with a few details he thinks are amusing. The girl, at any rate, laughs happily at his descriptions of himself—alone and unable to find his way on the mountain paths, completely lost.

"You are a fortunate man." The young woman in the novel also often says "you are a fortunate man" to the old writer. More than the declaration itself, he's surprised by how seriously she says it, the depth of the young American's feeling when she speaks the phrase, and when he asks her why, she says, *"Don't know, I just think so,"* but gives him no other answer, it's just the impression she has.

He wonders if he shouldn't turn the engine off.

The American girl says she's heard that the northern Basque Country is very beautiful. She wants to go there. He could reply that he'll take her there whenever she likes, but he doesn't think it very sensible, and what's more, almost as soon as she says it, almost without pause, she says herself that she's planning to go there. "I will go," she says with great conviction, which leads him to think that she isn't looking for someone to take her. And much less an old doctor, the father of a son that he knows is the same age as she is, even though he doesn't remember his exact birthday. They had the boy late in life, very late in life—it's complicated to explain the reasons for that, and it would involve mentioning Pilar's bicornuate

219

uterus—and because of that, his son is younger than is normal for a man of his age.

"DOES YOUR SON LOOK LIKE YOU?"

"DO THE TWO OF YOU GET ON WELL?"

"WHAT DOES HE DO?"

"WOULD YOU LIKE TO HAVE HAD A DAUGHTER?"

On other occasions, too, he's gotten the impression that it's easier to tell foreigners intimate things. For one thing, you care less about what they may think about you and about what they might do with the information you're giving them. For another, you feel protected by their limited understanding, because you think that they won't comprehend everything you say or that they'll take things you put badly to be the result of their own problems of understanding. Something like when you stay up late drinking.

It often happens, especially when it's obvious that the questions are being asked out of politeness and that the contents of what's being said are not the most important thing and instead it's being comprehensible and grammatically correct, like in a conversation class. However, even leaving aside the fact that the American girl gets by pretty well in Spanish, Abaitua would like to express himself with precision.

People say that Loiola looks exactly like him, a clear case of biological determinism. If the question is whether he likes that, on the other hand, the answer is no. He finds it disappointing to see himself in him, and sometimes, when they quarrel—the boy holding his chin, which is weak like his, looking at him with hatred—he thinks that his son blames him for making him as he is. In short, without even bothering to give a smile to let her know that he's saying too much, he tells her that because he doesn't like himself all that much, he isn't particularly proud of his son, either. And he doesn't say it as a *boutade*.

The girl doesn't smile, either.

He thinks the borrowed French "*boutade*" must be used in English, as well. But he doesn't ask her. He could specify that what he really dislikes about the two of them being the same and both of them knowing that they are is the fact that they both try to hide what they're really like. But he thinks it would be difficult to explain and, in fact, out of place. And there are easier questions for him to answer.

He isn't a doctor. He studied business, probably because he wanted to do something different. He thinks his grandfather probably conditioned him, as well, asking him if he'd like to be the skillful manager his clinic really needed, but he works at an NGO and spends long periods in Latin America and says that he plans to work there in the future. He probably wants to be loyal to the ideals that he—his father—has betrayed, also differentiating himself in that way. His son is at the radical age, whereas he, the old doctor, is at the age of frustration. Although on the scarce occasions they do talk about his son's plans for the future, he tries to hold back his egoism as a father, to emphasize the need to have coherent principles, the importance of being able to choose your way of life freely, and using noble ideas to do so. But his son's unpleasant attitude, his arrogance—similar, if not identical, to his own arrogance when he used to get up from the table and walk out on his own father in mid-sentence—and his belief that he knows everything drive him up the wall; he's often come very close to asking him just what he thinks he's doing in Latin America, to shouting that he's a paternalist, a missionary, and that the only thing he does there is gobble up in a day as much as a whole indigenous family does in a week, and he's wasting his time in the name of fucking principles and he'll never make the world change. For some reason, he's never said all that. But it's as if he had.

So it's not an easy question to answer.

The night before, in fact, when reading the novel that the American girl left in his office, he thought about how different the main character's approach to fatherhood was from his own. Because of what he says about a conversation he had with his daughter. A daughter the same age as the girl he's spending the weekend on Long Island with and who, as a child, he abandoned when he split up with her mother. The daughter sends him a postcard from Scotland to tell him that she's going to marry a German man she's met, and when he visits them, he's already a grandfather. The writer says it was about time he visited them, because his grandson had already started talking, and he said the visit was "neither easy nor difficult." Abaitua is sincere when he says he envies relationships like that. He thinks it's good for the children, above all because it helps them to be freer. In our culture, on the other hand, dependence is encouraged—parents make sacrifices for their children but then pass them the check later on. An unfair check, what's more, because the costs are exaggerated. Some parents—though more in the past than now, that's true— torture their successors, reproaching them for how much they had to

221

give up for their sake, perhaps wanting to reinforce their awareness of their obligations for the future.

The pelican strategy. Apparently that's the name for the behavior that Iñaki Abaitua has intuitively described. The young sociologist explains that the name comes from the myth that pelicans feed their chicks with their own flesh. The basis for the myth is that the chicks peck at food that's kept in a special pouch in the mother's bill, food that's often splashed with blood, and because of that, it was believed to be the parents' flesh. She explains it in a simple but serious way, in the way she normally explains things, without showing off or talking down, making it clear, once more, that she knows all about the type of things that the old doctor might tell her about. Everything's already been said, he remarks, amused. Everything that we think, all our clumsy reflections, have already been precisely and properly explained, usually by some short phrase in Latin.

He'd say that he's never used that strategy, the pelican strategy, no way, at least not consciously, even though his son is still feeding off his parents' flesh.

The young girl says it's clear he loves his son a lot.

Something difficult to deny, even though he doesn't see many things with such clarity, but which he does know without any doubt, is that if either of the two of them were to be the target of a hit, he would prefer to be the one to get hurt. No doubt about it. He's thought about it every time he's been frightened by the thought of a terrorist attack. An altruistic feeling, preferring one's own death to that of another, something hard to feel without being a parent. But it isn't something that he thinks of as being noble, or that makes him feel he's a better person. It's a primitive instinct, derived from some gene for the best interests of the tribe, and like most primitive, instinctive things, he doesn't like it. He's sure that if he told her about it, the young American sociologist would give it a technical name. But he thinks he's spoken enough or too much about himself already. What's more, he doesn't think it's right to mention his fear of becoming the object of a terrorist attack, and by not mentioning it, what's already a hypothetical matter can become even more theoretical.

THERE'S A TRAIN GOING BY.

The young woman is half facing the door and puts her left hand on the handle, as if she were just about to open it. He would like her

222

to, because the situation is becoming uncomfortable, but he's also afraid of her doing so. As afraid as he is of her inviting him to come in for a drink, which isn't probable but can't be entirely ruled out. He puts his foot on the clutch and reaches for the parking brake. He even puts it into first gear, ready to drive off.

He doesn't notice the giant excavator until its driver starts knocking on the car window. *"Tocándose los cojones,"* he hears the man say, grumbling about him sitting there scratching his balls. So it's obvious he's complaining about having to do his work with the machine while a couple of bourgeois parasites lounge around laughing in their large car. He's angry, and he'd gladly get out and tell him he's just spent ten hours standing up in the operating theater, but he contains his rage, not so much because he doesn't want to put on a show in front of the young girl—he'd actually quite like to put the guy in his place—but because he somehow feels he's been caught in an embarrassing situation: an old man with a young girl, putting off the moment of saying goodbye like some adolescent kid. He moves the car further back toward the house's iron gate and waits there with both hands on the steering wheel and the engine on, like before. The young girl still has her hand on the door handle but still doesn't open it. He wonders if the girl would misinterpret it if he invited her to lunch. The Barkaiztegi grill and cider house is just a few steps away, and it's a place entirely above suspicion—he would never take a lover to a cider house. He could say that it's too late now to go have lunch at home. But he knows he won't. And even so, he suddenly regrets the fact that she's going, inevitably, to open the door and say *"see you."*

One English expression he likes is *I miss you.*

Will she realize the ridiculous old man is nervous?

The young woman leans over the dash to get a view of the house and, turning back to him, says it really does look like a witch's house. He also leans over to see it, even though he knows it perfectly well. They've never been so close. He smells her perfume once more, it seems quite acidic to him, very different from the one Pilar uses. He sees the hairs on her neck that are too short to be tied up—they're curly, as shiny as copper. He agrees it looks like a witch's house, with its slate roof and conical tower. The girl's happy that she's found a really cheap apartment, a bargain, *un chollo* in Spanish, and he finds it strange to hear that word, which is difficult for her to pronounce, on her lips. He doesn't know much about rental prices, but the figure she tells him does sound cheap. She's been lucky. Very lucky. That quick smile of hers, just enough to stretch her lips. "*Well*," she says, now putting her right hand on the door handle, and although she makes no further gesture to suggest that she's going to open the door, the man knows that the time to actually say goodbye has at last arrived. He decides to keep quiet, with his left hand on the steering wheel, his right on the parking brake, waiting for her to open the door. She doesn't do it immediately. First she looks out the windshield for a moment, she's quiet, too, and after opening the door, she waits a moment longer, as if unable to find the right way to say goodbye. Finally she turns toward him, and lifting up her index finger, like a schoolmistress to a naughty child, she reminds him that he has two promises to keep. When the man says he isn't aware of having promised to do anything, she says that he has, and not just one thing —two things. The man remembers them only too well. He remembers that joke he's supposed to tell her, the one about the woman whose vagina gives off a terrible smell and who puts an ad in the paper seeking a man with anosmia for oral sex. The other promise is to do her portrait. It was meant as a joke when he told her, a little earlier, about his drawing hobby. He accepts that commitment, but not the commitment to tell the joke. He can't tell jokes, he says in his defense. Even if he finds them funny when he hears them, he forgets them immediately, but she won't let it go: "A joke about discharges," she says in a natural way, as if trying to help him. "Remember?" He can't keep saying no, but the mere thought of having to tell such a vulgar thing—and such an unamusing thing, at that—makes him feel nervous. He moves his foot onto the accelerator once more. He steps on it, the engine's two hundred horses whinny to express their strength, and the young woman puts one of her feet on the ground, almost certainly taking it as a sign that he wants to go. She threatens to remind him once more the next time they meet. There is no sign of anger on her face or distrust in her voice. "*It was a pleasure,*" she says, sticking her head into the car once more. "See you," says the man. And the girl, "*I hope so.*" And then she closes the door.

PILAR IS SITTING READING THE NEWSPAPER, which is spread out on the coffee table, with her breasts almost resting on her thighs, as usual. She sits up when she realizes Abaitua's there. He thinks she must be wondering where he's come from so late, but she doesn't say anything. There's turbot in tomato sauce for lunch. It's an unusual way to cook the fish, but a good method, according to one fisherman's wife, and ever since first hearing that, they often prepare it that way. Pilar knows he likes it a lot and has been waiting for him to begin lunch. She hasn't laid the table, the kitchen is tidied, and the turbot's still in its pot, untouched. But she says she isn't hungry. Normally she doesn't have a proper lunch when she's alone, not wanting to heat things up just for herself. A piece of toast, a simple omelet. He prefers to say that he, too, has already had a sandwich and isn't hungry. He couldn't stand her sitting there watching him eat. He goes back to the living room. The prospect of not having lunch doesn't make him feel any better. On the television, which has the sound turned down, a woman of around fifty is talking with tears in her eyes. What's wrong with her? Pilar turns it off with the remote control, stretching out her arm unnecessarily to do so. He thinks she looks gloomier than usual and weighs up asking her if there's some problem. He doesn't need to ask. Without looking up from the newspaper, she says her father's dying. Her voice sounds more angry than sad. Why does she say that? Because she's sure, she answers. But she doesn't have any objective facts to back her up. It's just what her mother says—he isn't eating properly, and he looks tired to her. It could be any little thing, he says to cheer her up. She shakes her head. She's convinced he has esophageal cancer. She wants him to have it looked at, but he won't let anyone come near him. Abaitua doesn't know what to say and so he says, once more, that a lack of appetite can be caused by many different things. Pilar answers that she has a better clinical eye than he thinks.

On top of the bureau, there's a framed full-length photograph of Pilar and her father standing in front of the big palm tree at the clinic. They're both flashing their excellent teeth as they smile. The old man's wearing a blue beret and still has his thin white moustache, which Pilar had always said he should shave off, because it made him look too right-wing, and then finally, some years ago, he did shave it off. It's from less than ten years ago—Pilar is wearing her red jacket. The one she was wearing that time when she came home in the early hours and sat on the side of the bed in silence.

The window is open, and the sound of the waves is very clear. It's more than a vague sound. Two white lines are continually advancing toward the beach. When the first wave peters out on the sand, the second wave starts coming in behind it. When it fizzles out, the next one starts, and so on. He would miss the sea if he ever had to live in a house you couldn't see it from. That's why he bought this house. Sometimes Pilar insinuates that he accepted an "incentive" from her father—in other words, money from his business of "trafficking in pain"—to be able to buy the house, which is far beyond the reach of a doctor employed in the public health system, a house close enough to the beach to see the waves breaking on the shore.

She says that Loiola called to ask if he could keep the car for a few more days and that she said yes. Nothing more than that. Not even a word to suggest she might be nervous about the approaching trial date for those boys. She turns the television on once more and seems to go back to her Sudoku. He says he has to read a bunch of articles.

The photocopies of *Montauk* are on his desk. He begins reading randomly. "1972, I've never met a Lynn before."

Suddenly, he has the impression once more that he's bored the young sociologist. Like one of those people who tell you all about themselves when you've only asked them out of politeness how they are.

He can't get to sleep. He realizes that when he gave the girl her file folder back, he said, *"Here's your carpet."* A "carpet," he'd said, *carpeta* being the Spanish word for "folder." *A real Turkish carpet.* He's so embarrassed he feels queasy.

7

IT'S NINE O'CLOCK. A van parked in front of the iron fence is honking its horn nonstop. Julia is putting on a sweater to go out and open the gate when she sees the writer coming down the spiral staircase. He's elegantly dressed, all in white. A white polo shirt, white linen pants, a white sweater knotted around his shoulder—he looks like F. Scott Fitzgerald. *Orratzetik hara*; *de punta en blanco*; *se mettre sur son trente et un*; dressed up to the nines. He says that he'll open the gate and hurries into the yard.

It's a cardboard box the size of a closet, and he tells the delivery guys to take it into the library. Even though she doesn't ask him anything about it, he tells Julia that it's a surprise, and also asks her to help him move a revolving bookcase and a table covered in books and to take a couch out of the room. It's clear that he needs some space for whatever it is he's had delivered. But it's a surprise, he says once more, and he asks her to go back into the living room. He'll tell her when he takes it out of the box.

She rules out the possibility of it being a piece of furniture, because they already have a lot of furniture: the new modern light-colored and functional furniture Martin had brought in, and the original house furniture—heavy, dark, and clumsy—that they can't completely get rid of. But Julia can't think what else it could be. It springs to mind that they might end up acting out one of Ionesco's plays, the one called "The New Tenant"—the main and almost sole character is trapped in his chair, surrounded by furniture the stage crew keeps bringing onto the stage throughout the play.

It turns out it's a Ping-Pong table.

When he suggests they give it a whirl, she blurts out that he'll be able to use it with the *penthouse* girl. So she can't hide her indignation. She's promised herself a thousand times that she'll let him do whatever he wants to, that she won't judge him, won't interfere in his life, but she can't avoid her pain. It's obvious he's bought the Ping-Pong table to be able to play with his tenant, because in *Montauk*, the writer called Max also enjoys playing Ping-Pong with the young woman called Lynn. But what annoys Julia isn't that he wants to play Ping-Pong. Rather it's that being as he is, with his hesitation when it comes to making even the smallest of decisions, being incapable of even buying a pair of socks, he's mustered up the energy and the decisiveness not only to go and buy that great big thing and have it delivered but also to defy his mother's wishes by setting it up in the formal library. She hasn't forgotten how hard he found it to take her crocheted covers off the armchairs, even, and he's never brought himself to give her a birthday present—pretty or ugly, expensive or cheap—that he thought of himself, having noticed some whim or need of hers; often, although he hasn't ever gone so far as asking his sister to go and purchase something in his name, she herself has had to help him come up with ideas and even go with him to pick something out.

It's obvious that he's noticed she's angry, even though he's pretending he hasn't. He apologizes, even though he has no need to, by saying that the table was on sale, a real bargain, and that it will be good for them, running after loose balls will help them to lose some weight around their middles. She laughs. For him, nothing would be worse than the *penthouse* girl turning up and finding them in the middle of a quarrel, and because of that, she's tempted—not really tempted, but she does think of it—to kick up a big fuss about him bringing this new object into the house in front of the girl. It would make him sick. He would do anything to avoid having others noticing that they're angry at each other, and there's no way he could have a couple's argument with a third person there, either, not even if it were Harri. And Julia has to admit that she's sometimes taken advantage of this fact to put him in a difficult situation, because she finds it easier to have others notice her bad mood than to keep her anger in check. It's a matter of character, she thinks, and also of upbringing.

Martin, relieved, asks her why she's laughing, and Julia laughs more, reminded of a certain anecdote. "You have no idea," she says to him, leaving him with the Ping-Pong table and paddles. She's just remembered a quarrel that her cousin Koldo and his wife had. Martin knows the story well and has sometimes told it himself, as an example of the open nature of coastal people. Koldo's wife, being deaf, uses a hearing aid. But she turns it off when they quarrel, and that really annoys her husband, who then shouts every insult he can think of at her. Her cousin himself told her about it. Once, while he was shouting, his wife asked him to be quiet, otherwise all the neighbors would hear everything. "What will Don Hipolito say?" she asked—Don Hipolito was the village priest and lived on the floor above them—and her cousin, opening the window, absolutely furious, like a storm breaking over the sea, mocked the neighbors and the priest with a passion, it was impossible to shut him up, until he decided of his own accord that he was finished. "Don Hipolito can go to hell!" was what he shouted. Apparently, the next day he had to go and apologize to the priest, and he said the priest was quite understanding—these things happen from time to time, he said.

TEMPUS FUGIT. Her father often used the Latin quote, in a completely natural way and always appropriately—it seemed a sign of wisdom to Julia, and she was disappointed when she noticed it inscribed on the face of the clock in the dining room that they looked at so infrequently—and recently, without knowing why, she's started saying it, as well. It's taking her too long to translate *Bihotzean*, because in addition to the difficulty of the work itself—and it is difficult—she has a tendency to lose herself in her own thoughts about each clause without ever reaching any conclusions. As far as the writer is concerned, although he turns his computer on, he seldom spends more than two minutes sitting down in front of it. He gets up to go to the bathroom all the time, and to go upstairs, as well, though he tries to hide it from her; she thinks he goes up there to spy on the *penthouse* girl, to make sure she doesn't slip out down the tower stairs without going through the house. In fact, she regrets being mean to him on one occasion, asking him, on one of his reappearances from the bathroom, if he realized how much hair he's losing. "You shouldn't comb it so much." She could have said anything to him, even that it had forced her to clean around the foot of the toilet bowl again. The man ran both hands through his hair gloomily and told her he'd already gone to the skin specialist. "He told me I wouldn't die bald." Julia knew what would come after his short, forced laugh. He didn't know if he meant that he didn't have much hair but that it was going to last a while yet, or that he wasn't going to have time to go bald because he was going to die soon.

The *penthouse* girl at last. Martin goes up to her to tell her he's bought a Ping-Pong table. "I have a surprise for you," he says, leading her by the arm into the library, even though the young woman doesn't look particularly interested. But she doesn't have much choice, and she thinks getting a Ping-Pong table's a good idea—it's a great sport. That's what she says, but without much enthusiasm, to the writer's frustration. She waves her photocopies of Montauk in the air and says she wants to talk about the Spanish translation as she runs back into the living room. "*I'm so angry.*" She really does appear to be angry, flipping so energetically through the pages that it looks as if she's going to tear them right out of their spiral biding, searching for what is, she says, an unpardonable treason. The writer insists that they have a game, and the young woman agrees, but just to a few rounds, because she doesn't want to get sweaty. In exchange, he promises to give her his bank account number so that she can make her rent deposit, as per their agreement.

Naturally, the noise of the bouncing ball doesn't help Julia's concentration at all. In *Montauk*, the writer says that the click-click of the Ping-Pong ball in the empty room sounded funny. To Julia, though, the echoing noise sets her on edge. Aggressive thoughts. If she picked up a paddle, she could wipe the floor with both of them. But on a *pilota* court, against a wall, with a real paddle. She played the game a lot with the boys when she was young, bare-handed, too, with leather balls. The sound of a *pilota* ball hitting a wall is something else. That heavy, violent thump, of stone against stone.

Now the overriding sound is the ball hopping up and down—click-click-click-click—on the floor.

ENOUGH FOR TODAY. They finally quit playing. The young woman says she's sweating, though she looks impeccable. The writer is visibly out of breath, and he starts panting even more heavily when she insists he give her his bank account information. He stalls, tries to change the subject, and asks her what it was she was so angry about. But she won't be sidetracked, and she insists—she has to pay him. Martin finally gives in. It's one thing that's always impressed Julia, the fact that he knows his bank account number by heart, because it's the only thing he knows. He writes it down on an empty medicine box, despite being surrounded by index cards, papers, and Post-its, and Julia knows why. He's obviously hoping to tell the girl the same joke he told her last night. He said he'd decided to stop taking antidepressants and that he'd dumped the whole box out on top of the pansies, and it had perked them right up. Since the flowers did actually look a little less wilted, she found it funny—just as the American girl does, *of course*—but now she feels bad that he has no qualms whatsoever about repeating the same gag, as if she weren't sitting right there.

TRADUTTORE TRADITORE. The main reason she's angry is that according to the Spanish translation, when Max and Lynn leave the hotel at *Montauk*, the writer is furious that the girl isn't going to find out how much he's had to pay for their stay there. She points at the line Julia should read, like a teacher to a pupil, and Julia obeys her: "*Le irrita, luego, el pensamiento de que Lynn, que se ha encargado de hacer las reservas, apenas tenga idea de lo que él ha tenido que pagar por las dos noches que han pasado aquí.*"

But the real text, she complains, is quite different. It doesn't say that "he is then irritated by the thought that Lynn, who made the booking, will hardly have any idea how much he's had to pay for the two nights they've spent there." What Max is actually angry about, in fact, is Lynn *knowing* what an expensive bill he had to settle. Almost twice what the girl earns in a week. It's very clear in the English translation, which was revised and approved by Frisch himself, but they can't compare the Spanish version with it, because she's lent it to Harri, which she lets out a cry of frustration about, but she's sure that's what it says. She stands there looking at each of them. It seems to be a matter of vital importance that they believe her, and Julia tries to calm her down. She remembers well that she'd been extremely surprised by that passage when she read it in Spanish; that revelation of stinginess in the writer—wanting the girl to know how much it had cost him to sleep with her—would have been more fitting for an arrogant dirty old man, nothing like Max's respectful, natural attitude toward Lynn throughout the book, nor was it in keeping with his attitude about money, which he talks about extensively. It would have been more natural for the writer—with his guilty conscience about being rich—to feel ashamed or sorry that the girl might see him spending what was a lot of money for her in such a carefree manner. It also contradicts the paragraph as a whole—because Lynn made the booking herself, she must, inevitably have known what the rates were. Isn't that right? The girl is extremely grateful for what she says; Julia, on the other hand, is rather disconcerted by seeing how influential a translator can be, even though the mistake seems terrible to her, as well, and especially terrible considering she thinks of the Max in *Montauk*, with all his weaknesses, as being a noble, loveable man, and likewise, the mean, despicable attitude in the Spanish translation could by no means, it seems, be shared by Max Frisch the author, not from what you can gather from his diary and from what several people who knew him—she thinks of Reich-Ranicki—wrote about him.

More things about Max and money. The young American likes Max's approach to money. He's generous, but he also knows what money's worth. Even though he's become rich and can easily satisfy all his whims, he hasn't forgotten that he was once poor; he's suffered his whole life as a result of some badly executed dental work he had done in a low-cost clinic that employed apprentices. She also likes the way he acceded, as a young man, to his friend W.—whom he thought of as being above him in all ways: tall, rich, and well educated—giving him his high-quality jackets as hand-me-downs and lending him money to pay for his studies. Money that, in fact, he never in turn gave back, in order that his friend's generosity would remain unrequited, that is to say because he knew that W. liked to feel superior to people and have them in his debt.

Julia is in complete agreement with Frisch—everyone should live according to how much they earn. She understands him so well when he says that a particular restaurant is not for him! Like him, Julia is not drawn by material things that are not for her, and she's not attracted by store windows with expensive, exclusive objects in them, although she does allow herself something of the highest quality from time to time. They're things for rich people, and she isn't rich. But that's not a problem for her. She thinks that arriving at such an *état d'esprit*—such a state of mind—is the result of long years of training.

Martin gets up and ambles out of the living room. He gets bored listening to them talking about another writer with such enthusiasm, he feels jealous, and Julia prefers his leaving to seeing him sitting there doing his best to make sure they know he's not interested in what they're talking about. Now that he's left, she can tell Lynn about something that happened when she was little and that Zigor found very funny. As always, she's not sure whether it's exactly her own memory, something she saw herself, or if it's something she was told about later on. In any case, it happened one late afternoon on some holiday. Her parents, her sister, and she had gone to Donostia for a stroll, wearing their best clothes. She doesn't know how old she was, but she was holding her father's hand—she always held his hand—as they walked along Hernani Kalea, which is where Martin lived when he was young, and they were going to take the bus or the tram, she's not sure which, to go back to Martutene, and she saw that some men were opening the doors of the cars parked there, getting in without a care in the world, starting the engines, and driving off; she told her father to do the same thing, to take one of the empty cars in the row. They had to explain the crude reality to her, told her that those cars had other owners, and although she doesn't remember how the rest of that holiday afternoon they spent strolling around the Alderdi-Eder park went, she thinks she was probably sad, and when she went to bed that night, she must have wondered why some parents had cars and others didn't, and why she had to be the daughter of parents without a car. She suspects that sometimes, seeing her father sitting in the kitchen with his legs stretched out like the president of the United States, his feet resting on top of the coal box, happy and singing because he had had a good dinner—"I have a wife, I have a son / I have a daughter, too / Good health / Enough wealth / What more do I need?"—she would wonder what a man who had so little could possibly be happy about, and that picture of happiness made her sad, angry even. She used to think that her contented father was incapable of realizing that there were wonderful things in the world apart from those few that satisfied him.

When she sees a child in the street holding the hand of one of those men who look defeated by life, sometimes she feels indescribable tenderness and sorrow, because she thinks that the resigned child looking up at his or her father with love, and even admiration, is actually fully aware of what fate has dealt them. Even so, it's clear that children accept their parents with excessive conformity, more so than the parents do the children, although it should, in all justice, be the other way around. Now, however, she's of the impression that she had an excellent father. A fine father, a loving one, one who smelled good and admired knowledge. What she wouldn't give to be able to hold him in her arms just once. To hold him as the woman she is and feel his strong warmth.

In fact, she doesn't mind the American girl seeing the tears in her eyes.

They hear Martin's steps in the hallway, and both women keep quiet until the direction of the steps reveals that he's gone into the library. They smile at each other. It's obvious he can't hear them, but the girl lowers her voice when she mentions Martin. She's worried, because several people have told her, when she mentioned what she's paying in rent, that the conditions are a far cry from the usual market rate, a real bargain. The obvious answer would be that there's no need for her to feel uncomfortable, because the owner feels very well-compensated by her company. But she doesn't want the girl to feel her anger, and she doesn't want her to feel she's in debt to him, either. She admits that it really is a low rent but explains that Martin doesn't want just any type of tenant at the house—someone with children, or who wants to stay for a long time—because he doesn't have clear plans for the future of the building, or for himself, either.

She doesn't know why she feels like saying that Martin doesn't have to worry about money, but that's what she says. She explains that while she doesn't know all the details of his financial situation and assets, she does know that he has more than enough to live on. His basic income comes from the rent he receives on some apartments he owns downtown. She knows that he owns a lot of stock in addition to that, but unless something out of the ordinary happens, he just reinvests the dividends from them. She's heard him say that what he wants to do is give back everything he received from his family—a family he can't stand. Deep down he's a puritan, he has simple habits, he's proud of not having a car, and when he buys something—clothes, music, gadgets, and suchlike—even though he usually chooses the most expensive things on the market, he then

234

makes them last forever. He boasts about not caring about money, and sometimes it does seem that he really isn't aware of its value. But that style of his, which could be seen as a virtue, has harmful consequences for Julia, and two in particular: sometimes, having her feet more firmly on the ground, it's she who has to pay their shared bills, even though she's far from well-off; and secondly, she has to remind him more than she would like that he owes her money, and that, in turn, usually makes her feel that she's the stingy one.

MONEY IS FREEDOM AND SAFETY. Lynn says that Martin is very lucky to have the means to allow him the time to write what he wants with no limits, without the restraints of having to earn a living. There's something there that Julia isn't so sure about. It probably isn't in Martin's character to write at the rate that Balzac, for instance, was forced to in order to pay off his debts, but sometimes she thinks that it wouldn't be bad for him to have a deadline for finishing his pieces, in the way that professional writers probably have, because in his situation he can put work to one side whenever he comes across any type of obstacle. But it's even worse than that— he isn't capable of putting his work on hold and traveling, for instance. When he can't solve a problem, he's unable to put it to one side, either, it becomes an obsession, and he becomes trapped by it. Another result of his being able to write without any deadlines, except for in a few cases, is that his writing tends to have the dull taste of food that's been overcooked. "Looking for the adjective." Harri and Julia use that expression for the times when he gets nervous and ill-tempered because he's stuck in his work, times that find him going in and out of the library all day, in and out of the yard all day, literally like a mental patient, his head down, his hands held behind him as he walks along. When they see him like that, they say he's "looking for the adjective." Even now Julia sometimes gets bored of seeing him like that and can't resist saying to him that he should turn the computer off and go to the movie theater, or go for a swim. Very bad idea. She can just see him saying "What would you know about it?"—his body bent over, his arms crossed over his stomach as if he were in great pain. But in fact she does know something about it. She sometimes thinks she could write a thesis about it. But she knows that he doesn't say "What would you know about it?" out of the arrogance of a misunderstood artist, telling someone at a lower level that they cannot possibly understand the suffering of someone at a higher level. The fact is that he suffers with his obsessions, he's restless, because he's been condemned, for some reason he finds incomprehensible, to dedicating his efforts to something that he's incapable of doing. And when he finally allows himself to turn the computer off, he spends the following hours, until he goes to bed, in a state of complete dejection, unable to forget that the next day, he will have to face up to his inability once more. When he's feeling productive, however, he doesn't seem to write much more. He doesn't trust how easy it is, because it comes too quickly (*"Pégase marche plus souvent qu'il ne galope,"* as his beloved Flaubert says), and when he finds it easy to write, the fear that he'll have to check the next day if it's any good doesn't help him at all. In particular, when he used to write at night with the help of some Armagnac—his style flowing from his pen like the blood through young Flaubert's veins— and in the morning had to judge his pages of inspiration and admit that they were nothing special, he would become unbearably frustrated. Julia is now able to understand the extraordinary extent to which finding that out exasperates the writer. (As Flaubert said— more or less—lapsing from the intoxication of genius to a desolate feeling of mediocrity, with all the fury of a king deposed.)

And so, fear of failure making him reach for the reins and slow things down, he never goes along at full gallop, and if after reading something he's written it happens that he likes it, which isn't very usual, his productivity will suffer. For one thing, because he wants to prolong his enjoyment, and for another, and to the same degree, his fear of not being able to work stops him from working. He can spend days playing around with a paragraph, trying to make it perfect, like a cat playing with a dead mouse, adding a comma, changing a name, removing an adjective. Unable to move forward because of the fear of making a mistake, or of not achieving the same standard, and above all wanting to prolong the pleasure of being a writer with a good piece of work in progress. That's happiness for him. Julia doesn't need to look on his computer to see which days they are, they're the ones when he's talkative and full of joy, happy and amenable, quite pleased with himself, in fact, with that look of believing himself to be *"nel mio mestiere dunque sono re"*—the king of his craft. Until, of course, he finally becomes anxious that he hasn't written a single line for too long. Julia doesn't know how she's aware of all this, but she is.

TEMPUS FUGIT. And that's how he spends his life, seeing the time he doesn't spend in front of the computer as time wasted, complaining about how great his sacrifice is, moaning, just like his beloved Flaubert, about how tiring it is to write, comparing—again just like him—his enormous ambition with his lack of respect for anything other than writing, lost in a sad existence that means nothing without literature. In fact, the *piccolo scrittore* is seeming more and more like Flaubert—although they are completely different, she sees the Normandy writer reflected in Martin's watery blue eyes and in the bags that are beginning to form under his eyelids—and she wonders to what extent that image is influencing her, because sometimes she thinks that she herself is starting to look a bit like Colette. The Colette who complains that Gustav is avoiding his friends because he's always immersed in his work, because he thinks loving or being loved is a waste of time, and Colette feeling hurt because he forgets to give her the money that she so desperately needs, tired of his endless monologues about his art, bored of the one night every six weeks that they spend together at a hotel if his book's going well. That woman on all fours, picking up the scraps of warmth that fall from that obsessive, unpleasant man's table, jealous that he's taken a young woman into his house but ready to accept her if the arrangement helps to improve his mood and entertain him during his breaks.

She should cut back on that tendency of hers to make cruel caricatures of herself. She thinks it's self-destructive. What's more, it isn't true that Martin has her dominated. If she does give way to him, it's because she wants to convince herself that in some near, visible future—after the final family problem is solved, or when he finishes the story he's working on—the source of her bitterness will be cured. But this putting off of things is endless, a new problem always crops up, another story he can't finish, and her hope inevitably runs out. But sometimes, when she sees a little affection left in his eyes, when he laughs all of a sudden, she's taken over by the irritating belief that she could be quite happy, and she decides that whatever's keeping her from that happiness is of no real consequence, nothing compared to what draws her to be with that ironic, sarcastic man who can be tender and move her when he wants to but is ruled by stubborn energy. Vulnerable—as she is, as well—discerning, funny at times. *"Intellectually acute, a keen wit, perceptive."* Those are the adjectives that the young American uses to describe Faustino Iturbe. She says she's really enjoying *Ez du sekula atertuko*, a story of his whose title means "it will never clear up." They both laugh as they recall the start of the book. Faustino Iturbe is walking under a series of balconies on a rainy day, trying to keep as dry as possible, keeping all the way over to the right, just next to the buildings' façades. He's ready to move over to the middle of the sidewalk to let others pass, providing the person coming the other way is old, or even if it's a young woman who's just come from the hair salon or is wearing light clothes or high-heeled shoes that make her particularly vulnerable, but he is determined to protect his right to walk on the right-hand side from those going the other way who are also sticking close to the façades, but on his left. There are people who move aside out of politeness, people who respect his rights. There are inconsiderate people who walk on until they run straight into him, and others, too, who despite having umbrellas want to walk with their left shoulders brushing along the façades and do so, until, one step away from him, they realize that he's decided to keep on straight ahead and then they move aside with a look of contempt on their faces, many even challenging him by standing their ground, thinking it's he who should step out and get wet and not them. Faustino Iturbe hates those people. He thinks that the seed that makes the world vile is sown in their hearts. What wouldn't they do for their own well-being over that of their neighbors' in protected, intimate circumstances if they dare to behave that way in public? As Voltaire described them, they're people who wouldn't hesitate to set their neighbors' houses on fire in order to keep their own children warm. If they had to flee a public building that had caught fire, they'd be the first ones out, killing more people by trampling over them than the fire itself. It's also funny to read the precise, exact descriptions he gives of the methods people use for line-cutting, from absent-mindedness to that obvious, unashamed trick—"I just want to ask a question." Which is a way of saying that they have no consideration whatsoever for other people's time. These things drive the character wild, because he thinks that society is too tolerant, that being shameless is thought of as a rather charming quirk, and as if that weren't enough, protesting victims are thought of as intolerant, but he thinks it's something that shows a completely selfish nature and is, at the very least, a symptom of being anti-social.

God made Martin just the way he is.

And that's how Martin is. Intolerant, overly sensitive when it comes to what other people do, attentive to how people greet him, or fail to greet him, how they look at him, the tone they speak to him in. When he comes back into the house after running an errand, it's like the return of Ulysses. When he writes, it's a caricature of himself, but he's very much like the caricature. He complains about everything that people do—they speak too loudly, they honk their horns, they litter, they don't give way when they should, they push, they don't apologize when they bump into someone. The American girl says that those precise descriptions of the way people behave, for example when they're in a line to buy bread, are good examples of behavioral sociology, like those given by certain authors that she mentions but Julia hasn't heard of.

Julia's glad to hear that she likes Martin's book.

The young American just read that one passage this morning where Faustino Iturbe's in a city he's not familiar with, walking along an empty street, and it's pouring down rain. He has a date and is nervous, afraid that he'll be late. He wants to find someone to tell him the way, but the street is deserted. He's soaking wet from head to toe and is getting more and more worried as time goes by. Eventually he sees a girl at a railroad crossing and goes after her to ask her how to get to where he has his date, but the girl, noticing that he's walking behind her, walks faster, and so he does, too, in order to catch up with her, but when he's just a few yards away from her, she starts running fast. He thinks it's because the rain has started to fall even faster, and he starts running, as well; they both run fast along the lonely street, and when they finally reach a doorway, the girl presses all the buzzer buttons with the flat palms of her hands, wanting to raise a general alarm. She turns toward him with her eyes wide open in fear, panting like a wounded deer, and he's frightened by the fear that he himself has caused, incapable of saying a single word, and finally, when the door opens and the girl disappears inside, he doesn't get the chance to explain to her that he only wanted to ask her for help finding a street because he had a date at a bar there with a beautiful woman who, by that time, might have gotten fed up with waiting for him; he stands there in the downpour, upset, deeply unsettled, unable to catch his breath from running so much, and panting, to his shame, like some lustful animal.

Perhaps the description of Faustino Iturbe as a compassionate, remorseful writer affected by his abhorrence of violence against women is comic, in that young women end up running away from him down empty streets—he, noble and sensitive, who only deserves to be smiled at—because the media reports daily on the rape and murder of women. Everything that can possibly happen happens to him. In any case, the most important thing for him is how monstrous things that can happen to anyone affect him. The caricature he gives of the egocentric character may be merciless, but that peculiar exercise of confession, in which neither regret nor any intention of self-improvement are mentioned, no longer redeems him in Julia's eyes. And in fact, she no longer finds it so amusing, probably because something in her sense of humor—in both their senses of humor, most likely, in his as well as hers—has changed; in the end, she begins to doubt whether the caricature is a real caricature, and her having doubts about that, about whether or not she is interpreting the text in the proper tone when she reads it, is one of the biggest problems she has when it comes to translating his work. It's part of the trouble she's having with *Bihotzean min dut.*

She has other sources of trouble, as well, starting with the title. She thinks the literal translation in Spanish—*Me duele el corazón*, meaning "my heart hurts"—would sound too much like heart disease. Someone translated it once as *Duéleme el corazón*—my heart pains me—apparently trying to give it a literary feel. She's left it provisionally at *Me duele el alma*—my soul hurts. *My heart is broken? It hurts my soul?* It's Martin's best-known story, or *novella*, for those who prefer the term. The story starts with the murder of a Spanish policeman, his car is blown up with him inside it just as his daughter walks out the doorway of their apartment complex. The events he writes about actually happened, and Martin himself lived through them; at that time, he was a Basque teacher—his only real work experience, and short-lived, at that—and the policeman's daughter was a student at the private school he taught at. The policeman used to drop his daughter off at school every morning on his way to work; she was a smart, responsible student, and it was she who used to remind him to look under the car every morning just in case there was a bomb there. But that day he didn't, because they were late. She'd been running behind that morning, finishing off a piece of work she was supposed to hand in that day, and her father got angry with her. And then, to add misfortune to misfortune, she realized, as she was finally coming down the stairs, that she'd left her essay in the kitchen, so she had to go back up again for it. She grabbed it, ran down the stairs, and when she reached the doorway, she heard a loud explosion. Then she saw her father's body on fire; the entire chassis of the car had been blown up into the air.

Martin really liked the girl—she was respectful, sensitive, and loved literature. He was amazed that when she wrote about literature, she often picked up on ideas and details that he'd missed, and he often talked to Julia about her. The student must have really liked her unconventional and interesting Basque teacher, as well. Nobody apart from Martin knew that her father was a policeman; she let him know in one of her papers. She told him that her father had a false identity as a commercial rep for reasons of security, and also to make her life easier. However, even taking into account her father's need for security, it was starting to be difficult for her to live such a lie. To an extent, it didn't seem right to her, it meant denying her father, but above all, it was because she had the feeling that covering it up meant betraying her friends, especially when someone opened themselves up to her and told her intimate or secret things.

She lived with the fear of being rejected because of her father's job and the discomfort of hiding the truth, the fear of exposing her father to an attack and the discomfort of denying him as a whole. She used to say that she loved the Basque Country, its language and its culture, more than anyone else in the class, because she was a Basque speaker, and also that she understood the mistrust there was toward the Civil Guard and the police and even the deep hatred that still exists toward them today because of the role they played in the past, and because of the atrocious acts that continue to take place from time to time; but she couldn't help loving her father, because he was a good, loyal man, incapable of doing anyone any harm, and he'd promised her that he would never do anything outside the law. She said that her father, too, loved the Basque Country and tried to fit in there, not letting hate take him over, not letting fear cloud his intelligence. She had to tell someone, and she opened her heart to her teacher, knowing that he would understand her; he'd revealed his sensitivity in their literature classes, he understood people's feelings, and their failings, as well. It was a moving text, of course, because the girl put her trust in him, and Martin felt proud of that.

In Martin's usual style, the narrative is in the first person and the voice is Faustino Iturbe's. The extreme sensation he feels on hearing about the murder makes him want to throw up; it's nothing like the more manageable reactions of revulsion and despair he's experienced up until then on hearing about new attacks. That day, he knows that he will not be able to look away from the corpse, and he feels an absolute need to face up to his student's pain. He hesitates over whether to cancel the class, as a way of setting an example for his students and his more radical colleagues, but in the end he decides to go ahead with it and use the time to speak about "violence that only causes destruction." His students are upset by the murder and amazed to find out that the best student in Basque language and literature is a policeman's daughter. He sees serious, anguished, rigid faces. There are a few arrogant faces in the last row, a few wretches who think that justice has been done by killing a pig, and the teacher, like a good shepherd looking for a lost sheep that's strayed from the flock, speaks to them, for in the future, if someone doesn't prevent it from happening, they, too, will become victims of violence, even if they have noble aims, and he wants to convince them that violence achieves nothing. Then, bracing himself, he goes to the student's home to give his condolences. There's no doubt that it's a sincere text condemning ETA's violence, a text that addressed the suffering of victims at a time when it went largely unseen, but now that Julia's translating it, she sees in that grieving teacher the same Faustino Iturbe she's always seen—a man giving a detailed, precise account of his own experiences after the attack, a man who is always seeing himself as the main victim, on this occasion a victim of the terrorist group, because of the thousands of police objectives they could have gone after, they chose the father of one of *his* students. Julia laughs to make it clear that she's joking. She doesn't mean anything by it, she knows she's tired and that that's affecting her. It's a sign that Martin's suffering moves her less and less. For while it's true that he suffers because of everything (because of the wars that are destroying the world, the seals and whales that are being killed, the children who are being raised badly and litter the streets as a result, because he has writer's block . . .), Julia decides that his suffering does not excuse him for the anguish he causes her. Yet even leaving her subjective position to one side, it's undeniable that the story can no longer be read as it was at the time of its writing, because everything has changed since then. Everything has changed, just as Martin and Julia themselves have. Many, themselves included, used to see the consequences of violence as some sort of fatal, inevitable accident. And the victims, too, have changed. Everything has changed, and in order to protect the story from misinterpretations, Julia thinks it would be good to write an introduction, in order to place the story in its historical context. At the same time, in addition to this subjective problem that conditions her more than she would like, there is another serious problem with the translation: Basque and Spanish are both used in the original text, depending on the particular situation, and putting everything into a single language leads to the loss of many things. *Lost in translation.* Having the text in a single language smooths away details, while the decision to write in one or the other in certain moments can be even more meaningful than the words themselves when it comes to creating an atmosphere, and sticking in a footnote to the effect that some word or phrase was "in Spanish in the original" does not solve the problem. When the teacher reaches the house, which is full of people, all the expressions of grief, of anger, of consolation are said in Spanish, which is the language the main character also uses to introduce himself as *"el profesor de Ana"*—Ana's teacher. When thinking to himself, he uses Basque to describe the scene and his impressions of it. He has to say that he is *"el profesor de Ana"* two or three times in Spanish, while speaking inwardly, in Basque, he decides he'll say that he teaches literature if anyone asks him what his subject is—he won't say he teaches Basque. The first person who asks him is the one who opens the door to him, and who then knocks on another door and informs Ana in Spanish that her literature teacher is here to see her—*"Ana, tu profesor de literatura viene a verte."* He, her Basque teacher, trusts that his student will understand that it's only a minor deceit—he does teach literature, as well, when it comes down to it. It's the game they always have to play. His Spanish sounds peculiar to readers when teacher and student hug each other and he says *"pobrecita, cuanto lo siento"*—poor thing, I'm so sorry—that being the first time they've ever spoken to each other in that language; and they find it very moving when the girl, in tears, her voice broken, says to him in Basque *"min dut, bihotzean min dut"*—I ache, my heart aches.

Hearing those words by the Basque poet Xabier Lizardi in a Spanish policeman's house. Women standing up, holding hands, and asking why it happened, beating their chests with their fists, embracing each other without doing anything to hide their distorted faces, demonstrating what real crying is; men who stare at them, unable to do anything faced with that measureless expression of grief, smoking in silence, leaning against the wall, some of them in uniform, one of them sitting down and staring at the floor as he moves his cap from hand to hand, another unaffectedly holding his pistol in place as he gets up. Most of the men are dark, they speak in low voices, and in thick southern-Spanish accents, from Andalusia and Extremadura, and they stand aside respectfully so that the teacher—who is ashamed or afraid to say that he's a Basque teacher—can walk through, the daughter of the murdered policeman leading him to her room by the hand, probably because she's aware that the atmosphere must be very foreign to him. The teacher compares her room with that of one of his nieces of the same age. It's smaller and more childish. A lot of stuffed toys. A lot of pastel colors, and her mother's extreme tidiness and cleanliness in full force, so that the room might be shown to visitors. There are books, a shared space for literature and the books recommended to her by the teacher, some of which he himself gave her. On a small folding table, there's a copy of Lizardi's *Biotz-begietan*, whose title translates to "in the eyes of the heart." The teacher picks it up and glances through it to cover up how uncomfortable he feels. He doesn't know what to say, and the girl whispers, "I have pain in my heart, desperate pain." A parasitical thought: Could poor old Lizardi ever have imagined that around seventy years after his death, the daughter of a Spanish policeman who's just been killed in the name of the Basque Country would pick up a book titled *In The Eyes Of The Heart* and express her unbearable pain with a verse of his?

The girl takes some papers off the only chair in the room, so that the teacher can sit down on it, and asks him to excuse the untidiness. She says it's a mess, even though everything's very tidy, maybe even too tidy. She feels guilty, because she had to return to the apartment for her essay and that's why they didn't look beneath the car in the way they always did every other day—she feels guilty because she's still alive. The teacher tries to comfort her. It was his idea to replace the language exam with an at-home essay on Lizardi and his context— should he, too, feel guilty? He tries to convince her that the terrorists are the only ones to blame. *Blame* is the key word in the narrative.

Later, when the teacher says that he has to go, the girl puts the pieces of paper she'd picked up from the chair into a plastic folder and gives the whole thing to him. It's the paper she was supposed to hand in to him. "Xabier Lizardi and His Context." She tells him that she cried the night before while reading "Xabiertxoren eriotza," but that her crying for "little Xabier's death" in the poem was nothing like the tears of anger that she's shedding now. Last night they were liberating tears, almost happy tears, because of the poet's nobility and goodness, the subject of the poem being respect for the happiness of the boys and girls going from door to door because it's Christmas Eve, letting one of the groups in to sing even though little newborn Xabier is lying dead in his crib in the next room.

So Julia has to tell the young American something about what happens in "Xabiertxoren eriotza," in the same way that she's going to have to put in a few words—as few as possible—in the footnote to her translation so that Spanish readers know that Lizardi gets his wife, who doesn't want to hear the songs, to open the door so that the boys and girls can sing around the crib, telling them that they don't have to worry about the child, that he won't wake up, because he's in a deep sleep, and the American girl, with tears in her eyes, says, "*It's so moving.*" Julia now thinks it's what the girl's found most interesting of everything she's told her. She finds it moving and asks for details about the poem and about the writer. When did he live? Is it still a custom to go from house to house on Christmas Eve and sing? How long had the dead child lived? Her answer to that last question is "around a month and a half," although she's not sure. She's amazed by her own ignorance. She doesn't know how old Lizardi was when he wrote the poem, either, but he must have been young, because he died before he was forty. She says he was thirty-three, because that's the age Jesus Christ was when he died.

The young American is Jesus Christ's age, as well.

She has to use the piano to give her voice some support in order to recite Lizardi's "*Bihotzean min dut, min etsia.*" She's asked Julia to recite it, "*Just to know what it sounds like.*" It must have been years since she last recited a poem, since the days when she used to recite them for her father. They were often Lizardi's verses. He made her read them to people who came to visit, and when they were alone in the kitchen, as well, and apparently she didn't get as embarrassed about it back then as she does now. Her sister is constantly reminding her of it, resentful that she was their father's favorite.

Her fingers play that lively phrase that answers the orchestra's dark question in Ravel's Concerto For The Left Hand. Perhaps because it's the most difficult thing she knows and she wants to impress and move the girl, who's now sitting next to her and looking serious, following the movements of her fingers with great attention. She asks her if she knows the piece, wanting to lessen the concert's excessive solemnity, and the girl shakes her head. But she has heard about concerts written for one-armed pianists. What she doesn't know is that the pianist was Paul Wittgenstein, the brother of the good-looking philosopher, and that the most famous concert written for the left hand, more so even than those written by Prokofiev and Richard Strauss, is Ravel's. "Ravel, the one who wrote Boléro?" Julia's amused by her surprise, and also by the way she pronounces it "boh-LAIR-oh." But she must have just replied a little vindictively when she told her that she likes Ravel a lot and that he's one of her favorite composers, because the girl rushes to admit she's completely ignorant when it comes to music.

The part she plays best is when the thumb comes in.

And suddenly she realizes why she chose that particular part of the Concerto For The Left Hand. A little earlier, when they were talking about *Montauk*, they mentioned the natural way in which Max accepted the superiority of his friend W.—the tall, well-educated, rich man who passed his fine English wool jackets on to him—and how, to an extent, they'd stopped seeing each other because of Ludwig Wittgenstein. The writer tells us that he had been going out with a woman—there was no doubt she was the Austrian poet Ingeborg Bachmann—who studied philosophy and had written something about the *Tractatus Logico-Philosophicus*, a fact his friend W. didn't know; when he introduced them, W. found it unbearable that such an interesting girl, who knew so much about philosophy, was sharing her life with someone as pathetic as Max.

And a little later, when she was telling the young American about the misfortunes of the Basque teacher in the *Bihotzean min dut* story, she was reminded of Wittgenstein once more. Because a few days earlier, when she first realized what she's just told her—that there was something in the story that she wasn't comfortable with—and she worked up the courage to tell Martin that she thought it would be a good idea to write an introduction to guide the reader (now she doesn't know how she managed to be so daring) and shared an idea she'd had for it and asked him what he thought of it, he said, *"Don't touch my dream with your dirty hands."* Or something like that, a brusque reply. He said, in fact, that her job was to translate, no more than that. And as if that weren't enough, he compared her "shameless" behavior with that of the pianist Wittgenstein, "to put it in musical terms," because the one-armed pianist had wanted to adapt the concert Ravel gave him, and the composer, of course, wouldn't let him do that at all.

YOUR HANDS ARE BEAUTIFUL." Julia thinks that the young American has been listening to her out of more than just respect, but at the same time, she has the feeling that she's been talking too much. To bring things to a close, she says it's late and shuts the piano lid, without remembering to put the protective strip of felt in its place. The girl smiles. Without looking at her watch, without moving. She says that it crossed her mind the day she met her that she might be a piano player, because of her hands. *"Very beautiful hands."* As she says this, she takes Julia's right hand, which was resting on the stool. She likes hearing that, or at least she isn't ashamed to hear it, because she is indeed proud of her hands.

ECCE HOMO. Martin appears in the hallway once more, this time he's on the phone. Julia knows, from the way he strokes his hair back whenever he's nervous, that either his mother or his sister is talking to him about something to do with the care his father is being given. He'll listen to them without saying a word for a long while as he walks up and down the hallway like a wild beast in a cage. They love tiring him out with their moaning, and he gives way to all their wishes and commands, although they always allow him, in the end, to assert his masculine privilege to shout whatever comes to mind and reproach them for not respecting his work. They're always interrupting his work, day and night. That's what he's saying right now to whoever he's talking with. He's not shouting—the American girl being there prevents him from doing that—but not speaking too softly, either, standing in front of the large 1:50,000 scale map of Sicily, which is stuck on the wall with pushpins and measures at least six by four feet, and he's thinking of Syracuse, she imagines. At least in that respect he has clearer ideas than his beloved Flaubert, who, while resolved to pack up and leave if and when his mother finally died, couldn't decide whether to go to Rome, Syracuse, or Naples: "*Si ma mère meurt, mon plan est fait: je vends tout et je vais vivre à Rome, à Syracuse, à Naples.*" He's made a more precise decision than the genius from Normandy: when he's finally free, he's going to Syracuse.

The first reason he's angry is that his sister in Paris is demanding that he book a suite at the María Cristina Hotel "at all costs," even though it's absolutely full up right now with film festival crowds, for some Catalan friends she owes a big favor to. The second reason is that when he complained, and he thinks rightly, about how the caretakers they hired for their father are not very professional—treating him like a child, speaking to him with too much familiarity, and often holding their own conversations as if he weren't there—his other sister, the one living there at the family house, got upset and told him that one of them had actually just announced that she was going to quit working at the end of the month and that he, Martin, would have to take charge of finding, hiring, and paying her replacement, because she's sick of constantly hearing that she does everything wrong, and then she started sobbing as she always does, and that drove him up the wall.

He asks what the two of them have been talking about. It seems he hasn't realized until just now that the two women are sitting next to each other on the piano bench, and he looks at them with curiosity, as if suspicious of them. Julia is about to say that they've been talking about "women's things," but Lynn gets there first and says, in a completely natural way, that they've been talking about him and, more precisely, his literature. She repeats more or less what she said when the two of them were alone. Intelligence, precision, irony, acuteness, face-to-face interaction. Descriptive tools of an almost scientific nature to describe people in public places. "*A dramaturgical approach to human interaction.*" Goffman is one of the authors she mentions to explain what she's talking about. Goffman with two *f*s. Martin hasn't heard of him but seems to be glad to hear that his story is connected in some way to what is apparently called *the sociology of interaction.*

WHEN HARRI ARRIVES, SHE FINDS THEM TALKING about *Bihotzean min dut,* about the impossibility of translating the ways in which languages interplay. At one time, Martin had been thinking about writing a bilingual novel, and *Bihotzean* was a sort of rehearsal for that. His intention was to address the linguistic reality in which the two languages coexist in greater depth. Julia thinks that part of that idea was driven by his wish to demonstrate that as far as he was concerned, there were no ideological obstacles, or obstacles of any other type, to his writing in Spanish. A pretty dumb aim when it came down to it, because only Basque speakers could read a bilingual Basque and Spanish text. So the question would be why doesn't he just write in Spanish—it's the more widely spoken of the two languages, and "everyone" understands it. The question is taboo, but Julia's very interested in it. Some angles are very clear. For instance, the idea that abandoning Basque would be betraying the Basque linguistic community, and the consequences of that— although she doesn't know what exactly those would be—would have to be faced. Martin certainly doesn't have any objections to the idea and admits that he finds it easier to write in Spanish than in Basque. Young writers, on the other hand, usually say that for them, choosing Basque is something quite natural, among other things because it was the language they used at school, and at university, as well. Julia doesn't know whether to believe them. One of the real masters of the Basque language, Anjel Lertxundi, says, "I'd happily change Basque sentence structure if the strength of the language could be preserved, and then I'd be able to write with the security that writers in hegemonic languages have, rather than having doubts all the time." But apparently, ease is not the only factor, not even the main factor, when it comes to choosing to use a particular language for literature. And Basque, too, offers certain advantages, features of its own that are more functional than the equivalent resources in Romance languages for those who know their secrets, and in particular for poets, offering them "a path less traveled." Among other things, virgin words—words that have not been worn down and disfigured by centuries of misuse.

NAÏVE LOGIC. So, if he finds it easier to write in Spanish, why does he write in Basque? It's easier to believe the question's being asked in good faith when it comes from a foreigner. There are clearly social, cultural, political, and economic factors involved. Recently, in order to sidestep the question, Martin has taken to saying that writers don't choose the language, it's the other way around, and usually the person he's talking with doesn't dare to ask how exactly that happens. "*I see*," says Lynn, thoughtfully, not understanding him, or so it seems to Julia. But Martin has other joke answers to the question, as well, some of them perhaps not without a firm basis. One thing he mentions is that Beckett chose to write in French because his writing ability being more limited in that language, he was freed from the need to pay attention to his style. Another thing he brings up is how the sculptor Eduardo Chillida spent a period using only his left hand to draw, finding it too easy to use his right hand, because he went too fast with it. The third thing is Conrad's choice of language, which he explains by saying that although the author had a perfect mastery of the French language from childhood, "he would have been terrified to have to make the effort to express himself in such a perfectly crystallized language." Of course, Basque has additional difficulties (some of which are intrinsic and stem from it being an agglutinative language, and then there are the many consequences of its never having been the language of power and authority, of its having become linked to culture at a comparatively late date, of its lacking a strong written tradition, and of its having limited rhetorical resources, mostly catch-all terms and fillers, which both Spanish and French, the languages that Basque has had to survive between, have in abundance, being as they are among the most rhetorical languages in the world), although the bulk of the tests to which Basque is put in terms of its usefulness and precision involve being in the difficult situation of having to use it to explain what politicians and civil servants have said in Spanish, and not the other way around. It is true, in any case, that Martin expresses himself with greater ease in Spanish, letting himself be carried away by his sentences, even falling into the trap that many Basques who write in Spanish do by using *too many* of the rhetorical resources that Spanish offers and that aren't available to them in Basque. Julia thinks that only a few Basques actually prefer to use Baroja's short, direct style. But she also thinks he writes better in Basque.

POLITICAL CORRECTNESS. The Basque grammar system's lack of gender signifiers, which the young American sociologist thinks may be very helpful when it comes to political correctness, is what gives him the most difficulties, Martin says. He says it makes it hard for him to refer to his characters with any apparent sense of objectivity or distance, to be able to describe them in the French narrative style of his youth—which he is still so attached to—by

250

making use of pronouns. *Il parle, tandis qu'elle écoute. Elle et lui. Lui e lei.* She and him.

They talk, above all, about Basque being judged by people who are more used to Spanish. A Basque speaker, however, would also find it difficult to understand why a question such as "How many sons/daughters do you have?"—which seems perfectly natural to their ears—should sound so strange to someone accustomed to Spanish.

Harri is not interested in the linguistic side of it. Content is what matters, and *Bihotzean* would be good in any language. To make the American girl realize how important a piece of work it is, she tells her that Martin received death threats when it was published. The writer waves it away—just some poor madman. But Harri insists—whether from a madman or otherwise, he did receive threats. Martin, quite roughly now, tells her to drop it. It could seem to be humility on his part, and that's probably what the young American takes it to be. But it's a tricky subject, and they haven't brought it up for some time. Almost since it happened. The reason for this is that when he told his fellow writers that he'd received anonymous letters, the rumors that they were made-up began spreading immediately. Julia thinks they doubted whether Basque literature in general and Martin's work in particular could have any influence on society. He was putting himself forward as being more than he actually was by letting on that ETA members were angry about one of his books. Martin heard about the rumors from Jaime Zabaleta, who had the nerve—or the good will, or the sadistic desire—to tell him that nobody in the profession was talking about anything else, and then he took the occasion to say that he didn't believe him, either. Harri had never liked the man much, and ever since then, she's hated him. But Martin didn't mind hearing it. He seemed to accept as a matter of course that people would think the anonymous letters were fake, and Julia doesn't know why, but she thinks he believes that to be her opinion, as well. And is it? She doesn't know. She wouldn't be too surprised if they were fake, and she wouldn't mind if they were, either. There are certain things that lead her to suspicion. He gets worried by anything, and yet he wasn't particularly concerned by the threats. He didn't report it to the police, though that's under-standable to an extent, because he wouldn't have achieved much by doing so, but it is likewise surprising that someone who never throws away a single piece of paper hasn't kept a single one of them, if only as a souvenir. But what is most significant is his enormous sense of guilt, which is limitless and on display for all to see, and which he calls "the syndrome of coming out of it alive," whenever they talk about it, the clear need behind it to be redeemed, to be able to approach victims as a victim himself, and those anonymous letters, whether genuine or fake, are just the absolution he needed. Perhaps he thought that it wasn't his fault if the ignorant ETA members didn't read, or didn't know how to read, or chose not to care about what he sees as the direct criticisms leveled against them in *Bihotzean*. And if he—who pays so much heed to the opinions of those around him, who would rather die than look like a fool—accepted the rumors so easily, then Julia supposes it was because he knew that nobody would take the falsified letters as a ploy to garner fame for himself but rather, in the worst case, as an expression of the need to redeem himself and, through him, Basque literature as a whole. When it comes down to it, Julia thinks it's just as dignified to feel the need to invent death threats as it is to actually receive them. She thinks Jaime Zabaleta may be of the same opinion. With Harri, of course, you can't question the veracity of the threats.

Harri realizes that Martin doesn't want to talk about it, and she tells the American girl that he also receives fan mail and that he'd get even more if he listened to her and wrote a few stories of a different type. Julia is sure that she wants to talk to them about her own story, her search for the man from the airport. Wanting to be good-willed, she shows an interest, asks her if she's heard any more, and Harri in reply lets out quite a dirty laugh as she asks if they haven't read the newspapers. They're amazed that the press has sought to report on the developments in her story. Julia says she's only glanced at the headlines, Martin gave up reading the papers a long time ago for reasons of "mental hygiene," and Lynn doesn't say anything. After quite a long silence, Harri takes a copy of the *El Correo* newspaper out of her green leather briefcase and holds it out to Martin. He flicks through it, and nobody says anything for a while, until she takes it off him again, roughly, as if exasperated by his inability to find the right place, opens it to the personal ads, and reads the Spanish text aloud.

"I saw you in the departure lounge at Heathrow, and I fell in love. On the plane, after your little accident with the bag full of books, you offered me *Montauk,* and I stupidly declined to accept it. I hope you give me another chance." And after reading it, she says, *"¿Qué te parece?"* She looks straight at them, as proud as a magician who's just put a handkerchief into a hat and pulled out a dove.

Martin says she's gone crazy; Julia doesn't know what to say. She isn't sure why Harri goes to such lengths to make them enjoy her airport story. Finally, she asks her what chance she thinks she has. First, will the man read the ad? And second, if he does read it, will he even remember—and she doesn't think it very probable—that *Montauk* was the book he offered her and thus realize that it's he she's looking for?

She chose the newspaper and the language for statistical reasons, but even though she can't calculate the probabilities of the man reading the ad, she's sure that if he does, he'll understand her message. She looks at Julia angrily, as if to say "you always try to spoil things," and when she asks Lynn's opinion, the American girl, after thinking for a moment, asks—and Julia doesn't know how serious she is, but she does at least look completely serious—if it wouldn't be easier and more effective to go straight to the airline and give them some excuse or other and try to get in touch with the man that way.

The main problem is that she doesn't know anything about the man, not even what seat he was in.

Still, they play around, like in a game of I-spy, with different possible reasons she might allege for having to get in touch with him. They agree that if they do get the airline to contact him and bring up *Montauk,* it's essential for him to know they're calling on Harri's behalf; but they don't think the airline employees will help much if it's just a matter of getting a book back to someone, people won't go to so much trouble over a simple book, so they decide that it can't be just the book itself, she has to be trying to get back something she had between the pages, something extremely important, a check, for instance, a long-lost friend's address that she'd finally managed to get ahold of, her only photo of her dead mother, the poem her husband wrote for her just before he took his last breath. Something of vital importance, something you would keep between the pages of a book. I-spy. They think the best thing is to tell the airline people about the bag that broke, that she helped him to pick up his books and in the confusion the man or she herself put one of her own books, the one with the important thing between its pages, back in with his. Obviously the man hasn't realized about the book, or hasn't opened it—otherwise he would have gotten in touch with the airline himself to tell them he had found the important document—and they have to warn him as soon as possible not to lose it or give it away to anyone or, worse still, throw it out. An indispensable condition, as much as the airline's willingness to help, is that the man must understand not only the details about the bag breaking and so on but also why she's looking for *Montauk*, and the hypothesis that he *will* understand is the only one that Harri is interested in, otherwise it would mean that the man isn't especially smart, which she doesn't believe to be the case, or that the feeling between them wasn't mutual, which she doesn't believe at all, and what's more, if either of those were the case, then why should she even be interested in the man? Lynn suggests that for all sorts of reasons, it would be much better to tell the airline people that she wanted to return a copy of *Montauk* rather then get one back—when the books fell out and she helped him pick them up, she had unintentionally kept one, which she now wants to give back, because she thinks it may be important to him, and she can easily come up with any old excuse she likes to explain the supposed importance. That way, it would be easy for her to slip a message into the book and there wouldn't be any chance for the man to misunderstand why she's looking for him. She would very gladly offer her own copy of *Montauk* for the operation, although she also hopes to get it back once Harri's found the man, she says, laughing. Is Harri serious about doing this? It seems she is, and Martin also seems to be when he says that he thinks the second option is better. Although, in general, he's skeptical. He thinks that even if the man fell in love with her at first sight, like Harri, and remembers everything just as she does—the bag breaking, her helping him to pick up the books, and, above all, *Montauk* being the book he offered her—it isn't likely that he'll work out who it is that's looking for him and why, not even if he's the smartest man in the world. Obviously, before that can even happen, the attitude of the people at the airline is crucial—if they simply ask him if he lost a book on his journey from London, it won't be easy for him to realize, as Harri wants him to, that a woman who is in love with him is looking for him. And then there's a problem even before that stage, because the people at the airline, even if they want to be as helpful as possible, have to follow strict confidentiality norms. But Harri doesn't want to hear any of this. She says they're always trying to spoil things for her. That's how she says it, in the plural. She accuses all three of them of being spoilsports, because they're all sure the man won't answer the ad in the paper. She asks the American girl, who is holding the newspaper, to read it aloud, she wants to know what it sounds like, and nodding as she listens to it, she says it couldn't be clearer and that if the man from the airport reads it, she has no doubt he will reply.

What catches the American girl's attention—Julia supposes it's because she's a sociologist and anthropologist—is the fact that there are so many advertisements for prostitution, and that they're so explicit, in a center-right newspaper that seems to be a more or less serious publication. She reads a few of the offers, which really couldn't be more vulgar, and makes them laugh with her comments. "Select Spanish Miss. Absolute Novelty. Pour your cream into my little mouth and I'll swallow it up." What's the point of the girls specifying where they come from, when one assumes you have to pay for the ads by the word? "Friendly, fun Catalan girl. Hot Basque chick. French-Basque girl first time. Cuban girl wet pussy. Japanese girl loves Greek style. Russian girl golden showers." Do they know what a golden shower is? What happens to the mattress? Do they do it in the bathtub? Do they wear shower caps?

"*I mean it, seriously.*" She holds her hands together as if she were praying, the others laugh, and Julia tells her, equally seriously, that she, too, has always wondered about that. They don't usually talk about sex, and she's surprised when Harri interjects and tells them to hold on a second—"*Pero vamos a ver,* haven't you ever felt the need for someone to piss on you, hit you, bite you, spit at you? You don't know what passion is."

As usual, she doesn't know if there's a comic intention behind that apparent seriousness or whether she's actually saying what she really thinks. The writer, who probably wants to seem prudent in front of the *penthouse* girl, tolerant but not dirty, uses liberal arguments— he thinks it's fine for couples to do what they want to, just as long as they do so freely and in agreement. An unimpeachable position that's been used a lot by people recently, and which Julia would add some caveats to if she weren't afraid of them taking her for a puritan and a reactionary. To her surprise, Lynn says what she was wanting to say, which is that she thinks sex is overrated; it's important, but nowadays people are obsessed with getting more out of it than it can really give them. And as far as women are concerned, she's convinced that many of them accept things that men like but that they themselves find mildly stimulating at best and only because their partner's excitement serves as an aphrodisiac for them, not because it stimulates their desire directly.

And the conversation stops there, because Harri has to go.

The house cats have been walking back and forth along the rail at the bottom of the French windows for some time. They walk toward each other with their tails up and meet exactly in the middle. Julia realizes she hasn't fed them. They come toward her, meowing pathetically, while a third, unknown cat lies down on the stone bench, waiting, watching them attentively. Lynn comes out behind her. She picks the kitten up and pets it. It's obvious she's used to cats. She says that her cat, Max, is shy, lazy, and clumsy but she forgives him because he's so handsome. She says she doesn't know what she'd do without him. She smiles. One of her fleeting smiles that means that she wants to be accepted, and Julia tells her that she agrees with what she's just said about sex. More laughter. "*I know.*" Even though she thinks she understands her reply, Julia feels the desire to ask, "What do you mean, '*I know?*'" She doesn't answer. Instead, Lynn asks Julia a question: Does she know that "golden rain" is the name of a very beautiful tree, *koelreuteria elegans*, a member of the Sapindaceaen family? More laughter. She says she knows more about trees than about sex.

It's been a long time since the neurotic thrush last paid them a visit. On the other hand, the greenish-brownish birds that turned up a couple of days ago are there. If they are the same ones. In any case, they perch on the same bush, and it's clear they aren't sparrows. They seem to be a couple. Although they are almost identical, the backs of their heads are different, one looks like it has a ponytail. Lynn points that out after putting her glasses on. They're horn-rims and make her look like a teacher. Being shortsighted, she should wear them always, but because she finds them a nuisance, she usually manages without them. Julia has the same problem.

Martin goes up to them. He says she looks particularly interesting with her glasses on, they make her look like a teacher. He, too, notices the one bird's distinguishing feature, although he thinks it looks more like a hat. There's no doubt the one with the ponytail or hat or whatever is the male; he says that in the animal kingdom, the males are usually the more elegant of the two sexes, and he says it as if he knew what he was talking about, which makes Julia laugh uncontrollably. She laughs at him as she looks at the sparse hair above Martin's forehead standing on end, and laughs even more when he says he doesn't know what she's laughing at, it's a scientific fact. Julia has to lean on Lynn for support, and Lynn, too, is laughing.

8

ABAITUA PARKS IN FRONT OF WHAT HE THINKS IS KEPA'S DOORWAY, in the Morlans district. He's changed apartments again, which he normally does to suit his financial situation, and he hasn't visited him here before. He decides to wait outside for him, the weather's marvelous. There's a gentle south wind, and that changes the color of Donostia completely—the horizon stretches further, and he gets the impression that his sight becomes more acute thanks to that. A perfect day to go walking in the hills.

The apartment buildings, which are two or three floors high, are modest, many of the balconies are full of flowers, and the atmosphere is peaceful and pleasant in spite of the ugly viaduct, but it's obvious the area must be damp and very different when the weather isn't so good. He reads the name of the district on a blue and white ceramic plaque. Morlans—like Urgull, Igeldo, and many other place-names in Donostia—is a Gascon word, he thinks, and that makes him slightly sad, though he's not quite sure why. He has a vague memory of the district, of when the Civil Guard had a house surrounded there for a long time with an ETA group holed up inside. He thinks that shortly after the radio gave the news about the Civil Guard's movements, he heard the shots and was scared by them, but he's not sure. In his mind's eye, it was a long shoot-out, and several young people were tragically, senselessly killed. He doesn't know how to place the events chronologically, but they seem far off to him now, perhaps because he'd rather forget them, but the traces they left on him, which senseless though they are still persist, must be from a time when he felt more closely associated with what was going on with ETA, when he felt sorrow whenever someone was killed, and also guilty, at the end of the day, because he hadn't met the same fate as those young people who had given their lives for him, for their ideas.

There are many places that have been marked forever because they were scenes of death, where the echo of machine guns can still be felt, and where it seems you can probably still see the indelible stains left by blood—and by long-shriveled memorial flowers, as well—and Morlans is one of those places.

He decides to go up to the third floor, which should be where Kepa's apartment is, and make sure he's remembered the building number correctly. When Kepa opens the door, Abaitua gets the impression he doesn't know whether to let him in or not. He's dressed for hiking and has a mop in his hand. "We've had a mishap," he says, finally moving to one side to let him in. There are books piled up against the wall all along the hallway, as if they were waiting to be taken to more noble surroundings. It's a shabby apartment, and there's a great contrast between the ugly furniture and the fancy decorative objects resting on the floor and waiting to be put in place, including several engravings—he recognizes some by Chillida and others by Balerdi—and polished tin maritime artefacts. The kitchen floor tiles are wet. Kepa says not to worry about it and to come in. His mother is at the sink washing dishes. She looks much better than she had at the hospital. She's a tall woman who was once very elegant, she has beautiful long gray hair that's gone a little yellow, a bit like her son's fingers, colored by smoking English cigarettes. Her son says she wets herself more and more often, and he'll kill her when she starts soiling herself. He says it as if he means it, without raising his voice, just as if he were saying he'd give her an acetaminophen if her temperature went up. His mother doesn't so much as flinch, but Abaitua gets angry with the son, because he doesn't think he should speak like that in front of her, even if she won't understand his Basque. "I know the theory: it's a disservice to us both." His gestures toward her, on the other hand, are full of love—he removes a speck of food left at the side of her mouth, holds her elbow to take her back to the sink. She says she likes cleaning pots. She scrubs them, leaves them on a towel, and then rinses them. And so on, without interruption. Her son puts a plastic apron on her, the type fishmongers wear. He calls her "*madre*," in Spanish.

Abaitua goes up to her when her son leaves to finish packing his backpack. "How are you?" "I'm fine, doing the dishwashing, as you can see, that's all I've done all my life." She tries to dry her hands on a wet cloth. "What about you?" "I can't complain." "Of course, you really did the right thing not going to war, Juan." Abaitua isn't entirely sure that he should say yes to everything and let her go on confusing him with whoever this Juan person is, it doesn't seem respectful to him, so he solves it by saying that going to war is never good. "But Pedro had to go," the old woman continues, "it would have been better if he'd died." Abaitua thinks she's talking about Kepa's father. He knows he spent the war in Jaen, in Andalusia, and subsequently emigrated to Bizkaia. "Yes, it would have been better if he'd died." Now she has her back to the sink and confirms her sentiment by nodding. If she had known, she wouldn't have prayed for him to survive the war, and that way he wouldn't have been so unhappy. He says she shouldn't say things like that. He feels more and more uncomfortable, she's opening her heart to him, confusing him with someone she must have really trusted. The war's over, he says, it's not going to happen again. Someone calls at the door. It's the girl who's going to look after her while they're away. Kepa's put a jacket on and is carrying his backpack over one shoulder.

"Enough with the stories about the goddamn war."

His tone is rough once more, but the old woman doesn't seem to be affected by that. In any event, she turns back to the sink that she's been leaning on to continue washing the dishes. Kepa says they can go. He goes up to his mother and rolls up her sleeves. This time he speaks to her more gently, "Forget that goddamn war."

He asks Kepa who this Juan is that she's confusing him with, but he has no idea. Abaitua thinks he does know but doesn't want to talk about it, and they remain in silence until they get to what used to be the gasworks. He asks if he remembers the gun battle that once took place in Morlans. Of course he does, as if it were yesterday. The operation was directed by General Galindo, and Luis Roldán was still heading the Civil Guard. This was back before they were arrested, naturally, the first for torture and the second on charges of corruption. The battle lasted for four hours, and three ETA members were killed. It was August 1991. Abaitua thought it must have been longer ago. 1991 seems very recent to him, but, then, twenty years is pretty long. They keep quiet again until they reach Antso Jakituna Hiribidea. Where are they going to spend the night? Kepa is always in charge of logistics. One thing he likes about going on trips with Kepa is that he takes care of everything: choosing the hotels and booking them, doing the same with the restaurants—and, extremely importantly, deciding how much to tip at each one—and figuring out which routes they should take. Abaitua's only responsibility is driving along the routes he's told to. He likes the arrangement, traveling as if he were a great lady.

They're booked into the Argi Eder hotel for the first night. In the town of Ainhoa, it's the best spot for couples, though not exactly for their sort of couple, although there's nothing wrong with that. They usually have a good time during the day, but in the evening, at dinner, the lack of women becomes too apparent for them, especially once they've had a glass or two of Armagnac each. When the nostalgia that they aren't always able to share takes over, they withdraw into themselves, each silently resenting the other for not being the company they would really like to be with, and they've even had arguments at such moments. It's wrong of them. Abaitua's aware of it, and he knows that Kepa is, as well. When they reach the Pio XII traffic circle, instead of turning off at the appropriate exit, he drives all the way around. Once, twice. Kepa lets him be and shows no sign of surprise.

He suddenly gets the idea of calling the young American. He's thought several times since they decided to go on this trip about how he'd like to show her Azkaine, Ainhoa, and Garazi, because she spoke to him about the northern Basque Country and said she wanted to go there. He would enjoy showing her the pretty parts of each town, taking her to good restaurants, and above all, they would have lively conversations in her company, they'd have to stay on their feet, so to speak. The third time they go around, he says, "How about if we invite a girl to come with us?" Kepa says it's fine by him—not really believing him, it seems to Abaitua. In any case, and to cover himself, he says he doesn't know if she'll be at home. He parks the car near the offices of the Spanish central government delegation and gets out to make the call, just in case the conversation is a disaster. While he waits for the call to go through, he feels his pulse racing—a sensation he'd forgotten, a state of anxiety he enjoys feeling.

He says both his first and last name to introduce himself: Iñaki Abaitua. His heart is beating fast, and he's afraid that his nervousness may be all too obvious on the other end. He starts by saying that he knows it's a last-minute invitation but that he'd told her that he was planning to go to the northern Basque Country with a friend. He thought she might like to see that part of the country. He mentions his friend and the mountains, to stop his invitation from seeming suspicious. Or so he hopes. There's a short silence, but he knows she's going to accept. Her voice sounds happy—she'd be glad to go with them, it's just a little out of the blue. She doesn't know if she has any suitable clothes for hiking. He says a T-shirt and some sneakers would be fine. They'll pick her up in half an hour. He starts the engine again and tells Kepa she's an American sociologist. A very smart, friendly girl. Kepa doesn't react, but Abaitua knows he's glad and will enjoy the company.

"MY NAME IS LYNN." She talks about her name's origins, the circumstances that brought her to Donostia, the good luck she had finding a house—it's a bargain, because of the price and because she can use the yard, and because Max, her cat, has the roof all to himself—things that Abaitua is familiar with, and now, hearing her tell them to Kepa, he has the agreeable feeling that he's known her for a long time, and that feels like a privilege.

When Kepa says "*o sea*—so—you live in that weird guy's house," Abaitua tries to make a gesture to him not to go on. Fortunately, he adds that although he's weird, he does write well. Then they remain silent while they drive through the more run-down districts of Herrera and Pasaia, trying to go as quickly as they can so the young foreign girl will see as little as possible of that embarrassing spectacle. The only one to say anything at all is Kepa, who mumbles that he can't remember what that name reminds him of. *Lynn*.

Until, suddenly, he clicks his fingers together. "The girl from *Montauk!*" he says in triumph, and Lynn seems to be delighted that he's made the connection. She's also amazed, but above all delighted, and that deflates Abaitua a little; he doesn't think it fair that Kepa—a devourer of books with the memory of an elephant—should get so much credit for knowing that. A twisted feeling, which makes him keep quiet for a while.

Lynn and Kepa are talking about *Montauk*.

Abaitua is amused by the fact that when they talk about the mistakes in the Spanish translation of *Montauk*, Lynn sounds as angry as if the translator had caused her some personal harm. But Kepa says she's right, and he's very angry, as well. So they talk about the translation, because it's something that Kepa, naturally, knows all about. He says that all of Frisch's work, including *Montauk*, has been translated into French very well. That leads them to talk about Julia, the writer's friend, and the American girl says she wants to convince her to translate the book into Basque, and Kepa, of course, thinks it's a very good idea, because it could be better than the Spanish translation and above all because that edition's long been out of print, and that woman, who he thinks is very beautiful, in spite of being that weird writer's friend, looks like a person who does everything well. The American girl openly expresses her happiness once more, because she shares his opinion completely. Kepa mentions that he only knows the writer's friend, Julia, by sight. Although he can easily satisfy the girl's curiosity by speaking about the character based on her, Flora Ugalde. Abaitua, on the other hand, is bound by professional secret and can't tell them that he treated her for a venereal infection and the writer most likely cheats on her.

FIRST STOP, BIRIATU, to see the cemetery. The plaque with the names that Unamuno transcribed for his poem *"Orhoit gutaz,"* or "Rememeber Us."

APRENDISTEGUY, CHARLES

ARISTEGUY, JOSEPH

EYHERAMENDY, JEAN JOSEPH

Etc.

Kepa starts reciting the Basque-born, Spanish-speaking writer's poem with great feeling: "You passed like oak leaves / blown down in a springtime / unseasonable hail; / you passed, sons of my noble race, / your souls dressed in your childhood Basque." Later, when they're having a bowl of soup in the restaurant by the church, Kepa talks to the young sociologist about the meaning behind the poem. In 1914 the prefect of the Basses-Pyrénées Département apparently complained to the minister of war that large groups of young Basque men were deserting and emigrating, and that it was because of the mentality of the local people, who knew no other homeland than the little corner of land they were born in and so viewed the war as a plague, something that should never have reached as far as the Pyrenees. Abaitua had to remind him that while that was true for the war of 1914, it was certainly no longer the case in 1944, because by then the République had taken good care to transform the French Basques into *vrais patriotes*—true patriots—and Kepa looked at him as if he were a spoilsport. He starts singing Gorka Knörr's "Morts Pour La Patrie," about people "dying for the nation"—not caring that a lot of people are staring at them. And the girl looks "*madly happy*" about it all.

SARE, just over the border in France, is almost exactly as Pierre Loti described it in *Ramuntcho*. On the outside of the church, there's a memorial plaque to Pedro de Axular that Bonaparte had installed there: *Euskaldun izcribatzalletatik iztun ederrenari ni Luis Luziano Bonaparte Euskaltzaleak au ipiñi nion. Ez dago atsedenik ta edoi gabe egunik zeruetan baizik* 1865—I, Louis-Lucien Bonaparte, an enthusiast of Basque culture, dedicate this plaque to the greatest of Basque writers. There are no days without clouds and no rest except in heaven. 1865.

THE LARGE STURDY CHURCH TOWER IN AZKAINE; the cemetery behind it with the famous circular tombstone dated 1657; the *place* with its Lapurdian houses. Kepa insists on having a glass of *pastis*. Unusual facts about Luis-Lucien Bonaparte, Abbadia, and Humboldt. But Kepa gets really excited when he starts talking about Agustin Xaho and Basque poets. He doesn't stop talking until they reach Ainhoa.

IN THE DINING ROOM AT THE ARGI EDER HOTEL, Lynn complains that she feels out of place there. She thought they were going hiking in the hills and has only brought underclothes, shorts, and a few T-shirts. She reproaches them for having put on very elegant clothes for dinner. Abaitua is wearing a raw linen jacket and a striking tie—black with large splashes of color on it, orange, yellow, and green—that Pilar brought him from Florence and that he doesn't normally dare to wear. And the one Kepa is wearing would be simply impossible back in Donostia. Abaitua picked it up for him in Rio, where he'd gone for a gynecology conference. From a distance, the gray and blue shapes on it look abstract, but they're actually a naked woman when you look closely. He, too, is wearing a jacket. It's what they usually do. Hikers in the morning and elegant night birds in the evening. The girl complains again that they should have told her. Now she looks out of place sitting between these two elegant gentlemen. Kepa says she looks very pretty.

Kepa is the one who talks most. The sociologist asks questions, and he gives her long, in-depth answers.

"So what they say about the Basque matriarchy is a myth?" the girl asks, looking disappointed. Her eyes are bright, her face flushed, and she laughs easily. It's very obvious she's a little tipsy. Abaitua likes women who let themselves be tempted by wine. Kepa asks for another bottle of Hermitage, saying something he probably read in a guidebook and hasn't forgotten (he never forgets anything): it comes from a winery that dates from the fifteenth century and can be aged for up to twenty years. None of that means much to Abaitua, but he thinks it's a very good wine. And he thinks it must be extremely expensive. He says the way to ask for more wine is to turn the empty bottle upside down in the ice bucket. Kepa doesn't stop talking, he has brilliant explanations for everything they see, an encyclopedia of anecdotes, and his observations are relevant and appropriate. He enjoys the young woman's attention, her admiration when he's able to make use of his knowledge, her loud laughter at the stories and jokes he remembers. And Abaitua, too, enjoys seeing that they're having a good time. It's a long time since he's seen Kepa so happy, so relaxed. That said, it isn't hard to amaze the young woman and get her laughing—that loud, happy laughter, which he sometimes finds too much—because their worlds and *backgrounds* are so very different. She is enormously curious and is interested in everything. So Abaitua lets Kepa show off, display his skills, and enjoy the young woman's interest, showing no envy in his eyes when he looks at them over his glass from time to time.

While Kepa is talking about matriarchy and mentioning someone called Goldberg, the sociologist interjects, calling the man he's just mentioned a sexist piece of shit—*"Ese machista de mierda."* It's funny the way she says it, and Kepa pretends not to have heard her, so that she'll say it again. *"Ese machista de mierda."* They carry on laughing loudly, and everybody in the dining room is looking at them.

Kepa usually talks quite loudly, especially after he's had a few drinks. The things he says about the Basques become more and more clichéd, and more and more sentimental, as they empty the bottle, and Abaitua, even though he, too, likes throwing a bit of imagination into things, despite finding himself somewhat repressed in that regard in recent years, is embarrassed by them idealizing history so much, and from time to time he asks them to calm down, maybe too often, because finally Kepa, looking angry, tells him to leave them alone. So he lets them talk. He doesn't know to what extent Kepa's use of medical examples is meant to provoke a reaction from him. He has heard that using biological models to express social subjects is a sign of not being able to explain them in social terms. He doesn't say that to him, among other things because he's been left out of the conversation. The Basque Country probably needed to have some of its myths overturned, but they've gone too far, Kepa says, they've left its innards nearly entirely stripped of gut flora. *"Do you understand?"* He keeps on repeating the question, with an incredibly bad accent. Bringing out the untruth in the myths in order to deny the Basque character. Myths are lies, nobody can deny that, but what makes Basques special is their ability and desire to make them believable. "It's all a lie, fine, but who else can say, with the same conviction as a Basque, that their language's words for "hand," "stone," "water," and "fire"—*esku, harri, ur,* and *su* in Basque—are the same ones used twenty thousand years ago? What's more, myths influence the people who believe them. The idea of egalitarianism may be a myth, but Basques believed that dignity knows no social classes, and so they convinced everybody else that they, the Basques, were all equally noble. That's why it was forbidden to beat up Basques in Castile, and disciplined observers such as Humboldt and Weber were amazed to see, as another traveler once put it, that "the poorest ox herd was just as proud as the governor of Tolosa."

It's easy to imagine him as a shaman from the Paleolithic Age when he says *"ur, su, lur"* in that deep voice of his.

The young American looks self-absorbed now, stirring the sugar at the bottom of her cup, and Abaitua wants to hold her thin-fingered hands. Just hold them. She sees his look and gives that fleeting smile that wrinkles her eyes and lengthens her lips. When Kepa says what fine hands she has, she puts her cup down on the saucer and hides both hands under the table as if she thought she'd been caught doing something wrong. She doesn't like them, she answers. Abaitua knew that, as well. Kepa, though, says they're pretty and makes her put them both on the tablecloth. He knows how to read hands. Love will soon come her way, he tells her.

OUTSIDE, A LIGHT SOUTH WIND makes the leaves murmur softly, and a little owl gives out its mysterious call. They also hear the harmonious chiming of animals they cannot see, close by though they are. The two men, Kepa and Abaitua, are alone in the gardens of the Argi Eder hotel, next to the swimming pool. The girl said that she was very tired and *"quite drunk, too."* She wanted to rest, so she wouldn't make a fool of herself up in the hills the next day. Kepa, on the other hand, said he'd have a last drink, and Abaitua preferred to avoid the frustration of saying goodnight to her at the door to her room. He, too, felt like taking in the night air. Kepa says she's a very interesting girl. They're both looking at the window, behind which the light has just come on. Abaitua's glad Kepa's said that. Yes, she's a nice girl, he says. It's the only window lit up on the whole façade, and the intensity and color of the light change at that precise moment—it's more amber now, and softer. She's obviously turned on some smaller lamp, probably the one on the bedside table, and then turned the main light off, and her profile is projected against the window for a short moment. She's probably looking out toward where they are. There's a smell of mint in the air and a slight trace of burned wood, as well. The shadow moves again, casts itself on the ceiling, appears and disappears two or three times. Abaitua tries to imagine her doing the things that women do before getting into bed. He thinks he can tell when she leaves the bedroom to go into the bathroom, which she does several times, and he also thinks he can probably tell when she takes the top cover off her bed and folds it up. There must be a chair by the window, as there is in his room, and she leaves it there. He clearly sees her leaning over to do that.

Then her profile stands out in the window once more, and for a few seconds, she stands there looking out the window. He doesn't think she can see them, there isn't a single light on in the grounds, but he wouldn't mind if she knew they were watching her movements. The wind has turned, and the leaves on the acacias make a sound like little bells. Then a long, sad howl that sounds like a wolf. Kepa, after listening carefully, says it's a tawny owl. Some not particularly interesting details about nocturnal birds. Abaitua didn't know that a young owl—*mozolo* in Basque, a word that also means "useless"—is called a *mochuelo* in Spanish. It should be pointed out that the white owl—*lechuza* in Spanish—doesn't have those upright feathers on its head that look like ears.

THEY SING THEIR SAD SONGS.

They lie on the grass for a long time after the girl turns out the light, looking at the moon and the patchy clouds that keep trying to cover it up.

Ene aberri laztana,
Jausi zara erbestepian,
zelan ondiño il etzara!
Zeure basotik atzo igoten zan
eskari ona zerura,
gaur erdeldunak sartuta
aixia emen biraoz bete da.
Obea eriotza da!

It means, "My dear homeland, you've fallen to the foreigner, you'd be better off dead! Yesterday from your woods, good requests were sent to heaven, today vile people have come, the wind here is full of curses. Death is better than this!"

Kepa, though, doesn't know the words to "*Ene aberri laztana*"— maybe that's why he likes myths. Abaitua, on the other hand, learned it from his mother, he thinks that's the only way you can learn it. The music is beautiful, very beautiful he'd say, as beautiful as the words are vile. He doesn't know why, but sometimes, when he's feeling particularly sad, the verses come to him from somewhere deep inside—*ene aberri laztana*—it comes out of his soul and lessens his sorrow. It isn't a song to sing solo, but he'd be scared to sing it with a group.

Later, back in his room, he's glad to be sleeping alone.

THE YOUNG AMERICAN SOCIOLOGIST comes into the dining room at precisely the time they agreed upon. She's wearing the green shorts she had on the night before and a sleeveless beige T-shirt. It's obvious she's happy. They ask each other how they've slept. *"I slept like a baby,"* the girl says, and then in Basque, *"Umea bezala,* is that right?" Kepa only ever sleeps about four hours; Abaitua's seen it before, a few times when he's had to share a room with him. He spends the night smoking and reading. Last night he read Tolstoy's diaries. He didn't just read them, Abaitua clarifies, he's learned them by heart, as well. The girl's hair is wet, and she keeps leaning her head from one side to the other, resting her ponytail on her shoulders. The two men, almost simultaneously, say that she'll catch cold. She laughs. She's used to it, she hardly ever dries her hair. *"What's the plan?"* She says she's ready to scale a 20,000-footer. Kepa's brought a great selection of hiking books and maps. And a sophisticated GPS and all the technological devices an expert mountaineer could ever want. He spreads a large map out on the table for them to decide where to go, but, he says, the weather's supposed to change, unfortunately— scattered showers. Abaitua's very surprised by that, because the sky's clear, there's no wind whatsoever, and everything looks stable. He suspects Kepa is hoping to avoid going out hiking, as he always does. What he likes is going on road trips, visiting towns, and looking for good restaurants. He's like Pilar in that sense. He remembers that the two couples once went together to visit the Great Dune. Neither Pilar nor Kepa wanted to walk, and he had to go the whole way, slowly, with Kepa's wife—it was like a procession she went so slowly. She was wearing an oriental type of headscarf—being so white that she was practically albino, she was scared of getting sunburned—and she talked nonstop about things only she was interested in, on the way there and on the way back. When they returned, Pilar and Kepa were sitting at a bar on the edge of the beach with a large tray of empty oyster shells and a bottle of Chablis in front of them; the bottle, too, was empty. *"Voilà nos explorateurs,"* said Pilar, looking very lively.

But Abaitua needs to walk and tire out his body. He likes hiking, reaching some town they've spotted from up in the hills, he thinks he discovers them in their intimacy when he reaches the first houses with their kitchen garden, and next the fields, and then little by little the streets begin to appear. Kepa says he only mentions it because he's heard it on the French weather forecast. He's trying to get over a sudden coughing fit, and Abaitua and the girl, a little taken aback, remain silent. When he recovers, and still with tears in his eyes, he says he's not going to stop smoking, he won't give up until he's quite sure what blame, sin, or perdition it brings with it . . . Something of Tolstoy's he read the night before.

CAFÉ NOISSETTE. "If you want a real *ebaki*, a real *cortado*, you have to ask for *café avec une noisette*," Kepa tells the young American. Spaniards really like asking for *café crème*, because it's mentioned in a lot of songs, and that's why they always end up drinking milky coffee. "And what about *café au lait*?" the girl asks.

Then, while Abaitua is trying to get Kepa to firm up their plans, the American girl says she thinks all their different suggestions are good. Just one thing, she dares to add, she'd like to go to a bookstore to buy the French translation of *Montauk* for Julia. She's going to have trouble finding it in any of the bookstores in the area. Even in Biarritz or Baiona. Perhaps in Bordeaux, Kepa says very enthusiastically, why don't they go to Bordeaux. The girl turns toward Abaitua with a sparkle in her eyes, like a child who doesn't dare to ask for permission. Her request is as clear as it is mute, but Abaitua finds it hard to hide the fact that he's put out. He says he doesn't mind. But there's a problem. The girl stands up, holds the sides of her pants, and stretches them out with a comic gesture to say that she can't go to Bordeaux dressed like this. Of course she can, she looks great, Kepa says. They're about to finish breakfast. The American girl eats with gusto, almost with zest. She puts the food into her mouth quickly, and swallows it quickly, as well. At the moment she realizes that the two men are looking at her, she holds up the horn of a croissant between her index finger and thumb and says, "*Un vrai croissant,*" with an expression of great pleasure on her face. They're very good, the pastry is flakier than the ones on the other side of the border, she says—"*más hojaldrados que los del otro lado.*" Kepa says it's because of the dough. Ordinary croissants have just enough butter, and special ones have four times as much. Butter only, no other type of fat.

When they find themselves alone for a moment, the girl tells Abaitua she's worried she jumped too quickly at the idea of going to Bordeaux and that it's spoiled his plans for going hiking in the mountains. He reassures her—any plan's good if she's part of it. He acts out the sentiment by making a gesture of reverence, and nothing could be closer to the truth. Everything seems fun to him, stimulating even, when she's there, he has to admit that, and he doesn't mind the girl seeing that. So he says, and suddenly speaking seriously for once, that she has nothing to worry about, he's going to be honest with her, and if he doesn't like something, he'll just tell her.

There's another matter, as well, the girl says, that she'd like to clear up once and for all so that they don't have to keep coming back to it. She has her old wallet in her hand and nods energetically toward the hotel reception desk. She wants to pay her share. Abaitua didn't expect that of her, and he likes it. He's always thought that what girls used to do in his day when it came time for a bill to be paid—pretending they didn't notice—was rude. And now this sign that the girl sees him as an equal companion—someone she splits bills with and not an aged old man who's expected to pay for her company with gifts and favor—cheers him. Impossible, he tells her. He has no difficulty improvising the explanation that Kepa and he have a joint fund for their trips and have decided to treat her. The two of them are treating her, he says, just in case it wasn't clear.

Abaitua can't stop thinking about different scenes from *Montauk* that seem to fit the situation. Even before the girl mentioned wanting to get ahold of the French translation, when she put her glasses on to see the woodpigeon blind they were pointing out to her up on the hill, he remembered that the writer saw the Lynn in *Montauk* as "*una mezcla de ondina y nurse*"—a combination of undine and nurse. He had to look up the word *ondina* in the dictionary: a nymph who lives at the bottom of the sea. Now, as they walk toward the car, Lynn has taken her glasses off again. She says his hiking shirt is very nice—it's brown with yellow checks, and Abaitua wears it over his shoulders as a light jacket—and he's reminded of something that happened to him long ago when he was wearing the same shirt, just as the writer does in *Montauk* with his own denim shirt.

At least ten years have gone by since then. Kepa and he were quite annoyed with each other. He'd refused to go for a drive as Kepa had suggested and instead left him sitting there doing sketches of houses in Bidarrai and, just as a matter of principle, went up to hike in the mountains by himself. After a good walk along a marked route, he reached mountain pass in Eguzki Mendi that he later found out was called Mehatxeko, and here, as on so many mountains in the Basque Country, he came across the disappointing spectacle of a large group of parked cars and noisy people. They were talking around a fire on which several large pots were being heated. Some of them came up to him as if he were a long lost brother—"*notre frère*"—and offered him a cup of soup. They also gave him a card with the Virgin Mary on it, the one from Fatima, he thinks, and told him they were from Bordeaux. They looked worryingly like members of some sect, and while Abaitua was thinking about how to get away from them, a young hiker appeared and after greeting them in French said seriously but politely that they were heating their pots on top of a megalithic monument. Those stones around their fire were part of a *cromlech*, a prehistoric tomb.

Because they took it as a joke, the young man told them again, not aggressively but angrily now, that it was a sacred place, probably a burial ground of their ancestors from thousands of years ago. And then the man who seemed to be the leader, full of the wrath of God, started kicking the stones and shouting that churches were the only sacred places and how dare he go around spewing such irreverent nonsense. Abaitua, looking at the perfect circle of stones around the fire, was ashamed. The young hiker was wearing a brown shirt like his. He was a typical young man from the area, not too big, but strong and agile. He looked at the members of the group in front of him, from one end to the other, and for some reason, his eyes stopped on Abaitua, who stammered, "I didn't know." He saw a brief sign of surprise in the man's eyes as he realized he was a countryman of his, and then his look changed and it was clear that he despised him, really despised him. Finally, his eyes moved away, he looked at the head of the sect and said that it wasn't surprising there were terrorist attacks against tourists. He turned around and walked away quickly. His words caused a great commotion in the group. They insulted him for saying that a pile of worthless stones were sacred. A few of them went after the young man, to take photos of him, and the leader said that he would talk with the prefect as soon as they got back to Bordeaux, he was a friend of his, and that young man was undoubtedly a terrorist. Abaitua took advantage of the uproar and went back down the hill along the same path he had come up it.

Kepa says it was eight years ago.

They're talking about megalithic monuments now. Cromlechs and the metaphysics of the void. But on the way to Bordeaux, and without any wine, their ancestors' voices are hardly audible.

He doesn't know which exit to take out of the traffic circle and, as he often does, goes around it twice. He took a wrong turning at a crossroads earlier, but neither Kepa nor the girl minded. We're lost again, the girl says, in the plural, and thanks to that wording, getting lost isn't as frustrating for him as it would be if he were with Pilar; he would have gotten angry with her long ago because she would have told him off for not paying attention. That makes him remember that in *Montauk*, the writer reflects on how different it is when the girl tells him off about something, because she uses his name—"*You're wrong, Max.*"

Even so, they still pull his leg a bit. Kepa says it's very exciting to go driving places with him—you never know where you're going to end up—and the girl, with a completely serious voice, says she doesn't think he really gets lost, he does it on purpose just in case anyone's following them, he wants to throw them off the track.

They've been on a flat, straight road going through an endless pine forest for more than an hour now. Kepa and Abaitua are singing French songs. Abaitua has a baritone voice, and Kepa sings bass. The communist Jean Ferrat's "*Ma France.*" "*Cet air de liberté au-delà des frontières.*" The voice of the Republic now fills their breasts. "*Celle du vieil Hugo tonnant de son exil*"—old Hugo's voice as he returns from exile. Lynn doesn't understand the words, and they translate them for her. They admit they're Francophiles. *La France*, back when Spain was a sad place, *au-delà des frontières*—just there beyond the border. Aragon's lyrics in "*L'Affiche rouge*"—that tribute to Manouchian and his comrades in the MOI, the *Main-d'œuvre immigrée*, the French Resistance's immigrant force, to the Armenians, Romanians, Italians, Poles, Hungarians, Spaniards, and Germans, too, who were executed at Mont Valérienen, *pour la France.* "*Parce qu'à prononcer vos noms sont difficiles . . . Ils étaient vingt et trois quand les fusils fleurirent . . . Vingt et trois qui criaient la France en s'abattant*"—Because your names are difficult to pronounce . . . There were twenty-three of them when the guns fired . . . Twenty-three who shouted "France!" as they fell. Ferrat himself was of foreign origin, and Léo Ferré and Aznavour and Moustaki and Montand and Reggiani and Sylvie Vartan and Marie Laforet and Carla Bruni and *le president*, Sarkozy. *La France*: churning out French people until very recently. Kepa talks about integration, assimilation, and multiculturalism. He says he's in favor of assimilation as long as cultural activities that don't harm republican principles aren't forbidden. The young American sociologist, on the other hand, defends multiculturalism, but they don't quarrel. Abaitua keeps quiet on the subject, as he often does, because he has a tendency to go against whatever he's confronted with, and right now he doesn't know who to side with. What he thinks is that you see things very differently depending on your culture's position, whether it's in a more dominant position or about to disappear. It occurs to him that Kepa's own personal assimilation has been perfect. The only thing he's inherited from his Andalusian culture, from his parents, is eating his olives with bread. And that's no bad thing. Pilar also likes eating olives with bread whenever she can; he remembers she picked it up from Kepa.

A hill of sand disappearing off on the horizon. If you only looked to the north and south, you might think you were in the desert. A dune almost two miles long and well over three hundred feet tall. The longest dune in Europe, Kepa says. To the west, to their left, it goes gently down to the sea, and to the east, meanwhile, it falls sharply down to the pine forest. Their feet sink deep into the sand, and Kepa starts panting after barely a quarter of an hour of walking. He lets himself fall backward onto the sand and takes out his packet of cigarettes. The other two had better go on, he'll wait for them and smoke a cigarette. Abaitua thinks that he, Kepa, must also remember that the same thing happened when they were out with their wives. Lynn and Abaitua go on. The girl goes first, and it looks as if walking doesn't require her to make any effort. The writer and the Lynn in *Montauk* also walked on the beach, the girl going first, the man following after her. The girl had a comb, one end of it sticking out of the back pocket on her jeans. He was surprised by that when he read it. At one time, tough guys used to keep combs in their back pockets. They would hold their heads to one side and run their hands over their occipital lobes. It really does look as if they're in a desert now. Really. Although she's very thin, she does have curves. The writer in *Montauk* says she's very thin but not bony. This girl's ponytail bobs from side to side, as well. She turns around, makes that gesture in which her lips lengthen and her eyes wrinkle; there's affection in her smile. "Thank you for asking me along," she says.

They listen to the radio. *Temps calme partout. Le soleil s'impose sur l'ensemble du pays* Calm and stable. Sunny weather all over the country. Kepa says that isn't what he heard that morning. But Iñaki

274

Abaitua doesn't care anymore. However, when Kepa mentions the idea of going to Archon to eat some oysters, he puts his foot down—it would mean reaching Bordeaux too late. Perhaps on the way back.

PORT OF THE MOON. World Heritage Site. Two thousand years of history looking out over this exuberant river. After Paris, it's the French city with the greatest number of protected buildings. Stone façades, sloping slate roofs. The girl's right when she says that it's a bit like the romantic part of Donostia. Obvious differences aside. The people of Bordeaux named the historical district the Quartier des Grandes Hommes, because it's bordered by the Allées de Tourny, the cours Clemenceau, and the cours l'Intendence. Kepa shows them the house where Goya died, in the latter street. They look into the store windows as they walk along, because the girl's said that she'd like to buy some clothes to wear in the city, but she steps back when the two men encourage her to go into a store that, they say, has "truly beautiful" clothes; she thinks they're too elegant.

Although the men stay outside on the sidewalk, they can see her through the store window. She comes out to the door twice to ask them what they think. Now she knocks on the window and orders them to come in. Kepa stays outside, because he's smoking. She has a small strappy top on, bright blue—Klein blue, says the retail assistant, a sophisticated woman of Abaitua's age who looks at him with curiosity, wondering if the girl's his daughter—and tight black pants. There's also a dress she likes, it's made of very fine cloth and has a pattern of large leaves. But she thinks it's too chic. The shopkeeper says she should try it on. The leaves are mostly green and yellow, colors that look good on *mademoiselles*, she says. The girl's barefoot. Her feet are very thin without being at all bony. She spins around with one hand over her head, the dress hem billows out. She asks what it looks like on her. Wonderful. She has perfect toes, unaffected by the ugly marks on so many women's feet caused by wearing the wrong shoes. The girl follows his look down to her feet and stares at them as if she were seeing them for the first time, and when she looks at him again, he thinks she's embarrassed. In any case, she puts her sneakers on again. She isn't going to buy the dress, beautiful though it is, because it's too sophisticated, and "*very expensive too.*" The shopkeeper quickly understands Abaitua's signal

275

that she should put the elegant dress underneath the other purchase, and he pays for his gift while the girl is getting dressed.

The enormous buttresses and flying buttresses propping up the sides of St. Andrew's Cathedral are so irregular that they look as if they've been put up in a great hurry. Kepa makes them count the apostles on the Porte Royale, and there are ten of them. He says there are eleven at Arantzazu, because the sculptor, Jorge Oteiza, left Judas out, and so on. He can't stop talking. Sometimes when Abaitua listens to Kepa come out with all these quotes, dates, names, and anecdotes about whatever it is they're seeing, he thinks he's just making it up.

Didn't Oteiza do thirteen apostles?

The bookstore smells of wax. A man who's older than Abaitua and wearing blue overall murmurs a greeting to them, "*bonsoir messieurs-dames*," almost without lifting his head from the book he's reading. The girl asks if they have *Montauk*. They have just one copy left. Beautifully published. Matte cover, beige, no photographs, drawings, or decorations, just "Max Frisch, *Montauk, a Tale*, translated from the German by Michèle and Jean Tailleur, NRF, Gallimard."

The girl reads, with her funny accent: "*C'est icy un livre de bonne foy, lecteur.*"

She's deeply moved to think they've just been walking along streets that Montaigne must have known, and she holds onto the two men's arms as she says so. And they walk through the streets like that, the girl between them, holding onto their arms.

THEY HAVE DINNER IN THE BRASSERIE at the hotel they're booked into, because there wasn't a free table at the bar Kepa wanted to go to. They've already drunk a bottle of wine, and the men can't stop talking. The girl listens to them attentively, one elbow resting on the table and her chin balanced on the palm of her hand, her eyes moving from one to the other. They talk, and the girl laughs. She's a receptive person. It seems she finds everything they say interesting, and they compete, trying to seduce her by being the smartest, the funniest, but then when he realizes what they're doing, Abaitua feels ridiculous and talks less.

Kepa teaches the girl how to taste wine. Hold the glass up, look at it against the light, stick your nose in. He exaggerates every gesture, especially the swishing of the wine inside his mouth, he opens his nostrils really wide, which even looks a little obscene.

Abaitua never tastes the wine. Pilar does, more cautiously than Kepa, but she takes in all the nuances of a wine in her nose and on her palate. She doesn't exaggerate her gestures, but she knows more about wine than he does, and more about gastronomy in general. She takes a little into her mouth, looks straight ahead, and then she can identify everything that was used to make the wine, however complex it may be. She obviously has a gift for it, but she's also been educated to do it. At lunch at her parents' house, there is complete silence when each dish is served. Everyone—except for her mother, who sits upright in her chair like an accused woman awaiting the final sentence, both hands firmly on the table—takes a first mouthful, and after a silence, which lasts long, drawn-out seconds, they start giving their opinions one by one. It's a sentencing process that focuses on the negative: "I don't think the full flavor of the truffle comes out"; "It could do with a little cream, just a touch"; "I don't think it should have the basil." It seems Kepa's reading his mind at that precise moment—pointing at him with his glass, he says that Abaitua's wife really knows how to taste things, she has an incredible gustatory memory. Abaitua doesn't like her being mentioned. The young woman looks at him with interest, though, and he merely nods. But his own wife, he says, wouldn't have been able to realize the difference between a very cheap Don Simón and a Château Cheval Blanc. He talks about his wife in the past tense.

The American girl must be about the same age as the waitress. Kepa says saucy things to her each time she comes up to their table, which she takes in good grace. "*Profitons donc*," she says this time. She's speaking about chocolate, inviting him to enjoy it while he can. The restaurant's star dessert is a "*tour de chocolat noir et de crème brûlée*"—a tower of dark chocolate and crème brûlée—and a bunch of other stuff, all served "*sur un soufflé de riz*"—on a soufflé of rice, and Kepa makes a show of wondering whether to order it or not, because "chocolate's a very powerful aphrodisiac." So much so, he says, that in the not-too-distant future, it'll be forbidden, just like smoking and making love. "*Profitons donc*," says the waitress, laughing. Only Kepa yields to the temptation of the chocolate. The American girl chooses strawberries, but it turns out that they, too, are aphrodisiacs. Kepa thinks they're an indecisive, ambiguous fruit, somewhat hermaphroditic, and that's why we like them. He says he's read that the aphrodisiac effect lasts longer than the strawberries themselves. Abaitua feels quite tired and punishes himself by not ordering any dessert. It's a way of distancing himself from Kepa's joke; he hates to think of the girl deducing that they go around paying court to young waitresses when they're out on their trips. But his refusal ends up looking ridiculous, it just leads to further joking, giving the waitress the chance to tease him for not wanting to take the risk—"*Monsieur ne veut pas se risquer alors*"—and she laughs again, with no inhibitions whatsoever, showing off her white teeth and pink gums. When she goes, the American girl says she envies those great teeth and complains that she herself has the teeth of a mouse.

EUROPE: the happy circumstance of having many different languages and cultures in one small area. And the unhappy one, Abaitua blurts out. Fortunately, the girl doesn't ask him why. He doesn't feel like talking about it.

BAS ARMAGNAC. Abaitua doesn't normally drink spirits. Only when he goes on trips with Kepa. The girl doesn't want to drink anymore, because she's "*pretty drunk*" today, as well. Then, just to try it, she takes a sip from Abaitua's glass.

Kepa looks melancholy, especially when the waitress comes up to them wearing her own clothes, to say goodbye and wish them sweet dreams. "*Faites de beaux rêves*," she says.

IN FACT, THE THINGS THAT ABAITUA IS LOOKING AT from his bedroom window—sloping lines, zinc roofing, stone façades lit by gentle yellow light, the reflections of streetlamps and the black dome of a public building trembling on the river—are quite like what he used to see from his parents' home as a child. There is complete silence, it's perhaps too quiet, and with the light off, he gets the feeling that he's plunged into the void. In the bathroom, however, he hears the sound of a shower. It must by the young American; her room is between his and Kepa's. He takes a shower, as well.

He's half asleep when he hears the door. Perhaps he's completely asleep. Fingers are tapping on the door, almost scratching it, and he knows it's the American girl on the other side. So he jumps out of bed naked and looks for the pajamas he has in his bag. It takes him a long time to put them on, among other things because the buttons on the shirt are still done up, and he's worried about what the girl might think.

The girl's wearing the same clothes she had on during the day, thick sweater and everything. He's wearing his blue silk pajamas with the darker blue piping, all very conventional. The girl says, *"Doctor, I'm not feeling well."* And then, with her hands crossed over her chest, she repeats Lizardi's words, *"Bihotzean min dut, min etsia."* She smiles sadly. And then in Spanish she explains that that's what she had planned to say, but it's so conventional, *"Es lo que había pensado decir pero es tan convencional."* Abaitua takes both her hands. He embraces her. "Let's keep it simple, all right?"

He feels it's a long time since he last embraced anyone.

IT'S THE GIRL WHO DECIDED to go back to her room. At around six, the time he usually wakes up. The curtains were still open, and the view, which the girl's figure was highlighted against, was bluish. He gets up, as well, and puts his pajamas on, even though the girl says it's still early and he should go back to bed and sleep a little more. She's only wearing her T-shirt and is holding all her other clothes, including her sneakers, in a bundle under her arm. He goes with her to the door, but she opens it, just enough to be able to squeeze through.

Abaitua feels a vague sense of guilt—which may be the result of some slight fear from having bowed to desire—but also the satisfaction of having seduced a young body.

KEPA IS IN THE DINING ROOM reading Tolstoy. "Interesting," he says when Abaitua asks him how he is, though he isn't talking about the book. He supposes he knows that he's slept with Lynn and is reproaching him for it. But he doesn't notice any change in his attitude when speaking with Lynn. In fact, he teases her again for having chosen strawberries. Lynn doesn't say or do anything that might point to her having been in an intimate situation a little earlier. They try to make plans for the day. They could take a quick walk around the city, set out early, and have lunch somewhere along the way, or they could stick around until after lunch. The girl doesn't mind one way or the other, "I'm sure either way will be fine."

Walking downtown is nice, the streets are fairly quiet. They see the *place* with the Grosse Cloche belfry, and Lynn gives two

279

fine Percherons that are yoked to a cart there an apple each. They see Montaigne's house in the Quartier de la Rousellen. They sit underneath the Café Régent's red awnings in the Place Gambetta and order a *café avec une noisette de lait*, a *café crème*, and a *café au lait*, so that they can compare them all. They count the columns— Corinthian, Kepa *dixit*— on the Grand Théâtre, and there are twelve of them. Twelve statues. Nine muses and three goddesses. Juno, Venus, and Minerva. They find the monument to the Girondins ugly and the Grandes Hommes market spectacular.

The girl stops in front of an elegant gift shop to look at amber figurines. It's the same shop Pilar bought a little jade dog in—it was identical to a fox terrier she'd had as a girl. In fact, she chose it and Abaitua paid for it. It's Pilar who controls their joint finances, but sometimes she likes him to pay, he supposes it makes her feel like a lady. There was a time when Pilar used to buy a lot of ceramics, figurines, and other decorative objects. She doesn't do that anymore. Now she says the only thing they do is pile up dust. He moves up to Lynn. He asks if she likes them, and she says she does, but she holds him by his sleeve when he makes a movement to go into the shop. She likes them, but that doesn't mean she has to buy them— we don't buy everything we like. He's already bought her enough things. They start walking again, Kepa out in front of them. They walk behind him, slightly separated from one another. Abaitua is worried the girl might think he had intended to buy her a gift as a sort of reward. She smiles when she tells him the dress was too much. It's the third time she's thanked him for it.

Kepa is waiting for them at the corner. At the door of a Crédit Lyonnais office. Abaitua guesses that it's the one his friend and Lynn's landlord once attempted to hold up. So he asks him, "How many years ago was it?" Not because he's interested, he just wants to see if he'll tell them the strange story, which is like something out of Laurel and Hardy. But all-knowing Kepa says he doesn't remember, it was ages ago.

WAR STORIES. Abaitua imagines it isn't because he's afraid of coming off as ridiculous that he doesn't want to tell the story, it's because he wants to show some discretion where Martin is concerned; he hasn't even mentioned that they used to be roommates in Bordeaux. But finally, faced with Abaitua's insinuations—he asks if it isn't true that the bank robbery of the century took place right there—he starts telling them about it, a quick summary, without going into details. He and Martin used to meet up in Baiona, Martin was studying sociology in Bordeaux at the time and would come down to Baiona most weekends, homesick, apparently. Kepa, on the other hand, lived in Baiona but wanted to get out; things had been tense for him ever since he'd left "the organization." The Basque refugees there didn't like Martin much, either, they thought he was weird, and some of them even thought he should be treated with suspicion. The two of them used to spend a lot of time together, and while Martin was thinking about what to do with his future, he invited Kepa to come and live with him. Kepa had the idea of robbing a bank, something he'd thought through before but the organization had never allowed, because there was a tacit agreement that they wouldn't carry out any operations in France. Kepa was experienced, he'd done three bank robberies with the organization, and the job he had in mind now was very easy. First, on the day of the robbery, they'd have to take a Polaroid of the cashier's little son holding one of their hands, with his face covered by that morning's newspaper, so that the father, on seeing it, would think that his son had been kidnapped. That bit was very easy, because he knew the woman who looked after the boy from speaking with her in the park—he'd told her he was a fine art photographer. And the rest wasn't difficult, either. They'd go to the bank, show the cashier the photo, and he, of course, would see that it had been taken that very day and recognize by his shirtsleeve that he was the same man as in the photo, and then there was no chance of him not believing it to be a real kidnapping, and he would give him all the money he had access to. Kepa would calmly leave the bank, and Martin would be waiting for him in a car they'd have stolen earlier, whose plates they'd have changed and hidden somewhere, and they'd make their way to Paris without any further trouble or anyone stopping them. Everything went well, he pretended to bump into the nanny by chance and, after taking some photos of her, asked her to take one of him with the child, which she did. She thought Kepa hiding his face behind the newspaper was some kind of artistic peculiarity. Then he went to the bank. As they'd planned, Martin was waiting for him, and he promised that he had the car in the nearby lot and would pull around at eleven o'clock on the dot and park in front of the door, because you could only park on that side of the street for ten minutes at a time. Kepa went into the bank at ten to eleven, stood in line, and, when it was his turn, showed the photo to the cashier, but just at the moment when he was going to explain that they'd kidnapped the boy, two policemen rushed into the bank, because they were being chased by a huge dog, one of those Great Danes, white with black spots, which was running after them and barking. There was an enormous uproar, and a few moments afterward, Martin burst in after the dog, which was his. Its name was Lagun, which means "friend." Kepa decided to run out of the bank; Martin, after getting ahold of the dog, did the same, and in the street there was another surprise: instead of the BMW they had lifted earlier, there was Martin's old Citroën 2CV. They jumped in, and after finally managing to start the engine—Martin was nervous—they fled. He explained to Kepa that he couldn't bring himself drive the stolen car, he was afraid he wouldn't know how to handle it. He claimed he was a one-car man.

He said that unlike many people who only need to know how to change gears to be able to drive any car they like, he found it very hard to get used to a car—by the way, some psychologists believed that particular inability to be a sign of monogamy—and so he'd decided to take his own car, which he was already completely familiarized with, in order to be able to make their getaway drive as safe as possible, which was important, seeing as how the bank robbery itself was already a nerve-wracking affair and he would probably be quite nervous. In addition to that, he'd decided to take Lagun with him because he, too, had psychological problems and couldn't stand being alone—the last time he'd left him alone at home, he'd destroyed all the furniture—and while he and his dog were waiting in the car, two gendarmes had walked by, and because the dog didn't like uniforms, he started barking. The gendarmes responded with some sort of unpleasant gesture, so he jumped out of the window and started biting them—he was a well-behaved dog, but threats made him angry. Although Kepa and Martin managed to get some distance away in the 2CV, they were soon tracked down. Not much happened to them, even though they found the photo of the cashier's son, which Kepa had dropped on the floor during all the commotion. They spent a few months in prison, and the worst thing about being locked up, he says, was having to put up with Martin. Kepa laughs loudly at that. He doesn't know how he ever asked Martin to be his accomplice. He laughs out loud again. Perhaps it was because Martin had offered to help without asking for any share in return. Even so, his help turned out to be very expensive indeed. But he says he thinks a lot of Martin, even though he hasn't seen him for a long time now.

PLACE JEAN MOULIN. The girl knows about the Resistance hero. A bronze angel with open wings, holding a naked, lifeless soldier in its arms; the soldier holds a broken sword. Both the soldier and the angel are very beautiful. A plaque on the ground says that the sculpture was made by Antonin Mercié, its title is *Gloria Vicitis, Gloire aux Vaincus*, and it's a copy of the original in the Square Montholon in Paris.

SWEET DEFEAT. The girl says the sculpture transmits the idea of a sweet defeat. It's very different from monuments to the victors, stuck on top of uncomfortable pinnacles or astride rearing horses with swords at the ready. In comparison, the death of that soldier, held there by such a beautiful angel, is sweet. "*Isn't it?*" Abaitua was brought up in the culture of defeat, he was taught that defeat is dignified. Soldiers who were proud of having lost the war, who'd never dirtied their swords killing unarmed enemies, who would rather die than murder, who lost in spite of being brave, who died because some rich, powerful nations got together to attack them from the sky with their fancy planes, when all the soldiers had to defend themselves were stones. They lost, but their dignity was still intact, unblemished. That's what his parents had passed onto him— defeat, if dignified, is beautiful.

CHEEEESE. Kepa tells them to smile for the photo.

THE ENDLESS LINE OF PINE TREES stands out against the mauve sky, and the low sun sends lively bursts of light through the gaps in the forest. They haven't spoken for a while. Kepa, sitting next to Abaitua, is breathing slowly, like someone who's about to fall asleep, and the girl is looking at the Frisch book in the back seat. Abaitua says he can't read in the car, he gets dizzy. She doesn't. She thinks she might be able to understand the text in French, she says, sticking her head between the two front seats. Because she knows the book so well.

"*Il est encore surpris de connaître son corps, son corps à elle. Il ne s'y attendait pas. Si Lynn ne lui signifiait pas de temps en temps qu'elle aussi se rappelle cette nuit, les mains de l'homme n'oseraient pas saisir la tête de la femme."*

Her pronunciation is not perfect, far from it, but it's intelligible, among other things because he, too, is familiar with what she's reading. Kepa says he likes her pronunciation—it reminds him of Jean Seberg in Godard's *À bout de soufflé*—and why doesn't she keep reading.

YOU'RE LAUGHING AT ME.

Abaitua cannot remember the girl's body. He just remembers that her contours seemed fuller to him when she was naked. He also remembers that her white skin was tinted blue by the light coming in through the window. Her laugh. You're tickling me, she'd said.

Abaitua thinks she didn't choose that particular passage—about how he's still surprised that he knows her body, and he hadn't expected to, and if Lynn weren't hinting to him from time to time that she, too, remembered that night, then the man's hands wouldn't ever have dared to reach out and touch the woman's head—by chance. He remembers another bit: "Lynn will not become a name for guilt."

Toward the end of the book, the writer drops Lynn off at her house in the early hours after spending their last night together—it hadn't been a melancholy last night, but the writer says that he hadn't felt well physically—and as he lies diagonally across his hotel-room bed, that's the thought that comes to him. Lynn will not become a name for guilt. His plane ticket is sitting under the yellow lamp where the girl had left her lighter the first time they met. Lynn isn't expecting the writer to change his plans, and he doesn't expect her to ask him to do so, either.

Abaitua feels envious of that relationship, which is based on sincerity—they both know there's no future for them together after their weekend together in Montauk. But while the narrative, which seems sincere, tells the reader that the girl shares the man's point of view—in other words, she has accepted that the relationship will not last—it does not explain exactly how they came to that agreement, the words they used to make it, or how they said them. It's true they both agreed not to write letters. Just a postcard every year on the anniversary of day they met—and the date is given—assuming, that is, that neither of them has forgotten about it by then.

Although Iñaki Abaitua doesn't remember his son's birthday, incredible though it may seem, he does remember that date: May

11, 1975. That very morning, when the girl asked Kepa how old his daughter was—she's sixteen—and he then asked Abaitua how old his own son was, he wasn't able to answer. Kepa quickly changed the subject, realizing that he'd put his foot in it. It felt as if they were both thinking, "around Lynn's age." Unfortunately, he can't forget her birthday.

THE WEATHER HAS TURNED by the time they reach Biarritz. There are large waves in the old port, and when they hit the seawall, they break into spray, falling like light rain. Kepa says that the grimy pier leading out to the Rocher de la Vierge had been an idea of Napoleon III's. Biarritz had its golden age and still retains some of that old splendor, but Abaitua thinks that Donostia was more beautiful back then and still is now. He realizes he's talking to himself and that Lynn and Kepa are a few paces behind him. They're looking downward as they walk, and the girl is talking. Abaitua doesn't want to know what they're talking about and continues walking.

They stop in front of the window at The Bookshop, a store near the Galeries Lafayette department store, also called the Dames de France. The girl has seen a book about Ravel and wants to buy it for Julia—he's one of her favorite musicians. Ravel, the one who composed Boléro and Concerto for the Left Hand. The other two go in, and Abaitua waits outside for them. On the cover of the book about Ravel, the composer is sitting on a rock on the seashore, looking straight at the camera. He looks to be a young man of around thirty, thin, agile, with sideburns that almost join up with his moustache. He's wearing a suit and a bow tie. His hands are resting on his knees, and there's an unlit cigarette in his left hand. But most striking are his white shoes, which stand out in contrast to the gray-black background, and his elegant black beret. He's very glad to then be able to tell her that Maurice Ravel was a countryman of theirs, from Ziburu, a Basque speaker. A yokel's satisfaction, a rather ridiculous sort of pride, but he's glad to have something to say.

Kepa's bought a bunch of books. He takes a wrapped-up book out of his full plastic bag and gives it to the girl as a souvenir—"*En souvenir,*" he says as he presents it. She is obviously excited to open it, but he stops her, saying she shouldn't look at it until she gets home. She thanks him with a kiss, and without having to stand on tiptoe to do so. She seems happier now. Very kind of you, and then she repeats her thanks in Basque—*Eskerrik asko*. Now they're getting in the way of the many people who are walking by, the three of them can no longer walk in line, and Abaitua, who's walking on the left-hand side, has to stop from time to time to let the people coming toward him go by, and on one occasion, getting stuck two or three steps behind the other two, he's tempted to let them go on, to see how long it will take them to realize that he's missing. Like a child. He knows it's what a little child would do.

When the two of them first met, Kepa already had a lot of gray hair, and he often used to wear it in a short ponytail. He still has a lot of hair, and it's still curly, but he has a bit less at the back of his neck, and it's much whiter. The girl adjusts her ponytail, and Kepa pulls it affectionately. Her hair looks darker in that light. They turn around and look at him. "*Oh, were losing our doctor,*" says the girl.

They cross another street. The cars let the pedestrians pass on the crosswalks, and there's no need to actively assert your right to cross the road. In Donostia, too, cars stop at crosswalks. Less so in Bilbao, and not at all in Gasteiz. He's seen that for himself, but he doesn't know why drivers behave in such different ways in cities across such a small area, unless, come to think of it, it's simply because of how far each of them is from France. He's also seen for himself that French people can be very poorly behaved when they leave their own country. *Terre conquise*—it's all conquered land for them. The girl, all of a sudden, and as if it were something she'd been thinking about for some time, says she doesn't know how to thank them for the wonderful trip they've taken her on, and Kepa replies that it's just a start to things, putting his hand on her back with what seems to Abaitua to be a very surprising degree of confidence, and then says that they're going to drink hot chocolate at the famous Dido café.

There aren't any tables free at Dido, and Kepa decides they should go to Miremont. Place Clemenceau. An old-fashioned tearoom in which the diligent waiters and waitresses move around discreetly and the floorboards, to their steps, make gentle noises. The customers drink their hot chocolate with measured movements, there are some old ladies in wide-brimmed hats with small dogs, and Kepa's voice is like a roll of thunder over the gentle murmuring and discreet clink of teaspoons. They're talking about music. Abaitua only knows classical music, maybe also a little jazz and blues, but only a very little. They mention names he's not familiar with, and so that the girl can have the chance to hear them, Kepa quietly sings a few songs in his deep voice, which, broken though it is, is quite pleasant. Abaitua, in order to remove himself from the situation, picks up the book about Ravel from the bag that Kepa's left on the free seat next to him. On the dedication page, it says, "*Voyez-vous, on parle de ma sécheresse de cœur. C'est faux. Et vous le savez, mais je suis basque et les Basques se livrent peu et à quelques-uns seulement.*" That explanation—"People are always talking about my having no heart. It's not true, and you know it. But I am Basque. The Basques feel deeply but seldom show it, and then only to a very few"—is a cliché, and like most clichés, it has some truth in it. There are a lot of photos in the book, and in most of them, the older Ravel we're all familiar with can be seen clean-shaven, without either a moustache or sideburns, and, as always, with a cigarette in one hand.

UN CHOCOLAT CHAUD, *recouvert de son exquise chantilly maison*— hot chocolate, covered in our exquisite house Chantilly. He says that this time, they have to let him have everything—whipped cream to top his hot chocolate, and some vanilla éclairs. The only thing he does not have is a *bolado*. The girl doesn't know what a *bolado* is, and Kepa explains that Alexandre Dumas discovered them in Tolosa in the nineteenth century and describes them in great detail in his book *De Paris à Cadix*. It was the first time he ever had them, and he thought they were very good, as good as the hot chocolate itself. On the other hand, he didn't like the place so much, and the waiter seemed rude to him. They look like big stones, Kepa says, they're made of sugar, and the sugar, of course—and Abaitua was previously unaware of this—is mixed with egg whites. As children, they used to like watching them dissolve in glasses of water. Abaitua doesn't want anything but the hot chocolate, and he tells Kepa that he, too, would be better off eating fewer sweet things. This tendency he has to cut people off is something he inherits from his mother. "Can it be good for you to eat so many sweet things?" she would have said to him in her soft voice. Kepa has thick elastic lips, they move a lot when he chews food, and it isn't the first time that Abaitua's thought they look a bit obscene.

Kepa, as if he hasn't heard Abaitua, says that they should show the girl the town of Donibane Lohizune and then stop in Ziburu to pay homage to Ravel and his Boléro; after all, countless people have used that particular piece of music to improve their sexual performance. He laughs again, his whole body shaking as he does.

Abaitua would like to be home already. More precisely, he'd like to be in bed, in the dark, not thinking about anything, after having gotten through the moment when Pilar will look at him inquisitively and he'll tell her that the trip was a success and throw in some anecdote or story he'll make up as he goes along. Even so, after the girl touches his hand with one finger—quickly, as if it were a fish—and says she doesn't know whether "our doctor" is in a hurry or not, he says that he isn't, that there's no hurry, although he says it without any conviction, without making any effort to sound convincing, even though behaving like that makes him feel mean, and the girl, obviously, doesn't believe him. After saying something in English that Abaitua doesn't understand, she takes her old coin purse out and waves the waiter over.

The two men try to stop her from paying by mentioning their joint fund, but she gets her way—they have to let her repay their generosity, even if only to that modest degree.

ON THE ROAD AGAIN. While Abaitua drives, the other two play games to keep themselves entertained. Kepa has to answer the battery of questions the sociologist asks him with only a yes or a no. She doesn't ask him how old he was or what year it was when he got married, just if he was young at the time. He says yes. Was he in love when he got married? The answer is yes. She knows that he's separated. In fact, it was practically the first thing he told her when they picked her up in Martutene.

Abaitua concentrates on driving. He works out that if they stop in Ziburu, he won't be home by ten o'clock.

When she asks him if he wanted to marry a woman who was Basque—ethnically Basque, she specifies—he says yes, which is something that surprises Abaitua. Really, he wouldn't know what to say if he were asked the same question. And in any case, he would find it very difficult to keep his answer to a simple yes or no. He doesn't think the ethnic question would have been a conscious condition or obstacle for him, but he would probably have preferred a Basque speaker, if only for practical reasons. He's had relationships with women who weren't Basque speakers, for example with Bárbara, the Port-Royal pharmacist, but it never crossed his mind that he might ever have a child with her. To an extent because although she met the conditions to be his ideal woman—she was educated and very beautiful, had blue eyes, a long neck, long soft blonde hair, she was elegant, affectionate, and sweet—their relationship ended when his residence ended. When it was time for him to go home. He's thought more than once that if she'd been Basque, they would have returned home together and their relationship would have continued its course, which is what happened later with Pilar. But it never occurred to him back then. Just as it never did with any others back then, because of the circumstances, because it wasn't the right moment. And although his parents wouldn't have been happy to see him going steady with a girl from another culture—he's not sure to what extent the ethnic factor would have counted there—they wouldn't have had any difficulty accepting her, above all if the girl showed signs of wanting to integrate, especially if that included learning Basque. Racism? It seems too extreme a word to him. What's more, as someone once told him, Basques can't be racists, because they aren't a race—they're a species.

RUE GAMBETTA. SAINT-JEAN-DE-LUZ. Tourists from Paris enjoying the light, the happiness, and the picturesqueness of the south. Tourists from Madrid enjoying the discreet, elegant picturesqueness of the north. Different colored berets, different colored espadrilles, tablecloths with white, red, blue, and green stripes, oxen yoked together in pairs. Macaroons from Maison Adam, *muxus* from Pariès. Iguzkia, Txiberta, Maïtia, Hegoa. The girl says, "*It's beautiful, really beautiful.*" Some children in the Place Louis XIV are wearing traditional clothes and singing "*Urso luma gris gaxua.*" Specks of rain. They wait stoically in the damp until the children finish their song about the poor little gray-feathered pigeon.

They only have to go over the bridge to get to Ziburu. Abaitua mentions that it's difficult to park, trying to scupper the plan they've made to stand in front of the house Ravel was born in and hum the Boléro there in tribute. The rain helps him. Kepa asks him to at least drive past it as slowly as possible. The house is made of stone, it's noble looking, like the ones bordering the canal in Amsterdam.

There are gaps on the top floor on both sides of the balcony, to be able to stick canons out. According to Kepa.

They soon reach Sokoa. Its beach and the remains of its fort, the round tower—a good place for shooting a pirate film. The girl says "*it's really nice*" again, and Abaitua's afraid Kepa might suggest having dinner at one of the little restaurants where the tablecloths are made of those striped fabrics they sell on the Rue Gambetta. There's a backup on the road, some campervan that's broken down, and they have to wait. On the beach, in the middle of the sand, there's a completely circular restaurant with a tall mast, on which a Basque flag is shaking in the wind. They've eaten some memorable *paellas* there, just as if they were tourists from Paris. Kepa also remembers them, "We sure have had some good *paellas* there." Back then, although it was some time ago, they were as good as the *paellas* from Valencia. They've put away their share of Sauterne there, too, the white wine that Pilar likes, though Abaitua did use to put a limit to how much they could spend on wine. For his own personal preference, out of a sense of moderation, and also because Edurne, Kepa's wife, didn't drink and hated seeing money being spent on expensive wine and not at the Dames or the Biarritz Bonheur department stores. She didn't like the sun or the beach, either, being afraid of burning her white skin, and after lunch, at siesta time, she used to lecture on and on to them about the dangers of ultraviolet rays and the polluted sand; she wouldn't leave them alone, until finally Pilar would say, "Let's leave these two here looking at tits and go and see some shops," doing them the favor of getting her off their backs.

It seems to have stopped raining. Kepa gets out to see what's happening on the road and smoke a cigarette. The girl goes with him.

Abaitua has another memory from further back in the past. It's a memory of disappointment and sadness in the outdoor dining area of the very same restaurant, a scene that unfolded next to the mast that the Basque flag is flying from right now. There's a man in the scene, he's well dressed—either a suit or an overcoat, he'd say—and he's telling some boys and girls where to stand for the photo he's preparing to take of them. The man's extremely excited. Abaitua's not sure what language he's speaking in, Spanish or Basque, but he's clearly come up from the south and hasn't seen a Basque flag for a long time. At the same time, there's a group of waitresses looking on, as young Abaitua is also doing. They're wearing black uniforms and white aprons and they're nudging each other, playing around, laughing, mocking what they see as the incomprehensible excitement of the man from the south. Abaitua doesn't know what he was doing there at that beachside restaurant, but he doesn't think it had anything to do with the man. He knows he felt sad that those women—or perhaps they were young girls—who were Basque, as well, just like the man and himself, didn't understand the man's excitement and were mocking him; Abaitua, though, did understand him, he'd even drawn a bunch of *ikurriñas*, Basque flags, which were still illegal at that time, on the inside covers of several of his books. He knew that such demonstrations of patriotism could be severely punished, but he wasn't prepared to see them being made fun of, and still less so by fellow Basques (his father used to say that the people on the other side of the border weren't French, that they, too, were Basques).

He believed his father, despite what his teachers at school and the textbooks said, when he told him that Franco was a murderer and was oppressing the people, and that the language that they used at home, which almost nobody in the whole neighborhood spoke apart from the milkman when he came with his donkey, was the oldest and the cleanest of all languages, the language spoken on both sides of the border, because all Basques were brothers and sisters. But that scene left a mark on him that had never gone away. Since then, painful, sad reality had prevailed over his father's wish not to see what he didn't want to. He has another memory connected with the flag that is also highly significant. He's drawing cyclists, probably the multicolored snake of them all on the Tour de France. In this case, he can in fact figure out how old he was at the time, because it's always possible to work it out with the Tour—that year, the Spanish team wore a gray top, which wasn't typical, and it had a thin Spanish flag going all the way around the chest. At the time, cyclists used to wear their nations' flags on their tops, and children would draw them that way. Young Abaitua knows his flags. He draws French, Italian, and Swiss cyclists but doesn't know whether to draw Spanish ones or not, because he would have to draw the Spanish flag for them. The boy has his doubts. The reality is that Spaniards do take part in the Tour, and so do some Basques, such as Loroño, and obliged by their circumstances, they, too, have to have the Spanish flag on their tops.

So he decides to reflect the reality he sees in photos in the newspaper and on the roads from time to time, as well, even if he doesn't like it. And that's what he's doing when his father comes up to him. He puts a hand on the shoulder of the boy, who then feels his father's thick beard up against his cheek. The father says nothing, but the son knows he doesn't like what he's seen, and he regrets that. His father takes his pencil and colors over all the Spanish flags on the cyclists' tops. He makes no sign of reproach, he makes the correction gently, not at all like the way he corrects his mistakes in arithmetic, and the child, though convinced he's in the right, does not dare to defend his decision, because he's so upset at having hurt his father by making him look at things he didn't want to see.

They've hardly spoken since leaving Ziburu, probably checked by the thought that they're about to say goodbye to each other. Kepa's breathing is deep once again, as if he were about to fall asleep once more, and the girl rests her head on the window, looking out onto the sea. Abaitua can't think of anything to say, and he doesn't think it appropriate to turn on the radio or play music.

A SPORTS FIELD lit up brightly in the middle of the darkness reminds him of pictures of the Bronx. Dirty areas, the shame of the city. It seems Abaitua isn't the only one who wants to get through the area as quickly as possible; the traffic speeds up where the different roads join up and go into the tunnel together. The Intxaurrondo barracks with their sinister mist. First he'll drop the girl off in Martutene. The beltway there's quicker, but above all it's because he doesn't want to be left alone with her.

It's a sad goodbye. Kepa is serious but also affectionate. When he kisses her goodbye, he puts his arms around her. Now it's his turn. The two of them kiss each other on the cheeks, and he smells her scent. A slightly acidic perfume, there's some lemon in it. He and Kepa wait by the car while she jogs across the yard, to not make them wait too long, he thinks. There's a light on over the door, and in a window on the second floor. She turns around at the top of the stairs and waves to them. A nice girl, Kepa says.

AFTER PUTTING THE KEY into the lock, he waits before turning it. On the one hand, he'd like for Pilar to have already gone to bed, in order to avoid her inquisitive look; on the other, he'd be glad to get that step over with as soon as possible. There's light in the living room, and the television's on. Pilar's sitting on the sofa with the newspaper spread out on the coffee table, she's leaning over it in her usual position. Did he have a good time? He says it wasn't bad. They went all the way up to Bordeaux, because Kepa wanted to get a book all of a sudden. Tell the truth as far as possible, that's the strategy. His wife, though, takes a quick glance at him, and he doesn't know how to interpret it. "Bordeaux?" Her tone suggests she's a little surprised, or curious. He supposes she's wondering what two men on their own could be doing in Bordeaux. But it's too late to put it right. He says he's tired. They've been eating and drinking nonstop. You know what Kepa's like. It's the second time he's said that. He tries to remember something he might be able to tell her. She's normally interested in knowing where and what they've eaten, but he can only remember the waitress laughing at Kepa's silly comments about the aphrodisiac properties of chocolate. He thinks it could be amusing to say that as they get older, waitresses treat them better and better, but he changes subject to avoid the possible risks there. They'd been thinking about going to Blaye, but in the end they didn't. They both like Blaye, and the restaurant in the castle with its spectacular views of Gironde.

"And what about you, what have you been doing?"

He can't avoid asking the question, even though he knows it will mean having to face up to her reproachful look. The answer in the way she looks at him is, "And what do you think I've been doing?" He, too, can tell what she's thinking. Pilar looks back at the newspaper and starts turning the pages sharply, almost hitting them, noisily, as she usually does when she's nervous, and it drives him up the wall. Finally she says that she spent Friday and Saturday putting some papers in order and Sunday with her father. She lifts her eyes once more on finishing the sentence. This time she holds his gaze, wanting to see how he reacts to hearing that she's wasted another weekend. Abaitua, too, takes his time examining her expression of bitterness, unable to avoid seeing that her cheeks droop downward to either side of her mouth, until he realizes that she's seen what he's thinking. He imagines she's thinking, "See my wrinkled mouth, my bitterness—it's your doing."

They spend some time sitting there in silence, watching the television with the sound turned off. There's a commercial on. Pilar

293

changes channels two or three times, but there are commercials on all of them.

She says she's spoken with Loiola, he says he'll come by and see them soon. Abaitua thinks their son is avoiding them, avoiding the atmosphere of tedium and sadness in their house. As with so many things, they don't talk about it, but he knows that Pilar, too, has that sensation.

He went through the same thing as a child. He liked having people come to visit. When they did, his parents, above all his father, were able to control their irascibility, there would be a better atmosphere in the house—at least apparently—so that their visitors wouldn't notice their usual malaise. Thinking about that doesn't make him especially sad. He says, maybe for the second or third time, that he's very tired and is going to bed.

She says she's going to bed soon, too.

He turns the light out right away. He thinks about Lynn. How she said "*bihotzean min dut*" when he opened the door. He'd taken her by the hand and led her to the bed. What else could he have done? He remembers how he followed her lead and, playing off her "*doctor, I'm not feeling well*," said, "Let's see what we have here." Not much more than that. What's more, Pilar's left the living room, and although it's improbable, almost impossible, that she'll come into his room, the mere thought of it makes him nervous. She normally walks past his room to leave something in the ironing room or to go to the bathroom they both use, which means going down the long narrow hallway. Often, like now, she walks around with an electric toothbrush stuck in her mouth as she does the final chores before going to bed—lowering the blinds, putting a pot or two in the dishwasher—and he hears the sound of the brush's engine as she walks up and down, and that always makes him slightly uneasy.

He knows that she got undressed without any particular ceremony, as people do when they're alone and preparing to hop into bed or the bath. He remembers seeing her sitting on the edge of his bed, and himself wondering whether he should take his pajamas off before hugging her. Her skin was bluish in the moonlight. He was surprised that her breasts were larger than he had thought. She laughed when he dared to kiss her feet, because she found it ticklish. That's what he remembers. And he regrets not having been more patient. The girl put a hand on his chest and said, "*Just relax,*" and he wasn't able to keep his desire in check, and that kept him from committing to memory the details he needed now to be able to relive the moment. So he goes back a bit, to the moment when she first scratched at his door.

In *Montauk*, the writer says that each time you're with a woman for the first time, it's always your very first time again. *"Toute première fois avec une femme est de nouveau la première fois."* He also remembers what Bárbara used to sing about being able to open your arms a hundred times to someone and always have it feel like the first time: *"Tu peux m'ouvrir cent fois les bras, c'est toujours la première fois."*

NEVERMORE. There won't be a second time. There are very few women he's only made love with once. One of them is now a good friend of his. An old friend with whom he does not mention the chapter they turned the page on. What would be the point? Problems always arise on the second occasion. He doesn't want that to happen with Lynn. He doesn't regret anything, but he promises himself that when he sees her at the hospital, he will behave normally with her, as if nothing's happened between them. In reality, nothing has happened, he tells himself. Lynn is an open, uninhibited American girl who's willing to have experiences, and he's a man who's still in his prime. As the Spanish say, *quien tuvo retuvo*—he's still got it. It's true. The thought makes him feel good.

9

It's around nine o'clock. Julia doesn't need to look at her watch to know that, because the Romanians are already on the platform with their shopping trolleys and their sticks for poking around in the trash cans. The train they're waiting on is the same one that the Catholic schoolgirls arrive on, wearing their ugly green uniform sweaters and pleated maroon skirts, when classes are in session. There aren't many people waiting, mostly elderly individuals with very few obligations just trying to squeeze the most out of their public transportation passes—they won't mind too much if they miss the 8:47.

Finally, when the convent bells ring out nine o'clock with their tinny sound, the writer says, "The girl upstairs must have really tired herself out up in the mountains." He says it with some irony, but his irony doesn't cover up the fact that he's not entirely pleased. He got up early today, and it's the third or fourth time he's mentioned that the American girl hasn't come down yet. Then, heading toward the stairs, he makes that gesture of his, patting his pants, hips, and buttocks with both hands as if he were looking for something, which normally turns out to be right in front of his nose, whether it's his wallet or the coffee pot. Julia realizes he's bandaged up one of his hands completely, presumably so that when his tenant asks him what happened to him, he'll be able to say that her cat scratched him. In fact, the cat had been meowing on the roof, and thinking it wanted to come down, he—the cat-rescuer who's never even touched a cat before in his life—put a hand out to it from the tower window, and the animal, scared, clawed him. The scratch was just a surface wound, and Julia thinks it probably didn't even draw blood, but she resists the temptation to tell him that the bandage is much bigger than the wound. She asks him what he's lost, even though she already knows that searching around in his pockets like that is no more than an excuse to go upstairs. Going up and down the stairs is all he's done for the last half hour. "A piece of paper," he says—it's almost always a piece of paper that he's lost— and he goes toward the stairs once more, but when he puts one foot on the first step, the girl's feet can be heard upstairs, and he rushes back to sit in his chair, like a pupil who doesn't want to be caught away from his place.

"*Hi.*" They give each other two kisses, something they don't always do. Julia's truly glad to see the girl, she's eager to hear about her weekend, how it was, where she went, what she saw; she's more curious than usual. "*Hi.*" Her cheeks are cold, and she's changed perfumes. The one she's wearing now is sweeter. "You're wearing a new perfume," but what she doesn't dare to tell her is that just for a moment, as she passed in front of the window when she was coming down, with the magnolias and hydrangeas behind her and the glow from her copper-colored hair, she looked like a Pre-Raphaelite model. She's very beautiful in her flowery dress; the blooms are large and leafy, mostly green and yellow. And upon hearing this praise, the girl takes ahold of one edge of the dress, stretches it open, and lets it fall. The cloth is thin, like muslin, it falls gently. It was a gift. She turns around and makes it float in the air, her arms held up like a dancer. "*Isn't it wonderful?*"

The girl is glad to see them, as well, you can see it in her face. She says she has the feeling she's been away for a long time. She's brought them gifts. Three bottles of a wine she's been told will be very good to drink the next time they have beans; a *gâteau basque* from Dodin, also for them all to share; a book about Ravel, and *Montauk* in French, both for Julia; and a poster of the first page of the manuscript of *Madame Bovary* and Frisch's *Récit I et II* for Martin. On receiving his gifts, Martin shows her his bandaged hand, and she asks what happened to him. "Just a little accident," he answers with a pitiful smile but unable to hide a glint of satisfaction in his eyes. As if trying to make light of it, he tells her it happened when he was trying to save her cat from danger—it was stuck up on the roof. Julia's ashamed to listen to him. He tries to calm the girl down, saying that it's probably nothing, but then he shamelessly goes on to say that the doctor's recommended he get an anti-rabies shot.

Julia is pleased with her gifts. It's not hard for her to find the paragraph in *Montauk* beginning "CHECK OUT: *Car que faire après le petit déjeuner? Se promener avec un parapluie? On pourrait rester assis dans la loggia et regarder la pluie tomber sur la mer . . . Puis il s'irrite de ce que Lynn, étant donné qu'elle s'est occupée de la réservation, sache à peu près ce qu'il est en train de payer pour deux nuits. Elle est déjà assise dans la voiture. Il paie presque le double de son salaire hebdomadaire : l'argent de l'homme, qui dans le contexte marital devient si naturel . . . .*"

As for the "*velluda y blanca chaqueta*," the shaggy white jacket is a "*veste blanche à poils*" in French. The young tenant guesses what part she's reading and says in a low voice, but with her eyes wide open and her index finger held upward, "*You should translate it.*" She looks like a strict teacher giving a pupil work to do, so Julia happily answers, "*Yes, teacher,*" because she thinks she's up to it, although, of course, the girl has no way of knowing that. The writer, on the other hand, says nothing. Julia figures it's because he's jealous of the way they understand each other, and she finds that funny.

She didn't recognize Ravel at first sight, but there he is, with his piercing eyes. He must be around thirty in the photo. He looks handsome, the moustache and sideburns make him look a little arrogant, he's as elegant as ever, wearing a suit typical of the period—a short, wide jacket and tight pants—and pointed white shoes, probably made of canvas. He's wearing a bow tie and a beret that look great on him. Cosmopolitan Ravel with his Basque beret on. You want to know if I love the Basque Country—"*Si j'aime le Pays Basque?*"—he once said. "*C'est-à-dire que je n'aime vraiment que le Pays Basque, mais je voyage beaucoup et j'essaie d'être Russe en Russie, Espagnol en Espagne et Chinois en Chine,*" he'd gone on—the Basque Country is the only thing I really do love, but I travel a lot, and when I go to Russia, I try to be Russian, and Spanish in Spain, and Chinese in China. Julia hadn't heard of the book and can't wait to read it. (Above all because she was very disappointed by Echenoz's fictionalized biography in which the musician is portrayed as being stingy with money and unlikable in general, only really interested in his clothes.) Perhaps it's because the writer thinks her gratitude for the gifts she's received is over the top, but it's clear he's not well pleased. She thinks it could also be because, among other things, he already has two of Frisch's diaries. In any case, seeing him there with his arms folded and the two volumes sitting in front of him—to make it clear he has no intention of opening them—she suddenly thinks he's like a spoilt, envious child glaring at everybody else's presents. It seems the girl, too, has thought something like that. She asks him if he already has them, he disappointedly confirms it with a nod, and she says she's sorry and adds that because she bought them in Bordeaux, she can't exchange them, to which the writer, quite astonished, almost shouts, "In Bordeaux?!" He thought she was going to the mountains. Like a suspicious lover? Or like a father worried because he doesn't know what his daughter's been up to? Julia is about to tell her there's no reason she should tell the silly man anything at all, when she starts explaining that they were planning on going to the mountains but had to change their plans because bad weather had been forecast.

They spent the first night in Ainhoa. She liked the village a lot, it was so neat and tidy, so pretty, it seemed like something out of a fairy tale to her. "*Fuimos . . . estuvimos . . . vimos . . .*" She can't stop using the first person plural, perhaps because she's talking about more than two people. We had dinner and spent the night at a small hotel.

ARGI EDER. Julia and Martin spent three days in that hotel seven years ago, during the period of time he refers to as "her infidelity," the crazy days following his discovery that she'd been in another relationship. "When you got together with that young poet" is something he also says. Remembering that turbulent phase is a nightmare. Martin hadn't been paying her any attention, and so she felt free, until finally someone she met at a writing workshop and had hit it off with realized that she felt alone and managed to get her to accept his continual requests. She liked the young man, he wasn't very complicated, was even a bit simple, and to tell the truth, they enjoyed spending the afternoons together, talking about any old thing and listening to Leonard Cohen songs. She didn't feel that she was being disloyal, because she didn't feel loved. It could have become a fond memory, but he, the cuckolded writer, tried hard for that not to happen, and he hated the other poor guy, because he was part of the nightmare, like Argi Eder, which is where they took shelter after her "infidelity" was uncovered, in the hopes of starting a new phase in their relationship.

Suddenly the writer seems more cheerful. He says that it was at Argi Eder that he wrote *Beroki gorria jantzita ohe ertzean jesarria dagoen emakumea*. "The Woman in the Red Jacket Sitting on the Edge of the Bed"—do you remember?" he says with a false smile. Julia usually tries to avoid any word at all that might remind him of all that, in order not to give him any excuse for continuing to punish her, or himself, with those memories. She still avoids words that could be interpreted as having even a very distant connection with that short tryst, so that the writer cannot latch onto them as an excuse to recall that day he cried aloud so bitterly. She was really moved by his pain. He was incredibly distraught when he heard about the relationship she was having with the younger man, and Julia, in her innocence, believed it was no more than frustrated anger at her clumsy betrayal of their love, when in fact it was simply anger at someone daring to use something that he considered to be his own. Although it didn't take her long to realize that, it was too late by the time she did. She agreed, dazzled by his manic rage, to start a new phase in their relationship, a phase in which there would be no secrets, and she innocently answered the questions he maliciously asked her, convinced that he had a right to know and without realizing just how much he despised her. He wrote nonstop, as if possessed, for two nights and two days—except for the time he spent having wild sex with her, which was something that caught her completely off guard, and with an intensity that he had never shown before and never has since—until he filled the lined composition book he'd bought at a stationery store in Ainhoa. He gave it to her to read. What he'd written was moving, and at the same time desolating. She realized too late that he was going to make her suffer, punish her terribly, and in a display of weakness, she asked him to destroy the notebook. If that was what she wanted, she should destroy it herself, he told her.

"Do you remember?"

She brusquely tells him to stop fooling around. She's not worried what the young American might think. She's learned that she mustn't give him any openings when it comes to this issue. A simple no. She will not accept his digging up the memory of what happened back then even in jokes, because she knows, even though years have passed since then, that he'll take advantage of it to punish her. And to torture himself, as well. She remembers him crying, shouting that she was a whore, walking continually from one side of the room to the other while she sat there on the edge of the bed with her red jacket still on, wishing she were dead. She felt like a whore.

The girl seems lost, she doesn't know whether to continue telling them about the trip or not, and Julia asks her to go on. She liked Bordeaux. A lot. She says it's a very beautiful city and she had a great time eating, drinking, and walking through the streets there, maybe too good a time, she says, moving her hips from side to side comically; it reminded her of Paris. But what she was really impressed by was "the other side"—the green hills, and the villages of white houses with red peppers hanging on the balconies to dry, the *pilota* courts, and the churches. She speaks with enthusiasm, mixing Spanish and English, as she always does when she's excited. She talks about the beautiful Basque they speak there (she knows how to say *iguzkia, maithia,* and *atherbia*—sun, dear, and inn), and the charm of Ainhoa, Sara, Azkaine, and Donibane Lohizune. Saint-Jean-de-Luz: "*She had the chance to see her happy in the sun and melancholic under the rain.*" It's no wonder Borrow, Humboldt, and so many other Romantics fell in love with those special places.

Until the writer suddenly stops her enthusiastic list by saying that she sounds like someone from the Syndicat d'Initiatives—the tourist bureau. He wants to tell her that he was only joking, but the girl picks up on his disdain and looks at Julia for her protection. The poor girl doesn't know that the sensitive writer feels put out by hearing that she's had a good time—"Maybe too good a time," and moving her hips around, what's more—and even more put out at hearing her call the French Basque Country "the other side" and linking Bonaparte with Azkaine, Abbadia with Hendaia, and Unamumo with Biriatu—the latter being information that hints at the fact that her guide for the weekend is someone who knows about Basque culture in the area, is an educated person, and is of a certain age, among other things because they went for hot chocolate at Miremont—and now he lays into whoever the man is, really angry now, saying that the picturesque things they've seen are all made-up traditions for Parisian tourists, and he attacks this man from his own cultural background who took the young American girl along the Corniche and who, he thinks, maybe shared more than hot chocolate in Biarritz with her, maybe even a bed in Argi Eder. He rails against the unknown man who used the same tricks he would have, who did and said exactly the same things he would have if he could've.

Sometimes, against her will, Julia finds it moving when Martin behaves, as he's doing now, like a spoilt, capricious child. The girl suggests they play Ping-Pong, as if she had to make it up to him somehow for having gone on a trip without him, and he turns her down. The girl, too, realizes that she's talking to a child with a hurt sense of pride, and it doesn't take her long to win him over by asking sweetly, "Are you angry?" So they go to the library to play. Neither of them are skillful players, it turns out; what Julia hears mostly is the sound of the ball bouncing off the floor.

When Ping-Pong is mentioned in *Montauk*, Lynn is a good player but doesn't know how to smash the ball home, which is what Max does to win. Julia decides that because the sound of the ball makes her nervous and distracts her from working, she'd better go to the library, as well, and just watch them play, but they've finished their game by the time she gets to the hallway. It seems Martin has won. A sweaty Martin is showing the unruffled loser a portrait of his father. His father was a good-looking boy, he's wearing a beret and a woolen jacket, and the portrait is by the great painter Olasagasti, to whom Celaya dedicated those two verses of his: "*Es terrible Jesús, no nos dejan ser niños*"—Lord Jesus, it's terrible, they won't let us be children. The girl says the boy's eyes are clear and tender at the same time, and they are. There aren't many books worth showing her, even though some of them have luxury covers. One exception: A first edition of *Biotz-begietan*, signed by Lizardi himself, and a volume of Diderot and D'Alembert's *Encyclopédie*, with notes by Altuna—Rousseau's friend from Azkoitia—which Martin values highly, he says. He always shows off that engraving depicting a gentleman seated with a woman on either side of him, both of them holding his penis, from the Bécquer brothers' book whose title, *Irurac-bat*, meaning "Three in One", is also the motto of the Royal Basque Society of Friends of the Country; and also a book of nineteenth-century illustrations with scenes of peaceful-looking bourgeois living rooms that have little flaps you can open up to reveal beautiful young girls and licentious old men involved in spicy, obscene activities. That's what Martin is showing the young girl, and Julia is unnerved by the sight of the two of them leaning over the book and opening the paper doors to look at the bawdy scenes in the illustrations, above all because, without having planned it this way, the little window where she's standing at the end of the hallway—a window whose purpose is entirely unclear to her—allows her to see them without them being able to see her, and so she is momentarily struck by the scene that the three of them are forming right then—a horny old writer showing a young girl dirty scenes while his longtime partner looks on at them from a small window in the hallway, a picture of voyeurism just like the ones in the book. At first she wants to make them aware of her presence by coughing, but, fortunately, she decides not to, and she moves away from the window and back into the living room on tiptoes.

Some years earlier, Martin told her something that happened to him in that library when he was an adolescent, and she recalls it now. She thinks it's rather terrible, although depending on how you look at it, it could also be taken as comic. The small window is something like an old-fashioned ticket office window, and there's a wooden sash blind that closes it from the library side. It's usually closed, except when, as now, it's been opened in order to show someone around the room. Because there are wooden shelves on both sides, you might think it was designed for returning books to a hypothetical librarian, or for her to give them over to you, which could, in turn, lead you to deduce that Martin's grandfather acquired the furnishings from some large library somewhere. What they do know is that he used to take his siestas on the leather couch that's still sitting underneath the window, and that a cup of tea was always waiting for him on the shelf when he woke up from his doze. Apparently, Martin got into the habit of spending time in the library, which his mother put up with but not without keeping an eye on the situation, sometimes going in when he wasn't expecting her in order to see whether he was studying or just wasting his time with the novels of Blasco Ibáñez, Valera, Ricardo León, and so on that he always had near, and when he heard the door opening, he would quickly hide under the table. On one occasion, when he thought his mother was not at home, he came across that book with the illustrations on a shelf and found the pictures very exciting, to such an extent that he was unable to resist the temptation to lie down on his grandfather's divan and masturbate. He was doing just that, apparently, when he heard his mother shouting, asking what was he doing, and then saw her stick her head through the window. Julia doesn't understand how Martin could have answered here, he who was so careful and secretive about his private world, especially when it came to physiological matters. It must have been incredibly embarrassing for him. She often feels sorry for Martin the child, the victim of such a terrifying mother, when he tells her stories like that. She's often asked herself how she would feel if she came across Zigor masturbating, but she's sure that, unlike Martin's mother, she would retire, in the same way she just has, without saying a word.

The girl asks if she's bothering her. The writer's had to go upstairs to change shirts, and the girl, who's perfectly composed, not sweating at all, has sat down on the edge of Julia's work table. She asks about her translation of *Bihotzean min dut*, and Julia has to admit that she's not making any progress. She's at the part where the student hands the teacher her essay on Lizardi and he says "the terrorists are the only ones to blame." Now it reads like an attempt to lessen the responsibility of those who, without participating in the murder directly, helped the killers by keeping quiet themselves. And so she, in translating, has to silence her own voice. She'd rather write about what she's translating than translate it. She'd like to write the story of what happened to her and people like her. The terrible admission that some people make nowadays—that they turned a blind eye—makes her profoundly uneasy. She'd like to know how such a thing could happen, if it really is what happened, and she thinks she'll never be able to know unless she writes about it.

Has she really just said that she wants to write? It makes her laugh.

WHY NOT?

HARRI DOESN'T LOOK BAD, and she's very elegantly dressed in gray. A jacket, a tube skirt, and a low-cut blouse, and when the American girl says she couldn't look more elegant if she tried, she juts her hip out to the side like a model, one hand on her hip and the other in the air, her green briefcase dangling from it, a very similar gesture to the one the girl made just a few moments ago when she said she had "a good time—maybe too good a time." Martin says that they're going back the nineteenth century when it comes to necklines and that she doesn't have all that much to show off anyhow. But she doesn't seem to care. When she gets her breasts remodeled after her cancer, she's going to get huge ones. They find this morbid attitude distasteful. Julia says she'd be better off getting an appointment with a doctor rather than saying stupid things like that.

Harri replies that she wants to find the man from the airport first. As always, she starts making jokes to avoid the serious issue. Even if looking for him by placing that personal ad doesn't work, she won't mind—quite the opposite, she almost prefers it not to work, because that would mean he doesn't spend his time reading that particular section of the paper, which is really for crazies anyway. She tells them she has a plan to actively search for him, but she gives no details. The others don't ask her for any, either. Furthermore, when she realizes that the American girl has a packet with a large red ribbon around it in her hand—"*Here's a little souvenir for you*," she says to her—she remembers about her trip and, taking her hand, makes her sit down on the sofa by her side and tell her everything, without leaving anything out.

The present for Harri is a crystal ball, inside of which snow is falling down on the red roofs of the little houses in Ainhoa, and Julia envies the young American's ability to show—in such a simple, uncomplicated way—that she's thought of everybody. The snow globe, which she thinks looks cute in Harri's hand, would have been corny and inconsequential if she, Julia, had given it to her.

SNOW IN AINHOA. It's said that Basque shepherds used to have several different words for snow depending on the size and consistency of the flakes. Martin replies that shepherds all over the world do, the word *snow* by itself not being descriptive enough, but the girl doesn't seem very interested. "*Elur*," she says pensively, repeating the Basque word for snow. Then she tells them about the sensation she has when she hears certain words such as *su*, *ur*, and *lur*—fire, water, and earth—which were the same words used many thousands of years ago. Primitive words. She looks at them, smiling, but they don't say anything. Julia's moved, that's the only way to put it.

She also knows that *haitz*, *aizto*, *azkon*, and *aizkora*—rock, knife, lance, and axe—have the same root. Peculiarities that natives tell visitors to demonstrate that their culture is of value. A language that has no Cervantes or Shakespeare but is so old that it was spoken in the Paleolithic Period, when people had only stones to put around them, and that's why they chose *stone* as their key word. Julia can't help feeling a liking for the man who told her those things, and she feels sorry when she sees the girl dismayed by the writer's loud laughter at her as he tells her that it's all a bunch of absurd speculation—why shouldn't *harri*, which also means stone, be the root instead of *haitz*? And he mentions the contemporary Basque linguist Lakarra, and others. Julia thinks the poor girl's about to cry. But she stands up to the myth-shattering writer, firm, although with a slight tremor in the back of her neck, and what Julia finds moving now is how loyal she is to the man who told her these peculiarities about their national language. She says that the most scholarly textbooks on prehistorical anthropology are full of far less substantiated theories. What's more, the most interesting thing about Basque is what a fertile language it is for speculation and fantasy. It isn't possible to have such far-reaching dreams about Spanish or English. The girl smiles again. It's obvious she would rather avoid the debate that the myth-destroying writer would like to carry on with. He says she doesn't know how short-lived dreams can be. Dreams become nightmares. And so on and so on. Until Harri tells him that's enough, stop talking.

Julia makes tea to go with the *gâteau basque*, and she asks the girl to serve it. The milk first. At Harri's request, she tells them about her trip again, where they spent the two nights, the towns they visited, what she thinks of Bordeaux. This second time it's even more apparent that she doesn't want to say who she went with, it's obvious that having to refer to her friends indirectly makes it more difficult for her, and it's impossible not to deduce that it must be someone they know, and finally, worn down by Harri, she implicitly admits it, and that only increases their curiosity.

Someone from the hospital? The girl laughs and says she isn't going to give any more clues.

But when she serves the *gâteau basque*—which the hurt writer refuses to taste—she goes and talks about the cake and its ingredients, saying that the cherry filling is inauthentic, the original cake was made with sweetcorn flour and pork fat, and this, unwittingly, gives the myth-destroying writer the opportunity to go on talking about the invented traditions that are built up to satisfy tourists in the north and nationalist sentiment in the south. None of the things that are sold as being Basque—*béret, maison, linge, gâteau,* and so on—are at all Basque. Does she really think that they ever made anything like this—he points at the cake from Dodin—in the *baserris* around Ainhoa?

"Tell her, tell her how you used to eat dessert at Etxezar."

Julia once told him that at her mother's *baserri,* after eating their daily portion of black beans, they used to clean their plates with bread, turn them upside down, and eat their daily baked apple on the underside. It must have impressed him greatly, because he's asked her to tell people about it more than once, or told them about it himself while chatting after a meal, thinking it could be a curious peculiarity as far as the other people at the table are concerned, in the same way that he thinks it worth mentioning that the plates and cups they're using are the remains of a large crockery set that used to belong to the wife, mother, or daughter of a Carlist general, or to all three of them. Julia feels more humiliated than embarrassed that something that's so natural for her is so strange or comical for him; she doesn't like it, even if his intentions are good, and in fact she doesn't think he means any harm. In any case, she dislikes having to talk about the intimate kitchen details of Etxezar whenever he wants to entertain someone. She also thinks it goes against the family's dignity, although she worries that she may have this idea because she's reserved and untrusting, and she wouldn't like to keep quiet out of embarrassment. So she tells them about it against her will, to avoid problems, and because otherwise, he himself will tell them about it. Every day, her grandmother used to bring out and put on the table a dish of beans—which are now so highly thought of—and another of cabbage with pork fat and pork ribs, and on holidays, there would be white beans or garbanzos instead of black beans. She knows from her mother that in some *baserris,* everyone used to dip their spoons into the pot without using plates and pass the wine from hand to hand to everybody, everybody except the farmhand. Not at Etxezar. But she only tells them what Martin wants to hear: after eating the beans, cabbage, and pork, they used to turn their dishes over when it came time to serve dessert, and dessert was never anything like the *gâteau basque* from Dodin, it was always a baked apple.

But what great baked apples they were. Harri seems to want to praise the cooking at Etxezar when she talks about the excellence of Errezil apples. Julia is glad that he then praises her recipe for apple pie, because she knows he means it. Martin agrees it's the best dessert he's ever eaten, and he included the recipe in one of his Faustino Iturbe episodes. At the same time, the recipe couldn't be simpler: apples, sugar, the pulp of a lemon, half its rind, and pieces of ladyfinger sponge cake. But the apples have to be Errezil apples, because of their wonderful flavor, and so that the dough comes out with the right texture without having to add any sugar.

All of a sudden, the young American lifts her hands up toward the ceiling and laughs. "Oh, your exquisite, your delicious, your unique Errezil apples!"

So she's heard about Errezil apples. She's even been told about Flora Ugalde's recipe. But who exactly did this girl spend the weekend with?

The poor thing must realize that the silence that falls after her ironic words is a question that requires an answer—she blushes up to her ears. A freight train going by gives her a brief respite, but after that, she has no choice but to say something about Flora Ugalde's wonderful apple pie recipe, and embarrassedly turning to Martin, she admits it was a friend of his who told her about it. Harri and Julia also turn toward Martin, as though they think he will be able to solve the mystery, and he holds both hands up to point at the middle of his chest and, amazed, almost frightened, says, "A friend of mine?" The girl nods. "Yes, Kepa," she says. Laughing from ear to ear, as if saying the name of her friend on the trip were a relief, and Martin incredulously repeats his friend's name, which she confirms by nodding again and again, apparently not realizing how stirred up the writer is. They spent some time together in Bordeaux, he tells her, but they haven't seen each other since then, and she thinks he feels very nostalgic about it.

I FIND OLDER MEN VERY INTERESTING, YOU KNOW?

She says it with the gesture of a naughty girl answering back. She says Martin's friend is great fun. He's going through the process of getting separated right now, and he's feeling quite sad, but he's a happy person per se. Something she remembers makes her smile. *"He is so funny."* She continues praising him. He's an understanding man, sensitive, he knows a lot of things, but above all, he's gentle and he's fun. The memory of something else makes her smile. She thinks he's a comfortable man. *"Comfortable."*

Harri and Lynn have to go to Donostia for something to do with work, but they don't move. They're enjoying trying to define what a *"comfortable"* man is. Meanwhile, Julia puts the tea things away. Harri doesn't need a comfortable man; she thinks she's got more than enough with her husband when it comes to that. She says she needs a man with passion. Julia is never sure if she's being serious. The writer, on the other hand, seems livelier, as if he didn't think his friend could possibly outshine him, and he asks the girl what type of man she would need. She avoids answering. What a question, how should she know . . . Julia takes his cup of tea away even though he hasn't finished it yet, a way of telling him to leave the girl alone, and also an excuse to disappear into the kitchen. But he doesn't give up. From the kitchen, Julia hears him saying that "need" isn't the right word and that he's going to ask her the question another way, but the girl interrupts him and says she doesn't think there's anything wrong with needing a man. There's a short silence. A few seconds later she says she probably needs someone brave. A brave man.

Julia thinks that she, herself, could do with an easy man.

Eventually, they start to get going. Martin suggests they come for lunch; he'll fix up something simple. What he wants is an excuse not to have to sit in front of the computer. Now he's like a child who wants people running around the house so that he can break his routine, and there'll be a special dessert, and his parents won't remember to tell him to do his homework, even though later on he'll regret not having written even a single line, complaining like his beloved Flaubert that he's only written fifteen pages in the last seven weeks, and none of them are good—*"depuis sept semaines j'ai écrit quinze pages et encore ne valent-elles."* But their work won't give them time to come, and they'll have to make do with a sandwich. What's more, Harri wants to go to the hairdresser's, "to look pretty in Bilbao tomorrow." More jokes about looking for the man from the airport. She says she feels he's close. And now Martin, wanting them to forget how unpleasant he's just been, challenges the girl to a Ping-Pong rematch before dinner. If Julia were to make her famous apple pie for them, he'd happily buy the apples and ladyfingers. He asks Julia what she thinks. While he asks, he puts his hand on her shoulder, and she doesn't dare to take it off, although she'd like to somehow exteriorize the anger he's pretending not to notice. She'd like to tell him that she feels immediately relegated as soon as a third person comes along. Julia needs problems to explode in order to stop the routine of time from leaving them behind and forgotten like trash in the wake of a ship. What they have always, always done has been to start talking again without explicitly mentioning the real reason for their quarrels, not just the pretexts Martin usually reproaches her with to explain his anger. At the beginning of their relationship, and later on, as well, she used to feel doubly guilty, first for getting angry and second for being unable to keep her anger appropriately in check. She has accepted that her way of reacting, that need of hers to pop the pimples, so to speak, is a function of her culture, as well as a sign of bad taste, and she's made an effort to adapt to his way of doing things, getting over quarrels without sinking deep into the mud at the bottom of each issue.

"What do you think?" Again. She thinks he gets bored with her. She's never been so completely sure. She's felt hate, anger, sorrow, love—even a lot of love—when looking into those blue eyes on occasions when they've been asking for a truce. But what she feels now is boredom. She isn't going to stay. She says that she has to go, too, putting the first thing she picks up into her bag, without bothering to think up an excuse. She decides she'll go to Donostia with the other two and then come back by train and go to her mother's house.

It looks as though the American girl may be feeling sorry for leaving the writer alone, because she not only promises to play the rematch some other time but also says that she wants to finish his book of short stories that night, and he says, meekly, that he'll go with them to the iron gate. Maybe he's hoping for an opinion about his book, an opinion that, for the moment at least, he doesn't get. They walk in silence. When they're in the car—and Martin, behind the bars, looks as if he's in a cell—the girl says that she has a complaint for his publishers, as if she's suddenly just remembered it. In Ainhoa, she was reading his book in the bath, and the dye of the bookmark ribbon washed away upon coming into contact with the water. She laughs. A way of saying that he was there with her in Argi Eder, with her in any circumstance. "This girl's a real artist," Julia says to herself. The writer stands frozen in astonishment at the gate, probably imagining Lynn naked in the bathtub with his book in her hands.

On the drive, Harri wants to get some more details out of the girl about her trip. "So how many people were there? Did you hook up with anyone? Who's the guy?" And even though she gives indirect answers as far as possible at first, Harri doesn't give up, and finally Lynn asks her, firmly but without being harsh, not to ask any more. "He might not like anyone to know. You know what I mean?"

HARRI, very excited: "So it's someone I know, then!"

LYNN: "Oh, come on. You're misunderstanding me, that's all . . ."

HARRI: "So is he interesting?"

LYNN: "Very." She covers her face with her hands. "Oh my God, I'm completely in love. *¿Qué te parece?*"

HARRI: "You want the truth? I think you're going to suffer."

RIVERAS DE LOIOLA. A sign pointing downtown. It's really easy to get lost on this bit, Harri says to cover up the silence. But Julia deduces that Harri's guessed who the man is who might not like his name being known.

When the lights turn red at the Maria Kristina *zubia*—or bridge—she wonders whether to get out and go straight to the station and catch a train back to Martutene, but she thinks that would make it all too obvious that she only wanted to get away from Martin, and so she stays in the car. When Harri asks where to drop her off, she says somewhere near Bretxa Azoka—the Brexta market. At the bridge, at Kursaal Zubia, that would work.

LA BRETXA IS NO LONGER the same place as when Olasagasti and Celaya, both nighthawks, used to come across the early-rising farmers from Igeldo, Ibaeta, Martutene, Astigarraga, and Altza on their donkeys, laden with containers of milk and baskets full of fresh fruits and vegetables. Almost everything sold there now comes from greenhouses, and some fruits and vegetables may even come from the central market, exactly the same ones on offer in the grocery stores, but more expensive because they're passed off here as being local products. Aitor still sells Errezil apples. Their appearance is better than it used to be, but they no longer smell as sweet; she thinks it must be a new grafted variety. She buys a few, because she's decided to make an apple pie for Zigor, and she'll take the American girl a piece.

You can still read the word *Pescadería*—fish market—on the façade of the classical-looking building, but now it houses a multi-screen cinema and the franchise pubs, sausage restaurants, and candy stores that you see in any suburb. She's not going to go straight back home. She's going to have a coffee and a pastry and then go to the movies. Something a free woman might do. She likes going to the movie theater by herself. First she'll stop in at Otaegui, the pastry shop, to buy the ladyfingers for the pie.

She decides to buy a notebook, as well, and while she's doing that, waiting at the counter inside the store, she feels something like what she used to always feel whenever she got a new notebook as a child, excited because she was going to fill it with her careful calligraphy and beautiful drawings, and worried about what the new school year would bring. Rather silly excitement, she admits, and now she's worried, because she's going to use it to write down her own ideas, not to translate other peoples', which is what she usually does. She asks for any color except red, because there's a book written by a woman called *The Red Notebook*, and she doesn't think she needs to ask for it not to be gold, she doesn't think they'll have one that color.

PEOPLE STILL LOOK with curiosity at women like her, she thinks, who go to the movies by themselves. It's as if they wonder what type of lives such women must lead, don't they have friends, or anything better to do than stare at a blank screen or sit around all alone waiting for the phone to ring?

The movie's about an American writer. She's a woman with writer's block, and her friends send her on a trip to Italy to help clear her mind. She falls in love with a house in the beautiful countryside of Tuscany and decides to renovate it and live there. Julia isn't surprised that more and more people are feeling the urge to write novels when doing so is portrayed as being the type of job that makes you famous and earns you a lot of money; the way writing's presented today is so far from the Romantic idea. She doesn't think the movie interesting, but the countryside's very beautiful. The time passes quickly as she sits there thinking. She knows now why she found it so painful listening to Martin question the notion of Basque uniqueness. It's obvious: it was because he wanted to hurt her. It's because of this sort of desire to hurt that she often feels personally attacked when myths and superstitions that should rightfully be destroyed are attacked, and she sees something like that in Unamuno's complaint when he said that the Basque language should be abandoned—he was applauded not because people thought he was right but because what he said hurt his countrymen. She admits it's an irrational feeling, one that she should have gotten over by now, but at the same time, rationalists' over-simplifications and arrogance drive her up the wall.

With regard to the mythical status that some people give Basque, she thinks it's fairly clear that it's a reaction, at least to an extent, to the idea, which until recently was commonly held, that it's a vulgar dialect, a useless relic, and an obstacle to cultural development. A reaction to the need for self-esteem, in fact.

TWO BEDS, CENTRAL LOCATION. Women in the train station advertising rooms for rent. A spectacle she has not gotten used to; she can't believe anyone doesn't have a bed in her city. Lots of people are coming off the trains, mostly young people, retired people, and women with children, on their way back from the beach. She decides not to bother trying for a free seat and hangs back on the platform for a few moments instead. It's very rare to hear anyone say "excuse me, please"; people just push their way through. A stocky, swarthy man of around fifty—wearing a thick gold chain around his neck and rings on his fingers—doesn't take his eyes off her. It's a habit of hers, probably not a very healthy one, to guess people's ethnic origin; she imagines this man is from eastern Spain. Because she's embarrassed to turn around and sit with her back to him, she spends the whole journey looking at the digital display that's announcing the names of each of the train's coming stops.

SHE HAS ALWAYS THOUGHT that it's extremely difficult to combine the rhythm of the drum with the *txistu* flute. She can hear it from downstairs—an *arin-arin* dance, and very well played. She opens the door without making a noise, to catch them by surprise. Zigor is playing, sitting on the kitchen table, and her mother is dancing. Her arms raised to the level of her head, no trace of tiredness, elegantly, on tiptoes, marking the movements with great precision, a certain heaviness only noticeable if you look at her feet, but that isn't the impression you get in general, quite the reverse, that wide-hipped body gives off an air of agility, and even though she's overweight, she moves with incredible ease through the air to the fast rhythm, dancing with her inner self, dancing with her bones and her very essence. That sad woman, with her bun undone, her hair down to her behind, looking like the image of death itself, that old woman, who always complains about her rheumatism, is incapable of keeping her feet still when she hears a *fandango* or *biribilketa*. She thinks her mother must be one of the last examples of Voltaire's vision of the Basques, "a people who sing and dance at the foot of the Pyrenees."

She lets her arms drop when she sees Julia. Zigor stops playing, as well. "You're early," Julia's mother says. She replies that since she had to go to Donostia, she took the chance to buy some things. She's going to make them a good dinner. Her mother: Are we celebrating something?

THEY TALK ABOUT THE ETYMOLOGY of the name of the village of Errezil. Julia's mother is peeling the Errezil apples, the three of them are sitting around the table, and she says that the name comes from *errez hil*—meaning "kill easily." It isn't the first time Julia's heard this, of course. The Basques found it easy to kill the Romans who were trying to get to Azpeitia, they simply threw stones at them from the slopes of Mount Ernio, and that, she says, is where the name of the creek, Errezil-erreka, comes from. It isn't the first time Julia's contradicted her, either, and she does so again now, not in the hope of convincing her to change her mind but so that Zigor won't take her seriously. There's no way that's the etymology of Errezil. While she's trying to fix on the best way to contradict her—she wants to be pleasant and pedagogical when she breaks the myth— her mother shrugs her shoulders and says to her, softly, "That's what my dead father used to say." Sometimes she'll say, in a regretful voice, "I'm ignorant, and you went to school." Sometimes, to Julia's despair, after this declaration of faith—"That's what my dead father used to say"—she wraps herself in silence like a Christian about to give herself up to the lions. Maybe what Julia's saying is very wise, but she won't listen to things she wasn't taught at home.

Julia's main pedagogical concern when it comes to her son is showing him that it's possible to disagree without getting angry; although it's something that she herself seldom achieves. While her mother washes the dishes—distant now that she's said all that she had to say—she tries to convince the boy that the theory about the place name is unreasonable. If the Romans didn't go all the way up to Errezil, it would be because they didn't want to eat any apples. They were quite capable of going wherever they pleased, for instance to Oiartzun, because there was silver there, and because the Basques, unlike many others, did not oppose them. Quite the contrary—they seem to have been fascinated by Roman civilization and they fought for the empire. She tells him about the Cohors I Vardulorum regiment, which helped conquer Britain, and which left an inscription to the "mother goddesses" at what is now Rochester, on Hadrian's Wall; it's the only known case of a dedication to female deities and also the only one put up not by an officer but by the whole corps. She talks to him about the Cohors II Vasconum Civium Romanorum unit. It was the Basques themselves who defended the passes in the Pyrenees, and it was after the fall of the empire, when the Barbarians sought to invade, that the Basques became warlike.

The boy listens to her with attention, happy with this new vision of pragmatic Basques who know how to make friends with power rather than uselessly throwing stones against it. He says very seriously, "You know what? We did the right thing. It was much more sensible to get together with the Romans than to go against them." In fact, although Julia thinks that valuing pragmatism and playing down the importance of rebelliousness is a step in the right direction, she's aware that she's been a little bit too enthusiastic in her telling of history, and that she's still left out the most important lesson of all: the members of those Basque tribes were their own people, their ancestors, and so whatever they did—throw stones at the Romans or sell them Errezil apples and Idiazabal cheese—was fine, and a reason to feel proud.

Her mother continues washing the dishes in silence, and when Julia goes over to help her, she doesn't let her. "I'm almost finished." She clearly thinks her daughter is a traitor. She doesn't know just how loyal she really is. Mother and daughter are watching television—the daughter forces herself to watch it so that her mother won't be alone—and the boy is reading in his room.

WHAT'S AN ANAGRAM? he shouts from his bedroom. He's gotten into the habit of looking up words he doesn't know in the dictionary, and he doesn't ask her for definitions so much anymore. Julia wonders if he no longer trusts her knowledge so much, because all too often she hasn't known what to say. *Anagram*—this time she does know the word. When it comes to examples, however, the only one that comes to mind is the one she was taught at school—*amor/Roma*—but Zigor needs them in Basque. She can't think of a single one. But she does think of another one in Spanish—*azar/raza*. On the last day of her writing workshop, the teacher mentioned how difficult it is to translate sentences containing anagrams and, as an exercise, gave them a poem by José Miguel Ullán. "*Diles / que no hay más raza que el azar / que no hay más patria que el dolor*"—tell them that there is no other race than chance, that there is no other homeland than pain. A sentiment that expresses so well what she was trying to get across to Zigor a short while before. Finally, she thinks of *ate/eta*—the Basque words for "door" and "and"—and Zigor comes up with *ogi/igo*—"bread" and "to rise"; *gora/garo*—"up" and "fern"; and *ore/ero*—"dough" and "crazy." After hitting upon the first one, the rest come easily. *Erraz/zerra*—"easy" and "saw."

On the television, some well-known people are all answering the same question: "When have you ever wanted to disappear from the face of the earth?" A famous chef doesn't mind saying that once, when he was waiting for his girlfriend, he was feeling uncomfortably flatulent, and after attempting to relieve his discomfort, he suddenly felt a trickle of liquid running down his legs and he had to tuck his pants into his socks, as he did when riding his bike. "That's when I wished I could disappear from the face of the earth!" and he laughs happily as he tells the story.

Julia's mother says nothing. She really likes the uninhibited chef.

Julia remembers the last lines of Jules Renard's *Journal*, which had such a great effect on Beckett; according to one of his biographers, after reading it for the first time, he then spent hours sitting in front of the fire repeating it: "Last night I wanted to get up. Dead weight. A leg hangs outside. Then a trickle runs down my leg. I allow it to reach my heel before I make up my mind. It will dry in the sheets, the way it did when I was Poil de Carotte." Apparently Beckett thought the natural way in which Renard dealt with physiological matters was admirable. Julia would like to know what he would have made of today's dominatingly natural approach to things.

She hears her mother's radio from the hallway. She goes to sleep with it on, and her loud snoring accompanies the programming, which is mostly talk shows. She opens Zigor's door. The light's off, but he tells her to come in, he's awake. She sits on the side of the bed like her own father used to do. A man who was proud to belong to a noble, hard-working race, who taught her about egalitarianism and the importance of keeping your word. The poor man, humble and loyal as he was, saw himself as no less than a Montmorency.

"What we talked about earlier." She wants to tell him that he doesn't have to feel obliged to be loyal to any real or notional ancestors. Who knows if he might not be descended from some Roman legionary who turned up one day in Oiartzun? All they really have to do is try to be honest and live without hurting anyone, respecting the culture and the countryside while being faithful to knowledge, which is one of mankind's most important achievements. She'll try to express it better in writing. Do you know what I mean? The boy says he does, no need to go on about it.

Julia feels like talking. She's interested in the interviews he's doing about the Spanish civil war. He isn't very happy about them, all the old people say exactly the same things—the war was terrible, they went really hungry, the Germans and the Italians helped Franco. An old woman told him the same story he's heard his grandmother tell a hundred times, the one about the woman running away from the bombardment and looking for shelter and suddenly realizing that the child in her arms is dead. He sits up in bed, lively all of a sudden. He speaks lower and asks if she believes the story of his grandmother's about how the Falangist leaders asked his grandfather during the war what he would do if the *lehendakari* turned up and he answered that he would do his duty and hide the Basque government's president. At first she doesn't know how to answer, she's had the same doubt for years. If it's true, it seems too daring for a person who was in charge of cooking for the Falangists and never once tried to poison them. She thinks that must be what Zigor's thinking, and it's what she used to think herself when she listened to her father. She knows her father used to tell the story, but she doesn't remember him telling it.

"Why wouldn't you believe it?"

"It seems a bit dumb to me."

"He wanted to show them just how loyal and noble Basque patriots were."

Zigor lies down again, but his eyes are wide open, she sees them shining in the dark. Julia doesn't know whether to tell him her theory about her father's hypothetical act of bravery. She thinks that what he said happened could have happened. It could be true that Colonel Urroz once asked him the question and that her father replied that he would hide Lehendakari Agirre because he was sure that was what the colonel wanted to hear. Because he knew, somehow, that Urroz—a member of the gentry of Navarre, who loved late nights and was a good man at heart—liked people who lived up to the model of noble, incorruptible townsfolk, and her father had taken the risk and told him what he wanted to hear. It's significant that, according to her father, he made him repeat his daring expression of loyalty more than once. She's sure about that, and because of that, she can imagine the colonel, with some of his comrades-in-arms, sitting around after lunch, and after drinking a lot of brandy, calling for her father to come out so that he could show him off like a circus monkey, asking him the question again so that the others could see just how humble, loyal, and dumb these Basque farmers were. She wonders if she has the right to share that theory with him. She isn't sure, and what's more, her mother has woken up and is telling her off from the adjoining room. Let him get some sleep, she shouts at Julia, he has to get up early tomorrow, you know. A voice without teeth making a mess of the *s*'s. She always sleeps with the door ajar. And you go to bed, too, daughter. She's seldom seen her without her teeth in.

A piece of library furniture with an oak plywood finish that has a folding table that comes out of it and isn't very stable anymore, because the screws in the arms are loose. She tries to tighten them but can't. It's the plywood that's loose. She takes the French translation of *Montauk* that Lynn gave her and her still unused blue notebook out of her bag and sits down at the table. She feels tired.

Traduit de l'allemand par Michèle et Jean Tailleur. The Montaigne quote is written in old French: C'EST ICY UN LIVRE DE BONNE FOY, LECTEUR. The text is easy to read, there's nothing to make you think it was originally written in another language. MONTAUK. 11.5.1974. *L'écrivain redoute les sentiments qui ne se prêtent pas à la publication*—the writer is wary of feelings that may not be appropriate for publication. She reads aloud a few scattered passages that she's already familiar with, to see how they sound in French, and comes across the part

Martin mentioned to her, the one he said she would identify with. It's almost at the start of page 87: "JE N'AI PAS VÉCU AVEC TOI PUR TE SERVIR DE MATÉRIAU LITTÉRAIRE. JE T'INTERDIS D'ÉCRIRE SUR MOI"—I have not been living with you to provide literary material. I forbid you to write about me.

Julia has never dared say anything like that, it would be arrogant of her, and unfortunately, she thinks he has the right to use anything he wants to. She's also never said "your shit literature" as Flora Ugalde did.

The six-foot-wide bed is too narrow. Even though she normally sleeps curled up, when she can sleep, she always likes rolling over, stretching out, and feeling how fresh the sheets are. She would rather have a wider bed. It would be tight, but a double bed would fit if they took the bedside table out. But she's never thought of having one brought in. She supposes it's because she doesn't want to bother her mother. It would be an unnecessary expense, an extravagance, something that a serious woman wouldn't do. And yet her mother would like her to dress more provocatively—deeper necklines, shorter skirts—and wear makeup. Use her womanly charms. Using one's womanly charm isn't something for sluts, or at least it isn't only for sluts. In fact, what her mother reproaches her for, though not openly, is being a slut but without getting any benefits from that inclination of hers. A vocational slut, so to speak. Depraved.

She remembers Martin teasing her, "So you've always been like this!"

She'd never told anyone, and yet she told him. Why? To recip- rocate, clearly. She felt obliged to open her heart and share a confidence of the same caliber with him. Telling her about the scene in the library, just admitting that as a boy he had masturbated to dirty books, must have required a great effort from him, embarrassed as he was by things like that, and so when he asked her to tell him something intimate and risqué in exchange, she thought it would be healthy for their relationship to share good things, bad things, and even terrible things, and she would actually say she felt glad to have a story of sexual abuse to tell him, something on the same level as the information he'd just trusted her with.

It was the first time she ever described that event in her life as "sexual abuse." Although it was a secret, she never thought about it very much. It was something that had happened a long time ago, something that was far from pleasant but didn't, she believes, do her too much harm, either. After telling Martin about it, she wondered if having kept it silent until then might not have been due to the tendency children have to feel guilty when they go through experiences like that. She isn't sure. In fact, she's never taken an interest in reading about the issue, and it seems to her now that perhaps that very lack of interest was a subconscious effort to avoid the subject, and a sign that the events were more traumatic than she ever wanted to admit.

She doesn't know exactly how it happened, but she does remember a few details. She knows the man seemed old to her—although he probably wasn't, because he was a friend of her father's; she figures he must have been younger than forty at the time. And he was ugly. She can't bring him to mind, but she knows he was fat and had some sort of problem with his eyes, maybe a lazy eye, or one he couldn't fully open. His lips were licentious, meaty, the lower one bigger than the upper, and he had something on them, perhaps a black lump, probably a small angioma. She doesn't know how she knows that, since she can't recall his face, so to an extent it's as if someone told her about it. However, although she probably reconstructed some of the repulsive physical image later in life, she's sure she would recognize him if she saw him in a photograph. She isn't sure how old she was, but at least ten, because she and a neighbor who was a year older than her were allowed to walk alone down to the provincial government building to see the man, who she thinks must have worked there as a civil servant. They used to go to the building in the evening, by which time there was nobody there. She doesn't know how they would get in to see the man, but she thinks he used to be sitting behind a wooden table in an anteroom or some sort of hallway, and he wore a dark suit, a white shirt, and a black tie, and because of that she knows he was a concierge, although she isn't sure if he had gold braiding on his sleeves.

The man used to lower their panties and touch their vulvas, hers more than her friend's. In fact, the man didn't like her friend going, because when he touched her, she started laughing and squirming; she, on the other hand, stayed still and serious, so that the man would finish quickly and she could take the pencils he used to give them and run out as soon as possible. They were good pencils. That detail about their reward is something she could have kept quiet about, but she found it difficult to lie, back then even more so than now, and she thinks she wanted to be very honest at the time, because it was back when she and Martin were starting their new phase of trusting each other more. So she told him that she usually had to convince the other girl to go with her, because she didn't want to go alone, and so, apparently, she also didn't want to renounce the possibility of getting the pencils. Her decision to be sincere probably led to her putting too much emphasis on her interest in getting the pencils and, at the same time, made her look worse than her friend. And in fact it's true that she was more interested in pencils than her friend. Being a hard-working pupil, she kept beautiful notebooks, and her friend, on the other hand, didn't much care about them. She was more interested in talking about boys. She was a year older than her—and still is, because she's still alive—and she was much more awake to certain things and, without doubt, more aware of what was going on with that man. Julia was more innocent, and because of that, she would feel pleased when that revolting man told her, while fondling her small breasts, that hers were going to grow bigger than her friends'. She thinks that's accurate, that she used to feel proud, and that's how she told Martin about it.

Those caresses came to an end when her friend told her parents what was going on. Of course, they told Julia's parents, who asked her if it was true. She doesn't remember how that went, either. She thinks she was annoyed that her friend had betrayed her, and a little frustrated, too, perhaps because she wouldn't be getting those pencils any more. She doesn't think her parents hearing about it had any serious consequences, and she's sure they didn't get angry with her. They didn't reproach her for anything, and even kept quiet about it. She's always wondered why she and her friend reacted to the abuse in such different ways. She certainly wouldn't say it was because she was in any way more malicious. She wasn't, quite the opposite, she was probably purer and more loyal, as well; they'd promised the man that they wouldn't tell on him, and so she kept her word. She thinks the basic reason was that her parents knew the man, and at the same time, he'd made it very clear that he wanted the relationship to be with her, he didn't like the other girl going, and so her friend realized that she was no more than a backup for Julia as far as he was concerned. That was why it was easier for her to reveal what was happening. (At the same time, her mother wasn't as religious as Julia's, she was more open and modern. She used to wear makeup, for instance. She didn't speak Basque, she listened to all the radio soap operas, and she let her daughter and Julia listen, as well—unlike Julia's mother—and that must have made it easier for her friend to open up to her.) She thinks that the young version of herself must have been hurt that her friend didn't confide in her that she intended to make the situation known. She must have felt betrayed, but she doesn't think she minded giving up that particular way of getting pencils, and she was relieved at not having to continue seeing that revolting man. She has the idea that the fact that her friend, unlike her, told her parents what was happening made her wonder, even back then, if there was more trust in their familial relationship than in the relationship between herself and her parents, and that seemed sad to her. Her parents, too, even though they never said anything about it to her—not even a single "Why didn't you tell us about it?"—must have drawn the same conclusion. That thought makes her sad, especially with regard to her father. She'd say it's something that still makes her sad. The most serious consequence of what, today, would be called sexual abuse was her regretting having caused her father sorrow.

She stayed friends with the other girl until their adolescence, but they didn't see much of each other after that. The friend became rather forward and started going out with older girls than her, from the factory she worked at, while Julia, on the other hand, kept her friends from school. Once, she bumped into her while out somewhere and asked her if she remembered that old man who used to touch them, but the other girl didn't want to talk about it. The subject never came up at home, either, and, of course, she never saw the man again. She's always thought that when her father heard about it, he must have given that vile man a really good beating. She's always hoped he did. From time to time, she's been tempted to ask her mother what happened, what they did when they heard about it, but she's never dared, for her own sake and for her mother's, as well; she knows it would be tough for her to talk about it.

Martin was not disappointed by the story. He probably hadn't been expecting anything like that, and he was moved. He held her in his arms as she told him, and she remembers well that he caressed her and said "poor thing," as if the dirty man were still abusing the child, and that it comforted her.

Even so, not much time was to go by before he made use of what she told him in that moment of weakness. One day, he allowed himself to joke that she'd been a Lolita; on another occasion, trying to be ironic, he said that the old pervert had been wrong in his predictions about how much her breasts would grow; and finally, in the episode he titled "Worse and Worse," he wrote, in order to complete her psychological portrait, that Flora Ugalde had had an "unfortunate sexual experience" in her childhood and that as a result of it, she'd "always had a guilty conscience for having sold her little vulva, and she lived in fear that the calculating little girl who'd let a dirty old man touch it in exchange for pencils was still somewhere there inside her."

THERE ARE EXPENSIVE BRAND-NAME NECK SCARVES that she never wears lying in a drawer in her closet, all given to her by Martin, her mother, or her sister. Flasks of eau de cologne and perfume that she's never worn, all of them Christmas or birthday presents. There's also fancy lingerie, particularly expensive and uncomfortable, which she seldom wears, and only ever for Martin, on the occasions when she decides to overcome the embarrassment of revealing her wish to be desirable. The times she's daring enough, or humble enough, to say "I want you to desire me." On the other hand, when she met up with that other young man, she would always wear her usual panties, those completely comfortable, flesh-colored ones that go up to her waist and that men, apparently, can't stand.

(She likes the fact that in *Montauk* they don't use any strategies for seduction, that everything seems to come about easily. Max can smoke his pipe in Lynn's kitchenette as if he were in his own home, while the girl does her daily relaxation exercises. She likes the fact that Lynn has no trouble saying to him one evening, *"We can't today."* When they go to bed together, she turns down the sheets just as she would if she were going to bed by herself on any normal day. That's what it had been like for her with that young man, as well.)

Why does she have the suspicion that her mother's been prying in her drawers, the same way she snoops in Martin's computer? She thinks she must be looking for something to tell her how her relationship with Martin is going and will draw her conclusions when she sees that she isn't using her lacy lingerie.

Julia hasn't opened the red notebook of his since she read it in Ainhoa. Now, prompted by the sentence she's just read in *Montauk*, she opens it: *No he vivido contigo para servirte de material literario; te prohíbo que escribas una sola línea sobre mí. Je n'ai pas vécu avec toi pour te servir de matériau littéraire. Je t'interdis d'écrire sur moi.* I have not been living with you to provide literary material. I forbid you to write about me. She found what he wrote to be denigrating, and she begged him not use it. He got on his high horse, something she hadn't seen him do for a long time. He seemed, once more, to be that domineering man who was always so sure of himself. "I have no intention of using it," he said. "I wrote it for you." And he threw the notebook down onto the bed of the Argi Eder hotel in Ainhoa. The next morning, when they were leaving, she put it in her bag, and ever since then it's been sitting in her drawer.

THE WOMAN IN A RED JACKET SITTING ON THE EDGE OF THE BED.

Flora Ugalde is sitting on the sofa in the living room wearing a red jacket. Like someone ready to rush out of the house as soon as the clock strikes one. That's how Faustino Iturbe saw her, and that's what happened in reality. Normally, she would kill time until the 16:40 train, because she always met up with the young man at five o'clock, and after the six-minute journey, it was only another five minutes to his apartment if she walked quickly. She might well have been reading a magazine, "like someone in a waiting room," just as in the description, because she no longer felt at home there, and she made a show of that by not looking after things there in the way that she had done before.

That scene—the two of them sitting in the living room one afternoon while she waited for her 16:40 train—had played out in exactly the same way every day for the last week, not much longer than that. Since the day the young man first invited her to dinner on the way out of their writing workshop. They'd seen each other every day since then, and she left the apartment at the same time every day without giving any explanation—Martin didn't ask her for one, either—and came back at nine o'clock every evening. Martin would make his own dinner, and she would skip it. She would already have had a little something to eat at the young man's apartment.

That day, the day she was wearing her red jacket, was the last day she went to the young man's apartment. By the time she came and sat down in the living room, she realized that it wasn't going to be a day like all the others. There was something disturbing in the atmosphere, and Martin's face was not, as it usually was every day when Julia started getting ready to go out, the picture of seriousness and indifference. He was obviously nervous, he was looking at her furtively from the behind the book he was pretending to read, he had her under surveillance, that was the term for it, and he seemed to want to break the silence but without knowing how to do so, and she, even though she was already wearing her jacket and ready to leave, decided to stay sitting there and let the 16:40 train go by without her.

She doesn't know what she would have answered if he had asked where she was going. "What do you care?" perhaps. She thinks her answer would have depended on the way he asked the question. She has the idea that if he'd suggested going to the movies, she would have accepted and broken her date with the young man. Because as she sat there waiting for the next train departure time to roll around, she was also waiting on some miracle that might get the two of them speaking to each other once more. But nothing like that happened.

At that point, they only ever broke their silence to say words that were strictly necessary—"You got a call from the doctor's," or "Someone's coming by to fix the antenna tomorrow"—a very few sentences like that, and, of course, they said them angrily. They'd both returned to this practice after a period of strict silence in which they hadn't even given each other messages or told each other things, a phase that had led to many practical problems: the new washing machine was taken back to the warehouse three times, because each of them would hang up whenever a phone call came in for the other; and Martin's insurance policy lapsed for the first time in twenty years, which was a very serious matter for him. And there were even times when they pretended not to know each other in front of other people, in order to prolong their standoff. But then there was a new circumstance that made Julia especially angry. It was Martin himself who told her that he'd once read an interview with Gabriel Celaya, or with his partner, Amparitxu, or maybe he'd heard it on the radio, in which he talked about a tactic the couple had for preventing their quarrels from becoming disastrous. They said they long ago agreed that whatever the situation was, even if they were incredibly angry with each other, every day, at a certain

325

time, they would stop whatever they were doing and get together at a particular place in the house—they even gave the place a specific name, which he doesn't remember—and drink a whisky together. Martin suggested that they should do the same thing, and Julia, although she didn't think that admittedly sweet-sounding method would work with her, accepted the idea as a show of good faith.

She promised she would always keep the appointment, and they decided to make it nine o'clock in the evening, in the formal library, and they would drink a gin and tonic together. However, the agreement did not last for long. Stopping what you're doing at exactly nine o'clock to have a gin and tonic that you don't always feel like drinking isn't the best way to guarantee a good time, and the day came when they just emptied their glasses in one big swig without saying a single word to each other—it reminded her of the words she'd read in a children's book on religion, "You have finally drunk the Chalice of Martyrdom"—and then they each went back to their own activities without saying anything at all. It has always been a matter of debate between them who usually gives in first by breaking the silence. Julia is convinced she does, but she could be wrong. What she doesn't have any doubt about is that it's Martin who usually stops talking, and then, faced with his silence, she does the same thing and goes mute. Be that as it may, it was he who broke their gin and tonic pact. She wouldn't have stopped going into the formal library with the two gin and tonics in her hand every day for anything in the world. But he would have, and he did. That day, they'd quarreled because of a decision her son had made about music. Zigor told her that he wanted to stop taking piano lessons in order to concentrate on the *txistu*, and Julia didn't like the idea. Because of that, and, more precisely, because she almost hated the *txistu* in any other context than at village festivals, she found it hurtful to listen to Martin, who as well as ridiculing the boy's choice also said that she was to blame for having brought him up in an atmosphere of "patriotic, *abertzale* folklore." She answered him aggressively, saying he was just an elitist and had obviously joined in with that unpleasant, fashionable craze of attacking anything even remotely Basque. Things like that. It was a terrible quarrel, and they fell into silence afterward.

It was almost nine o'clock, and she was preparing to go into the library, with her gin and tonic in her hand and ready to admit that his words had hurt her precisely because of the fact that she found her son's decision frustrating and assure him she was going to do all she could to get the boy to change his mind. She was even ready to confide to him that she wasn't sure if their Basque musical instruments were of any use as an outlet for musical talent or whether they in fact relegated people to less productive or expressive pastures. She was expecting him, too, to admit that he was nervous because he hadn't written a line for over a month; she knew that was the case, even though he was telling everybody that he was making progress with his novel. But the clock struck nine, and she heard the door to the gallery bang shut with a force that made the glass windowpanes tremble, and then she heard the sound of his steps on the gravel path outside.

It had been a long time since she'd last cried. That day she did, because she understood, without any doubt in her mind, that Martin could never be the man she needed, a man who would console her by saying that her son's playing the *txistu* wasn't that bad, that a nice *biribilketa* tune can be quite beautiful—she'd have laughed if he'd said that—and that, when it comes down to it, it's something that might make him very happy. The man who would take advantage of his sway—Zigor greatly admires him because he's a writer—to try and influence him as Julia would like him to, inviting him to the house and encouraging him to play the piano there, at least so he wouldn't give it up completely. Martin was not that man.

So why didn't she leave?

It hurt her to admit that when it came down to it, she was constricted by a material need, which is something that makes her feel lousy. There was nowhere she could go. Renovation work was being done on her mother's house. There had been a flood, and because the floors were going to have to be ripped up anyway, they decided to renovate the whole place at the same time. Her mother and Zigor were on vacation in Otzeta, there wasn't any more space for her there, and she would have found it humiliating to ask her sister for refuge. So she made the worst possible decision—staying put until the work at her mother's house was finished.

But the relationship was over for her, and she was sure that Martin thought the same thing. In fact, she was convinced that he'd made the decision and that he was putting up with her at the house only until she found an alternative. To such an extent that she would have been prepared to restart the relationship if he had shown some sign of good will, but that didn't happen. Or she was never aware that it did. He used to spend the whole day in his pajamas and slippers, wrapped in his robe, sitting in front of his computer without doing anything, looking depressed, and that must have meant something, but he still had writer's block and wasn't prepared to talk about it. She, on the other hand, started going out more, among other things so as not to force her presence on him. She started saying yes to having a few glasses of wine with friends, and that's what happened that one day as she was leaving the writing workshop. It's easy to go from literary matters to personal ones, which is perhaps why people read. Be that as it may, her friend from the workshop figured out that she was lonely and invited her to dinner. He was a young man, quite a lot younger than herself, and at first she only liked him because he was nice and easy to get along with. He wasn't at all complicated, and she didn't have to worry, as she did with Martin, about him taking what she said the wrong way or making her feel ridiculous for giving her opinion on certain subjects. She felt that he was not her intellectual superior, and the young man himself accepted that and admired her. He wrote poetry and had even been published in some magazine or other, but it was nothing out of this world. The truth be known, he was a pretty average poet. Once, before Julia and Martin's last quarrel, he had asked her to give Martin some of his poems, because he looked up to him a lot and wanted his opinion of them; but his opinion was so negative that she didn't dare pass it on to the young man. She told him that he'd liked them. That's what she told him every time he gave her a poem for Martin to read, even when she didn't actually show them to him. Martin is as strict and destructive with writers he doesn't like as he is with himself. He used to tease her about the writing workshop, saying that the participants were fools because you don't *learn* how to write, putting sentences together isn't writing. Julia, in fact, was pretty much in agreement with him, she had no doubt her friend was quite naïve and not very smart. She accepts that it may be for that very reason that she felt good by his side when compared to her stormy relationship with Martin; she never felt domineered, despised, or denigrated when she spoke with the young man from time to time, which was usually on the way out of the workshop.

The evening they had dinner at Casa Cámara in Pasaia Donibane, he invited her up to his apartment to see what he called "a visual poem"—slides of flowers with drops of dew on them—and although that wasn't anything special, they did end up in bed together. She didn't feel uncomfortable with a man ten years younger than herself, even though she hadn't gone to bed with anyone apart from Martin for many years, and she was delighted to feel desirable once more. What she most enjoyed was not feeling ashamed of the cellulitis on her thighs or her saggy breasts. Less so than with Martin, at any rate, who was a perfectionist, selective, and who couldn't stand ageing or deterioration.

After that, they saw each other every day. Time passed easily for her without doing anything in particular, she talked about whatever came into her mind, however silly it might be, never worrying about bringing it up. She was grateful he didn't see things in such a negative way, and she enjoyed planning trips around Greece and Turkey, listening to the music he liked. She didn't think about the future, she lived for the moment, and the young man's feeling when he'd open the door to her and stand there happy as a dog seemed to rub off on her. They hardly went out, they didn't need anyone else, and also because she wanted their relationship kept secret until she could move out of Martin's house. He suggested she come and live with him, but she'd had enough of living in one man's house for lack of anywhere else to go and felt no desire to go straight into another man's home for the same reason.

She never found it hard to talk to the young man about the difficulties of her situation, although she didn't explain all that much to him. She told him that Martin was a complex man, and difficult to live with because he was obsessed with writing. They talked a lot about Martin. The young man would ask her questions, and she was glad to answer as far as she could, because he listened to her with attention. They were usually questions about his habits when he wrote, his routines, and his obsessions, what he was working on, what his timetable was, whether he listened to music.

These are, apparently, things that interest a young writer about a seemingly more experienced one. In that sense, the young man respected Martin a lot—he thought he was a very talented writer, one of the most talented Basque writers, and Julia was glad to hear that. He told her that it's called *writer's block*, being afraid of the critics, not publishing for fear of failure; and she was indignant that some jerks in a bar said Martin was finished because he was blocked, and she defended him. She was sure he would write a good novel sooner or later, he'd always found writing hard, because he was very demanding with himself, perhaps excessively so, and she told the young poet as much, and also, by the way, that she was fed up of them always talking about Martin.

The last day she went to his apartment—"the day it all happened," as it said in Martin's story—she was late, because she missed her usual train. In fact, even before she'd realized that Martin was watching her from out of the corner of his eye and behind the book he was holding up, she was thinking that he must be wondering where she went every day at the same time, even though she didn't think he cared too much, and what she least expected was for him to come across the poem that the young man had sent her.

It had been her birthday four days earlier, and she'd had the remote hope—perhaps the remote fear—that Martin would break his silence and suggest they go out for dinner. If that happened, she was going to take it as a chance to say that in spite of the inevitable delays, the work on her mother's house was going to be over within a couple of weeks and then she'd be able to leave, but she'd say it in a civilized way, and they would become old friends, people who really appreciated each other, who were even able to tell each other about their feelings and amorous adventures. But it didn't happen like that. The young man sent a red rose to her workplace, and a card with "The Poem of the Red Moon" written on it. She had no idea why he wrote "you are loyal, more loyal than anyone" on it—something she was going to have to hear uncountable times. It's always nice to get flowers, even though she finds such flattery makes her feel sick, and she thought that tearing up the card would be a lack of respect.

She put it in her bag, inside the envelope with the Villa Flores logo on it, and there it stayed, until Martin, who must have been looking for clues about where she was spending her afternoons, noticed it easily. Her bag was completely open at the top, and depending on how it was set down, it was easy to see what was inside. It couldn't have been difficult for him to work out that the card had been sent along with some flowers; he was curious to see who'd sent them, and he held onto the card. He says that's how it happened, but she never noticed it missing. Among other things, because she had no interest in the poem. She has sometimes wondered if that carelessness of hers wasn't due to an unconscious desire for Martin to find out about her affair.

Strangely enough, on "the day it all happened," when it was so obvious that the expression on Martin's face had changed, it took a long time for her to see the most obvious sign of all: he had hung up his pajamas and his robe. He was wearing the clothes he normally wore at home, some light shoes and an old plaid hunting jacket, clothes he could also wear outside. She remembers that she even tried to work out how old the jacket, which still looked good, was. Suddenly she was sure that he'd dressed like that in order to follow after her when she left to catch the train. She thought that must be why he looked nervous, because he'd decided to tail her and see what she did when she went out.

When she began to suspect—rightly, as she'd soon discover—that that was what he was going to do, it occurred to her that she could take the next train, and she worked out that if she hurried out as soon as she saw it pull in and just managed to catch it, Martin wouldn't have time to follow and get in after her. And that's what she did. As soon as she heard the 16:55 train, she got up, ran across the garden, and in fact got to the platform quite a while before it left. So in the end, Martin did have time to get to the train, and at a brisk walk, he didn't even have to run. He got into another carriage. She felt really bad the entire ride to the Atotxa stop. She stepped out onto the platform, and he got out of the last carriage. They both remained standing there on the platform beside their respective carriages for the two minutes the stop there lasted, but she got on again just when there was no time for anyone else to get on or off, like in action films, just before the train started up again, and once it had, she saw Martin standing there on the platform. He could have caught up with her if he wanted to, but he didn't. He says he knew the trick she was going to pull but thought it beneath himself to get back on the train again. She went as far as Ategorrieta and backtracked from there, reaching the young man's apartment later than usual.

Because the railroad line, which goes over the road, passes in front of his apartment complex, at the same level as the fifth floor, which is where the young man lives, you could hear the trains go by there, too. She sometimes got to thinking about how the train she was hearing at the apartment would pass by Martin's house a few minutes later, as well, and how he, too, would hear it; what she didn't imagine was that Martin would later write about just that, about how the train he was hearing in Martutene had, seven or eight minutes earlier, gone past the window where she and her friend were.

He described himself standing on the slope above the tracks, watching the window where Julia and the young man were, and she's never dared to ask him if he really did that. After reading *The Woman in a Red Jacket Sitting on the Edge of the Bed*, you might think that he did, but when she got back to the house the following day, he asked her, "Who is he?" as if he knew that she'd spent the night with someone, or had worked it out, but didn't know with whom. She finds the same to be the case with almost everything—she doesn't know what's real and what he's made up. At some moments in the story, she has the impression that it did actually happen, that he'd been in the apartment itself, listening to what they were saying, and seeing what they were doing, until she realizes that what he wrote is what she told him. Back when she used to answer his questions, believing he had the right to know, without thinking how he might make use of what she said, back when she used to think it would be good for him to know, until she realized—after he spent days pestering her, asking her questions all the time, questions that seemed to be made in good faith but that, in fact, had a hidden purpose—that her answers only served to increase his need to know and his desire to later be able to throw everything he found out back in her face.

He remains on the slope for a long time, hours standing there looking at the young man's apartment, "wanting to embrace you when I see you at the window and feeling as though I've lost my arms," waiting for her to come out of the front door and take her by the arm as if nothing's happened and go back home together. But the time she normally goes back home has gone by, long since, and he's shivering with cold, and then, startled by the noise of a train, he loses his balance and falls over. He moves his observation post to the front door of the building, but it soon becomes hard for him to explain what he's doing there to the curious occupants coming and going, and so, a little after ten o'clock, he rings the young man's bell—his plan is to announce, "I've come for Flora"— but there's no answer, so he rings all the bells until someone opens the door for him, then he goes up to the fifth floor, the young man's floor, and after knocking on his door, waits there. He stays there by the door, still thinking he'll say "I've come for Flora" and that when Flora hears that, she'll come back home with him, no doubt about it, they'll definitely go back home together, but he wouldn't mind if something else happened, really wouldn't mind having to take the young man on and give him a good punch, or getting hit by him, getting the chance to tell him he's a bad poet, but no one comes to the door, and he rings the bell again and again, knocks loudly, until finally a neighbor comes out and threatens to call the police. None of that's true, Julia never heard anyone knocking on the door, and the young man never told her about anything like that happening. Although she did sometimes hear the bell and get startled by it, and it may be that it's something that also made the young man nervous, because he always took the precaution of closing the living room door before answering and looking through the peephole first to buy a little extra time, but as far as she remembers, he always ended up opening the door and it would be the man from the electric company, the gas man, or a neighbor wanting to ask him something.

In the story, after his run-in with the neighbor, he decided to go and wait on the front stoop again, putting up with the cold, until he noticed a few windows opened up and he heard a siren, which he thought must be the police, summoned by neighbors suspecting he was up to something, and he started running toward the center of Gros, where, breathless, he mingled in with the people coming out of the Trueba movie theater. Sometimes the story seems so pathetic that it becomes laughable. She thinks anyone else would find it comical, but she finds it sad; it makes her feel anxious, because she has the feeling that what he's telling is true. In fact, there's no doubt that some of the things did actually happen. She imagines he really did go back to Martutene in a taxi and wait for her in the living room.

He waited for her all night. That is true.

In fact, on "the day everything happened," she told the young man that she wanted to leave early—the memory of Martin, standing there in his plaid hunting jacket and looking at her on the platform at Atotxa, was making her nervous. She felt uncomfortable and decided that it was time to sign on the dotted line of what was already a fact—the end of the relationship—and tell him that she was going to her sister's house, because theirs was an absurd situation, but each time she said she wanted to leave, the young man

333

held her back. "It's so good being together right now." And it *was* good being there in that apartment. It felt like a student's apartment, but it was clean and tidy—the home of a man who knew how to live by himself. There were a few decorative, feminine touches, left behind by some previous companion, who he talked about openly, even their intimate details, without holding anything back. In fact, he talked about them more than Julia would have liked. He liked showing her photographs. He also told her about a very beautiful girl that he'd been going out with when he and Julia met but who he wasn't seeing anymore because he felt better with her—Julia—than he ever had with anyone else. He often said that, "It's so good being together." She remembers him saying it with his arms folded and a look of satisfaction that she sometimes found contagious and that she at least tried not to spoil. Julia agreed to have sex, although there wasn't much passion in it; she didn't find him especially attractive, and less so that last day, because she'd made her decision—she wanted to get back to Martutene as soon as possible and face up to Martin.

There were no particular complications to sex with him. Sometimes the young man would fall asleep, and she would get dressed in the dark without waking him and leave the apartment. But that day, for the first time, she, too, fell asleep. When she woke up, because of the light and the noise of the birds that had taken over a cypress tree in the street, it was seven in the morning. She got dressed in a hurry. The young man got up, as well, but he didn't try to stop her from going. He just put his pants on and leaned against the bathroom door, barefooted, while she washed her face and combed her hair. He offered to drive her back, but she didn't want that. She was sure she'd get there quicker by train, and just at that moment, she heard one go by. (The young man used to say that there was something romantic about the sound of a train, like ship's whistles, something that emphasizes the mood we're in, and he was thrilled, not put out at all, to know that Martin used to say the same thing.)

He always went with her to the landing and waited there with her until the elevator arrived. He would always open the door for her. He'd wave goodbye to her with a fairly childish gesture, never giving her a kiss, just in case someone was looking out through a peephole. "Go back in, you're going to catch cold," she probably said to him that day; because they'd come out in a hurry, he was still barefoot, and she got nervous having him there in front of her while she waited for the elevator, which was as old and beautiful as it was slow—Martin described it as being made of mahogany. Clearly he'd taken the trouble of going to the building door once, using the elevator, and looking at the landings in order to gather details to illustrate where things happened, and she found that fact alone, the idea that he had gone sniffing around like a hunting dog, worrying. And there were also things that she couldn't have told him, because she would never have been so talkative, even in her craziest moments, and even so, she's convinced that things happened as he told them, and those things make her feel real anguish, because she has the impression that he was watching them as she said goodbye to the young man and told him to go back to bed, he was barefoot and was going to catch a cold. The young man insists on waiting with her—he tells her again and again to wait, he'll drive her there—but she becomes more and more impatient, puts her hand on his chest, and tells him she's made up her mind, he shouldn't complicate things, he should go back to bed, he can sleep a little longer. Put like that, it sounds as if she resented him because due in part to him, she was now having to face up to her problems, but she doesn't believe that was the case, at least not yet. She doesn't think that the young man was at all worried about her facing up to Martin by herself, about him making a scene, and still less about him getting violent. She'd taken care to tell him that there was no feeling left between Martin and herself, that it was all over, and that they'd both decided to end it. What's more, Martin was supposed to be a liberal, modern man, and nothing could have led them to think that he would be as affected as he turned out to be by her having a relationship with another man.

She wasn't afraid when she got out of the taxi, though she was quite nervous—she was going to have to break off the relationship once and for all. All the lights in the house, or almost all of them, were on, and that shattered her hope that Martin would still be asleep as he usually was at that time those days; lately, he was reading and writing at night, or at least trying to, and didn't get up until well into the morning. She would have preferred him to be asleep, according to his version, in order to get rid of the young man's smell on her skin, but she could have just gone to her sister's house and she didn't. She could have lied, denied that she'd had another relationship, and prevented her "infidelity" from being the reason for their splitting up, which was something that, in reality, they had already done. But she didn't. It didn't occur to her. She doesn't remember seeing him when she went in, so she almost certainly walked across the living room without taking her jacket off. There was an acrid smell of cigarettes in the living room, the stench of several ashtrays full of butts, empty bottles on the tables, the signs of a wasted night, but that, she was later to find out, he had put there to decorate the scene. She walked across the living room, up the stairs, and into the bedroom, thinking he would be there, but he wasn't; she sat on the edge of the still-made bed. She didn't look for him or call him, she just sat there waiting for him, her jacket still on. Something made her think that the farewell was not going to be peaceful, she already felt like a disloyal woman, a woman who had come from another man's bed, regretting that she hadn't been braver. When he appeared in the doorway, she was still in that pathetic posture, quite downcast. "I fell asleep," he wrote that she said, and that, too, could be true, she thinks. It could be what she actually said. Martin didn't seem to be nervous, or down, or tired, even though it was obvious he hadn't slept. "Who is he?" he asked, even though he knew by then, and she meekly told him his name. No more than his name. She would have felt ridiculous if she'd called him "the poet" instead of saying his name. She normally called him "the poet" on the occasions when she couldn't resist the stupid urge to talk about her friend from the writing workshop, driven on by the happiness that feeling admired by him brought out in her, always mentioning his sentimentality and overly precious tastes, mocking him a little to cover up her feelings and for Martin not to suspect anything.

She wasn't surprised that the name was enough for him.

What comes next fits in well with the facts, although there are a few details she isn't sure about. "I'm going," she says, unable to bear the silence, but she doesn't get up off the bed. She stays there sitting on the bed, looking at her hands, head down, and with the deceived man standing next to her. He doesn't speak a word, but he softly puts one of his hands on her shoulder, and on receiving that first kind gesture in such a long time, something breaks inside her, and she says, in a low voice, "I felt abandoned." Her pathetic appearance is reflected in the mirror, and there's a suitcase on top of the closet. She murmurs, "I'm going," but now it's he who stops her from getting up. He kneels down in front of her, puts his arms around her waist, and presses his face into her lap, begging her not to leave him. It's the very picture of pain, of sadness. She's amazed by it, and moved to see such great desperation. Such great pain. He grabs her wrists with great strength and pushes her back onto the bed, and, just as he wrote it, possesses her, without giving her time to even take off her jacket. She remembers that she had wanted to clean herself, the idea of him ejaculating inside her right after she'd come from another man's bed was really revolting to her. He remembers it, too. "I haven't washed," she must have said, and he replied that he didn't care. That must have been how it happened, because she had the feeling, a very real physical perception, that she had the young man's sperm in her vagina, and that Martin's went in to join it, two sperms mixing together in her vagina—an image, the crudest image of promiscuity, which she found revolting, for herself and even more so for Martin, who had gone into the other man's remains and dirtied himself.

The next day, she couldn't go to her date with the young man, because Martin didn't leave her alone for a moment. Somehow she hinted that she would have to give him some type of explanation, so that he wouldn't sit there waiting for her in vain, to which Martin replied, "Tell him I'm *ta plus grande histoire d'amour*," as if admitting that she could have had others, but he didn't leave her alone for a single moment, until one day, taking advantage of the fact that Martin had to go to his parents' house, she called the young man and agreed to meet up with him, not at his apartment but at a bar in the Sagues neighborhood, to have coffee together. The young man was very understanding when she told him that Martin was her main story—a feeling the song *"Ma plus grande histoire d'amour"* put so well—and that they had been together many years and she couldn't break up with him just like that. He took it well, perhaps a little too well, and he wished her happiness, even though he was skeptical about the future of her relationship with Martin, and they agreed to meet up from time to time, to carry on being good friends. Julia isn't sure to what extent the young man's skepticism prompted her to make a greater effort to save her relationship with Martin, but from then on, it was with it in mind that she made space in her life to spend more time with Martin, leaving her job, accepting the opportunity to translate his short stories.

She met up with the young man in a café a couple more times, to talk about everything and nothing—he wanted to know how things were going for her with Martin, and she replied they were going well—but she soon decided not to see him anymore; having secret meetings made her nervous, Martin wouldn't be all right with her meeting the other man like that. Obviously, there was no way she could have suspected he would have such a pathological reaction and suffer so much because of it—he had sudden mood swings, going from fervent love to rough attacks, and that compulsive sexuality of his was not normal. But she had to admit that, to an extent, she was glad that her short relationship with the young man had had such an impact.

For the first time in a long while, they started going out every day, even though it didn't always suit Julia. He would hook his arm into hers, which he hadn't ever done even in their best times, and he talked to her nonstop, as if they had just met. Julia deferred to him in everything, only making one request—that they not go to Sagues, which was a neighborhood he liked going to, because the young man—and she had told him this, obviously—frequented the bars around there and it's where she and he had gone the one and only time they'd gone out together. So they started taking their walks along the Pasealekua Berria, in order not to risk running into the young man, but one day—an afternoon with a south wind, a sea as flat as a plate, and a sky so clear you could see as far as the Matxitxako headland—they saw him standing right beside the Oteiza statue. He was with a young woman, and Julia didn't mind that. Quite the opposite, she was glad that the young man had restarted the relationship he'd told her about. Martin said hello to them with a smile, and Julia thought that he even started to move toward them, but she took his arm in a mute request for them to continue walking. "Well, your poet's rebuilt his life quickly," she remembers he remarked ironically.

They went walking on the Pasealekua Berria three or four more times, and they always came across the other couple, who seemed glad to see them—they both seemed glad, the young man and his girlfriend, as well—and said hello as if they were old acquaintances who often went out to dinner together and wanted to exchange the simple words that couples say to each other when they happen to meet when out for a walk. It was obvious that Martin didn't like that attitude of theirs—once, he said, "I hope that idiot doesn't want the four of us to go out dancing together"—and Julia, too, thought that being so very courteous was a bit much, even though being civilized was fine by her. She doesn't know how many times it happened, because she also sometimes dreamt about it, and in Martin's story, as usual, the time factor is far from clear. In fact, it seems to her as if everything that happened—from the day she ran to catch the train on that last afternoon, and the only night she spent in the young man's apartment, to when Martin gave her *The Woman in a Red Jacket Sitting on the Edge of the Bed*—took place in a single afternoon.

The last time, they came across them in more or less the same place as always. They were right in front of them, the man leaning against the railing and facing away from the sea, holding the girl by the waist. They saw them from a distance, and Julia was tempted to suggest to Martin that they turn around, but thinking that might be insulting, she resisted. Forward they went, seeing the other couple smiling, as usual, as they got closer, and when they were almost up to them, Martin muttered, "Fucking wannabe." In the story, the young poet didn't even stop smiling. Julia only knows that she pulled on Martin's arm and managed to get him to keep walking. They didn't say a single word until they got home, and there, making himself the center of the universe as always, he started calling her a fool because that so-called poet had seduced her without her ever realizing that the young man hadn't been attracted by her mature beauty but by the fact that she was his, Martin's partner; he had taken her to bed to humiliate him, to humiliate Martin. Those words really hurt her; she began to realize that there was some truth in them, and to feel guilty about having fooled around so unthinkingly, without considering the pain it might cause Martin, pain that seemed to grow as the days went by, and then she couldn't take it any more. She started crying. It was she, now, who kneeled down in front of him to beg for forgiveness, for him to forget what had happened, and she might even have spoken that one sentence—"Don't spoil the story for me"—because that was exactly what she felt just then.

But what she asked for just made him insult her more.

He made fun of her, using the details that she herself had given him. Ridiculed her for cheating on him with a premature ejaculator who smelled of garlic (she'd told him that though he wasn't quite a naturopath, he did believe firmly in that particular plant's therapeutic effect, and also that he'd told her, to excuse his lack of sexual control, that he always had difficulty whenever he'd gone a long time "without being in a relationship"). For feeling proud that a man young enough to fuck whoever he wanted hadn't turned his nose up at her cellulitis-covered behind. For allowing a pathetic wannabe to fuck her "because men apparently can't go without it" (she had told him that, as well). For making plans to go off to Turkey in a van. For putting up with his corny poems.

He shouted at her that he would have accepted her cheating on him for some noble passion, but not just because she didn't know how to spend her afternoons.

Julia let him insult the young man, insult her. He shouted at her that she was a whore, and she sat there just as he described Flora Ugalde, curled up on the sofa with her hands over her ears and begging him to forget the whole thing. Why even bother pointing out that he'd also had affairs? Those were only men's affairs. It's peculiar how she came to believe that men's and women's infidelities are different. He was so moved, displeased, and angry, and she was so surprised by it all that, to an extent, she grew to accept that her silly little affair—which, when it came down to it, had been a result of her pain—had been an enormous sin in terms of disloyalty. What's more, the affairs he undoubtedly had were always kept hidden, including the one that led to her having to take antibiotics, because she closed her eyes to his fooling around rather than spying on him. He, on the other hand, had evidence, as well as her own confession. How many times had he held that Villa Flores card in front of her and sarcastically recited those clumsy lines—"You are loyal, more loyal than anyone"? He asked her what those words meant, but she couldn't give him an answer, she didn't understand them, either, didn't know what they meant. Once, she dared to answer that he would have to ask the poet, and he hasn't brought it up again since.

She even ended up hating the young man for writing that stupid line.

And she's also often thought that what Martin really finds insulting is the fact that she went to bed with a bad poet.

He suggested they should go spend a few days at the Argi Eder. They would rebuild their relationship again, from scratch. Julia

340

knew that wasn't possible, but she accepted anyway. It started raining the day after they reached Ainhoa. The Parisians fled, but she didn't dare cancel the reservation they'd made for the week. There wasn't much to do there. Martin went into the village one afternoon. He brought a composition book back with him and started writing with an intensity that Julia had never seen in him before and has never seen since. He spent five days writing nonstop, night and day, taking care to write legibly, not at breakneck speed but also never stopping, as if his inspiration only dried up on the last line of the notebook, or as if that were the exact length of his story. He gave it to her to read. It was the first time he'd ever done that. Until then, he had always read her his manuscripts. She thinks he likes using his intonation to bring out certain passages and make sure the text is well received, and in fact, he does read aloud very well, in particular his own texts, and when it comes down to it, she always finds it disappointing when other people read his texts. "Read it," he said to her, "but not while I'm here." And he went into the village.

When he came back and went into the room, he saw that reading the notebook had made her cry. She asked him not to use it, and he answered that he had no intention of publishing it, he had written it for her.

"I fell asleep," Flora says, as if she were arriving late from work. He couldn't have chosen a more painful, bitter, hurtful sentence.

"Who is he?"

"I felt abandoned."

The red jacket had a large hood. She never wore it again.

Now, having read that pathetic version of events, it's clear to her that for Martin, it isn't so much a matter of any love he might feel for her, it's about him feeling like a wronged owner, and that wrong will never be redressed, and the young man was right when he said that she would never be happy with him.

SHE CAN'T GET TO SLEEP.

Memories that she should reject keep coming back to her, and none of them are pleasant. Why did she usually distrust the stories that her father told her as a child, she wonders. She remembers very well that he spoke to her about whales, about their incredible bodies, nothing else like them in nature, their majesty, and with such imagination and eloquence as she has only ever seen replicated by Michelet in *La mer*, when he described how all fear and anguish gave

341

way to limitless emotion as he moved past those incredible bodies heaving with the joy of life. She thought that they were fantasies, stories, and she never believed him when he said it was possible to sail among whales. But it was true. Even the posters for the Bilbao-Portsmouth ferry mention whalespotting as an added attraction. Some years after her father died, she asked a friend who'd spent time at sea if it was true that you could see them, and he said it was. A few miles from the coast—she doesn't remember the distance he said—they'd passed right by them; but he didn't tell her that with the excitement her father had. (Michelet says they're shy and sometimes even get frightened by a single bird). Perhaps she felt sad then that she hadn't believed him. She thinks she probably did, but she also thinks that it must have been his fault, as well, to an extent, that she doubted the truthfulness of his stories. Be that as it may, the story about the whales is the only one she's been able to confirm.

10

ABAITUA IS DRESSED AND READY to leave the house when he goes into the kitchen. Pilar is holding a piece of toast balanced on the fingertips of one hand and has a cup in the other. She looks straight at him and, after putting the piece of toast down on the plate, says, "I'm not going." As if it were a decision she's just made. There isn't much for her to do at the clinic. That's a good idea, he replies. And adds that he'll come back for lunch. Pilar picks the piece of toast up again and, as she spreads some jam on it, tells him she's going to go out to lunch with Loiola. They haven't seen each other for a long time, and what's more, he has to give them the car back. Abaitua doesn't know if it would be appropriate to say that he'll go along, as well, but he'll be leaving the hospital too late for that. In any case, the fact that she doesn't suggest it to him doesn't encourage him. He decides to ask her to tell him that he, too, would like to see him one of these days.

THERE IS AN UNBEARABLE NOISE OF CROCKERY in the café, and on top of that, everybody there is talking at the same time. Apparently there's an article in the newspaper about the increase in the number of complaints being filed against doctors. That's what they're all talking about, and about the ways it negatively impacts doctors at work—the ordering of unnecessary tests, the increasing obsession with therapeutic issues, the mechanical application of protocols. In other words, doctors' main aim has become protecting themselves from vulture-like lawyers and lawsuits as for-profit enterprise. He feels no desire to join in the conversation in order to tell them that they keep mixing up the concepts of human error, negligence, and incompetence. In his experience, when a doctor makes a mistake, it's a matter of recognizing his or her responsibility and apologizing for it, which usually brings an understanding reply. The problem is when those errors are repeated. A doctor cannot make important decisions alone, decisions that are literally a matter of life or death, without being supervised, without discussing what he or she knows and his or her experience with a group.

For some time, he's thought that certain things, or, more accurately, certain realities have become clear to him, things that seem normal and common but tend to go unnoticed. For instance, he is completely sure that if he looked at the people around him, he would see someone who will soon do something they shouldn't, or not do something they should, something that in the near future, in a few days' time, will kill someone. It's undeniable. He looks at an individual wearing a white coat and dipping the end of a croissant into a cup. He's an anesthesiologist, and he probably can't read an electrocardiogram. He knows that the director of medicine is aware of that, as well. How many operations does he prep patients for every month? he wonders to himself.

This particular morning, however, his problem is Lynn.

The supervisor says that "that American girl" is looking for him. He finds it hard to look into her blue-eyed stare. Although she's his age and at the same professional level as him, she frightens him. She has an aura of dignity—a serious, responsible woman—and he also feels guilty, because her nephew is in prison. Abaitua knows that she feels unfairly treated because his own son hasn't shared that fate. When he's faced with that woman, he feels the same thing he did when he was with his mother as a child, that sensation that she was able to read what was going on inside him, and that she could tell when he wasn't going to keep the promises he made her, and when he'd lied to her. Every time he sees her, he thinks she's going to nod her head slowly, regretfully, and say, "You're a piece of work, you know that?"

So Lynn is looking for him. As for Arrese, he still calls her "the American sociologist." He doesn't like her sticking her nose in the service and going around asking questions. He imitates her voice and accent—"*It's crazy.*" It seems that she had a run-in with one of the midwives, saying that she wasn't treating some sick person properly. It wasn't a sick person, it was a pregnant woman, Abaitua corrects him, wanting to say something. He's already heard about the incident, down in the cafeteria. "The thing is, I don't want her going around sticking her nose in." He has to sit through an outburst about stuck-up, ridiculous feminists who now want women to give birth sitting down. "Although this one's pretty cute." Arrese looks around with a smile of complicity as he says that. And once more, Abaitua has that feeling he had with the supervisor, feeling like a little child standing in front of an adult who knows everything. Arrese knows that he's more pusillanimous, and that's why he treats him so patronizingly. He puts one of his hairy hands on his shoulder. He also knows that he has some weakness when it comes to women, that he gets "mixed up very easily by those bossy women" from time to time; Abaitua's occasionally opened himself up to the man's jibes for getting himself into situations he always ends up regretting. Arrese, on the other hand, would never put the partnership of material interests and affection he shares with his wife in danger.

He realizes that Lynn was right when she said that he spins his wedding ring around constantly when he talks.

"*Hi.*" From her greeting, she sounds pleased and surprised. Her smile is happy, as well. She's been looking for him everywhere. "*Too busy?*" Abaitua tries to use a measured tone—he's been in surgery, and he still has a bunch of reports to write. He particularly hates that last job; writing is really difficult for him. He finds it harder to pick up a pen than a scalpel. She's smiling the whole time as she listens to him, leaning against the wall, holding several files against her chest, one thin-ankled leg crossed over the other. He tries to argue that writing up a report properly is important while the girl listens to him carefully, and while he talks, he notices that his reservations are disappearing. He thinks there's no reason for them to talk about the weekend they spent together, it must be something normal for a young sociologist from New York to go to bed with a man unexpectedly, and there's no reason for him to regret it or to worry. Even so, he promises himself it won't happen again.

The material her dress is made of is light, and it hugs her body. He can't believe he's stroked that belly.

They've talked about writing on some previous occasion. Difficulty in writing usually comes from not being very sure about your ideas—when they're no more than soapsuds, they don't hold onto the paper, they just fade away. The work involved in putting something that's a mess in your head onto paper. They walk away from the surgery area as they talk in circles about this obvious observation, and now they've reached the spiral staircase that almost nobody uses. Even so, there's a flood of people walking down the hallway toward the exit. It's almost three, and he could say that as well as having to write his reports, there's someone waiting to have lunch with him, but he decides that there's no longer any point in running away. He'd been thinking about saying that it was a mistake, that he regrets what happened, but now that seems too dramatic to him. Really, nothing at all has happened.

The girl, on the other hand, tucks a strand of hair behind one ear, a decisive gesture that means she wants to get down to the matter at hand. She says they need to talk, and although she says it in a soft voice, almost sadly, even, it hits him like a blow. It's a terrible sentence, one that a few other women have said to him in the past and that makes him think about how, sooner or later, inevitably, the moment of truth always arrives. Experience tells him that, in the long-term, there are no sins without punishment and that the moment of judgement and penitence is unavoidable.

Right now he feels an urge to run away that's difficult to control; he leans against the shiny brass handrail in order to better face the onslaught. He can't move any further back. His thoughts, as always when he feels trapped, dwell on senseless details. The cleaning staff always put so much effort into polishing the metal on the handrails, even though they don't have time for the most basic cleaning tasks. Sure, they can talk whenever she wants—what else can he say. The girl stretches her lips a moment without actually smiling. What does he think about meeting somewhere outside the hospital, and she nods toward the exit. Looking that way, he sees a corner of a waiting room, a soda machine with brightly colored lights, a man connected to a drip sitting next to a woman who's knitting, both of them calm. To the left there's an empty bed at the end of the corridor. Sure, they can meet up wherever she wants.

He doesn't find it easy to choose a place for their meeting. Abaitua doesn't like bars, the ones he knows are noisy, uncomfortable, designed for ordering rounds of drinks, wolfing down food, and aren't right for talking about intimate matters. And he also has to take into account the idea of being seen in public with the girl, although he's not too worried about that. When he does think of somewhere that might be appropriate, he finds it hard to explain where it is to the girl, and finally, after a pretty absurd conversation, they agree to meet at a tavern called Mesón Portaletas. He'd told her about Portaletas when they were having dinner in Bordeaux. The sea gate in the city wall. A place to shelter if it rains. As far as the time of their meeting is concerned, he decides to set it for tomorrow, at eight, which allows him to take her out to dinner if that's how things are going but doesn't commit him to anything.

So that's what we'll do, then, the girl says—"*Quedamos en eso entonces*." "*En eso quedamos*," Abaitua repeats—we'll do that—and he turns back around on the first step when he says it, because he's already started down the stairs. He has to sort something out in Administration, he says, so that he won't have to go past the nurses' station with her. They are face-to-face now that Abaitua has moved down to the second step, and he can see into her eyes very clearly— they're damp, and she has yellow sparks in her pupils, like pollen. She tucks a strand of hair behind her ear with her left hand now, and this time he thinks it's a sign of hesitation or nervousness. Then she puts her hand on the brass handrail. Abaitua has his right hand on the handrail, and, leaning on it, he moves his head forward a little. He thinks saying goodbye with a kiss is the right thing to do, he doesn't want her to think he's being distant. A sign of weakness, as befits a weak man like him. "A kiss," he says, moving his head forward, and the girl, too, moves forward, but further, to face the stairwell, offering him her right cheek, which is a gesture Abaitua thinks overly genteel, and his lips don't touch her skin, he feels held back by that gesture of hers denying him her mouth; he hurries down another step, and he can clearly see how desolated the girl looks, but he ignores it, turns his back on her, starts going down the stairs, running down them, not stopping, even though the girl calls out his name twice.

STOLEN KISSES. Those girls back in his day, the ones who wanted to be sure of boys' intentions, and who administered their charms with merciless cruelty. They weren't going to give out sex in exchange only for sex, they made it very clear that it was something they weren't interested in, and at best they would "let them do it to them"—that's how they put it—only when the guy agreed to commit himself to a lasting relationship. He understands the reasons behind that behavior, of course. There were many things to be concerned about, not least pregnancy, and the fact that guys tended to look down on girls who agreed to sex as a matter of course, because they were "easy." Perhaps the girls' attitude led him to be less sincere than he should have been, to use twisted strategies that made him feel guilty, to the extent that he sometimes saw himself as a wolf on the prowl for innocent creatures, to see sex not as something fun or playful, as a way of having a relationship with another person, but as foul, animal impulse he should repent for every time he managed to get some. The priests couldn't have put it better when they said that ten minutes of pleasure led to an eternity in flames.

There's even a joke about it: The astonished girl says to the priest, "Ten whole minutes?"

PILAR IS READING THE NEWSPAPER. He isn't sure if she's wearing the same scrubs she had been in the morning. These ones are a pale violet color. He asks her how lunch with Loiola went, and the answer is, "We didn't have lunch." Apparently, their son had something he had to do, and they postponed their meeting for another day.

To break the silence, Abaitua tells her they have a thirty-year-old woman who went into septic shock as the result of a clandestine abortion and then not being operated on soon enough. "In this day and age," says Pilar. It's clear she's not very interested in the subject.

On the television, there's a couple sitting behind a kind of school desk. They must be around fifty, and their appearance is far from refined. (The woman, in particular, has very neglected teeth.) They each have a nametag stuck on their chest. Paco and Juana. The presenter asks them questions, and they take turns answering. Abaitua has seen the show before. Prizes are given to the couples that know each other best, they have to give an answer matching the one their partner has written on a board and kept hidden from them. They kiss each other gently on the lips and applaud when they get it right.

Pilar looks up at the screen when he gives her his opinion about the teeth you tend to see on television. He doesn't think they match Spain's overall economic development. Just at that moment, the man is flipping his board around and showing what he's written on it: "*Que se ponga ropa interior más sexy.*" He wants her to wear sexier underwear. They give each other a kiss.

They could talk about whether such a show would be possible on Basque television. They would conclude that it wasn't. "Fortunately, don't you think?" He could argue either side, but he would probably end up being the one to defend the positive side of the matter: they, Basques, don't have that easy openness, they're much quicker to feel embarrassed.

What most surprises him is seeing people of more or less his own age, who were therefore subject to the same repression he was and who on top of that never had the same opportunities he did to access a more open world (when it came down to it, he went to Paris and read *Modern Sexual Techniques* and *Le Nouvel Observateur* in 1968), shedding their inhibitions to an extent that would be unthinkable for him, not just in front of a television camera but even in the intimacy of his own bedroom.

The woman's written "*Bailarle el baile de los siete velos*" on her board—she would do the Dance of the Seven Veils for him. She holds her hand in front of her mouth to hide her teeth when she laughs.

"You should call him yourself," Pilar says, right after Abaitua says goodnight. Obviously, she's talking about Loiola. It seems as if they haven't said a single word to each other since he came in, since she told him that the two of them didn't meet up for lunch in the end. He remains silent in order for her to explain what he thinks she wants to tell him. Her words are failing her. Apparently she's afraid that something might happen to him, someone might want to get back at him for not being in prison with the rest of them. She says she would feel better if he could go back to the States, at least until the trial is over. What can he say to her? Basically, that he thinks her worries are unfounded, but that he'll speak with him and try to convince him.

He's in bed with the light off, even though it's too early for him to go to sleep. He's remembering Lynn's gesture—offering him her cheek and twisting her lips in the other direction like an old woman. And he doesn't mind having gone down the stairs without turning back when she called his name. He wonders if she might have interpreted his behavior as a cancellation of their appointment. He wished that were so.

He doesn't want to think about Lynn.

He hears Pilar's usual noises from the bathroom next door. The sound of the electric toothbrush going up and down the hallway at intervals. The sound of the various pots of lotion being set down on the shelf. He remembers how soft her skin was the first time they made love. An exact memory of her skin's softness and freshness. It never occurred to him that they might make love in that Ford Taurus as soon as they arrived from Zaragoza, the day after they met each other. Reaching that objective usually required several months of complicated preliminary maneuvers. He was amazed at how receptive she was; the young men at the time were programmed for being stopped by the girls, otherwise they would fulfil their biological destiny, which was to go all the way. Pilar had wanted to maintain her dignity, it seems, and live up to the expectations of a progressive man of Abaitua's age. That was how she lost her virginity, by believing that there was no place for excessive modesty with a dyed-in-the-wool leftist man such as himself.

His first time with a woman.

350

11

JULIA LOOKS AT THE MESS, the same one she finds in the living room every morning. Piled-up books, and on top of the piles of books, glasses, plates with scraps of fruit on them, yogurt containers, dirty little bits of kitchen paper everywhere. Sheets of newspaper spread out. His index cards get everywhere, they're on chairs and on the floor, rather like a plague. His output of index cards is in inverse proportion to the number of words he puts into his story—the more cards he fills in, the less he writes. She picks up a handful of them and tries to decipher them. She understands little more than the odd word. Two quotes from Botho Strauss on the same card: "The Mohave Indians"—she thinks it says *Mohave*—"usually carry on talking even long after the person they are talking with has gone away." "It's today again. What part of what whole?"

The main character in *The Man in Front of the Mirror* had woken up with that phrase in his head the day before—"It's today again." The weather was good, and he didn't feel bad, no pain; two nights before it had been torture taking a piss, and now there was no trace of those horrible spasms, which had become a far-off, pleasant memory. (He likes bringing his suffering to mind, it allows him to enjoy the awareness of no longer feeling any pain). Even the concierge's wife, who'd been looking at him with pity recently, although charitably holding back the obvious comments she usually made, said he was looking healthy today. He thought he looked good, as well. When he put his hand on his forehead and brushed his hair back, he even thought he saw some new hairs there, fine ones, almost transparent. The dermatologist assured him that hair loss isn't the main worry when it comes to going bald, and he's certainly losing hair, as he can see every time he washes it down the drain—hair is supposed to fall out, in the same way that leaves fall off trees. The main worry is hair not growing back, no new hair growing; he doesn't want to lose the hope that he does have some soft new hair, and he checks to see that it isn't an optical illusion created by the light flooding in. After eating breakfast eagerly, he decides to go for a walk through the neighborhood around the hospital. He often does that when the weather's good, even though it's uphill on the way there. He walks around the hospital complex and often goes as far as the research park. Sometimes, though, he goes into the hospital and walks along the corridors, has a drink in the cafeteria, which is usually full of very noisy people, or even goes to sit in the outpatient surgery lounge when there's a free spot; it's usually as busy as the cafeteria, even though it isn't as noisy right now. It does him good to spend time there, with none of the anguish he feels when he has an appointment, no need to worry about whether he should knock on the door or wait for the nurse to come out and call his name, and above all, no need to worry about what expression he's going to see on the doctor's face after spending several anxious minutes watching him or her sift through a pile of files looking for his test results.

He feels comfortable among that group of patients and the people who've come to the hospital with them, he looks at them with curiosity, not having anything to worry about himself. As if he himself were healthy.

He's just gone for a walk around the Maternity and Pediatric Ward, following the blue line on the floor, and he stopped at a large window to look at the rows of newly born babies, which also made him feel better, improved his mood for some imperceptible, idiotic reason. In Orthopedics, he sees people plastered up, they're past the worst and usually very lively. He avoids Infectious Diseases, for obvious reasons, and Internal Medicine, as well, afraid that some doctor or other might recognize him. He goes to Cardiology. It's completely calm there. He thinks visitors there must be very strictly controlled, unlike in Orthopedics, to make sure that when patients are discharged, they get the tranquility they need—they're not up to much celebrating. He sits down on one of the chairs lined up against the wall at the end of the corridor, next to a couple of patients and their visitors. The patients are easy to distinguish, because of their gowns, but he would know who they were anyway, even if they were wearing their street clothes. The patients are men and the visitors are women, their wives, in fact, as he quickly deduces from their conversations. At that moment, one of the patients admits that he's not looking forward to going home, he feels safer at the hospital. He says being more than two steps away from a defibrillator makes him afraid. The four of them recall the day they first came to the emergency room, and while he listens to them talking about the alarming symptoms, the fear of arriving too late, and the tests the man had to go through, he suddenly feels like dropping in at the ER.

While he wets his face in the washbasin in a restroom just outside the entrance to ER, he doesn't think he'll be able to go in yet. In the mirror, his face looks worse than it did in the morning, he doesn't know if it's because of the light or because he's nervous, and he doesn't even look to see if the new little hairs on his forehead had been an illusion or not. He doesn't plan his next move. In the ER reception area, he tells the first person he sees walking by in a white coat that he's feeling bad. Without being too dramatic about it. He's broken into a sweat, he's dizzy, he feels a pain in his heart, and he has pins and needles in his left arm. As they take him away in a wheelchair, he feels something shake in his heart, the excitement caused by the role he's playing, he imagines. He feels sure about his heart. In fact, it's the only internal organ he doesn't have any reason to worry about. His pulse has always been stable, and he tends to have low blood pressure. He tells that to the nurse who's putting suction pads on him to run an electrocardiogram. She's around sixty and is wearing blue latex gloves (he wonders whether she wears the same pair of gloves all day and touches everything with them). It's a small, dark room. There's just enough space for the stretcher, a small table, and the EKG machine, and the only window faces out onto a wall that can be no further than three feet away. He says to the nurse that it must be hard to spend eight hours a day in that miserable little room putting suction pads onto sick bodies such as his and then taking them off again. The woman smiles at him with gratitude. He doesn't know the half of it. She admits that sometimes, when she leaves, she feels disorientated, mixed up, and often walks all the way down to the city just to clear her head. The man commiserates with her, it isn't a very nice street to walk down with all that traffic. That leads him to the subject of Donostia, and he talks about how it's being drowned in concrete and cement while the device he's connected to noisily scrapes along the paper. The man is enjoying talking, and so is the woman, he can tell. The man says that Mount Urgull is an oasis in the city, a paradise that few people visit, and the nurse admits it's been years since she last went there, but this weekend she'll go and she'll think of him. She asks him if he's nervous, putting a hand on his shoulder—a gloved hand, the man is pleased to see. He says no, he feels fine, and it's true. There's a vase on the Formica-topped table with several many-petalled white flowers in it—they look like chrysanthemums. He decides he's going to send her a bunch of flowers.

A BUNCH OF FLOWERS.

He writes various notes under that heading:

A MAN is going to jump from a sixth-floor balcony. He's holding a bunch of flowers firmly in his right hand. He decides not to let go of it, he wants the bunch of flowers with him when he hits the ground. He holds them with great concentration, like a pole-vaulter in a stadium readying himself to break a record.

THE MAN GOES INTO THE ROOM where his wife is receiving hospice care. They've just given her Dormicum to sedate her. She lies there with her eyes closed, calm, her skin white like wax, more beautiful than ever, like Atala. *La belle morte.* A large bunch of red roses at the head of her bed. On the card: "I will love you forever. Juan." The man, who is not called Juan, has never given his wife a bunch of flowers.

THE MAN GOES INTO A FLORIST'S, planning to send one of his coworkers a bunch of flowers for her birthday. They get on well together, but he's never dared to tell her that he's in love with her. There's another customer in front of him, a tall, elegant man who's giving precise instructions for how he wants his bouquet made up. It's obvious he knows a lot about flowers. He chooses them with care, calling each flower by its name—petunias, gladioli, jasmine. As the florist is putting the bunch together for him, he gets her to take a few of the flowers out, because they don't look good in the arrangement. He gives her his business card and tells her where to send the bouquet. It's for his coworker. He doesn't know what to do when his turn comes and ends up asking for a plant that's not too expensive, a geranium, to give to his mother.

THE HUSBAND VISITS HIS WIFE, who is convalescing after a life-saving operation. Her illness has enabled him to see just how much he needs his wife, he feels completely in love with her and regrets having been a disloyal, careless husband. So he is fully determined to change, to be more responsible and agreeable, and that's why he's so sorry to see the large bunch of flowers on her bedside table—he regrets not having thought of that himself. He's been thinking about more practical things. Tidying up the house and painting their bedroom, as his wife had long wanted him to do, arranging a trip—he hasn't quite decided where—for when she's fully recovered. He figures her coworkers must have sent the flowers—someone usually goes around to all the desks collecting money for such things—but when he asks her, she gives him an ambiguous smile and says she doesn't know, there wasn't a card with them. There's a sticker on the cellophane around the flowers with the florist's name on it, and the husband decides to call after he leaves the hospital, and the urge to find out makes him cut his visit short and, above all, prevents him from being as open with her as he had wanted to be. When he leaves the hospital and telephones to investigate, they answer him politely but firmly that they are not allowed to give the information he's asking for, because they have a strict privacy policy, and after listening to an uninteresting lecture on client confidentiality, he decides to call their friends and relatives to tell them how she is and casually drop in a thank you for the roses. All the people he calls deny having sent them and sound embarrassed, because they think he's reproaching them for not having done so, all except for a neighbor woman and a brother-in-law, both of whom say it was the least he could do, his wife had always been so good to them, although the man is sure they cannot possibly have sent them, because of the sheer quantity of flowers—he counted four dozen roses—and because both of them are incredibly tight-fisted. And then, feeling jealous, he goes to the florist to investigate further. He buys a bunch of flowers, neither very cheap nor very expensive, as an excuse to establish contact, and then he goes back again, becoming a regular customer, in order to gain the florist's confidence; she's an agreeable and beautiful woman. He buys flowers every day—not as many as the ones his wife received in her bouquet—and the florist treats him exceptionally well. A man who enjoys buying so many flowers for his mother, aunt, and sister—that's what the jealous man tells her—just has to be affectionate and caring. In fact, he starts giving flowers to everyone, to his wife, as well, because he thinks it's a pity to throw them away once he's bought them, though he sometimes has no choice but to do so—and here the writer intervenes in a friendly way to reflect on the things that the man is, unfairly, not allowed to do—because he's afraid that people might think something strange is going on.

MARTIN IS STILL AT BREAKFAST, even though it's very late. He's wearing pajamas, one of those pairs that's completely shriveled up and that Julia hides from him whenever she finds them. She doesn't really need to ask him what sort of mood he's in, that's clear from the expression on his face, and even more from the state of his hair, ruffled and standing on end as if he's had an electric shock. She thinks that if she were to hold a small piece of paper to the tuft of hair standing up in the middle of his head, the paper would stick to it, like the bits of paper they used to get to stick to pens at school by rubbing them, but she doesn't dare to do it.

So when she asks him how he is, it isn't because she's holding onto some remote possibility that he'll say he's fine, instead it's to let him know that she's ready to listen to his reasons for feeling low so early in the day. But he only answers that he's had a nightmare, a reply that's almost become a proverb and that he uses to say there's nothing for her to understand, she should just leave him alone.

The phone rings. A game of suspense to see who will be the one to get up and answer it. Because it's always for Martin, Julia's decided that she won't pick up the phone ever again, tired as she is of having to guess if he's supposed to be "at home" or not for different callers, and of him reproaching her for being a bad liar when she says he's out. Martin gets up. It's someone from his family, she can tell just by his "hello." He goes to the library for some privacy, as if Julia cared about what he discusses with his mother or his sister.

She picks up the pieces of paper, notebooks, and loose index cards and puts them on a corner of Martin's desk. She's picking up plates, cups, and yogurt containers when Martin appears again. He'll do it. Astonishingly, he even starts dusting off the coffee table and, while he does that, asks if she'd like him to make her some coffee— he has a delicious fruit cake in the kitchen. Julia doesn't know why he's being so considerate. He says he hasn't seen Zigor for a long time and he'd like to have lunch with him one day. She soon finds out the reason for his change of mood when he says, as if he's suddenly remembered, "By the way, speaking of food . . ." and tells her that he has to go to his parents' house for lunch. In fact, he's arranged with his mother or sister on the phone that they'd both go, and now he's worried that maybe she won't go with him or won't behave as he'd like her to—*comme il faut*, in other words—in a way that will demonstrate they're an exemplary couple.

Suddenly she feels an almost sadistic urge and takes advantage of the importance of the moment to mock him, asking him about his *penthouse* girl. Isn't he afraid of what she might think if she catches him in those ugly pajamas and robe, and she's amused to see that he's still irritated with the girl, still feeling betrayed, or left out, perhaps. "She went out very early," he says, with a note of disdain in his voice.

THE EXCITEMENT OF OPENING A PACKAGE. The mailman's brought the original version of *Montauk*, and another book by Frisch called *Fragebogen*, which she hadn't heard of before.

Montaigne sounds like this in German: *Dies ist ein aufrichtiges Buch, Leser, es warnt dich schon beim Eintritt daß ich mir darin kein anderes Ende vorgesetzt habe als ein häusliches und privates.* So the book is *"aufrichtig"*—sincere.

Ein Schild, das Aussicht über die Insel verspricht: OVERLOOK. A sign promising a view across the island: OVERLOOK.

Being familiar with the Spanish and French translations helps a lot when reading it in German. The shaggy white jacket is *"la velluda y blanca chaqueta"* in Spanish, and in German it's *"weißliche Zotteljacke halte"*: *"Als ich ihr später die weißliche Zotteljacke halte."* She doesn't know how she would translate that. She imagines she'd prefer the Spanish version of "shaggy"—*de pelo largo*—to *velludo*, meaning "fluffy." In any case, that wouldn't be the most pressing problem.

DIES IST EIN AUFRICHTIGE BUCH, LESER
und was verschweigt es und warum?

357

This is a sincere book, reader,
and what does it reflect, and why?

LYNN SHOWS UP loaded with file folders. She's come from the hospital with Harri, but Harri stopped in at the pharmacy to buy something for her headache. She's glad that the German copy of *Montauk* has arrived, it seems to confirm to her that Julia is going to translate it into Basque, and she wants to look for the passage titled *"Check out,"* the one that has Max reflecting on how much he spent for the two nights at the hotel, the passage whose Spanish translation made her so angry. But the writer, who she finds still in his pajamas, is determined to explain to the girl why he's still dressed like that and to describe the nightmares that have been spoiling his sleep for years now.

It always starts with him standing in front of the door to a room. For some reason, he doesn't want to go in, but someone forces him to open the door, and there, inside, he comes face-to-face with a couple, a man and a woman. The woman is sitting on the side of a bed, and the man is standing next to her, a hand resting on her shoulder. The man is wearing serious-looking clothes, dark clothes, a black vest and tie, and the woman is only wearing a negligée. He says that he's aware of some things even though they aren't made clear in the nightmare. For instance, the woman is young and beautiful. He says he doesn't see her face, or the man's. But he does see some other things in great detail. For example, the woman's negligée is made of satin, it's salmon pink, and it had bows on its edges; she has long nails that are painted bright red. He says once more that he doesn't want to see what there is on the other side of the door, and Julia thinks he looks like a madman from an old-fashioned asylum sitting there in his shrunken, striped pajamas, his hair standing on end, his eyes closed, gripping the arms of the chair with all his strength to demonstrate how he is trying to resist being made to go into the room, but someone is forcing him, pushing him and dragging him. Finally, just when he can't take any more—and here he puts on an expression of being absolutely defeated—seeing the couple makes him feel incredibly frightened, and then he wakes up sweating. The girl, after listening to him seriously, says it's probably a trauma from his childhood. What else could she say to him?

Julia wonders where some people get the idea that their dreams, whether good or bad, might be of any interest to the rest of humanity.

DANN IRRITIERT ES IHN. As was to be expected, what Max is irritated about is the fact that Lynn "*da sie die Reservation besorgt hat, ungefähr weiß, was er da bezahlt für zwei Übernachtungen*"—that she made the booking and she therefore knows how much he had to pay for the two nights.

As soon as Harri comes in, she tells Martin that he cannot receive people at home dressed like that, and she sends him upstairs to get dressed. She says her headache's nothing serious, she just isn't sleeping much, because she's in a state of permanent excitement, "because I'm still looking for the man." Julia's beginning to feel bored by the whole story, and in fact even more so by Harri's insistence on telling them stupid stories, as if she were a teenager, and at the same time, she dislikes her own weak personality, which leads her to always allow other people to impose their stupid topics of conversation on her.

She'd like to share with Lynn her impression that she will never be able to read another novel by Frisch, and how arriving at that conclusion has been one of the saddest confirmations she's ever felt of the fact that life is limited. A foolish thought that moves her in the same way that some sunsets in the countryside do. She's sure Lynn would understand her. This whole line of thinking came about because of her disappointment at learning that *Fragebogen* is not, as she had thought, a lost Frisch novel but, as its title—which translates to "Questionaire"—suggests, a recompilation of questions that appeared in *Tagebuch 1966–1971*. Ten questionaires, with twenty-five questions each, except in the fifth one, which has one more. Two hundred and fifty-one questions altogether—a new and unusual way of approaching the concept of an essay. Questions about the human condition (about marriage, hope, property and money, friendship, country, death, and many other subjects), some of which seem dumb, most of which are unanswerable but unavoidable, simple, and frightening; the publishers' presentation says they "challenge the reader to recognize the fragility of the world we live in and to acknowledge the false assumptions upon which the human condition is constructed."

She translates a few at random:

DO YOU LOVE ANYONE?

Would you change places with your wife?

You find out that someone has an incurable disease: do you give him or her hope that you know to be false?

Have you ever embraced a dead person?

When you think about death, what comes to mind:

What you're leaving behind?

The international situation?

A particular landscape?

The idea that it's all been in vain?

The things that won't get done without you?

The mess in your drawers?

Have you ever found yourself without any friends, or lowered your standards for friendship when faced with the possibility?

Now Harri's complaining that they're talking about *Fragebogen* rather than paying attention to what she's telling them about her efforts to find the man from the airport. "You're awful, you could stop reading for a minute," she says to her, and Julia, overcoming her desire to tell her that she's bored of her silly stories, closes the book. And then, all of a sudden, she sees Harri touching her armpit, and she asks her if she's gotten an appointment with Abaitua yet.

It isn't the first time Harri's called her an embittered old woman. So when Harri starts telling her story, Julia has no choice but to pay attention to her. At first, when she says once more that the man not answering her ad only seemed like a setback at first glance, Julia is sure that she's pulling her leg, but when she starts telling them about her trip to the Iberia offices, she realizes without a doubt that she actually has gone down there and told them that she unwittingly picked up something of someone else's on a flight back from London and now wants to return it. What she wanted to do was return the object, she felt it was her obligation. The object, of course, was the English edition of *Montauk* that Lynn had lent her. On the dedication page, she wrote more or less the same thing she had put in the newspaper, asking the man for a second chance, and adding her cell phone number. She went to the offices, showed them the dedication—which she deduced must have been something very personal for the owner of the book, seeing as how it had someone's telephone number on it asking for a very important second opportunity—and told them she felt very bad about having taken the book into her possession, absolutely accidentally—she underlined that—because the man had dropped a bunch of books, she'd helped him to pick them up, and apparently she put the last one into her bag, because she, too, had had a book in her hands, which, it seems, she must have given to the man somehow, because she can't find it now, but that isn't what she's concerned about, that isn't the question, the other book is the question, the one she showed them, and it was irreplaceable for the man, she had to give it back to him. She said that she hadn't realized during the journey, because although she always takes a book with her, she never reads in planes, her fear of flying spoils her concentration, and instead she'd entertained herself by glancing at magazines; she only realized that the book in her bag wasn't her own when she got home in the evening. Apparently, the people in the office passed the copy of *Montauk* around, at least half a dozen people looked at it, and all of them read the dedication without seeming impressed. Stupid women—the type of women who think they're beautiful and elegant just because they're dressed like flight attendants—who didn't realize what an important problem it was. They started saying that, when it came down to it, it was only a book and if it really mattered to him, he would take the trouble to try and find it. And after listening to all they had to say, she asked to speak with the manager, and when he came out, she repeated her request to him, word for word, with a whole crowd of people listening to her, office workers, customers, and even a courier. She tried to convince him that there was no doubt that the book was more than just a book—mentioning the message and the telephone number once again—and she also said that the man might not have realized where he'd lost the book, and because of that, she was asking them to do all they could to get in touch with him, to tell him they had the book. The office manager was very strict—they didn't have time, they didn't know the man's name, they didn't know what seat he'd sat in, and all of that theoretical effort just to ask him if he's misplaced a novel called *Montauk*. But Harri didn't give up. If they gave her the passenger list, she would be happy to take care of it herself. She was just trying to do a good deed, to give the man back something that could be of vital importance to him, and give some woman the second chance she was so urgently asking for. She said that they couldn't possibly ignore such a request, and an older woman who was standing next to her said that she was right. Perhaps the two lovers would never see each other again if the book didn't make it back to its owner. The issue of confidentiality came up. Nowadays, it's the first thing you're told when you ask for information at a counter. She's convinced that passengers' data is sent from computer to computer, from phone companies to insurance companies, from travel agencies to banks, and that all of it probably goes through the Civil Guard and the CIA, as well, but she has no choice but to say that she understands.

"*¿Qué te parece?*"

Happy that they have listened to her with attention, she starts using pauses. To an extent, her habit of telling things in the present makes everything take longer. Julia's talked about it with Martin, because he also tends to do that with the verbs in his writing. You could say "rabies drove him mad, and he killed everyone," but if you said it in the present, you would need more details. And she gives them. Harri plays the part of each person in the conversation, doing their voices and expressions, too—herself trying to convince the office manager, speaking slowly but seriously and emphasizing her words, saying that love has to be given a chance; the under-standing, sympathetic elderly woman behind her saying that she's beginning to rethink her trip to the Canary Islands; the office manager, more understanding now, as well, perhaps taking the other customer's reaction to heart, saying he's sorry, he would love to help, but as he said . . . and Harri, once more, saying she's not asking this for herself—she points a finger at her chest—but for a couple that undoubtedly has problems. But the office manager, against his own will, sticks to his story and says that tracking the man down might put him in a difficult position. What would happen, for instance, if the book guy is married and traveled without telling his wife about it to go and see a lover of his, and the wife, on reading the letter that they would have to send the man, finds out about his affair that way? He says that some women are very jealous, real control freaks, and he knows what he's talking about. Harri didn't like him calling the man "the book guy," but in any case, to counter those unhelpful observations, she tried to argue that if they did it intelligently, they'd be able to avoid that problem. There's no need to write a letter, it would be better to phone, and if a woman answers, they could say it was for a market survey. But the office manager was inflexible. Theirs is a serious company and they can't deceive their customers by doing fake surveys, and it was then that Harri realized that the old woman who had come out in her support had growing doubts as she listened to the office manager's objections, and the situation got even worse for her when he asked whether the "book guy" had sat next to her, and when she had to say no, he hadn't, he took out a seating plan for a 727 and asked her to please point out what seat the guy had been in, and she couldn't tell him that, either. It was then that she realized, by the way everybody was looking at her, that she couldn't do anything. As if what had happened thus far weren't enough, the manager said that she should leave the book with them, just in case the man came and asked them for it, and, of course, she had no choice but to do so.

"*¿Qué te parece?*"

That wasn't the end of the story. She was completely depressed when she left the travel agency—"I had no hope whatsoever"— and she started wandering around with no particular destination in mind—"no hope whatsoever, *truly hopeless*," she added for Lynn— when, after crossing just a couple of streets, her phone rang. "I want to give you another chance." A man's voice said it to her, and for a moment, she thought she was going to faint. The man didn't tell her his name when she asked who he was, instead he asked her—or ordered her, really—to wait for him in the bar at the nearby Hotel Ercilla—he'd be there in ten minutes. And how will I know who you are? He said she shouldn't worry about that.

She spends more than ten minutes describing the situation, even though all three of them, who are curious, ask her to tell them what happened once and for all. A description of the bar, soft armchairs, the dark lighting, men standing around in suits, the type of men that look like they follow bullfighting, a couple of good-looking women very elegantly dressed and made-up, perhaps excessively so—a nervous scene, exciting, even, for a woman by herself. Her nerves, her emotions, her heart like an unbridled horse, incapable of thinking. She orders a gin and tonic, something she hasn't drunk since before the Holocene Epoch. Then the man appears. He's young, around thirty, quite good-looking, his black hair slicked back with shiny hair gel, he's wearing a burgundy-red jacket and a blue tie with the red and yellow of the Spanish flag on it in narrow, diagonal stripes. He has a gold-colored nametag on his lapel: Adolfo Aróstegui. That's what he tells her when he sits down in the armchair next to hers, he's Adolfo Aróstegui, he works at the airline, he's heard what happened, he understands the situation very well and wants to help her. Harri orders another gin and tonic, and drinking it down in one gulp makes her feel very good. The young man, like the office manager shortly before, asks if she doesn't remember what seat the man had sat in, putting another 727 seating plan in front of them with a cross where she had sat. The young man makes her feel more relaxed, he's more patient than his boss had been, is at least able to narrow down the area he must have been sitting in to a dozen seats, and the young man says that's enough to go on, that information will save them a lot of work. The young man is very considerate, and he has a nice voice. The voice of an accomplice. He, too, is very much aware of the magic of unexpected meetings, and you can see he's being sincere by the way he looks at her. How did he know she was the woman who was offering the second opportunity? Because he knows about women. He says it without puffing himself up. What's more, the obvious thing would have been to call the person who had written the message in the book and tell her that the man had lost it. Elementary. His boss hadn't thought of that, because, like most bosses, he was an idiot. Harri is embarrassed that she herself never realized that her strategy had that small error in it, but finally she laughs with the young man as they imagine what would have happened if the office manager had been smarter and had called the number on the dedication page of the book and her phone had rung right there in front of everyone at the airline counter.

"*¿Qué te parece?*"

The gin and tonic was flowing easily though her veins, and she enjoyed telling the young man about her meeting with the man at the airport when he asked her to tell him the real story in full detail. He listened to her with great interest. The young man was the very opposite of the type of men she likes, she says—in fact, he must have been somewhere there at the airline counter when she was, but she hadn't noticed him—he looked right-wing and vain, with that gel in his hair and the Spanish flag on his tie. A bit overly touchy, one of those people who are always putting their hand on your shoulder and moving their faces too close to yours. She was a little bit dizzy and completely relaxed there in that comfortable armchair at the Hotel Ercilla, leaning far back in the intimate semi-darkness; then the young man said he had to go back to work. He said once more that he would do everything he could to give her a second chance, he would call her as soon as he found something out, and then he went, and she was left alone, happy, her heart full of good sensations.

"*Qué te parece.*"

This time, the way she says it, without the intonation of a question, makes it a full stop. And it's late. The writer says that as he stands up, patting the inside and outside pockets of his jacket, or rather, the parts of his anatomy where those pockets would be if he were dressed, and the front and back pockets of his pants, which is what he always does whether what he's looking for would fit into them or not. For some reason that Julia can't fathom, he does the same thing when he wants to go somewhere, it's his way of saying that he has no choice in the matter. On this occasion, he says he's running late and has to go to Hernani and buy a puff pastry tart at Adarraga. They're old fashioned tarts, made using good butter, and his family is addicted to them. He tells Lynn that she has to try them, even though they're very rich and filling, and, suddenly enthusiastic, he suggests she come and meet his family, "*a meeting that might be of great anthropological interest,*" (Julia doesn't know why he says things like that in English), but the girl says she isn't sure how much time she's going to have. Martin presses her; he'd be pleased if a busload of tourists came along, anything to make sure the conversation at the table didn't revolve around personal or family matters, anything to keep his mother entertained, to keep the atmosphere from getting too intense. Julia being there is no longer enough to guarantee that lunch will go by with relative normality and without anyone getting angry.

JULIA TAKES A DEEP BREATH before going into Martin's parents' house, in the same way she would fill her lungs with air before diving into the water. She really feels like some out of place element there. Everything is dark, closed, heavy. The furniture, the carpets, the wallpaper, the paintings hanging from the walls, the atmosphere that sticks to the walls. The mahogany table with its gray marble cover, the cut crystal sweet wine glasses, the soggy Adarragaren tart, the porcelain place settings with the baroque designs. Their first duty, almost before introducing anyone, is to speak about Father, without worrying about him sitting there smiling, as if he weren't there, to discuss his senility, his incontinence, the need to have two people to look after him at all times. Martin's mother raises her hands to her temples, which she then massages with the tips of her fingers, just as her son does when he complains about his nightmares. Or the other way around, rather—he does it exactly the way his mother does. She says she can't take any more, she's exhausted, as if it were she herself cleaning him, feeding him, and putting him to bed. Good Lord, Good Lord, she keeps saying. She's thin, tall, large-boned. Her hands, above all, look huge, which is an impression that's increased, perhaps, by the arthritis that's deforming her joints. She wears little jewelry, but the little she does is unmissable: an enormous ring with a huge stone on her little finger; a thick gold bracelet, which looks like an anchor chain; a pearl necklace that goes around her neck four times. Curiously, wearing so much gold does not stop her from looking austere, it does not seem to embellish her; it's a sign of status, quite simply. She has thick gray hair that's lightly sprayed, combed up, and held in a bun. Her nose is pronounced, her eyes small, and her mouth delicate. Julia knows from old photos that she was beautiful as a young woman, and Martin and his sister think of her as a great beauty. They don't take after her.

Martin's sister, the eldest, the one who humorously refers to herself as the old maid, usually gives Julia clothes. Good clothes, ones she's hardly ever worn, or hasn't worn at all, and thinks don't look good on her, but all the garments are very classical and not to Julia's liking. Every time she goes to the house, the sister takes her to her room as though it were some secret between the two of them and gets her to try something on. Everything looks good on her. Sometimes she puts that down to having "a poor person's body." Today Julia's wearing a printed Hermès scarf, so that the sister won't think she doesn't appreciate her gifts. In fact, she likes being given used clothes, just like Frisch with his friend W., and the only problem is that, not being her style, she doesn't feel comfortable when she wears them. She usually tells her they'll be wasted on her, she won't ever wear them, but the sister doesn't give up and insists, telling her that she has to take the things, because they're Prada, Loewe, or Gucci. What's more, the reasons she offers for passing her clothes on are wholly reasonable and never make her feel like she's in debt to her—it's Julia who's doing her a favor by taking them off her hands. The sister feels guilty about keeping clothes that she doesn't wear in her closet, and giving them away means that she can buy new things. Of course, she recognizes the Hermès scarf, and she pulls it down over her shoulders—Julia just had it tied around her neck—and says it looks great on her.

JE M'EN SOUVIENS—I REMEMBER. In that house, with its gloomy atmosphere, Julia used to keep herself amused by talking with Martin's father. They would sit out on the enclosed balcony off the living room and look out over the Alderdi Eder gardens and the bay. She found the old man entertaining; even though he was a long way gone from reality, he was able to talk about his own worlds with coherence and a great amount of detail. More so than people who hadn't lost their minds, as if not being completely stuck in the present made it easier for him to situate himself in whatever place and time they happened to be talking about. But it's obvious he's gotten much worse since she last saw him. He gives her a foolish-looking smile. He speaks to her in Basque, as affectionately as he can, and in French when he talks about things that happened in his childhood, when they were exiled in Hazparne, which is his favorite subject. "*J'étais un exilé, moi*, that's the truth." He normally laughs when he says that. They had to go into exile because his mother's family were Basque nationalists, in fact his uncle was a member of parliament for the EAJ—the Basque nationalist Euzko Alderdi Jeltzalea party—a friend of the famed and ill-fated Jesús Galindez, also exiled under Franco. Apparently he's even mentioned in one of his books—he put his own life in danger by saving a large number of people from the Reds, particularly priests and nuns and right-wing folk, including some fifth columnists, in Donostia as well as in Madrid. His own father—Martin's grandfather—on the other hand, was from a liberal family, enterprising people, professional people (both of them, father and son, were civil engineers), with a lot of money but of no political significance. The old man's father must have been a republican, although he was also a Basque culture enthusiast, like Martin's father, and like him, he spoke the basic Basque that he had learned from his wet nurses, and he was a great *pilota* player. He'd taken charge of organizing the exile of a large part of his wife's family; although they were from an old, illustrious

Bizkaian line, they had little economic wealth. Martin's father used to speak ironically about his mother's family's contradictions, their being so nationalistic and yet none of them speaking Basque, being so far removed from the canons of Basque tradition—whether nationalistic or otherwise—which his father, on the other hand, so typified, in his habits, his loyalties, and his code of honor. The old man thought that his mother's family's nationalism, and his wife's, too, amounted to little more than folklore, and he used to joke about his extended family's enthusiasm for Bizkaia: they were very nice, and well-learned, even, but terrible parasites, and he used to say that they would have stayed in exile in Hazparne forever if his father hadn't decided to come and get his houses and businesses back. It was curious that he, too, Martin's father himself, had done the same thing when he married, because his wife's family was also a traditional nationalist mainstay—they had their family seat in Bergara and were related, they said, to Telesforo Monzón, the great folk leader himself—and they had come down in the world and were now, among other socioeconomic incoherences, no longer skilled at speaking the language; in the case of Martin's mother, for instance, her Basque was scarcely good enough to allow her to converse with maids, small children, and dogs.

Martin's mother is telling the American girl that the house in Martutene, in which Martin lives now, used to be the family's summer home, back when going to the beach wasn't thought of as all that attractive an idea and swimming in the sea wasn't considered particularly healthy. Things the girl already knows, because the woman's son has told her: the current owners of the building now housing the San Luis Clinic had stolen it from them—an accusation his father never mentions—and the Goytisolos were all a bunch of evil Carlists. She sticks in words and short sentences in English from time to time. It's to practice, she says. She normally does the same thing with Basque, dotting in little phrases here and there. Her use of that linguistic resource, which writers often employ to show that a conversation is actually being held in a language other than the one it's written in, probably results in her believing that she is, in fact, conversing in English.

In any case, she keeps on talking. She's giving Lynn the recipe for Adarraga tarts, which the poor girl writes down in her black notebook as if she were a hard-working student. The mother says they often used to make them at home, because they had a pastry cook who worked at the Adarraga shop before being employed at their home, and she stayed working in their kitchen for many years. She married when she was quite old, and both of her sons ended up in prison. "There's been a lot of suffering here. *Very, very much,*" she says. "This one grew up in exile"—she points at her husband—"and this one"—pointing to her son—"was in prison for collaborating with ETA. Back when ETA was something different. He's already told you that, *I suppose.*" The girl says yes, she knows about it, probably because the signs that Martin is making at her—raising his chin and stretching his neck out as if some invisible tie around his collar were too tight for him—lead her to think that he finds the subject uncomfortable and that agreeing with her is the best way to get the old lady to stop talking about it.

Martin's father, on the other hand, is actually wearing a tie. And a brown suit, which is quite loose on him. He looks thin now, but he hadn't just a few months earlier. Short hair, crew cut, gray, but plentiful, so Martin can't tell him he's going bald. His eyes are very light colored, like his son's, but they aren't cold, perhaps because he's always looking into the distance. It's obvious he isn't following the conversation, and he smiles in a slightly absent way when people look at him. When Lynn asks about the trophies on the mantel, he picks up one of the paddles resting against the wall and reads, "35-22 over Balda and Baleztenari." He picks it up in his right hand—it must weigh a ton—holds it upright with his arm outstretched behind him, and then brings it around in front of him, balancing it on his open palm in an easy, elastic, aesthetically pleasing gesture. Then Martin's mother shouts for someone to take the racket out of his hands, he'll break something, and Martin has to use a lot of force to get it off him. It's an unpleasant scene.

Now that the old man has spun around, he's completely disorientated, and he leans forward, with his arms held out wide, and Julia thinks that he wants to sit down and so she offers him a chair, but Martin's sister quickly moves to take the chair off her. "That one isn't his," she says, and the old man almost falls over, because he'd already started to sit down on it. The sister says he's been having "more and more accidents," explaining that she moved that one to protect the seat's upholstery, and her mother says it's "just a mess, *a lamentable situation.*" Martin's sister looks just like him. She's beautiful. A large woman, like Harri, still shy of fifty. She tends to support her mother's points of view and statements and provide evidence to support them. She's also the one who gets the stories started. "Tell them what he did in front of the girls the other day. Tell them what he did with the custard." Just as Martin does. They tell a long series of sad little stories—they're quite depressing, in fact, even though some of them are quite funny, as well, such as him taking off his diaper and putting it on his head—switching off turns as if it were a competition; all the while, the old man is looking at the light coming in from the enclosed balcony and Martin's doing that gesture of his that makes it look as if he's trying to loosen a tie that he isn't wearing. It's obvious he doesn't like them telling people these things about his father, and he tries, rather pathetically, to change the subject by asking suddenly, and with great enthusiasm, if they know why you pour the tea into the milk and not the other way around, and his mother, after asking who could possibly think something as stupid as that, carries on with her stories. They've had to reupholster all the chairs—"*absolutely all of them*"—because there were traces of urine on them. It really was embarrassing when they realized. Doesn't she think it's a terrible punishment, she says to Lynn, and she says she does, and what a trial, she says, looking at Julia now, and the two younger women have difficulty not laughing.

One of the situations they describe reminds her of something Simone de Beauvoir writes about in *The Farewell Ceremony*. Beauvoir mentions the stains that the philosopher often left on the upholstery of the chairs and says that once, in Rome in '72, when they were walking back from the Pantheon, poor Sartre tried to explain away the wetness on his pants by saying that a couple of cats had just pissed on him—"*des chats viennent de me pisser dessus.*" Back when she read it, she thought, as Martin is thinking now, that it was something there was no need to tell, and that it was ill-intentioned to do so. A little act of vengeance on the part of Beauvoir, who must have had plenty of reasons for it. Julia doesn't know what she would think if she read it again now, but she imagines her memory of that passage helped her to find the figure of the writer more approachable, more loveable than the writer who used to sign everything the Maoists put in front of him and allow himself to be bowled over by any student kind enough to light his pipe for him. She thinks that Simone de Beauvoir loved him dearly. But she still finds the scene in which she asks to be left alone with Sartre's corpse and then lies down beside it and falls asleep worrying. She knows the final sentences by memory: *Sa mort nous sépare. Ma mort ne nous réunira pas. C'est ainsi; il est déjà beau que nos vies aient pu si longtemps s'accorder*—His death separates us. My death will not bring us back together. That's the way it is and it is fine enough that our lives have been lead together for so long.

Harri often says that she's just like that Simone woman, and also, as she told her a little earlier, that she's embittered.

She'd rather be at home reading a book.

"*Oroitzen al zara Hazparnez?*"—Do you remember Hazparne? The old man's eye light up—"*Bien sûr, je m'en souviens*"—as he replies that of course he remembers. Julia has never been to Hazparne and doesn't think she ever will, because she knows she would be disappointed. She has a mental image, which is false, of course, of good-looking young men like Ravel dressed in white linen clothes, the girls wearing floral-print dresses, sitting on blankets in a circle, in green fields under cherry trees, around baskets full of white bread, Beloke cheese, good pâté, and Baiona ham. The older men are looking for field mushrooms. There are boys wearing berets and playing *pilota* against the church wall "*tandis qu'un crépuscule verdâtre agonise derrière les fenêtres*"—while the greenish twilight expires behind its windows. A Finzi-Contini garden scene, almost, with a Basque Coast touch. That's what everything she's heard about the exile in that house makes her think of, that image—nothing to do with what she's heard about her uncles, two on her father's side and two on her mother's side, who lived just a few miles from Hazparne, making a living cutting down pine trees in Les Landes while waiting for their chance to board a cargo ship out of there, Luis and Tomas to Argentina, Joxe Miel and Jesús to Venezuela.

"*Bien sûr, je m'en souviens*," the old man says again, his eyes lighting up once more. Julia's seen things similar to what Martin's father always tells them about in many movies, and has read about them in many books, but his story always breaks her heart for some reason, it's his story that moves her especially. Perhaps it's because she realizes that she's looking at the child who witnessed the scene himself. "*Je m'en souviens du bruit des bottes des allemands*," he usually whispers—I remember the sound of the Germans' boots—and at that moment, she thinks that she, too, can hear the frightful noise that had terrified the boy. Although it was something that happened often. He talks about how the town would be thrown into a frenzy all of a sudden, you could hear the echo of people coming together during the German occupation. The boy goes up to them to find out what the noise is all about and sees, between two rows of local people who are shouting insults, a group of men and women pushing forward a seventeen- or eighteen-year-old girl with her hair cut short. They've found her with a German soldier in the woods, and they are angry. But what's heard above all the terrible insults and demands for cruel punishment is an indignant man's voice next to him, and the old man now opens his eyes very wide and murmurs again and again the thing that had most affected him: "*Elle était à poil*"—she was naked. As if that were the worst fact in all the war.

Why is he so moved when he tells them about that scene?

In fact, what he's talking about is his awakening to sex, which is something as moving as the worst realities of war for many children. Julia regrets not having talked about that with the old man while she could have. She thinks that now—now that she can't—is when she might have been able to. Does she tend to regret more things she's done, or things she hasn't done?

The old man smiles again. His smile seems ageless somehow. In other words, it's easy not to take his age into account when he smiles. His smile is pleasant, happy, a little cheeky, as well. When Lynn says that he looks very good for his age, Martin's mother says that he still has all his own teeth, perhaps a bit contemptuously, or perhaps with envy, because she herself has false teeth and maybe she thinks she would make better use of her original teeth than he does. That's what it seems like to Julia. Then she thinks that it's his teeth that make her forget his age when he smiles. His hand, however, is that of an old person. He puts it on her knee; it's cold, long, very white, and with fine skin so delicate that she thinks she would tear it if she touched it with the tip of her finger. She takes it in her own hand, not wanting the old man's gesture to be misinterpreted, although she knows she's running the risk of being overly genteel.

Martin's mother: "You have to be with him day and night."

They don't touch each other. At least, Martin and his mother don't; she has sometimes seen the daughter giving her mother a kiss on the cheek. In fact, Julia herself would never take the mother's hands into her own in the same way she has just taken ahold of the father's. She's convinced that Martin likes her being affectionate with his father, just as he likes saying that she's his father's favorite. She, too, thinks that his father has always liked her; he thinks she's beautiful, but above all, he likes her because she comes from a world different from his own, a world he admires, because she comes from the world of Basque working people, she belongs to the type of people he has always known and respected, serious men and women who run their homes well. He's sometimes told her that he's proud of her, that she's the best possible match his clumsy, stuck-up son could possibly have. (His wife, too, who has now lost any hope for her son, doesn't think she's a bad match, knowing that Martin's peculiarities and lack of relationship skills make him a low-value product.) "Now that's a proper lunch." Sometimes Julia lies to him to keep her image up. For instance, when he asks her what she's going to have for lunch, and always with the idealized image of pots bubbling away on top of an old-fashioned stove in mind, Julia often makes something up: black beans with cabbage and blood sausage; beef with tomato and red pepper sauce; cod in a green sauce with potatoes and fresh peas. And he smiles with pleasure—now that's a proper meal.

When they start suggesting that they're going to have to go soon, the reproaches begin. Mother and sister ask Martin for information. Is he writing? They don't see him on the television or in the newspaper, and they do see Alberdi on the other hand, every day. Julia feels sorry for him, he's like a child who gets angry because he's gotten bad grades at school, and she sees him moving around nervously in his chair. He has no interest whatsoever in going on television, he defends himself. And it's true. In fact, she's sure that on the occasions on which he's made a great effort and taken some Propranolol before going on to some show, it's been for their sake. She knows he's sorry that they feel frustrated on his behalf, that he'd like to give them reasons to be proud, for their acquaintances to say that they've seen him on the television or in the newspaper, and for people they don't know to ask them if they're related to the writer when they give their names, which, it seems, has in fact happened to them sometimes. But he can't. He complains that it isn't fair that writers and artists have to be good not only at their work but also at selling it and being affable and photogenic (opera singers can no longer be fat, he always says). But his mother and sister pay no attention. What's the good of being a writer if nobody reads you? He should go on the television more. Julia has to bite her tongue to stop herself from saying that there's not much point in him being well-known, since they haven't read a single line of his. (She knows that Martin isn't bothered by that. Quite the opposite, in fact, he probably couldn't write at all if he knew that someone from the family was going to read it.)

Lynn is more loyal. She tells them that Martin needs all his energy for writing. It's moving. Her voice shakes a little, and she makes that gesture she does when she's nervous, tucking her hair behind her ears. She says she knows people who are interested in literature and who think a lot of Martin's work, and the old lady, interrupting her, asks if she knows a lot of people here. She doesn't ask it ironically—as Lynn, who feels she has to admit that she doesn't know all that many people, might think—but because she would really like to know what type of friends the American girl has, if, that is, she actually has any. Martin, too, prefers to take the conversation in that direction, and holding on to the slight pretext the American girl has offered, he says that she has mysterious friends who whisk her away on weekend trips, before realizing that that line of conversation will take them back to Bordeaux. Because now his mother wants to know where she went, and of course, when she hears Bordeaux mentioned, she's reminded of the bad memories about when her son was in trouble there and they had to visit him in prison and they managed to get him out thanks to her Paris daughter's contacts, and speaking of her, Martin has to repay the favor by getting her a suite in the María Cristina Hotel—Martin quickly promises he'll do all he can, even though it's going to be hard with the Zinemaldia festival going on—and then she says, for the American girl's benefit, because she's already told Julia as much plenty of times, that they've always had to get Martin out of trouble, like the time they found a box full of *ikurriñas* he was supposed to give out shoved under his bed, and they, mother and daughter, had to go, along with their two maids, and distribute them in the market, and the parish church, and wherever else they could. "Do you remember?" the mother asks her daughter from time to time; to which she replies, "Do I ever." (And one time, when Julia hears that "do you remember?" of hers, she thinks for some reason that she's going to ask "do you remember that time I caught you masturbating in the library?" and then she has to make a great effort not to burst out laughing.)

"Now where's he gone off to?" says Martin's mother, as if her husband might have gone to the moon, and at that same exact moment, he appears in the doorway. One of the legs of his pants is soaking wet from his fly to his knee, she makes her typical gesture of disgust and says, "Goodness, goodness, what's he done now?" and he complains that one of the faucets in the bathroom is too tightly closed and, because of that, he's gotten all wet. Mother and daughter leap up together to stop him from sitting down and cry out "Belen! Itziar!" and the two maids rush in, shyly greet everyone there, and sweep the old man away with them. It all happens in an instant.

Julia is sorry that Lynn has had to meet Martin's father like that, that she didn't get to meet him when he had his intelligent eyes, when the man was still attractive, as she once knew him to be. He used to say that he was only any good for making money. Perhaps his intelligence deserved a better fate than looking after the family's wealth, but he, like his father before him, had accepted the task with humility. It meant that others could spend their time on more noble callings, and even though he must have had reason to think that those others didn't come through on their part of the implicit deal—his writer son is the only one in the family who's created anything—he doesn't seem to have held it against anyone.

Finally it's the mother and daughter who show them out of the house. "It's lovely being with you, but you must have other things to do." As Martin predicted, they're getting them to leave before the television show they're addicted to starts. "Take care of yourself," Martin's mother tells him, as she folds his shirt collar over his jacket collar, "if you don't want to end up like your father." And then she says to Lynn, *"He is like his father,* they don't take care of themselves, his father never has." And to Martin again, "And you started much earlier." She turns a flushed cheek toward Julia for her to kiss it and says, "Take care of him." And Julia doesn't dare to ask what she's supposed to be protecting him from, why she should take care of him.

SINCE THEY DON'T HAVE ANYTHING ELSE TO DO, Martin tells the girl they'll go with her, and they walk along Hernani Kalea toward the old part of town. Martin, wanting to say something, makes the observation that it's one of the most expensive bits of land in the world per square foot, not realizing that the comment might make him come off as petulant given that they've just left his parents' house. Then he talks about the senselessness of building more parking lots downtown and how good taste and quality suffer every time the city council undertakes a project. It's very dull stuff, especially for anyone who's already heard it dozens of times before. They follow Lynn, since it's she they're accompanying, but Julia soon realizes that she isn't walking in any particular direction, and the second time they reach the boulevard, she decides to say that they have to go, because it seems obvious to her that Lynn doesn't want to take them to where she has her meeting. Martin, on the other hand, doesn't seem to realize there's a problem, he repeats that they aren't in a hurry, and finally, Julia says that they are, in a big hurry, in fact, and she holds onto his arm and drags him away. She wishes Lynn good luck.

MARTIN SAYS THAT HE DIDN'T REALIZE the girl didn't want them to see who she was meeting, but Julia doesn't know whether to believe him. They go back home in silence. Sometimes she likes the train's rhythmic clatter, it helps her to think. She thinks that she'd like to be in another train, one going somewhere a long way away. She overhears stupid remarks from the people chatting around them. Talking for the sake of it. She asks Martin why his mother always says that he has to take care of himself if he doesn't want to catch his father's illness. She's not worried about it, his father's disease is clearly degenerative and connected with old age, but she doesn't understand why she says he started earlier. They've talked about it before, and his conclusion is always the same: "Just my mother's strange ideas." She also often mentions a fever he had before adolescence, a long delirium. One morning, his bed was soaking and they found him almost in a coma, and he stayed like that for several days before coming round again. Nobody knew what diagnosis to give. His mother normally gives evasive answers if pressed for details. She says the only thing she knows is that the same thing happened to her husband, a soaking bed and a delirium that lasted almost a week, the only difference was that he was much older when it happened to him. Sometimes Julia thinks that Martin's mother knows more than she lets on. "You always think that, but it's all just strange ideas my mother has," Martin says. He doesn't want to talk. In fact, the train isn't the best place to talk, above all because when the subject isn't to his liking, he tends to raise his voice.

After getting off the train, they go up the slope and stop by the iron gate, as if they were saying goodbye. Martin says, "Who do you think she's going to have dinner with?" Julia had been going to stay the night with him, because there's no one at her house, but now she decides not to. She just shrugs her shoulders. She doesn't think the girl said anything about having dinner. He says, "It has to be someone we know, and someone married, that's why she wants to hide him." What does it matter to him, she suddenly replies, more tired than bored. After that, Martin makes no effort to convince her to stay, and without bothering to come up with an excuse, she says she's going to her place.

LA CÉRÉMONIE DES ADIEUX:

Page 27: "*Contre le socialisme centralisateur et abstrait, Sartre prônait 'un autre socialisme, décentralisateur et concret: telle est l'universalité singulière des Basques, que l'E.T.A. oppose justement au centralisme abstrait des oppresseurs.*'"—In opposition to centralizing, abstract socialism, Sartre favors "another type of socialism, decentralizing and specific: such is the singular universality of the Basques, which ETA sets in contrast to the abstract centralism of its oppressors."

Page 52: "*Il faut être modeste quand on est vieux.*"—You have to be modest when you're old. Yes, imagining Sartre answering that, with his pant leg soaked through as Beauvoir asks him how he's doing, gives her a better, more likeable image of him.

She wonders if Simone took her shoes off when she lay down beside Sartre's corpse.

12

THE PORT IS STILL one of the nicest places in Donostia, even though Abaitua thinks it's lost all its personality. Fishing has almost completely disappeared as a way of life. He knew the dock at the foot of Mount Urgull when it would fill up with ships, especially during anchovy season. It smelled of salt water under the arches and of tar and burlap on the docks. Anchovies, which are now about to become extinct, would be piled up everywhere, waiting to be taken away to fertilizer plants. During the tuna season, on the other hand, the smell was like *marmitako*, because the fishermen would gather around their pots on their boat sterns and eat the potato and tuna stew right there. The sardine sellers with their hair up in buns, dressed entirely in black, wearing earrings and necklaces, standing up straight—he remembers their arrogant way of walking was brought out even more by their wearing clogs. They used to mix Basque with Spanish, and they looked like gypsies from Andalusia. While they waited for the boats to come in, they would play cards on top of great overturned barrels, and they were continually fighting, accusing each other of cheating. Their swear words and curses were terrifying, and their shamelessness often frightened the big young men from Orio and Getaria who, barefoot, unloaded the water-laden anchovy baskets. He knew the coastal fishing docks at another time, when coal and wood were unloaded from boats and Rezola cement was loaded back on.

One of the fenders on his motorboat isn't where it should be, and he doesn't know whether to go down and put it right while he waits for Lynn or not. He does have time, because it's a quarter to one according to the San Pedro clock, but afraid of getting dirty, he decides to leave it for later.

He goes toward Portaletas, which is where they're meeting.

There used to be a barometer hanging there, protected by nothing but a thin iron mesh, and sailors used to go up to it and tap on it to get the needle to move and find out if they were going to have good weather or bad. His father used to do that, as well, and that gesture proved to him that his father was in possession of what he thought was very important knowledge. He's had some very good times here.

He sees her walking toward him along Portu Kalea from a distance. She's wearing a denim skirt, a dark turtleneck sweater, and a long jacket, which is also dark and looks like a sailor's. That's what he says to her, wanting to seem natural, that she's dressed absolutely right for the place, and she, laughing, says it's difficult to measure up to the standard of such a wonderful place. She seems glad to see him, and he's glad, as well, although he does feel nervous, because they're going to have to "talk about us." He tells her there used to be a barometer there. The girl turns toward where he says for a moment and then replies that she was afraid he might not show up. He thinks it best to pretend he hasn't heard. She's done her hair up in a bun, and a few shiny locks are hanging loose. He thinks it's the hairstyle that suits her best.

They stand in front of the plaque put up in honor of the *arrantzales* —the fishermen—and talk a little about people's tendency to become sentimentally attached to things that no longer exist. He says they should knock that ugly building down, it's just in the way, or otherwise find some different use for it, it's completely unsuited to what it's being used for now. Nostalgia for the primary sector. We want to believe that it's still the essence of our ethnic purity. We still talk about "our *arrantzales*," but at this point it's really only a few Peruvian and Senegalese guys scraping up the Bay of Biscay's last remaining fish stocks. The real locals are all civil servants now.

Any tourist who wants to see them will have to go to the regional government headquarters.

The girl would like to see his fishing boat.

He has to explain to her that the small boats, like his, that don't have a cabin and look more like skiffs than fishing boats are actually more expensive than most things that look like yachts. That's what our things are always like, good quality but humble appearance. Discretion above all. Our elegance is manifested in the same way when it comes to clothes—we'd rather wear high-quality suede jackets than cheap suits and ties. But, then, everything's changing very quickly.

His boat has a bait tank, a sounding line, a Volvo motor, sixty horsepower—real horses, not like the ones in some family sedan, the ones real boats use. He hardly takes it out anymore. He used to enjoy fishing, when there were still fish around, and above all he loved letting the boat drift on summer evenings, the sensation of freedom it used to give him. But you have to love a boat, and he's lost that love. Ever since he found out that some friends of his son's were using it for transporting explosives. After transferring the stuff from at least two other ships out at sea, they went up river and stored it all in his father-in-law's mastless yacht, which was less anchored there than it was run aground.

He could probably come across as a daring man if he told her what happened on the boat, but he doesn't want to talk about it. Unfortunately, it's too late to keep quiet, because the girl now wants to know if they suffered any consequences afterward. Nothing, happily. Father and son had to go through some unpleasant interrogations, particularly his son, but they themselves reported what was going on and were able to prove that those madmen had forced his son into it all. The trial will be held soon, and he hopes they won't even be called as witnesses. That's all there is to it. He isn't sure if it's the first time Lynn's asked him if his son is like him. Everyone says they're identical. Straight hair, round, soft faces, vulnerable characters. He doesn't like them being similar, it makes him feel guilty. But he doesn't mind him not having studied medicine. What he would like is for him to go back to the States as soon as possible.

He decides to raise the mooring rope on the bow a little and put the fender in the right place, so after going down to the bilge, he jumps from boat to boat until he gets to his own. He has to keep his balance, and he needs strong legs to not look ridiculous holding onto things with his hands. He knows the American girl's watching him, and like an adolescent in front of his girlfriend, he makes a show of moving with agility and strength, even at the risk of falling into the water. After completing the easy, precise task, he lifts his head up and there the girl is, sitting on a bollard, and next to her, Jaime Zabaleta and his bodyguard. "That's quite something, you're in shape," says Zabaleta cheerfully.

At first Abaitua doesn't dare introduce them, but as time goes by, he finds it increasingly difficult not to do so, and the situation, with the girl sitting just a step away, becomes more and more uncomfortable for him. Jaime Zabaleta asks him how things are going at the hospital, how he's getting on with Arrese. He seems to know all about what's going on in the department. Abaitua's always found him to be quite a gossip. Now he doesn't know how to get rid of him. He tells him the first thing that comes to mind, but there comes a moment when it becomes impossible for him to go on pretending he doesn't know the girl, who's still sitting there, because Zabaleta doesn't take his eyes off her, and Abaitua can't find the right way to say that he's with her. Until, finally, Zabaleta says, "I see you're in good company," showing off his large teeth when he smiles, as if he's just caught a child doing something naughty, and he walks away with his bodyguard after openly inspecting the girl.

DONOSTIA IS VERY SMALL. It's so small that there's every chance of a victim's mother bumping into his killer's mother. Iñaki Abaitua feels the need to tell the girl that Jaime Zabaleta used to have a boat he talked about as if it were a yacht, he christened it *Nire aberria*— meaning *My Homeland*—and he used to moor to the starboard of his own boat. But the police advised him not to go out to sea in it, because they'd gotten word of a plot involving a boat, and since the objective may have been to kill him, he ended up deciding to sell it. He doesn't have much contact with him, and he doesn't particularly like him, but the memory of running into him from time to time and exchanging hellos during the so-called "years of lead"—the bloody years—in the eighties and nineties does make him feel he has some type of connection with him. He's sure they both used to think about the possibility of someone coming up and shooting him in the back of the neck as they stood there talking on the corner of the avenue and Andia Kalea. Sometimes he even arranged to run into him when his son was young, for the boy to realize how absurd it was for a man like that—a Basque speaker, a much better Basque speaker than many people who consider themselves to be nationalists, a man who had a boat called the *Nire aberria*, who was friendly and polite—to require the protection of a bodyguard, and Zabaleta always tried to fulfil that pedagogical mission, being a friendly, polite, genuine Basque to the best of his ability.

The American girl didn't realize that most of the bollards for tying up the boats were actually canons stuck nozzle-down into the ground.

They go along the city wall toward Mount Urgull, one of the city's treasures; he would like to show it to her but doesn't know if that's a good idea. It's too romantic. They only go as far as the Paseo de los Curas—the old priests' promenade at the foot of it— where there are views of the bay and the smell of grilled sardines from the quay. The girl praises the view, and he can't stop himself from mentioning how it's changed over time. She should have seen it when he was young, without so many buildings, when there were elegant houses around the Kontxa rather than those great ugly buildings. The girl jokes that it can't have changed all that much over just two centuries. Abaitua's sure that if he went up to her and opened her jacket to put his arms around her waist, she wouldn't object. But he's promised himself that nothing will happen.

He shows her Chillida's marvelous alabaster cross on the baptistery wall in the Santa María Basilica. The girl speaks with enthusiasm about how well the old and the new combine together when both are beautiful; she strokes the warm, luminous stone with both hands. Abaitua puts his hands in his pockets. In any case, the church smells damp, like it hasn't been ventilated enough.

On what at the time was called Trintate Kalea, one of the few houses to survive the fire of 1813. It's one of the dates he knows— August 31, 1813—because it's the street's current name. That day, the English and Portuguese allies liberated Donostia, which had been fairly peaceful during its six years of French occupation, the high command having previously ordered the Gipuzkoan battalions to withdraw, and to celebrate the liberation, the allies pillaged the city and set fire to it in an orgy that lasted for six and a half days.

The Donostians who didn't manage to escape were put to the knife. They raped the women, including children and old ladies. A record of the events, written by a group of responsible citizens, referred to the city in the past, saying that Donostia "ceased to exist": "*San Sebastián dejó de existir.*" Perhaps that explains the Donostians' lack of bellicose enthusiasm the next time a war broke out, having learned that the difference between an ally and an enemy can be far from clear.

KONSTITUZIO PLAZA. Apparently, Le Corbusier said its measurements were perfect. Abaitua presumes that half the plazas in the world meet those criteria. They're standing in the middle of the square, and the girl says that she shares the Swiss architect's opinion. In the past it had other names, as well, the Plaza del 18 de Julio, among others. It was Plaza Berria, meaning "New Square," when they first opened it to the public, and that seems a more appropriate name to Abaitua. There'd been a guillotine there when the French were trying to spread their revolution southward. The numbers painted on the balconies draw people's attention—they used to be rented out back when bullfights were held there. The square's current name reminds him of an anecdote about when they changed the name of the hill from Ategorrieta Gaina to Konstituzio Gaina. Apparently, an English general who'd been invited to the ceremony said that from then on, the place would be called Constitution Hill, and everyone laughed out loud at that: "*Konstituzioa hil, konstituzioa hil!*" The American girl isn't aware of the homophony between the English word "hill" and the Basque *hil*, meaning "kill" or "die," but she laughs and says, "*Aberria ala hil*"—homeland or death. She does know that expression.

Everything he tells her seems interesting to the girl, and he doesn't have any trouble finding things to talk about. Everything he sees brings a story to mind, and the American girl listens to him with attention, but he gets the feeling that he's making use of that parliamentary obstruction technique known as filibustering in which, to prevent others from speaking, you never stop talking.

They go from street to street—she likes the street names, Bilintx, Perujuantxo, and so on—until they reach Kanpandegi Kalea. They can see the bay on one side from the walkway that crosses over Portu Kalea, and one of the gates into Konstituzio Plaza off in the distance on the other side. There are people walking around below them, but not many anymore at that time of day, "because we've become European," he says. They look for traces of fossils in the paving stones for a while. An almost perfect fern leaf, it looks like a red fern. The girl sits down on the stone bench and leans over the handrail to look at the people below. It's a situation that even with the most charitable interpretation possible is compromising. It's true that he doesn't mind if some acquaintance or other sees them, unconvincing though his explanation would be—the young American sociologist and anthropologist is taking part in a research project at the hospital. But if such an encounter has to happen, he would rather it not be on a dark, empty street, as if they were teenagers in love. Sitting on stone is a good way to get acute cystitis, he says, and the girl leaps up as if on a spring and salutes him, "*Sir, yes, sir.*"

Now they're walking along the empty street in silence, like a couple with nowhere to go. They will soon be back where they started. Kokotxa, the restaurant, is on the corner across from Santa María. A fine restaurant that experiments with new recipes, it's just the right choice for taking the American girl to, and he thinks there's little risk of coming across any friends there. His friends prefer more traditional places. He decides to invite her to dinner. Contrary to what he thought just a short while before, it seems to him that having dinner together will give their meeting purpose, while without having dinner, their sole, unavoidable reason for meeting up would be to talk about "us."

Kokotxa is a nice place. "*I like the wine,*" says Lynn as she raises her glass.

They talk about gastronomic societies. (He can see Gaztelubide through the window.) A space of freedom for men to get away from their Basque wives, who usually have very strong characters, despite the fact that it's the women who always do the cleaning, and often the cooking, as well, he admits. He's never been a member of one himself, but when he does go, he prefers the traditional ones, ones that women aren't allowed in. The anthropologist doesn't think there's anything wrong with that. Abaitua thinks that men don't speak much about women when they're at these traditional clubs, despite what many people believe. The men, in general, talk about things of little importance, they become like children in order to avoid the arguments that would arise if they talked about serious matters. As far as different social classes mixing together is concerned, which Kepa talked a lot about on their trip, he wouldn't like to spoil this idealized view of it all, but he doesn't want to lie to her, either. It is true that in the past, more than now, business owners and workers, shipbuilders and fishermen would get together at the same table and, as he's just said, forget about serious matters that could lead to disagreements. It's also true that their bourgeoisie was discreet, they didn't say much about their own status and either shared or knew how to adapt to the working men's culinary tastes and, especially, to their financial limitations. And the proletariat, in that context, were able to maintain their dignity and their punctiliousness about paying for their rounds.

The girl suggests toasting Kepa's health. Her eyes are shiny, and her cheeks red. It's clear that drinking makes her more emotional. He's very lucky to have such a good friend, she says, "*You are a fortunate man.*"

It's difficult not to mention Bordeaux. Abaitua thinks that the memory of it is hovering in the air, it's something that would be coming up again and again in their conversation if he weren't making an effort to talk about things far removed from it. Now, for instance, when they're served their coffee and some truffles, there aren't any jokes about chocolate's aphrodisiac qualities.

"WE'RE LEAVING, THEN."

THE GIRL KEEPS QUIET IN THE CAR while he talks about the places they're driving past: the Bellas Artes building, where, on Thursday afternoons, they used to go to watch double bills. He doesn't tell her that he also used to go there in order to feel up the servant girls, who, like the schoolchildren, had the day off—anything to avoid talking about sex. They would sit up in the highest seats in the wooden amphitheater. As soon as the lights went out, they would go down, step by step, to the lowest level, where the girls sat, and touch their breasts from behind. Normally the girls let them. Later, on the way out, they would pretend not to know each other, and in fact, you couldn't really say they did. They were mostly slightly older than the boys, from Extremadura for the most part, and he was occasionally embarrassed on exiting to see how ugly the girl he'd just been fondling was.

Where those red brick buildings are, the ones that stretch out from the park to the hill the hospital's on, there were once marshes. He used to go around them by boat. Now Lynn turns toward him and says that must have been back in the Holocene era. It's the second time she's made that same basic joke, and Abaitua is aware that he's to blame, because he refers to his age all the time, as if it were a matter of style. He uses the expression *in my day* a bit too much.

In my day. The American didn't know what *in illo tempore* meant. *In illo tempore Jesus dixit discipulis suis . . .* Blessed are those who haven't had to learn the Latin verse by heart.

He stops the car in front of the iron gate, having already turned around to be ready to go back to the road. He does not turn the engine off. Lynn opens the door but not completely. He makes sure the parking brake is on by pulling it up with more strength than is really needed and doesn't take his hand off it, ready to let it down again. "*Eskerrik asko afariagatik,*" she says, thanking him for dinner. She learned to say that in Ainhoa. She says it was very nice and smiles at him. It's no longer the same smile she had just half an hour ago when they raised their glasses in the restaurant, now there's a shadow of sadness in it. She's so grateful. She puts one hand on her chest and says "*I . . .*" twice, as if she were in pain, before completing the sentence. "*I feel very grateful.*" She has a few freckles where her full breasts start. He knows about that nasty scar of hers, too. And knows that her body, which looks so discreet when she's dressed, is exuberant when she's naked. She sits up just enough to be able to kiss him on the side of his lips. He doesn't move, he holds tightly onto the steering wheel with one hand and onto the parking brake with the other; he looks at the hydrangeas. She opens the door a little more and keeps it open. "I don't want you to do anything that's uncomfortable for you," she says, and she turns toward the house, in which there are many lights on. Now they're both silent and looking at the house. The flickering of a television can be clearly seen through one of the windows. The writer seems to be a nighthawk, he says, to say something, but she doesn't pay any attention to the comment and looks at him so seriously he gets frightened. He'd say the youngest thing about her is the soft, curly hair that sticks out from the base of her neck below her bun. When she asks if he wants to come in, he doesn't answer. "I don't want you to do anything that might cause you problems," she says again.

A BEAUTIFUL GRAY FLUFFY TOMCAT appears at the door as the girl is opening it, but it runs away to hide as soon as it realizes there's a man with her. "*Come on, Max, you're really antisocial*," she says. He's easily frightened, she says. She offers him a coffee. Abaitua is no longer worried about caffeine. He'd like one. She leaves the living room and goes to make it. You see almost the whole house from the entrance—the bathroom, the kitchen, the bedroom, and the living room. The latter has a wide window, and through the blind, which is not wholly closed, you can see the naked white light at the train platform, which makes everything inside bright enough to be able to see without any difficulty. Going up to the door, he can see a bit of the kitchen, which is very clean—the sink, a bit of the table with a plate full of fruit on it that looks like it's been put there as decoration, and a refrigerator with colorful magnets on its door. He'd say she doesn't cook a lot. The coffee maker is a French press. She puts the grounds in carefully and presses them down with a little spoon. She says she doesn't know how well it's going to turn out. In the living room there's a big sofa and two armchairs upholstered in light-colored cloth, a triangular wooden coffee table, three chairs made of the same wood, and a bookshelf. On the wall there's a small engraving of a flower, a water lily whose phallic calyx is blue rather than yellow. In general, it feels very minimalist and clean, very uncluttered. He knows many of the books on the shelves, especially the latest issues of the *Perinatal Survey*. She has the American and the British issues together on one shelf, which seems to be exclusively for work-related books.

It's obviously an educated woman's house, comfortable and welcoming.

He's in the dark, the girl says as she brings in a tray with the coffee things. She asks him to turn the lights on, but he says they're fine like that. It's a ghostly light. A few books on the shelves are placed so that their covers are showing, resting against the backs of the other books as if they were pictures. They could be the ones she likes best, or the covers she thinks especially pretty. Virginia Woolf, *To the Lighthouse*. A slip of land under the horizon, a lighthouse on it. A dinghy by the waterside, children playing. In the foreground, at the edge of the beach, on the grass, three or four people wearing hats, one of them with an open umbrella. Henry James, *The Bostonians*. Two women wearing long, elegant dresses while sitting and talking on a sofa in a rich person's living room. Two slim legs wearing tights with horizontal stripes, fastened with clasps, perhaps. Angela Carter, *Wise Children*. He picks that up, not knowing what to do. He's looking through it when Lynn says that the coffee's getting cold. She asks if he wants milk and points at the small jug. A small milk jug, the coffee pot, white and brown sugar, two small truffles, embroidered napkins. He thinks she knew he was going to come up and tells himself, without much conviction, that he's still in time to say that the coffee's good, that he's operating tomorrow morning, and then get out of there. The best thing to do, no doubt about it.

He asks her about the cat. She says he's very shy and has hidden under the bed. Apparently, he doesn't trust people until he's been with them at least a dozen times. She asks if he wants to listen to music, and he says yes. He doesn't listen to much music, generally just classical music while reading, and when he operates, too, almost always sonatas, but it's in order to isolate himself from other sounds. He could listen to the same sonata twenty times without realizing it. He thinks that must be insulting for anybody who really likes music. Words, on the other hand, move him, so they distract him. For that reason, with just a few exceptions, he doesn't listen to vocal music. The girl puts a CD on and sits next to him on the edge of the sofa, her legs together—a very different posture from the one she must adopt when she's wearing pants, he thinks—her body straight, stirring the coffee inside the cup that she's holding on the saucer in the palm of her hand. They listen to "Mad about the Boy." He ventures the opinion that in addition to their technique, those black women must have something special, something physical, attributes that allow them to be able to sing so clearly, make themselves so easy to understand.

The girl now looks at her hands, folded in her lap. She has long thighs, and they look very white in the shadow play projected by the light. The movement he would have to make to take her in his arms and kiss her wouldn't be very natural. He hasn't been in a situation like this for a long time, and he feels like a young boy who's supposed to give the first kiss. He stands up to put the book back on the shelf and his attention is attracted by another one. He can't help laughing when he reads the back cover. She asks what he's laughing about. He's embarrassed to read aloud in English, but he does: "*The lives of these men and women come together to give a fascinating portrait of the Basques, a strange and fiercely independent people to whom principles sometimes mean more than life itself.*" Margaret Shedd, *A Silence in Bilbao*. So that's what brought her to the Basque Country. "*Exactly.*" She walks up to him in her bare feet, takes the book off him, and throws it onto the sofa. She tells him to forget about principles for a bit, puts both her arms around his neck, and kisses him lightly on the lips. Then she takes him by the hand and leads him into the bedroom.

She says she's going to the bathroom for a moment, and Abaitua stands there waiting for her, looking at the starkly lighted train platform through the gaps in the blind. Stations at night have always seemed gloomy to him. Despite the music, he can hear running water and wonders if she's taking a shower. He, too, should go to the bathroom, but he feels awkward about going into the intimacy of other people's restrooms. He's afraid to move, too, because he knows he shouldn't be in that room that has nothing other than a bed in it. A room for sleeping in. A low bed, no headboard, a comforter with geometrical blue designs on it, two bedside tables, with a flex lamp and an alarm clock on one of them and two or three books piled up on top of one another. And a small Matisse engraving on the opposite wall. She bought it in New York for next to nothing, she says when he asks if it's genuine. She takes it with her everywhere, like Max the cat. She seems to be proud of that purchase.

Abaitua leans down to look for the cat, because he can't even bring himself to sit down on that untouched bed. He sees its eyes shining, he wants to get it to come out, but the cat pays no attention to his calls. "Don't go getting ideas, Max won't trust you for a long time." She comes in and closes the door behind her. She turns the music off, as well, and Abaitua is astonished that she does so in the middle of a song. To him it seems like an insult to the artist. She tells him about the cat as she takes off her blouse. Then she takes her skirt off and clips it onto a hanger. As if she were alone. And she opens the bed, too, folding it down with care. Just like the Lynn in *Montauk*. He decides to sit on the side of the bed and take his shoes off. It wouldn't be good for a man of his age to appear to be embarrassed, and in any case, the girl knows his body already.

The girl's naked, she has the alarm clock in her hand, maybe she's turning the alarm off. He doesn't normally need an alarm clock, most mornings he's already awake by the time he has to get up.

The girl smiles when she realizes he's looking at her. He would like her to have gotten undressed more slowly. He smiles at her, as well. She has very little pubic hair, just a thin strip. Women arrange it now, sometimes into peculiar shapes. He asks her if she does that, as well, trying to sound natural, even a little daring. She looks at him for a moment and says no, that's just how her body is, she doesn't have much hair. She doesn't seem to care about it, she's certainly not embarrassed about it. Abaitua's always been amazed at how naturally women move around in the nude after they've done it with someone for the first time. She comes up to him and undoes his shirt buttons.

Another memory from *Montauk*: "Her body is younger than her face." When he read that, he thought that the writer might have had that impression because he hadn't seen a young naked body for some time and so was amazed by the characteristics of youth that he'd forgotten. He doesn't know why, but it's a fact that bodies and faces often don't age in harmony with each other. Just as internal organs don't. Normally, because we're more used to looking at faces than at bodies, it can be easier to notice the first signs of decrepitude there. But Abaitua could tell a woman's age as well or better from her vulva than from her face.

What could be said about this Lynn is that she has a lot of expression lines—horizontal lines rather than the vertical lines, which come with age—because she moves her face around continually. As is to be expected, she smiles when she's happy, but she also does so when she asks for something or says or does something that she doesn't want people to take the wrong way, and her face wrinkles up completely. She frowns when she's worried or paying attention or listening to someone. Thousands of tiny tightenings on her forehead every day, between her eyes, and they've left their marks around her eyes and lips. But her breasts, too, firm and robust though they are, speak of the proximity of maturity; the equilibrium of her body's good form is precarious. As far as her belly, which may be the youngest part of her anatomy, is concerned it's flat and comfortable; her *linea nigra*—the line between the belly button and the pubis that darkens during pregnancy—looks as if it's been sprinkled with gold dust. However, he also sees a trace of suffering in her youthful beauty: a wide scar, more than two inches long, the result of clumsy surgery.

It would be enough for him to see her naked, just being as intimate as that with her would be enough for him, but the girl's fingers are skillful, and she turns him on.

He tries to stop her from standing up, but she's agile and strong. She moves away from him and, after locating a thin blue cloth on one of the bedside tables, covers the lamp with it. He's lying face up, and she sits on top of him, her legs to either side; she holds his wrists and forces him to keep his arms open. She bends down toward him and whispers, "*Relax, just relax,*" into his ear.

She squeezes her legs around him like pincers, and he feels her moisture on his waist.

The cat gets onto the bed and sniffs at him with curiosity, it seems to consider him an outsider. Lynn shoos him away, "*Get out of here, Max!*" The cat stays there looking at them from the floor. The girl takes the man's hands to her breasts. They're swollen and firm, he strokes them. Her nipples get harder and harder, she asks him to do it stronger, and he does, until two drops of milk come out, very white, thick, they stay there without running down, he spreads the milk around with his thumbs, strokes her nipples with it, and then licks them.

The girl is breathing through her mouth as if she couldn't get enough air, and she stretches away from him to enjoy her own pleasure, a pleasure that moves and frightens him at the same time. She grips the sheets with both hands, her body curves and tenses, she has spasms in her belly, her eyes go white, she groans, and, finally, she falls back, exhausted.

The sound of a train roughly breaks the silence, and its wake, like that of a scream, stays in the air. Then they clearly hear the echo of a television, which they hadn't noticed until then. He feels as if he's suddenly recovered consciousness, and he finds it hard to come back from something so pleasurable. Lynn is curled up against his chest, and he feels the cat's smooth angora on his back. He pets it, and the animal replies with a grateful purr. "Oh Max, you've given yourself on the first day," she says without opening her eyes. "*I don't blame you; this man is irresistible.*"

The shadows are dancing on the ceiling; the wind, which blows strongly from time to time, moves the top branches of the trees that are in the path of the light coming from the train stop. Abaitua sits up to see if Lynn is asleep, and she opens her eyes and smiles at him. Before closing her eyes again, she asks him what he's thinking about, and he says he wasn't thinking about anything. He thinks she's going to say that she doesn't believe him, but she doesn't. She says a sentence from *Montauk* has come to her. So she's been thinking about *Montauk*, as well. Amazing though it is, he doesn't tell her about the coincidence. He doesn't know why. What the girl remembers is something Max says: "*Every first time with a woman is the first time all over again.*" She asks what he makes of that. He doesn't know what to say. In any case, he wouldn't like to talk about other first times. He says that maybe that effect, that impression, if you like, is always the same whenever you become intimate with someone for the first time, and it's a feeling that can drown out everything else. There's a short silence in which a man's voice is clearly heard, though they don't understand what it's saying. That's the way men think, says Lynn. The first time, they don't realize what's going on at all, they don't see anything, they're fucking something ideal. *To fuck the ideal.* She says, standing on top of the bed, that that's what happens the first two or three times, in fact, and that's why she doesn't mind being naked. Because she knows he still can't see her. She laughs. In a short time, she says she doesn't know when, because it varies from one man to another, he'll start seeing her, and then he'll realize she has stretch marks—she pinches her hips—and saggy breasts, and she'll look ugly to him. And he'll run away from her.

He says that's not true. He holds her by the waist and makes her lie down on the bed again. He isn't blind, and he's certainly seen her ugly scar; that alone would be enough to ever prevent her from being a model. She tells him the worst thing about it is that her chances for a career as a stripper were ruined all because she once pretended to have a stomachache to get out of school. She's sure she didn't have appendicitis when they operated on her. Doctors really are terrible, he says after trying to bite her scar, and the girl stops him by holding onto his head. How insensitive, pointing out my defects when it's just our second time. She gets up and leaves the room on tiptoe, followed by the cat. She says there's another sentence in *Montauk* she likes a lot. She comes back with a book in her hands and lies next to him, resting on her elbows and belly, her feet crossed up in the air, leafing through the book for the page she wants. It's the French edition. She doesn't have the English one, and she's afraid she may never get it back. She laughs, and when he asks why she's worried about that, she says it's a long story. Pointing at the lines, she asks him to read aloud. Abaitua isn't embarrassed to read in French for an American: "*Après elle reste nue, Lynn dans la kitchenette, tandis que lui, l'invité habillé, est assis à table et parle, maintenant content de la langue étrangère qui lui donne le sentiment qu'il dit tout pour la première fois.*" It says that afterward, Lynn stays in the kitchenette, naked, while he, the guest in his clothes, sits at the table and talks, happy now to be speaking in a foreign language because it gives him the feeling that he's saying everything for the first time.

Talking about *Montauk* is talking about an uncommitted relationship between a girl and an older man, a relationship with no future.

WHAT IS LYNN THINKING ABOUT NOW?

She looks at him slowly and laughs before she speaks. She often does that, and he thinks it's so that he won't be put out by what she's going to say. That gesture of tucking her hair behind her ears. She says she, too, has that feeling, that feeling of always saying things for the first time. Feeling them for the first time, too. "Oh dear, I'm frightening you." Abaitua suddenly feels like saying "*I love you.*" If he told her he loved her at that moment, it wouldn't be a lie, but instead he has to tell her as quickly as possible that he can't stay the night, he has to go.

The sensation of fleeing from the scene of the crime.

Lynn is standing up, the cat in her arms, watching him get dressed, until she realizes that it makes him uncomfortable. He hears her turning the faucet on in the kitchen and talking to the cat. There's the sound of voices from the lower floor, too, and he thinks that they must be able to hear them talking, as well. It's two o'clock in the morning. He sees a box of medicine on the bedside table when he looks at the alarm clock to check the time. Amitriptyline. He isn't shocked by the young American taking antidepressants, but he is surprised she's taking something other than Prozac. He leaves the subject for a more appropriate moment and gets dressed in a hurry. He doesn't put on his cufflinks or his tie. He looks around to see if he's forgotten anything, as if he were leaving a hotel room. Lynn is leaning against the wall and waiting for him; she bends over and puts the cat on the floor. The cat walks toward him, tail up in the air. He sniffs at Abaitua's shoes and rubs against his pants. He can't resist leaning over to pet it, and when he does so, the cat offers him his belly. The greatest purrs of contentment he's ever heard. Lynn: *"You insatiable cat."* She opens the door. Does he really feel like going outside? They give each other a short kiss, as if they were two people who've just met. Abaitua thinks she's making an effort not to try to keep him there, so that he won't feel bad. They'll see each other tomorrow. Today, that is, at this point.

On his way down the spiral staircase, as he goes past the ground floor, he hears the voices clearly, although he still can't tell whose they are, and he has the uneasy feeling that he's walking through someone else's living room. It's a narrow, difficult staircase, and he has to walk down it on tiptoe to make as little noise as possible, one hand on the handrail and the other against the wall to avoid falling down. A pretty ridiculous scene, he thinks. He doesn't turn around until he reaches the yard. There are still lights on in three of the windows. It's clear the writer is awake, and if he's nosey, he'll look through the window and recognize him. Abaitua doesn't care.

It isn't the first time he's walked across a yard at night trying to keep the sound of his steps on the gravel to a minimum. When he was young, he used to go and visit a girl who lived in a house in Ategorrieta and got turned on by hearing her parents in the downstairs living room while they were together. At that time, Abaitua hardly used to have any dinner, because of the anxiety that his nightly clandestine activity made him feel; in addition to the parents, the girl's elder brothers lived there, but he'd been unable to give up the privilege of her favors even though it meant having to leave by the window and in total silence.

There's a smell of hyacinths in the yard. (He thinks it's hyacinth.) He feels good walking with his jacket over one shoulder. Healthy, younger, although he knows that it wouldn't be the same if he stopped to think about it. It's better not to think. He puts his tie on in the car and both cufflinks, gray pearls connected with thin white gold chains. A present from Pilar on his birthday last year. That's what Pilar's been giving him recently, cufflinks; she isn't very imaginative.

He's glad he left the car positioned to drive straight out onto the road. And that he didn't say *"I love you."*

It isn't the first time he's gone to the hospital in the middle of the night after going out to dinner and before going home. He likes the hospital at night. It's also a way of purifying himself, of course. It's occasionally been a kind of weak excuse. People, especially people who are sitting through the night with a patient, are grateful to see a doctor coming in at unscheduled times to see if everything is going well, and he's also sure that it's because of that habit of his that the nurses think he's one of the good, old-fashioned doctors, even though they can tell what he's been up to. He doesn't try to hide it: coffee and alcohol are keeping him up. Even so, it is true that he's managed, thanks to these unexpected visits, to save a few lives, and that gave him something noteworthy to tell Pilar when he arrived home just as she was about to leave for the clinic.

At the nurses' station, the duty nurse says everything's quiet. He sees there are some files with lab results on the table. He looks through them to see if there's anything about his patients and is glad to see the results of the additional biopsy on Room 207's lymph gland in the neck is negative. A good piece of news that's been locked away for almost twenty-four hours. News that could put an end to outpatients' worries often takes days to become known, because of appointment timetables and safety margins. His suggestions for improving the flow of test result notifications, at least in hypothet-ically serious cases, have come to nothing; they would, it seems, lead to insuperable administrative difficulties.

The carcinoma case in 207 is awake. She's amazed to see him at that time and without his coat on. He tells her he has good news, everything's all right, and the patient sheds a tear. She takes his hands and strokes them. Five, ten hours less anxiety for that grateful woman. Some other cases have to wait in vain much longer. She says that the young female doctor told her not to get her hopes up. That doctor with the bad expression on her face enjoys making people scared, he's seen it himself, just as he likes letting this patient believe he had something to do with her news being good. Two different forms of pleasure, conditioned by different neurotransmitters?

The front door of the house is locked with two turns of the key, a sign that Pilar isn't at home. Very surprising. It could be, as has happened sometimes, that she's heard some frightening piece of news on the television, gotten frightened, and locked herself in. He makes the least noise possible and goes slowly down the long hallway. On tiptoes once more. He keeps as quite as possible, more in order to not scare himself than because he doesn't want to possibly wake Pilar. In situations like this, he sometimes remembers the Léo Ferré song, "*Il n'y a plus rien.*" If your wife is sleeping, slap her as you would someone who's fainted or having a panic attack and shout at her, aren't you ashamed to be lying there submerged in your liquid decadence like that? That's more or less what it says, and it usually cheers him up. He stands motionless outside her door, listening for sounds to confirm whether she's in there or not. He doesn't hear anything and doesn't dare open the door to check if the bed's empty.

He doesn't know whether to brush his teeth or not, because of the noise of the electric toothbrush. He looks for a normal one, but the bristles on all the ones he finds are too soft.

He has to fight against the impulse to go and see if Pilar's in her bed. He remembers how nervous he was that night when Pilar arrived in the early morning. He doesn't know how many sleeping pills it took him to get to sleep, and when he woke up at dawn, she wasn't there by his side. They slept together back then. He'd gotten up and gotten dressed. He didn't think that anything bad had happened to her, that some problem had prevented her from coming home. It didn't even occur to him. She'd been speaking about the new neurosurgery resident doctor for weeks, because her brother-in-law was treating him unfairly and excluding him from the operating theater. He was a good guy, smart, someone who deserved better. Suddenly it was clear to him that Pilar was with the young neurosurgeon, and he sat down in the living room to wait for her. He heard the key in the door about an hour later. When she came in, she didn't look left or right, just walked straight through the living room without saying a word. He remained there, sitting in the living room, seconds, minutes, he doesn't know how long, and then he got up and went to the bedroom himself. She was sitting on the edge of the bed, wearing her red jacket, her gloves still on, as if she were ready to leave again. "I fell asleep," she said. And he was amazed by her saying that. He gets the impression she didn't realize what she was saying. He saw in her only sorrow and ruin. That's what she looked like, the very picture of sadness and desolation, when she said those words. He had never felt so unhappy; he felt every bit as bad as his wife. He put a hand on her shoulder. It was an impossibly sad moment. He wouldn't say that Pilar was running away from him when she stood up and walked toward the window. It was cold, and the windows were steamed up. They spent a while like that, the husband standing next to the bed, the wife at the window, with her red jacket and black gloves still, at least the one on her right hand, which she raised slowly. After that long moment, he went up to her from behind, still not knowing what to say to her, what was going to happen. The young neurosurgeon's name was written in condensation on the window. It was moving and meaningful at the same time. Funny, too, if you looked at it that way. He remembers that everything you could see through the letters was gray, everything except for the white foam on the waves.

SECOND PART

SECOND PART

13

WHEN MY LEFT KIDNEY STOPPED WORKING, TOO, and it all became clear to me, I went straight to a private clinic to have my tests done. At private clinics, they give you your results in an envelope, and you decide when to open it, you choose the best surroundings and conditions for it—lying alone in your bed, for instance, without anybody looking at you. I knew I wasn't going to be up to hearing the results from the doctor at the hospital without fainting, there in his cold office, the naked strip lighting in my eyes, the nurse standing by, complaining over the phone to someone about her shift having been changed.

Because that's what happened the first time, when I found out I had a deadly illness for which there was a treatment that could guarantee a reasonable expectation of life. The nurse sang out my first and last names from the doorway, the doctor greeted me, trying to see me not as a human being but as a hypernephroma case, I thought, and looked at my lab results with concern, tilting his head to one side and then to the other, while the nurse listed the various inconveniences that having her shift changed was going to cause her. And I, trying to decipher the way the doctor was moving his head—more and more—and the unknown secret in the wrinkles appearing on his forehead, waited for him to give his judgement.

It lasted forever. I thought I could hear the starter in the lamp, in spite of the nurse talking so loudly. It was the blood in my head, pulsing in my temples. Finally, after muttering a quick *"malas noticias"*—bad news—in Spanish, the doctor, who had enough medical knowledge to have earned his position even without knowing Basque, gave his judgement, and the blood froze in my veins, I suddenly started sweating, I lost my vision for a moment and thought I was going to fall out of my chair. They must have noticed; the doctor looked at me with distress, I think he liked me, and the nurse, without taking the phone away from her ear, looked on with curiosity as I loosened the knot in my tie.

Having had that experience, I don't feel up to going through the same or worse again, which is why this time I've decided to request the tests myself and at my own expense. (Even so, it wasn't easy. I had to overcome the laboratory staff's reticence to do the tests without a doctor's prescription, and it was even more difficult to get them to give me the results. I had to proclaim, and even raise my voice in the process, that the sample of blood they had taken was mine, just as the crazed cells they had taken out of me were my property, as was the money I had used to pay their bill.)

When I got ahold of the results, I didn't open the envelope straight away, I held onto it. I didn't open it on the train, either. I made the most of a sort of false control over my destiny. The judgement was in my pocket, and it wouldn't become final until I wanted it to. I thought about giving myself a few days, pretending I was ill—technically speaking, at death's door—preparing a short trip, to Syracuse, for instance, to which I'd always wanted to return, in order to enjoy the sun, to eat pasta with those famous sardines, *sarde a beccafico* and *cassata allay siciliana*, as if I thought myself to be eternal, which is the same as not thinking, just like the other people on the train, who themselves aren't free from the risk of dying in some stupid accident before ever reaching the point of being diagnosed with hypernephroma.

That's what I should have done, but I'm not like that. And after all, what if the results weren't all that bad? Saying that hope is the last thing you lose isn't enough; you practically never lose it, even when there is no hope. I was tempted to take the envelope out of my pocket and open it, but I put it back in again, and then took it out once more, that's what I did as far as Txominenea, where I decided to leave it until I got home, to the intimacy of my bedroom, because I was afraid that if the results were as bad as I feared, I would lose all my strength, not even be able to get off the train, and then what would I do when I got to Zumarraga, the last stop on the line?

She was in the house that afternoon. I went into the bathroom to open the envelope, but I didn't open it, because afterward I would have had to face up to her look and hide my tears if I wanted to cry, which was highly probable. I would wait for her to leave the house. As the minutes went by, my desire to be alone, to lie down on my bed and be able to open the envelope, increased. Finally, she realized she was in the way. She told me off from the living room, because I kept on coming in and going out again with a cigarette stuck in between my lips, since I'd started smoking again. "That's how you're going to end up," she said to me, pointing at a picture of a blackened lung on one side of the cigarette pack, and I answered her sarcastically. She, too, got irritated. She said I was a self-destructive person, my despair was worse than AIDS, because you could catch it in the air, and she didn't want me to infect her, so she left and slammed the door. A few seconds later, right after closing the door, in fact, she came back in and immediately whispered sorry, she hated seeing me like that, and did I want her to stay. "Do you want me to stay?" she asked me, and I managed to keep calm and answer that I'd rather she leave.

As soon as I saw she'd gone, I smoked a bunch of cigarettes, one after another, to try to calm my nerves, but without managing to avoid the feeling of guilt smoking gives me. Then I went up to my bedroom and lay down. I opened the envelope with great care, took out the piece of paper with the results on it, and sat motionless with it in my hands for a moment, my eyes closed. Then I opened them and closed them again. It was bad news, as my doctor would confirm to me a week later. As expected, the treatment was killing me; it would affect me more slowly than the illness itself, but it would be more painful. I felt the same sort of sensation as when the doctor diagnosed my illness a year before. A tingling in my head, a roaring in my ears, my sight distorted—I'd explain it if I were up to it, I don't know why I seem to recall, though I must have read it somewhere, that flies' sense of vision is supposed to be something like this—profuse sweating, the feeling of being drained of blood, but all of that was quickly alleviated because I was lying on my bed, and so there was no risk of me falling out of my chair.

I lived through the following days in a dignified way, knowing that death was close. I'd say the hardest thing was when some neighbor would ask how I was and I would have to suppress the urge to answer "at death's door." (Sometimes I would reply "still alive," but they always took it as a joke and said that keeping alive was the most important thing.) I didn't tell her anything, because I was sure I wouldn't be able to resist the temptation to use my situation to blackmail her, and in fact, I would have preferred to make her feel anger or revulsion than to make her feel sorry for me. My intention was to wait until the results were official before saying anything, until the Department of Public Health ran the tests for me again. Meanwhile, I tried to be more agreeable. Let's say I started to worry about what she'd think of me when I was gone, what kind of memory she'd keep of me, and I tried to not leave things lying around the house and to use her name more when I spoke to her. (I remember I once asked her, "Flora, have you seen my glasses?" and she looked at me with tears in her eyes, and then, too late, I had the feeling that our relationship could have been saved.)

Sometimes, just for a very short while, I hoped that the laboratory results from the hospital might contradict those from the private clinic—that does happen occasionally—but I didn't let myself get my hopes up, and when the day of my appointment arrived, I was ready to confront the situation with dignity. I won't say I found the situation amusing, but strange as it may seem, I went through it as if somewhat removed from it all. To start with, when I walked into the room and the doctor shook my hand—the nurse who was always on the phone was looking for something in a drawer and hardly lifted her head to glance at me—he didn't know that I already knew that this story was nearing its ending and that he was going to have to break it to me in the right way.

I found it surprising that after asking me to sit down, the doctor needed so much time to work out that I had hypernephroma. He took some time to find my medical record, and that meant he hadn't been interested in finding out the verdict before the very moment of giving me my sentence, which is amazing to anybody who isn't a doctor, because it seems as if it wouldn't be a bad idea to find out beforehand—even if it's only the slightest information—so that you would know, before the person involved sits down at the desk in front of you, what expression to have on your face, because it isn't the same thing to say "good morning, have a seat" to somebody you're going to then go on to tell something pleasant to as it is to say the same thing to somebody who you're about to tell they're dying; in the latter case, it's best to avoid saying things like "it looks like we're going to have a lovely summer this year." It's true that the waiting room is normally full and that the patients, and even more so the people who come with them, don't normally say nice things about having to wait so long, and because of that, or because he just isn't much of a talker, the doctor doesn't usually chat much before getting down to business. It's also true that looking for paperwork and examining it takes a lot of concentration, and he does that in silence, without making small talk about the weather.

And then, finally, when he realized what my situation was—my liver and kidneys destroyed by the disease, and my pancreas by the treatment—he lifted his eyes up from the paperwork, and I noticed a gesture of compassion. I also saw that the nurse was looking at me, in the same way, to see to what extent the doctor's words were going to affect me. I think something in the doctor's expression must tell her when things are going badly. In any case, she stopped talking on the phone, and, finally, there was complete silence.

I could only hear my own body's sounds, it was as if my ears were blocked up, and I wondered what would have become of me if I hadn't known about my condition beforehand—in other words, if I hadn't known what was going to happen to me—and even though I knew what I was going to hear, I held on tightly to the arms of my chair, just in case.

"*Malas noticias*," he said, just like the first time, and I deduced that he was going to use one of those techniques they teach them for giving patients horrible diagnoses. He avoided looking at my face, and I was convinced, once more, that he felt compassion for me. He told me that the figures were the same as those from the private clinic, and after putting them into a file folder—by the way, nobody knew where the rest of my medical record was—he added that they were going to do everything scientifically possible. He recommended that as soon as I started to have problems urinating, or if I noticed any hematuria, I should check straight into the hospital, which would make everything easier. There was no need to ask what it would make easier, and I didn't. Although the doctor's discomfort was obvious after a certain point, I decided to force my presence on him a little longer, something which, just shortly before, I wouldn't have been capable of. I was even so bold as to tell the nurse—who had started opening and closing drawers again—not to worry about misplacing *historias* because I could tell her some new ones, but she didn't laugh. Perhaps she didn't realize that the word means both a medical record and a story in Spanish, or perhaps she just didn't find my play on words funny.

Back home, and even though I had decided to give up smoking once and for all—not to have a healthier death but to at least have one without coughing up phlegm, a smoother death—I sat in front of the television and smoked all the cigarettes I had left, one after another, influenced by the petit bourgeois spirit I had inherited from my mother, which meant not throwing anything away.

JULIA WOULDN'T BE ABLE TO SAY what she felt after reading that. Disappointment, sorrow, anxiety. Disappointment because while she didn't expect him to come up with anything sublime, she had hoped to find something a bit different from his usual stuff—a story, characters who think of things and to whom things happen, life. Sorrow, as in all his texts, because it's him and only him in them, only he suffers. Anxiety because she doesn't know how to take what she's read, whether to take it seriously or not.

She's ordered the original version of Frisch's diaries—his *Tagebücher* —published by Suhrkamp. And she's photocopied *Fragebogen* and the second volume of the French edition of *Verhör*, to look at them all together. *Fragebogen*, *Questionnaires*, "Questionaires," and *Verhör*, *Interrogatoires*, "Interrogatories," she'd say. Unlike the *Questionaires*, the *Interrogatories* include the author's answers and some political contents, in the widest sense of the word.

FIRST INTERROGATORY

What is your attitude to violence as a tool for political struggle? There are bespectacled brainiacs like yourself who would personally rather avoid confrontation but who accept violence as part of political struggles.

Theoretically.

Do you think social transformation is possible without any recourse to violence, or do you condemn violence categorically, like Tolstoy, who you are reading right now?

I'm a democrat.

Julia thinks the interrogatories are as interesting as the questionaires in *Tagebuch 1966-1971* and deserve to be compiled in a book. In the interrogatories, we see the author on the other side of a false mirror, powerful spotlights shining into his eyes, forced to give short, direct answers, and seeing that makes us anxious.

"Apart from in extreme situations when seized by blind anger, have you ever wanted to kill somebody?" Julia would have to answer yes.

She vaguely remembers that Frisch confesses in one of his books that he once felt guilty about not having killed a German man. Julia leafs through *Journal II* again and again, she thinks the passage has to be there somewhere, but when she can't locate it, she goes through his other books, truly anxious now to find it. She thinks she's got it when she sees, in *Pages from the Bread-bag*, that on a car journey through Ticino Canton, he says he sees some German troops. But in the end, it isn't there. She gets confused, because the passage she's trying to remember also takes place during the World War on a mountain in Ticino, and she thinks Frisch had been called up. If she isn't mistaken, the writer is walking up a snow-covered mountain when he comes across a strong-looking German. The German asks him about the paths in the surrounding area. At the time, because of the war, both the sale of maps and their public use were restricted for security reasons, to make things harder for spies. Frisch gives the German the instructions he politely asks for, in the normal way any hiker would, but later on, when he spots him from above walking through a gorge, it occurs to him that he could be a Nazi spy, and that he should catch him from behind and throw him off the cliff. Then he loses sight of him and regrets not having done it. Although Julia can't find the passage, she's convinced that he mentions his feeling of guilt at not having killed the German in at least one book, and probably in more than one.

So when Martin appears, he finds her flicking through *Tagebuch 1966-1971* furiously, obsessed with her search, unable to master her urgent anxiety to find the text, and when he asks her what she's doing, she says she isn't doing anything, because it seems to her that he's reproaching her for not translating *Bihotzean min dut* at that moment, and she looks above his eyes at his scarce, weak hair, which is nevertheless miraculously stiff, standing on end as if electrified, because she knows he can't stand that, and when he realizes where she's looking, the poor man lifts both hands up to his head and pulls his hair backward to try to make it stay flat.

He says he hasn't slept a wink.

"Have you been having your nightmare again?"

"It's the girl upstairs that's the nightmare."

He says Lynn's the reason he hasn't been able to sleep. She came home with a man the night before and kept him awake all night. He says she howled like a cat in heat, it was scandalous. He whispers it, as if he were scared or truly scandalized. He says again and again that she made an incredible noise, and Julia beings to think he's not joking, he really is shocked. He says her lover left in the early hours. He admits he got up and went to the window, but he only saw him from behind, and not too well at that, because there wasn't much light. It could have been Abaitua, but then it could have been anybody else, too.

He asks, "Do you think it could have been Abaitua?"

Julia thinks not, she can't imagine him with her, even though Harri says Lynn's in love with him and there's no doubt it was him she spent the weekend with in Bordeaux. She says she doesn't care who Lynn's lover might be, but it isn't entirely true that she's indifferent.

"I don't care who it is, either," he says with an expression of disinterest, of looking down on the whole matter, "the problem is, she keeps me from sleeping."

He sees his reflection in the balcony window and tries to comb his hair down with his hands. It's no use—his hair, weak, scarce, and longish as it is, goes straight back to its place, upright, after he passes his fingers through it. He shrugs his shoulders, which could be out of resignation. In any case, he'll soon know if it's Abaitua or not, he says with a cunning smile. Julia is about to tell him that she thinks his habit of watching people come and go is unsavory, but he doesn't give her the chance, because he quickly informs her that he's going to meet up with Kepa, that famous friend of his. She finds it hard to believe that after not seeing somebody for so many years, he could get in touch with them again just to find out who Lynn is sleeping with. She confronts him with it: it's strange that he doesn't care whether Abaitua is her lover or not and yet he's prepared to dive back into the tunnel of time to see if he can get something out of this Kepa. He hardly bothers to defend himself. He says he hasn't arranged to meet up with him to talk about Lynn; ever since the girl mentioned him, he's been missing that old friendship, and in any case, he's long wanted to see him again.

Fortunately, Lynn arrives in time to stop the storm that's about to break. She's wearing the green and yellow floral dress she was given in Bordeaux, which looks so good on her. He tells her she's very pretty, and she lifts her arms up and spins around, making the dress float in the air behind her, just like the first time he told her he liked it, with a dancer's charm. Her hair is loose, and in the light its looks like orange preserves to him, perhaps because the only thing he had for breakfast that morning was coffee.

"Did you have the nightmare?"

Lynn asks the question seriously, not joking at all; Julia finds it difficult not to giggle, considering what Martin's just told her about the real nightmare keeping him from sleeping, until finally, seeing a mute pleading in his eyes for her to be discreet, she laughs out loud. She finds herself in the awkward situation of having to say that she isn't laughing about anything specific, which, fortunately, doesn't last for long; Lynn is very interested in knowing whether Martin's had his recurring nightmare again—seeing his electrocuted hair must suggest that's a possibility, of course—because she has a theory about what its origin might be. She's convinced that every time he's told her about having his nightmare, he was at his parents' house the day before. That happening a hundred percent of the time, even on so few occasions, is highly significant, and she recommends that he look into it. Martin's face, which expresses absolutely clearly that he can't decide whether the girl's serious or not, and his hair, even more electrocuted-looking than ever, if possible, make it really difficult for Julia not to burst out laughing again.

A young man rests his shaved head against the glass of a window. It seems he's having trouble seeing into the house, although he's perfectly visible from inside it as he stands there with both hands open and resting on his temples to shield his eyes from the light. He's one of Zabaleta's bodyguards. The other one must be the man with the belt pouch leaning against the car by the iron gate.

"Perfect weather for mowing the lawn." Zabaleta, as well as speaking with an Otzeta accent, is always reminding people that he was brought up on a *baserri*. He also has a great imagination, a quick, malicious tongue—typical of the improvisational poets from his valley—and the ability to identify his opponent's weaknesses and provoke them in the cruellest possible way. It can be amusing, but if it goes on long, it becomes tiresome for people who aren't used to it. He has an incredibly thick Basque accent when he speaks in Spanish, and he doesn't do much to hide it. Julia even thinks he makes a show of it, perhaps to cover up some complex he may have had in the past.

They've already met, he says, when Martin introduces Lynn as an American neighbor. Down at the port, he says in Spanish—"*En el puerto.*" Maliciously, without saying who it was that introduced them, and Lynn nods quickly as if wanting to prevent him from saying anything more. Martin then adds that she's working at the hospital, but just for a time; she actually came over as a tourist with her friend Maureen, who, unlike her, travelled to the Basque Country for professional reasons.

They can't avoid talking about violence, because of the work Maureen is doing and because of the two bodyguards standing at one end of the garden snacking on blackberries. He says he wanted to do without their protection, but ever since his name turned up on a list penned by one of those madmen who don't want to let go of the war, he doesn't have any choice in the matter. He talks about his situation humorously, without ever losing his smile as he mentions sad or tragic circumstances, as if he found it all amusing, probably because he doesn't want people to pity him, but Julia finds his insistence on smiling worrying, that repeated grinning gesture that shows off his large upper teeth even when he's talking about his own fear.

He became a member of the PSE—the Basque socialist party, known by its Spanish name, the Partido Socialista de Euzkadi—after the assassination of Miguel Angel Blanco in 1997. Julia and he had been members of the Euskadiko Ezkerra coalition previously and saw a lot of each other at one time. She thinks the day he told her about his decision to join the PSE is the only time she's seen him looking truly serious. Since then, it's always seemed to her a decision that he's prepared to see through to the end, as if he felt he had to pay back a debt, but without reproaching those who remained—indifferently, understandingly, compassionately, disdainfully, or spitefully—on the other side. He's never said anything that could give the idea he feels morally superior to people who justify violence, nor has he ever told anybody that they should take the same step he has. On the contrary, he's always appeared to be understanding and tolerant, suspiciously so, in fact, of the people who should be his enemies. He seemed to understand and accept people looking down at him and seeing him as a traitor; perhaps, to an extent, he saw himself that way, too. Guilty and traitorous for being a victim.

He makes a point of showing his affection for radical nationalists, and he seems to enjoy their company more than that of the members of his own party. He makes continual references to the former (approving nods to their famed gruffness) and ironic statements about his relationship with the latter, many of whom, he says, seem like Martians to him. He often uses the word *españolazo* as a way of putting people down, of criticizing overly Spanish loyalties, tastes, or mannerisms, and after sitting down, he says he doesn't have much time because he has to go to a party social center on the outskirts of town for lunch, and he makes insulting comments about what he'll be offered to eat there, "You're better off going to a PNV center for lunch."

He hasn't isolated himself in his situation the way some other people have, nor has he given up the signs of his identity. He says it's clear to him that the heritage of Basque nationalist history and culture is common to all, like the Basque flag, it doesn't belong exclusively to one ideology. In fact, Basque patriotism is his natural environment, and he feels its presence within him, perhaps with the guilty resignation of somebody who knows himself to be marked but does not bend to fear and proudly holds onto his feelings and convictions. He still goes, along with his bodyguards, to the same bars as always, and all the same cultural events, and he gladly accepts his role in the expiatory liturgy, welcomes with open arms the people who come to see him in private and say how sad and unfair they think it is that he—he who is "one of us, at the end of the day"—should have to lead a threatened life. He absolves them, comforted by their remote feeling of guilt. It's funny and also regrettable to hear him telling them how yesterday, some old ladies came up to him to tell him how much they liked him and to advise him to stop fooling around and join the Basque Nationalist

Party once and for all. He must be used to putting up with looks of disdain and hate, but he doesn't complain; he understands that for many people, he's a traitor, and he accepts that traitors are to be hated. Julia has sometimes thought that an attack on his life would be a dream come true and a nightmare for him at the same time, because he accepts his role as a victim with hope, believing his hypothetical sacrifice would be the irrefutable proof that violence is absurd.

She's never heard him talk seriously about fear.

ANECDOTES FOR THE AMERICAN SOCIOLOGIST. Julia finds a story she's heard before even funnier when he tells it in Spanish. Once, late at night, "it was his fault" that all the neighbors in his building had to run out onto the street, because somebody left an unmarked package by his door and called the police. The police's first security measure was to get everyone out of the building except for him, because the package being next to his door, they thought that opening it might be dangerous. His touchy neighbors complained, because the police had gotten them out of bed and made them wait in the street in their bathrobes, pajamas, and nightgowns. The improvised, contradictory behaviour of different police forces: the Spanish police told them to prop their mattresses up against their doors and move back to the farthest point in the house; the Basque police, on the other hand, insisted on removing everyone from the building by bringing them down ladders and out through an inner courtyard. Apparently the argument between the two police chiefs lasted so long that Zabaleta and his wife had plenty of time to get dressed before they were finally given permission to leave the building through the main door, which was an additional reason for their neighbors—who were middle class economically and Spanish more than anything else in terms of sentiment—to look at them with dislike; as well as being to blame for them having to leave their houses, it was he and his wife who were the ones who'd been threatened by the Basque National Liberation Movement and yet they hadn't been made to come out onto the street in such an uncomfortable, undignified way, wearing bathrobes at best.

In that situation, and inevitably feeling himself to be responsible for it, he decided to call the owner of a steakhouse on the same street, another guy from Otzeta, and get him out of his bed to ask him to do him a favor and open up so that he and his neighbors—who were missing out on sleep, feeling cold, in an uncomfortable situation, and, above all, complaining about the lack of dignity—could at least get some hot soup and coffee. They spent hours in the restaurant, eating and drinking, getting livelier, and even really quite lively in some cases, until finally the municipal police located the messenger who had delivered the package and learned from him who had sent it. When one of the police chiefs accused him of being negligent and unprofessional, the messenger said in his defense that nobody had ever told him there was a "problem" in the building. That was how they defined it, apparently, in their jargon, and it was obvious who the "problem" was, so he ended up paying for everything his neighbors and all the policemen had eaten and drunk.

He also remembers that around the same time, his friends from Otzeta told him that if he wanted to continue going to lunch at the cyclists' association on Saturdays, his bodyguards would have to wait outside. They didn't want any policemen there. That was a long time ago. Apparently his friends believed that ETA couldn't attack a member of the Otzeta Bicycle Association—and certainly not at the headquarters itself—if he were surrounded by people whose patriotism was beyond doubt, thus he had no need for bodyguards. The police's instructions were very clear, he couldn't spend a single minute without his protection detail, but he managed to give his escort the slip and go down to the association's headquarters on his own. The anxiety of giving the police the slip, thus offering any madman an easy target, combined with lunches of garlic-covered chops eaten without ever taking his eyes off the door gave him an ulcer, so that his meals there quickly became lighter and blander. But at least on those occasions he had friends to take him back home, some of them over six feet tall and weighing over two hundred and twenty pounds.

What happened at La Kontxa beach, not far from La Perla spa, had been much worse—the night he suddenly realized he was on his own. He and his wife had had an argument, a stupid quarrel, as a result of which he'd slammed the door and stormed outside. The last day for handing in their tax return was approaching and, for the hundredth time, he hadn't gotten all their various receipts together as he'd promised he would. His wife was nervous, because she always liked to keep things up to date, and angry, because she always ended up doing all the work. He wasn't in the best of moods, he was tired, and his wife's obstinacy, even though she was right, made him fly off the handle, so he walked out. He talks about "the wife" in Spanish, *la mujer*, with the definite article and that vibrating letter R; it would be "the old lady" in Basque. A good wife, but a pain, he says, quite insistently, and he doesn't mind adding that all women are a bit—"*Todas lo sois un poco.*" In any case, he raised his voice because she wouldn't keep quiet, she started complaining that he never did anything she asked him to, and, fed up, he turned around and, just like that, slammed the door behind him and left the house.

He crossed the street and headed for the Kontxa Pasealekua to go and calm down. That's what he did. But he wasn't able to go more than a hundred yards before, all of a sudden, hearing the echo of his own steps, he became aware that he was alone in the middle of the street and it was the first time in years that he'd been by himself at night without protection, and he got scared. Not even ten minutes had gone by since he'd left the house. He panicked and ran back to the building's entrance, and after going in, he waited on the stairs behind the elevator and smoked a few cigarettes to pass the time and to be able to give the impression that he'd actually gone on his little walk and go back home with a little dignity. When he stepped out of the elevator on his floor, he didn't need to put the key in the door—his wife was there waiting for him, worried, and she cried and kissed him.

"*La mujer* still loves me a little." While he takes his glasses off and carefully cleans them with the end of his tie, his eyes unfocused—accustomed as they are to relying on thick lenses—he looks up intermittently. Nobody says anything during those seconds, and suddenly, as he puts his glasses back on, he smiles.

His bodyguards are still picking blackberries in the garden. Zabaleta realizes that Julia is looking at them, and he says they aren't policemen, they're private, thinking she must be interested to know that for some reason. What Julia would like to know is what he talks about all day long with young men like that, who have shaven heads and black leather jackets and are currently picking blackberries. "The *Ertzaintza* are only for the uppercrust now," he says sarcastically. Then, turning toward Martin, he asks him the question the poor man is always afraid of, "So when's that novel going to be ready?"

"When's that novel going to be ready?" Martin repeats the question very slowly, like a pupil caught daydreaming, trying, in vain, to buy some time. In fact, he explains, as he always does, he isn't sure if it's actually going to be a novel, and he tucks his hands inside his sleeves in that revealing gesture of his. He crosses his arms uncomfortably, stretches his legs out, and adds that he writes very slowly.

"We can't wait to read it."

Martin is an eternal pupil, always forced to lie about his grades, incessantly pressured to finish his work, as if it were a matter of urgency for a world suffering from some lack of novels. Julia doesn't have time to feel sorry for him, because he immediately turns his question to her—"And how's yours going?"—and she finds it hard to answer that she's going over *Bihotzean min dut* one last time, because she realizes she's been giving the same answer for too long.

Zabaleta thinks *Me duele el alma* is a good translation of the title, and he thinks it would be good to publish the story on its own with a longish explanatory introduction, which would be a good opportunity for giving some historical context. That way, among other things, she would have the chance to explain how it was one of the first short stories in Basque literature to deal with the victims' suffering. He says *short story* and not *nouvelle*, and also that it was one of the first works to talk about the victims' suffering, not the first. Martin doesn't like hearing that, and he seems to listen on in uncomfortable silence. As if that weren't enough, he puts his arm over Martin's shoulder affectionately and says that a long introduction would also allow him to tell people about the threats he received after publishing the story. His smile—that of somebody who has seen how vile society can be, understanding and playful—could also be that of a person forgiving somebody else. But Julia thinks it's suspicious that he brings up the subject of the anonymous threats in front of her and Lynn, and she doesn't like it. Just in case he's planning to make a fool of Martin, she decides to stop him there and asks if he'd like a coffee. It's obvious from her tone of voice that she might just as well have been asking him if he wanted a slap across the face, but even so, he says he does.

From the kitchen, she hears him talking about socially committed literature. Zabaleta says that he recently went to a roundtable talk organized by a victims' association; all the participants agreed that

Basque writers have been more interested in the killers than in the victims and that Basque literature has not yet reflected the latters' pain. Apparently somebody said that even writers who have publicly condemned violence have not expressed the degree of commitment and empathy that might be expected from them in their work and haven't done anything to help demythologize ETA. Zabaleta says he mentioned Martin's name, reminded them of *Bihotzean min dut*, in fact, and spoke against making generalizations. He says that accepting that the victims are always right will lead to trouble. Quoting Primo Levi, he says that the real victims are the dead; they should differentiate between people who accept the risk of becoming victims and people who are taken unawares—Julia doesn't understand exactly to what end—and between victims and heroes. Things which he, Zabaleta, can talk about. Martin keeps quiet.

What Julia would say is that it's very clear in historical terms. That Basque writers' social, cultural, and political origins are the same as those of ETA's members; that at one time, the empathy between them was complete, and, in some cases, people were both things at the same time—members of ETA were writers, and vice versa. That those who started to see ETA's activities as a mistake began to show some empathy, their aim being to convince people close to home. That they found it hard to see certain things as atrocities and to take in the victims' pain, which is what usually happens when you're part of a particular social and cultural world. That it will take years for their memories to ferment, and that only then will they begin to produce literature with nuances, with more than just black and white, literature of a kind much more interesting than what's being offered at present in response to political opportunism and market demand, adding little to the already plentiful and at times excellent prose on the topic that you get in the press.

Lynn's telephone rings. It's Harri, and Julia guesses that she's on her way back from Bilbao. Lynn goes down the hall to speak, halfway between the living room and the kitchen, not wanting to bother people with work matters, and the two men talk more quietly now.

Although she can't hear him well, she knows what Martin is telling Zabaleta: literary works have to be left to themselves, and contextualizing introductions are surplus to requirements. He always says the same thing.

"Be careful." When Lynn tells them that it was Harri calling to say that she's been delayed in Bilbao, Martin can't resist the temptation to joke about it and say that what she was delayed by was finding the man from the airport. Because it's obvious this remark might make Zabaleta curious, Julia intervenes once more and, this time, stops Martin from talking, in order for him not to make Harri look silly. So she asks them what they've been talking about while she's been making the coffee. They say nothing of great interest. It's clear from his tone of voice that Zabaleta's realized there's something they don't want him to know, and he says he's got to go. But Martin, politely—perhaps too politely—says there's something he wants to show him and takes him into the formal library.

"HE'S IMPRESSIVE." When they're left alone, Lynn nods down the hallway, and that's how Julia knows she's talking about Jaime Zabaleta. It isn't the first term that would come to mind if she had to describe him. What impresses her so much? His humble stoicism, his discreet heroism.

Julia was just reflecting on exactly the same thing a few moments ago, but without thinking he was *"impressive."*

Lynn has to go up to her room for a moment to change before Harri arrives. She says it with a cardigan wrapped around her, as if she were cold, although it's actually rather hot. Julia asks if she isn't feeling well; Lynn replies she's extremely well. *"I feel really good."*

There's no trace of the bodyguards in the garden. She thinks they must have gotten bored and moved over to the iron gate; there, at least, they can watch the people walking by.

Barbellion (in *The Journal of a Disappointed Man*): "Am writing an essay on the life-history of insects and have abandoned for the time being the idea of writing on 'How Cats Spend their Time.'"

She doesn't remember who said that the problem is you have to stop thinking in order to write and that writing is as tiring as thinking is invigorating.

Come to think of it, there are voices that are ashamed and remain in silence in the Basque-speaking world. Embarrassed voices that think it's too late for them to join those first ones that made themselves heard, daring and dignified, back in the day. Arrogant silences of those who don't want their voices to be the last ones to join the chorus. Hypocritical voices that choose not to speak up so that it won't be obvious they've been silent. But there

417

are also the voices of those who, after falling off their horses and even before taking the time to shake the dust off themselves, attack those who used to ride with them, loud voices that hate all those who were their friends until recently. Extremely loud voices that don't want to admit they were ever wrong, and silences that speak of no regret. An old, long silence imposed by the bullets that killed López de la Calle and by the disdain that drove Imanol Larzabal to his death in Torrevieja; and that silence lives on. Silences brought on by weariness, as well. And there are silences that consider themselves to be dignified. Respectful silences, from those who don't feel they have the right to make use of pain. Prudent voices, who don't believe it's time yet to say everything about the absurd tragedy we've been through; let the noise not drown out the voices of those who have suffered.

She knows she would have to write about it to find out what she really thinks.

THE ROOSTER'S CROWING. It's been doing that for several days now, in some shed down by the railway, and it sings at any time of day. It hardly ever stops, but Julia doesn't mind. In fact, she enjoys that remnant of the *baserri* world. Even though she remembers that she hated the sound of crickets as a child. At one time, people used to get cricket cages, and her mother always kept one or two. She would feed the cricket lettuce, and some bread soaked in wine, too, so that it would "sing" more as it got drunk, and she could never understand how her mother could like that cockroachish beast with its unpleasant noise. Her mother could never explain it to her. Now she suspects that it must have been a need for the presence of the abandoned pastureland around the house she was born in, a need to hear what she used to hear when she opened the window at Etxezar.

Lynn comes back wearing a dress very similar to the one she was wearing shortly before. She asks Julia what she's doing—she seems to be very surprised to find her just looking out the window like that—and Julia answers that she's listening to the rooster.

Basque roosters go "*kukurruka,*" something halfway between French birds' "*cocorico*" and the "*quiquiriquí*" of Spanish ones, but she doesn't know which language the one down by the tracks is crowing in. It sounds like a different version each time, and sometimes like a combination of the three. Lynn says it's "cock-a-doodle-doo" in English. She imitates a rooster crowing, and they laugh; it doesn't come out so very different from the one down by the railway.

Even though Julia laughs, Lynn thinks she looks sad.

"Not sad, tired."

She's tired of always thinking about the same thing. There's a strange silence, which only the distant murmur of Martin and Zabaleta's voices breaks. Lynn says she understands.

She says so very seriously, looking into Julia's eyes. Julia isn't sure just what she's understood but thanks her for saying so.

"That's what I like best about you, there's nothing human you don't understand."

They laugh again.

Regarding understanding. The truth is that sometimes Julia finds it hard to accept that they've been able to live with so much horror—general indifference toward fellow citizens being shot dead on the pavement in front of their houses—and even so, she gets angry when she hears people saying that they don't understand it. She gets the feeling she's being addressed from some superior moral status, from another phase of evolution, when she hears people asking how they've managed to reach such a situation. And that hurts her.

"How did you come to this?" Step by step. Until the end of the '70s, being a member of ETA was a natural thing. Even in Madrid, people took off their sweaters and threw them up into the air in joy when they heard that Carrero Blanco, Franco's number two, was killed in 1973. The tortured ETA member who was gunned down as he tried to escape, who'd gotten his start writing *Gora Euskadi*—long live the Basque Country—on walls and then gone on to planting bombs, was that brother, that neighbor—or someone who could have been that brother or that neighbor—who did what other people couldn't, not because of ethical reasons but because they weren't brave enough, and he was accepted as a hero for having put his life at risk and given a whole community's dignity back to it. The martyr of a community proud to be considered resistant. She talks about dignity, because just like abused women, she felt despoiled every time she was overcome by fear, and that happend a lot, all the time. How can she tell Lynn about that feeling? Uncontrollable fear each time a secret policeman would ask for her ID on a train. It

419

made her feel mortified; an uncontrollable fear that humiliated her. Other people managed to control it better.

When the Civil Guard took her to the station at Ondarreta because they'd found a piece of paper with her address on that redheaded boy, and Sergeant López said "let's take this little whore down to the basement," she knew there was a carpenter's workshop down there and that they used to tie the people they arrested to the bench and turn the circular saw on while interrogating them.

Several residents on neighboring De Zumalakarregi Hiribidea—the type who consider themselves to be pillars of society—complained about the horrible screams they used to hear at night.

So when she saw her sister with her face and blouse splashed with a motorcycle-mounted Civil Guard member's blood and brain matter, she was terrified of what might happen to her. She called her from a phone booth in Ergobi to bring her clothes and money. The Civil Guard had stopped her friend and her at a crossroads, and when the officer put his head in through the passenger-side window, where Julia's sister was sitting, the boy ("the killer"?—even the police hardly ever used that word) shot him at least twice. Then he fled, fortunately after making Julia's sister get out first, and a few miles later, at a checkpoint near Bentak, he was gunned down. Julia felt very sorry for him, she cried for him, even though she didn't know him. She knew that he was sweet on her sister and, from the photo in the newspaper, that he was handsome, and she knew that he had overcome his fear.

She supposes she found out about the Civil Guard officer from the newspaper. She's never met a Civil Guard member or a policeman personally, outside their work; in other words, she's never seen one without feeling frightened. So whenever she's around one, she still has to remind herself that she lives in a democracy, although that doesn't entirely stop her from distrusting them, but at one time they were enemies, and her heart was like stone when she saw the spectacle of those Andalusian women throwing themselves on top of their sons' coffins and screaming out their sorrow.

(A memory connected with that: In Otzeta, a woman who's lost her young son and is at the summit of her pain is urged by her sister not to lose her composure. "Come now, woman, don't start wailing like the mother of some Civil Guard member.)

FRAGEBOGEN: Have you ever felt avenged by the death of a policeman?

She'd have to say she has.

Obviously, not all the victims were policemen. There were civilians, Basques and even Basque nationalists, and children, whose innocence was unquestionable, but they were collateral damage, and canceled out on the other side of the balance sheet by noble, brave acts: people who risked having the bomb blow up in their hands as they tried to deactivate it because they realized there was still somebody in the building they were going to put it in; people who would try to resuscitate some bank clerk who collapsed during a raid. They were heroes and martyrs, and she couldn't see them as murders right away. And the victims' pain didn't become apparent to her overnight, either. She thinks the two things are connected.

She still can't think of Melitón Manzanas, the infamous Spanish police torturer killed by ETA in 1968, as a victim. From that death, which most people considered a just execution, to the murder of Miguel Angel Blanco, which almost everybody saw as a clear case of evil and madness, each person, depending on their individual circumstances, needed a different amount of time to be able to open their eyes, to see the victims' blood, and be able to share their pain.

"St. Paul on horseback on the road to Damascus. You know?"

Deceptive though they can be, it's tempting to use parables. Most horse riders manage to stay mounted and hang onto the reins, because falling off's hard and because it's always too late to dismount. And there are people who've been traumatized by falling off, people whose amnesia prevents them from remembering that they've successfully ridden the craziest horses, people who are incapable of separating violence and a love for Basque culture, of accepting that their brother or friend, or somebody who could be their brother or friend, is a murderer, incapable of recognizing that they've supported the madness themselves, justified the crimes, incapable of admitting that their morals have been impoverished, that everything was a chimera. The victims themselves, at least the ones who had no connection with the state apparatus or its security forces, were discreet, not wanting anyone to take their admission of pain to mean they were on the bad guys' side. But the day comes when things can no longer continue to go on as they have, because the facts take over. What should always have been clear finally becomes so: terrorism, as well as causing suffering for its victims and for those who make use of it, also becomes harmful for the cause it's defending. Julia thinks they've already talked about that.

FRAGEBOGEN: If you are one of those who fell or got off your horse, how did it happen?

Suddenly?

Little by little?

EXPLAIN, BRIEFLY, THE MAIN CAUSE OF YOUR HAVING FALLEN / GOTTEN OFF YOUR HORSE.

AFTER GETTING / FALLING OFF YOUR HORSE, HAVE YOU HAD ANY OF THE FOLLOWING EXPERIENCES?

Keeping it to myself for fear of losing my friends.

Ditto, because of physical fear.

Not attending protests because it would have meant going along with Spanish nationalists.

Starting to feel repelled by anything Basque.

Lynn asks if ETA has killed any of her friends. Not friends, but they have killed some friends and relatives of people she knows. The first was the father of a friend of hers from school, Teresa Hoyos. He was in the army, and they killed him in 1980. She hadn't known him well, but he must have been a good man, and she knows for sure that he respected his children's extreme left-wing ideas. She can still see Teresa Hoyos dressed entirely in black—and by then people no longer observed such mourning customs, or not so strictly, anyway. It was a hard blow for Julia, she had seen the effects of violence first hand. They'd taken away the beloved father of somebody close, a good friend of hers, and she was very much affected by it all. She felt guilty about it. Although she told herself that she had nothing to do with the murderers who planted the bomb, she found it difficult to continue seeing Teresa Hoyos. She didn't have the courage to talk about what she felt, and they grew apart; it was partially Teresa, too—she started spending more time with other people, with members of the victims' association that had just been set up. She started seeing her in photos in the newspaper with those small groups of people who would get together to denounce violence, which she herself didn't go to, even though she felt more and more obliged to do so.

Until one day when she decided to go to one of their demonstrations. There were at most fifty people outside the regional government offices in the Plaza Gipuzkoa. She felt quite embarrassed standing there in the gardens; apart from the dozen or so people in the middle, it was a loose group, and she was at the edge of that silent gathering, while from the arches around the plaza, the few people walking by looked at them with indifference.

She would prefer Lynn not to ask why she was embarrassed, because she wouldn't know quite what to say. Embarrassed, to start with, about standing there silently in the middle of a square with just a handful of others and knowing that any people coming past the square as they went about their business would inevitably see them, and that reminded her of how she always felt whenever she would see those pairs of evangelists knocking on people's doors—all those passersby must now have been thinking the same thing about her. Embarrassed because she was alone there and wanting the demonstration to be over as quickly as possible. And embarrassed, above all, because somebody might have thought she was a Spanish nationalist, an enemy of Basqueness.

Fortunately, Lynn does not ask her any more questions. So she sticks to telling her what she does know: when the rally finished, she only dared greet Teresa Hoyos from a distance, because she was surrounded by people, apparently the center of attention, and when Julia turned to leave, quite pleased and above all relieved at having done what she thought was her duty, another old classmate came up to her, someone she hadn't ever talked to much back then, and said she was very glad to see her there. "Because you used to be such a fanatic," she said to her, "always going around handing out pamphlets." She said it condescendingly at best, as if she were saying "you used to be a real troublemaker," and Julia found the comment offensive.

She's ready to admit that much of her involvement in politics when she was young may have been rather impulsive, but it was sincere and noble, and at that moment, she was offended that somebody could see it as something to feel ashamed of or something to regret. The woman who said that to her had become a proper lady—"una señora bien"—and Julia could hardly remember what she used to be like when she was young. She thinks she must have been one of those people who never got involved in anything—like most people, in other words—who sensibly had no objective other than to finish school and find a boyfriend with honorable intentions, one of those people who has never had to get off a horse because they've never gotten on one in the first place, not for any ethical reasons but because they're cowards and easily manipulated. The worst of it is that individuals like that force her to wonder if things might not have turned out very differently if everyone had done the same, if everybody had stuck to satisfying their own needs, adapting as best they could to changing circumstances and living as well as possible without getting into trouble.

She could have told her that Franco had been one of the first to condemn ETA. (Her sister had said that to her some days earlier when she said that she regretted not having realized earlier just how senseless violence is.) But Julia didn't dare say anything to the woman. Although she agreed with her on the most important point—denouncing violence—it was as if she had nothing else at all in common with her, and she fled. She felt out of place at the next demonstration, too. To a large extent, the problem was that she always went alone, and so she would find herself surrounded by people she had no connection with, people of another style, people from another culture, when it came down to it. What's more, she had to listen to comments she found hurtful, remarks spoken against *abertzales* who were proud of their heritage that went well beyond condemning terrorism. And they started to treat her like a lost sheep.

She decided not to go to any more demonstrations, however justified they might be. She wouldn't pay them any more attention. She decided to act as if she had no information about them, to be prudent—"*in medio virtus.*" She didn't want to have anything to do with people who were increasingly claiming that the only way to solve the whole problem was to erase the nationalist chimera, to destroy the very ideas, feelings, and myths of that world that encouraged violence. Wasn't giving up her own ideas, however crazy they might be, in order not to have anything to do with violent people, wasn't that, in fact, a form of bowing to the will of others?

At the same time, she found that the reports of torture presented by the other side—and some of them looked real enough—moved her less and less. To an extent, they deserved it. When people started talking about cowardly equidistance, she thought it was deliberately unfair and paid no attention. What's more, the same people were calling for daring and bravery—*la gallardía* was the term they used in Spanish—and those were values she didn't find particularly attractive, not to mention the fact that she didn't think of herself as being overly affected by fear.

She was wrong. She was afraid, even if it wasn't physical fear; it was a type of moral fear, and it had been affecting her for a long time. She was very hurt to have to admit it. She remembers another funeral in Otzeta, an aunt's. Following custom, after the church service, her cousins offered a reception with light snacks in a gastronomic society nearby. The walls were plastered with posters of Mario Onaindia and Juan Mari Bandrés—politicians who quit the *abertzale* left to join the Spanish socialists—and the word *Spaniards*, or *traitor*, she doesn't remember which, maybe both, was scrawled across them. Her cousins are at the opposite extreme as her old classmates, but they, too, had had to keep quiet during the Franco years. Silent during the Franco years and, like many other people, vocal under democracy. Really vocal, in fact. Under the Franco regime, they were docile and well behaved, they avoided getting into trouble, as their parents had instructed them, and afterward, they traded in their bourgeois status in order to support the socialisation of suffering, began dressing in the combat gear typical of that crowd—ordinary-looking hiking clothes that were actually very expensive. They knew that she was in Euskadiko Ezkerra, but they didn't care; they felt morally superior enough to tell her that she, too, was a traitor, and she put up with that insult without so much as a peep, because she thought doing so was an example of politeness and tolerance. She was in Otzeta the day they found Miguel Angel Blanco's body in the trunk of a car, she was at a wedding banquet on that occasion. They were eating dessert when somebody came in with the news, and the rumor spread sadly from table to table; but then the voices got louder again and the party really got started, the dancing began, and she, too, stayed at the party, sitting at a table with the grown women, all listening to their children saying silly things, convinced—then, too—that the best thing she could do was to keep quiet in order not to spoil the party, not to spoil things.

Regarding collusion. A few minutes ago, when Zabaleta was talking about Basque literature and its treatment of violence, Julia got to thinking about how languages condition messages. She's written something about that in her blue notebook. Politicians don't say exactly the same things in Spanish as they do in Basque. It's very obvious if you watch the chat shows and debates in the media.

She has to think more about the idea, but for the moment she ventures to say to Lynn that "for whatever reason"—and what she's most interested in reflecting further on is what that reason might be—she thinks that Basque is used more for trying to convince people about things, probably because it assumes some degree of shared sympathy on the part of listeners. And she doesn't say so to Lynn, but she does think that in general—and it could be for technical reasons to an extent—people don't have the language skills required for debating in Basque, or, to put it another way, they are more talkative and speak with greater precision in Spanish.

But there's more to it than that, too, and she'd like to tell Lynn about it, something about it demonstrating the existence of a senti- mental attachment between those who speak it to each other, like when two people from the same country run into each other abroad. It was more apparent twenty or thirty years ago, when Basque created very close links between people. Not so much now, perhaps because more people have learned the language and it has some official status. She thought the subject could be brought up in the introduction to the translation of *Bihotzean min dut* and, at the same time, that it might even be possible to include the half a dozen articles Martin had previously written and collected under the title *Kale borrokako mutil bati gutun irekia*—or *Open Letter to a* Kale Borroka *Boy*. At the time he wrote them, Martin still believed it might be possible to convince and win over those young radicals. The letters avoid any mention of ethics, and she admits that their invocation of respect for human life as a supreme value is sometimes no more than hypocrisy. The person penning the letters is on the same side as them, understands the anger and passion blinding young people, but tries to convince his readers of the uselessness of blowing themselves up, pointing to the hypocrisy of the adults who are encouraging the struggle, noting, without in any sense forgetting the objectives, that there are less violent, more intelligent ways of furthering the cause. Letters written in the confident knowledge that they will be read, because they are in Basque, which is what their readers have in common. Julia thought the letters were beautiful, that their pedagogical purpose was intelligent, and she made Zigor read them. Later on they came to realize that this sort of pedagogical complicity, which tactically avoided all ethical issues, was useless.

Until very late on, they believed that the people in ETA were a bunch of young kids that could be convinced. She can still remember the voice of Chillida, the famed Basque sculptor, pleading with José María Aldaya's kidnappers to free him, and that was in 1995. She remembers the message that got played over and over again on the radio word by word: "This is Eduardo Chillida, I have a request for ETA. Show us that you are capable of doing something good. Release Aldaya. Make his family happy and work with us to make peace possible for everyone. I know that what I'm asking for is difficult, but I want to believe in Man."

Poor Chillida.

Nobody can deny there's been considerable tolerance for violence in the Basque-speaking world. Many writers and particularly our people's poets—the *bertsolaris*—have encouraged it. At the other end of the spectrum, there were people who rebelled against that reality, stating that identity—a murderous identity—was the real cause of the violence, people who made the Basque language the object of their hate, to the extent that they saw patriotism as being connected with guilt, and they lost all affection and loyalty toward Basque and began to favor Spanish. (It should be taken into account that this move from one language to another, apart from the few exceptions that prove the rule, always takes place in the same direction. That, too, gives Julia cause to think, and the questions she asks herself have answers that are more painful than they are difficult.)

She has to admit, at the same time, that her wish for the terrorists to listen to reason and let themselves be convinced had an ulterior motive: the desire and hope that there could be an end to the violence without having the concept of *abertzale* soiled. She wanted the violence to stop before Basque patriotism was completely ruined by it, before the cruelty and lack of dignity became clear for all to see, before their well-earned reputation as a noble community—sincere, hard-working, unconquerable, and also pacific—was dragged through the mud. The homeland of the oldest nation in Europe; the bombarded tree of democracy at Gernika; Agirre, Iruxo, and Beldarrainena; the soldiers who protected their enemies' lives behind the lines; Eustakio Mendizabal Txikia, who wrote, "Whatever I've done to them as an enemy / May they damn me for that"; ETA members who set fire to themselves in protest against Franco; the shameful last stand of violence in Europe . . . She wanted the violence to end before Basque society became a sad case of collective cowardice.

But it probably had to happen the way it did, so that future generations could make no mistake about it.

Drain the chalice to the last drop.

The fear that the baby will be thrown out with the bath water. Does she know that expression? *Throw out the baby with the bath water: Discard something valuable along with something not wanted.* Having to deny dreams and feelings that she thought beautiful, that were part of her character, just because they once fed some people's madness hurts her. She likes to think that there was no reason for those things to have been harmful; they're what made her father turn out to be such a sincere and hard-working man. But sometimes she wonders if it wouldn't be better to flush the Basque character and everything that makes the Basques special down the drain. She finds it brings her some relief to say *"merde à dieu, à la patrie, et à tout le reste"*—to tell God, homeland, and all the rest to go to hell. Accursed homeland. It's ruined so many lives, brought about so much suffering—like a fat sow eating its own young—suffering from which it will never free itself.

"Do you understand any of this?"

Lynn nods her head, as she usually does, several times. Like a diligent child.

"But how can you understand it, when I don't myself?"

JAIME ZABALETA AND MARTIN come in at the exact same moment that Harri knocks on the door. They greet each other in the usual Otzeta way, with provocative comments: Zabaleta asks Harri if she's just come from the hairdressers', because she's quite dolled up; and she asks him if his tie's shrunk, because the tip of it is hanging quite a long way up from his belt, what with the size of his belly. She'll give him a new one on his birthday. To which Zabaleta replies that he can't complain about presents, holding up a first edition of *Biotz-begietan*, which he says he doesn't deserve. At which Harri concludes, "Of course you don't deserve it." She looks at Martin, and then at Julia, without trying to hide her anger, and Zabaleta instinctively tucks the book away in his jacket. He's going, but first he has to call his bodyguards, and they position themselves on either side of the door, continually looking left and right. Harri's remark: "They've given you some pretty shoddy bodyguards, you must not be very important."

Harri doesn't like Jaime Zabaleta. As soon as they leave, she tells Martin off: whatever favors he may owe Zabaleta, they can't deserve such a considerable reward. A first edition of Lizardi's *Biotz-begietan*, for God's sake. She gives Lynn her take on Zabaleta and what his story is. They used to call his father Joxe *Gaizto*, or Evil Joxe, because he was a fanatic *Requeté*—"which is why that jerk was named Jaime," as if the girl could possibly understand that reference—and also a poor wretch, a man who did everything for the Goytisolos and took care of their house there, which they never used. Old man Goytisolo, Abaitua's father-in-law, had paid for Jaime Zabaleta to go to university. In other words, being Spanish ran in his family. Julia doesn't like this way of talking that Harri has—and her mother and sister, too—which involves invoking situations with family members to put people down. And she also always talks the same way they do when referring to somebody she doesn't like, as if she had some secret information about the person, something they should be ashamed of. "I could tell you a thing or two about that one," she'll say malevolently, her head cocked to the side and one shoulder raised.

"*Vive sin dar un palo al agua.*" Julia wants to find an English expression for that, for Jaime Zabaleta not ever wanting to work—she can only think of the French version, *ne pas en foutre une rame*—but Harri won't let her. She says Julia always gets hung up on words. Julia, on the other hand, doesn't know why Harri is so interested in telling Lynn about how Jaime Zabaleta has been aided by politics. Harri reminds Julia of her mother when she gets like that, and she can't stand it. Every time her mother hears the name of this one particular woman whose husband was killed by ETA, she can't help saying that they did her a great favor by getting rid of the man—now she draws who knows how many pension checks as his widow, and she, Julia's mother, has heard her say hundreds of times that her husband used to beat her.

The piece of iron sticking out of the angel's broken arm has a supermarket bag stuck on it, and it's blowing around in the wind. It's making Julia nervous, and she gets up to take it off, but Harri stops her by grabbing her hand. Apparently she thinks she's getting up to leave because she's angry.

"Come on, don't be like that. Aren't you interested in what happened to me?"

In fact, she isn't in the mood to listen to her stupid stories about café terraces in Bilbao and her search for the man from the airport. But she doesn't want to kick up a fuss in front of Lynn.

They aren't going to believe it. The same beginning as always, but now, after the usual steps she always takes to ask them to pay attention to whatever nonsense she may be about to tell them, she comes straight out and tells them something amazing—she's gone to bed with Adolfo. All three of them look at her open-mouthed, and this time, she doesn't need to ask them "*¿Qué te parece?*" because it's obvious they're astonished by what she's said. Martin's the first one to regain his speech, and he stutters, "How come you went to bed with Adolfo?" And Julia has to stop herself from laughing, because she doesn't understand who this Adolfo is, or why Harri's just blurted out that she's slept with him. "Who's Adolfo?" she asks, while Harri is still nodding slowly at them to lend gravity to her news, and after looking at Julia with wide open eyes, she shakes her head with a mixture of pity and disdain. It's obvious, she says, that she isn't at all interested in the things she tells her.

Julia realizes, too late, that Adolfo is the guy who works for Iberia, the airline.

Harri, with an offended look on her face, stands and picks up her bag to tell them she's leaving, complaining that they never pay any attention to her stories, but Lynn and Martin both protest, talking over each in an effort to tell her that she's not right about that, that they're dying to know, and then she sits down again and pulls a face like a child refusing to eat. After a considerable pause, she starts telling them about Adolfo, the Iberia guy. He called her that morning to give her some news about their search and asked if they could meet up at the Ercilla Hotel. They arranged to meet at midday, but apparently she had to wait a bit. He'd told her that it might be difficult for him to get away from work and that he might be late, but waiting made her nervous, and she ordered a gin and tonic. (A description of the atmosphere, the warm lighting, the discreet, shadowy corners, the respectful waiters and waitresses in old-fashioned uniforms, always on the alert, the murmur of conversations, the strains of *Strangers in the Night* coming from the piano, etc.) When he arrived, he asked her what the man from the airport had looked like, what his voice was like, and these were really the only two questions she could answer, though he also asked her about other details, some of which didn't seem to be particularly relevant.

When he asked her if he looked like he was married, she remembered the quarrel she'd seen when leaving the terminal, which seemed to indicate he and the woman he was with were breaking up. Although that was a very important detail for her, it had nothing to do with being able to find the man, but she told him about it even so, and her description of the scene that the woman with the dyed-blonde hair had made got them to talking about relationships between men and women. Adolfo told her again and again that her search seemed very romantic to him and that he sometimes got the impression he was in the middle of a movie. He said he was very romantic, too, and would do anything to be desired by a woman with such passion, determined to overcome all obstacles, like Harri in her search for this man, and that's why he wanted to help her, even if that meant doing things that were technically illegal. The Iberia employee's words made her nervous, she didn't know what he was trying to do. It occurred to her that he might be about to ask her for money in exchange for his help, and that idea made her feel really anxious, not so much because of the amount of money he might request as because it would spoil their relationship. She asks if they understand her, and all three say they do. She says she doesn't want to use alcohol as an excuse to explain what happened, not at all, but she did order another gin and tonic while Adolfo filled her in on the details of the search. He said he'd been telephoning all the men who sat behind her, right back to the last row. He'd been telling them, as she'd suggested, that he was looking for the passenger from the London-Bilbao IB 5545 flight whose bag full of books had burst open as soon as he got onto the plane, and on most occasions he hadn't had to say any more than that, because they'd hung up after saying that nothing of theirs had broken. Apparently a few of them had wanted to know what the reason behind the question was before they answered, and then he'd had to give them more information, saying that a lady had given him one of her bags—a Harrods bag, specifically, which she'd emptied and kindly offered to the man so that he could put his books, which had fallen onto the ground, into it—and she thinks she may not have fully emptied it before giving it to him, one of her own books may have still been inside it. A novel, which, for her own reasons, she was very attached to, a book called *Montauk*, and she wanted to get it back as soon as possible, whatever difficulties there might be. So he'd changed the story—Julia doesn't really understand how exactly he changed it, but she doesn't care, either—and Harri thought it sounded better this way. Be that as it may, he said he hadn't had to go into all of that very many times; when they heard the whole thing was just about a book, most people had lost interest and hung up, but—and here Harri puts on a triumphant expression—two passengers did remember the incident happening, the man's bag breaking and him spending a long time blocking up the aisle while he picked up all his books. One of them remembered that a woman had offered him a green bag, and that's what Harrods bags are like, green. Harri thought those two men remembering what had happened was very significant, because it made the story more believable for Adolfo.

He said that the biggest problem, unfortunately, and for obvious reasons, was that he couldn't phone from the office, or from home, either, not while his wife was there, at any rate, because she was very jealous and wouldn't believe the truth, and he couldn't think up any other story to tell her. So it was taking him awhile, but he didn't have many calls left to make.

Harri says that what she likes about Adolfo is his optimism and complicity, he's very understanding, and he doesn't think she's crazy—unlike some other people—for wanting to find the man. They spent some time drinking their gin and tonics and imagining what it would be like to find the man. They thought that when Adolfo finally reached him and told him the situation—that he was looking for a man whose bag full of books had broken and all the rest of it—he would answer straight away that it was him, although they couldn't be completely sure of that. Theoretically, if he tried to disguise the fact that it had been him, it would be because he thought they were looking for him for some other reason and so he preferred not to reply. In that case, it would all be over, but she wouldn't mind, because she wouldn't like to get involved with a man who was trying to hide something. But Harri doesn't think that will happen. She says the man didn't look as if he had many things to hide, and judging by the spark of passion she had seen in his eyes, she says that if he turned out not to be attracted to her—not remembering her at all was almost impossible—he would probably still admit that it was his bag that had burst. From that point onward, there were several different possibilities, which Harri wants to explain to them one by one, counting them out on the fingers of one hand, but Martin, a little irritated, stops her and asks her to tell them once and for all why she went to bed with the hair gel-wearing Iberia employee.

As was to be expected, Harri doesn't like the remark. For a moment, she stares at Martin with her right index finger resting on her left pinkie finger, frozen in astonishment at the very moment she was about to tell them about the first possibility, as if she can't believe what she's just heard, and then she gets up, threatening again that she's going to leave, complaining that they don't care about what happens to her, and Lynn is upset, asking her again to stay, using the affectionate tone you use to try to convince a child of something—of course they're interested in what she has to tell them, it's something about her, after all, and the story is so interesting per se—while Martin says that it's precisely because he's interested that he's asked her to come to the point and quit wasting time on pointless details.

Julia, on the other hand, keeps quiet, already quite bored of Harri's stories, and her hysteria, too. She knows Harri isn't going to leave. Now Harri sounds deeply hurt as she reproaches Martin, saying that it's incredible that a writer should be uninterested in details and what they mean. But instead of falling silent at that, the writer says that hypotheses are not the same as details. "*Facts, facts,*" he insists. *Déjà vu.*

Harri spends awhile going through a whole range of facial expressions typical of a spoilt child, but then, instead of telling them what they were interested in—in other words, what had happened with this Adolfo guy—she goes straight back to where she left off, talking about the possible reactions the man from the airport might have on receiving Adolfo's call, as if nothing has happened, and nobody dares to say anything to her, partly not to create a fuss and partly because she said she'd keep it to just three possible options.

A) The man doesn't remember that *Montauk* was one of the books he was carrying, nor that he offered it to her when he was crouching down there in the middle of the aisle. In that case, he would probably look among his books and then, after finding it, happily reply that it wasn't missing. She says she thinks it's the least probable option, and also the least interesting hypothesis.

B) He remembers that he had *Montauk* in the bag and that he wanted to give it to her. This was the most probable option, and it led, in turn, to two possible outcomes. Firstly, the man doesn't understand the message and, consequently, interprets it in different possible ways depending on his psychological profile. For instance, he might think it strange that somebody lost a book that he also has; it could also seem suspicious and irritating to him if he had a tendency toward paranoia and thought they were asking him to give them his copy of the book. C) The second outcome of the previous hypothesis is that when Adolfo tells him that a woman has lost her copy of *Montauk,* and that getting it back is a matter of life or death for her, he remembers the whole scene, the two of them kneeling down in the aeroplane aisle and him offering her the book and saying *"this book was written in good faith."* But in this option, unlike in the others, the man clearly understands that she is looking for him and knows why.

Option C is the only one she's interested in. She doesn't believe there are any other realistic options.

She doesn't know why, but she thinks the man will be the last on Alfonso's list and so he'll find him in a fortnight's time. He'll tell him he's sure he does have the English translation of *Montauk* and that he'll be very pleased to give it back to the lady he's unwittingly taken it from.

Adolfo told her that, in a way, he'll be sad when that happens. She tells them once more that she finds Adolfo's complicity moving, he takes her story seriously, and she mentions the care with which he had written down all the different possibilities on a paper napkin, many more of them than the three summarized versions she's just told them about. He seemed moved when he took her hand and told her they were going to find the man. She, too, was moved by him saying that he would be sorry in a way when they found the man because it would mean he wouldn't have any excuse for seeing her again. He said he enjoyed being with her, and she ordered another gin and tonic—that made three altogether—and they talked about all sorts of things.

She didn't mind having to pay for the drinks herself, even though it made her feel like an old lady. It did occur to her that somebody might think he was a gigolo and she his customer, but she didn't care about that, either. Adolfo was the first to stand up. He started walking away without doing anything about the plate with drink bills piled up on it; she quickly put some money on the plate and went after him. She promises them that when they got into the elevator, she thought they were going up to street level, she almost said to Adolfo that she was still quite capable of walking in spite of all the gin and tonics, but he pressed the button for the second floor. She didn't dare say anything and followed him along the corridor once they got there. She wasn't capable of thinking at all. She imagines that, mostly, she was embarrassed. Embarrassed to ask him what he took her for, or that he might think her old fashioned.

She continues talking about her impressions. She thought that for a young man, going to bed with someone was something completely normal, like having another gin and tonic, and so it should be that way for her, too. She said she was also worried about saying all of that to the guy from Iberia, and about the reaction he might have if she refused to go into room 222 with him after he finally managed to unlock the door with his magnetic card on the fourth attempt. She was afraid that if she didn't go in, he might be offended, get angry, and maybe say to her that she could look for the man from the airport by herself. That's what she thought refusing to go to bed with Adolfo would have meant, losing the chance to find the man, but in the end, she went ahead, and not only for that reason.

If she had to write a novel, she'd write that she was prepared to prostitute herself in order to get in touch with the man, but although that wouldn't be a lie, it wouldn't be the whole truth. She says she was curious, too. Apart from Martxelo, she's known no other man in the Biblical sense (to Lynn: "*Can you believe it?*"), and she hasn't done it with Martxelo for a long time, either, and it's been even longer since she's done it in a hotel. She stepped through the door and started laughing immediately, out of nervousness, she says, but then she quickly stopped. Apparently, this Adolfo guy took great care undressing, folding all his clothes over a chair so they wouldn't get creased.

No chance of him ripping off her clothes with his teeth, then. Everything very normal, maybe too normal. Adolfo's phone rang as soon as they finished, and he did nothing to disguise the fact that it was his wife, giving a string of *yes, dears* and *no, dears*—"*Sí, cari, no, cari.*" She was glad when he said he had to go. While he got dressed, she decided to show no more of herself and stay in the bed. She had doubts about paying for the hotel room, but he had none. He didn't have any cash, and since his wife looked at everything, it would be too much of a giveaway to use a credit card.

"¿*Qué te parece?* It could be a novel, couldn't it?"

Julia knew she was going to say that and wanted to be ready in case she asked it as a straight, non-rhetorical question. But she can't think of anything to say, and fortunately there's no need to answer, because Harri hasn't framed it as a real question and doesn't say another word. She just stands and picks up her green bag. She's late, she says.

Lynn's leaving, too.

As soon as they leave, Martin quickly turns the television on. It's time for Marie Laforet. Julia asks him what he thinks about what Harri's just told them, and he replies, "She's off her rocker." But off her rocker because of what she's done, or because she's started telling them her fantasies? It makes no difference. She's off her rocker.

In Marie Laforet's supposedly exotic Basque, every time she says *bertzalde*—or "on the other hand"—she draws out the last syllable and almost sings it, ending on a half note. One of her charms must be her way of speaking, along with her sand-colored eyes.

Julia has a headache again, just like earlier in the morning when she read about the ailing writer's stratagem for facing up to his doctor's judgement with dignity, not knowing whether the story was written in a humorous tone or not. Now, too, she is unable to determine what Harri's intention in telling them her story is, and that makes her feel dumb, like somebody failing to get a joke, which happens to her quite a lot. She guesses Martin is right when he reproaches her for not having a sense of humor. He, on the other hand, is capable of talking about the most absurd things while keeping a serious face; he calls that English humor.

Meanwhile, the wind continues blowing the supermarket bag stuck to the angel's broken arm around.

She's curious to know how Martin would react if she asked him if he's had any more tests done. She's absolutely sure he would never deduce from her interest that she knows anything about the man in front of the mirror, but the very idea of asking him makes her queasy. But she knows she's going to end up asking him, and so finally she does.

She asks in a neutral voice, "Have you had any tests done recently?"

Perhaps it came out too loud. He turns toward her quickly, and the look in his blue eyes is enough to know that he's astonished.

"Why do you ask?"

She has her answer ready.

"Cholesterol. You've been eating a lot of cheese lately."

When she goes out to remove the supermarket bag, the cats come up and greet her.

14

ABAITUA IS ALREADY DRESSED when Pilar sticks her head in and says hello. She spent the night in Otzeta, she's come by to pick up some documents, and after taking a shower, she'll go back there. "Dying's a mess." She doesn't seem to be very moved by her father's death, she speaks about his final days in a neutral tone. Although she has been expecting it, it's true. She said the old man had oesophageal cancer long before anyone else realized, even Orl. She repeated that she has a good clinical eye when he, Abaitua, said that the old man not eating much and being weak wasn't important, it was just a passing depression.

She gets undressed in front of him. The new bathroom isn't working properly, the renovators did something wrong, and so she's back to using his. Her breasts are quite a lot larger than when she was young, and rather saggy. Abaitua leaves the bathroom and walks off to the living room. He doesn't like being in such an intimate situation with her, he can't stand being dressed while she's naked, he doesn't know exactly why. But it's clear Pilar doesn't care about that; she comes into the living room soon afterward, rubbing lotion onto her shoulders and her back with enviable agility, and gives him more details about the old man's death. She says he died in her arms, peacefully.

Even though Pilar says there's no need for him to cancel any of his operations, he just has to make it to Otzeta in time for the funeral, by the time he reaches the hospital, he sees clearly that he should have gone with her. So he decides to only do the first operation of the day—that way at least he'll be able to get there before lunch.

He bumps into Lynn and Harri Gabilondo on his way out. The latter's heard about his father-in-law. She gives him her condolences and asks after Pilar. Lynn, standing next to her, looks at him, as if wanting to know how affected he is by it all, he thinks. Sometimes she seems smaller, completely diminished, when she shrugs her shoulders. He thinks it happens to her when she's worried. Her arms are tightly folded across her chest, her hands tucked under her arms— one of her typical postures—her right leg crossed behind her left ankle, her feet the wrong way around. She holds a hand out to him while Harri is telling him the latest department gossip, and, without touching him, she pulls it away again, quickly, with a gesture of regretting having gone too far, and she crosses her arms again like a punished child. It's very obvious she's told Harri they've slept together. He has nothing to hide, and he doesn't mind. Women tell each other these things. Don't they? He hasn't told anybody about what's happened with Lynn.

DARK PINEWOODS and a narrow valley. An old church, Knights Templar style. The inside of the church, where everyone is gathered, looks as if it's falling down, some of the oval-based columns are completely crooked. The precarious condition of the building shows they have little respect for the past. As Pilar straightens his tie, she asks him, with a look, to be patient with the people coming up to them to give their condolences. He thinks she looks quite fragile now, and she has that air of sweetness she sometimes has. Of those who approach them, at least three people say that it was thanks to the old man that nobody in Otzeta died during the war. They say he didn't care if they were on Franco's side or Reds', their lives had to be respected because they were locals, and he helped everybody as far as he could.

REMEMBER YOUR SERVANT, OH LORD. The priest's hiking boots and pants are visible underneath his surplice, and it looks as if his hunting dogs must be ready and waiting for him for when the service finishes. He tells them he's in charge of four parishes.

It's a bilingual mass, as Pilar's mother requested, and Abaitua finds it strange hearing Spanish in church, he can't get used to it. Ugly hymns, bland words, and vulgar music. Basque, on the other hand, sounds as appropriate as Latin. Those *dies irae*s. That austere, tragic solemnity; large black and golden candles; the smell of incense; deep voices; full-sounding words. *Pompa mortis*. He thinks the religious ceremony is becoming redundant, losing its meaning, and that no lay equivalent has been found for it yet.

When the priest, in his short homily, says that they haven't come together for a social gathering but rather to declare their renewed faith, he has to stop himself from walking out. Our brother Luis. The priest, too, mentions how the old man never sought vengeance, in spite of having been on the winning side.

Abaitua remembers some other church services. The most solemn of them, no doubt about it, was Fernando Aire Xalbador's funeral in Donostia's Good Shepherd Cathedral in 1976. A year after Franco died. The entire Orfeón Donostiarra choral society sang at it, and there were enough people in attendance to fill the cathedral twice over. He's convinced that nobody, however important they might be, could ever again bring together such a varied group of people in terms of origins and attitudes. And that's because the Basque language is no longer something emotionally shared and treasured by all citizens of the Basque Country.

And he often remembers another funeral, one he himself didn't go to. That, too, had been held at the Good Shepherd Cathedral. It was for two people who'd been killed by ETA: a high-ranking soldier, and his driver, a young man who'd been posted to his detail as part of his military service. Abaitua doesn't remember the date. While they were going somewhere in the now-deceased officer's car, two men on a motorcycle drew up even with them, and the one sitting on the back stuck a bomb on the roof. The driver had time to break, but not to get out of the car. It could have been a bloodbath, right there in the center of Donostia, but in the end only the soldier and the young man died, although some others were wounded.

The funeral was for both of them, and Abaitua's mother attended it—the driver's father was a friend of hers. She often talks about it, because she was very moved by it, she says. She says the coffins were placed side by side in front of the altar, with Spanish flags laid over them. That was how the army organized it, and the family didn't dare to ask them to do it any differently. But according to Abaitua's mother, the young man's father wasn't able to stand seeing a Spanish flag on top of his son's coffin, and gathering all his courage, he asked the officer presiding over the funeral with him—Abaitua's mother doesn't know what rank he was—to take it off, and he did. She mimes the officer folding up the flag with great delicacy each time Abaitua asks her to tell him the story.

He also remembers the day of Teresa Hoyos's father's funeral. A clear, sunny winter's day. He wanted to go, but the neighborhood church was full up. There were army officers with thin moustaches and sunglasses who couldn't get in, and he felt out of place.

He doesn't want to think about how bad Teresa Hoyos must have felt.

Offer each other a sign of peace. He sees some old Franco supporters who his father-in-law always avoided during his final years. One of those guys on that one May Day, he doesn't remember the exact year, who stuck the Spanish colors in his buttonhole and started beating up the handful of demonstrators that had gathered and then fled in fear. (Jesús Revilla was one of them—a tall bald man who used to walk around the city streets with an arrogant expression on his face and without anyone ever daring to call him a fascist.)

Jaime Zabaleta is there, too; he has to have bodyguards for much lesser reasons. He tells Pilar that her father was a gentleman, and when he greets Abaitua, he looks as if he's amused by something. He thinks it's because the last time he saw him he was with Lynn down at the port.

The cemetery is next to the church and is very small. Old iron crosses, most of the graves without any sort of slab on top of them, only piled-up earth, and new marble gravestones with *lauburus*—Basque crosses—on them. The only thing that looks like a mausoleum—with a gray stone angel, its wings folded down and a finger on its lips asking for silence—belongs to the Goytisolos. Pilar puts a bunch of wild flowers she picked nearby on it. Just as the old man wanted it—no pomp and circumstance. She turns around and hugs Abaitua. He's moved to feel Pilar's body shaking against his. Like the only other time he's ever seen her crying from grief, that time she asked him not to leave her, without any inhibitions, not stifling her cries. Like a child.

IT'S LATE WHEN HE GETS IN THE CAR to go back home, because his mother-in-law invited the family and close friends to the Lasa restaurant in Bergara. It's what the deceased would have wanted. He loved that restaurant. A classic, as he always used to say, in spite of not getting all the media coverage some other places have. His brother- and sister-in-law compete to name the places where they've had their best meals, praising the dishes as works of art and bragging about their connections to the famous chefs.

A SOCIOLOGICAL REFLECTION. He remembers the Livy quote Kepa recited to him the first time they ate at Argi Eder: "The cook whom the ancients regarded and treated as the lowest menial was rising in value, and, what had been a servile office came to be looked upon as a fine art." They don't talk about the old man, but when somebody mentions the future of the clinic, there's a quarrel. Pilar seems to have recovered. In any case, she eats heartily. Everyone's eating heartily except for Loiola, who looks gloomily at his plate without touching it, as if he were reproaching them for behaving as if nothing's happened, and Abaitua, to set himself apart from the other, declines to order dessert, in solidarity with his son.

He finds the drive back, following Pilar in her car, difficult—she drives faster and better than he does—and it bothers him that Loiola, who's sitting in the passenger seat and can't take the wheel because he left his licence at home, can see that, even though he's the first one to laugh at himself about his driving and doesn't mind that he's seldom the driver when they go anywhere as a couple, joking that it just goes to show he's no sexist.

He has a hard time keeping up with Pilar as far as Elgoibar, and from there on, he lets her go on ahead. The boy, understandingly, says it's a very bad road and that it's crazy to go more than sixty on it.

He asks his father questions about the old man, and he tries to paint the same agreeable picture Pilar does. He was a good doctor, he loved his profession, and he was ahead of his time. Having been on Franco's side during the war didn't mean he was a fascist. He never accepted any of the many positions he was offered during the dictatorship. He was a traditionalist, and was definitely attached to the Basque Country. He doesn't tell him that his grandfather was more of a racist than his other grandfather, who was a nationalist, but he does tell him that he believed the objective of the Basques should not be to separate from Spain but rather to dominate Spain, through hard work and wealth, and that he consequently thought that Basque nationalism was a mistake.

And of course, he said what was always said about him: when Franco's troops entered Otzeta, they didn't kill anybody.

And if he loved his community and traditions so much, why didn't he pass the Basque language onto his children?

It's a question the boy has asked a thousand times since he started to think for himself. It's probably one of the questions Pilar feels most uncomfortable about, and she tries to answer it by comparing her father with Unamuno. They both loved Basque but thought it was an obstacle in terms of cultural development and that it had no future. And that's more or less what he says. But why does his son insist on asking the same question again and again?

It's a difficult question, and he finds it hard to be sincere about it. He compares Basque with archaeological finds that force engineers to stop digging tunnels or change the course of roads—a respectable relic, but one that causes problems. He isn't optimistic about the costly, hard-won initiatives undertaken by the education system and the public administration; the language not having expanded enough, the issue of Basque has become a disagreeable conflict for many people, and even many of those who know the language don't use it. For children it's a language to use at school, one they leave behind as soon as they step out of the classroom. (A friend's child once expressed his surprise at being addressed in Basque outside of his language immersion school, "Hey, we're not in the *ikastola* any more!") It seems it's going to be difficult to obtain a critical mass of speakers who are able to use the language with ease, but if imposing its use isn't the answer, it doesn't look likely that retreating to winter quarters and using Basque only in intimate circles or exclusively for folklore and patriotic acts will win over the non-Basque speakers, either.

What, then?

Languages are functional tools. It's often said that languages don't die because people aren't learning them but because those who do know them aren't using them, but that's like saying that life doesn't stop as long as there are signs of brain activity. Everything is born and dies. Apparently there are five thousand languages in the world, and every year, twenty-five of them die, but not a single person goes silent because of that. A reality that is much easier to accept for people whose mother tongue is an imperial language.

Not while I'm alive.

After passing the town of Zarautz, they ride along in silence.

When they pull up outside the building door, Pilar's there waiting for them next to her car. Her mother hasn't gotten out. She tells them she's going to spend the night at her place, she's just coming in to get some sleeping pills. She doesn't take them often. She gives him a fleeting kiss, just long enough to feel that her cheeks are cold, which gives the impression that she's been in contact with death. Loiola says he'll walk back to the apartment on Urbieta Kalea, where he used to have his private practice, but he doesn't move, and Abaitua gets nervous; he'd like to be left alone, and at the same time, wanting that—wanting his son to go—makes him feel guilty. Because he thinks the boy feels sorry to leave him alone. He decides to say that he's very tired and has to operate the next morning. He wouldn't want somebody to lose their ovaries because he isn't fully awake.

Another missed opportunity to talk about security, the need to take some basic precautions, but whenever he actually has him there with him, he doesn't think it's the right moment—why frighten him. He pats his back in farewell. He doesn't remember when they stopped kissing each other goodbye. Whenever it was, he didn't realize it was going to be the last one when he gave it to him. It's the same with everything. He doesn't know why he feels sorry for him when he goes. Sorry for his sorrow, because he knows his parents don't get along, and that makes him sad.

There's a travel bag of Pilar's inside the door to the apartment. He picks it up and leaves it on a chair. He's never opened a bag of Pilar's, not even back when he thought she had secrets to keep from him. The smell of her perfume in the bathroom. It's sweet but not too sweet, and also refreshing; he loves that smell, which is her body's smell, even though he's never told her. Lynn's has a touch of bitterness to it that reminds him of ripe grass. He isn't tired, and he sits down in the half-light. But not for long. He sees the white of the breakers through the window, and the orange dots of the streetlights on the promenade.

He would have liked to have driven back via Martutene, just to see if her lights were on. He even thinks about going over there and spending some time standing in front of her house, but he knows that if he did that, he wouldn't be able to resist calling on her.

HE WAKES UP WITH THE IDEA that he's going to see Lynn, and that makes him jump out of bed, the cheerful sunlight streaming in through the window, because he forgot to lower the blinds the night before, that being one of the tasks Pilar still takes care of. But then, later, after just a quarter of an hour, while he's making sure the toast doesn't get burned, he promises himself he won't see her, which will make it clear that their meetings are no more than occasional and imply neither obligation nor commitment.

He enjoys being alone in the bathroom.

He chooses some pointed black shoes he's had for years now. When he bought them, they told him they were made of kangaroo skin, and they have large silver buckles on the sides. Pilar usually tells him they look like cardinal's shoes and he should throw them out. Lynn, on the other hand, has told him they're very elegant. He remembers that moment. When she said *"your shoes are very elegant,"* he uncrossed his legs and moved reflexively to pull his socks up, few things embarrassing him more than showing his calves, the soft white skin he has there, hairless, a part of his body he's particularly unhappy about because it's already showing signs of his age. He thought that Lynn noticed his embarrassed gesture, and feeling ridiculous, he started explaining to her—Frisch says that when he likes a woman, he starts talking like an idiot—about the alterations that men's and women's bodies undergo as they grow older, making them more like each other once again, as they were in childhood. Men's breasts get bigger and women's smaller; women get more body hair and men's falls out; women's voices get deeper and men's shriller. Lynn told him that both old and young men lose the hair on their ankles because of socks rubbing against them all the time.

He remembered, however, that when he and Pilar once spoke about that exact same thing, Pilar pointed out to him that women's tights don't do the same thing, at least not in her case, and somebody should research whether it could be a system for permanent hair removal, perhaps they could patent it. Abaitua replied that it had never occurred to him to think that she had any problem with body hair; the truth was that until recently, he added, and perhaps rather sarcastically, he had always taken her to be angelical, always had that idea of her. And then Pilar, in an unforgettable moment, looked him in the eyes and said, "That's the problem, you've always thought of me as an angel." She wasn't joking. He thought it was an enigmatic answer, and without knowing why, he was convinced it was connected with something profound in their relationship, and although he dropped the subject, for fear of finding out more, he kept thinking about it and was worried it might have to do with her sexual impulses. Once, later on, taking advantage of a period of harmony in their relationship, he dared to bring up the conversation again and asked her what she'd meant when she said that his thinking of her as an angel was a problem, but it turned out she didn't remember what she'd said. He thought she didn't say that with much conviction. He didn't believe her, and he imagined that Pilar thought—just as she had when he'd given her a wedding ring twenty years or more after getting married—that the time for that was past.

AT THE HOSPITAL, HE'S GLAD TO SEE that a couple of colleagues have put relatives of theirs on his patient list and that he isn't going to have a free moment all day. He's proud to be the doctor of choice for other doctors, nurses, residents, and all of their relatives, although it does give him quite a lot of extra work. Even so, he can't resist the urge to go by Lynn's work area just before two o'clock, on the excuse that he has to look something up in the library.

On the stairs he comes across Echevarría, the resident working in the neonatology department. He's very angry, because Arrese wants to put all the research data together in such a way that the high infant mortality rates the hospital experiences for births taking place in the early morning will go unnoticed. To get rid of him, Abaitua says he needs an article from the library and wants to get there before the documentalist leaves. Echevarría replies that Lynn has just left, explaining in Spanish that she was feeling a bit under the weather—"*Estaba un poco pachucha*"—as if he suspected that Abaitua was looking for her; but he doesn't mind.

ABAITUA GOES ALONG THE PATH flanked by lilies and hydrangeas that runs from the clinic to the train stop. For a moment, blocked by the cypresses behind the building, the loud noise of the traffic stops, and he can hear the birds' happy song. In the area to the right, where there are several abandoned-looking industrial buildings, there used to be kitchen gardens, back when he first started going out with Pilar. It was reputed to be fertile land, and it had a bitter smell of tobacco, because they used scraps and waste material brought over from the cigarette factory in Egia as fertilizer. The earth is black there, and the tar-covered barge across from the clinic, which was previously used as a jetty, is hardly noticeable there in the spot where the boys struggled to anchor it, on the curve of the river right where it disappears from view of the bridge and the road. At the time, he realized that they'd moved the barge to make it more difficult to reach—it would be impossible without using a skiff or sinking down up to your waist in the mud—but that hadn't seemed suspicious to him.

He can see the edge of the writer's property. He goes through a small forest of reeds and comes out on the path that runs beside the railway in front of the house. It can be seen from most places in the area, at least the roof and the tower, but he doesn't know if it's visible from the train stop and decides to go there, with the sole objective of finding out. So he walks down and crosses the lines. The façade is easily visible from the first floor upward, as is part of the eastern side. He realizes they'll also be able to see him, from the window of theirs that looks out onto the railway. He would particularly mind if Julia were to see him and think he was a dirty old man spying on young women.

He spends some time sitting on the iron bench, he doesn't know how long. Not many minutes, because only one train goes by, one from Irun to Madrid, a long-distance train that, naturally, doesn't stop there. He starts to feel ashamed of himself, because he's behaving like an adolescent—an old-fashioned adolescent, what's more—and finally, when he starts crossing the lines again, he has to do so at a run, because he hears a train whistle approaching. The house's iron gate is directly across the street from the bridge over the railway. He sticks his head between the railings and doesn't see anybody there, but as the last rhythmic sounds of the train die away, he hears footsteps on the gravel. Then he hears Lynn's loud, very apparent laughter. It doesn't sound like a sick person's laughter.

Moving back toward the path to the clinic, he can see the bit of the garden Lynn is in, and at the same time, anybody could see him from the clinic building, including Pilar, of course, as he's right out in the open. But it's a very slight risk, and he's not overly worried. Lynn is crouching down in front of a flower bed. She's wearing gloves and seems to be weeding. She's wearing an oversized men's T-shirt that goes halfway down her thighs, and canvas shoes. The writer is standing next to her and moving his hands a lot as he talks. They remain like that for a while until eventually disappearing into the house.

"*Hi.*" He was about to hang up when Lynn answered. He'd already called twice and had decided that if she didn't pick up the third time, he wouldn't call again. He can hear her panting as she says, "*Great to hear from you.*" She's climbed the stairs from the garden and has had to run to get the phone. She says she thought it might be him.

He says he's sorry he's made her run. He knows she's wearing a men's T-shirt. He thinks about telling her, saying that he saw her in the garden and had a strong urge to go up to her apartment—telling her the truth. He knows he won't, but he doesn't try to find any sort of excuse to justify his call. Nor does he need to; Lynn lets off a storm of words, doesn't keep quiet a moment, as if she were the one who called him. She obviously thinks he's nowhere close, and she tells him she's been working in the garden, she's planted some very pretty bougainvilleas. Then she talks about work. She's seen some information in the data that's been sent that doesn't add up. She also tells him the resident's complaint about the data being grouped all together instead of being put into categories, and several other problems, things Abaitua couldn't care less about just then, until, all of a sudden, she says she's not letting him talk and asks why he's called.

"To find out how you are. Echevarria told me you weren't well."

"How nice!"

She had a bit of a headache but it's gone now.

The sound of a freight train in the distance makes him keep quiet, and for quite a while.

"What are you doing?"

Obviously she's heard the noise from the train and worked out that he's close. He says he just left the hospital.

"If you like, you can come over here for tea."

The anxiety in Lynn's voice calms him down. He'll drop by if she prepares something special for him. She says she'll do her best. They agree to meet up in half an hour or so.

SHE'S CHANGED OUT OF HER T-SHIRT. Now she's wearing a short dress with brightly colored flowers on a sea-blue background, and it makes her look younger. He knows that type of print is called *Liberty*, because he's had ties made of it. They don't greet each other with a kiss. She says hi and stands to one side of the doorway to let him through, but he doesn't go in. He leans down to pet the cat, which has come out to greet him. It purrs and lays down at his feet. Lynn says, "Sometimes you can be quite obscene, Max."

She goes into the kitchen. There's a large plate on the table with slices of ham carefully laid out on it, alternating with slices of brie, all arranged in a circle. All prepared with special care. She's facing away from him, leaning down in front of a cabinet. Her hair is gathered up at her neck in a large leather clip. The curls on her neck are shiny, a reddish mahogany color. She turns toward him, perhaps feeling his eyes on her, to say that there's only ham and cheese. She also has wine, and hopes that it's good. He's sure it is. She has a dish of almonds in her hand. Abaitua leans down, too, and holds her elbow to help her up. He decides not to suppress his arousal. He pulls her toward him and kisses her; some almonds fall to the ground. The girl moves away a little and moves her head back to be able to see his face properly, perhaps surprised by his passion, and says they'd better have their tea first. For a moment, he worries that she might think he's overly lustful, only looking for sex to calm himself down, but even so, he quiets her by kissing her on the mouth, and he carries on kissing her until he hears the plate shatter against the floor. He moves to bend down, but this time Lynn stops him, pulling him against herself.

449

"JUST RELAX." He gets excited when he hears that expression. She puts her hand on his chest and pushes him softly, making him take a step backward and sit down on the sofa. She's kneeling down between his legs. She starts taking his belt off carefully, as if it were something he'd asked her to do, slowly but with determination. It isn't easy for her to undo the inside clasp. The belt is only marked on one hole, the first one. He's glad he doesn't have a gut. Lynn strokes his belly, her hands look small on his pelvis.

He feels a surge of arousal again when he sees that. He puts his hand down the front of her dress and moves the fabric aside to expose one breast. Very gently, very pleased, too. It's a very serious movement, solemn, almost ceremonial. A small gesture of pain on her face when he squeezes her nipple, and relief when a small white drop comes out of it. He licks it with no trace of revulsion. She strokes his hair.

He feels the warmth of her breath on his neck. She breathes slowly, as if she were asleep. There's bright light on the ceiling, and the shadow of the top of a tree moving around. The cat purrs on the back of the sofa, and he feels its damp nose each time he stops petting it, asking for more. *"You're insatiable, Max,"* he says, imitating Lynn, and she says, "How embarrassing," with a trace of sleep in her voice. Her eyes are closed, her face calm. He's surprised by the urge to kiss her. The girl moves up close to him, and he feels her warm chest. He closes his eyes too, even though he knows that images lying in wait for him from some corner of his subconscious, images he doesn't want to see, will come at him from the darkness. In his house, too, there is full sunlight at this time of day, and Pilar normally takes great care to lower the blinds to keep the house in half-light. Half-light broken by the gleams from the blue engravings on the walls and from the glass coffee table Pilar does her sudokus on. Pilar must already be at home, or on her way back. He opens his eyes and hears the echo of a deep voice from the lower floor. Lynn says, "It's Martin," as if she's read his mind. They both listen, but they can't make out what he's saying.

Then she asks if he wants to have tea. He answers that it's a bit late for that, even though he doesn't know what time it is. He doesn't want to know. He's hungry, but he'd rather eat at home, even though it's a pity, because she must have gone out to buy the cheese and ham and seems proud of the neat-looking plate she's prepared. He repeats that he's not hungry. The light is no longer so intense, but the shadow movements are livelier. Lynn, too, looks up at the ceiling. She says you can see the breeze. They keep quiet for a moment, until she stands up and says she's going to get a beer.

The same impression he always has: her body is more opulent when naked.

SMALL PERVERSIONS. A Franciskaner with a slice of lemon in a gold-rimmed beer glass. She takes a long sip. Then she turns toward him. She puts her lips on his and fills his mouth with beer; it feels cold and warm as he gulps it down, and when he's finished, he feels an urgent desire to drink more from her mouth. She takes another sip and he looks at her, like a thirsty dog watching his master fill up his drinking bowl. Once more, the beer feels cold and warm at the same time, and he wants to suck her all in. The bottle doesn't last long, and he's extremely aroused.

Lynn says she's going to put some music on, but she doesn't get up. She sometimes plays music, but only to listen to, not to accompany other activities—she says it distracts her. She has never, or hardly ever, put it on to make love; sometimes she gets up from the sofa or the bed to turn it off, irritated. Abaitua likes household sounds. He doesn't mind the echoes of the voices below, and strangely enough, the sound of the trains going by makes him feel he's far away. Sometimes Lynn talks nonstop, jumping from one subject to another, until she realizes and then says, "*I'm chattering like a magpie.*" She says it only happens when she's with him.

Now, leaning on his shoulder, she looks at his skin, which the doctor doesn't much like, and tells him about something she's read regarding home births. She was surprised to learn that, according to the statistics, it's a practice that stopped happening from one year to the next, and she wants to know if it was outlawed. He explains it to her. What happened was that after a certain point, children, regardless of where they were born, were allowed to be registered as residents of the town their parents lived in. Until then, as established by public health norms, children who were not born at home were registered as residents of whatever town the clinic they were born at was located in, which meant that many of them appeared to be residents of Donostia, and in order to avoid that happening, parents started saying that their children had been born at home. So in fact, parents from Hernani were working around the system to avoid their children having the dishonor of being Donostia residents, or parents from Hondarribia were trying to avoid having their children registered as residents of Irun, and so on; they would all just say they had been born at home, until the birth certificate law changed. So beware statistics.

The girl is curled up with her back against him, and he holds her around the waist. He ignores the question she asks him about the medicalization of birthing, and because he can't see her face, he finds it easier to tell her about tricylical antidepressants. Firstly, they are only for severe cases and they don't affect normal people. What's more, because they inhibit neoadrenaline reuptake, they can have major side effects, not just galactorrhea but also irregular periods, changes in libido, frequent urination, gynecomastia, pain on ejaculation, swollen testicles. And those are only the genitourinary effects. She turns around suddenly and looks at him as if not understanding. Then she laughs. "Do the testicles really swell up?" She stands up on the sofa, pretending to be frightened.

The music she likes isn't exactly avant-garde, and that suits him. Jazz and blues. She likes Bob Dylan more than he does. Because the stereo is up on a shelf, she has to stand on tiptoes to use it. She has strong calf muscles and very thin ankles. She's told him it makes it difficult for her to walk. She has firm, round buttocks. When she comes back to the sofa, he says she's robust, and she says he means fat. She curls up against him again, asking him to hug her. She's cold. He caresses her. She says he has expert hands. No man's caresses have ever aroused her as much. She stretches out, like a bow in his hands, she breathes deeply through her half-open mouth, twisting in the solitude of her absolute pleasure. She swears to him that nobody has ever aroused her as much.

Abaitua would like to reply with some ironic comment. He doesn't like compliments. He asks if she feels the need to flatter him, if she takes him for an old fool, and Lynn asks him in all seriousness if he thinks she has reason to do any such thing. He, too, admits seriously that she has no such reason. It's true that a gynecologist of his age could be expected to have a certain degree of expertise, but he's never thought of himself as being particularly gifted in that area, and the sex partners he's had in the past have never given him any reason to think that he is. His sex life has been discreet.

Perhaps more frequent than the average, but not incredibly so, at least not if you take into account the sexual explosion the country experienced at one point. Ironic reflections about Basques not having sex very often. The young woman is amazed that nobody before has told him he's sweet and sexy. *"Nobody's ever told you?"* she says again, and he says no, beginning to doubt whether it's true or not. Nobody has ever paid him that compliment before. The girl, looking annoyed, says he hasn't been properly appreciated—nobody has ever seduced her like this before. *"Ikusten?"* she says in Basque—"You see?" She takes his hand, and he meekly lets her lead. Just feeling his hand brush over her skin is enough for her. He keeps quiet, amazed by her arousal—she twists in his arms again, panting, her eyes flickering, literally going white, as if she were about to have a seizure—surprised, amazed by the spontaneity of this display of pleasure of hers, finally convinced that his hands do have some sort of power over her.

The cat, lying on the back of the sofa, looks at them with curiosity. He tries to shoo it away, finding its constant gaze unsettling, but it jumps down and sits between them, sniffing at them with curiosity. The girl swats it away. *"Get out of there, Max,"* she says without opening her eyes, irritated. He's never seen her looking angry before.

They're still lying naked on the sofa, even though it's suddenly gotten colder. The cat jumps up again to the arm of the sofa, where Abaitua is resting his head. He pets it under its chin, and it starts purring immediately. More loudly than he's ever heard it before. "He has miraculous hands, doesn't he, Max?"

"So tell me, do you believe me when I tell you that you drive me crazy?"

He lifts himself up on one side, leans on one elbow.

Yes, of course he believes her, he says as if it were part of a joke, even though he isn't at all sure. She, too, sounds playful when she says he doesn't have anything to worry about, there's no reason for her craziness to cause any problems. It doesn't put him under any obligation to her. She'll be his wife, his friend, his lover, his something on the side, his companion—he can call her whenever he wants her around, she'll come right away, she'll take care of him if he's sick, and stay by his side as he grows old. She'll be responsible for him and take care of him until his death, because it's a law of nature that he'll die first, although that's a long time off, because he's strong. There's no need for him to worry, and the only thing he'll have to do is hug her from time to time. She takes ahold of his wrists and pulls them toward her until he has one hand on her hip. It's only once in your life that you come across somebody and feel that that's the person who will make your love come alive and that the love will last forever. She puts her index finger on his lips so he won't speak. It's got nothing to do with you, you're separate from it. There's nothing you can do about it. I knew it the moment I saw you—I'd never been as attracted to anyone else.

"Does it frighten you that I say these things?"

"What things?" he blurts out, avoiding answering.

"The things I'm telling you. Do they frighten you?"

He supposes she wants to ask if they make him feel uncomfortable.

"They make me feel uncomfortable."

"They make you uneasy?"

"I don't like it."

"*Why not?*"

It could be something to do with culture. They've already talked about that. In fact, it was Kepa who talked about the timidity of Basques and all that when they were in Ainhoa and Bordeaux. They laughed a lot. When he imitated Edurne telling him not to get all Andalusian with her. They don't trust the hidden agendas that might be lurking behind the compliments they're paid.

Pilar, when he would say she was beautiful: "Don't be ridiculous, I do look at myself in the mirror, you know." Sometimes, just occasionally, he's managed to get her to say she's glad when he says she looks good, to really believe, at least to an extent, that he actually feels what he's saying. But in general, she doesn't like such enthusiasm. He's always thought it was because she was distrustful by nature; although very different from Kepa's wife, she is equally reticent of pretty, flattering words—he might just be saying them to ask her to forgive him for ruining her life. To put it another way, she would prefer something more than just words; but now, and from what he can gather from the feelings he himself has been experiencing just now with Lynn, he wonders to what extent it is his inability to respond to such statements of affection that makes them so awkward for him.

Lynn says, "I think I understand your problem now."

Kneeling on the sofa, he can see the barge and his father-in-law's mastless yacht anchored on the river through the sash window. And the clinic, too. They're both quiet, silent, sitting elbow to elbow, looking out the window, and Abaitua has the sensation that they're up in a tree house, which is something he would have liked to have had when he was a child, and when he was older than that, too. Lynn says it makes her sad to see such a beautiful boat. And so it was, made of beautiful varnished Burmese teak. He thinks he's already told her it was his father-in-law's.

She's learned to say *zorioneko gizona zara*—meaning "you are a fortunate man." She says Julia taught her. The Lynn in *Montauk* says it to the writer at least once—"You are a fortunate man." This Lynn says it to him all the time. When he complained to her one day that he'd been in the operating theater until late, hadn't had time to eat a proper lunch, and was really tired, she said he was fortunate because he was able to cure sick people and was healthy himself and was able to sleep peacefully on soft sheets when he was tired. Or times he's told her he went for a walk in Urgull and couldn't wrap his head around the beauty of the scenery, or that he fell asleep reading *Archives of Gynecology*, or listening to *La Bohème*, or that he was having trouble writing an article about cervical dysplasia—whatever he tells her, she tells him again that he's a fortunate man. And he usually asks her why, sometimes a little irritated by the comment, because he doesn't think whatever he's just told her has anything to do with being fortunate but rather just the opposite, or at best that it's something anyone might say. And she replies, quite seriously, *"Yes, I think you are a fortunate man,"* and then, to prove it to him, she repeats the trivial things he's just told her about, going for a walk in Urgull, or reading *Archives of Gynecology*, or whatever it was. Last week she told him he was fortunate because he has a well-modulated man's voice, and ever since then, Abaitua's been listening to people's voices carefully, realizing that there are voices that really make your hair stand on end, and comical voices, too, and perhaps he is fortunate to have a gift he's never been aware of before; his voice, at least, doesn't make people's hair bristle.

She tells him he's fortunate—twining her fingers with his—because he knows how to caress a person so well, because he's so sweet. Nobody's given her so much pleasure. He's got to believe it.

Lynn lies against the arm of the sofa again, with the tartan travel blanket wrapped around her feet. The two of them just fit under it. The cat, on the seat back, looks at them, purring whenever they touch it. "Do you think it's possible to die of love, Max?" And then, completely seriously, "Are you not answering because you're ashamed we'll think you're a sentimental old fool of a cat, or because you want us to think you're skeptical about it all, or because you haven't thought about it, which is more or less the same thing?" Abaitua remembers the title of a film from back in his day, *Mourir d'aimer*. It was based on real events. A high school teacher, an older woman, falls in love with a pupil and finally, afflicted by society's incomprehension of her situation, the poor thing commits suicide. The pupil or the teacher, Lynn asks. The teacher, he thinks. He remembers it was Annie Girardot that played her.

Lynn turns around to give him a quick kiss. Everyone knows what the French are like, but she's a young American, healthy and sensible, and she believes in life above all else. They're arm in arm again, and they stay that way, the silence broken only by the cat's contented purring, watching the gray shadow of the magnolia tree on the ceiling. Abaitua thinks about the dichotomy of Lynn, which so often amazes him: she uses gushing phrases that would be more at home in some cheesy *bolero* with just the same ease as she uses precise terminology to express sensible points of view. He remains in stoical silence while she, her arm raised to pet the cat, says, as if addressing it, that she loves him madly, she would kill, she would die for him, but that he shouldn't be afraid, she won't. He shouldn't be afraid because of her loving him so passionately, it's her problem, she's happy to feel what she feels, and he doesn't have to do anything he doesn't want to, doesn't have to take on the responsibility for anything.

Lynn turns around quickly to look at him, hoping to catch some expression on his face unawares. She looks whiter in the half-light. *"You don't believe me, do you?"* He dares to say he doesn't completely believe her. "You don't believe me, or you don't want to believe me?" He can't help moving around rather nervously, and there's no doubt she's picked up on that. He notes that her hand is cold as it moves across his forehead, and he closes his eyes. "Why are you afraid?" And she kisses his eyes. "There's nothing for you to worry about."

He wants to get up, but she forces him to lie down again. *"Just relax."* He realizes his desire is returning as she strokes his belly. The girl's fingers are very fine, precise, they seem to be retractable, just a touch from them is enough. "Do you like it more like this?"—her fingertips stroke him from the inside to the outside of his penis— "Or like this?"—now pressing and rubbing his foreskin in circles with great care.

She talks to him while she strokes him, and he lets her go on; each time he tries to touch her, she makes him lie back down and keep his arms by his side. She says she loves his body, it's welcoming. She sits on top of him with a leg to either side and strokes him with her hair. She likes his smell. She says she lost control when he sat down next to her in the meeting and she caught a whiff of him. Harri had warned her that he was attractive, but she hadn't believed her, because Harri talks before she thinks. "You know all the women there are in love with you, right? So am I." He jokingly asks if it might not be a simple case of gerontophilia, and as soon as he does, he realizes he uses that joke too often. She makes a gesture to say no. He shouldn't say silly things. He only just feels her weight on his belly. He holds her gaze. He wonders if they won't get fed up of making love, grow sick of it. She shows signs of being tired, her eyelids and lips are larger than usual. She leans further down and moves her body from one side to the other, tempting him with her nipples, first one then the other, just letting his lips touch them and moving them away as he opens his mouth. "Seductive old man who drives me crazy," she whispers in his ear, "with his skillful hands," she takes them in hers and caresses them, "hands that give me more pleasure than anybody else ever has." He only has to move his hips a little, and she lifts her arms up, hands clasped together, her head to one side and resting on her shoulder. He lifts his hands up and strokes her breasts. She asks him to squeeze them more, but he doesn't dare to. He doesn't want to hurt her. "You don't hurt me." She likes everything he does to her. But he lets his hands drop. He doesn't want to hurt her. She takes ahold of one of her breasts. Her right breast in her left hand. He looks at her bluish-white skin. She makes very soft movements, for him, for him to see, smiling sweetly. Then she squeezes her nipple between her forefinger and thumb.

Abaitua almost gives in and says that he loves her, too. It wouldn't be a lie. He thinks he's loved all the women he's made love with, more or less. That's why he has nothing against the expression *to make love*. There's always some trace of tenderness, some element of love, when you offer your naked body and take somebody in your arms. But it goes unsaid. He didn't say it to her, even though he wanted to. He was afraid he would call out her name, and he felt— he feels—tenderness toward her, gratefulness that almost brings tears to his eyes.

He thinks it says "neither of them has ever said I love you" in *Montauk*.

"I'M GOING TO GO PEE," she says, and he doesn't understand her. "I have to go pee," she says into his ear, but loudly, as if to somebody hard of hearing. He holds her back and licks her wet nipples, he'd like to make love with her again—don't be crazy, says the girl, laughing; she seems happy to him—he pretends to bite her belly, and she protests that he's going to make her pee all over the bed, is he looking for a golden shower or something? He lets her go, and she stands up.

He'd like to go to the bathroom, too, but he feels too lazy. Lazy or ashamed, or both at the same time. He looks around for his pants. They're on a chair, and Max is curled up on top of them. The cat lifts its head up and stares at him challengingly when he tries to shoo it away, and it doesn't jump down to the floor until he pulls at one of the pant legs. It escapes down the hallway, as if to report the way it's been treated to its mistress, and he goes to catch it. She hasn't closed the bathroom door. She's sitting on the toilet, there's the sound of her peeing, and she has an elbow resting on one of her knees and her chin pressed into the back of her hand, the expression of Rodin's *Thinker* on her face. Since they're going to live together, she wants to get over having a shy bladder, she says. But it's obvious she's embarrassed, and to cover it up, she shoos away the cat, which is looking at her from the doorway. "Get lost, Max, don't be such a peeping Tom." Abaitua doesn't turn around, he's embarrassed to be seen from behind.

"Do you think we'll live together some day?"

They're in each others' arms as she asks him that, her standing on top of his feet with her head tilted up. He hardly notices her weight. He say they will, making it obvious, with a gesture of displeasure, that he's only saying yes to keep her happy. He decides to go. He moves away from her and looks serious while she carries on with her joking remarks about how they're going to distribute the limited space there in order not to get in each other's way. Abaitua thinks he's made it perfectly clear to her—even rudely so, in fact—that he doesn't like this game of hers, although it's true he's never said it to her explicitly, in words, only indirectly, as he just has, by remaining silent and putting on unhappy faces. "This will be enough space for us, won't it?" He says it will be, more than enough, as he reaches for his keys. Seeing him do that, she asks him if he doesn't want to go to the bathroom to wash up first, while at the same time hurriedly putting on her checked shirt that looks like a man's. Then she stands there watching him dress, the cat in her arms, leaning against the wall. Studiously, Abaitua thinks, as if she were drawing conclusions, and he wonders if she's often been in that same situation, watching men get dressed.

She puts the cat down on the floor and helps him do up his cufflinks. "*Oso politak*," she says in Basque, "very pretty." Pilar gave him those, as well; he thinks the green stones are jade.

She says she's sorry he has to go. She watches him knot his tie with her hands held behind her back. She's sorry for him, she adds quickly, for having to go outside, get into his car, and get back into the hurly-burly of things. Even though there won't be all that much traffic anyway. Abaitua doesn't know what time it is and prefers to overcome his impulse to look at his watch. OK, he's going. Lynn flattens herself against the wall, a gesture to communicate that she isn't going to do anything to stop him from leaving. She picks up the cat again. It's a fine animal. Abaitua pets it, and it purrs deeply again. Words of farewell. She's the one who takes ahold of the doorknob, but only just enough to release it, and when she takes her hand away, the door doesn't swing out, so he has to finish the operation of opening it. She stretches her neck out, and he kisses her on both cheeks before leaving.

He trips on the spiral staircase and is about to fall down it. Lynn had warned him—it's treacherous. He waits a moment, just in case somebody's heard him and opened a door. He readies himself for the possibility—he'll act naturally, as if nothing were going on. The automatic light turns back off, and as if the sudden darkness made his hearing sharper, he clearly hears the writer's voice: "It doesn't seem to be anything." He walks down in silence, in complete darkness, thinking what a fine ending it would be to wake up at the bottom of the stairs with his skull broken. Finally, he reaches the garden. The air feels good, and he smells a flower he can't identify that reminds him of the perfume María Amor, the Dominican woman, wears. He tries to cross the lawn without making any noise, although he knows there's no point, because the person who might see him already has.

"You are a fortunate man." He blends in with the others at the train stop. Tired-looking men and women. He feels wonderful after making love on a sofa with a beautiful young woman for six hours. It's half past nine, he's still in time to have dinner with Pilar. Fortunately, he doesn't need any excuse for arriving home at this late hour—she would never lower herself to asking where he's been.

In the car, he worries about the way he smells, but he didn't feel up to sharing a shower with Lynn. He also feels a shadow of guilt and makes a firm decision not to peer any more deeply into it.

He has two things to feel good about: he overcame the temptation to tell her he loved her, and he dealt clearly with the matter of the tricylical antidepressants.

Pilar is sitting on the sofa wearing lilac-colored operating scrubs, leaning over the coffee table as usual. The television is switched on with the volume down. She turns toward him as he comes into the living room and greets him with an *hola* devoid of any special intonation, or so it seems to him. When she's happy, she emphasizes the first syllable and draws out the second. She doesn't do that today. Then she adds that she's been calling him all afternoon, looking down at the coffee table once more. She isn't doing her usual sudoku. She's going over a thick ream of papers in one of the leather-bound files with straps that they use down at the clinic for board-related documents. She says she's been calling him all afternoon because Loiola came and was waiting for him. He mumbles that he's sorry.

It's the truth. He would have liked to have spent time with his son, to encourage him to go back to the States as soon as possible. As he brushes his hair back with both hands, he adds that he's had quite a day, and as he says it, he realizes he wouldn't know what to say if she asked him what was so special about it. "Nothing specific, just all of it," he thinks he would say. Pilar glances at him again, but not at his face, and he feels as if she's seen inside him. He thinks there's only a very remote chance that she'll ask him what he's been doing or where he's been. She's far too proud for that. The few times she's done that, he's asked her if he needs to ask for permission to leave the house, and she won't make that mistake again. When she looks at him for a third time, which makes him do his jacket buttons up, it occurs to him that he could tell her, "I've been making love with a young woman." "There's some battered hake," she says as she looks down at her papers again, and Abaitua heads off to the kitchen to get away from her.

His intention is to have a bite and then say he's not hungry, so he can go straight to bed. Perhaps to punish himself, too. What's more, the light's too bright in the kitchen, and he wouldn't like her to follow him in there to tell him something or help him get his meal ready. That's what she used to do when he got home late and had dinner alone, sit across from him and watch him eat while telling him about what had happened during the day, filling his glass and attentively setting his place for him. But he thinks that's no more than a remote possibility, and it would be suspicious for him to go to bed so early.

The battered hake looks excellent, and he almost prefers it cold to reheated. Pilar knows that. He just has a couple of pieces, not wanting to tempt fate, but he can't resist the urge to have a glass of wine. There's white wine in the fridge. There are two glasses on the drying rack, and when he picks one of them up, he knocks the other off, and it smashes to pieces on the floor.

They struggle momentarily over who's going to sweep it up with the brush, and finally Abaitua gives in, mostly so that Pilar won't notice his smell. A scene of domestic submission: the woman kneeling down to pick up the broken pieces of glass while the man looks on, a glass in his hand, leaning against the door frame. The same parasitic idea comes to mind again—the thought of telling her that he's spent the afternoon having sex with a girl—and he remembers back to one particular schoolday afternoon, just as he always does each time he's tempted to play with fate. It was a Saturday afternoon, because they'd been singing the "Salve Regina" out in the courtyard, and that was what they used to do after the last class on Saturdays. He was standing with López and several others on the second-floor balcony, directly above the principal, who was conducting the downstairs singers, as well, from the bottom of the stairs. "Bet I can hit him with my spit," López used to say, letting some saliva dangle off his lip before sucking it back in again, doing that several times, until once, all of a sudden, he let too much out at once and it fell straight onto the principal's bald head. It was a dramatic event and led to the entire group spending the whole term without any recesses, because their system of loyalties included protecting even the worst-behaved, cruellest, most sadistic, bullying, and selfish classmates, and so nobody told on the culprit, who couldn't work up the courage to admit what he'd done.

"I wanted to tell you something," says Pilar, and Abaitua puts his glass down on the sideboard. They're in the living room. Pilar is sitting on the sofa with the file on the table in front of her. Her way of talking makes him think she isn't going to say anything about their relationship. He thinks it's probably going to be some family problem, something to do with the inheritance from her father, but even so, he's startled and can hardly keep his voice calm when he asks her what it is she wants to tell him about. The problem's the clinic. They've received an offer to buy it, and her siblings, brother- and sister-in-law included, want to sell. Her brother, Arrese, Orl, and many others are already at retirement age and don't have any intention of continuing to work. And they're all shareholders. So what sort of offer is it? He looks straight at her, as if he were seriously interested in finding out. She doesn't know whether the offer is good or bad, but she's going to oppose it, because it isn't what her deceased father wanted.

She says it with a firm voice, completely believing what she says, one hand open on the great book of papers in front of her, as if she were going to swear on it. He thinks it looks like a medical book, and that's what it is, a neurosurgery manual—*Manual de neurocirugía*, M. Greenberg, he reads—and after that, she rests her hand in her lap.

She's talked about the clinic with Loiola and gets the impression he'd be prepared to do a Master's course in hospital management in order to be able to take over at some point in the future. "To carry on the work," she says, in a way he still finds ridiculous. He feels sorry and to the same degree touched that she feels the need to idealize her father's business. On several occasions since his funeral, she's mentioned the conversations she had with the old man—she says he was lucid right up until the end—and it's as if she'd been debating with Plato, judging by the respect and admiration in her voice when she talks about them. She says she'd be willing to take on the responsibility, and thinks it would be a good option for their son, at least as good as working in some NGO, anyway. She wants him to help her convince him. Abaitua accepts, even though working at his grandfather's clinic isn't what he dreamed of for his

462

son. But above all, what he wants to do is retire to his bedroom and be alone. He rubs his eyes very obviously to give the idea that he's exhausted and, on doing so, gets a waft of Lynn's scent.

He thinks it was rather cruel of him not to pay more attention to the problems the old man's clinic is facing.

As he looks at himself in the bathroom mirror, he doesn't understand how Pilar can have missed the loads of cat hair stuck to his pants—even though the hairs and his pants are the same basic color, charcoal gray, the pants are a shade lighter.

15

THE MAN MOVES HIS FACE TOWARD THE MIRROR until his nose is almost touching it. His lower eyelids aren't swollen, but his eyes are very yellow. When the concierge's wife arrived with the newspapers, she pointed it out to him and speculated that it might be a consequence of eating too many eggs. He decides it's time to stop the treatment and let nature—the illness, in other words—get on with its business with no impediments. He supposes his bilirubin levels will go up if he stops taking the medicine; the color of his eyes will improve in exchange for his kidneys shutting down. He hopes he'll stop losing his hair, too. Repetitive ideas about Jacques Rigaut and his book *Je serai un grand mort*.

A memory from childhood. He's standing on the kitchen table. He must be very small, because they've put him on the table to be able to dress him more easily, and he sees his mother's and his nanny's faces at the same level as his own. It's very surprising that his mother is dressing him, and that she's in the kitchen, where she hardly ever goes. She looks nervous, and it's obvious she's in a hurry. She hurts him as she pulls a wet comb through his hair, but he doesn't cry. He feels uncomfortable, and there must be clear signs of that, because his nanny, who's the one who usually takes care of him, says, "This boy isn't well, there's something wrong with him," and she says it several times, but his mother tells her to be quiet, to stop saying silly things. His mother makes him stick his tongue out, looks under his lower eyelid to examine his connective tissue. "There's nothing wrong with him," she says, "his eyes are just a little swollen because he's slept a lot." The boy knows that isn't true.

It seems the concierge's wife forgot to bring his mail in, and there she is knocking at his door again. He thinks she does it on purpose, to be able to talk some more. Whenever he sees the couple at the front door of the building, the husband is telling his wife to be quiet. This time the woman recommends he go out and enjoy the good weather—"Wonderful autumn weather." He thinks it would make a good title—*Wonderful Autumn Weather*. They talk about the seasons. Now that she gets hot flashes, she doesn't find the winter so harsh. "Do you know what I mean?" It's because of the hot flashes, of course. He hates the winter, that's why he plans a getaway to the southern hemisphere every year. Midwinter. The painter Ruiz Balerdi titled his mural at the entrance of the Kutxa savings bank headquarters *Las tres estaciones—The Three Seasons*— sensibly leaving winter out. He agrees with the concierge's wife, summer is the best season in Donostia. Spring is short, and it isn't a sudden explosion of colors, there's no swift rush of magnificence as there is in places where the winters are cold and there's snow. But autumn is wonderful, *délicieux*, peaceful, and cosy, with the perfect light for bringing out the full range of different ochres. He says, without any affectation, that if he had the choice, he'd like to die in the middle of the autumn, when the wind is blowing the leaves of nostalgia around (he remembers "*les feuilles mortes se ramassent à la pelle, les souvenirs et les regrets aussi*"—the dead leaves being raked up along with memories and regrets—from a song made popular by Yves Montand), sometime before the first signs of harsh winter appear, and when spring is too far off to wait for.

The concierge's wife says that poets like him—he can't get it into her head that he isn't a poet, he writes prose—are madmen and they'd be better off paying attention to what they eat.

Then he remembers that song of Brel's that talks about how it's hard to die in the spring—"*C'est dur de mourir au printemps, tu sais.*" Brel managed to live on until the autumn. De Quincey, on the other hand, thought it was terrible to die in the summer, because the body loves days full of light. Barbellion, on the other hand, in *The Journal of a Disappointed Man*, found cemeteries generally harsher in the winter and thought that his old bones would take to the land better in the summer, when the earth is warm. Barbellion also says that the first night after the funeral is the worst. A tomb under the rain. Dying on a rainy day would make death even more melancholy, and the sight of a blue sky, on the other hand, would be a painful contradiction. He has these types of thoughts one after another, thoughts that are morbid, "but inevitable in someone with the hand of death on his shoulder, hearing a voice telling him that it's almost time. What else could he think about?"

The sky is lit up with sunlight at the moment. Light is an invitation to live. I say this with no bitterness.

She stays in the gallery for a while watching Lynn weeding the flowerbed. Then watering her bougainvillea. When Julia goes out into the garden, Lynn is raking up the leaves on the path. She offers to help by holding the basket and apologizes for not having pruned the hydrangeas earlier. She used to look after them, but little by little, taking care of the garden became just another duty she was forced to carry out. She thinks it's another symptom of her loss of affection for Martin and everything around him. She doesn't say that. What she does say is that he doesn't know anything about flowers and he's no good at gardening. Lynn, on the other hand, knows a lot about it. What most people take to be the bougainvillea's flower is actually a type of leaf, and the real flowers, which are small and white, are inside those leaves. Julia tells her she's like an encyclopedia. She laughs. She says she never knew that before, either. Kepa, Martin's friend, told her.

It was Kepa, too, who told her that the chubby birds with the round heads, one of whom has a sort of crest, are melodious or polyglot warblers, and that they have that name because they imitate other birds' songs. The one with the pointed crest is male, so that dilemma, too, has been sorted out. Julia thinks that Lynn doesn't know how to explain the fact that Kepa's been at the house—she says it was a dinner party to celebrate the three month anniversary, so to speak, of their trip—without her having mentioned anything to them, to Martin and herself, beforehand. She seemed to have hidden the fact. But the reason is obvious: she can't bring up Kepa without mentioning Iñaki Abaitua as well. Julia thinks that's why she normally feels the need to refer to him as "Martin's friend," separating him from Abaitua in order to make the connection legitimate in some sense. In fact, she only mentions Kepa's name when talking about the dinner party—what a good cook he is, how delicious everything he makes is, the strange stories he tells, how much he makes her laugh—until Julia works up the courage to tease her: she doesn't believe the shine in her eyes is all down to Kepa. She laughs. He really is an incredible man, fantastic. As well as having the erudition of an encyclopedia and cooking like an angel, he's running a bookshop and taking care of his mother. The latter doesn't make him a very attractive man, Julia jokes, but Lynn, for once, doesn't continue the joke. His mother is seriously disabled, and he takes care of her by himself, feeds her, bathes her, everything, and without ever playing the martyr, always good-humoredly. He doesn't put himself across as a victim, and although he wants to put his mother in a home, he hasn't found a place for her yet.

"You have to meet him. You'll like him."

"I have enough of men with mothers with just Martin."

She isn't embarrassed to show her bitterness, quite the contrary, she feels a sort of exhibitionist pleasure in complaining to the girl. She tells her they quarreled first thing that morning. His mother and sister kept calling and calling him to tell him about their problems, until he finally lost it, and then she had to put up with his complaining for an hour about how the whole world is against him and conspiring to prevent him from having the even minimum degree of tranquillity needed to be able to write. It irritated her. The final straw was his telling her that her obsession with tidying things meant he couldn't ever find anything. Even though she sometimes manages to take quarrels like that with a sense of humor, knowing that not paying him any attention and waiting for his anger to pass is the best thing to do, she wasn't able to do that today, partly because she was having trouble with the translation of a particularly difficult paragraph she wanted to finish. She was furious because of his complicated, dark way of writing, and then he just kept going on and on about how nobody ever helps him and he always has to sort everything out himself. He was hurt because she hadn't helped him find someone who could go to his parents' house and look after his father. Finally, fed up, she said she had no intention of helping him with that, she wouldn't put her worst enemy under the orders of his mother and sister. She knows she hurt him, that family's still family however much he hates them, but she couldn't take any more—the fact that he gets overcome by so little drives her up the wall. Could she imagine how he'd react if he ever had to bathe his mother? Lynn doesn't answer. They keep quiet for a moment. Then the girl smiles, takes Julia's hand, and asks if she'll invite her in for coffee.

Nobody would have guessed that she's spent an hour tidying up the books, pieces of paper, index cards, and notebooks lying around. There are work materials on the tables, the floor, and the chairs, everywhere. She'd picked up a dozen of his little notebooks alone. She shows them to Lynn. Useless notebooks with illegible writing scribbled all over them. The worst of it is that Julia's started doing the same thing, uselessly filling notebooks.

"*¿Qué te parece?*"

"As Harri would say," they chant in unison. And they laugh out loud.

A little later, when Lynn mentions Kepa again, they say "Martin's friend" in unison and laugh together once more. Lynn told Kepa that Julia was planning to translate Frisch's questionaires, and he thought it was a good idea. Apparently, he said he'd be able to find her a publisher to finance the project, and also that in any case, he thought her own *Fragebogen* would be a much more interesting read.

Julia is embarrassed that Lynn's told somebody about a project she wouldn't dare mention to anyone herself. What's she up to, acting like her own personal Celestina? They have to look it up in the dictionary. Celestina. Old women in classical theater pieces who serve as matchmakers. *Celestina, alcahueta*, procuress, bawd. She says she doesn't mind being a matchmaker, because she's sure she's going to like "Martin's friend" a lot.

Lynn looks at her watch. She says she has to tidy up her apartment. Julia doesn't want her to go—she can tidy it up later. She'd beg her to stay if she had to. She tells her she doesn't feel like doing anything. Perhaps what she's feeling is that emptiness you get when you finish a piece of work that's taken you a lot of time and effort. Lynn asks her if that means she's finished *Bihotzean* and sits down next to her, happy. They'd said they were going to celebrate it. Julia doesn't feel like celebrating anything, she feels as if she's lost an arm. Finally, she has to admit that she doesn't like the story, the novella, or whatever it is; reading it now, it seems really dated to her, it oozes with that self-satisfaction sentimental people feel because they know they're sensitive, which she finds so repulsive, and it will probably be even more obvious in the Spanish translation because of her. She doesn't want to tell Martin that she's finished the translation. She'll tell him in a few days' time, and she won't ever translate any of his work again.

Sometimes, she doesn't know what she's going to play until she hears the first chord. The book about Ravel, the one Lynn gave her, is on the stand. *Dans tout ce qui est basque, il y a un peu de musique—* there's a little music in everything Basque. Her fingers start playing the Adagio from the Concerto in G Major. Ravel was planning a concerto for piano and orchestra titled *Zazpiak bat*, meaning "The Seven Are One." An expression defending the unity of the Basque Country and its seven provinces, dating from at least 1906. In 1913 he wrote to Stravinsky that he was working on it, but then he left his notebooks in Paris in 1914 and never started working on it again, using pieces of it in other works instead. *Fragebogen*: Why did Ravel never finish *Zazpiak bat*, the concerto for piano and orchestra that he started? She thinks she's going to buy another blue notebook to reflect on that. First off, she thinks that a concerto for piano and orchestra, just like a symphony, needs a story and that, unfortunately, Ravel never found one. He had the music, but not the words. Nonsense she wouldn't dare say to anyone other than a foreigner, and not to anyone who didn't know a lot about music. So the Basques never got their *Zazpiak bat*, and she misses a work that has never existed. "*¿Qué te parece?*" "As Harri would say," they chant again in unison.

THEY DON'T REALIZE that Harri herself is there, knocking on the gallery door. They don't know what to say when she asks them what's so funny, and then, when she asks after Martin—"What's the boy up to?"—Julia tells her that he's gone to his parents' house and thinks that Harri can tell there's a connection between her good mood and Martin's not being there.

She says "poor Martin," with a voice full of pity, when she hears that he's having trouble finding somebody to look after his father. Julia doesn't like him being seen as a martyr. "What do you mean 'poor' him?" she says. "Poor everyone else around him," she moans like a wife. She'd like to see Harri spend more time around him and then hear what she has to say. But Harri says she's always complaining, she should be more understanding about all his problems, his wanting to finish his novel, his need to look after his family. Lynn is afraid they'll start quarreling, apparently, and so she starts talking about Martin's recurring nightmare, in order to say something. She's told them her theory on other occasions, saying the nightmare must be connected with something that happened to him as a child. She's realized that when he talks about problems connected with his family, or when he's spent time with his relatives, or his sister's come to visit, or he's gone to see them, he always complains the next morning that he's had the nightmare. So they have to watch out, the same thing could happen tomorrow. She says it in a completely serious tone, with no sign of it being a joke, just as seriously as when she's doing research work at the hospital. Harri, too, listens to her completely seriously, agreeing that the poor writer's nightmare must be linked to some trauma from his childhood.

To change the subject, Julia brings up her cousin in Sagastizabal. Her mother said that the guy's girlfriend is Peruvian and that she doesn't want to give birth at the hospital. Apparently it's a cultural tradition, children have their roots in the houses where their mothers give birth to them, they become part of that place, and that's why the girl wants to give birth in the cabin they have out there in Sagastizabal. Her mother doesn't approve. She says they shouldn't let foreigners impose their customs, quite the opposite, they should be made to integrate. Julia disagreed, and as is always the case whenever they disagree, they ended up getting angry.

Harri agrees with Julia's mother. She has no time for immigrants from underdeveloped countries and their backward cultural traditions, among other things because they usually harm women. We already have enough work overcoming the obstacles our own culture creates. Just when we've managed to make miniskirts acceptable, now we have to accept people wearing veils. Lynn says that cultures other than our own can make positive contributions. What's more, giving birth at home is something some people are demanding in today's society, and they want to do it in the most natural but also the safest conditions possible. In her opinion, the Department of Public Health should guarantee the option of giving birth at home for those low-risk patients who want to. Harri doesn't agree. She says it would be too expensive, and in any case, who is it that's demanding it? She can't stand all this alternative medicine, philosophy, and so on, or put up with those people who speak in low, soft voices about the goings-on in their intestines; she hates brown rice and soy milk, she finds women who don't shave their armpits and placenta-eating bald men revolting. Who knows how long she would have gone on if Julia hadn't stopped her with a loud "that's enough!"? She shuts up and looks at her with a smile. She, too, knows that she gets hysterical.

She docilely asks her what she wants to talk about, and Julia says why doesn't she tell them about her search for the man from the airport, just as she might have asked to talk about Lynn's bougainvilleas, or any other old thing, but Harri starts talking without realizing it was a joke. Unfortunately, she doesn't have much to tell them. The Iberia guy from Iberia is still looking into it, but so far his calls have led to nothing. It's going slowly, but she's placed her trust in the Iberia guy. Now she defines him as "one of those young people" who are exactly what they seem to be, not like people back in her day, who seemed forward-thinking from the outside but deep down were sexist and retrograde.

Julia doesn't know if Lynn is taking Harri seriously; at a glance, she seems to be. She listens attentively, as if it were the first time, to what she's saying, which has little new to offer, and she asks the same questions to show that she's interested, as if the whole thing were a routine. Now what she wonders is what the Iberia guy is going to say to the man who's going to admit that it was his bag that broke on the aeroplane, assuming he ever manages to find him. Harri looks at her as if she hasn't understood the question. He won't have to say anything. The guy from Iberia will give Harri his phone number, and she'll be the one to call, and then she'll repeat more or less what she wrote in the book: she's the woman who helped him to pick up his books, he offered her a book called *Montauk*, with a beach and a lighthouse on the cover, but she hadn't dared to take it, and now she regrets it.

Lynn asks how she thinks the man will react.

Harri looks irritated and asks if Lynn doubts he's going to remember her.

She says she doesn't, she didn't mean that.

Now the dreamer, Harri, admits that she's thought about hundreds of possibilities for when she meets up with the man from the airport, and Julia shivers imagining that she's going to tell them all of them. Does Harri realize that? Of course she does, she tells them right away not to worry, she isn't going to bore them with her imaginings, and they both ask her, beg her, to tell them, Lynn with particular passion, perhaps repentant because she had the same thought. Harri doesn't want to tell them anything, they don't take her seriously. Julia would love to tell her that she's not at all interested in the airport adventure and would she please keep it to herself, but for the sake of peace, and hoping to introduce some humor into the conversation, she asks Harri if she's considered, among her different theses, the possibility of disappointment—they finally get to meet up, and, for some reason, the man disappoints her. For instance, what if he says *"hola, muñeca"*—the Spanish equivalent of "hey, baby"—when he sees her? Harri is not amused. She shakes her head—as if thinking, "You poor fool, how could you possibly understand?"—and finally answers by asking whether she thinks she, Harri, would go to such lengths to find a man who looks as if he would be the sort to say "hey, baby." Harri looks genuinely hurt, and Julia has to say once again that she's only joking. How does she imagine the meeting? She uses all her effort to look as if she's really interested. Harri does not answer immediately. She looks at her sharply, inquisitively, but doesn't seem wholly convinced by what she sees, answering without much enthusiasm that she thinks he must be shy. She says that when she imagines it, that's the option that keeps coming to mind, again and again. The man comes up to her and says "Hi"—no *hey*, and certainly no *baby*—and he's shy and not very expressive. And she would be glad if he turns out to be like that. They sit in silence for a long while, until it becomes apparent that she doesn't want to say any more about the man from the airport. Although the link is only indirect, they start talking about the Basque character, with Harri's last remarks as their starting point. Are they really so cold? Lynn is very interested in the subject, because she's a sociologist, of course, and Julia tells them what she just read in the book about Ravel: *On parle de ma sécheresse de coeur. C'est faux. Et vous le savez. Mais je suis basque.* The Basque themselves accept the cliché. With pride, in fact; it isn't a shortcoming—it's elegant moderation.

An anecdote about the Basques' proverbial miserliness when it comes to affection is the one the famous linguist Mitxelena used

472

to tell. After spending eight years at war and in prison, when he got back home, his mother said, "So, you're back then?" Nothing more than that. She tells it for Lynn's benefit, knowing that Harri is familiar with the story. According to the linguist, he didn't need to hear any more than that to understand that his mother loved him a lot and to know how glad she was to have him back. Lynn laughs. A sad laugh that expresses sorrow rather than disagreement. She says that sometimes you need to hear more than that, you need to hear that someone loves you. There's a short pause, as if they're embarrassed to go on talking. Or you feel the need to express your own love but you have to suppress that desire in order for the other person not to feel uncomfortable. Lynn says all of this without removing her apologetic smile. Of course it's not for her to say, but she thinks that Basque men might be inhibited when it comes to expressing their feelings. Perhaps they're too reserved.

Then Harri says, "So he's one of them, too, is he?"

Lynn goes as red as a tomato.

"Don't be naughty."

Something Julia didn't mention when she was telling the anecdote about the linguist coming back home after the war: though her own mother, just as Lynn's put it, is inhibited when it comes to expressing her emotions, Julia couldn't stand it if she were more open in that sense. She remembers that her mother used to say "don't be silly," seemingly angry or uncomfortable, whenever her father was acting affectionately toward her. One day her father wanted to carry her mother up the stairs in his arms, but she didn't let him; Julia must have been very little, and she thought that her mother was being mean.

Harri, on the other hand, doesn't mind telling them that her husband is a true Basque but is nevertheless very open and affectionate, even too much so, and she's beginning to find him somewhat cloying. But then she adds that she's not really sure, she doesn't know if the same behaviour would irritate her coming from somebody else. Sometimes Julia is moved by how transparent Harri is. Then Harri opens her green leather briefcase, and the clasp makes its usual dry sound. She's just remembered that she's brought back the English translation of *Montauk* that Lynn lent her. Before giving it back to her, she apologizes for having spoilt one of the pages by writing a message on it for the man from the airport. She thought about rubbing it out with an eraser, but in the end she left it as it was. It's on the dedication page, written clearly and expressively: *Fui tonta rechazándolo en el avión. Espero que me des otra oportunidad.* Translation: "It was silly of me to refuse it on the plane. I hope you give me another chance." And then her cell phone number.

As she flips through the pages, Lynn says that she prefers it like that and it'll make for a great memory. Julia knows what she's up to, she's looking for the passage in which the couple is leaving the hotel and Max regrets the girl finding out that he's just paid twice her weekly wage for the two nights they've spent there, and not the other way around, as it says in the Spanish translation.

It couldn't have been any other way: *"It irritates him that Lynn, who made the booking, knows more or less what he is now paying for their overnight stay."*

Lynn says once more that she has to tidy up her apartment and that she has to go to the store first to get some beers and something to eat. So they can deduce she's going to have a visitor. "Come here," Harri says to her. She hugs her tightly around the waist. Lynn has her eyes and mouth wide open to say that she's strangling her. She's breathless. Harri says, "*Ikusten?* You see? There's no pleasing you two." Then Lynn says that they'll understand her eventually and hugs her back, but without touching her body.

She asks them if they know the tale about the porcupine. They don't. She says it's a German fable. One cold winter's night, a group of porcupines all decide to sleep together to keep warm. But their prickles make it impossible for them to sleep, and the next night, they move away from each other. It's terribly cold, and they move together once more. The porcupines have to move around like that from one day to the next until, finally, they find the right distance in terms of manners and decency.

Lynn has just disappeared up the stairs when she comes back down a few steps again and tells them, "Don't forget to stop in at the bookshop when you go to the university so you can meet Martin's friend."

She almost forgot to take her copy of *Montauk*.

The Montaigne quote reads like this in English: *This book was written in good faith, reader. It warns you from the outset that in it I have set myself no goal but a domestic and private one.*

Even so, on page 136 it says: *This book was written in good faith, reader, and what does it keep concealed? And why?* Julia thinks it would be interesting to know Lynn's version. The Lynn from *Montauk*.

When they're alone again, Harri asks her about "our boy" again and whether he's writing. Julia doesn't know what to say. The only thing she can think of is that his character has jaundice and spends a lot of time in front of the mirror looking at his own decay. Finally she answers that she thinks he is writing. "You know how it is, he doesn't say much." They talk about the Basques' famous reticence and, once more, draw the conclusion that there are all sorts. Although the train they hear leaving the stop is only the 19:02, Harri says they'd better get going.

BUT THEN, LATER, THEY HAVE TOO MUCH TIME. In Ibaeta, being a fairly newly built area, like any other recently developed district in any other town, Julia doesn't mind sitting at the bar's outdoor terrace as Harri suggests. She doesn't like sitting outside in places where she thinks people she knows might walk by. Obviously she'd rather go into Martin's friend's bookshop, but Harri doesn't seem to remember about it, and without knowing why, she doesn't dare to suggest it. She doesn't want to show any particular interest and has been hoping for Harri to suggest it herself. In fact, she's very surprised Harri hasn't suggested it, because she's a person with a lot of curiosity, in fact she's something of a gossip. She feels ridiculous when it occurs to her that Harri might have a tendency to steer her away from other men in order to make sure she sticks with Martin, but that's what she thinks.

HITZ BOOKSHOP. *Hitz* is Basque for "word." From where Julia is, on the other side of the roundabout, she can only see its door and its single window on the corner of the squat white building that houses it. She doesn't know what to order and asks for a shandy. Harri orders a gin and tonic; she says it tones her up.

Harri likes outdoor bars. She says they're good places to go. Julia remembers how enthusiastically she spoke about Bilbao's—apparently, she spent a lot of time sitting at different ones, hoping the man from the airport would walk by. Julia wonders if she really did do that.

Harri enjoys sitting there in the sun with her eyes closed. They don't say much. Julia keeps the bookshop door in sight—it hasn't opened once since they've been there. Which isn't long, in fact. Harri sits up in her chair, perhaps because the sun has gone behind a cloud, and asks if she's going to go back to work at the regional government office. Julia is almost sure she is but says she doesn't know, in order not to say that she wants to split up with Martin, even if only professionally.

"I'd like not to have to work."

"What would you do if you won the lottery?"

She's never asked herself that common question. She's never dreamed of having money or thought about the possibility of living without having to work. But recently she has allowed herself to fantasize: Write a history of the Basque Country for young people in the style of Gombrich's *Short History of the World*; translate Frisch's *Fragebogen*, his questionaires, into Basque, his *Verhör*, his interrogatories, in other words, and *Montauk*, perhaps; organize the notes she took while translating *Bihotzean* about peoples' attitudes toward violence and do more work on them; and write about writing, about writing in Basque. Take a trip to Cuba.

Harri would be astonished, of course, to hear that she has ideas about writing. Martin is the writer. Julia's sure that if she told her about her plans, she'd tell them to Martin, and then she'd have to put up with him teasing her.

Young people come and go, most of them with shoulder bags. A girl on a bike, riding it with style.

Julia says that if she won the lottery, she would go to Cuba, to which Harri says, "Honey, it's degrading to have to go all the way to Cuba just to have a little fun." She laughs at the joke. But it's a fantasy she has no trouble telling her: She'd go with Zigor, she'd like to look for the old black gentleman that used to work as a servant for one of her great uncles. Apparently, he knows how to sing "*Gernikako Arbola*" and even say a few sentences in Basque, too. Her grandfather's brother is dead now, but he used to own a restaurant in Havana, a place called Centro Vasco, which is still open although it's now state-owned. The old black gentleman must be very old by now, if he's still alive. She knows that half a dozen years ago, a journalist visited the Centro Vasco, he met him there, and when he said he was from the Basque Country, the black man spoke to him in Basque—and also sang him "*Gernikako Arbola*"—but unfortunately, the journalist didn't understand him, because he didn't speak Basque himself. The black man told him about how her great uncle used to send him to the *pilota* court with messages in Basque, which he would learn by heart in order to deliver them, and he would bring back the replies using the same method. The black man didn't know what the messages meant, he just passed them on like a parrot, although he did still remember some of them. What were they about? Were they to do with bets? Was he just asking them what they wanted for dinner after the game? So why did they use Basque? Julia doesn't know, and she'd like to find out.

And what would Harri do? She shrugs her shoulders. She pushes her empty glass to the middle of the table and says, "I've got an appointment with Abaitua tomorrow. Do you mind coming with me?"

They don't talk much on their way to the university. Julia decides to accompany Harri there and then go back to the bookshop, if only for just a brief minute, and even at the risk of arriving late for the roundtable talk. She's curious to meet this friend of Martin and Abaitua's. They give each other two kisses goodbye. Harri puts her hand on Julia's cheek, "Take care of him."

HITZ BOOKSHOP. It looks like some local neighborhood stationery shop, and the volumes on display in the window make it look like a second-hand bookshop. There aren't that many books, either, and a beautiful model of a sailing ship takes up a large portion of the display window. So because of that, it also looks like a shop specializing in maritime matters. But even though *The Nigger of the 'Narcissus'* and *Moby Dick* and Alberto Fortes's *Memorial de a bordo* are there, there's also Escoffier's *My Cuisine* and an encyclopedia about watercolor techniques. Her attention is drawn to *In the Face of Death*, by one Peter Noll, because its subtitle is *Funeral Oration by Max Frisch*. So she has an excuse she can confess to for going in.

Inside there's only a girl behind the counter; she lifts her head from the book she's reading when a bell hanging from the door rings as Julia opens it. There's a curtain behind the girl, separating the storefront from the back. Julia tries to spend time looking at the shelves, and she has the sensation she's looking around the books

477

at somebody's house while dinner is being made. *Under the Volcano*, Malcolm Lowry. *Beneath the Wheel*, Hermann Hesse. *Bakakaï*, Witold Gombrowicz. *Balizko erroten erresuma*, Koldo Izagirre. *Botoiletan*, Antton Luku. *Bluebeard*, Max Frisch. *Bartleby, the Scrivener*, Herman Melville. *Baudelaire*, Jean Paul Sartre. There's no sign of movement behind the curtain, and it's getting late. A failed mission, though not completely—at least she's come across something about Frisch that she wasn't aware of. The phone rings, and the girl answers it before taking Julia's money. She says, "I'm sorry, Kepa's in London. Please call back next week."

THE MAUPASSANT TRANSLATOR is a man with a beard and a deep voice, with the tender, melancholy look some Basque men have in their eyes. Julia likes his explanation, it's very practical, he talks about several specific passages and the difficulties involved in translating them. He chooses a paragraph, compares it with the students' versions, and they talk about it. The problem is that they keep going beyond the text's linguistic characteristics and talking about the contents. A problem only in relative terms, in any case, because most of what's said is interesting.

"*Soudain Jeanne eut une inspiration d'amour. Elle remplit sa bouche du clair liquide, et, les joues gonflées comme des outres, fit comprendre à Julien que, lèvre à lèvre, elle voulait le désaltérer.*"

A young girl, probably the youngest in the group—Julia is the oldest, of course—doesn't stop talking, even though she blushes each time she speaks. She says that some of the things in the book are strikingly daring, "this part about quenching his thirst lip to lip," for instance, in a novel that's otherwise said to be "*une peinture remarquable des moeurs provinciales de la Normandie du XIX siècle*"—an exceptional portrait of provincial customs in nineteenth century Normandy. And this, as well as making everyone laugh aloud, livens up the debate.

At moments like this, everybody has something to say. The French, now they really knew how to have a revolution, nobody else guillotined their kings; and the men make ironic remarks about French women's famous brazenness; and then the women point out

478

that people are the same the whole world over—"*en todas partes cuecen habas*"—which takes them back to linguistic matters. In Basque, you say *irin adina lauso leku guztietan*—flour is just as smooth in everyone's house—or *etxe guztietan laratza beltz*—the cauldron chain is equally black in everyone's house. Suggestive interpretations of the line from the famous song that has Bartolo asking Marixu where she's going looking so beautiful— "*Maritxu nora zoaz eder galant hori*"—for example, the idea that Bartolo's girlfriend might have been a reader of Maupassant. They all laugh. They wonder if every generation thinks it's invented sex: a) because parents keep quiet about it, hide it, and repress their children; and b) because children find their parents' sex frightening or revolting.

Julia works out that Maupassant—whose mother was a friend of Flaubert's, and maybe something more than that, too—was a contemporary of her great-grandmother's. She knows that her great-grandmother was once a messenger for the Carlists—apparently they used women for such tasks because they raised fewer suspicions—and she took messages between Otzeta and Oiartzun. Around forty miles over the hills. Julia did get to know her grandmother. She was a very loving woman who combined a belief in magic—she had blind faith in the *lamiak*, the river nymphs of Basque myth—with the darkest, most frightening parts of the Catholic religion. She remembers well that once, when she was very small—but as always, she doesn't know what exact age—and she and her grandmother were coming down from Etxezar to Otzeta, her grandmother, with a shawl on her head and a missal in her hand (which, now that she thinks about it, she might never actually have read, she might have been illiterate), suddenly stopped and sniffed the air the way animals do and said there was a smell of burning oil in the air, and that it must be the souls in purgatory asking for help. She knows that when she tells that story, people think she's exaggerating, but it's the pure truth. She also remembers that her grandmother told her that one of her uncles had seen the Basque goddess Anbotoko Dama herself, brushing her hair with a golden comb, completely convinced that it was true and that she was passing on that conviction. After her came her mother, and then it was herself. The first person in the family to read Maupassant.

It's probably the bright light in the carriage that makes everybody look tired. Whenever she takes the train, she looks around to see if anybody is reading. She'd rather sit next to them. Rainer Maria Rilke: Ah, how good it is to be among people who are reading. There's nobody. She hasn't opened the book she just bought, either, she's waiting to open it greedily at home. She keeps herself entertained by wondering which of the people around her looks as if they might quench their thirst by putting their lips against somebody else's in the way Maupassant describes. She glances at a man, neither young nor old, neither ugly nor good-looking, who then looks back at her, and that forces her to take her book out and start reading the first page she opens to. "*¿Qué es lo que más se ama en una mujer y por qué se enamora uno de ella?*" it says—What is it one most loves about a woman, and why does one fall in love with her?

She has the impression that her journey to the rational, modern world has been long and difficult, that she hasn't been offered any shortcuts, that moving forward in order to overcome obstacles has been hard work for her compared to others who've had their parents' and ancestors' shoulders to stand on.

FRAGEBOGEN: Would she have been different if her mother had read Maupassant?

AS SOON AS SHE GETS HOME, Martin tells her he's found somebody to look after his father. He seems happy. He appears to be quite excited as he tells her that, contrary to his normal custom, he was going to catch the train in Gros—he'd gone to Kursaal to buy some tickets for his sister—when who should he bump into but Abaitua, who was there with quite a full-bodied young woman. He was going to walk past them discreetly, without saying anything, but Abaitua said hello to him, and he had no choice but to stop. He had the impression that Abaitua wanted to justify what he was doing with such a striking-looking girl, and he started explaining so that he wouldn't get the wrong idea. He introduced the girl, and it just so happens that she's a nurse specialized in geriatrics and looking for a new job. She seemed like a very nice person to him, and he said he'd call her to arrange things. He's sure she'll take very good care of his father.

Julia had forgotten about the map of Sicily. Now she remembers it as Martin looks, perplexedly, at the wall where it previously hung. She says she tore it down accidentally—she has no idea how such an accident might have happened—it got ruined, and she'll buy him another one. Then, mostly so that he won't say anything about it, she goes straight on to tell him that she went to Kepa's bookshop but he wasn't there and that she'd bought a book because the epilogue was written by Frisch. When he asks her what it's about, she tells him what she read on the back cover: the author had been a friend of Frisch's—a famous professor of law in Zurich—who refused treatment when he was diagnosed with cancer of the bladder, because he preferred a dignified death to gaining a little more time. During the nine months he remained alive, he gave a daily dictation of his reflections on death and dying, the world, and himself.

Martin, of course, is interested in the subject, and the interest he shows so obviously, especially compared to the scarce attention he normally pays her and which she finds so hurtful, makes her want to provoke him. Using the book as an excuse, she talks ironically about poor people who think they have something original to say about death. Something she's been wanting to say to him for a long time: if displays of narcissism are pretty laughable in general, those of people who are inspired by foreseeing their own deaths seem particularly pathetic to her. Unfortunate people, mesmerized by the nobility of their own thoughts; saddened about how their absence will affect other people; worried about what will become of their corpses, whose cold touch they can feel as they draw their fingertips along their oval faces, like his character did when looking at himself in the bathroom mirror the last time she checked to see what he was up to, just over a month ago. Martin looks at her with his blue eyes wide open, a look of fear on his face that moves and frightens her. She tells herself it's impossible for him to know that she goes onto his computer, in order to stick to her intention not to confess it to him and to stand up to Martin's stare. They stay like that for a while, perhaps for quite a short while, but it seems like a long time to Julia, and finally Martin, destroyed, says, "You're probably right." That makes Julia feel sorry, but it's too late now.

She tells him what she thought about the bookshop, how it's quite special but doesn't look like it's a particularly successful venture. Martin says he doesn't think Kepa is any good at business. She thinks he says it with regret. Then he turns the television on. So, it's Marie Lafôret time. She doesn't have to look at her watch to know that's what time it is, she'd even say it's marked on her biological clock at this point.

481

MAX FRISCH'S FUNERAL ORATION: "Our circle of friends among the dead keeps growing."

He used the same idea in some of his other writing. *Fragebogen*: "*Möchten Sie wissen, wie Sterben ist?*"—Do you have any friends among the dead?

After Marie Laforêt, Julia sits next to him on the sofa to keep him company. Actually, it's so that he won't feel guilty for watching such trash, because she's occasionally thrown it in his face: "How can you stand seeing such garbage?" In any case, what he usually says seems to be true—after the first few minutes, he becomes saturated and doesn't pay much attention to what's happening on the screen. He also often says we spend time in front of the television in the same way that our ancestors used to watch the fire—the light attracts us, and it gives us an excuse to think our own thoughts in silence.

The two of them are sitting in armchairs, each with their arms crossed, looking at the screen. The remote control is on the coffee table, in the no man's land between the two chairs, and neither of them is using it, not even to find something else when the commercials come on. Julia would say their situation looks pretty pathetic, and it reminds her of a scene Martin described long ago. After his father had an operation, he and his mother went to the private hospital to take care of him. Apparently, his father was asleep and his children were all sitting, their arms crossed, watching the television, just as the two of them are now, not having anything to say to each other. All sorts of things were happening on the screen, but Martin didn't notice any of them, until one of the announcers said, "And now we're going to see an unforgettable film, one that broke all the taboos," and he realized he was seeing the opening credits for Nagisa Oshima's *In the Realm of the Senses*. Martin had seen it before, and he remembered the scene in which an enormous penis, framed so that it's taking up the whole screen, ejaculates and then the sperm slowly moves down like lava on the slopes of a volcano. He says he allowed himself to be ruled by fate. He could have changed channel, saying, "I've seen this film, and it's revolting," but he didn't. And he doesn't know why. Even though the very idea frightened him, he wanted to see how it would affect his mother. The film started, the scene with the large, erect penis letting out an endless stream of thick sperm, and his mother didn't say a word. He'd heard her shout things like "*por Dios, quitad esa porquería*"—meaning "for God's sake, turn that trash off"—at much less before. He didn't say a word, either. They both carried on watching indifferently and sat there in silence until the film came to an end. Not a single word. What was she thinking? Why didn't she shout at him angrily and tell him to turn it off? Why didn't she faint? That's what Martin wondered, completely dismayed by the experience. Obviously, the son was wondering whether what his devout mother had just seen might not be new for her.

Why did he make his mother go through that, and what exactly did he learn from it all?

Martin's been nodding off for a while. It happens to him more and more often.

DROPS OF URINE AT THE FOOT OF THE TOILET. From time to time, she's ventured to tell him that he should be more careful, but normally she keeps quiet, because she knows any mention of physiological matters makes him uncomfortable. She could say what Beauvoir wrote about Sartre in *La cérémonie des adieux*: "*Il ne faisait jamais allusion à ses fonctions naturelles et s'en acquittait avec la plus soigneuse discrétion*"—he never mentioned his bodily functions, and carried them out with the greatest of care. Once, after she mentioned something about it to him, he replied that from then on, he was going to pee sitting down, giving up the only thing men do with more dignity than women: peeing standing up, the masculine way. But that didn't last long. Julia didn't like him sitting down to pee, it was obvious he was giving up a natural way of doing things, so to speak, for her sake, and that made her feel guilty, especially after reading Werner's caricature of the subject in one of his novels, where he tells the story of a disappointed man whose wife makes him sit down to pee and then suddenly, "after four years of submission," he realizes that mean-spirited demand could be grounds for divorce. So whenever she draws his attention to drops of urine around the toilet, which isn't all that often, and he replies humbly and hurt that he'll do it sitting down from then on, she always ends up saying he doesn't have to take any such extreme measure, just be a little more careful, that's all. She's the one who always ends up having to apologize.

When she goes back to the living room, he's no longer sitting in front of the television. She looks for him on the lower floor, but he isn't there.

He's in the bedroom. There's very little light, he's sitting on the side of the bed, and when he realizes she's there, he asks her to keep quiet by putting one index finger on his lips and pointing at the ceiling with the other. The murmur of a man's voice reaches them from there. "They're up there," says Martin, and Julia shouts, "What are you doing?" surprised at her own anger. But Martin doesn't react, he just looks at her, his hands resting on his knees, and she feels as if she's the castrating mother who's just caught her son masturbating. "What are you doing?" she repeats, now trying to sound nice, and she lifts her head up to look at the ceiling. She doesn't understand the words, but it's clearly Lynn talking now. Then the man, in a lower voice, and Lynn laughing.

There's still some light coming in through the window. The light is dying, but it brings out the trees, the houses, and the far-off hills—they all look as if they've been drawn on the same level, with no depth, as if they were all part of a theater set. They've put music on upstairs. Julia recognizes Bob Dylan's "When the Deal Goes Down." Lynn likes it a lot, and she gave a copy to her, for no apparent reason, a few days earlier. They hear them on the left-hand side, where the upstairs living room is. She works out that the upstairs house is not much wider than the room she and Martin are in at the moment.

She envies Lynn's laughter.

Martin is still sitting on the side of the bed. His face is hardly visible, just the reflection of the light in his eyes. "You can hear everything they say," he says, pointing at the ceiling again, his head cocked to one side in what looks like an effort to make out who the man is, but Lynn's voice is clearer. She tells the cat off—"Enough for today, Max"—and it seems to jump onto the floor from somewhere high up, they hear a quick thud as it lands. They both listen out during the silence that follows, until the girl's wild, loud cries begin, which they hear with absolute clarity. Julia finds them terrifying, frightening. The shame of listening to other people's intimacy mortifies her, but she doesn't want to make any sort of gesture that Martin might find offensive, and so she holds a hand out to him and is going to say that they'd better go downstairs, when he pulls her roughly toward him and lays her down on the bed. She lets him, because otherwise he would feel offended, or hurt, or both at the same time.

But the knowledge that Martin's seduction is prompted by Lynn's cries puts her off. That's the way she is, the slightest trace of perversion turns her right off. It's obvious she's a puritan. She lets him do it to her, remaining passive, until she thinks her attitude is mean and she regrets it, even stroking him where she knows he likes it, and Martin breathes heavily on the dip in her neck in gratitude.

She's never turned him down. Martin did once, and she thinks it was the only time she ever explicitly offered herself to him, but he did it in a fairly nice way. "We men have a less complex mechanism, but it's more fragile," he told her. She didn't press him, she didn't want to find out any more. In any case, the reasons she doesn't take the initiative in bed date from before that. It started almost at the beginning of their relationship, in Faustino Iturbe and Flora Ugalde's first episode. Faustino was unnerved by Flora's clumsy insinuations while still wrapped in her bathrobe after a shower, and he found the smell of her body gel particularly off-putting. Of course, he mentioned the brand of gel, and, naturally, it was the one she always used. The one she used up until then, that is.

Sometimes, without Martin asking her to, she lies face down on the bed and lifts her buttocks up to offer them to him, because she read somewhere—could it have been in Horney's *The Neurotic Personality of our Time?*—that neurotic people like to do it from behind, and she thinks that he may be repressing that desire.

They don't hear the man's voice often, but it's modulated, whereas Lynn's isn't, even though it's loud at times. The voice of somebody who would like to shout but can't, somebody about to fall down a cliff, and the man's cries blend together with her broken voice, and they seem to Julia to last forever, she feels her heart beating wildly. When there is silence again, she only just manages to stop herself from laughing.

Martin is lying next to her, his eyes wide open and looking up at the ceiling.

THE USUAL HOUSE SOUNDS TAKE OVER. The sound of traffic from the east predominates, because the sash window isn't properly closed. However, the noise isn't very loud, and she guesses it must be late already. She thinks she hasn't heard a train go by for a while, but perhaps they have and she just hasn't heard them—that often happens. There's a murmur of voices from upstairs, slower now, quieter. Two voices, a man and a woman's alternately, but she thinks the woman is talking more. Next to her, Martin is breathing regularly, with a whistling sound, which means he's asleep.

Julia doesn't mind getting up. She doesn't like the dampness of the tissues she's stuck between her legs. Martin, on the other hand, doesn't understand why she bothers to clean off his sperm. They've talked about it from time to time; in fact, it's the only thing they have talked about in connection with their sexual relationship. Julia's need to get up and wash between her legs seems, to Martin, to mean that she finds him physically repulsive. She thinks he's wrong. Back when she found him physically attractive, even very physically attractive, she couldn't get to sleep if her thighs were wet, and she's amazed that there haven't been other women who've felt the same among those he's been with. She's always felt a little guilty about having to get up to clean herself, and she normally solves the problem by surreptitiously sticking a few paper tissues down there. She's also always found it frustrating not to be able to go to sleep with her head resting on his shoulder. She doesn't find it comfortable. She's occasionally made an effort to try it, but she never manages and always ends up saying it's just a movie pose.

As far as cleaning her vagina is concerned, she doesn't think she has any friends she could talk to about it, which immediately seems foolish to her when she realizes that she could talk about it with Harri and that, in fact, Harri would be delighted to talk about it. But she herself is the one who doesn't want to; it would require a lot of emotional effort, and it wouldn't be worth it.

"You're terrible," she hears Lynn saying.

She's asleep, of course, when the sound of steps on the stairs wakes her up, and whoever it is is already downstairs. She sees Martin's profile, in sharp contrast against the cobalt blue sky, standing on the balcony that looks onto the garden. Watching life. He used to stand the same way at the back window, watching the young guys coming and going on the barge.

The sound of steps on the gravel, then the screech of the iron gate. Martin comes back from the window, and she closes her eyes so he'll think she's asleep.

16

BY THE TIME ABAITUA leaves the bathroom, Pilar is already wearing a sleeveless beige linen dress. She looks at him from the corner of her eye, an instant, an indivisible moment in time, and then stands in front of the mirror. She starts putting lotion on her face, apparently unconcerned, opening her mouth and eyes wide to tighten her skin, but he knows she's noticed something. And so she has. Just as he manages to escape into the dressing room, he hears her calling after him that he's got something on his neck. He guesses what it is and checks in the closet mirror—a small love bite. It's at the bottom of his sternomastoid. "Let me see," says Pilar from the bathroom, apparently innocently, but he doesn't trust her. Without answering, he tries to find a high-necked sweater on the shelves but finally decides to wear a normal shirt, because any sort of turtleneck would do no more than confirm her suspicions, and if it comes to that, he'd rather just not let her look at his neck. If necessary, he'll tell her he doesn't like being examined.

To an extent, he also likes playing with the idea of telling her that it's the mark of a young woman's passion, and as always when he toys with some crazy thought, he remembers that classmate of his spitting on the principal's bald spot from up in the gallery. Fortunately, he doesn't have to say anything, because Pilar doesn't come into the dressing room, she waits for him in the hallway. She has a jacket made of the same cloth as her dress in one hand and a large black leather bag hanging from her other hand. She looks elegant. This time she looks into his eyes. She doesn't look angry, quite the opposite, he'd say she looks conciliatory—he knows all the nuances of her different gazes very well—and he tries to show no feelings. Fortunately, he already has his pants on, and he does his shirt up slowly, trying to give the impression that he has nothing to hide. Perhaps that's why she says "I'm in a bit of a hurry," but she doesn't let any anxiety show in her voice. Recently she's been trying to be the first one to get to the clinic, she says. She's operating today, too. "Simple things," she says, and adds that she's more worried about the shareholders' meeting at midday. That's how she tells him there's a meeting.

She puts her large bag down on the floor and slips her jacket on. "You could come."

Déjà vu. He thinks of several mean-spirited responses. Asking where, acting hurt because he would have been happy to go with her if she'd told him further in advance, but finally he just says he can't go. In fact, he's pleased she's so busy.

When they reach the hall downstairs, Pilar tells him about how an old woman who worked as a cook at her parents' house in Otzeta used to cross the street when she left the house. She would cross herself and, without looking left or right, walk straight out into the heavy traffic on the avenue, causing the drivers to brake angrily, honk their horns, and swear. Abaitua doesn't know why she's telling him this now.

He's about to go into the operating theater when Arrese appears and says he wants to speak with him as soon as possible. Unusually, he's wearing a suit and tie, probably because, like Pilar, he's going to the shareholder's meeting later on. The patient is already on the operating table. An easy case, a myomectomy, so the most important thing is to keep the preoperative bleeding risk to a minimum. But there was an unfortunate accident the week before, and he wants to show the residents how to do it. Arrese promises it won't be more than a moment, and Abaitua has no choice but to take his smock off and follow him. He has no idea what Arrese might want.

He's only slightly surprised to find Orl in Arrese's office. He's sitting behind the desk, which is typical of his tendency to take the place of authority wherever he goes. There's something about him that makes Abaitua uneasy, frightened even. His eyes, hidden behind the flashes of light glinting off his always spotless rimless glasses, suddenly appear, small but lively, as if to say they know something about him that not even he himself knows. Sometimes, to get over the nervousness Orl makes him feel, he tells himself that if he had to, he could take ahold of his pastel-colored tie with his left hand and knock him to the ground with a blow from his right. He isn't proud of these remains of savage, macho primitivism, but knowing that he is physically stronger than some worrying interlocutor helps him to keep calm. Having that final recourse.

The opening chitchat, which can never be dispensed with, is about golf. He doesn't understand them, because they always use technical terms and he's never bothered to ask them to explain them. They encourage him, as always, to join the Basozabal golf club, and while they explain the membership fees to him, he tries to think of a sufficiently all-encompassing and silencing response to shut down the subject he thinks they're undoubtedly going to bring up. Problems at the clinic are Pilar's concern, and she's quite capable of taking care of them herself. What's more, as they know, he's never gotten involved in the clinic's business. Orl's lenses reflect the window, the ventilation device, and the incinerator tower. He puts one of his fingers, which is the width of a scalpel, alongside his nose as he starts in on the subject. He says they want to tell him honorably—in their name and in the name of many of the members of the board, as well—that Pilar's position, much as they all respect her wish to be loyal to her father and all that, doesn't make any sense. The sale they've been offered is a deal they can't turn down, what with the crisis in the construction sector and the high speed train line and other infrastructure projects that are going to make the future of the entire area uncertain. Likewise, the conditions the public administrations are going to impose over the next few years are going to make it impossible to earn even the smallest profits, and they aren't prepared to make the investments they would have to make in order to be able to compete in the new market.

Abaitua thinks he knows now why Pilar brought up the cook from Otzeta crossing herself and not looking left or right before crossing the road. He gives them the answer he had prepared, though not as forcefully, and without saying that Pilar is intelligent enough to sort out her problems on her own. As they know, she is very much her own woman, and he doesn't think anything he might say will change her mind. In fact, the opposite could happen. In many of their discussions, instead of changing her opinion, she sticks more firmly to her own, often with an unwavering "And another thing!"—jumping at the chance to load up on new arguments. He feels pretty ridiculous, because he's the only one who laughs at that. He takes his surgical cap off. In any case, the easiest way to get out of the situation is to tell them that he'll try to convince her. He turns toward Arrese, because he prefers to say it to him, and just then there's nervous knocking on the door. It's the head midwife, and she's obvious shaken up. There's a problem in the operating theater, and they need help. "A resident's having trouble," she says, looking at Abaitua. He starts to get up, but Arrese puts a large, hairy hand on his shoulder. Abaitua would have a harder time with him if it came to a fight. Arrese tells the midwife that they're busy, without taking his hand off Abaitua's shoulder. He tells her to look in the cafeteria, she's bound to find somebody there. The head midwife, after hesitating for a moment, straightens her cap and leaves.

Abaitua wrings his own cap between his hands. He says he'll do what he can to convince Pilar but he can't promise them anything. Pilar is very much her own woman. Orl says, "She loves you more than you think." He leans back in the chair, and the intense sky blue reflected in his lenses wipes out any meaning his eyes may have held. Then he talks about the benefits of golf—it's a sport you play against yourself, and also one in which players of different standards can compete against each other—and after explaining all of that to Abaitua, he goes on to tell a joke about clubs and balls that he doesn't get but that makes Arrese laugh out loud. They also talk about a golf website, and some sort of forum. Then all of a sudden, he spreads his hands out on the table—very white hands, very thin hands that could fit through the hole of a stitch—and says, "That's all."

They get up and go out to the hallway. "By the way, I forgot: Teresa Hoyos's husband's been admitted." Arrese tells him with an air of confidentiality but so that Orl can hear, too, and the latter nods to confirm it. He's in the ICU, in a coma. "By the way," he said, as if it were in some way connected with what they've just been talking about. "By the way, Teresa Hoyos's husband's been admitted." He's just been with her, and she's distraught; her husband's prognosis is bad. Abaitua tries to work out how old the man—who he hardly knows—must be.

They've reached the nurses' station. Beyond it, at the waiting room door, a man is making energetic gestures, and the head midwife and a resident are trying to calm him down, but Abaitua shows no interest in finding out what's happened. He shows more interest in the contents of the file he's just picked up from the counter. It's made of blue cardboard, with elastic straps to close it, and there's a yellow Post-it note on it. Abaitua sees his name on the Post-it, and the supervisor tells him "the American girl" left it there for him. Arrese looks at the file, turns it over to check the other side of it, turns it back over again, and lifts up the Post-it to see what's under it. He doesn't seem to want to give it to Abaitua, who takes it out of his hands. He knows what's in it, a questionaire for him to correct, and he isn't sure whether to open it or not, so that Arrese can see it's work, but he thinks it's beneath him to have to do something like that. In fact, he'd rather not take the risk, improbable though it is—highly improbable—that Lynn might have put something in there that would hint at their non-work relationship. "By the way," Arrese says once more. "By the way, that *gringa*'s got a good head and all that, but her tits aren't bad, either." He laughs out loud. When Orl asks who the foreign girl he's talking about is, Arrese has to tell him. A young sociologist they've sent to the department to get in everyone's way. "And to trail around after this one," he says, pointing at Abaitua, "just like all of the rest of them, young and old." He laughs again. Now it's Orl who puts his thin-fingered hand on his shoulder. A paternal gesture that doctors are particularly good at and particularly hate having done to them. He should take care, Orl says, you never know what these floozies might be after.

IN THE BIRTHING ROOM, half a dozen people in white smocks stand pale and sweating around a young woman who looks calm. She asks them again and again to tell her husband that she's OK. The man Abaitua saw at the nurses's station, apparently. He was kicking up a fuss because they made him leave the room. Abaitua takes her hand and promises to speak with him. The resident tells him she's a first-time mother, thirty years old. They admitted her half an hour earlier with a painless hemorrhage and a blood pressure of 140/90. No albuminuria or glycosuria. Good fetal heart rate, 144 beats per minute on the mother's right-hand side. Judging from her sanitary towels, they estimate she's lost around 150 ml of blood. But she's still losing blood. They think it's abruptio placentae, even though her abdomen is flexible and palpable, she's been in no pain, and there's no sign of uterine contraction. Fortunately, they say, the problem has been reduced to almost nothing, and she's hardly losing any blood now. The resident who tells him smiles. It's just a trickle. He's a young guy from Otzeta, he has kind eyes and looks honest. Abaitua is sorry it's him it's happening to. It's vasa previa. The blood vessels of the placenta, fetus, or umbilical cord have covered over the entrance to the birth canal beneath the fetus and are being torn. It isn't the mother who's losing blood, it's the fetus. And it's already lost too much.

The blood volume of a full-term fetus is around 250 ml. He orders a cesarean section, which should have been done an hour earlier.

He remembers Lynn. The nurse on the poster with her index finger held up to her lips to ask for silence reminds him of her. "Just relax"—that same finger held up.

After piercing the amniotic sac, no meconium comes out, but there's 100 ml of fresh blood along with the amniotic fluid. The fetus's heart rate slows down all of a sudden. A minute later, it's undetectable.

The resident is at his side and cleaning up; he can't hide his tears. Abaitua comforts him—the death rate in cases of vasa previa is very high, between sixty and ninety percent. It's never diagnosed until afterward. That's the way it is. The young guy knows that. "If you'd been there when she was admitted, it wouldn't have died," he says. It's half criticism, half praise.

He remembers the first time he ever lost a life. Many years ago. He never thought it would happen, and nobody ever prepared him for it. He had to learn it for himself. That's what's happens with all of the most important things in life—how to find love, how to face up to death—and everybody seems to accept that that's the way it is.

Arrese shoves open the door, and it swings back and forth for a long time. It's a habit that drives Abaitua up the wall, even more so now, when he's just told a stretcher-bearer to please respect the tranquility befitting of the setting. Arrese wants to know what's happened to make the man in the waiting room so shaken up, and Abaitua feels a trace of satisfaction when he tells him. A vasa previa we got to too late.

Arrese's expression doesn't change. He shrugs.

"Shit happens."

"Somebody's going to have to tell the father."

There are only two residents remaining, the rest have all left at some point—the chubby neonatologist resident, who'd been there shortly before, isn't there any more—and they both take a step backward instinctively. The anesthesiologist and two nurses are looking after the mother in silence, and another nurse is gently cleaning the dead baby. Abaitua knows that in the end, he'll be the one who has to tell the father, but he doesn't think it fair to accept that fact right away, just like that. He isn't to blame. He's about to say that his myomectomy patient has been waiting for him for a long time now, when the supervisor comes in. The father's kicking up a real fuss, and they can't calm him down. The supervisor, too, is highly agitated, beside herself, and Arrese asks her to calm down. He orders her to calm down. "*Calma al pueblo*" is what he says—let there be peace. Abaitua is certain about what Arrese is going to tell them. He's going to repeat once more the recommendation given to him by his professor of obstetrics at Zaragoza for this type of situation. And Abaitua is right, that's just what he does. If a child dies in birth and, consequently, the father shows signs of getting overexcited, the thing to do is to tell him, with all the seriousness one would expect from such circumstances, that they've done everything humanly possible to save the baby's life but, unfortunately, they haven't managed to, and that now it's the mother's life that's at risk and so they would like him to settle down, to let the doctors and nurses get on with their work, and if he is a believer, he should pray for science to achieve a miracle with God's help.

"*Mano de santo*," he says—hand to God, it works. And he mimes washing his hands. Fortunately, nobody laughs. Without waiting any longer, Abaitua says that he'll tell the father.

Stick to the truth and admit mistakes, if there are any. When you behave like that and share people's pain, they understand and forgive. He thinks that's what the residents should be told. He asks the young guy from Otzeta if he's up to speaking to the father, and he nods in reply.

SOMETIMES, AS HE WALKS PAST THE ICU, he thinks he'd like to lie down on a bed right there. The atmosphere is calm, the lighting is low, the slow beeps of the various electronic devices make it even more peaceful; a murmur of voices is all you hear, and the only thing you have to take care of is your own breathing. When he tells the head of the department this, his reply is that the ICU isn't always as peaceful as right now, he should come back when there are people running around during emergencies and shouting hysterically, when the alarm sirens don't stop ringing out. "We had four just this morning". His face expresses his regret. Four deaths. Four cases that will do nothing to improve his statistics. Death, at the end of the day, is a professional failure for doctors.

Abaitua asks after Teresa Hoyos's husband, but his colleague doesn't dare give a prognosis.

Teresa Hoyos is sitting in the ICU waiting room. There's another person there, too. An older woman who's staring down the corridor. He's in the bay farthest from them, and he observes them through a gap in the blind. Teresa Hoyos is reading a book. She's dressed in black—a blouse and pants, and light, open shoes, which are also black. Shoes that are almost like slippers, to be more comfortable in the hospital. He thinks about going to say hello but doesn't feel up to it.

IT'S THE SECOND TIME ABAITUA has walked past the library. Lynn is in there. He knows that because of the chubby resident, who told him when he walked past him in the hallway, as if he already guessed he was looking for her. Finally, he ventures to stick his head around the door. Lynn smiles at him, and he guesses she's said "*hi.*" She's wearing a pistachio green dress with a zipper running from top to bottom on the front of it.

He thinks, just for a moment, about opening her dress. It's short and rises halfway up her thighs when she sits down. Her peach-colored down shines in the sunlight. As does the braid of steel smokestacks he can see through the window, pushing out thick smoke that dissipates only very slowly in the blue sky. He's often wanted to find out what type of smoke it is, but he never has. He thinks he's heard that white smoke isn't harmful. The nearby hills. He tells Lynn their names: Adarra, Onddo, and Aballarri, but he isn't sure which is which. He tells her about his hikes, stopping for a break at the small megalithic site at Mulisko Gaina, where he still sometimes feels like one of the successors of the people who first placed those stones there, and where his feeling that he's part of the surroundings becomes much stronger. He tells her—even though he admits it's nonsense—that from time to time, he thinks he'd like to give himself up to the melancholy that identifying with that landscape inspires him to feel.

She asks if he'll take her there one day. Of course he will. They could drive to Besabi that very afternoon, but he prefers to say that he has to have lunch with Loiola, even though it isn't true. That had been his intention, but the boy called to say he couldn't make it because he had to go to the US consulate in Bilbao. He was determined to speak to him once and for all about taking security precautions. He had that idea in mind, and so, before hanging up the phone, he told him to be careful. "What do I have to be careful about?" his son asked him, but he responded evasively "Everything—driving, life . . ." He didn't think it was something to talk about on the phone.

"So we won't see each other again until tomorrow." Abaitua doesn't want their meeting up to become a habit. So he says that's right, he doesn't think they'll see each other before that, and she shows her disappointment by shrugging in such an exaggerated way that it's comical. She says she doesn't know if she'll be able to last that long. Then, after looking toward the table where the librarian is sitting, she puts her finger on her lips to ask for silence, like the nurse on the poster, and whispers that she knows a place.

Surprised by his own daring, he follows her down the stairs to the basement. Somewhere he's never been before. They only person they walk past in the long corridor is a single blue-coverall-wearing man; he's pushing a trolley full of bags of clothes. There isn't much light. They only thing they hear is the continual sound of machines, perhaps a pump, and the atmosphere is gloomy, almost sinister. After looking carefully left and right, Lynn opens the only door without a sign on it and takes him into a space that's barely as wide as his dressing room at home. The dim light inside it comes from the neighboring room through a gap at ceiling level. There's white clothing on the metal shelves that run along the three walls. Abaitua teases her for knowing about the place, and Lynn teases him back by saying that he's the only doctor who doesn't know about it. They hold each other and kiss while leaning against the door, she smiles happily seeing he's getting an erection. Impressed too, he'd say. He's astonished by the heat of his own desire. It's easy to open her dress. She, on the other hand, has trouble taking his pants off, first the belt buckle, then the catch inside the waistband, and she seems to be losing her patience. He doesn't know if she really is. She says "shit!" But when he tries to help her, she hits his hand away. "It's like you're wearing armor." And Abaitua has his doubts again about just how annoyed she actually is at his lack of foresight in choosing pants that are so difficult for her to get off—and she really wants to take them off—but just in case, he tells her seriously that he'll never wear these pants—which she's pulling off his ankles at last—again.

He's really turned on. About to lose his balance, he grabs onto a shelf with both hands. There isn't space enough to lie down. When he hugs her, she whispers in his ear that she's getting turned on. He gets the same message from her swollen labia, open, lubricated vagina, and erect clitoris. When she reaches down to his penis, her cold hand makes him cry out. She whispers "Shh!" in his ear, but he can't keep from moaning. He has to cry out—he needs to. He could shout, he's never felt so full of desire. He doesn't mind covering the hand over his mouth with his saliva.

He falls down on his knees, sobbing, and she goes down with him, asking him to stop the laughter he's unable to silence, because they can hear voices on the other side of the wall, at least those of a man and a woman. He has trouble breathing, he has to open his mouth to breathe and manages to tear her hand away from his mouth using considerable force. Now she tries to silence his cries by putting her mouth over his, happy about the amount of pleasure she's giving him, but that only livens his flame, and she strokes his face, covered in sweat and saliva, whispering that they're going to be heard, but he doesn't care. That's the main thing he's feeling—he wouldn't mind if the door opened and the whole hospital saw him fucking this girl.

Lynn wraps her legs around his waist, her arms around his neck, and he holds her up with one hand on her back and the other on her ass. He doesn't think he'd be able to hold Pilar like that.

KEPA'S CALL FROM LONDON. He's been book hunting and is very pleased. Among other things, he's bought a facsimile of the first book on obstetrics ever published in Great Britain, back in the sixteenth century. Another one about medicine in the Middle Ages. He says they're very interesting books and seems to have read them already. He tells him about various passages and gives a lot of details. Apparently, at one time, in order to induce labor—because there was no oxytocin back then—they used to beat women, literally, with whips. He suggests Abaitua should look into developing the technique. Or, otherwise, the variant used by a German empress who, in order to make her own labor process easier, had twenty men whipped—also literally—during the dilation and delivery phases, and two of them were whipped to their deaths. Abaitua says he'll have to tell him all about the various techniques when he comes back, because it doesn't sound like he's finished. He doesn't seem to have any awareness that talking on the phone costs money. "OK, OK, I won't disturb you anymore." Abaitua feels guilty and asks him if he's made any good deals. He answers that he's on the trail of a very important discovery, about which, for obvious reasons, he can't say any more over the phone.

The stairway down to the river is made of gray granite. The last two steps are covered in very thick, almost black moss. Several balusters are missing, and only one of the four fruit basket-shaped iron capitals that once decorated the first and last pairs of shafts are still in place. Some small violet-colored flowers are growing there. It reminds him of an expression in *Montauk*: "obstinate nature."

Ignoring everything he sees to the left and the right and only looking forward, he could almost mistake the part of the baluster that's still standing, and the vegetation dangling down over the river and lying on its surface, for a boat on Lake Como, though one in very poor condition, that's for sure.

They're coming from the parking lot. They are around a dozen of them, he recognizes Pilar among them immediately, because of her beige suit. And Arrese, too, and Orl. He thinks they must have had lunch at Miramon. He finds it very strange to see Pilar talking with other people without realizing that he's there. Without any connection to him, without him, in the middle of her own life. She takes the arm of somebody whose face he can't see, and they move away from the group to do something in private, to explain something—that's what it looks like. The others go in, and Pilar and the person with her are the last to follow.

At one time, he used to wait for her on occasion on one of the benches at the entrance to the parking lot. Never at the clinic itself. He always had the impression that she was glad to see him. Even the times when she would come out with the young surgeon—when she realized that he, Abaitua, was there, she would quickly say goodbye to the young surgeon and run to greet him. He never had the sensation that she was put out by his turning up there.

Once, from the same slope he's on now, he saw the two of them come out of the building together, as on other occasions, and instead of walking up to her to greet her, he hid behind the high voltage shed. The pair walked down the stairs and over to a VW Beetle, talking in a lively way as they went. They carried on talking for a while, each from opposite sides of the car's hood, and then they got in and left together. That night, she told Abaitua about him without him even having to ask her. He was a good kid, a little naïve, but charming, and she was sorry that her brother-in-law wouldn't let him try out the new surgery techniques he wanted to.

Something else he read in *Montauk*: "A man who does not notice that a woman has come to him from another bed is no truly amorous man."

Going around the blocks of houses and along the riverbank, he reaches the train stop in less than ten minutes.

Lynn is in the garden, bending down behind some plants with a watering can in her hand, that's what it looks like to him. She's wearing a wide-brimmed straw hat and blue denim overalls. Suitable clothing for gardening. She seems to take everything she does very seriously. She's frowning and has her serious child look on. He sees her from up on the old road, sheltered by the reeds. He doesn't hide himself. If she were to see him, unlikely though that is, he would say hello and then tell her the first thing that came to mind—Loiola cancelled their lunch; he left the clinic to go for a walk . . .

SHE GETS UP, LEAVES HER FLOWERS, and greets the writer, who's just appeared in the doorway, by taking her hat off. He's wearing a bathrobe and is holding an open book in both hands. They speak—mostly it's the writer speaking—and it looks like they're talking about flowers, because they point at them from time to time and lean over to look at them. Lynn is just as tall as Martin.

Her hat hangs down from one hand, and she holds her other hand up to shield her eyes. Her copper-colored hair shines in the sun. He thinks she really is beautiful, and he likes thinking about how he's embraced that body, drunk from her breasts. He could go up to her into the garden and kiss her right on the mouth, to the writer's astonishment. And Lynn would laugh. *"But what is this!"* That's what she said in the hospital laundry room. *Che passione!* He finds the idea amusing.

He walks back the way he came and decides to go as far as Okendotegi to kill time. When he gets back, if she's still speaking with the writer, he'll go home.

Due to his weak but persistent intention not to see her in the afternoon, they never set up their dates beforehand. But he always phones first to say he's coming, so as not to just barge in on her. And also to make sure that she's alone and will open the tower door for him, which doesn't have a bell, so that he won't have to go along the glass gallery. And to give her the chance to say that they can't meet up, if need be.

While he waits for her to pick up, he imagines the cat lying on the green travel blanket on the sofa, looking at the telephone ringing on the triangular coffee table in the middle of the room. He wonders what he would feel if she didn't pick up, or if she told him she couldn't see him because she had friends over. He's ready for that and doesn't think he'd mind too much. He doesn't want to see her all the time, either, and he doesn't always tell her the truth. Perhaps being turned down would hurt him a little bit, his pride would be hurt. He's thought more than once about the fact that the day will have to arrive sometime, the day when they, like Frisch and the Lynn in the novel, will say goodbye and promise to send each other a postcard once a year, both knowing that they probably won't.

He sometimes fantasizes about the idea of seeing her holding hands with another man, with the young man she really should be with, the man she'll have children with, and when that scene comes to mind—it's rather abstract for him, probably because the man has no face—he doesn't feel sad.

"Hi." Happiness in her voice. His son had to go to Bilbao, so he's free in the end and felt like stretching his legs, and so on. He's in the neighborhood and could come by if she wants to make coffee. She

tells him to come right away. He sits down at the train stop to delay himself a little. Not too long, because it's not a very agreeable place and he doesn't have anything to read, and when it comes down to it, he doesn't mind if she finds out he was lying.

LYNN STICKS HER HEAD OUT after opening the door completely. They do not give each other a kiss. It isn't a habit of theirs, perhaps because they don't want to feel like strangers when they greet each other with other people around. What's more, as soon as she opens the door, the cat lies down at his feet, offering its gray, almost white belly for him to pet. It starts purring immediately, making a noise like a saw, like some device that starts up as soon as you press the button. Lynn, leaning against the wall, watches him, glad he gets along well with the cat. "The doctor's got great hands, doesn't he, Max?"

She squats down to join in petting the cat. *"You're insatiable, Max."* Abaitua takes his hands away, so that they won't brush against hers. He knows that if they touch, their fingers will link together, they'll hug, and, holding each other, he'll lead her to the sofa and, once there, quickly take her clothes off. Sometimes they find themselves naked on the sofa as soon as he puts his foot in the door, without even speaking a word. That youthful energy is a fine memory for him, to look at it one way, but he doesn't think it's appropriate for her to let him always have his way, he doesn't want her to think he's some horny old man whose only reason for seeing her is to satisfy his sexual drive, for her to think that's the only thing about her that interests him.

Now they're standing up again, face to face, and she asks for his jacket. He gives it to her, and she caresses the cloth after folding it. She says it's soft. He bought it in London a long time ago, in one of those glass-fronted galleries near St. James's. Sometimes he remembers that type of thing. They stand by the door as if they were each waiting for the other to make the decision to finally go in. Lynn's changed clothes. She's taken her overalls off and is wearing a short dress with flowers on it, it's made of something like silk and has large vents on either side. Liberty pattern. He thinks she wears it more often since he told her he likes it. He tells her again, and she thanks him. He's always thought that particular form of politeness is too much, thanking others for praising something you've bought, or somebody you've invited to a meal in a restaurant for praising the food or the good service—as if you had something to do with it. It isn't part of his own culture, certainly. He tells this to Lynn, and she argues that what you're thanking people for is appreciating your good taste in choosing things. "You're a piece of work, you know that?" Many people have said that to him, but Lynn seems to find it amusing.

He feels good like this, the two of them just talking. Just as in the meetings they both attend, he's able to observe her measured gestures—she moves her hands more, her arms less so—and how she chooses her words with care, apparently unaware of his itching desire, which he'd like to keep in check because otherwise he'll feel guilty afterward and run away.

So they go on talking, each at either end of the sofa. Even the clumsiest observer would see what they are, because while he is correctly dressed—only his jacket, which he's hung on the back of a chair, is missing—she's barefoot, and her flowery dress comes halfway up her thighs. An older man visiting a young woman, going through the necessary ritual of talking about whatever before getting down to other things. He also thinks he could be imagined to be a parent visiting his daughter. In fact, he's often thought that they could be taken for father and daughter, an idea that probably isn't very healthy.

Iñaki.

When her questions are genuine ones, when she really wants to ask them, and actually wants to find something out, she normally says his name first. "*Iñaki, what do you think about it?*" *Tell me* is another expression she uses. "*Tell me, what do you think about it?*" As to why she always asks him in English, he thinks it's so he won't find her questions so direct.

Her question now: "*Iñaki, how do you say 'home birth' in Spanish?*"

He thinks she's asked him before what he thinks about home births. He isn't against them but doesn't approve of promoting them "artificially" either. If, for some reason, there were a lot of demand for them, he wouldn't disapprove, but the system would have to be adapted to deal with it—the telephone and ambulance emergency services would have to be adjusted—in order to offer the best conditions for birthing. Why does she ask?

"Somebody told me."

He thinks it's another way she has of bringing up a subject, first mentioning a purely linguistic side to the topic she wants to discuss so that when they get into it, it seems to be a logical continuation.

To cut a long story short, if there is a story, Julia's family used to have a *baserri* called Sagastizabal, much of which has now been lost, taken over by the Elektra electricity plant, and one of her cousins wants to recover part of it and use it for growing ecological products. So far, he's done up the old shed, planted apple trees, and built planting boxes. The thing is, his spouse, an indigenous woman from Peru, is pregnant and wants to give birth at home, because according to her traditions, it's a way for her to become part of the new family home. That's what she's understood. As far as the Sagastizabal man is concerned, apparently he wants to combine respect for his Peruvian spouse's superstitions with his son's right to have the safest possible conditions for birth. So Abaitua suspects that Lynn has volunteered to sound him out about delivering the baby in a farm shed in who knows what sort of conditions in order to respect some useless, outdated cultural tradition. Suddenly he's angry that Lynn has accepted this role as intermediary and, above all, that she's made their relationship public knowledge. Surely she doesn't think he'll go supervise a birth in some farmhouse shed, he says, making no effort to cover up the fact that he's angry. She says no, that it hadn't even occurred to her.

She already knows what he's like when he gets angry.

Forcing herself to smile, she asks what sort of morning he's had.

It's been quite a hard day. The change of subject reminds him of the vasa previa. He considers telling her about it, telling her about his annoyance at not being able to reach the birthing room earlier, saying that if his diagnosis had been quick and correct, a quarter of an hour would have been enough to save the child's life. He wouldn't like to give her an incomplete explanation by covering up the reason why he got there late. But even so, as a way of apologizing for his bad mood, and with Lynn curled up on his lap and asking him to tell her what happened, he can't think of anything better than to tell her about the events in the birthing room, though without much enthusiasm. He realized what was happening right away, as soon as he saw the woman, something the resident from Otzeta wasn't able to pick up on because of his lack of experience. Now he doesn't know which of the two feelings is stronger: his sorrow for the parents who've lost their child—real sorrow, he has no need to fake it—or his sorrow at the death itself, the young guy's first, knowing how horrible he must feel about it. He thinks he can be sincere with Lynn about that, he doesn't think she could interpret anything untoward from his telling her about this doubt.

He also mentions to her—seeing how moved she obviously is by what he's been telling her—that he decided to take the young guy with him to inform the father about his child's death. It was something very sad to see and, in a way, beautiful. It was very touching to see the two young men embrace. So much so that he found it hard to keep back his tears. Lynn has the same difficulty as she listens, her eyes go shiny and she says "*pobrecito*"—poor thing. Abaitua doesn't know who she's saying it about. And he doesn't ask her. Poor him, too, having to admit his own cowardice. Suddenly the urge to open his heart to her, tell her how it all happened, without omitting the fact that he'd meekly let Arrese drag him into his office. When, in order to lessen the resident from Otzeta's sense of guilt, he told him that there's a long chain of responsibility behind every mistake, he felt the urge to admit what he'd been hiding—in other words, the fact that he himself was the main culprit. He doesn't know where that urge comes from—perhaps it has something to do with his Catholic upbringing—and it's an urge he distrusts somewhat, because it would also be a way of behaving aggressively toward Lynn, a way of testing to what extent she would be able to stand seeing the real him.

But then he would have to tell her why he's afraid of Arrese, and about Teresa Hoyos.

Instead of revealing all his shortcomings, he decides to come clean about another issue, which, in fact, was where this whole thing started, and so he goes back to the story of the Peruvian woman in Sagastizabal. He admits, without trying to excuse himself for it, that demands and requests made by people from the Third World, not to mention their proclamations about their identity, make him uncomfortable. He has sometimes wondered why and thinks it may be connected with the structure of his character, which is intolerant, when it comes down to it.

It also ocurrs to him that the fact that culture tyrannizes the individual, (and it's easier to see the speck, not to mention the beam, in your brother's eye than it is in your own), that fidelity to sacred traditions is a form of submission, and that pride in one's own culture may be simply pathetic, forces him to question his own fidelity to his parents' culture and wonder whether being rooted in something, being attached to something, might not be overrated, might be no more than an underground version of beating around the bush, as somebody once put it. Confronted by extreme fanaticism of a foreign variety, he is forced to ask himself whether he has the right not only to impose his own traditions, whether genuine or invented—that's the least important part of it—but whether it's legitimate for him to even bother the majority of people, who are not part of his culture, with them. In other words, resisting new minority groups' exotic needs unavoidably brings with it a questioning of the reasonableness of his feelings about his own origins. And perhaps he should be grateful for that lesson, which breaks his heart in two. That's definitely too extreme a way to put it, but they're the only words he can find to say it. He has to make a joke. Their own voices fall quiet, embarrassed by the anachronistic voices of others come from afar, and in fact, when he sits down underneath the Eteneta menhir, they only speak to him now about the decay of the landscape.

But Lynn laughs and says that at least they'll be speaking about it to him in Basque, and he answers "*of course*," even though he isn't sure. Because Unamuno's is one of those voices (and he, too, is an ancestor of his, when it comes down to it), but even though he used to try not to listen to it, it hurts him less and less.

Lynn hasn't heard of Unamuno. She knows of Baroja, because of *Zalacaín el aventurero*—Zalacaín the Adventurer—which Julia gave her to read. She remembers a sentence she particularly liked: "*Mi patria es la montaña*"—my homeland is the mountainside. That reminds Abaitua that one of Baroja's characters said somewhere that he would love to be descended from a humble Pyrenean shepherd. Which he himself almost certainly is. He is almost without a doubt descended from a shepherd who came down from the Pyrenees after the glacial period and settled in Otzeta. As Unamuno said, a people who arrived at culture late on. He was practically the first in his line to come down from the mountains, and it took him two hundred years to assimilate the universal values of the French Revolution. And because of that, in contradiction to his feeling of belonging to a small people and their small culture, he's a late convert to and fundamentalist of the Age of Enlightenment. It's part of the character of those descended from shepherds to be fundamentalists in everything. He hates cultural relativism, the idea that all cultures are flowers of different shades on a field of the same color, just as much as he hates the ecological fundamentalism that holds that everything in nature is wise and good.

Lynn isn't in favor of cultural relativism, either. She doesn't think traditions should be tolerated if they go against fundamental values, but it must be admitted that cultural traditionalism does have positive sides to it, as well. Then she talks to him about the virtues of tolerance and the failure of cultural integration policies—Abaitua doesn't agree with them, either—and the richness of diversity, the advantages of interculturalism compared with cultural diversity, and so on. Very little he didn't know already, but expressed with a degree of clarity and precision he himself is incapable of. He'd forgotten that she's an expert on the subject and is embarrassed by his own attitude, so typically male, of feeling himself qualified to speak about anything at all in front of women.

The record finished a long time ago now.

"CULTURE IS STRONGER THAN LIFE *and stronger than death.*" The quote —she's forgotten who the author is, but it's long, and by the way it reads, it could be a poem—refers to the untameable power of culture, culture being something that can lead men to slice themselves open with swords, to refuse sex for life following a vow of chastity, and a whole stream of strange things she doesn't fully understand, and finally—after making a gesture like somebody closing a picture book and giving Abaitua a soft kiss on the forehead as if he were a pouting child—she adds that it's that which makes an unfortunate indigenous Peruvian woman want to give birth in a farm shed just five hundred yards away from a hospital. She smiles and then holds his chin and kisses him again.

"My intolerant old man."

It isn't the first time she's called him old. On the dunes at Pyla, she called out from a distance, *"Hey, old man."*

Obviously, he has become an intolerant old man, and one who's come to the conclusion that that particular virtue—tolerance— much like elegance, is easier for the rich to nourish than it is for the poor. And as he's told her before, he was poor until recently. This descendent of a shepherd from Otzeta has only just left religious fundamentalism behind. He's seen people cross themselves as they go past churches; seen them run to kiss the cords of every Capuchin, Franciscan, and Carmelite that walked by, and there were a lot of them; had a deaf priest hit him on the head for speaking too softly in confession (speaking in a normal voice would have meant that everyone in the church could hear about his sins); he's seen frightening Holy Weeks, heard furious sermons, *dies irae, dies illa* . . . sometimes he would wake up in the middle of the night, frightened by nightmares about burning for eternity. He's been humiliated, threatened, punished, scared, sexually abused, and mistreated by friars, and although the damage done is irreparable, just when the tyranny of the Church—his church—seemed to be at an end, new fundamentalisms and superstitions belonging to other religions appeared on the scene, new superstitions that are sure to rekindle the intolerance of the religion he was brought up to view as the one and only true one. Only somebody who has recently left poverty behind hates poverty more than the poor do. But Lynn is old money and can afford the elegance of tolerance, to feel sympathy for the poor. Even so, he thinks it's a paternalistic type of tolerance, it seems a bit dumb to him. He remembers what Claudel said about there being special houses for tolerance: "*La tolérance? Il y a des maisons pour ça.*" He's always thought it a good joke, but it isn't funny after having to explain to her that a "*maison de tolérance*" means "a house of ill repute" in French. And instead of laughing, Lynn says she understands.

A little later, she wonders whether it isn't more a matter of patience than tolerance. Holding the cat against her naked chest, her head leaning down toward her right shoulder, her face half hidden by a curl of hair, and Abaitua, just like every time he sees something that moves him, feels he'd like to draw her. The Virgin of Patience. He supposes she must be right, but he doesn't have that virtue. He's impatient, as well as being a xenophobe.

"AN UGLY WORD." She asks the cat, but looking at Abaitua, if it thinks Abaitua can really be a xenophobe. "*What do you think, Max?*" The cat looks at him, too, as if proud to be in its mistress's arms. Now Abaitua has to defend himself from an accusation he's just cast against himself. He is xenophobic, but only a little. Now she looks at the cat while she talks. "But that's not serious. Is it, Max?" Apparently, Lévi-Strauss said a little xenophobia is a good defense mechanism. She thinks that protective reflex, which has its origins in social biology, shouldn't be confused with racism, thinking that we are better people than our neighbors or foreigners. The most important thing, she says, is how we treat each person. It's a question of whether we see a person or an outsider when we see somebody from another place.

She asks if he doesn't agree. She lets go of the cat—it jumps down heavily—and takes ahold of his hands. He has his back against one arm of the sofa, and she's sitting between his legs, facing away from him. She wraps his arms around her and holds his hands on top of her belly. She's sure that if he were to come across the Peruvian woman, he'd try to help her. And she can tell, from the way he holds her hands tighter, that he's felt her urge to move away.

She turns around and smiles at him. *"Would you like a coffee, or anything else?"*

He jokes and asks if she knows how to make anything other than coffee, and she pretends to get angry. He watches her filling the French press from the doorway. The kitchen is clean, perhaps too clean, in fact. That's what Kepa said when he was there. He doesn't want to become part of the daily life of the house, he's trying to avoid that. Kepa, on the other hand, walked all over the place and opened the fridge, the closets, and the drawers as if he were in his own home. It's true that he was busy making the dinner, but then, looking from the doorway just as he is now, he had the impression, even though he'd just made love with Lynn on the sofa, that Kepa was becoming more intimate with her than he was.

The writer's voice, calling to Julia from the floor below, silences them. "Julia, Julia," the voice calls loudly, which makes them guess she's on the ground floor. *"Martin da . . .* it's Martin," says Lynn, obvious though it is, perhaps because it's something she knows how to say in Basque, and that gives him the chance to say he thinks Martin is a strange guy. He's been wanting to talk to her about him. It gives him the chance to tell her about his concerns over the fact that Martin has hired María Amor—indirectly and unwillingly, to put it one way—to take care of his father. Lynn laughs out loud; she already knew that María Amor was a prostitute when he started talking. She asks for details about how it all happened, and somewhat relieved by Lynn's laughter, he gives them. Some days earlier, in Gros, as he was leaving the dentist's, he came across María Amor—more or less bumped into her, in fact—and he asked her out of politeness how things were going with her; she started telling him about her life, saying she felt really bad, degraded, and wanted to stop being a prostitute and all those things some prostitutes say—others say it's a dignified profession and compare it with nursing—but she seemed especially sincere to him for some reason, although he found it pretty uncomfortable speaking with her on a street corner, but then again it wouldn't have been any better inviting her to go to a bar. There he was, listening to María Amor with great patience, when he saw the writer a couple of steps away. They gestured hello to one another, but the writer didn't move, just stood there waiting for his conversation with María Amor to finish, but she, too, became aware of his presence and stared at him, so Abaitua had no choice but to take a step toward him and introduce them. He introduced Martin as a writer and María Amor just by her name. He was about to say she was a nurse and let him think what he would, but he didn't feel it was right to do that, above all because he would have realized what she actually was as soon as she started talking, that was why he had only said her name to introduce her, and she added that she liked people to call her Maite. That was new. And then the writer apologized to them, fairly formally, for having interrupted their talk and said he had a serious problem because his father needed someone to take care of him twenty-four hours a day and he was having trouble finding a good nurse to fit in at his home—he explained that his mother and sister were unusual, difficult women—and on seeing Abaitua, he thought that perhaps there was some sort of list of professional caregivers at the hospital and that he might be able to give him the name of somebody trustworthy. Abaitua was absolutely amazed that Martin should stop him on the street for that reason, and he was about to get out of it—he didn't know anybody, and he wouldn't have dared to expose anybody to him even if he did—when María Amor clapped her hands together and said that he, Martin, had been sent by the Virgin of Mercy, protectoress of the Dominican Republic, herself, because she was "*una enfermera especialista en viejitos*"—a nurse specializing in old men—and she had just been telling the doctor that she was looking for work, and the writer, delighted, asked for her telephone number so that they could arrange a meeting. Abaitua didn't know

508

what to do. The Dominican woman gave him two big kisses and walked away—she, too, was pleased—and he almost went after the writer to explain the confusion, but he left it at that, thinking it would be easier to sort it out over the phone, but later he found it more and more difficult and didn't know how he could possibly explain it to him and just hoped that the writer wouldn't end up getting in touch with María Amor because there must be plenty of other women available for looking after old people.

Lynn's laughter makes him feel better about it again—when it comes down to it, the whole thing's comical. It's a good idea to let prostitutes look after infirm old men. Her laughter ends up being a bit excessive. She doubles over and says, *"I can't believe it,"* again and again, and he has to wait for her to calm down, that's how funny she finds it all. He thinks they must be able to hear them very well from the floor below, and imagining the writer wondering what Lynn is laughing so much about makes him laugh, too. Lynn has fun imagining how the story might end, and she laughs even more as she pictures the possible scenes, and that goes on for a while, until she asks him if she can tell Julia, so that she, too, can have a good laugh at the idea of a whore being hired to work in Martin's parents' house. He doesn't have to say he thinks it's a bad idea, it's obvious from his expression. She promises she'll keep quiet and tries to reassure him, using the same argument he himself already arrived at: being such a showy woman, it isn't very likely that Martin could ever think her a good fit for his parents' home, and he probably just took her number down out of politeness.

It must be late, although it's still light outside. The top of a tree—he doesn't know what type of tree it is, but it doesn't have many leaves on it—is swaying around in the wind, and the sound comes in through the gap in the sash window above the sofa, which isn't very agreeable. He isn't what you'd call particularly handy, but he thinks he would be able to repair it if he had a screwdriver.

Lynn has that screwdriver. She gives it to him and kneels on the sofa while she watches him fixing it. He thinks she's happy that he, the man, is taking care of repairing something in the house. Domestic life. He manages it halfway, changing the position of an iron fitting that had been preventing the blind from coming down completely. But she congratulates him for having solved the whole problem, even though now, because the crack is smaller, the sound of the wind coming in is even shriller. They're both kneeling naked on the sofa and looking out through the window. The meander in the river, the clinic roof and its almost empty parking lot, the reeds, the mooring place, and the mastless yacht, which looks as though it's been shipwrecked.

Lynn asks him what he's thinking about.

About the boat. He once hoped to repair it, too, but has never gotten around to it, partly out of laziness, but also because he didn't want to ask the old man for his permission. So when Loiola told him that he wanted to repair it enough to be able to take it to a shipyard in Pasaia and that he had his grandfather's permission to do so, he was glad, but at the same time disappointed, because he'd been left out of it. When Loiola started using his motorboat without asking him first, he had mixed feelings: on the one hand, he was glad his son had taken to the sea, and on the other hand, he found it frustrating that he had done so in secret. One of the other people who used the mooring told him that his son had been going there along with some friends of his, but Abaitua had already realized from the way the motorboat was moored. Why did he pretend not to notice? Answering that question was the most difficult thing for him when the police interrogated him. How could he say that he felt fulfilled by his son using the motorboat and that he wanted the boy to tell him about it himself, because it would have been a way for him to free himself from an old regret. The police, understandably, asked him the same question time and again. Why hadn't he done anything when he realized that the boat was being used secretly? Why didn't he do anything to find out what the boys were doing on the old yacht? How was it that he didn't show more of an interest in what his son was up to? What kind of father was he? They were hours of great anxiety, and he was very worried about the consequences it might have for them. He broke down. The police interrogated him with some degree of respect but also made it clear that the atmosphere could change completely depending on his answers, and in fact, he felt the urge to tell them the most terrible things he could think of, even if they were completely irrelevant. So he told them things that would have been more appropriate on a psychologist's couch, saying he felt incredibly happy on the afternoon he first saw, because of the way the moorings were tied up, that his son had been going out to sea, thinking it meant he had gotten over an awful thing that he, the boy's father, had made him go through on a fishing expedition when he was a child. It was one morning when the seafaring conditions were excellent, and they saw a school of mackerel almost as soon as they got past the breakwater, and the fish went for everything they threw at them. He kept on reeling them in, fired up because the mackerel were biting, and that brought out his primitive instinct, he kept on casting out and hauling them in, and his son, meanwhile, was sitting next to him, bent over a tangle of lines he was trying to undo. He ordered him to stop that and use his rod, he'd grab another one for himself, but Loiola tangled that one up, too, and he got angry at his son's clumsiness. They were going to lose the fish. He shouted at him that he was useless; there he was, standing and surrounded by bloodied mackerels that still hadn't stopped jumping around, covered in blood himself. The boy started sobbing and mumbling that he felt sorry for the fish, which was the last straw for him. Beside himself, as frustrated as he was angry about that sign of weakness, he started throwing the mackerel overboard, not worrying about cutting his hands on the fins, furious, swearing, until he became exhausted by what he was doing. And then he saw himself, surrounded by mackerels, their white bellies shining in the sun, and the child with a tangled up line in his lap, crying. Then he realized that he would never forget that scene, and neither would his son. If there was one event in his life he would never be able to get out of his mind, that was going to be it.

Lynn says she'd like to meet his son. It isn't the first time she's said that. He finds the idea of seeing Lynn and Loiola together frightening and attractive in equal measure. They're almost the same age. She offers to help Loiola if he needs contacts in the States. She asks if he'd like to go to Nevada.

No way. Abaitua would rather he went to Georgetown, or any other Jesuit university. It would be pathetic for him to decide to go to the States and then take shelter in a Basque community there, if there is such a thing. They talk about Nevada. Since neither of them have ever been there, they talk about what they've heard. Abaitua isn't at all moved by the survival of a Basque community that's supposed to be protecting his identity there. He isn't really sure of his opinion, but that's what he says, perhaps in order to be consistent. Having expressed his reticence when it comes to immigrants remaining ensconced in their cultures of origin (to the extent to which that means refusing the local culture), he doesn't think he can praise his compatriots for holding on tightly to their own. People tend to be highly contradictory about that. The Spanish don't want to be invaded by English, but then they seem pleased that more and more Spanish is being spoken in Times Square. He thinks that Basques—except when it comes to missing certain things, particularly the gastronomy—tend to integrate quite well, and in fact, he doesn't feel particularly sympathetic toward the cultural synthesis between Basque shepherds and barbecue-loving, Republican-voting cowboys that gets showcased so often in Basque Television documentaries. He has no doubt that he has more in common with educated people from Madrid or with Parisians than with that Basque community in Nevada. He's never admitted as much, and he thinks it's terribly scornful of him, but because he can say anything to this American girl who's sitting there listening to him so attentively, he follows his urge to go further and says that he has less and less in common with his friends from his summers spent in Otzeta as a child—each time he sees them, their fingers as thick as blood sausages, they ask him, in their village Basque, which becomes cruder year by year, if he couldn't use an assistant.

(Lynn, who doesn't seem to want to contradict him, says what they both already know: there are going to be fewer and fewer people with singular identities. In the future, it will be normal to be like her, someone from New York who feels Basque. She says this in Basque, and quite good Basque at that.)

They hear the writer calling out to Julia again. Julia doesn't answer him, or they don't hear her because of the train going by, one of the ones that don't stop there. Then there's silence as Lynn breathes over his moist belly. "*Maite zaitut,*" she whispers, "I love you."

He doesn't find sperm revolting, at least not as much as Lynn thinks he does; she thinks he's more of a prude than he really is. From what he's read, finding sperm revolting, like not wanting to ejaculate, is because spilling the seed means the death of desire. It seems logical to him. While Lynn pretends to provoke him by playing with his fluid, he expresses more revulsion than he really feels. He isn't uncomfortable about her playing with his penis, which is tired and soft, though he does feel the need to excuse himself, so he apologizes for his situation by using a Spanish cliché: "*Dura lo que dura dura*"—a somewhat vulgar adage that basically means "love only lasts as long as *it's* long." The expression cracks her up, and her loud laugh, which must be heard throughout the building, goes on for a long time, until she tires. Then, seriously, she says that it isn't true, it's a complete lie. She continues repeating it while she kisses his belly.

Now Lynn has her head resting on his shoulder and her hand on what is still, fortunately, his flat belly. He smells her skin, intense and sweet at the same time. The coffee cups and milk jug shine on the small triangular table. The glass in the frame of a painting on top of the closet is shiny, too. She says she has to show it to the writer, she thinks it might be valuable. An antique, she says. Abaitua doesn't think it is. Everything looks old to Lynn. She didn't know it was Our Lady of Mount Carmel. Apparently, bliss being ignorant, she thought it was the Immaculate Conception, and he has to explain to her that the Immaculate Conception is usually depicted in a white tunic and a blue shawl with shafts of light coming out of her hands—or, at least, he thinks so—while Our Lady of Mount Carmel, on the other hand, is dark-skinned and has scapulars dangling from her hands. She doesn't know what scapulars are, and he explains, more or less. And, of course, she teases him for knowing so much about virgins.

Inevitably, he remembers that there was a large painting of Our Lady of Mount Carmel on the wall across from his bed in his grand-parents' house in Otzeta where he was sent to stay in the summers. She hovered over several souls in purgatory that were surrounded by flames and had expressions of fearful suffering on their faces, their hands clasped together and begging her to take them out of there and up to heaven. Things were always very strict in his grandparents' dark house, he would miss his mother a lot, and because one of the suffering souls in purgatory looked very much like her, the picture made him sad and he'd have trouble sleeping. What he tells her seems to really move Lynn, she sits up on the sofa and puts her arm around his shoulders—just like Our Lady of Sorrows around the recumbent Christ—and she kisses his eyes and says poor, poor thing. It's the first time anybody has ever comforted him for that childhood suffering, and he feels that an old sorrow has been laid to rest. Poor little thing. Abaitua has realized that Lynn likes him to talk about his childhood; whenever he tells her about any memory from the distant past, he sees how moved she is when he looks in her eyes. He wonders if that might be what he most likes about her.

He isn't sure if it was John Paul II who abolished purgatory, so to speak. He read somewhere that the Catholic Church inventing purgatory, somewhere between heaven and hell, was its most profitable innovation, opening the way to a highly lucrative market in indulgences. The disappointing thing for him was that the abolition of purgatory didn't make him feel any better. It was as if he'd already been through it.

And even so, he finds it strange to say that he isn't a Christian; perhaps he is, to an extent, because officially he's still a Catholic. It seems his atheistic convictions aren't strong enough for him to go through all the administrative steps involved in officially declaring his own apostasy. In any case, he doesn't like the word *apostasy*. He isn't a dogmatic atheist or rationalist; atheist fundamentalists seem almost as mean to him as religious fundamentalists—people who, in their humble arrogance, believe they can solve everything just by arguing that two and two are four.

It's pretty easy to explain how he gave up religion. Come a certain moment, he decided that being a Christian was too difficult, and he gave up trying. Then, after taking that first step, and as happens always, the easiest thing was to keep on going. He gets on well without God. He seldom feels any need to think about the meaning of life or the universe. On the occasions he's tried to read about astrophysics, cosmology, black holes, stellar infinity, and such matters, he feels truly anxious, sincerely feels the danger of falling into madness by getting sucked into unfathomable voids. As far as religion is concerned, it was never a consolation for him, though it had been a source of sadness and suffering with regard to both life and imagining death. He thinks he was an emotional boy, sensitive, to put it tactfully. He had a bad time at the religious boarding school he went to. He doesn't think he's ever felt as miserable again as he did at that school, though he can't reproach his parents for it, because they thought they were doing what was best for him by sending him to such an expensive place. It wasn't cheap, and because of that, he had to put up not only with being mistreated at school but also with hearing his mother say how much they were sacrificing on his behalf. He has to admit that some of his classmates didn't seem to have any trouble with that type of education; they took in the friars' threats of eternal flames, in addition to the terrible illnesses they would suffer beforehand, without being overly worried by them, and they'd carry on masturbating happily, even though the consequence if they, the masturbators, were caught by the friar on night duty was that they, along with everybody else, would be dragged out of bed and forced to run around the playground in their pajamas in the middle of winter so that they'd be too tired to give in to the temptations presented to them by the devil.

Pilar is astonished that he suffered so much at the friars' school, and from what she says, she didn't have such a bad time at her boarding school with the nuns. She often says she finds religions aesthetically attractive—prayer books with covers in mother of pearl, silver rosaries, tulle veils, medals, lighting candles and offering the Virgin Mary flowers, singing in processions and passing around piggy banks to collect money for poor Chinese families. When she went to confession, for instance, she used to decide which sins to confess to, making sure they were ones the chaplain would like, including some things that weren't even sins, things like breaking a promise not to eat sweets all week. She found the sinister side of it fun, too. For instance, sometimes she would wear a spiked belt, out of a strange sense of curiosity—she only wore it very loose, of course—and because the nuns liked her wearing it. She never worried about receiving communion after eating a large breakfast or even, in fact, after committing a sin, which was something—something no short of sacrilege—that he wouldn't even think about doing, even now. He knows what it is to have sat alone on that long bench while the others lined up for communion, thus making it very obvious that he'd committed some sin after going to confession the night before. Why were all those wretched masturbators able to ignore all the cruel threats and take the blessed sacrament in their two hands with their heads bowed and he couldn't?

He thought it was amazing that when he bumped into old schoolmates, many of them, though not all of them, had happy memories of the place and made light of all the cruelty and mistreatment and abuse they'd been subjected to ("We used to call Brother Aniceto 'Mittens,' because he was always copping feels), and he found it impossible to understand that they were now sending their own sons to the very same school, even though they had other options, saying that a bit of discipline would do them good.

It's often the ones who used to play soccer. He preferred drawing, he was introverted, and the friars didn't like that. He guesses he wasn't very quick-witted, either. He remembers that once, in class, a friar had given them what seemed to him to be irrefutable evidence of the existence of God. He drew four trees inside a circle. The fourth had grown from a seed from the third. Right. The third from a seed from the second. Right. The second from one from the first. But who made the first? The unavoidable answer was that it had been God. He thinks it's Saint Thomas's second proof, the proof from efficient cause. He, Abaitua, wasn't intelligent enough to ask who created the creator of the first tree. He didn't think of the question until he knew there was no answer to it. Which was after he was quite a bit older, he thinks.

He was probably also quite a bit older at the time when he found himself still worrying about the mysteries of life. He has a vague memory that a friar—perhaps the same one who demonstrated God's existence—told them about the birds and the bees. He doesn't know how old he was then, but he'd reached the conclusion on his own that parents had children because they ate the same food. Apparently, he thought that his parents eating at the same table was more significant than them sharing the same bed. Sometimes he comforts himself by thinking about how he came up with that theory at quite a young age, an age when the others weren't even thinking about the issue, and about how that must mean that he was a bright, thoughtful kid. But in fact, it must have been a much later thought process, because he also remembers the arguments he came up with to counter his theory—why did some people not have children even though they ate together, and the other way around, why did some people, even though there were only a few of these cases, have children even though they didn't eat the same things, or even eat together—and this leads him to think that he must have reached some degree of maturity by the time he came up with the idea. So he had been an inward-looking boy who didn't have anyone to ask questions of, and those religious dopes, many of whom used their long arm of authority to hit the boys or stick their hands down their pants, didn't help him much. "*Poor little boy,*" Lynn gently whispers to him again, and he feels he could easily start crying.

As if coming out of deep, silent depths, he gradually starts hearing noises coming from around the house again—the echoing sound of a television, the hum from the fridge, the whistling sound still coming in through the window—and yet he's sure he hasn't been asleep. Did Lynn just make those cries of pleasure? He tells her he's been far away, and she tells the cat, "The thing is, we're too noisy, Max, they must hear us all over the neighborhood."

She's sitting back on the sofa with her legs in the lotus position. She's so white that in the half-light, there's a bluish tone to her skin. In a typical gesture of hers, she raises her chin, shakes her hair backward, and then puts her hands back on her knees. Matisse's drawings. The scarcely sketched figure of a woman. Spirals of hair, fine lines showing strong hips, the zigzag of hands crossed over her knees and short curls between her legs. He'd like to draw her at that precise instant. In fact, he's sure that if he had a pencil and paper, and the nerve to say that he wanted to draw her, he could do a good portrait of her.

She moves her thin-fingered hands away from her knees and, at the same time, straightens up. She leans toward him. She has a serious expression on her face now, a decisive look that makes him uneasy. An unarmed man. Crazy thoughts: if he were to draw her, her chest would be the easiest part. He catches her smell once more and feels her cool skin as she snuggles up to him. She takes his hands for him to hold her. *"Just hold me, for now."*

He still finds it amazing to be next to her naked body, naked himself, too, talking about all sorts of things, as if they were in a bar. *"Do you know what?"*

Now the doctor knows why she's gone serious all of a sudden. She wants to talk about the hospital. She finds it surprising that while most of the professional people in the department—doctors, nurses, and auxiliary staff—do their work well, a few others are allowed to avoid working, some of them actually doing their jobs very badly. She can't understand how that situation is so calmly accepted. She speaks gently and softly, as if afraid he might be offended by what she's saying.

She says that Arrese lets doctors do whatever they want so that he doesn't have to deal with them. Whenever anybody brings him a problem, he normally starts shouting like a madman, particularly at young nurses. Just yesterday, he drove a nurse to tears.

Everyone knows that the X-ray technician feels people up.

She talks about doctors who insist on showing sonogram footage to poor parents who are in danger of losing the child. Comments inappropriate in such a bleak situation, like "look, see his little hand, he's waving at us."

About midwives who can't get Kristeller's method out of their heads. About the habit of sitting on women who are about to give birth in order to "help them along," the foul language used to encourage them to push—"Push like you're trying to shit," and so on.

But, then, she can't tell him anything he doesn't already know.

Even so, as he listens to Lynn, he finds it amazing that pointless suffering and injustice take place without anybody complaining about them, as if it were just part of everyday life. It's clear there's an underlying criticism in her words and that she thinks he should do something about these types of behaviour.

But what could he actually do?

DÉJÀ DIT. He's often told her that he made a decision long ago to be as honest and effective as possible in his work and to concern himself only with his own affairs, without looking too much around him, in order not to waste his energy and get burned out. When he was head of the department, he found out that it was very difficult to change even the smallest things without getting into all sorts of difficulties. There were too many vested interests for it to be possible to influence things with mere good will. In order to change anything in an institution such as a hospital, everything would have to be rearranged from top to bottom, and to do that, political will and a mature, informed society were needed. That's why he gave up being the department head, he was tired of wasting his time listening to complaints he didn't know how to respond to. He's embarrassed to have to use such arguments to excuse himself, but he doesn't see any other way out of it, passing his pure cowardice off as elegant, disinterested skepticism.

What would Lynn say if she knew the real reason that had prevented him from confronting Arrese? If he told her what was behind his inability to act? He knows that he would find it liberating to shed his deceit, he'd like to do it, but the mere thought of it terrifies him. As usual, he's as proud as he is cowardly. So he says what he always says—he doesn't want problems, he just wants to cure his patients—when Lynn insists softly that any alternative would be better than Arrese. He repeats that he doesn't want problems and says he'd be grateful if she could forget about the hospital in their free time. He can't control his anger. The poor girl's seeing his irritability once more, and she stretches her lips out in a weak smile that's a request for peace and says that she knows he does all he can.

It isn't the first time he's seen her rubbing her temples. When he asks if she's all right, she admits she has a slight headache and smiles to play it down. She's having trouble with her sight, and that's probably what's behind it. She has an appointment with the ophthalmologist. She's also got premenstrual pains, the ones some male doctors don't believe exist but many women obstinately continue to have, she says humorously. Abaitua protests that she's taking what he said out of context, even though he knows she's not being serious. He doesn't deny the existence of premenstrual problems, what he says is that because of the influence of drug companies, more and more women are being led to believe that their normal physiological discomforts are symptoms of some illness or other. They've already talked about it, he thinks it was in Bordeaux. As Kepa usually says, instead of inventing new medicines, the laboratories look for illnesses that the old medicines can be used on, look for new uses for their old products. If possible, chronic illnesses that many people suffer from, in order to maximize their profit intake. Fluoxetine, known commercially as Prozac, has been found useful, among other things, for treating PMS, which is something that, depending on the statistics you look at, between thirty and eighty percent of fertile women suffer from. The problem is that before long, most women will be taking antidepressants to treat the emotional changes associated with the onset or conclusion of their menstruation cycles and, in most cases, it won't be any use to them. But he doesn't deny the fact that there are serious cases. He's glad the subject has come up, because it gives him the chance to say that he thinks taking antidepressants doesn't make sense, especially tricylicals, if only because they cause galactorrhea. But she doesn't let him go on. She takes ahold of both his hands and shakes them to get him to keep quiet and pay attention to her, frowning to pretend to be angry. Does he think she's sick? she asks, after moving his hands around again as one might to a child in order to get an answer out of them. There are little pieces of dry skin on her lips. He says yes. She frowns again, her forehead damp. "*Benetan*? Really?" She says the word in Basque as often as she does in English. And she always puts the accent on the first syllable, instead of on the second or last. He finds it funny. *"Really, yes."* *"So you do believe me, don't you?"* She says, in a loud voice, which even cracks a little, that she has a serious illness for which there is no cure. *"Mad about you."* She goes on shaking his hands after each thing she says to him. *"Maite zaitudalako.* Because I love you." She says she has an incurable illness. He thinks she's being serious and tries to protect himself—could she please stop saying silly things and tell him what illness she has? Does she have a temperature? Taking his hands out of hers, he puts one on her forehead and takes her pulse with the other, but Lynn stops him and pretends to get angry. She absolutely forbids him to treat her like a patient. She holds his waist between her legs and pretends to punch his chest. If she needed a doctor, she says, she'd definitely go to Doctor Arrese. She wants Abaitua for other things. He feels the murmur of her voice warmly tickling his ear and asks her not to be mean, it's his turn to pretend. He's old. Doesn't she realize she could give him a heart attack? What would happen if death took him on this sofa, or while he was going down the spiral staircase in the dark? Has she thought about that? She answers completely seriously that she has. She has thought about that eventuality. He takes one of her hands and caresses it. He thinks she's telling the truth, that she has thought about his death.

They're both lying lengthwise on the sofa, he's on the inside with one hand lifted upward to pet the cat, watching the shadows from the tree on the ceiling. She's on the outside edge of the sofa, on her side, her arms crossed. She says that since he's older, the normal outcome would be for him to die first. He knows that sometimes she says what she really thinks as if it were a joke. She asks him some unexpected questions, which he answers with single words, without joining in her game, resignedly saying she's right.

"TELL ME." Doesn't he think it would be normal for him to die before her?

She says he can't expect her to jump onto his funeral pyre like some Indian widow. She asks if he understands that. She'll look after him with love, and when he goes—Abaitua really hates that euphemism, *when you go*—since she'll still be quite young, she'll remake her life. It won't be the same, but she'll be all right. He doesn't have to worry about her at all. *"Tell me."* Is he worried about dying first? He should tell her. Touching his ribs with her fingers and nibbling at his neck, she says that although she's not sure, she thinks he's going to live for a long time and that if she outlives him, she'll be a little old lady by then.

He asks her to stop saying silly things.

"*Tell me.*" How can doctors be incapable of seeing what's right in front of them?

Sometimes he gets furious when people lump all doctors together, and politicians, too. As if sociologists or architects were any better. But he'd rather talk about that than love. One example of doctors' inability to see things is the fact that none of them ever paid any attention to the problem of pregnancies lasting more than forty-two weeks until Clifford described the postmaturity syndrome in 1954. And, he says, that's despite the fact that millions and millions of women since the Holocene had been insisting that they'd given birth to children after more than ten months of pregnancy, children who were obviously different—wrinkled, long-nailed, and undernourished as a result of having been linked too long to a placenta that had become no more than a dry sponge. But still nobody paid attention to the evidence. It was the women, the poor fools, they just didn't know how to keep track of their missed periods.

"JUST ONE QUESTION." Even when he's talking about medicine, she often doesn't know to what extent to believe him. "*Please, don't laugh.*" She asks him to take her seriously. When they were first set up, Christian hospitals' main objective was not to make people healthy again but rather to give caregivers the opportunity to save patients' souls with their charitable work. Taking into account the fact that even after a long process of evolution, getting patients healthy again and lengthening their lives was still only a secondary objective, she has a question: What is their main objective nowadays?

This time he's the one who says *really*. Even though all doctors are pigs, blind, and incapable, the most sensible thing for a sick person to do is still to go to the doctor's, and he asks her to promise to go to one as soon as possible to find out what's behind her mysterious problems. He holds her wrists to emphasize what he's asking her to do. She should go to any doctor except for Arrese, and she, trying to break free, says she's crazy but not crazy enough to put herself in the hands of the sort of faux gynecologists they have at the hospital.

He sits up and takes her hands again to repeat his request and says he would even agree to her going to Arrese if there were no alternative. "Surgical midwives." She sits on him, a leg to either side of him, trying to keep him from moving, as she recites the stream of Spanish epithets Kepa taught her, and her difficulty pronouncing them makes them even more comical. "*Vendimiadores de vientres, pasteleros de úteros, segadores de monstruos, hurones de pocilgas humanas, ladrones de la herramienta de parir. . .*" she says—harvesters of abdomens, pastry-makes of uteri, reapers of monsters, ferrets of human pigsties, thieves of birthing instruments. He tries to stop her from moving, which takes some effort. Holding her tight in his arms, rolling around on the carpet, he says she should go see a psychiatrist about her gerontophilia—he knows she doesn't like that joke, but he comes out with it anyway—and her premenstrual irritability, anxiety, and other emotional disturbances, which often have psychiatric origins.

Lynn says, "*The girl who went mad with love.*" At this stage, no psychiatrist could possibly cure her of her madness. "*Too late?* Is it '*berandu*'?"

Abaitua nods.

But does he mean yes that's how you say it, or yes it is too late?

Abaitua shields himself in silence, knowing that a cycle of declarations of love will follow. Lynn waits a long time for him to say something. It seems like a long time to him, at least. He sees bits of broken skin on her thick lips, and then, looking as if she can't take any more, she asks him, regretfully, if he believes her when she says she loves him. She says she isn't asking him to say he loves her, she just wants him to believe her when she tells him she's in love with him. He patiently says he does. How could he not believe her when she's told him so many times? So he says yes, he does, but without adding that he loves her too, even though that's what she really wants to hear, even though, in fact, he finds it hard not to say it; "*Neither of them has ever said I love you.*" That's what Frisch says at the end of *Montauk*, pleased they've never declared their love for each other. So why has this Lynn said it to him in three different languages? Why do things always get so complicated for him? The silence lasts a long time, but he isn't going to be the one to break it. The fridge motor suddenly starts up and makes a lot of noise. It sounds old. Lynn asks him what he's thinking about. It isn't a question asked out of desperation, it seems like a request to break the silence, and he says the first thing that comes to mind. When he was talking about the postmaturity births that had gone unnoticed until Clifford opened his eyes to them, he remembered that Kepa once told him that Eskimo dogs can put off giving birth for up to two weeks if the weather conditions are especially adverse.

Really? She falls back against the sofa with her eyes closed and one hand on her forehead, as if she were fainting. She says she can't believe he was thinking about that. She sits up again and holds both of his hands. *"You don't want me to say I love you."*

He now works up the courage to tell her no. And he's decided to tell her why he doesn't like it if she asks him. Because he feels obliged to tell her he loves her, too, and he can't. He has trouble holding Lynn's clear, serious stare. She doesn't ask him anything more. She sighs and lovingly strokes his hand. She can't promise she'll manage to do it, but she'll try to repress her urge to tell him how much she loves him.

A beer? The question makes his heart beat a little faster. A conditioned reflex. He wonders whether she realizes that. She's sitting on folded legs—he sometimes thinks she's made of rubber—and she rises to her knees, pushing herself up with her hands. A beer?

He hears her moving around in the kitchen, and there are increasingly loud voices coming from the floor below. He knows they're women's voices but can't make out whose they are. Lynn could. Now she's standing in the middle of the living room holding two long glasses with bits of lemon in them and two Franziskaner beers, all on a tray, and she's listening carefully. That's Julia, that's Martin's sister. She says Harri's there, too. She's able to identify their voices.

She pours the beer as Kepa taught her, tilting the glass a lot. After pouring a little, she livens up what's left in the bottle by rubbing it between her hands and then adds it slowly to the glass. He watches her impatiently, surprised that his tired body replies so obediently to that conditioned reflex.

Lynn sits on the floor with her back against the sofa, her hands resting on the floor to either side of her. Her head is leaning slightly to one side. Her mouth is half open in an expression of tiredness. *"You drive me crazy,"* she murmurs, as if she really has lost her mind, and Abaitua covers her mouth to stop her from talking.

Don't be silly.

She asks him to let her say for the last time, whispering in his ear so that nobody else will hear, that she loves him.

He lets her put his hand on her vulva, and he feels its dampness. She holds him there, whispering in his ear that just touching her there drives her wild. "*Zer egiten duzu niri?*" she says, attempting to wonder aloud what it is that he does to her but getting the grammar wrong. He'd like to escape from the situation, because he doesn't like exaggerations—he's afraid they might be real. He isn't sure. He corrects her Basque, and she makes a gesture of impatience in reply. She opens her eyes. He sees sorrow and disappointment in them. She doesn't know what language to use to make him believe that his mere touch is enough for her to lose her mind. She holds tightly to his arm, shaking as she repeats, correctly now, "*Zer egiten didazu?*" with insistent groans, her voice more and more broken, and he feels his hand has exceptional powers. Or he feels that for a moment, at least.

He lies down. He feels the cool wood on his back and intense pleasure all over his body. He's tired. She's still sitting with her back against the sofa, her head leaning toward her right shoulder. He sees her lifting her left hand to her opposite breast, holding it in her palm and squeezing her nipple, as she usually does, between her thumb and forefinger. He tells her not to, she doesn't have to.

It's a moment in which it seems the pleasure is only for her. He moves away from her, fascinated by the scale of her pleasure—a pleasure in no way connected to him, something he has nothing to do with, is not familiar with—and a little alarmed. He sees her stretch out in an arc, her arm going over her head and holding onto the bottom of the sofa, her eyes roll up into her head; he thinks she's about to start trembling.

Abaitua starts to become aware of the sounds around them once more, identifying them one by one, regaining his perception of them as if he were coming out of a deep, silent pit. He wonders if he himself has ever felt as much pleasure, and whether he's ever wondered about such a thing before. He isn't sure. He isn't sure whether he's gone through life convinced that he's been enjoying his sexuality to its fullest or whether, as in other areas, he's had doubts about whether he's explored all the possibilities or remained satisfied with just enough. It's been enough, he thinks, at least he's never felt frustrated about not being able to go further in that respect. It's true he doesn't have anything to compare his experience with, since sex isn't something people around him talk about. Only jokes and sarcastic comments about the failings of age and spousal shortcomings. He remembers a dinner party with his best friends at university. They all had dates except for Juan Aguilar, who was divorced for the second time. He'd started seeing a Cuban woman thirty years younger than himself and was talking about that with the enthusiasm he always showed for any new relationship. And then he said something that surprised them all: he'd learned how to kiss from her. He realized that the moments of contact between lips and tongues that he had experienced with all his girlfriends, fiancées, and wives up until then weren't real kisses. They were nothing like the exciting kisses he shared with this young Cuban woman.

As well as being the only divorcé in the group, Aguilar is also the life and soul of every party, for both the men and the women. They all really enjoy hearing about the trips he's made around the world and the adventures he's had since recovering from his depression after splitting up with his second wife. He says he thinks the men envy him, and he's right to an extent. He's small and chubby, but he's lively and dances a lot; he's romantic and prone to falling in love, one of those men women find attractive. He doesn't bring his lovers to the group dinners, and that makes it easier for him to talk openly about sex.

Talking about his thirty-years-younger Cuban friend, he said he regretted having lived more than half his life without knowing what real kissing is, taking for granted that it was the same for the rest of them. There were some nervous giggles. They could have told him that they had nothing to learn from a young Cuban woman, but nobody said anything. Out of shame, and partly out of pity, too, because the fact that Aguilar's love life was in its second or third youth made them feel a little sorry for him. Perhaps some people there had once had the same experience as him and had to keep quiet because their spouses were there. Perhaps some people also started to wonder whether they were missing out on something, something they'd have fewer and fewer chances to put right. On their way back home, Abaitua wanted to bring it up with Pilar. He said something to her, something about Aguilar being horny, and she said, "He's a little naïve," that's all. Now he wonders if he understood what she meant. He thinks she meant that, like Aguilar, everyone realizes too late that they haven't led a full sex life. But being more reserved that Aguilar, they don't say anything about it. Pilar, too, knew what it was to kiss somebody much younger than herself. They didn't talk any more after that, because he remembered Pilar sitting on the edge of the bed, her forearms resting on her legs and her head down, as if she were looking at her hands. He'd put a hand on her arm and asked the young man's name. He didn't want to think about it.

Lynn is asleep. He can't even hear her breathing.

When he and Aguilar drove to Milan together, he hardly stopped talking about his first wife, all the way from Donostia. How much he missed her, how they used to "kiss each other like lovebirds" as soon as they woke up. Abaitua hasn't forgotten how striking he found it that after having been married for several years, he was still so much in love, and he was even more surprised by his not being embarrassed to talk about it in such a corny way. He's sure he said "like lovebirds." He'd like to know if now that the Cuban pediatrician is history, too, Aguilar still remembers or misses those lovebird kisses.

He thinks it was in *Montauk* that he read that the first time with a woman is always the first time. Whoever said it, it's true, and in fact, the basis of promiscuity is probably rooted in that desire to have another first time.

He regrets being so clumsy in some of the relationships he's had with women —he's even ashamed of a few particular memories— but he still feels affection for all the woman he has ever made love with. And so what is he worried about? His pleasure has very seldom, or perhaps never, been free of a feeling of guilt.

A TRAIN. Some other trains must have gone by, too, without their hearing them. The wind is now blowing from the south and is much noisier because of that, it makes the noise from the rails last longer, as if the train were never going to completely disappear. Sometimes Lynn bets on which of them will guess what type of train is passing, and they run along the hallway to the balcony to check, him letting her go first so that she won't see his back. He should get up and pee now, but he's feeling too lazy and stays lying down. He tries not to use her bathroom.

The reserved space under the streetlamps at the entrance of the clinic's parking lot, where Pilar's little car had been shortly before, is now empty. There are many lights on in the apartment buildings, most of them white kitchen lights. He realizes from this fact that it's dinnertime; he's got to get going. Lynn leans on his back with her arm around him.

Frisch says he wants Lynn to be the last one. Abaitua knows that's how it's going to be for him, this Lynn will be the last one.

The light traffic also means it's late. Lynn is asleep now, her head on his shoulder, curled up against his ribs, giving off damp warmth and that intense, sweet smell of hers. She whistles slightly as she breathes out. He decides to take his arm out from under her, get dressed silently, and leave her there asleep. Before doing so, he'll have to shoo the cat away, which is curled up on his pants and staring at him as if it wanted to know what he's planning to do. He frees his arm very carefully and stretches out enough to be able to touch his pants with his fingertips, but Lynn sits up as if she were on a spring. Is he going?

Doesn't he want to stay and have some dinner? She can offer him some stuffed peppers from the shop over at the Culinary School. He's tried those frozen peppers, stuffed with swordfish instead of cod and with a dubious cocktail sauce made with a lot of cream. He can't, he has to go, and he doesn't want to stay. He's also decided to be merciless on matters like this, telling her his decisions without cushioning them, giving his diagnoses and prognoses the way the American school recommends—beating around the bush is never any help. She doesn't discuss his decision. She doesn't lift a finger to make him stay; she never does. Although when she stretches her lips out, almost like a smile, she looks very sad to him. "*Bazoaz*," she says—you're going. Pronouncing the *z* perfectly, and he follows the cat, which has jumped heavily off the chair and disappeared down the hallway. He tries to put his pants on as quickly as possible, because he doesn't like her seeing him in underpants, either. When he goes back in, she's wearing her green pajamas, the ones with little drawings on them that look like children's pajamas and, inevitably, make her look like a little girl.

He wouldn't know what to say if she asked him why he had to go.

As always, she leans against the wall and looks at him, petting the cat in her arms at the same time, and she helps him when he has trouble getting into the right-hand sleeve. Then she wants to brush his pants down, because she's seen him trying to shake some hairs off them, but he doesn't let her. He thinks it's too attentive of her, and what's more, he doesn't want her to think the cat is a problem as far as he's concerned, and even less so that he's worried he might have to face up to Pilar's scrutiny when he gets home. But she gives him a brush and insists he do it himself. He obeys her, and she points out where there are hairs.

She's barefoot. Her feet are small for her height, and her big toes lift up as she steps. She walks in front of him to the door and looks through the peephole to make sure there's nobody there. She moves to one side to let him past, almost hiding herself between the wall and the door. The cat jumps from her arms and rubs itself against his pants and, after sniffing at his shoes, lies in front of him with its belly up, asking him to pet it. No, Max. She picks it up again. He says it's Saturday tomorrow. A way of saying that they won't be seeing each other at the hospital. He says vaguely that he'll call her. And then an innocent kiss on each cheek.

By now he's used to the smell of the jasmine and the sound of the gravel. When he opens the iron gate, he realizes he doesn't have a car and will have to call a taxi.

It's around ten or eleven at night. The taxi driver is listening to a sports program. He says Donostia's Real Sociedad is doing badly and that he's started to get bored of soccer. He doesn't know whether the good moments are worth all the suffering. Abaitua says life's like that, and the taxi driver looks at him in the mirror. He probably wants to know where somebody wearing a tie has come from at that time of night. Abaitua would have to tell him he's been fooling around with a young woman for the last six hours. He feels at one with the night. The taxi driver says no when he asks him if he's been getting a lot of business today—Donostia isn't a lively place at night.

HE FINDS PILAR ASLEEP in front of the television. Her laptop's on the table and turned on, along with some files from the clinic and some books. She has one open on her lap. His first impulse is to wake her up, but then he leaves her there and goes to brush his teeth and get ready for bed.

Techniques in Neurosurgery. When he gently takes the book from her hands, she opens her eyes and looks at him for a moment, confused, as if she didn't recognize him. "You're back," she says, and then, "I fell asleep," as if she had to excuse herself. The sides of her mouth have drooped over the last few months, since her father's illness and death, and some of the vertical wrinkles around her mouth are deeper. Abaitua lets her scrutinize him, glad he's put his pajamas on.

He feels obliged to say that he's bumped into Kepa, she knows what he's like, and as soon as he says that, he thinks he might have told her that morning that Kepa's in London. He doesn't care. He's used to sticking to lies even when there's evidence to the contrary. But his wife's wrinkled lips speak and tell him she's made scorpionfish for dinner. He's seen it, with thin potatoes and small peas in a green sauce with finely chopped parsley, all inside a clay cooking pot. In order to avoid the risk, distant though it is, of her sitting down with him as she used to do when he would come home late and asking him how his day went while he eats, he prefers to say that it's a pity but he's already had something to eat. What's more, not having dinner is a way of punishing himself.

He says he's dead tired, as a way of getting ready to make his escape.

Then his wife puts on her reading glasses. They look good on her, they don't make her look older, which is what she thinks; they make her look like an active, interesting woman. She says she's half asleep, too, but she has to study. In spite of what she says, she suddenly looks wide awake. She tells him she operated on a guy called Chiari, who was on the waiting list, without telling her brother-in-law, even though that'll lead to a quarrel. She's pleased with the work she's done and determined to keep the clinic going. For the first time in a long while, she talks to him until she sees that he's bored, or tired, and then she tells him he'd better go to bed. With no resentment.

He's no longer tired.

He reads in *Montauk*: *Il est encore surpris de connaître son corps, son corps à elle. Il ne s'y attendait pas. Si Lynn ne lui signifiait pas de temps en temps qu'elle aussi se rappelle cette nuit, les mains de l'homme n'oseraient pas saisir la tête de la femme.* He prefers to turn the light off, since he's told Pilar he's dead tired.

He remembers Lynn as he struggles to take his pants off— "you're wearing armor," she'd said.

He remembers Ayllón. The Galician colony in Donostia's Trintxerpe neighborhood was the last stronghold of home birthing in Gipuzkoa, and Ayllón was the doctor in charge of most of the births. Many doctors didn't approve of the work he did, even though they didn't question his being a good doctor, and the fact is that the care he provided was better than that given in many maternity wards.

He, too, had his reservations about Ayllón's work, because the man was helping those Galician women to carry on with their backward traditions instead of encouraging them to give birth in a hospital, with the necessary advances; however, as time went by, he ended up deciding that agreeing to accept those women's cultural criteria had managed to prevent several unfortunate events from happening. And now, years later, nobody gives birth at home in Trintxerpe anymore. He could have told Lynn about it, but he hadn't remembered about Ayllón when they were talking about the Peruvian girl giving birth at home.

A fantasy: He goes to Lynn's house at midnight and knocks on the door. She opens the door ajar, sticks her nose out, and says *"hi"* happily. Then she opens the door wide for him and, like always, with her back against the wall.

The sound of an electric toothbrush going from the bathroom to the living room. And back to the bathroom.

17

WHEN HE COMES IN, LYNN OFFERS him a Ping-Pong rematch, but Martin goes up the stairs without bothering to answer her. "It must be a bad time," she says, as the writer disappears, her eyes wide open, her mouth, too, an expression of fear on her face and shaking one hand around in the air. She asks what the expression was in Spanish but then remembers it herself, you say "the oven's not ready for buns," *buns* being another way to say "trouble," "drama," or "commotion" in Spanish: "*No está el horno para bollos.*" The oven's cold. Her gestures of astonishment are as funny as the way she pronounces the saying. She's getting used to the writer's rages, and apparently she finds these explosions of his funny. It's better this way. Julia, too, takes it with a pinch of salt, although she's finding his tantrums increasingly unbearable, and after he slams the door, making the fine family crystal on the sideboard tremble, she tries to explain to Lynn the reasons for the writer being particularly angry with women today.

It all started because a call from his sister in Paris had woken him up. She wanted him to make sure there's a bouquet of flowers waiting for her friends when they reach their suite in the María Cristina Hotel; as if that weren't enough, apparently she also told him that instead of the conventional welcome message on the little accompanying card, it would be lovely if he could send them one of his books with a "charming dedication." When Julia arrived, she found him having a nervous breakdown about this new commission, swearing about his sister, and she thought what was exasperating him was having to write a "charming dedication"; she knows he doesn't find it easy when people politely ask him to do that, and from what she's read, many other writers feel the same way. In fact, Martin has a good collection of passages he's underlined in which writers are put out by having to write dedications, including writers who you wouldn't normally think of as being easily put off their stride—Joyce, for instance. So he was walking up and down nonstop, swearing about all the trouble his sister always gives him, until she convinced him that the best thing would be to sort out the problem as soon as possible rather than obsessing about it. So he decided to go to the hotel, see that the reservation was all correct, and, at the same time, check that they were going to send him the bill, and then see what to do about the bouquet of flowers. It seems things went well at the hotel—the staff would take care of the flowers—and then, finding himself with renewed energy to complete the task, he went to the bookshop on Okendo Kalea, almost directly across from the hotel, with the idea of asking for the Spanish translation of his *Beti euria ari du*, which was titled *Siempre está lloviendo*, meaning "It's Always Raining." Since there weren't any copies of it on display, he had to get over his embarrassment and go up to the counter, afraid of the not very likely possibility that someone might recognize him, and he asked for *New York–Bilbao*, too, even though that was actually on display, in order not to seem so egocentric. It was something like buying Tylenol along with a pack of condoms. Even though the clerk told him at first he didn't think they would have it—"It was published quite a long time ago"—he then saw on the computer that in fact they did have a copy. Julia has to ask Lynn not to laugh, because that's exactly what Martin told her, and she knows how precise and vociferous he tends to be when he's been insulted. He told her that while he was waiting for the copy of his book, he saw that there was a woman of around forty in the guidebook section—she was completely anodyne, he wouldn't recognize her if he saw her again, he emphasized that—speaking in Catalan with a boy who looked to be her son, and suddenly he saw an easy solution to his problem with the dedication: a few conventional words, but written in Catalan, would handsomely meet his sister's request. Apparently, the vocation itself is what makes it so difficult for authors to write dedications, which isn't the case for artists and athletes, who usually just sign their name, because writers can't just put down some clichéd sentence. That, she thinks at least, is what Martin's problem is—he usually feels obliged to write something original or personal, because he thinks that's what people expect from somebody they think of as a writer. He could never write *With affection* or *From the heart* or anything like that, because people would be disappointed. Julia understands that, and so does Lynn, although she still doesn't stop laughing. But Martin thought that writing something in Catalan would give it that special touch, at least display his desire to be friendly with his sister's friends, who were Catalan. He could have written *Amb simpatia* or *Abraçades*—Catalan for "with affection" and "hugs"—but he thought that if he asked the "ordinary-looking woman" who was flicking through the guidebooks with her son for help, he would be able to sketch something a bit deeper. Can she, Lynn, imagine how nervous the writer must have been about going up to the woman and asking her to help him find the right words? "*Of course.*" Naturally, he wouldn't have been able to introduce himself as a writer who wanted to dedicate one of his books in Catalan. That would have been showing off. He was thinking about the best way to do it, when the mother and son left the bookshop without buying anything. Apparently, it had taken the bookseller some time to find a copy his book, which, to tell the truth, wasn't in very good condition, and because of that, they were out of sight by the time he left the shop. But all of a sudden, as he was crossing the street—and Julia has to ask Lynn again not to laugh, because the tragedy is about to unfold—he sees them both, the mother and son, sitting on a bench and speaking Catalan, and probably because it was such an unexpected encounter, he went straight up to the woman without thinking twice and asked her if she was Catalan, and even though she looked at him with mistrust when she had answered that she was, he just came out and asked her if she could tell him a few words in Catalan, at the same time taking out his pen and his Hemingway-style notebook with its elastic band—Julia promises Lynn he told this to her with precisely those words—and when the woman, who by this time was looking at him with even greater mistrust, asked him what words he needed, he couldn't think of anything better to say than "with all my affection," and as soon as she heard that, the woman sprang to her feet, said she was in a great hurry, and fled, dragging her son behind her. Martin was still upset when he got home, distraught, because now women were taking him to be the sort of depraved man who goes for women in front of their young children.

"*Gizajoa*," says Lynn, poor man, using Harri's intonation, emphasising the first syllable and almost whispering the other three.

Julia felt sorry for him, too, and to make him feel better, she told him that the woman couldn't have been that bright and that it was incomprehensible that she could have taken him to be one of those men who go up to women on the street. She told him he was right again and again. She must have been a bit of a goody-goody, as well, because when it came down to it, it was ten o' clock in the morning, they were in the middle of town and surrounded by people—there wasn't any reason for her to be frightened. He should just forget about it. But he wasn't prepared to do that, he carried on criticizing her, because he was hurt—how could such an ordinary-looking woman think that he, the seduction king, who had more difficulty than anybody else steering clear of all the women who were after him, could possibly want to ensnare her in his net? He kept on grumbling, walking around and around, until she, fed up, told him what she really thought: he, too, should have been more careful and understanding, because at the end of the day, that anodyne woman was in an unfamiliar city, and in addition to that, he had to admit that his question, which was suspicious at best, put her in an unusual situation. He flew into a rage, accused her of always being very understanding with people who insult him and never being on his side.

"*Gizajoa*," Lynn said again.

Julia can't think of an equivalent expression in Spanish to *one does the harm, and another bears the blame*. *Pagar justos por pecadores*, maybe—the innocent pay for the sinners. She can't think of an equivalent in Basque, either. The closest thing she can come up with is *ardien hutsak pagatu behar bildotsak*—the lambs have to make up for the sheep's mistakes. Lynn says that sometimes women are unfair to men, and Julia, on the other hand, says she thinks Lynn is fairly critical of women and very understanding with men. She says it as she thinks it, and Lynn bursts out laughing. Julia doesn't understand what she's laughing so much about. She says she's glad Lynn's in such a good mood. She sounds as if she may be annoyed. Be that as

534

it may, Lynn becomes serious. "Not all that good a mood, believe me," she says, and when Julia asks her what's wrong, is she unwell, Lynn answers vaguely.

Nothing serious, just "*disorders*," she says, wanting to avoid the subject. Julia thinks that by "disorders" she means the ones some women have before their periods, and she is just about to tell her that if that's the case, she's in good hands, but in the end, she keeps the pleasantry to herself.

Lynn asks if she knows what she was just laughing about. With an air of confidentiality, she lowers her voice and moves toward Julia until their knees touch between their two chairs, and she says that she's had these "disorders" for a long time, they're not serious, just pretty uncomfortable, and she doesn't pay much attention to them, but since she has a health insurance plan now that's much better than the one she had in the States, she decided to go to the doctor's last week. She was told that one of the places that accepts her insurance company is the San Luis Clinic, and she won't deny that finding that out did to an extent influence her decision to go ahead and make an appointment for a general checkup. Smiling, she looks at Julia inquisitively to check that she's understanding her—"*¿Me entiendes?*" Julia says that she understands, even though she isn't wholly sure, and Lynn asks her if she thinks it's wrong, unhealthy. Without waiting for an answer, she adds that she's incredibly curious to see what Abaitua's wife is like and that when she stepped into the clinic's reception area and saw her name on the directory board, she almost fainted. "Pilar—*a harsh name.*" Doesn't Julia agree? She doesn't have an opinion about the name, but she doesn't have to say anything, because Lynn carries on talking without letting her answer. Lynn was convinced that if his wife saw her, she would guess she was her husband's lover, and while she was getting all her tests done, many of which really weren't necessary, her only worry—a mixed feeling of fear and hope—was that his wife would suddenly appear. While she sat naked under her little gown on the examination table, she fantasized that Pilar would come in, covered from head to toe in surgeon's clothes without saying a word, and she, Lynn, would only know who she was because of the name on her smock. Later, when the tests were over and she scanned the directory board again, she decided to go up to the floor where her office is, just to see her name on the door, nothing more, and she was about to reach the landing when she bumped into her. She looked younger than she had expected her to, and above all, more beautiful. "*Oso ederra da?*"—Isn't she beautiful? So she is. Lynn thought her very elegant in her violet-colored scrubs. She took her cap off and shook her hair loose; she had some gray in her black hair, but she looked young and strong. She was with another female doctor, who was wearing a white smock, but Lynn had no doubt that she was the one who'd just taken her cap off. She wanted to make sure, put her glasses on, and stepped closer to her to try to see her name. Lynn says she found her attitude peculiar. When she went up to her, Pilar looked at her and asked in a very particular voice—cocking her head to one side in a gesture of displeasure, with a "confoundedly" soft but firm voice—if she needed help. She asked it with the informal rather than the formal Spanish conjugation: "*¿Necesitas ayuda?*" She didn't have her name embroidered on her chest in the end, but Lynn was sure it was her. She answered that she didn't need anything. Luckily, the elevator was just a step away. She pressed the button and thought that Pilar must be thinking, since they were on the first floor, that she didn't lead a very healthy lifestyle. Pilar turned her back on her. She said that she was inundated with work, as if trying to get rid of the other doctor, and in farewell, she said to her colleague, "And don't you pay any attention to men." Remembering that was what made her laugh when Julia claimed she was too understanding with men. She'd said, "Don't you pay any attention to men," and she'd laughed—one of those clear, crystal laughs—before closing the door behind her. She envied that laugh. When the overweight, ordinary-looking woman who she wished would have been the one to have *Pilar Goytisolo* embroidered on her smock walked by, Lynn had only to stretch her neck out to see for sure that the sign on the office door had Pilar's name on it. She looked elegant and beautiful, had a soft voice and a happy laugh. "*I felt terrible.*" Lynn looks at Julia with her funny, happy smile. "*What do you think of that?*"

Julia is about to say "*I think you're a bit crazy*" when they hear Martin's pacing out in the hallway. Julia thinks he drags his feet more and more and wonders whether he'll join them in the living room or stop at the bathroom. The latter happens. He slams the door closed, as if to let them know that he's still angry.

Lynn points at the book by Noll on the table and asks Julia if she's enjoying it. So she wants to change the subject. Julia says she is, more than when she first started reading it. There's a lot in it about Frisch. She's marking the pages with quotes on them for Martin, so that he doesn't have to read the whole book. There are some funny observations in it. For instance, on page 97: "As long as [Frisch] has problems with women, he won't die." And on page 110: "Literary history would be making a serious mistake if it didn't see him as a thinker." And on the same page: "Frisch's work leads us to the mistaken belief that his literature, in terms of content and theme, is in some way connected with the writer's life and, in fact, that it is a description of it. It is often thought that Frisch's themes are personal: his own identity, his relationships with women, his problems with himself and with other people. In fact, he stays quite a lot further away from his own descriptions than the descriptions themselves might lead one to believe." Julia thinks it's an interesting observation, coming as it does from somebody who knew him. And she finds it moving to see how much Frisch enjoyed his relationship with his dying friend. On page 189: "Most visits make me think I'm fulfilling an obligation. Of course, it's not like that with Frisch, because he, too, finds our conversations interesting." And then there was his kindness in taking Noll to Egypt when he was really ill. It was a tough journey for both of them, for the sick man and for his friend, too, and the Swiss Air Force had to repatriate them. Frisch was as generous as ever. Lynn's eyes shine. She asks Julia to lend it to her when she finishes.

HARRI ON THE PHONE—she can't get the iron gate to open and can somebody come out to open it for her. She complains, by way of greeting, about the rain, even though it's long since cleared up. There are puddles everywhere, and she'd been wanting to wear some wonderful new sandals for the first time. She says hello to Lynn in the same way. It's still too early to go to the hospital, but she feels nervous waiting at home, and she would have ended up buying more clothes if she'd continued walking around town. Julia says she doesn't have anything to complain about and she'll soon enough regret saying such silly things. To which Harri replies that the only thing making her nervous is the prospect of Abaitua seeing her practically naked like that, whiter than white as she is. As always, it's not clear whether she's trying to make them laugh or not. Then she asks about the boy, and Julia, in order to keep her happy, says that he's been working for a while now. Julia also tells her about the bad experience he had that morning, and as expected, Harri comes out in his defense. The woman was real idiot, no doubt about it. The insulted man comes into the living room, like Diogenes emerging from his barrel, just in time to hear the last comment, and he takes advantage of the presence of an ally to accuse Julia of always siding with his enemies. "And somebody once said you were loyal." It's a comment neither Harri nor Lynn can understand, but they do understand that it's undoubtedly connected with some private thought of his, and an awkward silence descends. Until Harri complains once more that the bad weather has prevented her from wearing her new sandals for the first time, and Lynn recites: "*Mal tiempo dicen los veraneantes . . . ¡Ay qué buen tiempo sin tiempo digo yo!*"—summer vacationers say the weather's bad this season . . . I say it's unseasonably good! Julia is amused by Lynn making use of Celaya, as if she were a Donostian taking foreigners' complaints about the weather as personal insults. Martin asks her where she got that from, jealous, apparently, that somebody else has told her about *Rapsodia Euskara*, and Lynn tells him that Kepa usually says that when it rains. "*Con boina y con gabardina recorro el Paseo Nuevo*"—I walk along the Paseo Nuevo in a beret and a raincoat. She knows the whole poem by heart. She tries to explain herself: she prefers intermittent rain and mild temperatures to sweating in the shade in ninety-five-degree heat. A typical Donostian's statement. In any case, says the writer, it doesn't rain like it used to. He means it doesn't rain like it used to back when he wrote *Beti euria ari du*. In Julia's memory, too, the rain then would bring mist with it and last for weeks once it started. Back then, trying to find shelter until it cleared up was pointless.

They talk about climate change.

"*Anyway,*" says Harri, imitating Lynn. She says that the rain having prevented her from wearing her fine Italian sandals for the first time means that she won't be able to show off the part of her body she has most reason to be proud of. She stretches her legs out and uses her toes to take her shoes off and holds her feet up in the air. Julia is astonished to see that she's gone to the trouble of painting her toenails purple just to go to the doctor's. Otherwise, her feet are quite normal—they do have rather large bunions, but they aren't damaged and are very well looked after. What do they think of them, she says, holding them up in the air. It's obvious she's nervous, and she confirms it when she says there's still an hour to go. "What's there still an hour to go for?" The writer's forgotten that she has an appointment with Abaitua and that Julia's agreed to go with her. Harri makes great signs of disappointment. Is that what you would expect from a friend? How could he forget that she's got an appointment to get the carcinoma in her chest looked at? She puts on quite a performance about it all, until Lynn tells her to stop talking about tumors and that she'll feel better when the appointment's over. Martin, too, says he's sure that she'll feel better when it's over, but there's a hidden meaning to his words. And to make it clear, he adds that it seems the doctor has good hands—"*Badirudi doktoreak oso esku ona duela*"—and gives a pathetic, rabbit-like laugh. He isn't sure if Lynn understands him or not. Julia pretends not to have heard, and Harri does the same. Martin quickly tries to cover up for the fact that he's just carelessly mentioned Abaitua in Basque by saying that Abaitua recommended a nurse for his father and that his mother and sister are already unhappy. Martin's sure he's a good doctor, but apparently his nurses are prettier than they are competent, he says, completely seriously, to which first Lynn and then Julia laugh. They start laughing out loud, and Harri and Martin look on at them uncomprehendingly. Martin seems to be the more put out of the two. Lynn asks him to forgive her as soon as she can, tears in her eyes, saying she just remembered something else. Julia can think of nothing better than to say that she found Lynn's laughter contagious and suggests tea, so that she can get away to the kitchen.

To show that he's still put out, Martin uncouthly pours the milk in on top of the tea. Harri usually says thank you in French. *Merçi.* Lynn points it out to her, and they say that it's a custom in the Donostia area. It's a result of historical contact with French polite customs. People of modest means didn't use to say thank you in Basque or Spanish and started imitating the French. That's what Julia thinks. It's a relevant subject—today is August 31. That night, the burning of the city will be commemorated on the street named after the day, Abuztuaren 31 Kalea. Lights are switched off and candles are set out on all the balconies.

Something incredible: Martin suggests going to have dinner at Kokotxa, because from one of the restaurant windows you can see Abuztuaren 31 Kalea. It's incredible, because he hasn't left the house at night for a long time. It seems he regrets having been rude to Lynn, and in a way, it's a direct invitation to her. But she can't make it. She blushes and says she's expecting a call and can't make a new commitment. Martin pours milk into his tea again. It doesn't take much to make him feel insulted. Lynn, wanting to change the subject, tells Julia that the time has come for big decisions. *"The big decision."* Julia merely nods. Lynn then asks her how she's getting on with the translation. Julia doesn't want to talk about going back to work, but even less about how the translation's going with Martin there. She just says it's going well and, to stop her from asking any more questions, passes the baton onto Harri—how's her search for the man from the airport going? It's also incredible that Harri, for once, doesn't feel like talking about the dratted story she usually forces them all to take an interest in. She tells them not to tease her, she knows they don't believe her at all, and she pulls a face like a sulking child. However, there's no doubt whatsoever that she's completely serious when she reproaches them for not taking any interest in things that happen outside of novels. It's a reprimand for Martin, because he's never been inspired to use her stories in a book. She holds onto his sleeve and looks him in the face—"Tell me, what are you writing about right now, something more interesting than my story?"

The scene going on is quite pathetic, and that's probably why Lynn now literally flees. She's got the washing machine going. It sounds like an excuse. She gives all three of them two kisses—Julia envies her being able to give the annoyed writer a kiss on each cheek, too—and longer ones to Harri, wishing her luck. It's all going to go well.

As soon as Lynn leaves, Harri starts in on Martin for the way he's been treating Lynn like a wretched little girl recently. And don't think she hasn't noticed his way of serving the tea, either. "How could you?" Like Julia's mother, she shakes her head slowly. The writer defends himself like a child having a tantrum—she doesn't know how Lynn spoils his evenings. He talks about her lovemaking again and about how her cries can be heard all over the house. Isn't that right? Now he wants Julia to side with him. She could say to him that perhaps he wouldn't hear them if he weren't listening out for them, running up to the bedroom as soon as he hears Abaitua's footsteps on the gravel. "Isn't that right?" he insists. Really frightening cries, cries that drown out the noise from the trains, cries that must scandalize the nuns at the convent next door, he says, now trying to resort to comedy to help his cause. It makes Julia want to say that the calm murmur of voices and their happy laughter usually make her feel envious. Even though, at first, the cries made her a bit nervous, they don't any more; once, she almost sat down and started playing Ravel's Bolero on the piano, and she even ventured—she has no idea how she worked up the courage—to tell Lynn that, and Lynn found it funny, she laughed at the idea, and the memory of it makes Julia herself laugh now, right as Martin is talking about how he once caught Lynn with a jar of oil lubricating the hinges on the tower door for the sole purpose of making her secret lover's arrival more discreet. Julia had seen that, too, and she'd found it moving. In fact, she'd been envious. She gets jealous when she hears Lynn listening to Dylan's most sentimental songs and realizes she's waiting for him.

The howling. Harri tells them the results of a recent survey: 90% of women admit that they have at some point faked an orgasm. Young women, especially, shout because they've seen it in films and because men like it. She admits that she's done it herself, but normally she doesn't bother. But she can do it really well. "Do you want me to do it now?" She puts her face on Martin's forearm, her eyes closed and her mouth open. Martin makes a gesture of repugnance, which probably isn't entirely false, and Harri says, "One of these days, we'll have to get over the taboo of incest. You don't mind, do you?" Julia says she doesn't. What's more, she's still pretty sure they have gotten over it. Once, to be precise.

In the end, they're late leaving.

JULIA ISN'T USED TO SEEING the hospital in the afternoon, and it looks like a void to her. It seems Abaitua was doing Harri a favor by agreeing to see her in the afternoon. There are very few people in the waiting room. Two pairs of women, both made up of one woman of around thirty and another of more than seventy. She supposes that the younger woman in one of the pairs is the other's caregiver, because she's casually reading a magazine while the older woman stares straight ahead, mute. In contrast, she can make out from the other pair's whispered conversation in a Goierri accent that the younger woman is the patient, because she's worried about how everyone else will be getting on back at home and the older woman is giving her reassuring answers. It reminds her of the many descriptions Faustino Iturbe gives of hospital waiting rooms: the talkative women accompanying the frightened men and straightening their shirt collars, rubbing out the creases in their clothes, telling them off in a motherly way because they don't take care of themselves, because of something or other they've done or left undone. The young woman who isn't reading pats the older woman's hand, so Julia begins to doubt now which of them is sick. She wonders if the woman realizes that she, Julia, isn't the sick one of the two, and knowing that she isn't and that she's only accompanying Harri makes her feel happy, and also guilty. What's more, she hadn't felt any lumps in her breasts that morning when following the instructions in the pamphlet that arrived in the mail from the Department of Public Health.

She didn't have to come with her, Harri says; she's embarrassed about her wasting the whole afternoon, but before Julia can reply, Harri thanks her and says she'd be very sad if she weren't there with her. She mentions another survey according to which men feel reassured when a woman accompanies them to the doctor, whereas men's company simply irritates women. Julia lets out a laugh. Remembering what Lynn told her about her run-in with Abaitua's wife, she says, "Don't you pay any attention to men," and seeing the inquisitive way Harri is looking at her, she promises to tell her about it later.

From time to time, doctors walk past them, carelessly talking about their private matters. That's fair enough, in that the hospital is a workplace, too, as well as being a place where patients and their guests live out their anguish. Even so, they should be a little more careful. The thought comes to her—*Shouldn't they dress and behave in a way that gives the impression they're only thinking about their patients' situations?*—as she listens to a female doctor's high-heeled shoes echoing loudly all over the ward while she complains about her vacation being over. "It was so much nicer in Menorca." Without realizing that anybody who heard her would be happy just to be able to work and have a healthy body.

"People are a piece of work," says Harri. She's quite different when Martin isn't there, mostly far less histrionic. She says she woke up that morning with a feeling of distress, and for a while—she doesn't know for how long, but long enough for her to notice it—

she didn't know what was causing it. It isn't a new feeling. She often gets overcome by sorrow, pain, or anguish, and she usually tries to figure out what's behind it for that infinitesimal moment until it finally becomes clear to her. Her daughter's bad grades at school, her quarrel with her husband, having lost her purse with all of her credit cards and IDs. This morning, on the other hand, after that moment of not knowing what her unease was due to, it became obvious to her that it was because she might have breast cancer. And even so, her unease, sorrow, and anguish did not diminish. *"¿Qué te parece?"* It's the same reflection that Julia read in Martin's book a few weeks ago. Faustino Iturbe didn't know why he felt a tightness in his chest, until he realized he was condemned to death. He realized that in the past, any little matter—someone he knew not saying hello as they passed in the street, the roofer not properly fixing a leak in the living room—used to produce the same effect in him. The same sorrow, the same anguish. After that, he found it miraculous that he was able to lead a normal life, taking an interest in daily problems and handling the decisions that have to be made every day, even enjoying lots of small things, too, until the signs of his impending death would make themselves known once more. Julia thinks Harri would find it comforting to know that they've both shared the same reflection, but she doesn't get a chance to tell her.

It's Abaitua himself who comes out to get them from the waiting room. A show of consideration, something he does in a natural way but still making it clear he's going out of his way to be considerate. He gives them each a kiss, first Harri and then Julia, putting his hands on their shoulders as he does so, in a gesture that seems too paternalistic to Julia. He may have a little too much eau de cologne on, it smells of fresh citrus and has a masculine touch of cedar. Sometimes she smells a trace of it on the stairs going up to the tower. He and Harri talk about the research project they're working on and Lynn is taking part in, and about people Julia doesn't know. He says he's not very happy about things at the hospital, but he tries not to pay much attention to what's going on around him and just concentrate on his own work. So he's a resigned sort of man. She doesn't pay much attention to what he's saying, but suddenly, just when she's least expecting it, he turns and addresses her. How's the translation coming along? It's obvious he knows about her work from Lynn. She answers with more detail than is required for what was just a polite question. Talking so much makes her nervous, and she has to make an effort not to raise her hand to cover the mole on her neck. When she was getting ready to leave the house, she thought that the bad weather would have justified her wearing a neck scarf, but she didn't take one in the end, because it would have just reinforced her complex. He doesn't seem to be in a hurry, and the time he's taking to get on with examining Harri, which is perhaps just out of politeness, is beginning to make Julia nervous; she'd like him to find out what Harri's lumps are as soon as possible. Abaitua thinks that few people really appreciate translators' work; when people read translated texts with ease, very few think about the translator. With doctors, fortunately, the opposite is true. Normally, when things are going well, it's because nature wants them to, and yet it's we who take all the credit. An expression of humility that Julia doesn't know quite how to take.

Abaitua spreads his hands out on the desk—they're thin but strong, well looked after—and leans forward a little to say to Harri at last, "So let's see, what's troubling you?" Then he leans back in his chair and seems to be ready to give her all his attention. He's attractive and doesn't look his age. Definitely a man who looks after his appearance. He isn't wearing a tie, but his shirt would be right for one, it has one of those little straps on the collar for holding a tie from behind, although it's hanging loose right now. So it looks as if he's taken his tie off to look more relaxed but is still a little formal. His elbows are resting on the arms of his chair, his hands together in front of his face, his fingers linked together except for his index fingers, which are touching his lips. Suddenly Julia realizes she's heard him moaning with pleasure, and she's embarrassed to think that he's realized it, too, when he takes his eyes off Harri for a moment to look at her.

Harri tells him she's been feeling this lump of hers for more than a year now.

He stands up and says "let's see" once more.

Harri complains that the changing room's too small for her, and Abaitua agrees that it's very small. Julia remains seated on the other side of the screen, and Harri walks past her wearing a hospital gown that leaves her back exposed; she does a dance step, raising her arms above her head and stretching one leg out behind her. Julia still thinks she's overdone it with the purple nail polish.

Abaitua's occasional brief comments break the nervous silence. He keeps on saying "let's see," "that's it," "closer," and "very good." Short commands. The sound of latex. Other identifiable sounds: chair wheels on the tiles; tools on the tray; a spray; Harri's silence; the quiet ticking of an electric clock on the wall. Something of Noll's she read that morning: doctors protect themselves and not their patients, just as lawyers protect themselves more than they do the accused. Something Abaitua just said reminded her of that—he used different words, but the idea was similar—and she almost tells them the quote but doesn't dare to in the end, not wanting him to think she's being overly clever. And she wonders again whether he's aware that she knows he's sleeping with Lynn, but then she banishes the thought again, she doesn't think it's appropriate. Another quote, this time something Frisch said to Noll: literature's task is to obliterate the present. She thinks she understands the meaning of that, but she isn't sure. Abaitua keeps on saying the same things—"very good" once more, but in a different tone now, because he's finished examining Harri. The sound of latex suggests it, and the sound of water coming out of the tap confirms it. "You can get dressed," Abaitua says, washing his hands. Julia thinks he's going to give her a provisional verdict, because the test results haven't come in yet, and she gets the impression that Harri wants to put it off as long as possible, because she keeps up a steady stream of ridiculous comments from behind the curtain, one after another. She says that she's more worried about her breasts getting saggier than she is about the lumps. She's been telling the same joke for months now. She says she'll take advantage of her cancer to get some new breasts. Abaitua sits down behind his desk once more. He taps away on his computer with just two fingers but with great ease. It's strange the way he holds the keyboard on his lap. Without pausing in his typing, he says that he's seen some very sexy women with mastectomies, to which Harri says, "Oh, really? Are you saying that to keep my spirits up?" His sudden mortification almost makes him drop the keyboard onto the floor. Not at all—Julia is amused by the look of horror on his face—what he meant to say was that women worry too much about the aesthetics of their breasts and he doesn't think it's much of a problem as far as men are concerned. He looks at Julia for her understanding, which she tries to give him by smiling. All types of breasts have their own charm—large and small, round

545

and pear-shaped . . . But Harri isn't convinced. "That must be why you guys choose young women." Her delivery seems to indicate that she's unaware she's just put her foot in it, but Julia gets embarrassed. She wonders if Abaitua's typing more vigorously now.

She isn't sure, but she thinks he says "*anyway*" when Harri walks out from behind the screen. He waits for her to sit down and leans forward once more with his forearms resting on the desk. He holds his hands firmly together, fingers linked. As was to be expected, he doesn't give a verdict—they have to wait for her to get her tests, which should be done right away. "As soon as possible," he insists, when Harri mentions waiting to do them in the autumn. He gives her an appointment slip, which Harri tucks into her thick leather planner.

When they all stand up, Harri is the one who moves forward to give him two kisses. Julia, on the other hand, hesitates for a moment and then decides that he's the one who has to move toward her. He puts his hands on her shoulders as before and doesn't take them off after giving her two kisses. That feeling she always has, that he looks at her mole when talking to her, wondering whether she's had it looked at. She doesn't say anything. He says he bumped into Martin a few days earlier, he told him he was making good progress with his novel.

He seems to be one of those people who have real difficulty saying goodbye. He politely goes with them to the vestibule, leaving his office door open, as if to tell the women waiting that he'll be back momentarily. Julia finds the situation uncomfortable. Harri, on the other hand, seems calmer now. It's clear she doesn't realize she put her foot in her mouth just before; she keeps on talking about her theory that girls nowadays have larger breasts. The doctor seems to listen to her with attention, although his eyes go to the open door of his office a couple of times. Julia guides Harri toward the stairs, saying that Doctor Abaitua has people waiting for him.

As soon as they're out of his sight, Julia asks Harri how she had the nerve to tell him that men prefer younger women, and Harri doesn't flinch. She says he's a good doctor and an honest man, but that doesn't mean she'll let him take her for a fool—it's fine for him to say that women with mastectomies are sexy, but he himself is sleeping with a women thirty years younger than him with great big tits. Julia thinks Harri knows she was in the wrong but doesn't want to appear weak. Harri asks her to go to the university with her, which is just what she had been going to suggest. As Lynn would put it, she feels like going to Martin's friend's bookshop, if only to see it for the first time. She takes the risk of telling Harri that she's curious to see what the man is like, because of the things Lynn's told her about him. Apparently he's a happy man, a good cook, he knows about flowers, he changes his mother's diapers. She regrets saying that, because she knows that Harri will use it against her, and that's exactly what happens—she says to her, as if she'd heard her earlier conversation with Lynn, "If you need a man with a mother, you've already got Martin." She says that what the other guy probably needs is somebody to change his mother's diapers for him and that at least Martin has enough money to pay for however many nurses he needs to take on. What's obvious is that Harri doesn't accept Julia showing the least bit of interest in any man other than Martin.

"Poor Lynn," says Harri, as she starts up the car. Julia decides not to ask in what way Lynn is poor, because she knows the answer and doesn't want to hear it. And Harri says it anyway. The poor girl's going to suffer, because she's in love—that man's never going to break up with Goytisolo. Why isn't he going to break up with her, and even if he doesn't, what's wrong with enjoying what there is to be enjoyed while it lasts? "Beclouded" is how Lynn tried to put it in Spanish. She wishes Harri could hear the girl saying "*me tiene obnubilada.*" She can't help laughing as she remembers Lynn trying to pronounce the Spanish verb right. And in any case, who is Harri to say anything if what she's told them about her own undignified behavior during her search for the man from the airport is true? Although Julia doesn't use the word *undignified*. There's an enormous difference, Harri says, taking her hands off the steering wheel. The man she crossed paths with at the airport, with only the promise he had seen in her eyes—she puts a hand on her chest when she says "my eyes"—told that peroxide blonde to get lost.

The car is stopped at a traffic light, but it's green, and car horns start sounding out behind them.

After parking near the roundabout on the street next to the bevelled building where Martin's friend's bookshop is, Harri walks left, even though going right is the way to get to the university, the cafeteria, and, of course, the bookshop. Julia stands still in the middle of the sidewalk and points the other way—"We'll get there quicker this way." But Harri says, "It doesn't make any difference," and keeps on walking. When it comes down to it, Julia doesn't much care, she just wants to satisfy her curiosity and meet Martin's friend.

."And for you, a shandy?" The pleasing feeling of having the waiter know what you like. She likes sitting at that outdoor terrace—Donostia seems a long way off. There are drops of water on the table from the rain shower a few minutes ago, and they have to wait for a couple of chairs to be brought out from the bar. It doesn't look like it'll rain again. Clouds and patches of blue sky. Julia tells Harri that she's starting to like sitting at outdoor terraces. It's a custom from the south of Europe that's beginning to spread all over the continent, although the heat in other places, of course, is provided by those patio heaters that look like lampposts. It reminds her of when Harri used to say how much she liked the outdoor terraces in Bilbao. She no longer mentions them. Now she just says "that was a great time." She clearly isn't very lively, Julia thinks probably because of the tests she's had to have done. She takes her hands and dares to squeeze them gently. She tells her she's going to be just fine.

"It's not that."

She moves a hand away to take a sip of her gin and tonic.

"What is it, then?"

Now, all of a sudden, now that the chance to meet the man seems very close, she's afraid. She feels it could be the end, the end of everything. She says she felt something similar the day she saw Martin putting the new map of Sicily up on the wall with pushpins. She tells her she told Martin, teasingly, that he'd never have the energy to go to Sicily if it weren't on one of those one-week package tours with the flight, hotel, and rental car all included, and he didn't answer her. While they were still arguing about the map, she picked up a book from the pile of them on the table, opened it at random, and, incredible though it seems, read the following: "Our ships will always set sail for Sicily, although we know they're heading to destruction."

"¿Qué te parece?"

She doesn't believe her. It's impossible that she could have found that exact text, whose author is unknown to her, while Martin was fixing a map of Sicily to the wall. What could she possibly make of it, she answered. She regrets not having ordered a gin and tonic herself. Sometimes she's tempted to get slightly drunk in the afternoon, and that temptation makes her a little afraid.

Harri's finished hers. She picks up her glass and looks into it for a moment, as if surprised to see only bits of ice and lemon left in it, and then puts it back down on the table. She has the peculiar habit of talking about herself in the third person. The man at the airport and the woman—herself. She seems to be worried about the idea of the man and the woman meeting and nothing else happening, that being the end of it all. So now that she knows they're going to meet, now that they're about to see each other again, she's very afraid. "Do you know what I mean?"

How can she expect her to understand if she doesn't tell her anything? What does she mean she's about to meet the man? She tells her about it, but tells her so little that it's difficult to follow her. She wrinkles her face up, that unattractive gesture she makes when she tastes a bite of food she doesn't like. Why would she tell them anything, they don't believe her, they stop her in her tracks and think she's crazy. That complaint once more, in the plural, the reproach that they're only interested in things that happen in novels, which Julia thinks stems from her complex about not reading much. "There is life beyond books," she often says. She raises her glass to her lips once more and tips her head straight back in a rather vulgar movement, taking in all the ice, and Julia wonders if she hasn't started drinking a little too much lately. Don't be silly, of course she believes her, she says, putting her hand on her forearm this time, a way of showing affection that's more typical of men and that she finds easy to use. Apparently Adolfo's called her again.

"The Iberia guy," she explains unnecessarily—so Harri really does think she doesn't pay any attention to the things she says. He called her by surprise one day when she was in Bilbao and asked to see her at the Hotel Ercilla. Among many other things, the most important one he told her was that it was very clear which of the last two travelers he had not yet spoken with was the man. There was no doubt about it—when he called one number and said what he usually did, a vulgar woman told him that the jerk didn't live there any more and she didn't want to have anything to do with him. Just in case, Iberia Adolfo took the trouble of going to the other traveler's office—he was a businessman, and very well protected by his secretary—and managed to see him. (He'd done all this using some skill not relevant to the story, but something to do with his ability to seduce the secretary.) And he turned out to be nothing like the man Harri had described, not at all, in terms of appearance. To start with, he was bald. So the only thing they still had left to do was find the true man's new address, which, unfortunately, they could only do through his ex-wife, because his first and last names, which were very common indeed, wouldn't be any use to them in that sense.

"A bit of a disappointment." Harri smiles sadly, as if truly disappointed. But she doesn't know his first and last names, she only knows that they're very common, because that was all the Iberia guy would tell her. He refused to tell her, even though she begged him. As if being able to put a name to the man from her memory might almost be enough for her, but the Iberia guy wouldn't budge. He said he couldn't risk giving her information about a traveler without checking first that he actually wanted her to get in touch with him. First he, Adolfo, would have to speak with the man and check that *Montauk* meant something to him, that he understood what was meant by a second chance, and that he was interested in being put in touch with her. He couldn't be budged from there. In any case, he promised that he'd soon be in touch with her again, because he was determined to get the information out of the peroxide blonde. He didn't tell her how and she didn't ask him for any details, but it seemed the Iberia guy had some plan or other and was confident of his seductive powers over women—in this case a trashy abandoned woman. She made him swear that he would give her the man's name soon, and he swore on a photo of his son, a cute-looking boy called Borja. Then everything happened more or less like the first time. Adolfo stood up and started walking, and she followed him up to room 222. His wife called him while he was trying to fuck her for the second time, and he had to leave. She called Martxelo and told him that she was in a meeting in Bilbao, it was going to finish very late and she had another one first thing the next day, so it wasn't worth her going back home and he should get something out of the fridge for dinner. She ordered herself hot chocolate and pastries and fell fast asleep.

The next morning, on leaving the hotel, she had to pay not just for her chocolate and pastry feast and the room but also for the minibar, which Adolfo had emptied. She picks up her glass again, looking inside once more as if she's just realized for the first time

550

that it's empty, puts it back on the table, and pushes it away from her. Then she stares at it. The Harri who is sometimes a serious woman, especially when it comes to her work.

"Do you think he's trying to get money out of me?"

"I wouldn't trust him."

"So you'd let the whole thing go?"

Julia has her doubts. She's afraid Harri will say "silly you, I can't believe you believed me!" and she doesn't want to feel like a fool. She doesn't reply. Harri waits for her answer for a few seconds while she looks for some coins in her purse. Then, in the way she normally does such things, she puts the money carefully on the tray and says, "You guys are always clipping my wings." With neither anger nor sorrow. Not very nicely, though, either.

Julia could change the subject by asking her why she's using the plural, but she doesn't. Obviously, she must have told Martin about her affair previously, he probably thought she was crazy, and that's what's got her back up. That's why Harri's used the plural. She ends up saying, "What you have to concentrate on now are your tests." Getting back to cancer. Sensibly, as a mother would do, but it's too late by the time she realizes. Harri looks at her sadly, gives a laugh, and nods. The waiter's been attentive, and he gets a good tip. They both keep quiet, each waiting for the other to say it's time they got going.

Harri looks at her watch and says it's terribly late.

On their way back to the car, and because Harri's said it's so late, Julia doesn't dare suggest that they cross the street and have a look at the bookshop. When they reach the corner, it's Harri herself who suddenly stops and asks her if she doesn't want to go in and have a look at the bookseller, and Julia feels obliged to say no, in order not to come across as being as crazy as her.

SHE FINDS ZIGOR ALONE AT HOME, because her mother's gone to her sister's. He says grandma is sad, she's been crying. Apparently, a friend from Otzeta came by to visit and told them the latest news from Etxezar. It seems her great nephew is still selling bits of it to his neighbour, and several days earlier he was found lying in vomit on the kitchen floor with the dog chewing at the bills from the sale of the pine forest.

Zigor's sad, too, and Julia's angry the situation at Etxezar's made him so. He's sitting at his desk, a fold-down board like the one Julia has that comes out of the closet. She asks what he's up to. He's trying to finish his project about the war.

They spend a long while without talking, because the boy's reading, or pretending to, and while she folds some T-shirts, Julia tries to think of something to say to him about why her mother is so sad about losing Etxezar. Until he breaks the silence.

"Does Martin have a lot of money?"

The question doesn't surprise her much. She knows he's sometimes heard her mother saying that if she, Julia, asked Martin, he'd lend them enough money to be able to get Etxezar back, and Julia's even less pleased that her mother's made the boy her confidant for her absurd ideas.

"I don't know if he's got a lot. Enough to live on, I think. Why do you ask?"

He shrugs his shoulders.

"I just wanted to know."

She folds the last T-shirt, sits down on the side of the bed, and, seeing his *txistu* and drum cases, says, for the sake of it, "You haven't played your *txistu* in a while."

"I don't have any time."

Silence once more. Julia is thinking about the best way to tell him they can't ask Martin to lend them the money, and even less so in order to buy the old *baserri* in the hills around Otzeta for the sole reason that that's where her mother was born. She prefers not to seem angry and asks him what he's reading, to buy herself time, and he makes a movement to hide the pieces of paper on the table. Finally, he tells her he's gotten ahold of a book in the city library with some horrifying information about the war. In fact, it's a compilation of firsthand accounts that Joxemiel Barandiaran collected from people who fled across the border. The witnesses weren't all old people, he says, as if that point were important, but what they had to say was more interesting than what the people at the retirement home have been telling him. He photocopied what one woman said; her last name was Barandiaran, as well, and she, too, was from Ataun, but he says the whole book is horrifying. He reads that in the summer of 1936, some woodsmen had been working in the Eugi hills when one night, several Falangists turned up with four prisoners and told

552

the woodsmen to kill them. They didn't want to, but they forced them to take the rifles, otherwise they'd kill them right then and there. One of the woodsmen, Juan Galfarsoro, from the Tellerietxea *baserri*, fainted as soon as he picked up the rifle, and the rest of them shot and killed three of the prisoners. The fourth managed to flee through the forest thanks to the light coming from the headlights of the car in which the group had arrived. The Falangists ordered them to bury the bodies, and the woodsmen obeyed them. When the Falangists left, the prisoner who got away came back, said he was going to Gasteiz, and asked them to please tell him the way. They went back to the village and never told the whole story of what had happened, only saying that the Falangists made them bury the three shot prisoners. The rest of it came out later.

"The one who fainted was a nice guy, wasn't he?"

Julia's glad Zigor likes the woodsman who wasn't up to killing another person. She's moved, and she doesn't mind her son seeing that.

Zigor says he's thinking of including an imaginary interview with the woodsman who fainted in his project, but Julia tells him she doesn't think it's a good idea. The objective of the project they've asked him to do is to interview old people and, as far as possible, he's supposed to use firsthand accounts, find people who actually saw things. Zigor doesn't give in—the old people themselves haven't told him anything interesting. Even his grandmother has told him nothing more than vague platitudes, and when he asks for more details, she says she can't remember.

In fact, she doesn't even know where his grandfather spent the war.

Julia decides to leave him alone, let him do whatever he wants to. She's not going to be the one to criticize him for finding what he reads in books more interesting than what people around him have to say.

"I'd like to read it once you've finished."

Julia gets up, grabs the *txistu* and drum, and puts them on the table.

"Hey, can you play something? I'm feeling sad."

Zigor plays "*Intxaustiren Kontrapasa*," because it's the most traditional piece in his repertoire, and he probably thinks it's the most appropriate piece for his mother. Really, she'd have preferred a fandango, but as always when she listens to the *txistu*, she ends up thinking about how it's amazing what people can do with a simple three-holed flute.

After the short concert, Zigor puts the *txistu* back in its case, and while he does so, Julia says she understands Grandma feeling sad about Etxezar being destroyed but she can't ask Martin for money. She wouldn't ask him even if he had more than enough.

"Do you understand that?"

"Yes, *Ama*, don't worry."

18

LIGHT'S POURING IN THROUGH THE GAPS in the blinds when he opens
his eyes. Pilar's footsteps up and down the hallway mean she's getting
ready to go out. It's Saturday. For a moment, he wonders whether to
get up or stay in bed until she leaves; in the end, he decides to get up,
though not knowing why. Perhaps he doesn't want to come across as
being lazy.

Pilar sticks her head around the bathroom door to say good
morning. He'd forgotten she's going to Bordeaux. She has the look
she usually has in the morning, the look of being in a hurry. She
hasn't dried her hair, and she's standing in her bra, dressed only from
the waist down—a tight skirt and quite high-heeled shoes, a bit
more formal than most days—and she has a blouse, a jacket, and a
bag hanging from one arm. She disappears and then appears again to
remind him that Loiola's coming at noon. Will he take care of him?
She says she's in a great hurry and rubs her neck with a tissue. She's
just had a shower, and she's already sweating.

She'll call him as soon as she gets to Bordeaux.

SOUTH WIND TODAY AT THE BRETXA AZOKA. The intense blue
brightness and the golden sandstone of the buildings. People out for
a walk, happy to live where they do. The noble market building

turned into a vulgar mall. The farmers swept to small stands on one side. Hothouse runner beans and tomatoes; peas that should have been spring peas at this point in the season; year-round carrots, chard, and leeks; and shiny eggplants, all identical in shape and size, imported from Holland. People trying to use their Basque to get better deals from the farmers. The peas are incredibly expensive; they swear they're home-grown. It's a long time since anybody's bartered for anything, but the farmers still give the parsley away for free. The old woman fishmonger wrapping anchovies from Benidorm up in newspaper sheets. The escalator goes down to the underground market. Hake that isn't from Hondarribia, red seam bream that isn't from Orio, its best side flipped up under the strong spotlights. He has his favorite fishmonger, Jon Sarriegi, who never cheats him. But why is swindling accepted? Answer: because we are all of us sinners. For the same reason that the allopathic, scientific, official medical establishment tolerates natural remedies, homeopathy, and even witchcraft.

Many familiar faces. Doctors doing their shopping—it's well-looked upon socially on Saturday mornings at the Bretxa Azoka.

As soon as he sees her among the people at the flower stand, he recognizes her by her hair. She has it tied up in a small kerchief, it shines like bright copper in the light. She's wearing those rather loose blue jeans he's seen her in before, she uses a belt with them but places it beneath the loops, which shortens their length and brings out her buttocks. He doesn't know if he wants to go be with her. Or rather, if he wants to take the risk of some acquaintance seeing them together.

Now he sees her turning around, as if she's noticed him looking at her, a small bunch of violets in her hand and sunglasses half-covering her face. He doesn't do anything to hide himself and leaves her seeing him or not to chance. He'd like to go for a walk with her, show her places in Urgull and then have a glass of wine with her, but he has to admit that his reluctance to meet up with her is greater than his desire. He's reluctant to have some midwife or colleague looking at them maliciously; he doesn't want their being seen together out and about to be a confirmation of their relationship; he's afraid he'll get used to her being there; anticipated malaise about having to eventually tell her he has to leave.

He hardly has time to start wondering whether his doubts might be due to a lack of affection when somebody pats him on the back.

He turns around. It's the resident from the neonatology department, and he seems to be glad to see him. Beautiful weather, it's like being in the Caribbean. The shirt he's wearing certainly gives that idea, it's loose-fitting and has yellow flowers on a blue background. He's just come off night duty and is going to sit down at an outdoor terrace, read the paper, and have "*un cafecito*"—a little cup of coffee. Then he's going to meet up with some friends. "*Para tomar algo y echarse unos vinitos*," he says—to grab a bite and have "a little glass of wine" or two. He finds the childish satisfaction expressed by his use of so many diminutives supremely irritating. The baby with choanal atresia has been having some serious problems, he mentions in passing. Abaitua had forgotten all about that child. The resident looks away, following Abaitua's glance, and says, "*Mira por dónde*"— would you look at that—"it's Lynn." And he moves his arms as though swimming to clear a path through the crowd to her.

"*Hi.*" They kiss each other on the cheek, probably because they've bumped into each other outside the hospital. She gives Abaitua two kisses, too. "*Qué alegría*"—so great running into you. She tells the resident he looks good without his smock on. And his shirt's really beautiful, too; fatty blushes. She doesn't say anything to Abaitua. She takes her glasses off for a moment, just long enough for him to see how much her eyes lighten, and then she puts them back on again. What beautiful weather, she says, gesturing at everything with one hand. "Perfect for going for a walk." She turns to the resident again. "What route would you recommend?" Fatty hesitates, he's discon-certed. "The Kontxa could be good, but there're too many people." Abaitua listens to them in silence, full of the innocent satisfaction of knowing himself to be the chosen one.

They're in a crowd of people, and the young doctor suggests they have a drink. They could sit down at the outdoor terrace over there. Lynn thinks it's a great idea, and she looks at Abaitua as soon as she says so, as if to ask if she's done the right thing in accepting, and he says he'd gladly stay but he's in a bit of a hurry, he'd like to go by the hospital before noon. That gives him the chance to get away and also to make it clear that he's a hard-working doctor. The young doctor's face is covered in sweat, and he's definitely pleased. So that's it, then, he says—"*Entonces nada*"—as he takes Lynn by the elbow. She smiles naturally and pulls a purple flower out of her bouquet to give it to Abaitua. Then she lifts up her hand and wiggles her fingers in the air.

They don't give each other two kisses to say goodbye. After taking ten steps, he ventures to look back but doesn't see them, just a bit of Lynn's head, her blue kerchief and cherry-wood-colored bun next to the statue of Sarriegi. He isn't jealous of the biochemistry-obsessed resident. He's young, but too fat.

However, if Lynn doesn't decide to go back to the States soon, he'll end up having to deal with that before long. One day he'll see her holding hands with a young man, perhaps on the Pasealeku Berria at dusk. It isn't the first time he's had that thought. He's even come up with candidates. Young doctors at the hospital, ones he thinks attractive and bright, and he's thought that he would be glad for Lynn, and for himself, too—that way this story, which he can't decide what to do about, would be over once and for all.

He knows there's something pathological about the whole thing.

He's well aware that he can't be sure of anything before it actually happens. He would never have thought that Pilar's affair—if you can call it that—would have affected him so much. She had been sitting on the edge of the bed when he put a hand on her shoulder. He thought she looked troubled, and that moved him. That was why he'd put his hand on her shoulder, to comfort her. He still wasn't aware of what was going to happen, it was unthinkable for him that she could go to bed with somebody else, that she could even be interested in going to bed with somebody else; he wasn't furious yet. He was just sorry for her—she who was usually so measured in expressing her feelings—sorry to see her looking so inconsolable. On the edge of the bed, like in that painting by Hopper. The memory of that scene is more immediate and devastating for him at night. Now it's day, a beautiful day with a warm south wind.

THE NURSES AT ALL THE DESKS he goes past are only talking about one thing: the weather is more appropriate for going to the beach than for going to work. More than one of them is astonished to see him there—admires him for it, too, he'd say—outside his working hours.

So the weather's beautiful. A woman who probably doesn't have many days left to live says the same thing. Her husband is sitting next to her and holding one of her hands. It seems he hasn't given her much of a life. He admits as much himself. Abaitua convinced him to make up for it a bit by being at her side while she died, sensing that the wife loved him a lot and still does. Abaitua normally uses his intuition in situations like this where his medical knowledge is of no use and he feels he could use an expert's advice. Protocols don't cover everything. The woman tends not to complain, thinking pain is inevitable. "We're fine," she normally says when he asks. The husband doesn't say anything. A few days earlier, he asked for some sedatives for her, because he couldn't deal with the anguish of seeing her like that. Abaitua thinks his presence there helps the man to stay put. Abaitua makes her promise to call the nurse if she feels any pain; there's no need for her to suffer.

He still finds it surprising how important culture is when it comes to dealing with illness and death. There are too many people in the room. Children, nieces, and nephews, all competing to show their respect for the patient. If it goes on a long time, and it certainly will, signs of tiredness and malaise will begin to appear, desertions, instances of negligence they will blame each other for, anger. He advises them to take turns and relieve each other, to economize their strength. Patients mustn't be allowed to tyrannize people, either. She's happy to see her whole family around her. Unlike some others, she wants to experience everything right up until the end.

It's sad when there's nothing you can do or say, when your only worry is that the patient might realize that your only desire is to leave the room and close the door behind you as soon as possible. He doesn't feel very comfortable right now as the patient tells him about her urinary malfunction, with too many details—of course, for her, it's the most important thing in the world—while what comes to his mind is that it wasn't a good idea to leave the *txipirones*—the baby squids he just bought in the market—in the car in this sunny weather.

As he's about to leave, he remembers that before seeing Lynn at the Bretxa Azoka, the chubby neonatology resident was starting to tell him something about the child with choanal atresia. Curious, he decides to stop in at the maternity ward to find out. In the waiting room, there's a group of residents. On seeing him, they make no pretence about stopping their lively conversation. On the other side of the door, there's almost complete silence, broken only by the tired, exhausted crying of a child. The head nurse who looks like his mother is at the desk, the one who always gives him a hard look because her own son is in prison. Or that's what he thinks at least—she reproaches him or at least lets him know she's hurt because his son is free. Each time he sees her, that gesture of hers, nodding slowly with an expression of sorrow on her face, reminds him of his mother. He was planning to walk straight through, but a young nurse stops him. She had one of her ovaries removed a couple of months ago, and she's doing just splendidly now—"*de cine.*" But that isn't what she wanted to talk with him about. Has he heard the latest? It sounds mysterious. Abaitua is sure she's going to tell him about the choanal atresia patient, and he's right. After looking left and right, with a gesture of confidentiality, she quickly tells him what he already knew: the child was born thirty days ago—he didn't think it had been so long—and ever since then, all their requests for Orl's people to operate on him have fallen on deaf ears. It's an operation that can only be performed by the head of the department, and he's very busy. That was all the troubled ENT specialists who came to see the child dared say. According to what some of them have led her to understand, it's all because somebody wants to make the waiting list longer, in order to be able to do the operations that don't get done in the morning in the afternoon, so that they'd get to be paid overtime. So now all this time's gone by without anybody doing anything to stop what's happened from happening. And what's happened is terrible: unable to breathe through his nose, the child went blue in his mother's arms and they had to revive him, the reanimation took far too long, and the result was serious anoxia. The woman's air of confidentiality, arising from the fact that she's whispering, is increased by the feeling in her words and her constant glances at her other colleagues around them to confirm what she's saying. "The poor child's a vegetable now." That's how one of them confirmed the nurse's words, sadly nodding her head in just the same way as the head nurse and his mother do. There's a poster on the privacy screen behind him, one he hasn't seen before and must be new. The paper's shiny, which, with the sunlight on it, makes it difficult to see completely, but there's a beautiful child on it feeding from a swollen breast.

And what do they want him to do about it?

He keeps quiet and doesn't say that, of course, not with all of them agreeing that things can't be left at that, somebody has to do something more than just crossing their arms. A tracheotomy, at least. Or take the child to another center. Something. The one with the cysts on her ovary is the angriest. She's the most confident, she goes so far as to say that somebody should grab Orl by the ear and drag him out of the Basozabal Golf Club, even knowing that he's Abaitua's brother-in-law's brother. She talks about the tyranny within the service, doctors often remaining idle because they aren't even allowed to remove a pair of tonsils. Then it's Arrese's turn. *Clumsy* and *incompetent* are the nicest things they have to say about him. Always in a whisper, discreetly. They can speak with him about it, because he's different, a real doctor. He's sure that's partly why, but it's also because they see him as one of them, as being frustrated, to an extent, stripped of power, and he would rather not be their accomplices in that sense. He guesses their indignation is a result of personal bitterness, a secret desire for vengeance in their hearts, a despicable happiness stemming from a horrendous event that opens the way for them to take action against the people who don't value them as they should be valued. They want there to be disasters, so that they'll be given justice. He's often had to combat that dirty feeling.

They tell him that serious though the matter is, it isn't the worst of it.

He would rather not know any more, but he can't get away now. The worst thing is that Orl and Arrese told the mother that it was she who suffocated her son, while she was breastfeeding him. They all look at him to see how hearing those words will affect him. What does he think about that? He thinks it's cruel. But he realizes that's insufficient. It's insufficient in terms of their indignation, and so he repeats it, saying again that it's horrible, because that's what he thinks, but they keep on looking at him, as if expecting something more than just that simple statement from him, as though he had some special responsibility there, and that makes him deeply angry.

There's an explosion of light at the end of the hallway, which makes him close his eyes. The tired crying has stopped. He thinks about the resident, who must be having his little cup of coffee near the Bretxa Azoka with Lynn. He also remembers the squid he's left in the car, it's probably in the sunlight, and he tells them he has to go.

He could also add that it's his day off, but he just says he has to deal with an emergency, without putting much conviction into his words and without moving from where he is; finally it's the head nurse, who's been standing there with her arms folded listening to the others talking, who helps him get away by telling the girls they've got work waiting for them, and they all disappear into the newborn nursery. The head nurse then nods two or three times, as if confirming some thought she's had, with that mixture of disappointment and sorrow he knows so well.

That expression on her face that means *ona hago hi*—you're a piece of work.

She walks off down the corridor without saying a word, and Abaitua follows her, because that's the way he's going, but then she stops in her tracks after half a dozen steps, and he does the same. They're in front of a door with a small window in it. Through it, they can see the same poster as before, but now it's possible to read the slogan—Breastfeeding Is An Act Of Love. And they hear the child's tired crying again. He goes up to the door to widen his field of vision and sees them sitting there. He doesn't need anyone to tell him it's them. The mother has a white blanket on her lap and she's playing with the tassels on its edge. She looks quite distant, disconcerted perhaps, maybe wondering why there's nobody wrapped in the blanket. There's a man next to her, bending over and looking at his hands, who seems very far away. Abaitua steps aside. He doesn't' want them to realize he's there, and taking a step back, he looks at the head nurse. Her eyes are sad, full of reproach as well as tiredness. She asks him—with the moral superiority that being from his mother's town and having a son in prison lend her—if he doesn't think it's about time something was done.

Do something. As his mother would have said, "*Gizona, gizon denak*"—the man who's a real man.

He refuses to let this woman—who he'd happily strangle—make him feel guilty. He looks at his watch and says, "It's very late," and with that, he disappears quickly upstairs, the same ones he once fled down to get away from Lynn.

As he goes along the badly lit green corridor, he's ashamed to realize that he's spent half his life fleeing and the other half paralyzed by fear. He's not familiar with this part of the hospital but thinks it must be connected with the ICU. If that's right, he decides, he'll go visit Teresa Hoyos; otherwise, he'll leave the building. (Whenever he decides to let chance rule his decision-making, he remembers Saint Ignatius of Loiola on his mule—or had it been a donkey?—standing

562

there next to the Moor who'd mocked the Virgin Mary's virginity; he let go of the reins and decided that if his mount took the same path as the Moor at the next turning, he would kill him, otherwise, he'd let him live.)

The doctor on duty in the ICU says there's nothing new as far as Teresa Hoyos's husband is concerned. Apparently, she's reading a book by herself in the waiting room.

She's wearing a black or very dark-colored sweater and pants. She has one leg crossed over the other and a shoe balancing on her foot up in the air. The doctor tells Abaitua that if he's her friend, he should try to convince her to go home, she isn't going to achieve anything by waiting there. Even so, it's normal to be afraid of going away, to want to stay there in case her husband comes out of the coma. Wanting him to know that she's been there, that she hasn't abandoned him. She closes her book and puts her face in her hands. Abaitua says he'll try to convince her, but some other time, he's running late, he says, and he looks at his watch without seeing what time it actually is.

IT'S EASY TO CLEAN FRESH SQUID like that, so fresh it's still the same intense color of the sand at the bottom of the bay. Almost too fresh. He could put it away and take Loiola out to a restaurant, but he'd rather have lunch at home. He'll cook it in its ink, although it's not the best thing to eat straight away, because it's a stew. Modern people say it's a way to spoil the ingredients, but he likes to have that type of stew from time to time, and so does his son. Cut plenty of onion into small pieces, put it in the frying pan, and then cook the squid on medium. Pour in half a glass of wine, add the ink, an (optional) spoonful of tomato sauce, and allow to cook. He's not in the mood to put the sauce through a sieve.

To cook, just like to operate, he has to be relaxed, and he isn't. He's feeling unhinged by the way the nurses laid into him—"something has to be done" definitely meant *let's see what you're going to do about it*—and having to have lunch with Loiola doesn't make him feel any calmer, either. Things seldom end well when they meet, though not particularly badly, either, and less and less so, but their meetings never live up to his expectations. To an extent, it's because he always has something to say about what the boy has or hasn't done or should do. Because he gives him advice clumsily, he recognizes that. Because he doesn't accept him as he is. He thinks that's what spoils their encounters. That and his wishes, and his anxiety. Really, the fact that they don't get together very often means he feels the need to tell him all the things he's been thinking about and saving up to mention to him. So sometimes he decides to keep quiet, and then his son asks him if he's angry, and so he replies he doesn't have anything to be particularly pleased about. He also admits that he can't stop criticizing and correcting—his way of talking, his manners, the fact that he keeps his elbows on the table when he drinks, for instance—in a way he would never dare do to any other adult, in a way he'd never let anybody else do to him. Pilar's called him out on it. You don't tell an adult person you're eating with not to lean over their plate so much, or not to make so much noise with their chair, or not to open their mouth so impolitely. And he replies that even though his son is an adult, he's still his son, and he drives him up the wall. Every time he sees him, he has to make the firm decision to hold back and be tolerant. Pilar says that, too, that the important thing is to keep the relationship going and that his attitude is just putting that at risk, because it gets their son's back up. So he's decided to act sensibly, forget about trivial matters, and just deal with the important issues. The most important thing is to encourage him to go to the States, and in that sense, to make things as easy as possible for him. After that, he has to tell him that there's no need for him to commit to working at his grandfather's clinic, the idea his mother's suddenly had, against everybody else's opinion, shouldn't condition what he studies or his overall future in any way whatsoever. Without in any way criticizing the level of commitment that Pilar has taken on since her father's death or the romantic side of the whole thing, he has to point out to him that as well as the fact that he's free and shouldn't let himself be conditioned by others, it's very difficult to make a health center profitable while at the same time practicing medicine properly, and as if that weren't enough, the clinic's full of old sharks and his mother would be better off getting as far away from them as possible. In fact, it's just occurred to him that he wouldn't put it past those cold-hearted jerks to dump a corpse on Pilar's operating table in the hopes of getting her out of the picture. But he obviously isn't going to say that to his son. Nor is he going to say anything negative to him about the surge of loyalty that

Pilar's shown for her father's work lately, or anything that might give him the ridiculous idea that he feels he's been taking a backseat to Pilar's increased responsibilities and workload. Quite the opposite, he'll say he's proud, and that's true to an extent—what's more, her having a lot of work right now makes things easier for him—and he'll try not to be sarcastic or ironic, that's the main thing, because Loiola's very sensitive.

It's because they're identical, as Pilar often says.

And there's no doubt about that. He gets irritated when he sees his own flaws in his son—weakness, irascibility, laziness (he knows that he's lazy even though nobody else sees it in him, he's probably learned to hide it over the years)—and he can see them clearly. And his son, too, is aware of all those flaws.

Add the fried bread chunks at the very end.

His son sniffs the air and says it smells good—a lovely way to say hello. It's a pity, he says, after lifting up the lid and inspecting the squid, that he can't stay for lunch. Abaitua tries to cover up his annoyance at hearing this by keeping quiet, but he can't bring himself to continue cutting the bread and puts the knife down clumsily, and of course, his son notices. He thought his father already knew, because he told his mother this morning.

Abaitua excuses her by saying that she must have forgotten, she's had a lot of work recently. She's been feeling nervous about operating in Bordeaux with Giraud. "Boy, she really is busy." He says this as he goes into the room that he still considers to be his, although he doesn't use it, and Abaitua is sure that he's taking a quick look at what is now his mother's room as he walks past it, probably checking to see if they're still sleeping separately. What will he think of that? His father doesn't know how to make his mother happy? He isn't capable of leaving her? Does he despise him for that? Abaitua is sure that young people today are clearer about these things and aren't such hypocrites. His son's come to get some clothes, as he does sometimes. He usually takes some books and records, too, some of them Abaitua's, but he doesn't mind that. He's glad to be able to pass on some of his tastes in music and books, but it's to his son's credit that he's receptive to them. He has to admit that young people today have fewer prejudices than they did back in his day, they're more eclectic. They don't usually look down on things as he used to.

He asks him how things are going at school.

Does he want another bag? The one he's brought with him is almost full. He says he doesn't but still doesn't stop taking things out of the closet. Abaitua leans against the doorframe as he watches him. He couldn't be more damning about his university. From what he says, it's clear he does have reasons to be unhappy, but Abaitua finds it irritating to have to listen to him being so critical, so negative; with that sort of attitude, he'll never be able to get anything good out of it.

Just to give him an idea: there's a lecturer who doesn't know that Newton wrote *Principia Mathematica*. Loiola stares at him, and Abaitua, not knowing whether it's because he isn't as surprised as he expected him to be or because he wonders what he's doing there, staring around his room, decides to go back to the kitchen.

There are big gray bits of onion in the squid sauce. He doesn't know what to do with what he's made.

While he cleans up the squid ink that's splashed onto the kitchen surfaces, it occurs to him that he could have been having lunch with Lynn, but he doesn't find the thought annoying.

Now it's his son who's looking at him from the doorframe. He's a little taller than him, just by an inch or two. He asks him what he's going to do that afternoon, as if he were worried about leaving him alone. He'll use the time to study, he says, letting him know he likes to keep up to date in his profession. He always says *study*, never *read*. Then they're both quiet. Because there isn't much time, Abaitua doesn't know how to bring up the future. The bag at his feet is full, and any moment now, he'll bend down to pick it up and say he's going; Abaitua is both afraid of that and wanting it to happen. Loiola says he'll come by for dinner next week. Some day his mother's free. "Because she's working so much lately!" Talking about his mother's work again: Apparently, the operating theater's productivity is up by a hundred and twenty percent; apparently, two new services are going to be set up; apparently, she's managing to keep the vultures at bay. It's clear that Pilar tells him about her job and that he's proud of her taking charge of the clinic and trying to save the old man's work. Loiola looks at Abaitua with concentration. He wants to know whether he, too, is proud, and he says she's working very hard and in very difficult circumstances.

Abaitua's interested in the circumstances. It occurs to him again that those vultures, as Loiola's just called them, would be just the sort to drop a dead body on Pilar's operating table, but he still keeps quiet. He doesn't say it, in order not to frighten him, but also to avoid making the objective of saving the clinic not sound overly epic. To say something, and for his son to see what type of people they are, he starts telling him about the case of the baby with choanal atresia, and it's too late by the time he realizes that his son must be wondering what he's going to do about it.

He doesn't ask him anything. "What bastards," he says, and he leans over to pick his bag up.

What could Abaitua do?

Loiola's going. He goes up to the cooking pot and smells it and says he's sorry he can't stay to eat. He clasps his father's shoulder and says, "You're a great cook." Abaitua asks if he wants to take the food with him. "Glad to," he says, if he doesn't want it. He puts it in a tupperware container for him and says it'll be better the next day. He also gives him a jar of tuna and a bottle of white wine from the fridge.

Although he's said he's leaving at least twice in the last minute, he's still standing there by the kitchen door with his bag in his hand. "Are you really going to spend all afternoon studying?" Abaitua has the sensation once more that his son doesn't want to leave him alone, and he has a sudden surge of energy as he realizes he could tell him that he might spend the afternoon making love with a woman who isn't much older than him.

Is he proud of that? Sometimes, even though he knows it's dumb.

He pushes Loiola toward the hallway, saying he has to go once and for all. He's bigger than him, but also a bit softer than he was at the same age. He pats him on the back. It's been years since they gave each other kisses, he doesn't know how many years or why they stopped doing it. Now he finds being close to him repulsive, doesn't like his body odor, and supposes he must feel the same. "We should go out fishing one day before I go to America." Mentioning America gives him the chance, before he gets into the noisy old elevator, to tell him that he must make his decisions freely, without being conditioned by anybody or anything. "Think about yourself, your happiness, without any ties," he shouts at him as the glass door closes. "Don't worry." The boy smiles at him with one hand on the button, waiting for the iron grille to close. "In any case, in order to be happy, I have to be loyal, too." Behind the heavy iron bars, it

567

looks as if he's in a cell. Abaitua doesn't know if he's joking, but he smiles again and waves goodbye with his hand, and the elevator goes down. "*Nire amaren etxea defendituko dut*," he mutters once it's out of sight, switching the Gabriel Aresti poem around to say "I'm going to defend my mother's house" instead of "my father's."

HE WISHES THE STATION WERE BIGGER, like Austerlitz or Victoria Station, and he'd like to be able to get lost among the crowds, but he has to make do with what he has. There are no more than twenty people in the vestibule, and the newsstand is closed. He could call Lynn to make sure she's at home, but he doesn't. He likes the feeling of uncertainty, and if he knew she wasn't there, he wouldn't have any reason to catch the train. Nor would he like to be completely sure that she is at home; then he wouldn't have to decide whether to call or not. Although he knows it's no use, a voice inside him says he shouldn't. Inevitably, he'll call her from Martutene, and if she isn't in, he'll go for a walk in the area. He'll go to the spot with the rushes along the little road that runs through the apple orchard—the living room window and bedroom are visible from there. In fact, he doesn't really need any more than that, he doesn't think he'll be overly bothered if she doesn't pick up the phone. It'll have to happen some day, she'll have something to do and he'll hear her telling him she can't see him.

"TRAIN TO BRINKOLA." Taking a local train is something new for Abaitua, and he finds it amusing that he feels like he's setting out on a journey. He's impressed by how tidy the train is. Lynn's told him about that; she's a great defender of trains. She normally praises their punctuality, too. An old woman is having trouble dragging her big suitcase in and doesn't seem to trust the boy who's trying to help her lift it off the platform, maybe because he's got green hair. The boy holds onto the suitcase and the old woman onto his shirt; they both almost fall over.

He sits next to the window. There aren't any *E pericoloso sporgersi* signs on this train warning passengers not to lean out the windows, among other things because you can't open the windows.

A boy of around ten sits down next to him, and his father, who sits across from him, has to tell him to talk more quietly. They look very much alike. The child tells him, or shouts at him, rather, to tell the story about when he stole the shotgun. "*Aitá*, tell me about when you stole the shotgun." It's the second time he's asked him, or commanded him, rather, and the father says he'll tell him later. It must be some sort of exploit he's already told his son about and doesn't want to repeat in public. Abaitua never told his son many adventures, just a few things that happened at sea and that he exaggerated a little. As far as shotguns are concerned, he remembers that he used to be allowed to use an air rifle back in Otzeta. All men in Otzeta hunted birds. He tried his hand, too, firing at the birds but never hitting them. Until one day when he saw a robin perched on the branches of a walnut tree. He got it in his sights, fired, and hit it. He still remembers how it fell down like a stone. He clearly felt happy about his achievement, because he picked it up and went running to show his grandfather. He was surprised by his cold reception. He told him that robins did good things for them, ate insects, and that was why they shouldn't be shot. He didn't exactly tell him off, but he did say it to him very seriously, and he still, after so many years, hasn't fully recovered from his feeling of guilt. He remembers it every time he sees a robin.

The boy is eating pumpkin seeds and throwing the shells on the floor; his father says nothing about it.

He finds the journey very short. One of the advantages of taking the train, and one to really take into account, is that it removes the danger that anybody going into or out of the clinic on the old road might see his car sitting there in the only parking space that's usually empty, which is right next to the iron railings and quite visible.

From the train stop, there is no sign of her being at home. He goes over the walkway, taking the risk of being seen by anybody who might be in the garden. But there's nobody there. The idea of calling her from that very spot makes his heart race. She usually says "*hello.*"

No, he hasn't woken her up from a *siesta*; no, he hasn't interrupted anything; no, it's not an imposition on her at all. How could he think such a thing?

LIKE SOMEBODY STOPPING BY FOR A VISIT. He knows he looks ridiculous like that, killing time in the living room looking at books while Lynn is in the kitchen making the coffee. There's a framed photo of the two of them in front of the bronze statue of the angel holding the soldier with the broken sword in Bordeaux. He likes seeing it there but also finds it a bit worrying. If somebody comes there, they'll ask her who the man is. What will she answer?

When she comes in with the coffee things clinking together on the tray, he can tell by the way she looks at him that she's wondering what he's doing standing there "as if he were stopping by for a visit." He thinks she must realize he finds it difficult to be at ease there, and he's sorry about that. "Make yourself at home." But he can't shake the idea that he's like a man showing up at some sort of *pied-à-terre* he keeps for secret rendezvous. He isn't comfortable seeing himself as an old man visiting a young lady, and he doesn't like the idea of keeping a bathrobe and a pair of slippers here. She tells him to relax, takes his jacket to a closet in the next room, which she uses as a study, and, when she comes back, takes the photo out of his hands. He's very good-looking in it, but a little too serious, she says. And she takes him to the sofa. What a great time they had in Bordeaux, she says as she drops onto the cushions. And more than anything else, she's proud of having dared to knock on his door. Because he mustn't think she's in the habit of knocking on men's doors. She frowns comically.

But he did the most difficult thing, he took the first step. He was the one who took the initiative of asking her along for the trip. They play at arguing. It's less of a risk for a man. When it came down to it, he'd given her a completely innocent offer: a polite invitation to a foreign sociologist to go on a trip with two friends. On the other hand, there's only one way to interpret knocking on a man's door at night. It's Abaitua who protests now, reminding her that he's a doctor and that she pretended to be sick. He remembers it very well: "*Doctor, I'm not feeling well,*" she said in a theatrically weak voice. He tickles her, and she rolls over.

"HOW DID I ENCOURAGE YOU?"

He likes remembering the first several times they met, when nothing seemed to suggest they'd ever make love, but he finds it hard to share those memories in response to her implicit desire for him to do so. And if she asked him, he wouldn't know at what precise moment he became interested in her. For instance, he hardly remembers if he thought she was good-looking the first time he saw her; he knows he thought her bright and well educated. He isn't one of those old men who always goes for young women. In fact, when he called her, it was for company, to avoid Kepa and himself boring each other. It was in Bordeaux itself that something lit up, in that boutique where she called out his name to ask whether the dress he can see her wearing in the photo looked good on her. He says he doesn't know how it happened.

But she remembers it very well, all the details, even what he was wearing the very first day. Now she's gotten used to seeing him dressed a certain way, but at that point he looked incredibly elegant to her. She was expecting a lot from him because of what Harri had told her, and Julia, too, saying how interesting he was, but right then she saw quite clearly that he was the man who held the key to her happiness. She only had to look at his hands, listen to his voice when he went up to Harri to ask her so softly about her health, to know how sweet he was. "*Of course.*" She puts her hands together and turns her head with a gesture of resignation, as if she were talking to a third person—all right, she could see that he was a man who was tired of life and that she wasn't going to find it easy making him happy, but seeing him so tender and in such need of tenderness, she understood right then and there that her greatest adventure was going to be trying to get him to be happy. It was bad luck meeting as they had—he was already quite old—but finding the love of your life isn't something that happens to everyone. She makes a brief, comic gesture of regret when she says that, and he tries to silence her by covering her mouth, asking her not to tease, not wanting to believe her, and she protests. "*You don't want to believe me.*" Is it really true that nobody has ever told him how tender he is?

A very short, fast train goes by; the sound of its whistle, however, can be heard for a long time to the west of the house. Lynn looks up, perhaps wanting to see the time. Her head is resting on the arm of the sofa, and she has one hand raised to pet the purring cat on top of it. Abaitua finds it amazing how uninhibitedly the cat requests pleasure. There must be people who are a bit like cats. Lynn turns toward him with the inquisitive look of knowing that somebody's thoughts are far away, and he tries to come up with something in case she asks what he's thinking about. What comes to mind is the image of the parents of the baby with choanal atresia.

But Lynn hasn't asked him yet what he's thinking about. She kneels down in front of him and takes ahold of his belt. She finds it hard to take off; it's new and isn't very flexible. As usually, the sociologist's fingers have problems with the inside catch, but he doesn't help her, he just watches what she's doing. She takes his pants off seriously, without saying a word, as if she's just made an important decision; she always concentrates at moments like these. Half nurse, half undine.

An undine who no longer has to say "*just relax*"; he's learned to let himself go. He'd prefer not to be naked just yet.

Lynn gets out of his arms—"I have to go to the toilet," she says—and he moves his knees to let her past. He misses her warm skin. The cat jumps off the back of the sofa onto the seat, and from the seat onto the floor, with what seems to him to be a heaviness inappropriate for a cat, and follows its mistress down the hallway. Lynn turns around. "You see how agile he is?" knowing he's going to laugh. She has a multi-colored, striped shawl on her shoulders, which makes her nakedness look peculiar. He thinks she isn't very modest, much less so than the Lynn in *Montauk*, at any rate. The Lynn in *Montauk* tells the writer that she had a puritanical upbringing, and he thinks she makes the writer leave the room on one occasion so he won't see her in her nightgown.

And one night, she tells him they can't make love. "*Not tonight.*" Lynn's never told him "*we can't make love.*" He doesn't remember her period ever having been an obstacle, and that makes him reflect that it's been some time since she had her last one. He'll have to ask her. They aren't very communicative about the subject, but she shouldn't be careless when it comes to amenorrhea.

From inside the bathroom, she tells the cat she doesn't want it in there with her. You're distracting me here, Max. He hears the cat scratching on the door and calls it, but it doesn't come to him. Now he hears running water in the bathtub and wonders what she's doing. He imagines the bathroom with its small hexagonal white tiles, the copper tubes on display, something like an old-fashioned hotel, clean and full of light thanks to the large window that looks onto the garden and forces him to crouch down because there aren't any curtains. The cat's gone back to scratching at the door, and it cries out again, making a sound not so different from that of the trains as they run past into the distance. It reminds him of the cries of the cats in heat out on the patio at his parents' house that used to make him so nervous as a child, it was like the crying of children being tortured, and along with that, he remembers the crying he heard in the hospital corridor earlier this morning. He opens his eyes, not wanting to think.

Lynn runs back along the hallway, hugging herself as she does, shaking her head, panting because of the cold, and she curls up to him. But she really is cold, her feet are frozen—she asks if he minds as she rubs them against his legs—and he feels cold dampness between her legs and a faint smell of soap.

Another train. Because of how long the sound lasts—he counts almost thirty seconds—he thinks it's a freight train, one carrying cars; he's seen that they're the longest. Lynn says that because of the cadence it has, which is much more continual, it must be an express. He'd bet her something, but he doesn't feel like getting up.

The cat is curled up between them and begins purring automatically when he starts to pet its neck. "What hands, eh, Max? *Anyway, that's enough for today.*" She throws it onto the floor. Now it's her turn.

The cat stares at him as cats usually do. It gets onto a chair and finds a good place to curl up on top of his pants—Lynn doesn't see it—but he doesn't mind getting hairs on them today, because Pilar isn't going to be at home when he gets back. It's sitting there upright, its forelegs extended, its tail wrapped around its body, as if posing, aware of its own beauty. He tells Lynn that Max is beautiful; he knows she likes hearing that, and it's also to pay it back for having treated it badly earlier. It really is beautiful. Its eyes shine like agates in the darkness. Lynn knows a lot about cats. It isn't exactly true that they can see in the dark, but they can see in what we think of as total darkness. He likes the way she says that—"*In what we think of as total darkness.*" She explains how the reflective layer of proteins and zinc crystals, which form a type of triangular mirror behind the retina, work, and then she gets annoyed when she realizes he knows what the tapetum lucidum is and he's just letting her go on talking.

"*Zertaz pentsatzen?*" She asks him in Basque what he's thinking about, with almost no accent, her knees against his ribs, hands on his shoulders and the shawl over hers. In that position, too, her breasts stand proud. About using the iris in diagnostics. Yesterday he saw a woman a naturopathic doctor had diagnosed with uterine cancer and the man was now treating her for it. But she had no such thing. Lynn says it's incredible, leaning back against the sofa again. He doesn't know if she's referring to the naturopath or to the fact that he's said he's thinking about using the iris in diagnostics.

They're both quiet, close against each other, looking up at the ceiling. Lynn takes his hand to show she isn't angry. She says she knows why he's sad, and he denies her premise—he isn't sad.

She doesn't listen to him.

He's sad because of what happened to that baby, she heard about it, the neonatology resident told her about it this morning at the Bretxa Azoka. Abaitua denies it. He's decided not to worry about other people's mistakes and negligence and to do his own work as well as he can. He's told her that many times. He also says that he's told her he doesn't want to talk about the hospital, he finds her complaining depressing. He's all too aware that if he looked into most clinical stories, he'd find evidence of negligence, inattention, and oftentimes even negative intent. And since she's mentioned the resident, he tells her that what the fatty she had coffee with this morning is really upset about is that there's soon going to be a selection process for his position and he's not going to get it, because he doesn't fit in with the people in charge at the moment.

Like a jealous man.

She wraps him in her shawl. It's soft and gives off a lot of heat. The tassels around the edge are shinier than the cloth itself. She tells him Martin gave it to her when Abaitua says how soft it is in order to avoid thanking her for caressing him. It's very good quality, she says, looking at the label, "*Seventy percent pashmina, thirty percent silk.*" She's proud to own such a fine item. Of such high quality. (It isn't the first time he's heard her saying that Martin's given her something of great quality, and he thinks that he, too, should give her something.) She explains what pashmina is—after he promises he doesn't know— while she ties and unties the tassels on the edges of the shawl. And once more, he remembers the couple underneath the poster of the woman breastfeeding, the father looking at his empty hands, the woman stroking the white shawl on her lap. "Breastfeeding is an act of love."

She's leaning sideways against him, her head on his shoulder, a position Pilar wouldn't find comfortable. He opens his eyes when he realizes she's looking at him and then closes them again. Now he's the one who'd like to know what she's thinking.

She asks how to say *tender* in Basque. "*Samur.*"

Samurra zara. You're tender.

He believes her when she says he's a tender man. Believes that she thinks that. She asks him again if nobody has ever told him that, and he says no. How could he say yes? What's more, he doesn't think anybody ever has said that to him.

He likes hearing it.

Her breathing is slow and regular, but he doesn't think she's asleep. Her loose reddish hair, half-open mouth, slightly swollen lips, slightly reddened face (he wonders if that's because of his stubble), her very white body, and her long, thin fingers crossed over her belly remind him of Ophelia floating among the water lilies. He envies her being so relaxed, so calm. It's the image of a woman who has just experienced pleasure, and he's proud to have given that to her, as if he possessed a gift.

"YOU DRIVE ME CRAZY." Those words, and words like them, make him feel uncomfortable when she says them to him, with a trace of despair, outside of moments of pleasure. She tells him again he has to believe her, and he can't or doesn't and gives her the impression he takes it all as a joke, saying that all Lynns are gerontophiles—it's a joke he often uses—and she gets angry. Or she pretends to get angry. He isn't sure.

He says she just looked like Ophelia among the water lilies.

What do I look like now?

She puts the shawl over her head and turns toward him. She puts her right hand into the shape of a cup and takes it to her left breast, her head tilted slightly to one side, and squeezes her nipple hard with the thumb and forefinger of her other hand. Her gesture of pain is hardly visible, and then a small drop of milk comes out. He doesn't dare to tell her that she shouldn't do that. She smiles sweetly, holding her areola between her forefinger and middle finger, softly this time, and sits up slightly, moving it toward his mouth.

The cat stretches out on the back of the sofa and sniffs at them.

"Leave us alone, Max," Lynn says, looking angry.

"You leave it alone."

He takes ahold of the sides of the shawl and pulls them tightly together, immobilizing her. She doesn't try to break free, looks at him seriously, as if she's seen that he wants to ask her something. He doesn't know how she's guessed. He's already asked her if she takes antidepressants. He doesn't understand why she would need them, much less tricylicals. He asks her again, and she says she doesn't take antidepressants but she should take cyanide. She frees her arms and pulls him down by the ear to her belly. He imitates the cat and sniffs at her scar. He asks her if she's had any other illnesses apart from false appendicitis. What is this? An anamnesis? Lynn asks. Now she takes him by the ear again to draw him away from her belly. He tickles her. It's a very ugly scar, really ugly work; he himself does wonderful stitches. She knocks the hand stroking her scar away with a gesture of repulsion. *"You see, Max? He finds me ugly already."*

He talks to her about the bursting of the ideal image. Someone's told her the joke before: Men don't leave women *because* they look old and ugly; they need to see them looking old and ugly *so that* they can bring themselves to leave them.

He says he thinks she's very beautiful, and Lynn looks at the ceiling in silence. Her eyes shine in the half-light.

Lynn's questions. She wants to know if he's ever thought about testing her skin temperature while they're making love, checking the color or the texture of her skin, smelling her fluids or examining their density as a doctor would. She hopes he's never thought of doing anything dirty like that. She lifts a finger up to her nose in threat. She wouldn't forgive him for something like that. She wants to know if any woman has every complained to him about that, his hands touching them not as lover's hands but as expert hands.

He laughs, he'd have to think about it but doesn't think so. And the other way around? The other way around being has he ever felt eroticized while practicing medicine. This question is serious, even though she asks it with a humorous tone. He defends himself by saying it's still too common a fantasy. Playing doctor. A few idiotic acquaintances still ask him from time to time if he needs an assistant. But neither the women nor he play games at work.

From time to time, some woman tells a risqué joke while standing next to the examination table, and while sitting on it, too, but he's never felt eroticized, as she puts it. She looks at him with incredulity. She's often had that fantasy. She goes into his office and answers all his intimate questions and then, when he tells her to get onto the examination table, he makes her wait there with her legs wide open, listening to the sound of the metal instruments on the glass table and imagining him heating up the speculum. Now it's her turn to laugh. She's sure some other women have thought the same thing.

From time to time, some women flirt a little, doing all they can to give him a glimpse of some particularly seductive lingerie. That has happened to him. And some women wear too much perfume, but he thinks that's more out of embarrassment and fear than the wish to be desirable. Perhaps it would be interesting to research women's attitudes and behaviors on the examination table. As far as feet are concerned, there are women who can't stand revealing them and, at the opposite extreme, women who never leave their socks on, thinking they look ridiculous naked but with their feet still in socks. It's something that goes beyond the feet in themselves, something unconnected with whether they're pretty or ugly, or something not entirely connected with that. In any case, he still sees some very ugly feet, feet that have suffered inside shoes and haven't been properly looked after, but not as much as before. Elegant, very fine-looking women who have feet like birds of prey.

Lynn stretches her legs out in the air. She doesn't mind her feet, they're not bad, the only thing being that sticking-up big toe. She lets them drop. She accuses him of having changed the subject to feet; what she wants to know is whether some scheming whore has ever seduced him in his office. She urges him to talk by pushing a finger into his ribs. Then he immobilizes her by holding onto her wrists. He doesn't have anything to tell her.

TERESA HOYOS'S FEET ARE LONG but not bony, not too thin, either, her toes are well looked after, her nails shiny. They're very beautiful, and she knows it. She wore Roman-style sandals even before they were fashionable, those ones that show off the whole foot. He thinks she even adapted her hairstyle to match her feet—a Cleopatra bob with straight hair. Very black hair, dyed now, of course. He thinks she must have broken her nose at some point and that it never set well, he's never asked her, the bridge was a little asymmetrical, but that imperfection fits in very well with the rest of her face, particularly her lips, which are almost as thick a black person's.

He feels the urge to talk about Teresa Hoyos, to tell her about the stupid, squalid incident he had with her. More than a need for inner relief or a need to exorcise his guilt, what he hopes is that a pronouncement from a generous judge will make the whole thing seem less important. He knows that Lynn won't be as severe with him as he himself is, or at least not as merciless as Pilar. Once, when he told her about something that happened to him in the way these things often get told, attributing it all to a third party with "I heard about this one gynecologist who . . ." or some other similar comment, her first disdainful words were "What a pig!" It's true that he hadn't been able to explain any of the attenuating circumstances, because then she would have realized that he was talking about himself.

Does he not care that Lynn might despise him? He doesn't think that's the issue.

She lifts her head from his shoulder, apparently wanting to know why they are sitting there in silence, and he turns his head away from her on the pretext of wanting to pet the cat. He prefers not to look at Lynn when he tells her that he hasn't always been an honorable man. Quite a dramatic sentence to start off with. So, he's talking about Teresa Hoyos, who's around ten years younger than him. She was attractive, sweet, and timid, nervous, although he's not quite sure what he means by that; sometimes when they spoke, her voice would break, and he thought it trembled a little. He used to see her at the private practice he's long since given up. He enjoyed being with her, and because of that, he would spend time talking with her after her medical examination, just as he did with other patients who were also friends. He doesn't think he really desired her. He found her pleasant—her voice, that way she had of speaking as if she were frightened, her perfume, her distrustful, evasive attitude that held something mysterious behind it. Perhaps it was just that—he found her vulnerability attractive. He isn't sure.

He thinks it never even occurred to him to try to see her outside the office. Saying anything to her would have been unacceptable, because she was so vulnerable, but above all he thinks she didn't really desire him. It was nice to see her at the office, that was enough for him. He used the trick of giving her more appointments than she strictly needed. Of course, he tried to justify what he was doing and used an argument that was not very convincing—every time her test results came back, she was always within the theoretical limits for anemia. He examined her for several years, without ever increasing the frequency of her gynecological explorations, always remaining highly professional with her, never overstepping the mark, never taking their post-examination chats toward any dubious subjects of conversation. He paid her a compliment about her skin on one occasion. He said it to her quite simply, but it seemed to throw her off; on another occasion, he left his hand on her knee for what seemed like a long time to him. He never praised her feet, which seemed so beautiful to him, or touched them. There's no reason for gynecologists to touch feet. But once, one day when she didn't have an appointment—she had called to ask him to see her because her pelvis had been hurting for several days—and he doesn't know how or why, perhaps because he was seeing her outside the normal schedule, he went too far. Everything started normally, he asked her about her symptoms, told her to undress—normally, he insists, without any obscene intentions either then or when he helped her into the gynecological exploration position—but suddenly, when he sat down in front of her, between her wide-open legs, he was taken over by the desire to put his naked hands into her vagina. And that's what he did. No more than that—he put his index and middle finger in and left them there for a second. Nothing more than that. Fearing he might be painting too depraved a picture of himself, he repeats that it never happened again and that if he did do it, it was more out of affection than in search of any type of pleasure for himself, but he wishes he'd taken her hand rather than putting his fingers inside her. Every abuser's line, he thinks. But he has no idea whether Teresa Hoyos realized; it's impossible she could have told the difference by how it felt. She probably noticed he wasn't wearing gloves, didn't hear the slap of the latex, which is normally done very obviously so that patients feel safe in the knowledge that they are in clinical, aseptic surroundings. Nothing at the time gave him the idea that she was uncomfortable, particularly uncomfortable, he means, more nervous than on other occasions, and they said goodbye, as usual, after making a new appointment.

He suffered over it. He was depressed at having done something so dirty, and even though he told himself that nothing had happened, he never managed to convince himself it was true. At best, the difference between himself and the most repulsive of abusers was only a matter of degrees, it wasn't that he'd done an essentially different type of thing, and he felt despicable, foul. That was just the beginning of his punishment. He wouldn't say he started to forget about it as the days went by, but he did start to think that, to an extent, it was more of an impure thought than a case of abuse—and in any case, it was something he would never allow himself to do again—and he came

579

to believe that it was no more than an ambiguous incident, barely perceptible, even for the person who had suffered it. However, she called a few days before her next appointment to cancel it. Not to change it—he found that out almost immediately; when the nurse suggested another date, Teresa Hoyos quite simply turned it down without saying why. And that was when the real torture began for him. That cancelation proved something he already believed—he was to blame for a cowardly incident, because the woman was aware that she had been abused.

So Teresa Hoyos did know that he was some sort of pervert. Did anybody else know? Was he going to become one of those doctors that colleagues tell jokes about at dinner parties? He couldn't really imagine Teresa Hoyos talking about intimate matters in public, and at the same time, what she had to talk about was, in objective terms, very little. But there the fact was—she left his practice, and he didn't know why. He thought about all sorts of possible explanations, some of them as absurd as the idea that she was prejudiced against him because she thought he was a Basque nationalist. Because he'd heard that she began espousing opinions like that after ETA killed her father, a logistics officer, a man who'd been about to retire, that she'd become radical in her politics, staking out extreme Spanish nationalist positions. That could be what was behind it, he thought. A few months later, however, Arrese himself proved what an absurd notion that was; himself an open, proud Basque nationalist, he let him know that she had come over to his practice. Abaitua remembers well that he told him he knew she had been a patient of his; he said she was very good looking but also pretty strange.

Knowing Arrese, Abaitua is absolutely sure that he must have done all he could to find out why she'd left his, Abaitua's, practice, and judging by his insinuations, he's sure he found something out.

The end of his confession comes at the same time as a long, slow train to Madrid goes by. He's told her what he's never trusted anybody with, something he didn't think he'd ever confess to anyone. Lynn, too, is silent. She pulls her shawl around her, as if ashamed of her nakedness, and he notices it. It isn't that he doesn't mind what she thinks; in fact, he thinks he's glad to have shown her his worst, dirtiest side. That's all, he says, because she seems to be expecting something more, lying there silently staring at the ceiling. He'd like to see her face, see to what extent she's been affected by his confession, which he doesn't regret having given her, but he doesn't dare look. It's she who turns on her side and holds onto him. She strokes his belly, and he's relieved to find out that at least she doesn't find touching him revolting.

"FLY AWAY FROM HERE."

They stay still in the half-light, holding onto each other, until Lynn turns to rest on her elbows and looks at him. "*You know what?*" She talks without showing any particular feelings, as if she were talking about something unimportant. "*That poor woman.*" She says the poor woman ran away because she was frightened about what she felt for him. She ran away from him because she was in love with him.

Abaitua asks her not to talk such foolishness, his expression—not put on—says that he's had enough. He finds her excessive devotion to him a bit much; she seems to belittle his confession, make it banal by not acknowledging how important it is. He wants a more impartial judge. Could Pilar be that? Pilar would have called him a pig, asked him how anybody could sink so low.

And what if Teresa Hoyos had actualy been in love with him? Would that have made him innocent?

Abaitua turns around quite brusquely, facing away from her. They hear the whistle of a passing train, it sounds like Morse code and lasts quite awhile. "*Hey, man.*" She knocks on his back as if it were a door.

He's become more prone to showing his feelings over the years, he cries more easily. He likes feeling the tears run down his cheeks, showing his sorrow, at the same time as he realizes that it might be rather obscene to see a tearful old man. So he tries to hide it, hide his head, but she hugs him, makes him turn his head around and kisses his tears away. She whispers in his ear that she's sure the woman doesn't have anything to forgive him for.

He sits up, and she, on her knees, hugs him from behind. He should stop punishing himself. "*Believe me,*" she says. That woman knows he's an upright man. He disagrees; he isn't upright, he says, trying to break away from her, but she stops him by holding onto his neck. Then she holds onto his forearms and forces him to lift them up. She forces him to lift his arms up and then lower them as if he were flying.

"IN THE ARMS OF AN ANGEL."

Lynn takes ahold of him by the armpits and tries to lift him up. Obviously, she can't. Up on the sofa, crouching behind him to be able to use her strength, her arms under his armpits, she pulls him upward, and he slowly gets up, as if she were actually lifting him.

"FLY AWAY FROM HERE."

He isn't ashamed to look at her. He asks her to forgive him for having opened up to her like that, trying all the while not to cry again. She gives a smile. She stays quiet for a while and then takes ahold of his arms again, opening them up and making him fly with them again. He shouldn't let himself be weighed down by feelings of guilt, that doesn't do anyone any good. Hasn't her strength helped him?

She says she's serious, with a little impatience in her voice, as if she were telling off a child. He has to rid himself of that load, it's stopping him from living.

He says it's late.

He picks up the cat in both hands—he doesn't dare take it by its scruff—and puts it down on the floor so he can get his pants. There's no need for him to say that he has to go, but he does. She consents by putting her hands behind her back. It's the gesture of a child, meaning she won't do anything to keep him there. It's what she always does. Then she goes into her bedroom, and when she comes back, she stands against the wall in her green pajama top with the little animals on it and watches him getting dressed. He puts his cufflinks, tie, and watch in his pocket to finish quicker, even though he's in no hurry and nobody's waiting for him at home. In the hallway, too, she does as she always does and opens the door just enough to stick her head out and check that there's nobody there, standing to one side against the wall to make way for him as she opens the latch. They usually give each other a glancing kiss to say goodbye. He gives her the kiss, and she puts her cheek out for it. They say nothing.

Today is different. He doesn't want to leave without saying anything. He steps back onto the first step, but he doesn't know what to say. It's she who talks. He should try to comfort the mother whose child has been left disabled.

After he closes the iron gate, he remembers he came on the midday train and doesn't have a car. He has the impression that several days have passed since he went through the gate in the other direction. He isn't sure about what he should do but decides not to call a taxi and turns left to take the walkway over the railway line. It's night, and there's a warm south wind rustling the leaves. There's no traffic on the narrow road up to the hospital.

THE NURSE AT THE DESK, astonished to see him there, doesn't make much of an effort to disguise her curiosity. She seems to be wondering where he's come from at that time of night, and although he's only come a short way, it was up a steep road, and his shirt is stuck to his sweaty body. So he tries to improve his appearance by combing his hair back and says it's very hot outside. Inside, however, it's almost cold. He'll have to be careful not to catch a cold. She's very motherly. A young, healthy-looking blonde who stops smiling when he asks after the mother of the child with choanal atresia. She says the baby's been operated on, finally, and the mother won't leave his side. She says it sadly.

There's complete calm. The nurse confirms that it's a quiet night. She watches him with something like a smile as he takes his cufflinks, watch, and tie out of his pocket and puts them on. Then she offers him the towel and comb she has in the staff room. She makes a gesture meaning "you look much better now" when he gives them back to her. He asks her for a smock. She finds one for him without anybody's name embroidered on it and helps him put it on. It's too small for him, but not so bad if he doesn't do it up. The nurse wants to find a better fitting one for him, but he says he's fine like that and asks her to go with him to see the mother. She replies she'll be glad to.

The mother looks completely destroyed. She half stands up when she sees them come in and then slumps down in her chair again as if she didn't have the strength to get up. Abaitua introduces himself. He sits down next to her and offers her his hand. Her hand is small and very cold, like a dead person's. He holds it between his hands without knowing what to say. The nurse, standing by the door, mumbles something and starts to leave, but he tells her to stay. He needs a witness for what he's decided to do. He's going to tell the mother he's ashamed and deeply sorry about what's happened, about what's been done to her child. She in no way harmed the baby by breastfeeding him, and he promises that he'll do all he can to see that justice is done as far as possible. She puts her head down on her chest and starts silently crying. The young nurse starts crying, too.

When he goes through the birthing area, there is absolute silence. He's thirsty and goes to the vending machine in the hallway. He isn't sleepy, and he isn't tired, either. He doesn't have any coins; he never does, he finds carrying the weight around in his pockets a nuisance and usually puts them into a little box when he takes his pants off. Pilar likes using that money that seems to come from nowhere. It's typical of Pilar, in fact, to make large expenditures without a care while being careful about small amounts of cash. Something of a bourgeois attitude. There's nobody at the desk for him to ask for coins, but he sees a nurse going into a room and decides to wait. She doesn't close the door. From the hallway, he recognizes the little Peruvian woman lying down and the guy from Sagastizabal sitting next to her. They're both looking at the heat rate monitor with great attention, the red numbers on it dancing around the seventy mark, hoping for them to stabilize. The nurse impatiently tells them not to call her until it reaches around ninety, and she closes the door behind her. "A first-time mother with a long wait ahead of her," she says when she sees him, looking for his understanding. She can give him some coins, but the vending machine on that floor isn't working and he'll have to go somewhere else to get what he wants. The nurse has just gone to the ICU to get a soup. She recommends the soups from the machines. She looks at him as if weighing up his appearance—he can feel that his shirt is still stuck to his body—and, nodding as if some thought's just confirmed her suspicions, declares that he could do with a soup, as well.

A soup and then bed, she says, as she rummages around for coins, and while he waits for her to give them to him, he amuses himself comparing the situation with that of a beggar and some charitable soul recommending he not spend it all on wine.

What he does know is that if he goes to the ICU, he'll find Teresa Hoyos there. He believes in omens to an extent. He doesn't know whether it's a superstition, the remains of some magical thought process, or just a neurotic tic, but he thinks that the nurse just having gone to the ICU is a sign. In any case, when he sees her sitting there, alone this time, leaning over a book on her lap like the previous time, he isn't surprised. He knew it was going to be like that.

He bumps into the duty doctor outside the office. He has the impression, in fact he's sure, that he's more surprised by his appearance—the sweat from coming up the hill, his wrinkled pants all covered in Max's hair, and the remains of a long afternoon of love—than he is by seeing him there at such an unusual time, but he doesn't try to explain himself. He asks after Teresa Hoyos' husband, and the answer is that he's showing signs of waking up, in fact, he was just coming out to tell the wife. He agrees to let Abaitua be the one to tell her. In any case, she can't see him right away, he doesn't want to overwhelm the man and needs to run some neurological tests on him first. She'll have to wait a little. He tries once more to improve his appearance in the bathroom before approaching Teresa Hoyos, but looking now in the mirror, he thinks he hasn't improved matters; more than anything else, he looks like an all-night partier who's just run his hair under the faucet a little.

When he opens the doors after going through the ritual of counting to three, she's still sitting there, with obvious anxiety in her eyes. He tells her he has good news. He tells her what the ICU doctor's just told him, only leaving out a few technical details. They'll have to wait a bit longer. She lowers her head for a moment and covers her face with her hands, and then, raising her hands, takes ahold of Abaitua's left with her right. She puts her palm firmly on the back of his hand and thanks him. He replies that there's nothing to thank him for, and seeing that she has no reservations about touching him, he finds it hard to hold back his tears. He makes an effort to control his crying. It'll be the second time that night if he cries.

He thinks they're both sitting there trying to think what to say. He is, at least. He keeps his hands busy by trying to do up the over-tight smock, and she closes the book on her lap and crosses her hands over its back cover. She has pretty, well looked-after hands, smaller than her feet in proportion, and not as beautiful. When she sees him looking at it, she says the book's about victims and forgiveness, but she doesn't show it to him. She says the writer thinks forgiveness has to be asked for if it is to be given. But she wouldn't like to be put in the situation of having to answer a request for forgiveness. She doesn't need to be asked for forgiveness. She smiles and says that perhaps it's because she's feeling relieved, happy. What does he think about it? Abaitua isn't sure but thinks he would at least need an expression of regret for the harm done. He probably isn't as noble as she is. Then she laughs—she doesn't think she's noble.

She says she thought about him for a moment while she was reading the book. She looks at him, as if to gauge how much her words have affected him. She has quite a few wrinkles. At the corners of her eyes, and vertical lines above her lips. The skin on her neck, too, has started to loosen, but her eyes are bright and show no sign of sclerosis, not a trace, like a young person's eyes. She's still beautiful. "I, on the other hand, do need to ask for forgiveness. It's probably because of my religious education." Her voice is rather broken but sweet, too. She doesn't look away from her lap.

"I'm so relieved." She throws her head back. She looks at him from that position, and it seems to Abaitua that she's looking at him from a long way away. "Thank you very much for coming." She remains silent awhile between sentences, which she speaks alternately in Spanish and Basque. Her hands on the book on her lap, her head leaning backward against the wall, her face turned toward Abaitua after her last short sentence, and then she looks again at the spot where the ceiling and the wall meet.

It's meaningful that he's the one to give her this happy news after such a long time spent without seeing each other. How long has it been? she asks him.

He doesn't know.

"I had no choice but to leave," she says, her eyes bright once more. Does he understand? Then she leans her head backward once more. "Oh, don't make me spell it out." She found it very difficult going to his office and grasped at any excuse not to go, because she wanted to so much. She wanted to be very sick, so that he could operate on her and take care of her. "*Qué se yo*," she says, shaking her head—I don't know.

He's going to say something, but she puts her hand on his shoulder. She asks him not to say anything.

"My husband's a good man." It seems like rather a sad statement. After a long silence, she says they've been married for nearly twenty years, and that they've flown by. She goes quiet again. He says it's incredible how time races by—an inoffensive filler of a sentence. If she were to ask him, he wouldn't be able to say how long he's been married. But she doesn't ask him. Now she looks at him almost naughtily, lifts her chin a little, and says he still wears the same eau de cologne. So he does. He's been true to his eau de cologne, at least. He could tell her he's realized that she, too, is still wearing the same one as before, and that he noticed it once on a patient and felt tempted to ask what it was, in order to be able to buy it and thus remember her better; but he doesn't.

Instead of that, he says that he, in fact, does have to ask her for forgiveness. Right then, a nurse opens the door and sticks her head in. There is astonishment in her eyes at seeing a white smock in the waiting room. She tells Teresa Hoyos that they'll call her to come and see her husband in ten minutes, and then she leaves. Teresa squeezes his hand, lets go of it, and puts her hand back in her lap. "Don't say anything." It could be because the nurse's leaving the door open has diminished their privacy, but he doesn't think so. There's complete silence. He only becomes aware of the beeping of a machine when Teresa Hoyos says it's like an anxiety-making machine that she carries around inside her. He remembers the Peruvian woman and the guy from Sagastizabal listening to the machine marking out their child's heartbeats, and he feels sorry for them.

They've got ten minutes.

Because he doesn't know what to talk about, he tells her about the guy who wants to bring Sagastizabal back to life in the very center of Martutene and the Peruvian girl who wants to give birth there to show respect for her ethnic group's traditions. Teresa Hoyos seems moved by the story. She brought two children into the world via C-section, and now she regrets not having any memories of their births. The most important moments in our life are going to be presided over by that depressing beeping. Don't you agree?

Less than ten minutes isn't enough for him to say what he's thinking.

Teresa Hoyos says he's lucky to be a doctor.

They keep quiet. They stand up together when the nurse comes back. Teresa Hoyos takes ahold of both of his hands, which are hanging at his sides, and squeezes them tightly. Help that couple, she says.

THE COUPLE IS JUST AS HE LEFT THEM half an hour earlier, the girl lying on the bed, the guy sitting next to her, and both of them staring at the tomograph. When he asks if she minds if he examines her, she turns toward her partner as if to ask him for permission, and the guy gets up. Then he moves back to the wall. She has short, strong legs, her ankles and hips are thick, but she's supple. The baby has reached Hodge's first plane, the cervix is two centimeters dilated, uterine tone is normal, and the amniotic sac remains unruptured. There's still a long way to go.

He asks if she'd like to have the child at home, and she nods two or three times with a smile from ear to ear.

When Abaitua looks at the clock on the wall and sees that it's two, for a moment he doesn't know whether it's two o'clock in the morning or two o'clock in the afternoon. The place is artificially lit night and day, but that isn't the main reason for his confusion. In fact, it seems to him as if he left home days ago. The nurse signs the voluntary discharge and then reads aloud the list of medications and materials he's requested. Dressings, gloves, scissors, dissection tweezers, surgical tweezers, Foster tweezers, curved needles, local anesthetics, 5- and 10-unit oxytocin drips, Methergine. She looks at him after reading each item, and he nods. She quickly comes back with it all in a cardboard box. She's taken the initiative of adding a sheet, towels, and postpartum sanitary pads. There's a large group of nurses standing around the counter. They seem excited. One of them asks if they should call an ambulance, and he says no. The guy says their van's in the parking lot.

IT'S A SMALL HOUSE—it used to be the shepherd's shed, the guy explains—and even so, the coat of arms over the door wouldn't be out of place on a palace. When the *baserri* was knocked down and the property was expropriated, his uncle, the firstborn, put it into storage, and he's now dug it out.

They're obviously both proud of the house. The furniture is modern and functional, everything's clean and tidy. A room used for many different things takes up almost the whole floor. There are bookshelves in one corner and a table with detailed topographic maps on it. It's how they make their living. They take on just enough projects to be able to get by. They also have oil, rabbits, two pigs, and a goat. And fruit trees, several cherry trees, a walnut tree, and of course the apple orchard that gave the house its name, though it's nowhere near as big now as it once was.

Her name is Luz, but the Sagastizabal guy uses the Basque word for light instead, calling her Argi. He says it's only because he has trouble saying *Luz*, it's hard for him to pronounce the Spanish *z*. Luz would like some soup. What she'd really like is to make some soup, to pass the time by doing something, and she won't let the guy touch the cooking pot. She looks at Abaitua and asks if he'll let her, and he says she can do what she wants. It seems soup is a universal heritage—a couple of leeks, a carrot, a bit of bone, and a piece of meat. The two men go out to the stoop. It's a warm night, and the sky's completely clear.

HE WISHES LYNN COULD WITNESS THIS.

The couple don't mind him calling a friend to help him, it would be good, just in case the father can't manage it. The father says he shouldn't worry about him. The only problem is calling Lynn at that time of night might frighten her. While he waits for the line to connect, he remembers the first time he called her, from the Pio XII roundabout. He likes remembering his moments of daring. Lynn's voice doesn't sound like he's just woken her up. When he tells her he's at Sagastizabal waiting for Luz to give birth and that he could do with a midwife, she gives out a cry of joy. She won't be more than a minute.

"I'LL FLY OFF."

She says *maite zaitut* again, as well.

She gives Luz, or Argi, two kisses, and a minute later it seems as if she and Lynn have always known each other. Abaitua envies that ability—which is more typical among women than among men—to come together without any distrust. She's wearing a white T-shirt and jean overalls that make her look younger and more Irish. She's got a red bandana with white spots on it tied around her neck.

"HEY MAN." She ties the bandana on her head like a pirate and claps her hands in front of the father's face to perk him up; he seems to have taken fright since the contractions began growing more frequent. They have to heat the house up to around eighty or eighty-five degrees to make it comfortable for the baby. Lynn says that babies lose half a degree of body heat every minute. Abaitua cleans his hands in the sink and splashes her with water, saying she's too clever by half. They've never acted so familiarly with other people around before.

They talk about Couvade syndrome to tease the Sagastizabal guy; he's mimicking Argi's breathing without even realizing it. Abaitua thinks the term *couvade* comes from *cave*, but Little Miss Smartie Pants says that it's called Couvade syndrome in English, too, and that it comes from the French *couver*, to incubate. He isn't embarrassed about Lynn seeing he doesn't know something related to his own profession; on the contrary, he's proud of her knowledge. She also says that it's connected with matriarchal societies, and that, inevitably, leads them to a discussion about Basque women. The Sagastizabal guy's convinced that traditional Basque culture was matriarchal. The main beam of the house. They drink soup and eat boiled chorizo while they talk and almost forget about Argi.

It's amazing how short her delivery is. Argi sits up and pushes, holding onto her husband's and Lynn's shoulders, and a few minutes later, the child's head comes out. Abaitua cleans its face with a piece of gauze and then almost all he has to do is hold it.

AN APGAR OF 10. Fast heart rate, active tone, strong crying, pink color. No need for aspiration even. He puts it on the mother's belly.

"*Mi hijito*," she says—my son.

Argi takes the child to her breast. She's peaceful and crying at the same time, she hugs the Sagastizabal guy and, with wide-open eyes, shows him their child. "Welcome to the world, Peru," he says. *Peru*, but with the accent on the *e*. That's going to be his name. Lynn didn't know that Peru is how you say Peter in Basque, she thought it was Kepa. She's incredibly happy, he's never seen her so happy. She goes up to him and thanks him for calling her, and he hugs her. Abaitua hasn't cleaned himself, and he's covered in Argi's blood. "*I love you*," she tells him again.

They leave Peru with his parents in the room and go out to the stoop. They sit down on a long wooden bench and wait for the day to come. "*The small hours*." It's the same expression in Basque— *ordu txikiak*. That moment full of silence, waiting for the transition between night and day, the sounds of night gone and those of daytime yet to start.

Lynn says she's felt that profound silence that lasts only an instant, no time at all, but is absolute, until the birds' singing breaks it. He hasn't. The sun begins to rise behind Santiomendi, and a rooster crows.

He doesn't think he'll ever forget that day, and he'd say, as Lynn says, that he's a lucky man to have gotten the chance to live it.

"*A fortunate man.*" He admits that he does feel like it, and she snuggles into his arms. He's made her the happiest woman in the world. They stay there on the bench, Abaitua sitting and Lynn lying against his chest as they watch the sun come up. There's hardly any noise from the traffic, it's still early. When the Sagastizabal guy comes out, he seems a little embarrassed to find them like that, but Abaitua doesn't mind. With his hands in his pockets, he, too, looks at the sun and then suggests they have breakfast. He's added some tomatoes and peppers to the meat from the soup.

Argi wants to get up. She feels good and wants to feed the chickens. That's one of her jobs. The guy doesn't think it's a good idea and wants to see what the doctor has to say. He shrugs his shoulders. She shouldn't do anything strenuous, but she can do anything else she feels like doing. The man fills up a container with grain from a large sack, and the newly delivered mother feeds it to the free-range chickens. Lynn helps feed them, too. While throwing them grain, Argi calls to the hens in Spanish— "*Pitas, pitas*"—while Lynn speaks to them in English—"*Here, chick, chick.*" Abaitua says they're going to confuse them. You say *purra, purra* to Basque chickens.

The splendid Sagastizabal coats of arms looks out of place, strange to say the least, on the humble shed wall in daylight. The panoply around the shield itself is magnificent: a helmet with feathers on it, two dogs or wolves stretching to hold it up on either side, and a lot of leaves all around. The guy bets they can't make out its peculiar feature amid so much decoration, and indeed, they don't notice anything particular until he points it out. In the lower area there's a head, as large as the helmet at the top, opening its mouth above an erect penis. The testicles are very easy to make out, too. It's all very clear once it's been pointed out, and yet difficult to notice amid all the baroque flourishes. The Sagastizabal guy hadn't noticed it, either, until somebody researching local heraldry came to draw it and pointed it out to him. Before him, none of the family ever noticed it, quite clearly. Not his father, his uncle, or his grandfather, at any rate, because they wouldn't have put up with such obscenity, or perhaps they had found out but kept it a secret. An embarrassment for the family that they'd kept quiet by pretending not to see it. Something everyone saw and nobody admitted seeing. In any case, it's clear Basques haven't always been so serious and puritan, says Lynn, to which the guy says that it was almost certainly chiselled by a Galician stonemason. Then he says solemnly that factories are what make communities gloomy and sad.

With regard to the religiousness with which Basques have usually been associated, his opinion is that the Church has taken the traditional world that modern times have mercilessly destroyed to its bosom, that's the explanation for it. Lynn listens to him attentively. Abaitua, on the other hand, can't stop eating the strong aged cheese, and that in turn makes him drink more and more wine. He's been feeling sorry for the guy, ever since the moment he placed his hand on his little Peruvian wife's shoulder and said that he, being from Sagastizabal, was an aboriginal and should be considered a protected species. Like the autochthonous apple tree they grow. Abaitua has to go. Argi comes up to him to thank him for the thousandth time, but this time in Basque—"*Eskerrik asko laguntzeagatik.*" It's obvious she's rehearsed the sentence. Strange-sounding Basque. He tells her she's said it very well, and she complains—she's finding it hard to make any progress but thinks she'll learn more with Peru. Her partner, who's listening closely, says, "*Por la cuenta que te trae,*" joking with her in Spanish, in a mock threatening tone, that she'd better.

But when he says that Peru is going to be Basque—"*un vasco de verdad*" is what he actually says, a real Basque—he isn't joking, he's making a serious statement. Even so, Abaitua ventures to ask him what he means by "a real Basque," the early morning wine consumption having removed his inhibitions and the fact that he just recently helped his wife to give birth removing any suspicion that his question might be ill intentioned. The guy answers that he isn't very sure. Speaking Basque, of course, and then there are unavoidable conditions for being Basque, and also something that defines being Basque, but he doesn't know exactly what that is. A way of being, a style, perhaps—wanting to last. An insistence on continuing to be Basque, that's what he wants Peru to inherit.

Abaitua proposes a final toast, to Peru. The wine has a purple tone to it, the sky is blue apart from a sketchy white cloud or two. He predicts, in spite of what the Sagastizabal guy said, that it's going to be one of those wonderful, south wind, end-of-summer days. Lynn smiles as she looks at him and holds up her glass, and he can't believe he made love with her a few hours ago. She says he's a little tipsy, "*un poco chispa,*" and he does seem to be. When Abaitua toasts to Peru—

"¡*Por Peru!*"—he speaks first in Spanish and then in Basque: "*Para que sea un hombre libre, gizon librea.*" May he be a free man.

Even though the child is doing really well, he's going to send them a pediatrician to have a look at him. Argi puts cheese, eggs, walnuts, apples, and chorizo in plastic bags for them to take away with them. They don't want to, but the couple insists. They owe them much more than that. The Sagastizabal guy shakes his hand. He's bigger than Abaitua. He holds his hand tight for a long while, as if looking for the right words to say goodbye. His eyes shine damply. Finally, he says "*eutsi*" and lets his hand drop. It's a colloquial Basque term, both a greeting and farewell, that translates more or less to "stay strong." Stay strong against what? The women say goodbye, too. Lynn gives Argi her child back, and they embrace while holding him between the two. They both shed tears as they give each other two kisses, and then, holding each other by one hand, they look into each other's eyes and laugh.

SHE GOES FIRST along the path that runs parallel to the road, and when she turns around, she says, "I'm happy," as if she's guessed that he's thinking about her, and after a short smile, he says, "I know," not at all surprised by what she's said. They walk on until the electric warning system sounds to announce that a train's about to come through, and then Lynn turns around once more. She challenges him to guess what type of train will go by next, a local train or some other type. The one who guesses right gets to ask the other to fulfill one fantasy. She prods him to make his choice quickly—come on, come on, hurry up—and he bets it'll be a local train, thinking, probabilistically, that they go by more often. They both wait with their hands in their pockets, and a freight train comes out of the tunnel. Abaitua protests that she's won because she knows the timetable. Lynn denies that, and in any case, even if she did know it, she doesn't know what time it is, and so she couldn't have cheated. They have to raise their voices a lot to be heard above the noise.

She says she hopes he'll keep his word as a Basque. She's standing in front of him with a bag in each hand. Betting debts are sacred, and now he has to make her fantasy come true. When he asks her what the fantasy is, she turns around and continues walking. He'll know when the time comes. She sounds completely serious, half nurse and half undine.

It's the first time they've walked through the garden together. He, also for the first time, doesn't care if the gravel makes noise as they walk across it or even if somebody sees them from the gallery. He thinks Lynn is aware of this, and grateful for it. It's obvious, at least, that she's happy. With those bags in her hands, they look like a couple that's just done the shopping together and is now coming back home. Abaitua takes the bags to go up the stairs. A man's job. At the top, where he can't get away from his obligation to pet the cat, which is lying there on its back for him to do just that, Lynn tells him to hurry up or he'll get to the hospital late—an accomplice's order, as if she were talking to her spouse. So he isn't going to have any difficulty leaving. She loosens her overall straps, and he holds onto them by the bib to draw her toward him, with no sign of being ashamed at how badly he smells of sweat. He isn't going to wash, even though she says he looks dreadful. He has a large wine stain on his shirt. He doesn't care, he'll take a shower at the hospital, he has fresh shirts there.

At the train stop, he realizes again that he doesn't have a car and decides to walk up the old road to the hospital. As he walks up the slope, he has the impression that weeks have passed since he walked up it the last time, just the night before. The road is narrow, and many cars are going by at that time. Hospital people, of course. His phone rings. It's Pilar. She greets him with a happy *"Hola,"* emphasising the first syllable and drawing out the second. They've stayed the night in Bordeaux. That plural means her and the young neurosurgeon. That's no secret, it's work and nothing more. She says she's been at work since four in the morning. She says she's just completed a hydrocephalus operation, using a new technique for positioning the shunt, and it went really well. Professor Giraud said she has a very steady hand, and she's almost sure he'll agree to come operate on difficult cases in Donostia once a week. Do you realize what that means? She's delighted. And you, what are you up to? He says he's on his way to the hospital, and it seems she's realized he's out of breath, because she asks, surprised, if there's anything wrong with him. There's nothing wrong, he says, he's walking up the hill from Martutene, and he's just not in good shape. "And what are you doing there?" It's too late to go back on what he's said, and he can't think up an excuse. "I'll tell you later." To which she says, "Yes, we have to talk, you and I have a lot of things to talk about," without sounding at all worried. Her farewell is happy, too, and she sends him a goodbye kiss—"*Muxu!*"

It's obvious that the porter at the desk is waiting there for him. He goes up to Abaitua and tells him that the director has asked him to tell him to go up and see him. After wondering whether to first drop the bag with all his materials somewhere and change his shirt or not, he finally decides to face up to whatever it is as soon as possible. Because he's curious.

In the director's office, while listening to the inevitable preamble of complaints about having to reconcile the interests of different pressure groups and the limits imposed on him from above, Abaitua's spirit goes freely through the open window and flies down from the top of the hill and over the city and gets lost on the slightly choppy gray sea partially covered by clouds of the same color. The guy from Sagastizabal was right—the weather's changed in a matter of minutes.

Abaitua can't see the other man's face very clearly, because he's sitting in a high-backed chair with the light behind him—almost certainly a strategy learned at some administrative workshop in order to gain the advantage over the person you're interviewing—but the man is clearly nervous and unable to start in on what he has to tell him. Continuing with his preamble, he reminds him of the health speech they wrote together for an Euskadiko Ezkerra conference. "Healing Life" was the title they gave it, like one of the books Maspero published in the seventies, *Guérir la vie*, which argued that it's impossible to improve health standards without first changing production relationships and living conditions. "How innocent we were," he says with an air of nostalgia. Abaitua works out that the director must be ten years his junior, but he looks older than him.

"O TEMPORA, O MORES." Abaitua feels something like pity for this kowtowing individual who, in order to protect his job, has to pretend not to notice the wrongdoings of the shameless people who hold the real power at the hospital. He himself isn't so very different. He's tempted to open his heart to him and say, all of a sudden, that he's full of inner peace, completely calm, tired—because he does feel absolutely tired, a feeling that's heightened by having drunk all that wine—and, above all else, that he should be aware that he's

595

immune, that they can't do anything to him, because he's lost his sense of personal ambition, he doesn't need money, and women love him. He's really tickled by that wild thought and has to stop himself from laughing, a problem made worse by the fact that the director is sitting there with his mouth open and so he can't help imagining him as a fish stuck swimming around in circles inside a fish tank. But curiosity gets the better of him, as does tiredness. So he asks him to say what he has to tell him.

The director suggests unpaid leave for a couple of months. And that he tell the mother of the child with choanal atresia that he accused Orl as a result of the personal problems between the two of them, that the hospital was in no way to blame, and that it would be better to convince her, for his own good, not to report the incident to the police. The director's picked up speed and doesn't give Abaitua any time to answer. The alternative is immediate suspension for interfering with another doctor's work, for reckless endangerment, for enticing a patient to voluntary discharge, and all of that while being off duty, and, as if that weren't enough, using hospital material for private purposes. They would report him to the Board and to the Medical Council, and he would unquestionably be barred for several years. Personally, the director respects him a lot, he knows he's a good doctor, and because of that, he strongly recommends Abaitua accept the proposal and offer to try to call Arrese and Orl off himself.

The director puts his elbows firmly on his desk and leans forward to look at him from close up. In a confidential tone, he says that Abaitua can't deny his behaviour has been curious lately to say the least, and Abaitua thinks he's moved in close like that in order to check if the stains on his shirt are wine. He buttons his jacket and stands up. Let them bar him if they have to.

He's just taking his shirt off when Arrese walks into his office. He doesn't knock, and Orl comes in after him. "Eres un inconsecuente, un inmaduro," he almost shouts. He says that—that he's reckless and immature—in Spanish, more because he's angry than because Orl's there, Abaitua thinks. Orl doesn't raise his voice when he says that he's mad. Abaitua doesn't pay them any attention. He puts on a clean shirt and starts sticking papers into a briefcase, without looking at what exactly he's putting in, just wanting to make it clear he's leaving. He has to push Orl away from the door to get out. There are people standing frozen and staring in the hallway. He hears Arrese's voice behind him, "You won't be able to drag yourself out of this one." Abaitua turns around and points a finger at him, "But it's you two who are going to have to pay." White smocks move aside to let him through to the stairs. He doesn't see their faces.

THE FRONT DOOR HAS BEEN LOCKED with a single turn of the key, but he finds there's nobody there when he looks around. As he could have expected, there are signs that Loiola has been there—he's drunk a cup of coffee in the kitchen and gone through a couple of closets in his bedroom.

After the shower he's been so needing, he sits down in front of the television in the living room in his robe, because he doesn't want to go to sleep so early. There are a few photo albums on the table, and he deduces that Loiola's been looking at them. He's been looking at photos a lot recently, and has even taken a few away with him, and he asks questions about them—who's this or that, where are they, what are they doing? It's something Abaitua doesn't like; he's always hated photos, and they seldom suggest a happy past to him. Many are loose and out of order. In one of them, Pilar is wearing her red coat, which he remembers so well from back then. She's laughing with her mouth wide open, showing off her enviable teeth. Her eyes are laughing, too. But she told him that she always felt unhappy, extremely unhappy, whenever she wore that coat.

When he gets into bed, the room is in half-light, which he likes. He also likes having a big bed to himself, even though he hardly moves from his spot at one edge of it. He's about to fall asleep when the phone rings. It's Pilar again, telling him her return trip's been delayed once more. They're working really hard and learning a lot. *We are; we're doing, we're going* . . . All ways of saying once more that she isn't alone, her use of the first person plural stands out. She only uses the singular at the end, to say that she's tired and she wants to come home.

He's sure, with regard to her use of the first person plural, that her relationship with the young surgeon is purely professional. He's sure she's holding true to her promise not to have other relationships without telling him about them, without specifically breaking up with him first, without taking a purely implicit freedom for granted as she did back then. He remembers that when she came home, she was sitting on the edge of the bed he's lying on right now, and she was still wearing her red coat. "I felt abandoned," she said. Before that, she'd moaned, "I fell asleep," as if the worst of it was arriving home late, at around eight in the morning, he thinks.

He's never fallen asleep in another woman's bed.

He tries to shake that memory off and reexamine everything that's happened in the last twenty-four hours. He remembers Lynn. She's sitting behind him and hugging him. *"In the arms of an angel,"* she whispers in his ear, while moving his elbows up and down. *"Fly away."* He remembers her in her new dress, saying cheese and smiling, in the photograph Kepa took of them in front of the statue of the bronze angel holding the soldier with the broken sword.

He remembers that the statue is in the Place Jean Moulin and is titled *Gloria Victis*, and that the angel holds the fallen soldier up with its arms wrapped around his thighs, so that their two heads are close together, and the fallen soldier has his arms spread wide, the hand he holds up to the sky is empty and open, and the angel's wings are pointing downward.

19

AS SHE OPENS THE IRON GATE, Julia can't understand how they could have put up with the terrible screeching noise it made until Lynn finally put some oil on it. Another example of their increasing neglect of the garden—the poor girl's the only one who makes any effort. The sun is already heating up the side of the house that faces the train stop, but the blinds in Martin's room are still down. The shutters on Lynn's windows are closed, too, and that's really astonishing at such a late hour. As she walks toward the empty-looking house, she has no uncertain feeling that she's going to come across something bad there, and with the keys still in her hands, she pauses at the bottom of the stairs for a moment. She had forgotten about that bad feeling she sometimes gets standing in front of the house, the fear she makes herself feel by straining to see some sign of life. She admits that she's gotten used to Lynn being there, to the pleasant thought of seeing her there watering the plants or raking up leaves.

She walks around the house to check that all the blinds are down, and then an old image, one she thought she'd forgotten about, comes to mind. She's in the half-light of the living room, trying to see if there are any alterations to the usual chaos there, listening to the silence, which extends beyond the empty hallway, a silence broken by the sharp sound of the library door as she opens it and by the creaking of each step on the wooden stairs as she goes up them. She can hear her own heartbeats as she puts her ear to the bedroom door, and then she hears nothing, absolutely nothing, as she tiptoes into the darkness and feels rather than sees that he's not moving. She remains by the bed, not daring to touch him, hoping to get some sign that he's still breathing. Finally, she works up her courage, takes him under his arms, and shakes him; she starts screaming in horror and nobody comes to her call.

Julia breathes deeply to dispel the images, overcomes her hysterical fear, and opens the door. She raises the blind in the living room, just enough to be able to tidy up the room a little, picks up the tray on the armchair in front of the television with the remains of a dinner on it, and takes it to the kitchen, trying not to make any noise. It wasn't always like that. In the early days, when she came to the house so late in the morning, she would walk around in a natural way, perhaps even making more noise than usual so that he would wake up, thinking that he would like that, just as she likes hearing noises coming from the kitchen when she wakes up—the promise of a fortifying breakfast, the meal she most enjoys. And the other days, when she got there early, she would go up the stairs in silence, walking on the right-hand side, like now, so the stairs wouldn't make any noise, and then, too, she would put her ear to the door, but it would be with the expectation of hearing him say "I'm awake," explaining that he'd been up writing until dawn. Sometimes he'd ask her to lie down with him for a bit, and she would.

It isn't like that now. She hears him breathing regularly on the other side of the door, making a slight sound as he exhales—it isn't quite snoring—a sign that he's tired. Then she goes down the stairs, making some effort not to make noise on them, but not too much—she doesn't want to make herself nervous again.

Julia finds it a bit sad that she prefers him to be asleep.

But it's also true that knowing he's asleep makes it easier for her to go onto his computer, although she's not completely relaxed about it, because she hasn't yet gotten over her scruples, even though she tells herself each time that she's only doing it to see how he's getting on with *Gizona ispiluaren aurrean*. Her curiosity has never taken her beyond that document, and in fact, she doesn't exactly read it, either; she just has a glance at it to check whether he's made any progress, and, depending on that, to see what sort of mood he may be in. It's a habit that's similar in a way to tapping on the barometer every day to see whether the needle's pointing to poor or fair weather.

This time, she sees he's written quite a lot. The writer has decided to leave home for the first time in a long while to go and buy a beret. Apparently humans lose sixty percent of their body heat through their head, and it doesn't make any sense to wear thick jackets and coats and then walk around bareheaded, as people do here, even people who are as bald as a coot. The decision to buy a hat comes at the end of a long process of reflection, one Julia is familiar with because Martin explained it all to her when he bought a beret himself.

He thinks classic Borsalino style hats are pretentious, and going out of your way to choose an informal or sporty hat—whether one of those floppy ones that look like they're for going salmon fishing in Scotland, or hats with visors, both canvas ones (like baseball caps, which retired people seem to like so much) or those made of any other sort of cloth, above all British looking ones—is a denial of the beret, and that denial seems to him to involve obvious psychological, social, and political factors. From a certain age onward, a beret positions a man as he should be, making him look more like his grandfather. On the other hand, there is also some prejudice against them, fed by the fact that berets are still used nowadays to crown stupidity. Some people even say that getting rid of berets is the same as leaving atavism behind and embracing modernity—"*Que viajen, que se quiten la boina de una vez*," they say, telling them they need to travel and get rid of their berets once and for all. And in the Basque Country, the problem also has a symbolic side to it, with some people using it to stand up for certain things. Even though that's the case, or perhaps precisely because it is, depending on how you look at it, Martin chose to get a beret—even though he very seldom wears it—and that's what the man in front of the mirror decides to do, too. He doesn't want to renounce the beret just because some people claim it as their own or because of what some other people might think; he decides to humbly accept the fact that it makes him look the same age as his grandfather when he thought him very old, just as being naked probably does.

He gives his long soliloquy while trying on the wide-brimmed black beret that the lady in the Leclercq hat shop on Narrika Kalea hands to him. He would have preferred a smaller one, in the

European rather than the Basque style, to wear tight on his head in the way he's seen Sándor Márai and George Steiner used to, but the shopkeeper thinks quite the opposite. She says that a proper Basque beret, a real *txapela*, has to be wide, and even more so when the man wearing it is good-looking, like him. While he's trying on the beret, which he doesn't like because it's too wide, in the mirror he sees the shop door opening. It's Marie Lafôret. Julia's pulse beats faster when the character unexpectedly appears, and for the first time since she started her spying, she reads the progress he's made with special interest, curious to find out how such a promising meeting goes. He regrets their meeting taking place with him looking at himself in the mirror, looking so vulgar, and he steps out of the way and discreetly takes off the beret. Then he goes back to the counter and asks the Leclercq lady to show him some blue berets. He prefers blue to black, in spite of its historical connotations—the Falangists wore that color, and right-wing Donostians had, too— or maybe because of them, not wanting people to think he's somehow reaffirming his *abertzale* credentials. Blue berets also look more modern, less *txapela*-like, he says to the lady, who has to go into the back room to see if there are any blue berets there, because blue berets don't sell in Donostia. "It's more of a Bilbao thing," she says, with something like disapproval, as she disappears, and the two customers are left alone waiting at the counter. The writer ventures to look at Lafôret from the corner of his eye. She has that special aura about her, the one television personalities do when they suddenly appear in person, although she doesn't seem to be aware of it herself. She doesn't seem to mind having to wait. She spends the time looking at the hats and caps on display on the shelf across from them while twirling a black beret with a pompom around on the counter, until, suddenly, she turns to him and, her arms spread almost entirely open, says, "My goodness! Is that you? Is that actually you?" He doesn't know what to say, happy because he's met a beautiful television presenter, but feeling awkward, too. Her gesture—holding her arms apart—and her quiet smile show that she's friendly, and she moves in closer to him until she's almost touching him, as if wanting to show him that it's really her. They give each other two kisses. "What are you doing?"

He doesn't know what to say and is about to tell her that he's buying a beret, but she doesn't give him the chance, adding almost without waiting that she's heard that he's about to publish something, and he manages to stammer that she's right, he's about to finish a novel that's been taking him longer than he had hoped. He brushes his hair back with both hands, glad that he's stopped taking the treatment; at least he doesn't have yellow eyes now. "You don't know how many of your admirers are waiting for that novel." She seems to be sincere, and he feels proud again, but ill at ease, too. He doesn't know how to answer her, and finally, he tells her that he never misses her program. He also says that "at home"—he doesn't know why he uses that expression, but it's what comes out—they call her Marie Lafôret, and she accepts this without showing any surprise, saying it's not the first time she's heard it. *La fille aux yeux d'or.* She laughs, and even so, her wonderful eyes are still sweetly sad. Perhaps he doesn't know, she says, that Marie Lafôret's heritage is Armenian, like Silvye Vartan and Aznavour, and her real name is Maïténa, written with an umlaut, which is a coincidence, because she calls herself Maite. And she adds that like everything "genuinely French," she comes from somewhere else.

There aren't any blue berets at Leclercq. The lady from the shop repeats that it's a Bilbao thing and that he should try on the wide-rimmed black one again. He's reluctant to do that. He's embarrassed to try it on in front of the television presenter, but there's no way out of it. Both women are looking at him, both say complementary things, and both say he needs one size bigger. Sixty-one. While the shopkeeper goes into the back room, he talks about berets, about men being afraid that they'll make them look like their grandfathers. Because, in general, their fathers don't wear them. Lafôret listens to his reflections with attention, says he should write an essay about it—he would, he says, if he didn't have so much work already—and nods from time to time. But when Faustino Iturbe talks about the problems associated with them—the fact that many ethnic and religious groups use them as identity signifiers—Marie Lafôret says that's exactly why they should be worn, to stop those people from becoming their exclusive owners and turning their use into their own private symbol. A perfect metaphor. In fact, you could say that she's an expert on the subject of berets, because she made a documentary about them, and he's quite frustrated that she should know that beret colors have always been used to distinguish factions in the Basque Country and that even though Zumalakarregi, the

Carlist general, wore a red beret, the original Carlist version was white and the liberals' beret was red. She even uses her wonderful voice to sing to him that line about the girls of Azkoitia having plenty of reasons not to dance with the red berets—"*Azkoitiko neskatxak arrazoiarekin / ez dute nahi dantzatu txapelgorriekin.*"

He tries to overcome his embarrassment at having told her things he thought quite original but that she, in fact, already knew all about, and then embarrassed at still having to try on the beret with the two women looking on at him. They both say it really looks good on him, and the presenter doesn't hold back her compliments—he looks very handsome, extremely interesting. As far as the subject of whether he wouldn't be better off with a smaller one is concerned (and he doesn't mention Sándor Márai or Steiner, but a photo of Beckett comes to mind, wearing a beret like a bonnet), the presenter agrees with the shopkeeper—no way, small berets are incredibly ugly, only fit for farm workers from Extremadura. The two women, looking at him from their height—the Leclercq lady is very tall, too—stick to their opinion without expressing any doubt at all, and he doesn't dare to stand up for his own idea. The presenter's recommendation: the secret to wearing a beret with elegance, as with all types of clothing, is to wear it in a natural way, without prejudice, in the way foreigners do. Ian McKellen wore a black beret when he was awarded the Donostia Prize at the film festival, and she says he looked much more interesting with the beret on than bareheaded.

Defeated by these arguments, Faustino Iturbe has no choice but to buy the black beret. And he's going to put it on right then and there. While he's waiting for his change, the presenter picks a red beret up from the counter and shows him how to put it on, "using a single hand," and elegantly lifting up her chin, as if to draw attention to herself, she asks him how she looks, whether she looks more like a barmaid or an *Ertzainatza* officer.

He says she looks very beautiful.

He could leave then, but he decides to remain by the counter, and Marie Lafôret explains, seemingly as much to him as to the shopkeeper, that she always wears a black beret with a pompom, like a French sailor, but because the one she has is worn out, she needs a new one. The shopkeeper goes into the back room again to see if they have any left, and he wonders if it would be too daring for him to suggest to the beautiful presenter—who's looking at a

Danborrada hat, the sort worn during Donostia's drumming festival, and admiring the gold-colored cords all over it—that he could wait for her to finish making her purchase and then they could leave the shop together and go grab a coffee or a beer together. He's sure she'd accept if he suggested it, completely sure, more so than with any other woman he's ever met before. Her way of smiling tells him that, her agreeable way of talking and listening to him. Her easygoing, natural presence.

The Leclercq lady, who's found a beret with a pompom on it, proudly explains to them the detailed work that went into the making of the Danborrada hat—which, judging by its decorations, must be a general's—Laforet happily tries it on, with no inhibition whatsoever, and it falls right down to her nose. The lady talks to them as if they were together. Two old friends who've met up in the shop by chance, and she would certainly be surprised if he just walked out and left the television presenter there trying on the beret with the pompom. What's more, he feels very relaxed next to her— he's always admired her beauty, sweetness, and sophistication—but suddenly he realizes that they've met each other too late, that there's no future for them, and he feels the need to leave. So he says he has to go, before she tries the beret on, and just in case she might try to hold him back or something like that, he adds that he's very late for an appointment. They say goodbye, and he's already turned toward the door when he hears her say, "Are we going to see each other again?" Her voice has the soft, musical tone typical of Lower Navarre, and he replies that he hopes so. Give me your number, she asks, taking out her phone, and he gives it her. She presses the keys with a young person's skill, and his phone rings immediately. "Add me to your contacts," she says.

She makes a final movement with her hand to say goodbye. *"Txapela burian ibili mundian!"* She's used the old Basque saying— put your beret on and go see the world. He spends the rest of the afternoon in his study. He tries to get Marie Laforet out of his head; after making the firm decision not to call her, he also thinks about the possibility of not watching her on the television any more.

ON REALITY IMITATING ART. The writer looks in his archives. He always has the idea that he needs to clean everything up before it's too late. He has many duplicate copies of his documents, which he makes because of his fear of losing them, as well as different copies of the same pieces of work in different stages of completion. He dares to erase what seem to be exact copies—even that he finds a struggle—and destroying the remains of previous versions of his final documents is a relief. He has a lot of unfinished stories, most of them short sketches, things he's written, things from his imagination, "which reality has written new versions of." She's heard Martin say that a thousand times. "Love and War"—the story of a couple that ends with the husband throwing his wife off the sixth floor of a building. He finished the story and it had been published when, shortly afterward, a news agency in Valencia reported on the very same thing having happened. It wouldn't have been an amazing coincidence for a man to throw his wife out of a window—although not an everyday occurrence, it isn't all that unusual—if the only point in common had been it being the sixth floor. But the floor wasn't the only thing in common between the fictional and real events, there was more than that: the victim's name—Flora, as always—and the murderer's alibi and cover-up strategy—blaming his wife's lover—were also the same. At dinner parties, Martin used to have the rather infantile tendency to marvel at reality imitating art, and he would even go so far as to imagine, though only as a joke, that the police would take his story to be the Valencian killer's source of inspiration, although this hypothesis was far from probable, since it had only ever been published in Basque.

"*Zuk bai ulertzen nauzula*," another story of his, is also about the problems a couple are having. The title translates in English to "You Actually Do Understand Me." They both feel miscomprehended by the other, there's no communication between them, they hardly speak to one another. They both take refuge in relationships with online partners, looking for comfort. In both cases, the online couples open up to each other and talk about the harsh words, the bad treatment, and above all the lack of respect they each receive from their real-life partners, in full detail, and they say nice things to console each other. They understand each other. The electronic exchange lasts a long time, they come to feel close. They grow to understand each other better and better and, above all, are increasingly understanding with one another regarding the treatment they're getting from their respective partners, until finally it's obvious and they each realize that their confidant is actually their real partner. A news agency reported that the same thing had just happened somewhere or other in the world, but in that case, Martin wasn't able to demonstrate that he had had his idea before the real event occurred, because he had no more than a draft when it came out in the newspapers; he had the original contents, but nobody other than himself could confirm that, and he was really put out, because he was afraid that people wouldn't believe him. Julia could confirm his version, but not without admitting that she used to sneak onto his computer. Once, the subject came up when they were with some friends, and Julia took pity on him and ventured to say that he was right, that she remembered very well that he told her the story before it came out in the newspapers, almost giving herself away, because he had a strict rule about not saying anything about whatever he was writing while he was still writing it. He must have taken it for a white lie, and nothing happened.

In another story, titled "*Heriotza baino saihestezinago*", or "Less Avoidable Than Death," an army officer who's tired of life decides to commit suicide in his family's mausoleum, wearing the clothes he'd like to be buried in, his dress uniform, with all his many medals on his chest, simply wanting to spare his own corpse and his relatives the irritating procedures that go along with death; but what he doesn't take into account is that his decision is just going to make things more complicated, because they always do autopsies in cases of suicide, and so they have to take his body from the mausoleum to the morgue, from there to the funeral parlor, and then back to the cemetery, and in the end they bury him in an ordinary civilian suit because his dress uniform had gotten splattered with blood and the family didn't have time to take it to the cleaners. In this case, too, the newspapers published the story of something similar happening in Madrid a few months after he'd written his draft. According to the articles, a gentleman—who turned out to be an army officer—showed up at the Almudena Cemetery and asked to be cremated. After the employees told him that it was impossible, explaining that they were only allowed to burn cadavers, the man decided to shoot himself, and inside his family's mausoleum, no less. Another excuse for Martin to show off about reality basing itself on his ideas, but with the frustration of not being able to prove it, "*Heriotza baino saihestezinago*," too, being no more than an unpublished draft. It was pathetic to see him setting himself forward as an example when he spoke about reality imitating art, and one day, when Julia was in a bad mood, they quarreled about it. Tired of hearing him say the

607

same thing for the thousandth time, she came out and told him that reality was always better than what he called art, because the real officer's request to be cremated, something which isn't in his story, was amazing, she thought, and she still thinks so now—you just have to imagine the conversation he must have had with the people working there. He didn't speak to her for a long time afterward.

The man in front of the mirror has often thought about writing a short essay on the topic of reality and fiction, which would allow him to make use of the couple of dozen sketches and synopses of stories he has filed away without having to develop them any further, in order to do something with them before reality itself or some other writer is inspired by the same ideas; it would also be a way of insuring his ownership of the ideas. From time to time, he starts working on the stories, to complete and round them off in the quickest, most direct way possible, but he doesn't think he has the time to write an essay that could justifiably be published. He also considers the possibility of just publishing his ideas for the stories, under the title *Stories I Haven't Written*, but he doesn't think he has enough material to make it into a whole book. He's reflecting about this when his telephone beeps to tell him he has a message. It's her, of course, Marie Lafôret. "It was lovely meeting up like that. Your beret brought us together—another reason for you to wear it. What's going to bring about our second meeting? Will there be a second meeting?"

Faustino Iturbe doesn't know how to classify all the feelings the message brings out in him. They are many and contradictory. Agreeable, because the most beautiful television presenter is interested in him; frustrating, because the opportunity to meet her has arrived so late on; and perhaps for that same reason, thinking it so late on, he doesn't feel the nervousness he would have once in the same situation, it doesn't make him feel so ill at ease.

His answer: "I hope so." Without thinking it over much; it seems to him the only thing he can say. And he leaves it at that.

THERE'S A ROUGH WIND, and one of the shutters on the top floor breaks loose and bangs against the wall. It happens with the same window every time there's wind from the northwest. Julia turns her computer off and starts going upstairs to close it and stop it from breaking. She hears a cough. It's his way of saying that he's awake, and she isn't sure whether or not to open the door and say good morning. She decides to do so, pointlessly knocking on the door first and asking if he's awake. Then, as she raises the blind, he hides his head under the sheets. It's horribly stuffy. So she pulls the curtains aside and opens the balcony door. Because the room faces south, the wind is hardly noticeable, the only sign of it is the movement of the highest branch on the tree. She tells him it's very late and it's a beautiful day, like a mother trying to get her children out of bed, and he gives an excuse—he hasn't slept a wink. Julia imagines that Laforet must be the reason he hasn't slept, and to be nice, she asks him if he's had any nightmares. He mumbles his answer—how could he have nightmares if he's just told her he wasn't able to sleep? "The woman upstairs" stopped him from sleeping. He complains that she made a terrible amount of noise. Julia doesn't want to listen to any more, she starts to leave, so that he'll see that she disapproves of him keeping tabs on what Lynn is up to, but when she reaches the door, she hears signs of life from the floor above, and, unconsciously, she looks toward the ceiling. He must have taken this as a signal that she's interested, because he insists that she has to believe him. He sits up in bed and says it was scandalous, and he looks as if he's hallucinating; what little hair he has left is all in a mess and standing on end. "It's been a scandalous night." He protests with greater conviction and firmness than on other occasions and, above all, asks her to believe him. He'd been up writing until late, and when he finally went to sleep, he was awoken by the phone of "the woman upstairs." He heard her going around the house and opening and closing doors until, eventually, she ran down the stairs. Since he couldn't get to sleep, he got up and tried to continue writing, until he became exhausted again in the dawn light, but by the time he got to sleep, he heard them on the stairs again, the two of them this time, one running after the other to catch up, as if they were having a race. They were talking, laughing, sighing, groaning, and wailing, much more than usual, and when they stopped for a moment, he was so tired that he dropped off to sleep, but right away, once again, they woke him back up when her friend left, and he made an incredible noise as he went down the stairs, because he tripped a couple of times. He says they had both been drunk when they came back.

"At least this way they keep you awake to write your novel."
She laughs so he doesn't have any doubt that she's joking, but even
so, he looks at her severely. "How's it going?" she asks him then,
and he shrugs his shoulders. "I'm at a critical moment." He has to
do some thinking before he can go any further.

"Don't think too much, let it flow."

He looks at her in silence, measuring the meaning of her words.

"Aren't you ever going to tell me what it's about?"

"It isn't about anything. The thoughts somebody has while he
sits there with a pencil in his hand. Something like *Malone meurt*,
though not quite like that."

A reply that stops her from asking any more questions. But Julia's
sure he's met Marie Lafôret.

WHILE JULIA PUTS THE FOOD into the cats' bowls, the two house cats
sniff at it, while the non-house cat stays a few yards away. It won't
come up to its bowl, the guest bowl, until the other two satisfy their
hunger; it will sniff at it and sometimes even stir it around while the
others go off to digest their food by the woodpile or the flowerbed,
depending on the weather. Today the wind from the northwest has
brought some clouds with it. She sees Lynn looking at them from
her window. Who knows how long she's been there. She makes a
silent gesture that means "hi" and then asks her to come up—no
words with that, either, as if she didn't want the writer to find out.

The house is full of light. The top floor, which is higher than the
Indian chestnut tree, gets more light than the ground floor. Martin's
grandparents' dark, heavy piece of furniture rescued from the
basement, looks cheerful in that clean place. Lynn's very tastefully
placed objects around here and there, and she's even covered some
of the furniture with patterned cotton cloth—to protect them from
Max's claws, she says—the armchairs, for instance. The house Julia
never had, the house she'd like to have for herself, one where there
would be no excuses for not writing. Tidy, in order, with flowers
in it. She only has time to look at the books and the four or five
engravings on the walls, which, because it's a small apartment, take
up the whole space. Then Lynn, after saying that she wants to talk,
tells her to sit down next to her on the sofa. The wedding sofa.
She knows they make love there, and because of that, having to sit

there makes her feel something like apprehension. She'd rather sit in the armchair across from it, on the other side of the triangular table, which doesn't look like something belonging to Martin's grandparents. She asks her about it, in order to justify standing up, worried Lynn may guess what she's thinking. As Julia suspected, Lynn bought the table, and finally, Julia decides to sit next to her, closer than usual, not wanting her to think for a moment that she's trying to avoid being intimate with her.

Sitting on the sofa, they hear the very clear sound of a toilet being flushed, and she has the sensation that the space around her is familiar and unfamiliar at the same time, like on occasions when she's seen her own kitchen from a neighbor's window. The phone rings, and Martin doesn't pick up—she didn't tell him that she was going when Lynn asked her up—and they hear him quite clearly, his slow steps along the hallway, and the bedroom door opening. There's no need for them to say that they can hear everything. Lynn smiles with an expression halfway between that of an accomplice and that of somebody with regrets, and Julia can't help remembering Martin sitting exactly beneath where they are now, on the edge of the bed, pointing at the ceiling and listening to their cries of pleasure, and Lynn's angry voice, so unusual in her, shooing the cat away—"Get out of here, Max"—and the loud noise of the cat jumping down onto the floor.

By the way, where is Max?

Lynn apologizes for Max's naughtiness as she always does, as if she were excusing a shy child for not coming out to greet the visitors. He's just as shameless once he gets to know you as he is shy before that. Julia asks her about the cat, out of a stupid need to buy time and put off the moment when Lynn is going to take her into her confidence; she's sure she's brought her up here to tell her about her relationship with Abaitua, that she doesn't want it to remain a secret any longer. She knows that, just as she knew that the cat would run and hide beneath the sofa as soon as she came into the room. Why is that beautiful, elusive cat—which moves to the back of the sofa when she goes down on all fours to try to tempt it out—called Max? Lynn's attitude is like that of a teacher waiting for a naughty pupil to take her place so that she can start the class, and that makes Julia feel like she shouldn't ask her the question. So she gets back up and sits down on the sofa again, her back up straight, her arms determinedly crossed, acting the pupil, attentive to whatever it is Lynn has to say. Lynn laughs at the joke, opens her mouth a little, and looks as if she's going to say something, but doesn't. She covers her face with both hands, then takes them away and smiles again.

"THE MOST WONDERFUL NIGHT OF MY LIFE."

Julia's shocked that the story of the most wonderful night of Lynn's life starts off with the revelation that Sagastizabal still exists and that her cousin, the new *etxeko-jaun*—landlord—has had a child with a little Peruvian woman who's apparently called Argi, and that they're going to call him Peru; she thinks it's because of her amazement that she doesn't comment sooner, as Lynn would have liked her to, on how "wonderful and magical" the double meaning of the child's name is. And then doctor Abaitua's name comes up— except that he's no longer Abaitua, he's Iñaki now—and after saying his name, her words come pouring out, so quickly that Julia has to ask her to speak more slowly, so that she can understand what she's saying about how in the middle of the night on "that wonderful night," he called her from the hospital to say that he had come across the couple and, seeing them looking really concerned, taken pity on them and decided that that he would help the Peruvian woman— whose name he still didn't know to be Argi—to give birth at home, but above all, how he made the decision because of her, Lynn, because she had convinced him of the advantages of home births and of the need to respect different cultures. So he teased her—she was to blame, and she was going to have to be the midwife. It was moving to have the chance to take part in a birthing. She ran out of the house, and everything since then has seemed like a dream to her. There were four of them there—Argi, the owner of Sagastizabal, Iñaki, and herself—all waiting calmly for Peru to arrive; they talked about this and that and various Basque subjects, and finally, when the child made his appearance, it was all very easy, each of them knew just what to do, and she's never had such a moving experience.

Then, while mother and child rested, they watched the sun come up and went on talking, and everything seemed simple and easy to understand to her. Love, life, death—everything seemed beautiful to her—the river, the valley, the little Sagastizabal field, the goat, which was so white, the red rooster, and even the silent industrial buildings and the cranes surrounding them. Energy in storage, force, that's what they suggested. Then lights started coming on, the birds started chirping, noise coming from the road and the trains going by, and they gave a toast in the name of life, they ate boiled chorizo and cheese, drank soup, and she thinks she's still drunk, and she doesn't want the sensation to go away.

"I'M IN LOVE." She shakes her head slowly as she says it, giving the impression that more than anything else, it's an unavoidable fact that's been cast upon her and the only thing she can do is to give way to it. Julia isn't at all uncomfortable hearing about it, and she doesn't think it's because Lynn's told her in English. She's astonished to realize that it's something nobody else has ever told her—leaving to one side Harri's histrionic declarations about the man at the airport—and above all, it's the sureness with which Lynn says it that moves her, as if she were telling her that she was having her period, something that cannot be doubted—a known, undeniable physiological fact.

Although she looks darker against the light, there's a copper-colored aura around her, and the peachy down on her legs looks more golden than usual. She once told her that she doesn't have to shave her legs. What luck. Julia would say she's got full breasts, and she's realized recently that she always wears a bra, even when she wears informal T-shirts around the house. She admits to herself that she's even hated her at times because of her bare thighs and the way her breasts move from side to side as she walks down the stairs. She's very lucky, Julia says, and Lynn replies, after agreeing and moving her head slowly from side to side, that she doesn't know just how lucky—even if for no other reason, last night alone would make her whole life worth living. Then she keeps quiet, as if wanting to make sure that Julia is taking what she says seriously.

"Do you think I'm crazy, too?"

Julia could ask her why she says "too," but she doesn't get the chance, because Lynn immediately adds, "I think I'm crazy." She, too, used to distrust happiness. She used to think it would make her pay at some stage, abandoning her and leaving her with an unbearable vacuum. But she's no longer afraid, because she's seen real love. So it's no longer a matter of faith, she's actually felt it, its ability to transform things. She'd seen the man alone, weighed down by his circumstances, sunk in sad skepticism, and now her love has given him the energy to shake things out, to want to live. *¿Qué te parece?*

Lynn herself answers first. "You think I'm as crazy as Harri," she says, laughing, and Julia, too, laughs, relieved and hoping the joke will bring the moment of sharing intimate thoughts to an end. But she doesn't know why she's relieved, to what extent it's because of embarrassment and to what extent it's a matter of fear. And if it is fear, what is she afraid of? She thinks that Lynn has asked herself the same thing, she's aware of her, Julia's, discomfort as they both take advantage of a train going by to keep quiet. A while after it's gone by, Lynn says that the trains don't bother her at all.

Love exists, it's as simple as that, she says, before walking out of the living room.

While listening to the sound of water coming from the bath-room faucet, Julia wonders whether she's done the right thing pointing out to her that there were traces of dampness on her T-shirt near her nipples. She's standing up and looking at the books on the shelves. She doesn't have very many. Large anthropology volumes. Most of the literature is from the Penguin Popular Classics paperback collection, and Julia's amused to see Martin's *Beti euria ari du* between Margaret Atwood's *Cat's Eye* and Ian McEwan's *Enduring Love*. And English copies of *One Hundred Years of Solitude* and *If on a Winter's Night a Traveler*. She thinks it very surprising to see so many books about Max Frisch. *Understanding Max Frisch. Perspectives on Max Frisch. The Novels of Max Frisch. The Reluctant Modernist. Contemporary Male-Female Relationships in the Novels of Max Frisch.* She begins reading at random: "*It might be argued that Frisch's novels really are concerned not with love, but with the absence of love.*" "*Can a man's life be so described that it becomes visible and comprehensible to others?*"

Among the objects scattered around the shelves, there's a small, A4-sized watercolor—a house that looks like a *baserri*, a sloping red roof, blue windows and shutters, surrounded by trees; the style's quite naïf. The painter, who signs his name *Kepa*, has written "*To Lynn, a souvenir from Ainhoa*" at the bottom. Now Julia recognizes it: the front of the Argi Eder Hotel. On a sheet of square paper of the same size, there's a drawing of a cross section of a woman—she has to look carefully to see that it's drawn in pen and isn't a printed reproduction—with the organs numbered but without any notes to accompany each number. She recognizes Lynn's writing in the words "*The first time I saw him.*" A photo of the couple standing in front of a bronze statue. Abaitua looks serious, his hands in his pockets, wearing a light-colored polo shirt and pants. Lynn's wearing the dress with flowers on it that he gave her. She's standing a little apart from him, but her head is leaning toward him, almost touching his shoulder, and she's looking at the photographer with her eyes wide open, a humorous look. It's obvious that he doesn't like being in photos and that she isn't at all interested in looking pretty in it. The sculpture behind them is of an angel with its large wings spread open, holding a dead or unconscious young man who has a broken sword in his hand. It looks familiar to her. She imagines it must be a famous sculpture and that she's seen it in some art book.

She asks Lynn when she reappears wearing a new T-shirt and looking as if she's taken a shower. She doesn't answer right away. She takes the photo and, after looking at it for a while, says, "He's an interesting man, isn't he?" Then they talk about the sculpture, without Lynn waiting to hear Julia's opinion about him. She doesn't seem to need it. She says the sculpture is highly symbolic for her, even more so than what you can actually see, and she doesn't think that Kepa—she pauses for a moment, smiles, and gives the impression that she's about to add "Martin's friend"—chose it as the background for the photo by chance. When Iñaki suggested going on the trip with them, she already knew that he wasn't an elderly ladies' man, one of those men who like flirting with young girls, and when she saw the sculpture, she wondered whether she would have the strength to lift him up and take him with her. Now she knows she does. And they've taken flight.

She asks whether Julia minds talking about these things.

This time she says no, how could she possibly think that? But then, immediately, she feels the need to tell her the truth. It's true that she feels ill at ease. Lynn's smile encourages her to go on speaking, but she doesn't know what more to say, she has insuperable difficulty expressing her feelings. She knows very well it's not a matter of embarrassment, that's not what she feels about her inner life; it's fear. Fear that everything Lynn is telling her may be unknown to her. To get out of the situation, she tells her it's more a matter of envy than discomfort. "Hearing about what I'm missing out on. *Ulertzen?*" she explains, asking her in Basque if she understands. After looking at her for a while, very seriously, as if trying to measure to what extent she's telling the truth, Lynn laughs. *"Don't be nasty."*

The kitchen's immaculate. It looks as if various coats of white paint have been put on all the containers, and their contents, too, everything, for sanitary rather than aesthetic reasons. The blue cups and plates on the drying rack are the only exception. The containers on the shelf over the fridge, with different cereals and nuts in them, are transparent. And there, on the white marble table, is the real reason why Lynn's brought her up here: a large plate of *kokotxas*—hake cheeks—floating in bloodied water. They don't look good, probably because she kept them too long in the fishmonger's plastic bag. She says her plan is to amaze "the man who has her floating on air" by cooking it, and she wants Julia to teach her how to do it, and that's why she bought a third ration for her. *¿Qué te parece?* They both laugh out loud. Does she really want to know what she thinks. She nods. She shouldn't even bother trying.

The girl's look reveals that she's trying to figure out if Julia is attempting to tell her something more than what she's actually said, and while Julia's chopping up the garlic, because the girl's determined to at least practice with a few bits of the fish, and explaining how to cook the *pil-pil* sauce—don't let the garlic get burned, take the pot with the fish in it off the flame for the oil to cool down, take most of it out, and add it back in as the sauce thickens, little by little, just as you would to make mayonnaise, and keep on moving the pot around, shaking it with your wrists—she realizes that Lynn isn't paying any attention to her. Even so, Julia finishes cooking, though not without some difficulty—she has to shake the pot a lot to keep everything from sticking, because not much gelatine comes out of the fish—and the results are nothing exceptional, and then there's no parsley to put on top. Lynn starts laughing when Julia asks if she thinks she's got the hang of it. What's she's laughing about? She's remembered something Kepa said to her: the sensuality of Cuban women dancing the Rumba is nothing compared to that of Basque women making *pil-pil*.

They're laughing when they hear Martin's voice from the floor below. He's calling out for her, even though he knows very well where she is. What does he want now? She's embarrassed by him calling out to her like that, shouting her name, angry because she's with Lynn; she knows that's what's bothering him. Now the small entryway is the only area in darkness, and the young woman in love's eyes shine with a different color. The Max in *Montauk* says that Lynn's eyes are like slate under the water. That's what this Lynn's eyes look like now, too. "He needs you," she says, and Julia wonders whether or not to answer. She could tell her that Martin used to remind her of one of the characters in his *Naufragoen istorioak*—or *Shipwreck Stories*—trying to save himself by holding onto her neck, but that now she thinks his aim is quite simply to sink her. But she only answers that she doesn't know what he needs her for, hesitating whether to add the rest of what she's thinking, which is that she doesn't know why or what she needs him for, either. Finally, she says that he must have lost something and takes ahold of the door handle, and in response to that movement, Lynn makes way for her, putting her hands behind her back and leaning against the wall. As if to say that she doesn't want to stop her from leaving but that she's here for whatever Julia needs, and what Julia's needed for a long time is to cry. She doesn't know how it happens, but she falls into her arms, sobbing, in a way she hasn't done for years, not since she fell to her knees and begged Martin to forgive her for being unfaithful. She cries for all the days that have gone by, for every day her unhappiness has lasted, and Lynn accepts her tears in silence, holding her softly in her arms. She needed to get it off her chest, she says when they move apart a little later. It's a statement, not an excuse, because she doesn't need to apologize; she's not embarrassed. Now she really smiles, she really feels better, and Lynn smiles, too. She's sorry she's spoilt the moment, Lynn having been so happy, and she strokes her white cheek—perhaps it's too white—with the tips of her fingers, and Lynn returns the gesture. *"Don't be silly."* Their hands, which are still clasped together, separate when she says she's going. They give each other the usual glancing kisses and wish each other luck, as if they were going on a journey or had to do something really important. Lynn says in Basque that they both deserve it—*"Biok merezi dugu"*—as Julia starts going down the tricky spiral staircase. "You said it." She stops for a moment to let her know that she really is sure of what Lynn doesn't quite believe. "I really do envy you." Then, when she starts off down the stairs again, she slips and has to hold onto the bannister with both hands. She turns around and looks upward once more. "One day you guys are going to break your necks," she says, using the plural on purpose, and Lynn, at the top of the stairs, holds her arms open and pretends to fly. "I'm the angel," Julia thinks she hears, because she says it clearly but in a very low voice, so that Martin can't hear them from the gallery.

"WHERE WERE YOU?"

She tells him the truth—"Showing Lynn how to cook *kokotxas*" —overcoming the feeling of contempt that having to explain what she's been doing brings out in her. She doesn't know why she's told him that, and now it will give him the chance to roll out his sarcasm. Perhaps she hoped he would be moved by the girl's desire to please her man, but what he actually says is that he doesn't think the prospect of having *kokotxas* is what's pushing the delivery doctor up the spiral staircase. It's the same thing she herself thought a couple of minutes earlier, but hearing him say it makes her mad. That often happens to her. *Fragebogen*: Why do some observations about reality, or, more exactly, criticisms about it, which she would normally be in complete agreement with, seem like exaggerations when coming from him? (It's something she denies when Martin says it's due to her need to reaffirm herself.)

They don't have time to get angry at each other, because Harri arrives and makes one of her most classic entrances—she drops down onto the sofa, out of breath, as if she'd run there. They aren't going to believe it. What she tells them is what Lynn has just told Julia about the Peruvian woman having her baby, but she gives them the version that's going around the hospital. Apparently, everybody's talking about his strange decision to take the unfortunate woman who was about to give birth out of the delivery room and over to some farm building to have her baby there, and there are different interpretations of what exactly happened. Some witnesses have it that he turned up late at night on the maternity ward looking disturbed; some people say he'd been drinking. Other people say that before that, he spoke with a patient in the pediatric ICU, naming the doctors who were responsible for her son's terrible situation, offering himself as a witness, and encouraging her to sue them. All of them said that he was shouting as he walked up and down the hall, going on about the medical mafia, their insatiable thirst for money, about corporatism and cowardice covering up the blame for so much unnecessary suffering, and then he gathered up the materials he needed for the home delivery. Apparently, he's been temporarily suspended, and from what she hears, if some of the allegations are confirmed, he might even have his license revoked.

"*Qué te parece?*"

Julia is astonished, upset too. She says she's just been with Lynn, who doesn't seem to know anything about Abaitua's problems. She gives them some of the details of what Lynn's just told her: Abaitua called Lynn from the hospital to go and help him bring Sagastizabal Peru into the world; she was convinced that it was her influence that prompted him to his decision; being a midwife was a marvellous experience for her. Julia tries to convey some of the sensations she had listening to the story of "that wonderful night," and Harri is clearly moved. But Martin isn't, he's only interested in repeating what he already told her—they both tripped going up the stairs, drunk, at dawn.

"That's the strength of love, isn't it?" Harri says it only for Julia, as if Martin weren't there. When he comes out with a vulgar Spanish expression about tits having more pull with men than horse-drawn carriages—"*Tiran más dos tetas que dos carretas*"—Julia realizes that it's the first time she and Harri have ever understood each other so well in the company of Martin. Then she asks if it doesn't make her feel envious, and she says that she just said that to Lynn herself, that she's envious, although she doesn't know how sincere she was being. Why?

She thinks she would be afraid of somebody being so influenced by their feelings for her when making what might be important life decisions, and of the consequences those decisions might have. An argument it doesn't take Harri long to overturn, and which Julia doesn't go to much trouble to defend, either. In any case, whenever she's thought about Abaitua and Lynn's relationship, she's always seen Lynn as the victim, assuming there is one. A victim of his imprudence—momentarily lost on a one-way street she doesn't have any doubt he'll return to soon enough. Iris Murdoch writes about the injustices married people commit against those who come into their lives. It has never even crossed her mind that it could be a case of the older man being taken in by the belief that he has sufficient strength or energy to change his route and follow the steps of a young person who may be rather rash or naïve.

As far as Harri's question is concerned—why there has to be a victim at all—she doesn't know what to say. Why not an ending like the one in *Montauk*, without losers or winners? Lynn goes back to America, wiser and having promised to send him a postcard each year on the date she marked down as being "the first time I saw him"; the doctor is resigned, and relieved to be going back to his usual life with memories of what might be his last love affair.

She likes the way Lynn and Max say goodbye to each other—a final dinner the evening before Max goes away, to which Lynn invites their friends, so that they aren't alone, a farewell near a park close to the United Nations, the promise to send each other postcards on the agreed upon date, if they don't forget. Without any reproaches.

Harri: "There are people who bet on life and win or lose, and then there are others who don't take any risks and end up embittered." Julia thinks that must be the conclusion to something she's said previously, she doesn't know what, because she hasn't been paying attention to her, but something that has to do with herself. She doesn't mind. She's amused that Harri, after her search for the man from the airport—a story she really doesn't know what to think about—thinks of herself, the high-level Department of Public Health official, the wife of a doctor and the mother of a pupil at an English boarding school, as one of the most daring risk-takers in life. Julia doesn't mind. She wonders whether Abaitua having to leave work, even if it's temporary, might affect the tests Harri has to have done at the hospital, but seeing her so relaxed, she doesn't think it a good idea to ask her.

Harri goes on talking about the importance of betting on life. Julia suspects that she wants to tell them the latest developments of her own adventure, but she decides to punish her by not showing any interest. The writer doesn't ask her any questions about it, either. Then all of a sudden, he slaps himself on the thigh, says "*navigare necesse est, vivere non est necesse*," and gets up. It's one of the few quotes he knows by heart—to sail is necessary, to live is not—and he always underlines it whenever he comes across it in books. Very often, in other words. And when Harri asks him where he's going, he looks at her, amazed that she doesn't know. He's going to write, he says with great dignity. So, he's going to risk himself in the dangerous waters of literature, leaving life to one side. Harri says, "Let's see if you can finish it once and for all." She complains that he won't tell her what the novel's about, and to Julia, she says "Really, has he not told you anything, either?" Julia's first thought is to say she doesn't know anything, so that she'll leave her alone, but then she's tempted to say what it's about, giving the impression that it's something she's deduced from what Martin's just said. "It's about somebody who knows his end is near and is writing about his past and present." The mention of *Malone meure* could have brought her to that conclusion, but then she says something more specific. "Although I suspect he's going to meet somebody and he's going to have his last love story, a real love story, peaceful, complete, like a wonderful sunset." As she says it, she's amazed she's dared to, and she's quite alarmed by the question mark she sees forming between the writer's eyebrows. She's reminded of Gantenbeim. When Gantenbeim pretends to be blind, he puts his foot in it again and again by making remarks he shouldn't about things he sees through his dark glasses—"What a beautiful apartment," for instance, when a woman invites him to her home—but nobody picks up on it, because he's wearing dark glasses and carries a stick. "I bet there's something like that in it!" she ventures to say, knowing that Martin thinks his computer is protected by his password. He doesn't answer, and she doesn't want to take any more risks.

When he leaves them alone, locking himself in the formal library, Harri suggests they go up to see Lynn. She says she thinks they have to tell her what people are saying at the hospital, but Julia doesn't think it's a good idea. She thinks it's Abaitua himself who will have to tell her about the consequences of the "magical night." Harri doesn't look very convinced, but she remains seated. And she has a lot of questions. Could Abaitua really have been drunk? Could Lynn really be about to take that man out of his balanced, stable circumstances? Would Abaitua really be capable of leaving a look of astonishment on Goytisolo's beautiful face and then abandoning her entirely to go to America? Is Lynn some sort of Mata Hari?

The truth is, they don't know anything about Lynn.

She remembers how she had to change her T-shirt but decides, after a moment's reflection, not to mention that to Harri. She remembers that once, talking with Lynn about the other Lynn, the one from *Montauk*, she said that you don't find out much about her by reading the novel, but the real Lynn didn't agree with her. They listed the physical data given by Max: the color of her eyes (slate under water); her hair style (a ponytail that sways from side to side as she walks along the dunes); her very thin but not bony figure; the fact that she wears glasses, which Max once held by the temples, in the way opticians do, and placed over her eyes with great care;

621

and her looking half nurse, half undine. They also know that she's not particularly well educated—she reads books about dolphins—which is something Max finds reassuring, and that she hasn't been to Europe. She isn't very good at sewing, but she accepts her female role when she sews a replacement button on Max's old jacket. She has a complex about having small breasts. She's shy. Once, she refused to make love with him, "for justifiable reasons"—"*today I have my period*." She's had experiences with men, but not many, which is something the writer deduces from the way she takes off her clothes and opens the bed the first time they make love. All things that are in *Montauk*.

But Lynn gave more details, too: she was born in Florida, went to school in California, was a javelin champion, and had a puritanical upbringing. She was also married for a short while and lived in Sydney, where she used to ride horses. Details that in fact, now that Harri's pointed out that they don't know anything about Lynn, she isn't sure actually appear in *Montauk*, and unable to quieten her curiosity, she feels a strong urge to check, for example about whether the information that she was once married to an Australian man is actually included somewhere in the book. If it isn't, then it must be information she's gotten from somewhere else, information about the woman the character Lynn was based on, and so Julia gets up without realizing it, without paying much attention to what Harri's saying, either, and goes to look for the book.

Until she says, "You're not listening to me." Harri would prefer her to just say that she's not interested.

Julia apologizes, but it's too late. She admits that Harri's right when she accuses her of being more interested in what happens in novels than what's happening in real life. "I don't know what's important for you." She says sorry again, but it's no use. She tells her, in Spanish, to say goodbye to "that other one"—"*Despídeme de ese otro*"—to make it clear she's angry. At the door, she doesn't let Julia come with her to the car, but all of a sudden, her voice becomes softer, and she seems to be more affected by sadness than by wanting to tell her off. It's one thing to be a gossip—as she is, she admits that—but not being interested in what's happening to the people around you is quite another matter. Julia admits that she's right and asks her not to be angry. "How could I be angry? It's just the way you are."

WHEN SHE'S LEFT ALONE, she feels really guilty about not having paid her any attention. She admits she doesn't really care about what happens to people, and the more intimate the things going on with them are, the less she's interested; for some reason, people's private lives intimidate her.

There's a strange type of silence in the house. The cats seem to be asleep, and no birds have come. The leaves on the trees are very still, which is unusual.

She thinks she lets herself be influenced by other people's attitudes too easily. It's something else she should look into. And if she's thought of this now, it's because she has to overcome her scruples about picking up *Montauk* again and looking through it.

"MAX, ARE YOU JEALOUS?"

She asks him when they're on the desserts. It's Saturday, and Max's flight is on Tuesday; Lynn is trying to find out what his vices are—*laster* in German, meaning "loads" or "burdens"; *vices* in French and English; *pecados capitales*, in Spanish; *hoben nagusiak* in the old Basque. Both the Spanish and the Basque versions translate literally to "capital sins." They've decided not to meet again. They've also promised not to write—only a postcard on May 11, 1975, if they remember. But Max doesn't comply with what they've agreed to and turns up in her office in January of '75. He doesn't dare phone— "It would be like a voice from the past"—and when he asks for her at reception, pretending he's there for a business appointment, the black woman at the counter tells him, "*Lynn is no longer with us*"— words that astonish him. He thinks it sounds as if Lynn's died. The black woman, seeing him looking so affected, doesn't introduce him to Lynn's replacement and instead says, "*I liked her very much indeed.*" Later, when he's back in Europe, he receives a long letter she wrote while onboard a steamboat—she's unemployed, she was hoping to change the type of work she does anyway, she's spending a lot of time playing Ping-Pong, and she's reading the book he gave her.

So Lynn broke with what they had agreed upon, too, in her case with a long letter.

Julia can't resist the temptation to translate the ending. "*Lynn miró el reloj, yo retiré la mano de su hombro. Nos habíamos puesto de pie para besarnos. Imposible correr más que cuando bajamos por esa deslumbrante escalinata. No quedaba más que encontrar el sitio exacto en el que separarnos y prestar atención al tráfico; nos cogimos de la mano y tuvimos que correr para atravesar la avenida.* FIRST AVE / 46 TH STREET, *era a todas luces el lugar, dijimos* BYE, *sin besos, luego una segunda vez, levantando la mano:* HI. *Al cabo de unos pasos volví a la esquina, la vi, su silueta que caminaba; no se volvió, se detuvo y necesitó un buen rato hasta que pudo cruzar.*"

Why does she find it easier to translate *Montauk* into Spanish than to translate *Naufragoen istorioak,* she wonders.

And just then, the author comes in. She doesn't hear him until he's right by the table, and she hides *Montauk* under the *Diccionario de dudas,* like a student in an exam. He doesn't realize, among other things because he's looking out the window at the garden. The cats are as they were before, but a breeze is now blowing the leaves around. She asks him how his work's going. Will Marie Lafôret have answered his text message? She has to admit that she's genuinely curious at this point, although she doesn't know whether what she wants to know about is life or literature. She sees Martin from behind, and he shrugs his shoulders, "Not too well."

He turns the television on "to see what type of weather they're forecasting," and Julia throws herself into translating the third story in *Naufragoen istorioak.* A pair of former lovers meet up in a restaurant. He hadn't behaved very well when they broke up, and a few days earlier, when they bumped into each other with their different groups of friends, he suggested they meet up for lunch or dinner. He was a little tipsy and wanting to make up for their nasty breakup. She's put on weight and doesn't look good, but she's still the same woman as the one who used to go out with him. The same helpless look, languid air, sharp voice. If he ever loved her, he can't understand how it could have happened. She's rebuilt her life, and so has he, to an extent. She's the one who talks most, about her children, how things are going for them at school. She has a dog. She seems happy. After dinner, she insists they should go to the nearest beach for a walk and then get into the water, even if just for a quick paddle. He accepts, even though he doesn't particularly like the idea. At best, even assuming they don't get splashed by a wave, they won't be able to dry their feet, and their shoes will be full of sand. She starts talking about her children again. The problem is, in contrast to the impression he got during the dinner, that they're a complete disaster, they're doing badly at school and aren't grateful for anything. Only the dog loves her. Suddenly she lets her shoes fall into the water, starts crying, and raises her hands to her face.

She's very unhappy. She doesn't love her husband, she still loves him, she's never loved anybody else. When the man tries to pick up his former lover's shoes, he drops his own. A wave drags them out to sea . . . Julia can't go on. She turns her computer off and tells Martin that she has to go home, Zigor's waiting for her to help him with some homework. She's finding it easier and easier to lie. He doesn't take his eyes off the television when he says goodbye.

AT HOME, HER MOTHER'S WATCHING THE TELEVISION, too. Marie Lafôret is interviewing an old man with a beret on. It's a program on the civil war. Julia thinks about calling Zigor to tell him it's on— he's at her sister's house—but she doesn't feel like talking with him. The man being interviewed has a very high, faint voice, and it's hard to understand him. He's talking about the Durango bombardment, the one that happened before Gernika. He says that four bombs fell on the land around his *baserri* and that he wants to explain exactly where they fell. One fell on a pinewood he planted with his father when he was very little, just a few feet from a shed. Another fell near a drinking trough, on the slope by the apple orchard.

She goes to the kitchen to fill the washing machine. Zigor's underwear—men's clothing. She eats an apple and watches the clothes spinning around. Her son must have kissed a girl by now.

When she goes back to the living room, Lafôret is interviewing a man who says he's ninety-five and who's still bright and robust. His voice is strong, and his memory exact. He was a communist and had to flee from Santoña to France and then came back to Spain via Catalonia. He fought in a Basque division, first in Madrid and then in the Pyrenees. He escaped from two concentration camps, was condemned to death, and spent twenty-five years of his life in various prisons. One of the times he was locked up, Franco's troops would go in at night and choose three or four people to put up against the wall. He says people used to react in very different ways: some would hit their heads against the wall, desperately cursing their luck; others would cry; others were so dumbstruck they almost died on the spot. The old man, still tall and strong, stands up very straight, his chin proudly held high. His only fear was being stood up in front of the firing squad and finding himself unable to shout "¡*Viva la República, Gora Euzkadi!*" as he died, and he would practice every evening, so that when his time came, he would be able to keep his courage up.

Julia's mother says nothing.

For some reason, sitting there next to her mother, she suddenly needs to know what her father did when he found out that his civil servant friend had been abusing her. She doesn't know why she's never dared to ask before, but now her need to know has become unbearable. Without thinking it over much, she starts by asking if she remembers a friend of Dad's, a man who used to work at the regional government office, who used to give her and her cousin pencils and fondle them. Her mother looks at her and nods. Her chin starts trembling. She wasn't expecting the question, of course, and she's obviously affected by it. Julia regrets having asked the question, but it's too late now. "He wasn't a friend," she stammers. "His wife was our friend, he wasn't from around here." Julia doesn't say that she doesn't care where he was from. "What did Dad do?" Her mother shrugs her shoulders, about to cry. She doesn't know. "What do you mean you don't know? He must have done something!" Julia's never seen her so weak, so beaten up, so helpless. The feeling of pity she has for her doesn't stop her from asking the question again, and her mother shrugs again and puts her hand into her sleeve to look for her handkerchief, like a fragile little girl. "I suppose he told him that we didn't want to see him ever again. I didn't ever see him again."

Julia retires to her bedroom. She feels sorry for her mother, for having made her remember a bad episode, but she also feels sorry for herself. Now she knows that what had been stopping her from asking the question, to a large extent, was her fear that the answer might be frustrating. She's always nurtured the fantasy that her father must have given that foul toad-like man a violent punch in the face. Knocked him to the floor and stepped on the dirty old man's head. Her dad strong and handsome, because that man had touched his favorite daughter's body. She should have asked her father what he did.

20

Going up the stairs two by two, Abaitua's heart speeds up on the final steps to Kepa's house. He's fit, but when he hurries upstairs, he often remembers his colleague Basarte's death on the landing between the fourth and fifth floors on his way up to Agote the cardiologist's office. In order to test his heart, the cardiologist told him to go up the stairs as quickly as possible, and that's what the poor man did, but then he had a heart attack and never made it all the way up. Kepa's waiting for him at the door, and out of breath, he tells him the anecdote, which he doesn't think he's told him before, but Kepa replies that he tells it to him every time he walks up a flight of stairs. Kepa isn't in a good mood. He's nervous about some business matter, something important that has nothing to do with the bookshop, he lets him know, something to do with the sale of an unusual ancient manuscript. Abaitua thinks it's an imaginary excuse in order to shirk his duties at the bookshop, but he doesn't want to give any opinions about business or money. This time, Kepa says he's found a diary written by a musician from the court of Jeanne d'Albret in a second-hand store and that in a few days' time, he'll go there and pick up this priceless piece for a pittance.

Although he's concentrating on business, he hasn't forgotten about their plan to go to La Rochelle for a couple of days. The idea is to try out an amazing schooner he plans to cross the Atlantic in later on. Abaitua doesn't believe it at all really. He knows that the father of one of his friends is the owner of a shipyard in La Rochelle, because he's met him and even sailed with him, but the story Kepa's telling is too perfect to be true. His friend had built the schooner of his dreams, because there isn't much work at the shipyard, and on seeing it, one of those Americans who are loaded with money decided to buy it. Kepa's friend has to deliver it to some port in Florida, and needing a crew for the voyage, he's asked him to go with him on the trip and to find somebody else to come along who would be prepared to take part in the adventure, as well. Abaitua, who doesn't fully believe him, has fantasized more than once, since Kepa suggested it to him, about going to America in a real sailing ship. But before that, the plan is to go to La Rochelle and sail around for a couple of days—a plan that seems much more plausible. Abaitua doesn't have any trouble with dates now that he is, as he usually puts it, "a suspended doctor." Kepa, on the other hand, has to solve "the problem of his mother."

The old lady's sitting down in the kitchen, deep in her task of rubbing two bits of old bread together. Small pieces of the bread are falling onto the table, almost crumbs. She stops what she's doing for a moment to look briefly at the newly arrived man. "*Juan*," she says to him. Then she tells him, "*Ya ves Juan, todavía estoy viva*"—you see, Juan, I'm still alive. She looks at little bit like La Pasionaria, dressed in a black dress, a woollen shawl of the same color, sharp eyes that look as if they've suffered a lot, white hair with nicotine-colored stains combed back into a bun. Abaitua suspects that the severity in her eyes is partly because she's outside reality, but she smiles when he asks her what she's doing with the bread. "*Migas para los pajarillos*"— crumbs for the birds, she says. She still has a good set of teeth.

She has a urinary tract infection, which she often suffers from, and perhaps a bit of a temperature. She smells of piss. First he takes her pulse, and then, while he listens to her chest, to give the impression that he's doing something, Kepa gets things off his chest by telling him more or less the same things as always. She spends all day heating up *café con leche*, forgetting that she's just had some. She drinks gallons of the stuff and, because of that, spends the whole day urinating, and not always in the bathroom, less and less there, in fact, and she refuses to use diapers. But that's the least of it. The worst thing is the danger of her having some accident with the gas and blowing the whole house up. There's quite a high risk of her flooding the place, too, because she also insists on cleaning every-thing she sets eyes on. So he can't leave her alone for even ten minutes.

He's seen that antibiotics don't have any side effects on her and the only thing he can think to do is to give her amoxicillin. Abaitua doesn't know what to answer when he asks him, "But how long can she go on like this?" In any case, he doesn't think that what Kepa suggests—taking her to the ER—is the solution. They won't admit her, probably, and even if they did, it would only be for a couple of days and only to torture her with the same useless tests they've done on her so often, and then the Haloperidol might really knock her body for a loop.

Kepa's challenge: What would happen if she refused to go when they discharged her, if she refused to be taken home? Abaitua is sure that this idea, too, is a fantasy, but why does he keep on thinking about it if he knows he'd never be able to go through with it? Or would he? He asks him, and Kepa just replies that he feels suffocated. He can't go away even for a weekend, the check he gets from the city government doesn't help much, the girl he's hired for a few hours a week is costing him a lot of money. His mother starts heating up coffee again, and Kepa goes back to moaning that she could have an accident at any time. Finally, Abaitua gets fed up. He asks why he doesn't try to teach her to use the microwave, and Kepa doesn't like the question. Just write the prescription already, he replies sharply.

"So, more amoxicillin." There's obvious mockery in his voice as he reads back the prescription. What was he expecting, Midazolam 30 mg? Abaitua knows that Kepa could get ahold of something to cause irreversible sedation, and that he could get his GP to issue the death certificate without ever seeing the corpse. And of course, Kepa even knows a few of those doctors who smile beatifically whenever death is mentioned to them. They've talked about it before. It's possible that this woman who is now so engrossed in rubbing two bits of old bread together might express a desire to die when the moment comes. Probably, in the not too distant future, it'll be just as routine to finish off people who've reached the stage the old woman has as it now is to give children trivalente vaccines. They may even come up with some lovely ritual to regulate the practice, like nomadic tribes in the desert; Kepa says they used to leave dying people with enough water for the caravan to be able to move away and not see their actual deaths. He always mentions anthropological curiosities that speak in favor of euthanasia, as if he had to convince him. They've discussed it. Abaitua has additional reasons for being prudent in this particular debate; he can't help asking himself if he, as a doctor, would be prepared to take on the responsibility for putting an end to a human life. The difficulty is distinguishing between life and human life. Faced with useless suffering, in which there is no hope, Abaitua has no doubt, and he's taken action when he's had to. But he has the impression that people often make decisions too easily when it comes to whether it's worth it for sick people, even terminally ill people, to go on living. His experience makes him cautious, even when it's the sick person asking for an end to their life, because that request may be influenced by variable personal circumstances, particularly by depression, or by situations that might be changeable. He's aware that his objections are shared, as Kepa often reminds him, by those who describe themselves as being "pro-life" whenever abortion and euthanasia are mentioned but who—due to their own comfort, negligence, and ignorance—don't mind putting their patients at risk. But that's what he feels. He also thinks that people who are in favor of euthanasia or assisted suicide—as he is—often simplify the question, and they'd be more prudent about it if they considered the possibility of having to make such decisions themselves.

Before going to get the amoxicillin, Kepa asks his mother if she wants to go to the bathroom. He isn't very affectionate, and he uses the first person plural in the way doctors usually do with their patients. "Shall we go to the bathroom and pee?" But when Abaitua hears him talking inside the bathroom—how to sit down, how to hold on—he sounds more pleasant.

She's sitting down again, her arms forgotten in her lap, hands in her sleeves, her knees together; her black dress goes almost down to her feet, which are in black slippers. As if she were sitting by the front door of her house in Cadiz, whose name she is able to recall when Abaitua asks her. She knows that she isn't there, and she knows what season it is, too, but not what day of the week it is, or the month, or the year. When he shows her his watch, to find out if she can say what it is, she laughs. Why's he asking her that?

So he asks her why she's making bread crumbs, and after looking at him with mistrust, she says it's to give to the birds—"*para dárselas a los pajarillos*"—as if he were pulling her leg by asking her such

630

questions. She says she feeds them at midday. "Lots of sparrows come, and two robins. The robins have their own windows, one goes to the kitchen and the other to the bathroom, each one has its own territory. They're cheeky, and they fight a lot. Do you know what people call them here?" Abaitua pretends not to know. "*Txantxangorris*."

She continues calling him Juan. "You were really lucky in the war, Juan." He asks her why. "Because you got wounded so early on." He isn't sure whether or not to follow her lead or try to find out who she's confusing him with, and finally, he tells her he wasn't even born when the war was going on. So she asks him how old he is, and he tells her. She stares at him, as if to decide how he's looking for his age. For just a moment, her eyes are fully alive, paying full attention. Then, as if unable to understand, they lose their sharpness. He asks her if she's sad, and she says she is, quite sad. The reason: her memories of the war, the dirty war, the bad life Pedro had as a result of the war. She talks about the terrible thing that happened to Pedro. Abaitua knows that Pedro—the old lady always says "poor Pedro"—was Kepa's father and that he volunteered for a CNT battalion when he was seventeen. "*Pobre Pedro*," she says— poor Pedro. "It would have been better if they had just shot him." She talks about "*aquello que le pasó*"—the thing that happened to him—as if he knew all about it, and Abaitua wouldn't understand her if he didn't know that when Franco's soldiers captured enemies, they made them execute people from their own side. Apparently, that was what happened to Kepa's father, and it ruined his life. Kepa told him that his father took to drink. She tells him that he drank to forget. After drying her eyes with a cloth, she lays it out on her lap and delicately folds it, passing the back of her hand over each fold. Her story is short and to the point. Pedro used to say that he wasn't brave enough to kill himself, and he started drinking to forget. It got worse after the war, because he was afraid that somebody might know he had taken part in the firing squads. Somebody from their village or around there. But apparently he himself was the one who talked about it. He used to go from bar to bar to get it off his chest, telling everybody about his drama, how many people he'd killed after hearing them shout "¡Viva la República!"; but the day after, he would forget that he had admitted to it. "That's why we came to Vasconia," she explained, using an old Spanish name for Euskadi.

When Abaitua asks her if she only has bad memories, she asks him, surprisingly, to specify if he means from the war or just in general, and after he tells her he means in general, she says she has a few fine memories. She laughs out loud, and Abaitua sees that she doesn't have any wisdom teeth or premolars.

"*Pedrito, hijo, cuánta guerra te doy*", she says—what a lot of trouble I cause for you, Pedrito, my son. She lifts up a hand to stroke Kepa's cheek when he hands her a yogurt for her to eat with her antibiotics. He tells her to quit trying to sweet-talk him—"*Déjese de zalamerías.*" It's a shy, rough answer, a strange mixture. Abaitua thinks she's embarrassed about having called him *Pedrito*.

They agree to meet up another day to talk about the trip to La Rochelle. Kepa's suggestion is that they go up the coast as far as Nantes. There are different routes drawn in red and blue on the map he spreads out on the table. He has photos of the schooner, too. It's a really beautiful sailing ship, at anchor but looking ready to go, as if only waiting for some wind.

When Kepa says that it's outfitted for six people, Abaitua gets the impression that he's holding back from saying that they could ask Lynn along, and that impression grows as he keeps quiet while Kepa points to his mother and says, "I can bring her along with me. At least she'd be able to make us all *café con leche.*"

Abaitua doesn't want to mention Lynn, although he's not sure why. Something to do with Pilar, but he doesn't want to think it through. He tries not to take their relationship as a given fact, even with Kepa, though it's obvious he's fully aware of it, and when he asks after her all of a sudden, as if he's just thought to wonder how she's been doing, Abaitua blurts out that he hasn't seen her for a while. Kepa asks him to say hi from him.

But the truth is that she'll be waiting for him at home at seven. "At seven o'clock," she'd said, pointing her index finger upward as if to say that he'd be in for it otherwise. When she opens the door for him, she'll be wearing her green dress that goes down from her neck to her knees.

As he puts his phonendoscope and tensiometer back in his briefcase, the old lady gets up to say goodbye to him, and Kepa says it is time for them to have a bath. Abaitua smells piss again when he gives her two goodbye kisses. He'll come back to visit her. She tells him to come whenever he wants to, and her son, a towel over

632

his shoulder as if he were a boxing coach, says he'll have to see himself out and sorry for not going with him to the door. But then he does go with him. At the door, Abaitua has the sensation that he's running away and feels the need to apologize—Loiola's leaving for America, and they're going to say goodbye to him.

Kepa smiles. Tell him we'll visit him when we sail across the Atlantic.

His eyes are very dark and full of sincerity. Abaitua gives way to temptation and puts his hand on his shoulder and squeezes it. If crossing the Atlantic isn't enough for them, they can keep going all the way across the Pacific, he says.

What he doesn't say is that he understands him feeling suffocated in the situation with his mother, it's all right to want to be freed from that weight, but it has to be done in the right way. He'll try to find a place for her at the home. Kepa nods. Abaitua is already on the ground floor when he hears Kepa say what he apparently didn't dare to say to him face-to-face—he's glad he had the guts to stand up to the hospital mafia.

WHEN HE REACHES HOME, he's surprised to see Pilar's car parked in front of the garage with the keys in it, as if she were going to go out again. In the entryway, she herself confirms it. She seems to be in a hurry and carefully asks him, with that imploring look of hers he knows so well, to be nice, which allows him to deduce that Loiola has already arrived. There's been a change of plan. She speaks to him as she goes from one room to another looking for something, and he, in the living room, looks over the mail that's arrived. A letter from the doctors' association. They threaten to suspend him for at least two years and for up to twenty. The news doesn't startle him, and when Pilar stops running around and looks with curiosity at his reaction on opening the letter, he tells her it's nothing, just an invitation to a conference. He doesn't know if she believes him, but she doesn't ask him anything else. As far as the change of plans is concerned, she tells him that Urrutikoetxea called to say he was happy to talk about the assisted reproduction program and that when she told him about Loiola's plans to go to Harvard and that he was flying to Milan out of Loiu tomorrow and from there to New York, he said that he happened to be with a lecturer from that very university and why didn't they come up early so that they could all have dinner together. The lecturer is a very pleasant woman, and it would be useful for Loiola to have her as a contact. Loiola thought it was a good idea. He's going to spend the night in Bilbao, and that way he won't have to get up early the next morning and drive to catch his plane. Pilar doesn't know what she's going to do, it will depend on how much she has to drink at dinner and how tired she is, but she'll probably stay with Loiola. She says all of this quickly and naturally, even happily and with a lively air, to an extent, but without giving any impression that she might like him to go, too, which would have been natural, because it's he who's friends with Urrutikoetxea, and he finds it all quite frustrating, even though he has a date with Lynn at seven o'clock. What's more, he's sure it hasn't crossed Pilar's mind that he might want to go to Bilbao, and still less to have dinner with them, a dinner party at which the matter of what happened at the hospital would definitely come up and at which he would have to explain what his current situation is, and he knows that's why she doesn't suggest it to him. And the truth is, if she did ask him to go with her, he would refuse flat-out, and not just because of Lynn, who he could give any number of excuses to. Just thinking about traveling makes him nervous. Spending the night in a hotel. What would they do with Loiola there, ask for a room each? Impossible. Even the best option—having dinner without any wine and then coming straight back—would mean being together alone for a whole hour. It could be the moment he's been waiting for, the moment to talk about their life, but as always, he'd rather put it off.

"Where are you?" she calls to him, asking him to come to the bedroom, as if they'd never quarreled. He's here, he says again, and he goes to the bedroom and stands by the door. She's put on a gray skirt and a white blouse, which she hasn't done up yet. The skin on her neck is a little loose, and her lips are thinner than they once were, but he thinks she's still beautiful. It's the thought of a moment, like a spark, the image of something that can't be specified, something he finds attractive. He doesn't want to think about it and takes a step backward involuntarily. Pilar stops doing her blouse up and looks at him with sharp eyes, as if wanting to read his mind, and he worries she may actually do it.

While they're in the living room, she takes the towel off her head and shakes her wet hair in a movement that always makes her look young; she talks about the projects she's working on, and he envies her enthusiasm. Organizing the assisted reproduction service; the menopause treatment center; a well-run prostate unit. The future. The prostate unit's all arranged; she needs Urruti to help with the assisted reproduction project; and she herself is the best person to head up the menopause center. She doesn't seem to be joking, and she looks at him seriously as she says, "I really mean it."

She gives him the towel and asks if he wouldn't mind putting it in the dirty laundry basket.

Smelling her perfume. Out of curiosity, he lifts her towel up to his nose. It's essence of violet with a touch of cinnamon, but he's ashamed of himself and throws it into the basket.

Loiola's looking through an old box in the junk room. What's he looking for? He turns around to say hi. He likes looking through old things. A red *Requeté* beret with a lieutenant's star, yellow pompom and all—he puts it on. It even looks good on him. Suddenly he looks like his maternal grandfather, or perhaps the beret just reminds Abaitua of him even though he never saw him wearing it. He says it suits him and then Loiola takes it off. "He was a real fascist, wasn't he?"

Abaitua wouldn't say he was a real fascist. Sometimes his son seems to him like a child who always wants to hear the same story. He's tried to explain it to him hundreds of times. He doesn't think the word *fascist* is right for him—he believed in traditional values, he was religious, and he thought that Spain wasn't ready for democracy. England was, Spain wasn't. There are several medals in his boxes, faded leather folders, discolored hand-written letters tied up with bits of ribbon. They're the old man's relics, which Pilar hasn't dared throw away. He used to have two pistols, but Abaitua knows that he took them to Eibar one day to have them decommissioned. Yes, he thinks he wasn't a bad man. In some areas, Abaitua's father, who was on the other side of the war, was more reactionary. His father was authoritarian, intolerant, and racist by nature, more than Pilar's, but by chance, he'd been on the right side of the war. If his leaders had chosen to join Franco's "crusade," as they called it, he would have blindly obeyed them and fought against anarchy and disorder just as he actually did fight in favor of freedom. He tries to explain it to his son, even at the risk of shattering his perception of his other grandfather, whom he idolizes. It was he, Abaitua, who gave him that perception, proudly telling him of the deeds of the dignified losers at Intxorta, while Pilar, as though ashamed of her own father, listened on in silence. He remembers that shortly after they met, she told him, "My father fought with Franco during the war," almost challenging him, the admission taking a weight off her shoulders, he thinks.

Loiola rubs a medal against his chest to polish it. He says it looks like gold, and it probably is.

"What are you going to do now?" For a moment he feels as if they've swapped roles and now he's the son, about to start his degree in the States, worried about what type of lifestyle his father's going to have. "*Ama* says . . . *Ama* believes . . . *Ama* thinks . . ." He's surprised by him mentioning what his mother says, believes, and thinks all the time. When do they speak? Apparently, she's proud—even though she hasn't told him so— that he stood up to Arrese and Orl. As Loiola says the words, he looks at him, as if wanting to see how he reacts to them. So what are you going to do? He answers that he doesn't know, but he'll probably take advantage of being out of a job to cross the Atlantic in a schooner, so one day he may turn up in Boston on a sailing ship. He tells him about Kepa's plans as if they were his own, and his son listens politely but starts asking him questions as soon as he can. "What are you going to do about the hospital?" He pretends not to understand the question, so he frames it more specifically—Isn't he excited about his mother's plans? He answers that he doesn't know what her plans are. "You know full well."

He has to think about it. In any case, he's going to write to him, and he hopes he'll write back, tell him what he's up to. They're standing facing each other, an arm's length away. He feels that a serious, uncomfortable atmosphere, which he was hoping to avoid, has been created, and he's afraid of being moved by it, but Loiola bursts out laughing when he realizes his grandfather's medal is stuck to his chest. He makes the fascist salute, and Abaitua lifts his hand to knock his arm down. He doesn't know what to do and feels the need to say something clear to him; precisely, he thinks that if he says something to his son right now, it will stay with him for ever, just as he remembers saying goodbye to his father on the platform in Hendaia when he went to Paris for the first time. A memory in black and white. A friend of his father's had driven them both to Hendaia.

636

He got onto the train—which must have had a plaque reading *è pericoloso sporgersi*—and stuck his head out of the window. They, his father and his father's friend, the owner of the car, were on the platform. They didn't know what to say to each other and didn't say anything, just waited together for the train to set off. They heard the guard's whistle, and his father looked at him as if wanting to say something, but it was his friend who said with a firm voice, "And don't forget you're Basque." He'll never forget it.

He goes up to the boy to take the medal off him and says he's prepared a special speech for the occasion, but it's an after-dinner speech, it's solemn, it has to be delivered in a certain atmosphere, and so it's no good for a junk room. So he'll spare Loiola it, given that his son doesn't have much time anyway.

"*Ama* insisted," he apologizes.

The poor kid doesn't have much of a sense of humor.

It's going to be quite a frustrating farewell. Abaitua nods toward the door when they hear Pilar's voice from above telling them that it's getting late, but the boy doesn't move. "There's something I'd like to know," he says seriously. Abaitua sees he's nervous and realizes that he is, too. What does he want to know? He wants to know about when he found his friends with the boxes on the boat and he told him to call the police—had he actually wanted him to call, or had he just wanted to give them a scare? He doesn't hesitate and says that he wanted him to call the police, that it was what had to be done. Why does he ask? He answers that he's always thought he must have misunderstood what he wanted him to do.

Abaitua isn't sure whether his own father embraced him at the Hendaia station. He thinks he didn't, but even so, he'd say he was an affectionate man. He and Loiola do embrace each other, perhaps a little clumsily, although they don't give each other a kiss.

Have a good time, he says to him, enjoy life. What else could he tell him?

Pilar empties her bag onto the table to look for her keys. Loiola reminds her that she left them in the car. Abaitua had forgotten that, too. "This head of mine." Pilar slaps herself on the forehead and holds the boy by the chin. She smiles at him. "What on earth am I going to do without you?" Her smile looks happy. It's the only smile Pilar has—she doesn't know how to fake smiles. She's incapable of using her zygomatic bone to lift her cheeks up and wrinkle her eyes.

When she smiles, it's because some spark has touched her orbicularia oculia, a muscle that can't be moved voluntarily; according to Duchenne, it only serves to express emotions of the soul. It's a miracle that seldom happens, but it always moves Abaitua when it does.

Before leaving, Pilar asks him what he's going to do, as if sorry to be leaving him alone. He'll read for a bit, and then maybe he'll go out for a walk.

Lynn is going to be waiting for him at seven on the dot, wearing her green zipped dress that goes down to her knees, and nothing beneath it.

HE STOPS AT THE BOTTOM OF THE SLOPE, across from the train stop, because at that moment, Martin's opening the iron gate, and he waits for him to walk across the garden. He can go back or hide behind a sycamore tree a couple of yards to his left, but he doesn't, out of dignity, and also because anybody looking out from the house would be able to see his movements. Because he's the only person on the slope, it's probable, not to say inevitable, that the writer will realize he's there if he turns around to close the gate. Which is what happens. He opens the gate, turns around to close it, and when he recognizes him—Abaitua thinks he's recognized him, even though he doesn't give any sign of it—he doesn't close the gate but stays standing there looking at him, undoubtedly waiting for him to come across the thirty or forty feet between them. It had to happen some time, and now that it has, he doesn't much care. Even so, he decides that he's going to greet him when he reaches the gate, say whatever comes to mind, and then carry on along the old path up to the clinic, as if he hadn't come to see Lynn. It's ridiculous, since the writer and homeowner must already be very well aware of their relationship, but he's not worried about that. He doesn't want to explicitly recognize it, sanction it, so to speak, by walking across the garden with that man who, what's more, he likes less and less, among other things because he gets the feeling he keeps tabs on everything that happens in the house. By now, there's no doubt that he's waiting for him there, and out of politeness, he feels obliged to quicken his step, even though he stops a couple of yards away from the gate to make it clear that he has no intention of going in, less so now that he's remembered their last conversation in Gros, when the

638

Dominican woman offered herself as a nurse to look after his father. He's thought hundreds of time about calling her to beg her never to use his name when looking for work, but he hasn't done it.

He calms down a little when Martin, after dryly saying hello, talks to him about the weather. The summer's over. Yes, the temperatures have really dropped. The writer tells him he thinks autumn weather's perfect, because it gives him a feeling of melancholy and that, he says, is a sweet sensation. Abaitua, too, likes the woods in autumn. He takes advantage of the comment to say he's going for a walk, nodding toward the path up the hill, and the writer looks in that direction with great attention, as if he were looking for something specific. Then, unexpectedly, he mentions the old sailboat. "It's still there." They can't see it from where they are, only a little bit of the river's visible from here. He agrees it's still there, but avoids taking any responsibility for it. He doesn't know what they're going to do with it. His wife's family's things. That's what he means, he doesn't know what *they* are going to do with it. The writer looks at him with his lively blue eyes. He wants to make clear that it doesn't bother him. The thing is, there's a group of boys that go there, and they've started messing around on it again. It would be a good idea to take care of it. Abaitua promises "he'll make sure they know about it," without saying who will, and almost says he'll go take a look himself, it's just as easy for him to go one way or the other, but just then, the writer suddenly lifts one hand up to his forehead as if he's remembered something important, in the same way Pilar just has, and tells him he has to thank him for helping him find a nurse for his father. Apparently she's very sweet and affectionate. He says it without a smile. Although his report is positive, it doesn't reassure Abaitua, who's about to clear the matter up when Martin starts talking about the problem of old people in society today. Abaitua just stands there watching him bring his lips together, open them again, and stretch them all around as he trots out one cliché after another about ageing demographics, and all the time, he thinks, Lynn's there waiting for him as she promised in her green dress and without any panties on. Literally without any panties, and instead of finding it funny, it makes him worry. It's the second time he's had a specific date with Lynn. The first was when they met at Portaleta, and this is the second, at the house. At seven o'clock, she'd said to him, and he can still see her finger pointing upward, half nurse, half undine, and he can see on the writer's watch—which he keeps catching glimpses of as he lifts his hands up to his forehead in that typical gesture of his—that it's half past seven now. Ever since leaving home with plenty of time to arrive punctually, he just keeps bumping into people. So Lynn must already be bored of waiting for him, there in her zipped dress that goes down from her neck to her knees, because that's how she said she would come out to meet him, at seven on the dot, with nothing on underneath, and he'd have to open the dress very slowly when he arrived. That was her fantasy, the one he had to make come true because she guessed right about what the next train to go by was going to be when they were walking back from the Peruvian woman's birthing, and gambling debts are sacred.

What the writer is worried about is the fact that his family responsibilities are stopping him from working, from concentrating. And when it comes down to it, he's got plenty of resources. What must it be like for other people? He brushes his hair back from time to time. It gives Abaitua the chance to see on his watch that time's moving on.

He doesn't dare lift his glance to check, but he thinks he's just seen Lynn in the top window and that she's even signaling at him. He feels trapped by this man rattling off commonplaces about the unavoidable final destiny of humanity, feels like an idiot, unable to arrive for his date, and now even his date itself seems idiotic to him. Waiting for him without any panties on, which excited him as soon as he woke up in the morning and remembered about it, now seems just like complete nonsense to him, something out of one of those French novels where the girls ask the men to guess what color panties they're wearing and declare they want to see their willies— "*Devine de quelle couleur est ma culotte*" and "*je veux voir ton zizi*" and such like. He feels himself blushing, and the writer realizes.

Even so, in the end, the writer asks him if he doesn't want to come in, but he nods vaguely toward the clinic and says he'll finish his walk. A stupid way out, in any case. Now he'll have to wait a good while, in case the writer sees him on his way back, so that he can say he really has been out getting some healthy exercise.

When he reaches the reeds, he asks himself why he felt he had to keep up appearances. Why didn't he admit he was going to see Lynn? Why does he have to pretend? He can see a good part of the house from where he is, there's nobody at the windows, or in the clinic parking lot, either, which he sees surrounded by a metal fence, and right now it looks like a prison yard. He's tired of waiting. He really doesn't care if Martin or Julia realize what ridiculous manoeuvres he's been on, and he goes back in the direction of Lynn.

SHE MEETS HIM AT THE DOOR wearing her moss-green dress with its zipper at the front running from top to bottom. She pretends to be angry, frowns, puts her hands on her hips. What's he been up to, she demands to know. She's been here for two hours, with no panties on, and in danger of catching cystitis, and what's more, more people have knocked on her door than in the entire rest of the time she's lived there. The postman's come, the water meter reader, the gas canister delivery man's been twice, and she opened the door to all of them, in the best of moods, thinking it was going to be him, and she's sure they all realized she was waiting for somebody and not wearing any panties, and all for what, when he finally does arrive, he starts petting the cat and not paying her any attention. She's clearly trying to be comical, and she manages it, but Abaitua, who has the cat at his feet begging to be petted and who can't bring himself to deny its request, finds it a caustic type of comedy, and he feels ridiculous.

The dress gets stuck, he has trouble opening the zipper, and then he embraces her naked body. Lynn laughs and says it's too late now.

He doesn't want tea, coffee, beer, or wine, but says yes when she suggests putting some music on. She has traditional tastes in that area, although perhaps she's choosing music she thinks he'll like. She seldom puts Bob Dylan on, even though he's her favorite singer. Abaitua knows because she's told him, and he was inconsiderate enough to say that he didn't like him. He doesn't understand what the man's saying with that nasal voice of his.

Fly Me to the Moon is playing. He likes it—*and let me play among the stars*. She often plays it; she has a compilation of twenty different singers doing it. Tony Bennett, Anita O'Day, Astrud Gilberto, Blossom Dearie, Diana Krall, Dinah Washington . . . The same song again and again, endlessly.

From the sofa, he can't distinguish the names or the authors of the books on the shelves, but he knows what they are. *City of Glass*'s view of New York at night. *Wise Children*'s crossed legs. *Flaubert's Parrot*'s colorful parrot next to a black-and-white old woman. *To the Lighthouse*'s lighthouse and umbrella. He can't see anything on the cover of *Montauk*, because the light coming in through the sash window is reflecting on its protective cellophane cover, but he could draw the beach and the two deck chairs, the lighthouse in the background. He likes that cover. It brings him memories of a beach in Cadiz you can see the Trafalgar lighthouse from, wild and abandoned. There, too, the sand goes all the way up to the grass, and Pilar and he used to go to that boundary where the two meet, because she liked the sand—above all because she hated the bugs in the grass—and he, on the other hand, prefered the grass. He now has the impression that they were happy back in those days. They've often made plans to go back there.

Let me see what spring is like on Jupiter and Mars. It's Frank Sinatra singing now.

Lynn tells Max not to be so tiresome when he gets on the sofa and begs to be petted—"*Don't be such a bore.*"

But they've never gone back. They also made plans to go to Milan to see one of Modigliani's paintings, part of a private collection, because the woman in it looks a lot like Pilar. From time to time, he's said that he has to find out where it's on view exactly so that they can go and see it, but he hasn't. Out of negligence, and also because he knows that deep down, Pilar doesn't like things like that very much. She grew to accept that the woman in the painting looked like her, even that she looked like her a lot, but she's suspicious of him being so enthusiastic about it. In fact, she's always been suspicious of his sounding enthusiastic, and of his expressions of emotions, they seem delirious to her, and she's reluctant to go up, probably afraid that it will mean having to come down afterward. He thinks that's why she reacts as she does. Perhaps the most Pilar wants, with him, is to share a peaceful daily life.

He cannot imagine Pilar suddenly saying one day, "Listen: I love you."

Lynn gets up from the sofa, runs to the stereo on tiptoes, and remorselessly takes Peggy Lee off; "*please be true*" are the last words she sings. Music gets in the way, spoils her concentration; he thinks she said that to him on some occasion, and in any case, it's obvious. When she comes back, she slips between his back and the sofa. Now she's behind him, and she puts her legs around him to embrace him. He lets his body slide downward until his head is on her belly, and she leans over her and strokes him with her hair. There's a clear expression of pain on her face, and she complains, "It isn't coming out now," as she squeezes her nipples. He takes ahold of her hand—she doesn't have to do that. How many times has he told her?

Sometimes she tells him exactly what she wants, demands it, with a determination that seems rough in a girl, and on those occasions, the sex is short. He could look at her without any inhibition whatsoever, because she doesn't seem to be seeing anything. Her eyes are literally white, her body curved and shaken by spasms, suddenly possessed by an explosion of disorder, and he's in awe, as he would be if witnessing a storm at sea that you can only gaze upon in amazement, and he wants to hold her body, which is receiving all that pleasure, to embrace it, to be able to feel that need to explode that's moving, without being aware of his presence, toward some seashore where, on emptying its strength, it searches for him like a spent wave, calling his name, still sobbing.

In *Montauk*, Max Frisch writes about all women being similar in "the moment of greatest pleasure," but he doesn't agree with that.

"What is it that you do to me?" "You drive me crazy." "I can't take all this pleasure." She says these things that always make him feel uneasy, and to get her to be quiet, he says she can't fool him—three out of four women fake their orgasms. Usually with the best of intentions, to increase their pleasure and their partners' pleasure, but it's a put-on. She presses her shoulder to his chest and leans on him. Why doesn't he believe her? Why doesn't he want to believe her? And she moves off him again.

He doesn't answer her.

And in any case, being a gynecologist, you would have thought he'd be an expert.

What are you thinking about? He's hardly done anything all day, and even so, as is usual in him recently, he has the sensation that things are happening to him all the time. He feels sorry when he thinks about how he's just said goodbye to his son, who he probably won't see for another year. He'd thought for some time about what he should say to him when the moment arrived, but he knows it's too late to pass anything onto him.

The northeast wind blows up. The sound of thunder out to sea, the wind moaning through the closed windows, the panels in the sash windows trembling.

She asks him, for the second time, how he would define an orgasm; he says he didn't hear her the first time. It's true, he didn't. "An orgasm consists of involuntary contractions of the perineal muscles, the vaginal, womb, and Fallopian tube muscles, and the anal sphincter." Lynn sits up again and hits his chest with her elbow, saying its "*horrible*," but that doesn't stop teacher Abaitua from reciting his knowledge at top speed: "The erectile vascular tissue under the clitoris is activated by parasympathetic impulses." Until she puts her hand over his mouth.

He protests—it was her question.

ABAITUA GETS UP, using both hands to try to put the window in place. Outside, everything is gray, apart from the train stop's white wall. He sees himself about to leave for Paris once more, his head sticking out of the train window and his father's friend calling out "and don't forget you're Basque." A piece of advice that couldn't be made any shorter, tied to an implicit body of thought by the conjunction at the beginning. That order was as heavy a weight on his conscience as apodictic commands such as "thou shalt not kill." A good Basque, the friend had meant to say—hard working, noble, keeping his word, honest to himself and to the group, which is always more than the individual. And not to forget what we inevitably are. A weight of identity from which he has never felt completely free, which he couldn't free himself of without feeling guilty. He doesn't find it easy to talk about it. He did discuss it once, with a friend he bumped into in the washroom while they were both at a dinner party in a restaurant. So it was a toiletside conversation, like the ones where homosexuals used to reveal their sexual identities. Abaitua sounded his friend out while they were cleaning their hands, asking whether he was bored of being Basque. There had recently been a terrorist attack. They talked until another customer came in. His friend told him it had been more of a wrench for him to stop being a nationalist than it had been to leave the Church and, later on, to get divorced from his wife. Like many others from his generation, this friend had once been a priest.

Abaitua never studied at the seminary, but he hasn't spent his whole life boasting about that fact like some other people do, as if they'd been close friends of Voltaire's. When it came down to it, in many cases the real reason for not answering the call was a weakness of the flesh—that or they were just too foolish or lazy to be recruited. The same was true of people who spoke out against the armed struggle. Many people had never held a pistol in their hand not because they were convinced anti-violence militants or because they had moral objections, they just didn't have the audacity to put their lives at risk.

He's always found the wind disturbing. He isn't comfortable there at one end of the sofa with Lynn resting her head on his shoulder. She's falling asleep, she slowly opens and closes her eyes from time to time, and although he's tempted to stop her from falling faster asleep, in order to avoid being left alone with his thoughts, he keeps still and feels her cold, damp skin. He stretches his arm backward and picks up his jacket from a chair there to cover her with. She thanks him without opening her eyes and curls up against him. Shortly afterward, the cadence of her breath tells him that she's left him for sleep.

Pilar said "I fell asleep" the day she came back home in the morning and sat on the edge of the bed. She couldn't have said anything more hurtful. Since then, every time he remembers that sentence, he realizes that his pain and frustration and anger were more because she'd fallen asleep with another man than because of the fact that she'd copulated with him; she'd been able to let go of herself, confident and relaxed, and with him out of her mind.

Lynn stretches her lips to smile when she realizes he's looking at her. "I hope I don't snore," she says, sitting up, and Abaitua teases her and says that she does, making a gesture of resignation that he doesn't know to what extent he's exaggerating. "You're losing your ideal image," she says with regret. He didn't use to hear her snore, and soon he'll think she's ugly. A new gesture of regret, after which she covers her face with both hands, and Abaitua takes her by the wrists to move them away. He tells her to stop fooling around—"*No hagas el ganso.*" She doesn't understand what he means, and he finds telling her tedious, above all because he doesn't want to use the words *bird* or *clown* in his explanation. She puts his jacket on while waiting for him to explain it to her. Then she gets up and tiptoes to the stereo to turn it on.

She asks him again if he wants anything—tea, coffee, beer—and he says no once more.

Sarah McLachlan's *Angel* is what they're listening to now. "*Fly away from here.*" He likes being able to understand the words and finds it strange they're about flying. He thinks about making a joke—first *fly me*, and now *fly away*—but it's not appropriate. When she asks what he's laughing about, he says he's listening to the song and he likes it a lot.

The sky's still clouded over, but now the shafts of light breaking through are very clear, and they brighten up the room. Matisse's engraving, a mirror, in which he can see Max, and the shine on the books at the front of the shelves, which varies depending on their positions and the material they're made of.

"IN THE ARMS OF AN ANGEL / FLY AWAY FROM HERE / FROM THIS DARK COLD HOTEL ROOM."

The photo of the two of them in front of the *Gloria Victis* statue is too far away to be able to see what position its wings are in. He remembers the composition—a soldier holding a sword in his left hand and his right hand open and reaching up to the sky, the angel holding onto him by his thighs—but he couldn't say what position the wings are in. He doesn't know if they're completely open. The stupid need to clear that point up takes ahold of him, and he tries to get up to grab the photo, but she doesn't let him. What does he want? He owns up to it—he can't remember the position of the angel's wings in the photo of the statue in Bordeaux, open or closed. Does he really not know? Abaitua is amazed by the expression of sorrow in her voice and on her face when she asks him. What position does he think they're in, she asks, holding his face in both hands so that he's looking at her and not at the photo. It's no game. Her voice makes it clear that the situation's nothing like when she challenged him to guess what type of train the next one to go by would be. She lifts her chin up to ask him to answer, but he doesn't dare. He doesn't understand why the answer should be so important, but he knows it is, and afraid of not getting the answer right, he keeps quiet.

"OH MY GOD."

She covers her face with her hands again and murmurs "*oh my God,*" twice. Then she looks at him in silence, with the same expression of sorrow and disbelief. What position does he think they're in? She holds his hands when he tries to get up once more and smiles to encourage him to answer. He can't remember.

He's impatient now as he shakes her hands, which are holding him down. She tells him to imagine the position the wings are in if he can't remember. *"How do you imagine them?"* He realizes that the answer is important to her for some reason and wants to avoid the question, but she doesn't give up—*"Tell me, how do you imagine them?"* He dares to say that he thinks the angel's effort to hold the fallen soldier in its arms is more apparent than the strength of its wings. And in any case, he's sure it isn't flying, it's walking, and so its wings must be facing downward, or almost. Not completely open, in any case.

"OH MY GOD."

He sits up and looks at her face to check that she's not joking. She isn't. Her eyes are wet. What's wrong with her? She mumbles that she doesn't know, it's just a feeling—*"una corazonada."* She lets go of his hands. Or *"una descorazonada, más bien"*—or more like a letdown feeling. The effort of saying the words makes her seem more pathetic. She lies back and seems to tell him, with a wave of one hand, to get up and grab the photo to see just how wrong he is.

There's no question that the angel's wings are open. And pointing upward, too, the right one parallel with the ground and the left one almost vertical, but he thinks he could defend the idea that, in general, the weight of the vanquished soldier is more apparent than the angel's ability to fly. But he doesn't do that, fearing it would be throwing salt on Lynn's wound, disappointed as she is at his having imagined the angel's wings facing downward. He could get angry about her becoming sad as a result of such a banal thing, a very womanly thing to do, it's true, making a mountain out of a molehill, the tendency to seize on words, silences, gestures, forgotten birthdays, and similar mistakes and interpret them negatively. But he can't do that, either. He's aware that however absurd her method of arriving at it may be, she's reached a diagnosis: he's a lost case.

"LET ME BE EMPTY / AND WEIGHTLESS AND MAYBE / I'LL FIND SOME PEACE TONIGHT."

"YOU KNOW?" she asks with a sad smile. He keeps quiet and, already standing up, puts his pants on. "You know?" she asks again. She takes his jacket off and wraps herself in her striped shawl. Finally, he asks her what it is he should know, sounding tired. She stretches her lips out again, as if they were stinging her.

"Oh, nada," she replies—nothing.

They stay sitting on the sofa for a while, leaning against each other, she plays with the tassels on her shawl, and he, wearing only his pants, pets the cat, which is purring on the floor, with his bare feet.

She asks once more if he knows, but this time she doesn't wait for an answer and goes on to say that the first time she saw him, at the hospital, he seemed lonely and resigned. That caught her attention, and she let herself wonder about it. Why was a man who seemed so attractive, bright, agreeable, and gentle lonely? Why was he resigned, if he gave off such intelligence and energy? He was playing at being a skeptical old man. She was incredibly glad when he called her to go on that trip with Kepa. Perhaps there's no such thing as eternal happiness, she says she thought to herself, but it was a great chance to spend a weekend in the French Basque Country. But destiny took them to Bordeaux, and he took them to look for this one plaza because there was a marvelous statue there that they just had to see. She was suprised by how pleased he was when they found it, but she thought she understood it once they were standing in front of the angel holding the vanquished soldier with the broken sword in his hand. She lifts her head up as if to make sure that he's listening. It was like a premonition for her. Does he understand?

Abaitua doesn't believe in premonitions.

"I made you fly. A little bit," she says, smiling, holding her index finger and thumb slightly apart to show him, but it's clear she's fighting back the urge to cry. He wonders what he'll do if she starts crying, while instinctively putting his feet into his shoes, something she could easily interpret as his wanting to get away. He stays sitting there, fighting against that very urge, and keeps petting the cat lying at his feet, to avoid her eyes. He can't stand the silence but fears even more the words that might break it; an old feeling of anguish takes ahold of him, takes him back in time to when, as a child, his mother used to tell him to explain himself, upset because he'd disappointed her in some way, in some clumsy way, and she'd say, "Haven't you got anything to say for yourself?" He used to hate that, with a child's selfish hate, and he's still fighting against it.

What could he say?

If only he could love her. Abaitua remembers that other passage in *Montauk* when the old writer says that he doesn't love Lynn and that he's glad he doesn't. This isn't the same situation. He thinks he'd like to love her the way she doubtless loves him. Because he has no doubt about that. She's happy when he is and sad when she sees him worried. That interest in what he says or does, as if it were the most important thing in the world, is what he's seen in her. He believes her when she says she loves him. He also believes her when she says she's crazy about him. Now he knows that love does exist, at least Lynn's love, and he can't help wondering if anybody has ever loved him like that, and whether he's ever loved somebody like that. Whether he's able to love like that. It's true that he wishes he could allow himself to be carried away by her, that he's sometimes felt that her love might be able to make him fly and get him out of his dark, cold room.

He's relieved and feels that his punishment has been lifted when, suddenly, as if coming out of a heavy, long silence, and in a completely natural way, perhaps just a little upset, she tells him that her friend Maureen will be back soon. *"One of these days."* Abaitua had forgotten all about her. But her eyes question him again as she says that she'll have to take her in and the two of them will have to find somewhere else to get together, at least for a while. So it's only a momentary respite, because he doesn't know how to respond to this, either.

Leaning against the wall, Lynn watches as he does up his shoelaces —he tightens them so that not even a millimetre of the tongue is visible and tucks the ends of the laces in, as his father taught him.

"Is somebody waiting for you?"

He shakes his head.

"You're never going to stay over, are you?"

Her back is right against the wall, but her feet are quite a way from it, as if she were going to slide down and sit on the floor. It's something she sometimes does. Her arms are hanging down, still. Abaitua's tempted to answer her direct question with a no, and when she asks him again whether he's never going to stay, he finds he has no problem admitting it.

She asks if he would rather they not see each other again.

Even though he feels the urge to address the matter directly, now that he has the lancet in his hand, the look of sorrow on her face holds him back. She guesses this and whispers that there's no need for him to worry, she isn't going to cry, and to buy himself some time, he says, *"No se trata de eso"*—it's not that. A precarious exit, he knows she's going to ask him what he means by that, and he's ready to explain that he'd rather stop seeing her for a while but not forever; he needs some time to split up with Pilar, live alone for a while, and then decide what to do with his life without being conditioned in any way.

"*Tell me.*"

She asks him to tell her if he'd rather they not see each other any more. Her voice breaks and gets sharper, but there's still a reproach in it: "Tell me: you don't want us to see each other?"

He says, in English, and facing up to the challenge, that that would be best. Without beating around the bush. He doesn't add that it'll just be for a time, doesn't take refuge in the excuse that he needs some time to think. She looks at him. Her trembling lips are dry, there are drops of sweat on her forehead, dark areas around her eyes, her face is pale. Some strands of hair have gotten stuck in the side of her mouth, and she tries, unsuccessfully, to brush them aside with her fingertips. She looks at him with sadness, and he holds her gaze, resists the urge to stretch out a hand and try to free her hair, and decides to be firm, unwavering, like when he has to deliver a negative diagnosis, suppressing his feelings of pity, not giving any impression of a hope that's unjustified by reality. Indecisiveness can cause more pain than ruthlessness.

"*That would be best,*" he repeats, turning toward the window, through which the branches of the trees can be seen blowing around in the wind. Then she looks at him again and raises a hand to her forehead, as if trying to shield her face from the light and be able to examine his face better. At least tell her, she says, that it's not because he's old and doesn't want to force a life with no future on her or something stupid like that. He says no. He remembers that the old novelist in *Montauk* mentions a life with no future. He says no, and she, after looking at him for a few seconds to check that he's telling the truth, turns toward the window and says, "Because that would be stupid." She tries to take the strands of hair from her mouth once more and doesn't quite manage it, and he has to stop himself again from holding his hand out to help her.

He hears the fridge motor starting up.

"Well that's a drag, because I'm crazy about you."

"I know you're the love of my life and that I could be happy with you."

She keeps looking out the window. She's sitting sideways, her legs folded under her, her arms folded over the back of the sofa, her forehead almost touching the glass of the windowpane. He's sat back down too, but looking the other way, his forearms resting on his thighs and his hands together. He has to turn around if he wants to see her. Her neck, the start of her curls, her very small white ear, her eyes reflected in the window. He doesn't know if she sees him.

"I thought I could make you happy."

"So there's no hope for me, then."

He remembers himself counting the time between the flashes of light from a lighthouse.

"*Esan, zuk ni ez nauzu ezer maite?*" she asks—don't you love me at all?

He finds the question harder in Basque. He doesn't know what to answer. It would be hurtful of him to say no, and there's no point in him saying that that's not the issue, but that's what he says. That isn't the issue.

And then: "In any case, what is love . . . ?"

"Oh, I guess when you love someone, you know it, just as when you hate someone."

She turns back from the window, frowning, and he looks away from her.

"But you must love me some, because I've seen that you've been happy with me. Isn't that true?"

He says it is.

"We've had fun. We've laughed." She touches his shoulder for him to pay attention. "*¿Verdad que sí?*" she asks—isn't that right?

He says it is, with a tired voice, and she goes back to her previous position, almost kneeling, her arms crossed on the back of the sofa, her forehead against the window. He stays still, his head down, looking at his open hands, their fingertips touching each other.

The photo of the two of them in front of the statue of the angel in the Place Jean Moulin in Bordeaux is still on the triangular table. Abaitua thinks he looks old and pathetic in it, one hand on the shoulder of the smiling girl next to him, the same girl who's sitting by his side right now and making statements every few seconds, who turns toward him from time to time as if to make sure that he's still there.

"I won't be offended if you don't love me."

"You love her, don't you?"

He can't help thinking that his mind, which he needs in order to think straight, is zipping around like a trapped hornet banging its head into windows again and again. He thinks of Kepa's mother making bread crumbs for her robins. His father and his friend—the latter a much bigger man—at the Hendaia station, the same place where Franco and Hitler met, saying goodbye to him. Pilar smiling at Loiola as she says to him "what would I do without you?"

He thinks he deserves his punishment.

"What do you still see in her? Tell me. What do you see in her?"

When he doesn't answer her questions, she says, "*Oh my God*," the clearest sign of her frustration or lack of hope. Abaitua finds this moaning more distressing that her tone of anguish as she continues her questions: "Tell me. Do you understand me? Come on, I know you're not enjoying this, but it's so important for me, and you talk so little. I have to know. Don't you realize that?" She speaks forcefully but without any trace of anger. "Because you're the man of my life. Do you understand that?" She moves her face toward him, as if she doubted his ability to understand, as if she were with a little child. "Do you understand that I need to know? Do you still love her?"

"TELL ME."

And once more: "*Oh my God*."

Her eyes are shining, and the red on her cheeks looks like a temperature, he'd say. The dryness of her lips is even more apparent now. The sweat on her neck is shiny, too; a couple of drops have slipped down to her freckle-covered collarbone and toward her neckline. She adjusts her shawl and moves her face toward him, as if she wanted to whisper in his ear. "You looked so alone when I saw you, that's why I got close to you. I thought you wanted my affection, and I liked you so much. I'm never going to want anybody as much as I want you. I don't think anybody's ever going to love you like I do." Covering her face with her hands: "It's really bad luck to have gotten to spend just enough time with you to know that this great thing that I feel actually exists, and then to have it all go away."

NADA, NOTHING, DEUS EZ.

He stands up, and she holds onto his wrist for him not to leave. She does so softly and tries to smile. "Please don't leave like this," and a moment later she repeats it in Basque. "*Ez joan horrela, mesedez.*" He stays still, leaning down a little, because she's holding onto his wrist. She shakes his arm as if to ask him to pay attention. She doesn't mind if he goes on loving his wife. She doesn't mind sharing him, being his lover, she'll find a small apartment when Maureen arrives and they can meet up three times a week, or twice, whenever he wants. She'd be happy like that. Please think about it. He loosens his arm and tells her not to say stupid things, but she doesn't listen him.

"How very annoying it must be to have somebody love you and not be able to love them back."

Now he's the one who lifts his hand to touch her forehead, but she moves away resolutely, though not brusquely. Then she makes that gesture of hers, wrinkling her eyes and stretching her lips. She's all right, he doesn't have to worry about her. *"Don't worry, I'm not going to commit suicide."* She smiles.

They say goodbye like any other day. She opens the door and lets him past, then sticks her head out from behind the door and offers her cheek for him to kiss. Which he does, lightly. He's already gone down a few steps on the spiral staircase when he hears her say that she's going away for a while. He stops still. After thinking for a moment about whether to ask her where, he decides not to. He says he'll probably go away, too.

When he turns around to close the iron gate after crossing the garden—Lynn's living room, a soft amber color, is the only room with lights on in the house—he promises himself that he won't go into that house again unless he's a free man, with no ties, after sorting out his situation with Pilar. He's ashamed to be so mixed up, it doesn't seem appropriate for a man of his age. He doesn't feel like going home, either. He'd like to be sitting in a park in some other country, at the side of a lake, throwing bread to the ducks. The lights at the train stop aren't on, but there's a very intense bluish light in the gloaming. He takes a deep breath to relieve the pressure in his chest and takes a few steps. He crosses the rails and decides to sit on a bench at the train stop for a moment. There's nobody waiting; there are very few local trains at that time. He feels a long way from everything and surprisingly calm. What is he doing here? He wonders what his answer would be if he were to bump into an acquaintance and they asked him that. What comes to mind: He misses lakes with ducks and swans on them, and he's seldom sat on a bench in his own city.

He feels mixed up. He remembers Pilar's smile once more as she said "what would I do without you?"—something she's never said to him. By now she will have decided whether to stay over in Bilbao or not. What would he answer her if she were to call and tell him she needed to know whether or not he loves her? Not whether he feels affection for her, liking, or whether he's attached to her—whether he really loves her. Loves her according to Lynn's parameters. He hears the sound of a train to his left, from the direction of Txominenea, but a long way off and coming at great speed. Too fast to be a local train. That shaking sound of the whistle—he doesn't know what makes it do that—and shortly afterward, the sound of another train, coming the other way but already very close. They pass each other right in front of him. The light from their windows lasts awhile, he sees them as if they were blinking eyes. When they disappear, he tries to tell which train's noise lasts longer, but he can't make it out.

21

IT'S A FINE MORNING with a clear sky, the horizon slightly shaded in pink, no trace of wind, which doesn't encourage Julia much to start on her corrections. But the author is standing there in his ugly bathrobe, looking out of the window and not saying anything. "There she is," he says. He's talking about Maureen, Lynn's friend, who's just walked by dragging her wheeled suitcase. She thinks it's Lynn's case, and it's come in and out of the house two or three times since Maureen arrived. This times she's heading out, and her way of walking reminds her of a blackbird—forward and backward. She's had to lift the case up for a long stretch of the path, apparently because the gravel keeps stopping the wheels from turning, but that doesn't seem to tire her, she lifts it a foot and a half off the ground; maybe she's strong and there isn't much in the case. That's what Martin's deduced, and even so, because she seems to be equally at ease in both directions, leaving the house and coming toward it, he can't tell whether she's taking things out or bringing them in, and being highly interested in the question, the owner of the house doesn't take his eyes off her. But what he's really interested in is where Lynn is, because they haven't heard anything from her in the last six days. Julia, too, is very surprised at her having spent so long away without saying anything, but she doesn't take it the same way Martin does, she doesn't think it's rude of her. She's worried at her being away for so long and can't help imagining situations of greater and lesser misfortune, and that's why she doesn't find it funny when Martin says there's no doubt the fat woman's killed her and is carrying her body out in bits inside the wheeled suitcase. Martin no longer mentions her by name. He talks about "the woman upstairs," or "the American girl," or "the delivery doctor's friend." It's true that she didn't tell them much when she said she was going away for a couple of days, and he says maybe she's gone on another trip with friends. Julia, too, thinks it the most credible hypothesis, even though Lynn didn't look in the mood for that type of thing the last time she saw her, and in any case, that wouldn't explain her not telling them where she was after those first couple of days had gone by, and still less her not picking up the phone.

Martin calls Maureen "the fat one" for obvious reasons, and also "the side table," because she wears a long gathered skirt and a belt around her waist that make her look like she's got on a long, circular tablecloth. Julia is convinced that on both the occasions she went up to the penthouse—worried about not having any news from Lynn and overcoming her fear to be taken for a nosy *Spanish snooper*—she didn't open the door to her even though she was in there, and that she didn't make any effort to hide the fact, either; on the contrary, the second time, she clearly heard her closing a window while she waited to see if she would open the door. The following day, when Julia went out to meet her on the garden path and very politely asked her if she knew anything about Lynn, her answer was vague, even mysterious, perhaps taking advantage of the fact that she wasn't very good at Spanish. She hoped to see her *"con prontitud"* she said—which is more like saying "quite promptly" than saying "soon"—thanked her for her concern, and said she'd let her know as soon as possible.

THE WRITER, IN HIS INCREDIBLY UGLY BATHROBE, is still looking out at the garden. There's very little hair left on his head, which isn't the same for the man in front of the mirror, or if it is, the man doesn't seem to realize, as evidenced by the fact that he comforts himself, in his many reflections about his baldness, by saying that at least for the time being, it's limited to his hairline. The type of baldness he thinks most terrible is when it's a round emptiness that starts at the temples and draws a clear line all the way around the head, which looks even worse when the remaining hair is thick—something he calls bank clerk baldness or notary baldness—and he's much less worried about the other type of baldness, the one that widens the forehead but doesn't affect the back of the head.

He turns toward her with a look of fear on his face—a real look of fear, his eyes wide open, his eyebrows forming a circumflex—and Julia thinks he's read her thoughts, but it's the phone ringing. He makes wild movements with both hands for her not to pick up. They both know it's his publisher. The persecuted writer doesn't dare ask her to answer and say that he's sick, or even about to die; she's long since told him that she's not willing to lie for him anymore. As well as being disagreeable and difficult for her, it was obvious that he wasn't gaining anything by telling lies to put off the moment of having to face the truth. He, on the other hand, accuses her of having an indecent relationship with the truth, of being incapable of betraying her prejudices for him, of not being with him unconditionally, of not protecting him, of not being loyal to him.

The phone keeps on ringing mercilessly, endlessly, and all of a sudden, it brusquely stops halfway through a tone—*click*. The cease-fire's brief, and it starts ringing again; the publisher knows only too well that he's at home. Twice, three times. There's no more irritating sound than a phone you mustn't pick up. Why doesn't he answer and just tell him that there isn't any novel, and no novella, either, that he can't write, or doesn't want to, and that he's going away to Sicily?

Silence at last. The persecuted writer slumps down in a chair and pulls his bathrobe tight. But Julia wonders whether she's going to have to put up with him all day like this, in this state of negligence and desolation he deliberately subjects her to, knowing it's the harshest punishment he can give her. She can't stand his exaggerations, his overacting, his overblown statements about how he feels, and she can't help thinking that if Marie Lafôret were to call him and ask him out for a coffee, he'd run up the stairs like a teenager and get ready to go out. She almost says, "Why don't you call Lafôret and go out for a bit?" But she controls the urge and, in the most affectionate way possible, just says the second part, says he should go out for a while, it's a beautiful day. He looks at her with a combination of amazement and anger. How could he go out? He's the very picture of anguish, his elbows on his knees and his hands cradling his forehead. "Go out for a bit," he mumbles. Once, twice, three times.

She allows a long abandoned feeling of boredom and revulsion to take over, even though she knows it does her no good, but she enjoys giving herself up to it. She looks at the thin hair around his bald patch—standing on end in a mess—which he vainly tries to comb into shape by rubbing at it with his bitten-away nails. Why does he make everything so painful? His ankles are swollen, too. She stares at the skin on his calves, which is white, almost transparent, and there, too, he only has a little bit of long hair, and at his weedy, hairless thighs, the area between which, fortunately, is covered up by the lower part of his foul bathrobe. After finishing her inspection of him, she unintentionally uses the same tone his mother does when she asks, "So why don't you write some then?"

He stares at her with his blue eyes wide open, his hair looking practically electrified now, as if somebody's just given him a slap, but Julia hasn't had enough, and like a boxer wanting to finish off her opponent, she says, "So tell me, why can't you just finish that fucking novel of yours once and for all?"

He gets up and draws his bathrobe around him, his dignity wounded to the core. It looks as if he's going to say something, but he doesn't. He's too angry. Julia feels relieved for a moment, but she knows that she'll soon feel guilty for having let herself go. A moment of silence. "I'll finish the fucking novel sooner than you think," he says finally. He unplugs his laptop and holds it to his chest. His wounded dignity. He's obviously going to lock himself into the formal library, which is what he's been doing recently every time he gets angry. "I'll finish the fucking novel sooner than you think," he says once more, as if it were a threat, in a low voice, then he says it once again and slams the door behind him. Julia is left wanting to clarify that she didn't mean to say "that fucking novel," she was trying to say "just fucking finish it," but it's too late now.

NORMALLY, WHEN THE INSIDE STAIRCASE CREAKS SO MUCH, Lynn opens the door before she reaches the landing. As long as the music isn't very loud, at any rate—she says she likes to listen to Dylan's "Like A Rolling Stone" at full volume—and then she always knocks on the door. She doesn't think she's ever rung the bell; it's unpleasant sounding, and she doesn't think it's right when you get on well with your neighbors. Maureen doesn't open, and it's one of two things: either she's not at home, or she doesn't want to answer. So Julia dares to ring the bell, while trying to remember which way she'd seen her walking through the garden last time, toward the street or toward the house. She rings a few more times, but gets no answer. Although she's ashamed to do so, she leans down to look through the keyhole, but she doesn't see anything. She even gets down on her knees to try to see under the door and thinks the cat's there. It's sniffing at the crack. "*Hi, old chap,*" she says, as Lynn usually does.

A rough south wind has started blowing, and it brings dust from the construction being done on the neighboring buildings and shaking the branches of the acacias. She finds the noise of the trees frightening. She'd like it to rain but doesn't think it will. The garden needs rain. Especially the hydrangeas; before the wind started, there'd been more petals piled up on the ground than on the plants themselves. She wouldn't mind watering them but would prefer the writer not to find her doing something so frivolous if he came outside, and she only uses the watering can on Lynn's bougainvilleas.

When Martin's sister walks past on the other side of the French windows, she has the feeling that something's gone wrong; she doesn't normally appear at that time of day without announcing her arrival previously, nor does she normally look so down. The first thing she thinks is that something's happened to their father, and even as she prepares herself to hear that, she thinks that had it been her in that case, she would have phoned right away. In any case, those two women always like bothering them with things that turn out not to be so serious in the end. "Has something happened?" she asks as soon as she opens the door to greet her, with her still some distance away, but she doesn't answer. Not even as she crosses the threshold. All she does, and in a manner very much like her brother, with that same look of exhaustion, is to drop down onto the sofa and say "something dreadful," at which Julia deduces that it isn't anything as terrible as all that.

"Where's he got to?" she asks, after inspecting the living room for dust, and when Julia asks her again if something's happened and goes on to tell her that her brother's in the formal library, she just lets her know, in a whisper, that something unimaginably scandalous has happened, something she can't even talk about. But what she does tell her is quite funny: her mother has refused to go on living with her father. She's categorically demanded he leave the house before nightfall tomorrow and has called a lawyer to get divorce proceedings going as quickly as possible. The way she tells it is funny, too. Her eyes—the same blue as her brother's—wide open and her lips closed, almost murmuring her words from a small, twisted opening at one side of her mouth. A caricature of secret-sharing.

But it's clear she doesn't want to deprive her brother of the right to know first. "Is he writing?" She nods toward the end of the hallway as she asks, and Julia answers that he is.

She starts to feel tired. She supposes that her respect for the writer's isolation is more a matter of affectation than real respect, as is the case with Harri, who starts walking, whenever Martin locks himself in the formal library, from one side of the living room to the other on tiptoes, like some kind of long-legged bird, pretending not to make a sound but without stopping talking, her neck hunched down toward her shoulders, pretending to speak in a low voice and yet perfectly audible from everywhere in the house, including the library. Even though it's pure hypocrisy, sometimes Julia's offended by her show of only interrupting the writer's work when forced to and then having no trouble stopping her from working without the least consideration.

"Sorry to interrupt you," she says to her brother with a tone of great suffering, as he comes into the living room in his bathrobe like a ghost, tightening the belt and wanting to know what's going on. He's unable to hide the anxiety his sister's unexpected visit has caused him, but he also tries to show indignation at being drawn from his sacred task. Countless times he's told them the anecdote about the writer—he knows he's French but can't remember his name—who instructed his housekeeper not to interrupt him before lunchtime no matter what happened, not to knock on his study door until exactly one o'clock; however, when the housekeeper receives the news that the writer's son has died, she thinks it's important enough to make an exception, knocks on the study door, and tells the writer, who replies by asking her how she dares disobey his orders—she should have waited to tell him the bad news at one o'clock. Martin usually tells the story with a touch of humor but also, Julia believes, in order to express admiration for the French writer and proclaim respect for his sense of vocational duty.

"So what's going on?"

Brother and sister face-to-face. His sister is one of those people who enjoy giving bad news—she enjoys being able to hurt Martin, who is very easily wounded in any case—and it's clear she wants to put off the moment of saying what she's come to tell him. There's a flicker of malicious pleasure in her clear blue eyes, which appears at the same time as a look of foolish shock comes into her brother's identically colored eyes. "*Que tu madre se quiere divorciar de tu padre.*" She tells him this—that his mother wants to divorce his father—in Spanish, because it's a serious matter. She uses the possessive and the second person singular, as she always does when talking about their parents' problems. "*Ni más ni menos,*" she adds—there you have it. And then she keeps quiet to see his reaction. In the same way that Harri says "*¿Qué te parece?*" And then, when Martin says he's not in the mood for jokes, she says she's being serious and that it's not a new problem, although until now she hadn't said anything, not wanting to worry him. She repeats that it's nothing new, moving her hands around in the air several times, although his mother has started complaining more and more since he began wetting himself. She found it unbearable, and still does. Having to live with somebody who wets the upholstery is revolting, and she, his sister, sees that, too, but his mother finds it especially difficult to put up with, because she's convinced that what's happening to him is connected with his excesses from years ago.

But ever since "his" nurse—the one Martin chose—has come into the house, things have gotten noticeably worse. Apparently, his mother didn't like her from the start, and not because she was Dominican but because she spends the whole day walking around singing and moving that big behind of hers. She finds her affectionate nature irritating, her continually stroking the old man's hands and calling him *my love*— "*mi amol*"—in that Caribbean accent, whispering little things in his ear and then both of them laughing for no apparent reason. His sister says she doesn't know where he found her. Martin defends himself with dignity—Abaitua recommended the nurse, and as his sister said herself, it isn't a new problem. He tries to play it down. He says Dad's always been affectionate with women—"He's always paying this one compliments," he says, pointing at Julia—and as for Mom, she's been dementedly talking about his father's problems having come about as a result of his sexual activities for some time now.

His sister shakes her head again and again, in a way Julia finds exasperating. She doesn't think their mother's demented, and she thinks she's made a firm decision this time. Apparently, after what's happened, she's been insisting that she already forgave him once and that she's not going to forgive him again. She refuses, emphatically— *"taxativamente"*—to live in the same house as him and has said that she'll lock herself in her room for one day and one night and wants him out by the next day. *"Ese individuo y esa puta"* are her exact words—she wants both that man and that whore out of her house.

If they don't want to take the radical step of putting him into a home, which she wouldn't think dignified—that, at least, is her position, she says with a hand on her chest—they'll have to find a place for his father and his caregivers to stay. She says it while looking around the room, like somebody noticing where the furniture is in order to consider possible changes.

Martin admits he doesn't understand anything, now looking really rattled. Like a child, he shrugs his shoulders and tucks his hands into his bathrobe sleeves. Julia can't deny that she feels sorry for him, but it's sorrow mixed with tedium, and a bit of revulsion, too, which he realizes when he sees her looking at his thin legs, and so he covers them up, embarrassed. His sister, on the other hand, is very happy and smiles toothily, like a witch, unable to hide what she's feeling, and once again accuses Martin of being partially responsible, he having been the one who came across this—she pauses a moment and waves a hand in the air—incredibly attentive nurse.

It's clear that things could get bad—Martin stands up, infuriated, and says that it's his fault for not being able to just tell them all to get lost—and Julia, to stop that from happening, tells her to quit making accusations and tell them exactly what brought this all on, asking what it is their mother remembered having apparently once forgiven their father for.

When she and their mother got back from shopping, they couldn't see their father or the nurse anywhere, until finally, they thought of checking in his bedroom, and that's where they found them. Obviously, Martin and Julia want to know what they found them doing. After a few seconds' silence, his sister says they were *"en una actitud cariñosa"*—in an affectionate posture— and she links her fingers together, meaning that she doesn't want to tell them any more than that. So they have to ask for more information in the way that priests used to, and she answers them with euphemisms, saying it wasn't anything in itself, nothing big, but it affected her a lot, because it was the same scene they had witnessed as children and which had been so traumatic for her.

She talks to her brother with sincere feeling for the first time, saying she's glad that he didn't have to see that again. She says she was about to faint when she saw the nurse sitting on the edge of his bed wearing a slip of their mother's, light salmon colored with delicate swiss lace on it, and the old man standing up beside her—like this, she says, making a gesture to describe each movement—with one hand, his left hand, on her right shoulder.

"The nightmare," Julia blurts out, and his sister slowly nods. "The same scene as forty years ago." They remain in silence. Julia has to wait a few seconds to get her voice back before asking what scene she's talking about. Martin needs a lot longer before he asks the same question. "What scene?" With that idiotic expression he has on his face sometimes. His sister, unable to believe it, asks if he doesn't remember. She seems to be having fun with him again. Their mother, going against her usual practice—because she never used to tend to them herself—got them out of bed very early and made them get dressed without having breakfast. She dressed Martin herself, because he didn't know how to, and then took all three of them to a house on Urbieta Kalea. A sixth floor apartment that's currently for sale, across the street from the cathedral, and as narrow and long as a tube. Their mother had the key, and the four of them opened doors into empty rooms, one after another, until finally, in the third or fourth room, they found them, the young woman wearing a slip, sitting on the edge of the bed with her torso and head leaning over— she imitates the position—and their father wearing a dark suit and standing with a hand on her shoulder. *"Ahí tenéis a vuestro padre"*— there's your father for you—their mother shouted, pushing them into the room, and just then, the cathedral bells started pealing and making an incredible din. The girl was Martin's nanny, a girl from Otzeta, sweet and pleasant, who he loved more than anybody else as a child.

His sister asks if he's forgotten it. Martin appears to have gone dumb and nods. She seems to find that funny. How could he have forgotten something like that? Something as awful at that. *Si bouleversant, so shocking.* She also remembers that Martin was sick that

663

day, or at least had a bit of a temperature, and even though the maids objected, their mother still got him uncaringly out of bed, probably because he was the apple of his father's eye and, because of that, she needed him as a witness. He was always sick, she tells Julia, pointing at the anguish-ridden writer with an expression of resignation.

Apparently, their mother suspected that their father was being unfaithful to her, and when she found out about the apartment, she made a copy of all the keys. She also tells them that she recently took advantage of the apartment being for sale to visit it and find out if the bells really were as noisy as she remembers, and she thinks they weren't. Everything seems more intense when you're a child.

Julia feels calmer. Finding out what's been behind his sleepless nights and so many bad moods makes her incredibly happy, and she's astonished that Martin shows no sign of being moved by it all. He stares at the wall, as if he were looking for a specific point on the map of Sicily, shaken up, she imagines, until he starts nodding and saying, "I remember, I remember," seeming angry, wanting to shut his sister up because she insists on describing the scene again: furniture of poor taste; a girl with nothing especially interesting about her, young, almost a child, with light-colored soft hair and two or three curls going down to her neck; and their father with his hand on her shoulder as if he needed support, dressed in black from head to toe, with no hat on. She laughs. She thinks it's funny now, but in fact it was frightful, she's always blamed her mother for having used them like that to humiliate and punish their father. She thinks the poor man was wounded forever after the experience.

Martin keeps on looking at the map of Sicily, rubbing his hands together behind his back as his sister looks at her nails, half pleased and half moved, Julia thinks, to have managed to render her brother speechless, or because, for once, she's had something to say. Brother and sister stay quiet for a while, and Julia doesn't think she can be the one to break the silence. She waits for something to happen as she moves toward the window and looks out. The two cats are preening themselves by the statue of the angel, which is still pointing with its broken arm at the sky—in spite of the forecast of rain, there are no clouds—and the usual pair of warblers are in the bush and seem to look at each other attentively when it's their turn to sing. She counts up to six blackbirds—that is, if they are blackbirds—pecking at the bed of pansies.

Julia would like something to happen.

Suddenly Martin's sister cries out, "But hey!" and claps her hands together. "I forgot, I have some good news, too!" She's spoken with their sister in Paris, who's told her that her Catalan friends have decided to cancel their trip, so there's no need to make the booking at the María Cristina. Pleased to be able to give him such good news, until she's then frightened to see the effect it has on her brother, who's put out once again. "What, they're not coming?" he stammers, his face as pale as if he'd just been bled, one hand resting on the wall as if he were faint. His Paris sister hasn't taken the trouble to call him, she hasn't even had the consideration to tell him directly. Doesn't she know how much trouble he went to to make the booking?

His sister tries to play it down—she's sure the people at the María Cristina won't mind canceling the booking. She looks at Julia, hoping she'll back her up, but Julia decides not to pay any attention. Now it looks like all the blood's gone to his head—his face is red, his eyes look as if somebody's strangling him and they're about to pop out of his head. How can he possibly cancel something that he only managed to secure through a favour from Zabaleta and with the help of the mayor himself? What can be going through their minds? Julia knows that any attempt to make it seem less important—which is what his sister is doing—will only make matters worse, so she decides to go to the kitchen on the excuse of needing to empty the dishwasher. But when she gets there, she feels an incredible lack of energy and sits down at the marble table, which is like a tombstone, a big, thick one. She sees that the juice from half a lemon is staining it. She throws the fruit into the sink at the other end. She misses and doesn't make any movement to pick it up off the floor.

She listens to them talking. Martin's sister keeps on trying to play down the situation, trying to calm her brother. Martin is shouting that they always mess things up for him. They don't let him concentrate on his work. He has to get a novel finished. They go on for a long while like that in the living room, Julia in the kitchen, and his sister, sobbing, says that she, too, is kept from living as she would like to, saying that she had to leave home just to be able to complain about the problems there. She goes into the kitchen before leaving and, in tears, says to Julia that she doesn't know how she puts up with him.

Then, after his sister leaves, Martin stays in the living room for a long time, and Julia sits in the kitchen.

"WHAT DO I DO NOW?" He says it with deeply felt desperation and without turning his head away from the map when she approaches him. At first she doesn't understand what he's talking about, and then she'd rather not understand. She lets the hand she'd lifted to put on his shoulder fall. She, too, looks at the map. She doesn't remember anything about Messina. Some things about Palermo. She had a hard time persuading him not to go to Corleone. She remembers the difficulty they had paying a parking meter in Catania, its incredible fish market, and a bad restaurant in its beautiful square. Miles and miles in their Opel rental car, and she found the seat uncomfortable. Syracuse: restored churches, and mansions full of tourists like themselves, an incredibly hot weekend. "Do what about what?" she asks him, tired. "What do you think? About the booking at the María Cristina," he answers, amazed, and angry about having to explain it to her. She tries to add a touch of humor, "In any case, don't cancel the delivery of the flowers and the book to the room." Who knows, maybe with a bit of luck they'll find their way into the hands of some film star who'll be unable to sleep and start reading it and like it.

If looks could kill.

Seeing him sitting there with his elbows resting on his thighs, his hands pushing what little hair he has left toward the back of his head, murmuring to himself, she remembers the first night they got together, leaning against the railings on Pasealeku Berria. When Martin's glasses fell into the sea, she, having drunk a little, cried out, "Glasses overboard!" He wasn't amused. She was surprised at the time —and now she realizes that she was disappointed, too—that just as they were about to have their first kiss, he got so bothered about losing some glasses, and she was about to throw hers in, too, to iniciate a little lovers' ritual for them to laugh about together, but she didn't in the end. She just made as if she was going to throw them in, but she didn't yet realize that his not being able to see the funny side of the mishap was a bad sign. She just felt ridiculous, like somebody who can't tell a joke.

Now she doesn't take the trouble to repeat that his sister's right and that the people at the hotel would be perfectly accepting if he called to cancel, or to point out to him that the manager probably wouldn't even realize the rooms weren't being used as long as they were paid for. She tries to imagine what she would say if Martin were suddenly to tell her that he's going to use all his influence again to get a table at Arzak for the two of them to have dinner there together and that later, after having a few drinks in the hotel bar with all the film stars, they were going to make use of the king-size bed originally booked for those Catalans who had no idea what they were missing. She isn't sure. In any case, he doesn't say anything. He lifts his head up when the phone rings again and tells her not to answer. And then he hides himself in the formal library once more.

She's disappointed, that's the word. She's always hoped that finding out what was behind his nightmare would transform him. In fact, more than hoping that would happen, she's fantasized about the idea that becoming conscious of his subconscious would make his neurotic symptoms disappear, as happened to Gregory Peck in Hitchcock's film *Spellbound*. *Recuerda*—meaning *"Remember"*—was the title they'd given it in Spanish. Julia is convinced that the need to fill the gap in his memory is what's behind Martin's desire to write. He wrote to remember, to cure his neurosis, and paradoxically, that very neurosis was what often stopped him from making progress with his writing. Once he recovered his memory—which she thought would happen through writing—he would overcome his neurosis, become a happy man, feel free to either carry on writing or not, to go to Sicily or stay in Martutene. She's lost that hope completely.

IT'S RAINING HARD. There's no doubt it's just a shower, because the sky's still bright. The cats seem to have taken shelter in the woodpile, while one of the blackbirds continues pecking under the magnolia. She watches it for a good while, sitting on the step by the entrance, listening to the rain, breathing in the air with its smell of wet soil. She remembers Lynn again. During another rain shower, she took her blouse off and danced something like ballet, barefoot on the grass, around the one-armed angel. Shyness stopped her from joining in as she wanted to do. She remembers her with her chin resting on her arms crossed on top of the piano—she looked like a little Irish girl who could only just reach up to the piano—while she played Satie. *"Après la pluie."* Her accent like Jean

Seberg's when she read *Montauk* in French. How happy Lynn was when she told her she planned to translate Frisch's *Fragebogen* into Basque. "*I'm happy, so happy.*" Her thousand ways of saying I'm happy, so happy. When she told her she was in love with Abaitua, for instance.

I'M HAPPY, SO HAPPY.

To start crying, she need only remember a picture of herself as a child, a photo in which she's wearing a white dress with organdy bows on it.

ALEA JACTA EST. When cuckoos sing, rains turn to spring.

She's sitting in front of the piano again. She likes the stool high up, like pianists from Eastern Europe, to be able to play energetically like Liszt. She hardly ever feels free to play when she's not alone, perhaps because he's seldom asked her to play when they're together. Maybe even never. The sheet music for Ravel's Concert for the Left Hand, adapted for both hands, is sitting on the music stand. She remembers Lynn had trouble understanding why playing it with both hands is difficult. And there's a copy of the Boléro too, which he bought with the threat of using it to accompany Lynn's hot love sessions with Abaitua. And despite it all, she can't help laughing when she starts pretending to play it without touching the keys. C B C D, C B A C C A C B G. She knows she's going to miss the old Petrof.

Her sheet music and dictionaries alone fill up a bag she can hardly lift. Then she tiptoes up to the first floor. In fact, she isn't quite sure why she takes the few clothes she has in the closet out and throws them onto the bed. She doesn't even have an appropriate suitcase to put them in, but it's comforting to do things that would fit in well if she had to write the end of a novel. She picks up the bag and says, "I'll come back later for the rest of it."

She sits on the edge of the bed and waits for him; she knows he'll come up sooner or later and wants him to find her as she is in order to save on introductory explanations. Time goes by—she doesn't know exactly how long—without any trace of the writer. Downstairs there's complete silence. Upstairs, on the other hand, on the ceiling, she can hear Maureen's steps. She's come in without Julia realizing. Her steps are heavy and rough compared to those of Lynn, who used to walk lightly, almost always barefoot, so different. Julia gets up and listens with attention to Maureen walking around. She can clearly hear her opening and closing the closet and the drawers. And her nasal, authoritarian voice as she speaks on the phone. Julia only understands the odd word when she speaks near the window. *"I tell you"*; *"absolutely."* *"Come back,"* she says twice. Julia wonders if she's talking with Lynn.

IT'S CLEARED UP. There are some boys pulling ropes to bring the boat to the old mooring. They're younger than the ones back in the day, they don't look more than fifteen or sixteen. Years have gone by since then. Martin used to spend hours and hours watching them, wondering what they could be up to, complaining that they were on his property but incapable of taking any measures to deal with the situation. Like telling Abaitua about his suspicions, for instance, because it was his son who asked for his permission to move the pontoon to make it easier to work on the boat. He used to look straight past them when he came across them, or just not say hello.

Now a man from the clinic side shouts at them to stop mucking around. At first they don't obey him, but they give up after around three minutes more pulling the rope to no effect. A large white car—similar to Abaitua's, if it's not actually his—pulls out of the clinic parking lot. It goes very slowly along the old road and, after crossing the bridge, goes even more slowly toward the house. She'd have to run to the balcony on the other side of the house to see whether it parks next to the iron gate or takes the main road.

She can hear Martin on the other side of the formal library door, decidedly, ceaselessly typing on his computer in a way that's unusual for him. After wondering for a while whether to go in and tell him that she's leaving or not, in the end she can't summon up enough courage to do so. She has two books to take back to the university library, and even though there's still a lot of time left on them, because she has nothing better to do, she decides to take them back before forgetting about them. Just as she reaches the iron gate, she sees the white car start up and head off toward Donostia. Without knowing why, she tries to memorize the number plate.

THE TRAIN'S ON TIME. In the empty carriage, she starts thinking about why it could be that Lynn isn't giving any signs of life, apart from her allergy to the phone and her perpetual problems with keeping her battery charged. She completely rules out what Martin thinks, which is that this time, too, she's gone off with Abaitua, because she's almost sure she's seen him. She thinks it more probable that Lynn's fled from Abaitua rather than gone with him. When it comes down to it, she wants to believe that her being an independent woman, she has every right to go wherever she wants to go, but she doesn't manage to convince herself; surely she should have let her know something by now. She makes a firm decision not to let Maureen escape the next time; if necessary, she'll break down the door to ask her where Lynn is. She doesn't want to think about it any more for the moment.

She almost misses her stop.

THE BOOKSHOP IN IBAETA'S CLOSED. On her way back, she walks past the outdoor terrace where she sat with Harri and decides to stop and have something to drink there. She isn't sure if she's ever sat at an outdoor terrace by herself. It's empty, and the waiter, who recognizes her, talks about what a bad summer it's been. He asks her if she doesn't go to the beach, she looks pale, and she asks him, with a sense of humor, if he thinks she looks bad. Absolutely not, the guy replies, ashamed of himself, and trying to make things right, he says he thinks she's a very interesting woman. "A very interesting woman." She doesn't want to follow his lead and ask what he means by that; she doesn't feel like talking, she closes her eyes, and all she wants is for the sun to stroke her face. He's a nice guy, and he must be bored. He sits down at a chair at the next table, facing her. He talks on and on about various topics, and she finds it hard not to pay attention to him.

A phone call at just the right moment. It's Zigor. He says he can't find a T-shirt he wants to take to Otzeta with him. She says she'll come home. Since the waiter's disappeared, she can sit on the front edge of her chair, lift her face up, and close her eyes. She thinks about Martin and wonders what he's writing. It's curious what's happened to him since he met Marie Laforêt. She doesn't have any doubt that he has in fact met her—he did actually buy a beret at Leclercq—and that they exchanged telephone numbers and have sent text messages to each other since; although the way he describes saving her number isn't something Martin would normally do. He would have had to write her number down on a piece of paper, he wouldn't have been up to using the process he describes. She feels put out and irritated while she wonders how far they've gone. But not excessively so.

It turns out the sun really does get on her nerves.

She looks toward the bookshop once more, still a little phased by the sunlight, and sees a large, dark man carrying a stack of books under his arm. She sees him from behind. He has thick curly hair and is wearing a shiny green guayabera and loose white trousers—a carefree, tropical style. She doesn't have any doubt that it's Kepa and wonders whether wanting to come across him is what led her to sit down at this outdoor terrace in Ibaeta. She pays for her shandy— asking the waiter as she waits for her change whether she looks any more suntanned to him now—and then crosses the street. She doesn't go straight into the bookshop. She decides to walk around the block and rehearse meeting him. "You must be Kepa, Martin's friend— Abaitua's, Lynn's, and everybody's friend, from what I've seen." Then she'll tell him that she's worried not to have heard from Lynn, she keeps calling her and she doesn't answer, and has he heard from her?

The little bell at the top of the door rings as she opens it. The shop's empty, and quite a while goes by until the same girl as before comes out, says hello, and without asking her what she wants, sits down on the other side of the counter. She seems to be used to people looking around the shelves themselves rather than asking for what they want. And so Julia looks around, making time.

She has the impression she's spending a long time looking around the books. No other customers come in to make her presence stand out less, nor does the man wearing the green guayabera and white pants. Finally, she tries to choose a book so that she can go up to the counter and, as she pays, ask the girl if Kepa happens to be there; but she finds it hard to choose one. She already has the books she's interested in and isn't interested in those she doesn't already have.

When the girl looks at her from over the top of the book she's reading, Julia really feels that she's been there too long and is ashamed to think the girl may take her for one of those people who waste the workers' time in bookshops without actually intending to buy anything. But she wants to wait a little longer, buy some more time, and see if the man, who must be in the back room, comes out. So she takes out her phone to call Martin. It's a double strategy. She'll say that she'll be back after lunch—she's feeling guilty about putting her dictionaries into a bag and taking her clothes out of the closet and throwing them onto the bed—and ask if he knows anything about Lynn, not because she thinks Martin may have heard from her but because when the man in the back room hears her ask, she figures he'll want to know who's speaking.

But he doesn't come out.

She decides to go straight up to the counter and ask the girl. There are several piles of books on top of it that almost hide her from view. Julia picks a book up. It's a copy of *Zalacaín el aventurero*, an old Austral edition—the girl points out it's second-hand—and on the dedication page there's a drawing done in different-colored ballpoint pens. It's of a young man wearing a red beret, blue pants, and a white shirt and socks, he's walking, there's a black-and-white dog behind him and, in the background, some green hills. She likes it. It's quite naïf and reminds her of some of the drawings by Caro Baroja. She asks the girl if it's for sale, it would make a nice present for Zigor. "Of course," is all she replies. "With the drawing and everything?" "Of course," she says again, this time shrugging as if amazed by her question. "Kepa does them," she then adds, and Julia thinks she says it to explain the book being priced at just five euros.

She gets over being too embarrassed to ask the girl to wrap it up as a present—it's another way of buying time, too—and, while she does that, not very skilfully but making a good effort, Julia suddenly dares to ask after Kepa. He's just left and won't be back until tomorrow.

The girl says, "You almost walked past each other at the door."

IN THE END, HER MOTHER AND SISTER have decided to go to Otzeta and have lunch there. Julia isn't in a very good mood; she'd wanted to talk about things with Zigor, about the project he's working on about the war. She knows the feeling she has that they're taking her son away from her isn't fair—she's the one who's always asking them to help her out with him—but she can't help it. She's going to miss him, even though it won't be more than a few days. She's sad, and it's obvious Zigor notices, which she likes, but at the same time, it's an impulse she'd like to be able to control. That's why when he asks her if she's going to have lunch alone, she feels obliged to say no, she's going to have lunch with Martin.

The T-shirt Zigor needed hasn't turned up. They've looked everywhere, and now, as a last resort, while she looks in the closet in her room, just in case—sometimes she wears his T-shirts around the house—she tries to convince him that he shouldn't be so inflexible, he should learn to let things go, not get obsessed, one T-shirt's as good as another, all with that insistent, didactic tone of hers that she's incapable of avoiding, even though she knows that it does no good and that what really counts is her example, which is a true case of obsessive behaviour.

Eventually it turns up. She shows it to Zigor as if it were a flag of victory, but he, lying on his mother's bed, doesn't lift his head, which is buried in a book. Julia knows the book. George L. Steer's *The Tree of Gernika*, which was put away somewhere and he must have found when looking for his T-shirt. "It's really something," he says as he shows it to her, and then he reads her the start of the book, which she knows by heart. "The Basques, who are the subject of this book, are a religious, hard-drinking people who have no time for blasphemy, and who live in the mountains to the southwest of the Bay of Biscay." He asks if he can borrow it, and she says of course he can. She's never denied him a book. "But don't believe every word." He waves his hand as if to ward off tedium. "For instance, I don't know if I really believe that bit about not having time for blasphemy. We'll talk about it when you've read it."

She'd like to tell him how important it was for her to read the book as a child. She'd like to talk about that. The idealization of the Basque soldiers, the author's exaggerations about their courage and noble behaviour, which made what her parents told her about the war seem understated, and while she may have had reason to distrust what they told her, because they themselves were involved in it all, there was nothing to make her doubt an Englishman who had been an eyewitness, above all considering he was a correspondent for *The Times*. What she would like to tell her son is that now, when people are talking about the right to disinter the corpses that were buried by the roadside before the war, and during and after it—and every side, reds and blues, right-wing and left-wing, they all had, to some extent or another, brutal things they'd rather hide—she still believes that whatever idealization there may be, there's no reason to feel ashamed of the Basque troops, and she's proud of that. A pride she has no reason to feel—children are neither to blame for nor to be credited with what their parents did. But she does want to pass that feeling onto her son, and she's sorry, in a way she wasn't when she was young, that the old patriots have left that source of pride—the fact of having lost well, in the right way—behind them. But then his grandmother comes in and says they're late and her brother-in-law's been waiting in the van for half an hour.

Zigor gives his mother a hug.

There's nothing to eat in the house. She chops up an onion to put in an omelette, but takes the frying pan back off the heat as soon as she dumps it in.

She takes her shoes off and lies down on the bed, fully dressed.

Zigor's gone and forgotten his wretched T-shirt.

She finds Flaubert's letters to Louise Colet on her bedside table and looks over the sentences Martin has underlined.

"Je n'ai jamais vu un enfant sans penser qu'il deviendrait un vieillard, ni un berceau sans songer à une tombe"—I've never seen a child without thinking that it would grow old, nor a cradle without thinking of a grave. Julia does the opposite—when she sees an old man, she thinks about how he must have been a child once, curled up in the arms of a young mother.

"Qui sait? Tu me remercieras peut-être plus tard d'avoir eu le courage de n'être pas plus tendre"—Who knows? You will thank me later, perhaps, for having had the courage not to be more tender. Had he been thinking of her when he underlined that?

"Etre bête, égoïste, et avoir une bonne santé, voilà les trois conditions voulues pour être heureux: mais si la première nous manque, tout est perdu"—To be stupid, selfish, and have good health are three requirements for happiness, though if stupidity is lacking, all is lost.

"L'ignoble me plaît. C'est le sublime d'en bas"—I like the ignoble. It is the sublime debased. That's the quote Martin wasn't able to remember when he was trying to tell Lynn why he liked trashy television. On the same page: *"Tous les grands voluptueux sont très pudiques"*—All the most sensual people are very reserved.

"Pour vivre tranquille il faut vivre seul et calfeutrer toutes ses fenêtres, de peur que l'air du monde ne nous arrive"—To live in peace one must live alone and seal one's windows lest the air of the world seep in.

"La patrie, c'est la terre, c'est l'Univers, ce sont les étoiles, c'est l'air, c'est la pensée elle-même, c'est-à-dire l'infini dans notre poitrine"—The motherland, is the earth, the universe, the stars, the air. It is thought

itself, that is, the infinite within our breasts. She tries to memorize it to tell Zigor.

There's no underlining in the last letter, Martin almost certainly stopped reading by then, and every time she reads it, it seems increasingly cruel.

"*Madame:*

J'apris que vous vous étiez donné la peine de venir, hier dans la soirée, trois fois, chez moi. Je n'y étais pas. Et, dans la crainte des avanies qu'une telle persistance de votre part pourrait vous attirer de la mienne, le savoir-vivre m'engage à vous prévenir que je n'y serai jamais. J'ai l'honneur de vous saluer."

I was told that you took the trouble to come here to see me three times last evening. I was not in. And, fearing lest persistence expose you to humiliation, I am bound by the rules of politeness to warn you that I shall never be in. Yours.

Julia thinks about how her mother will react when she tells her she's going to stop seeing Martin. And how is she going to tell Zigor?

Once more, she wants to know what's going to happen with Marie Lafôret. She thinks it'll be the story of the man in front of the mirror's last love, the one he'll choose to be with him until death. Because it's clear that death is what it's all about.

She has to buy a present for Zigor's birthday, the book doesn't seem like much to her. She doesn't know whether to tell Martin and then take her things, or the other way around. She's tempted by the second option, which will put off the difficult moment, but decides on the first, because farewells in the afternoon seem harder.

THE HOUSE IS THE SAME AS WHEN SHE LEFT IT. There's no sign of life. She remains standing in the living room for a while waiting for him to come in; he must have heard her arrive. She cleans two plates and a teaspoon, and she's not sure if they were in the sink earlier or not. Then she goes up to the formal library door and hears him writing on his computer.

She goes up to the bedroom. There are no sounds from the upper story, from the penthouse. She sits on the edge of the bed and waits for him. The suitcase is open at her feet.

She gets up when she hears him looking for her on the ground floor, takes the few clothes that are still in the closet out of it, and starts throwing them onto the bed. She does it instinctively, not wanting him to find her doing nothing, and also because it's going to be the easiest way to start the inevitable conversation—he'll ask her what she's doing, and she'll answer that she's going, she can't take any more—but suddenly she wonders whether it isn't just a little too theatrical, childish, in fact. So she's hesitating, holding a white dress with red and blue spots, which Harri gave her, on a hanger in her hand.

What she would least like would be to go through the old scene again, Martin wrapped around her legs begging her not to leave him—she doesn't want to have to go through that again. She hears that he's looking for her downstairs and then, shortly afterward, the creak of the staircase. He walks silently along the hallway, as if wanting to catch her by surprise or not wake her up. He stares at her from the doorway. He also looks at the pile of clothes spread out on top of the bed, then at the open closet, and then back at her. He doesn't ask her what she's doing, just shows her a pile of paper; she figures it must be around fifty pages. Now he sits down on the edge of the bed, with the pieces of paper on his lap. "I'm finished," he says, without excitement, using a tone not very different from the same one he might use in any other situation, as if she were looking for something, any old thing, the dictionary he'd borrowed from her, for instance, and he were using the same tone as now, "I'm finished," as he handed it back to her. It's astonishing that he doesn't show any sign of happiness or pleasure. All she can do, on the other hand, is show as much surprise and happiness, or something like it, as she can muster.

"You're completely finished?"

He smiles. That happy, mocking smile that looks so good on him, and which he uses less and less. "I had no choice; I had to finish it."

He looks at her in silence, and she doesn't know what to say. She finds the idea that he might read it to her tiring. He used to always do it, more than anything else to hear himself, she thinks, and to make sure that the text would be well received, because he reads extremely well and his voice makes what he reads better, knowing how to underline the parts that work particularly well and pass lightly over what doesn't work so well; but for Julia, listening to him became torture, because she was so anxious that he would notice some inappropriate gesture of hers. He would lift his eyes from his papers from time to time, and when he looked at her like that, she used to be afraid that he might see her not looking as moved as she should be, or might think she was laughing at the wrong moment. In short, she was afraid of disappointing him. Even so, when he waves the pages in the air and asks if she wants him to read to her, she whispers of course she does. But he, playfully, says, "Don't worry, I'm not going to," and laughs, dropping backward onto the clothes spread out over the bed. "I know you hate it."

Then—with his feet on the floor, his knees bent, his bottom resting on the edge of the bed, and the sheets of paper in his hands on top of his body—he turns and looks into her face. She's still standing up by the window. "I'll spare you the torture," he smiles again. Then he sits up. After what seems like a moment of reflection: "The thing is, I have to read aloud to see where to put the punctuation, and I always feel like I'm off my rocker if I do it alone." He's looking at her seriously, without any trace of irony. He offers her the pieces of paper, which she takes. "You read them."

Now it's Martin who's standing up by the window and Julia who's sitting on the bed with the pages on her lap. *The Man in Front of the Mirror.* He has the palm of one hand on his forehead, pulling his hair backward to measure how far his baldness goes. She starts turning the pages over. She's familiar with most of the text, except, perhaps, for the last dozen pages or so.

"The sky is full of sun now. Sun that invites you to live. I say this without any bitterness."

Martin, turning around from the window, says, "I'd rather not be right here if you're going to read it," and she, relieved, puts the pages down by her side. "I get nervous," he adds. He suggests they have some tea.

Even though they have to walk across the living room to sit down on the sofa, he doesn't notice that there are two bags full of her books in the middle of the room. Or that her half of the table's empty. They both remain silent while they wait for the tea to be ready. And then, when Julia serves it, she asks, "What was that thing about tannin?" but he doesn't answer. "Where on earth is she?" He's talking about Lynn, of course. Silence once more. "I'm sure the fat one's kidnapped her." Silence. "She's a lesbian, and she's in love with her. Don't you think?" She manages to keep quiet while he interrupts the silence with various vacuous comments; she wants him to ask her why she's not saying anything, and at the same time, she's afraid that he will.

When he finally does, she wants to answer tactfully, and that's why she uses his name. So she says, "I can't take any more, Martin, I'm leaving." She thinks he looks at her quite confusedly, and maybe he's understood that she's simply going home just as she has almost every other day recently, and so she says once more, in a drier tone, that she can't take any more. Martin spends the long silence that follows scratching his fingertips along the glass table, as if writing on it, until suddenly, like a child fearing he's going to be told off for marking it all up, he quickly closes his fist and tucks it into his sleeve. A freight train goes by, one of those long ones carrying cars, and then there's silence again.

Julia picks up the two bags full of books and puts them in a corner. They're too heavy for her to be able to walk out with any dignity, so she decides to tell him that she'll come by for her things soon and finish correcting his short story in about a week. She manages to do that and sound natural, and she interprets the silence that follows as meaning that her having made the decision to leave is a relief for him. "Sometimes the stronger of the two doesn't have the strength to leave, and the weaker of the two has to." She doesn't know who said that. "Let's talk about it. Don't leave like this," he says finally, and she agrees. "We'll talk, but right now I have to leave." Neither of them makes any sign of moving when the phone rings, not even to see who's calling, and they let it ring, both staying as they are. When it comes down to it, it's the end of a long relationship. "Stay for a while," he insists, and she says no, she can't. It's Zigor's birthday on Monday, and she has to get him a present. He lifts his hands to his head and says he's forgotten all about it.

"Buy him something from me. I'll give you the money."

So why did he mark the thirteenth on the calendar, then? She's more hurt by him forgetting Zigor's birthday than she is by any other type of negligence; he knows how grateful she is when he gives her son a present, more than her son himself. And that mistake, if that's what it is, seems even bigger to her now. She's reminded him of the date a hundred times, because she set it as her deadline for going back to work. And even so, he's forgotten. So what was the point of marking the day on the calendar? To pay homage to the forty *Requetés* who took Donostia on that same date? She'd like to ask him that, but it doesn't seem the right moment for sarcasm, and she'd rather not get into a session of mutual reproaches. She

678

picks up the bags of books, to underline that her decision to break up the relationship is final. He looks at her without making any sign that he's going to help her with them, and although she would like to take her things with her right then, she realizes once more that she wouldn't even be able to make it as far as the iron gate with them. Not, at least, if she wanted to keep her dignity intact, and that's why she puts them down on the floor once more, this time leaving them under the coatrack by the door. It seems like the best place to her. Then, just to say something, and even though it's not yet six o'clock, she tells him the shops are going to close soon, and Martin asks her once more to get her son something from him. "To tell the truth, I've been having some really bad days lately," he says to excuse himself, rubbing his face between both hands.

"You always manage to make them bad." He looks at her as if he hasn't heard, with a sad smile on his lips, but then cheers up immediately. "At least I've finished this," he says, straightening up, placing his hands wide open on top of the pile of papers. He picks them up and goes toward the door, which Julia has opened.

"You're forgetting these."

She takes the sheets of paper and puts them in her handbag, wondering whether to remind him that she's going to come back for her things, making it clear that the breakup's final. She doesn't. She sets off along the gravel path until she hears his voice. "It's full of mistakes." Nothing more than that. But then, when she starts moving again, she hears him once again. "I hope you'll go through it for me." She nods, and he says, "It's Faustino Iturbe's goodbye." They stay like that for a moment, Julia lost in thought by the flowerbed, and Martin at the top of the stairs into the house; she waits to check that he's not going to say anything more before starting off again. She has to walk slower than she would like to, because her feet sink into the gravel, and when she turns back at the iron gate, he isn't there any more. Although the three cats have followed after her meowing, they never cross beyond the boundary of the property.

There are only a few minutes before the train's going to arrive, but she can't resist the temptation to pick up the story again, wanting to find out what happens between the narrator and the television presenter who met by chance at Leclercq on Narrika Kalea, after having left off reading at the point where he receives a second short text message from her, which says "Hi, are you still there?"

EVEN THOUGH LIVING UNDER THE SHADOW of death has killed his libido, she's not only beautiful, and more beautiful in person than on screen, but also an unquestionably bright woman—she got a couple of his ironic remarks right away and laughed at them—and as can be seen from her message, she's an uninhibited, open person who only deserves one reply: "Yes, I'm here, I can't wait to see you." What makes him hesitate is the idea that if they agree to meet, he may not feel able to keep the truth from her, to hide from her the fact that he's seriously ill and only has a short time left to live. How would she react to that? He wants to know, but not enough to risk making her feel sorry for him and, at the same time, risk putting her in a difficult, uncomfortable situation with a half-dead man "sunk in the abstraction he slips into time and again." On the other hand, he wouldn't have the energy he'd need to go out with her and behave as if nothing were happening, making an effort to be full of life and make her laugh, which is what women like. So he doesn't dare answer her message, and it hurts him to think that Marie Lafôret may take him for a rude or arrogant man.

He tries to forget her message, even tries not to watch the program she presents. He likes to think that one day she will understand his silence, although he isn't sure to what extent that will be a consolation for him. It will be, to some extent. In any case, there are some things he has to sort out before he loses all his strength. He has some possessions. He finds out that his personal situation moves his lawyer and his notary less than it does his doctor. He has some pretty interesting reflections about that. After a few days, he's tempted to glance at the message again, and when he looks for it on his phone, he realizes he's erased it. And he doesn't have Marie Lafôret's number, either. It's a complication resulting from having changed phones. His old one wasn't working well, and while he's stopped buying long-lasting objects, for obvious reasons, it wasn't a good idea for him to be without a phone, and so he decided to get a new one.

It was the girl at the phone company who took charge of changing the chip from his small old phone to the new one, and she put the broken old one into a big box for recycling. When he realized that Marie Lafôret's message and number had disappeared, he went back to the shop, where another girl told him that the information might not be stored in the chip, it might be in the telephone's own memory. He got her permission to look through the box of old phones for recycling. There were hundreds of them. He took them all out and looked at them one by one until he found his. He's indignant, he gets angry, he complains that they didn't give him the information they should have. "In all probability, there's somebody I'll never see again in my life because of you people," he shouts at an employee, who doesn't understand the scale of his indignation. He doesn't go so far as to say "a person I love," leaving it at "somebody." "So the incompetence of Euskaltel interfered in my decision. It's true I could have called the television station, but I was reluctant to—I'd have had to call the telephone operator, give my name, be filtered through by who knows how many secretaries and assistants. Although it wasn't objectively impossible, it was an additional obstacle that inclined the balance in favor of my doubts and against getting in touch. I went as far as looking up the station's telephone number, but not as far as using it. I didn't go any further. It seemed to me that losing the number was more than just a sign of the clumsiness of the people at Euskaltel—it was also an undeniable sign of fate. I stuck to seeing her on the television screen, but that made me gloomier still, because I thought she looked sad, and I felt it was because of me, because I hadn't called her, but I didn't have the energy to get the relationship going again. I thought it was better to break it off there rather than let it become something, and I stopped watching her program, too."

It was all pretty disappointing.

She can't continue reading on the train—the old lady next to her asks if it's still a long way to Donostia and then doesn't keep quiet, talking about just anything, out loud, not specifically to her, but in such a way that she feels obliged to listen to her. She must be around seventy, her hair is dyed blond, she doesn't have any lips, there's a little heart painted in bright red in the middle of her mouth, and she keeps turning around to the man sitting next to her and fiddling with some detail of his clothing. She tucks the collar of his shirt into his V-necked sweater, straightens his tie, folds his sleeve over, and the hard-faced man lets her do it. Now she takes a piece of thread off his pants and says, "There's some blonde after you, and it's not me," and she says it for Julia to hear, for her to laugh at the joke. In fact, the uninhibited woman's hypercritical attention and perhaps slightly scornful pretence in looking after the man, and his reaction—

between a frown and fright—remind her of a description Martin wrote of an outpatient waiting room. Women taking care of their silent husbands, treating them in an exasperating way to calm them down, as if they were children, telling them off for the things they did or didn't do that made them get sick, sharing all the details with everybody around them: "it started happening to him two years ago"; "they can't find out what he's got." They're from the province of Ávila, but the town they live in is close to Cáceres, and they've come to Tolosa to visit one of their sons. Julia would have guessed they weren't from here, not only from their voices and clothes and appearance in general but from their faces, too. And just like every time she thinks about people who are from here versus people who aren't, she isn't proud of herself.

THERE ARE MORE PEOPLE THAN USUAL AT THE STATION. Young people dressed casually, with backpacks and computers hanging off their shoulders. They've obviously come for the film festival. Contrary to what the Basque weather service predicted, it's a beautiful afternoon. The sun's going down, and there's a terrific noise coming from the birds in the trees across the way alongside the river. They're starlings, apparently, and they spend the night fighting for a good place on the branches. Then, suddenly, a whole flock of them takes flight, hundreds of birds rising quickly to go to the other side of the river. Immediately, another flock takes flight—who would have thought there could be so many birds in a single tree—and takes the same route as the previous one. Thousands of birds covering the sky, but nobody looks up to see them.

AT THE PUKAS SURF SHOP, she feels incredibly old as she picks out a sweatshirt and a couple of T-shirts. She wonders whether to buy him a surf watch, but it's too expensive, bearing in mind that she has to pay for Martin's present, too. She's long had her eye on a type of zippered case at the Tamayo stationery store—she isn't sure whether it's leather, but it looks it—fitted out with all the basic equipment for drawing and doing watercolors: pencils, brushes, the water colors themselves, around a dozen of them, a foldaway plastic cup for water. It's her fantasy. Traveling around with somebody, walking and stopping from time to time, drawing and writing descriptions of the countryside, shrines, and special buildings. She'd like Zigor to be able to do that. She remembers Lynn once told her that Abaitua and this Kepa guy used to do that, and of course, that the last time her son was at Martin's house, he really liked Danièle Ohnheiser's series of travel watercolors—*Promenade à Villa Borghese, Voyage à Rome,* and the rest—and that he was moved when he heard that you don't really see things until you draw them. He takes things Martin says to heart. She thinks the bag of watercolors is a good present to get on Martin's behalf, it's a little old-fashioned, in a serious, cultured way, and she knows he'll like it a lot, above all because he'll think it's from Martin.

There are two elderly women in front of her waiting to pay, both *très comme il faut,* and they're both buying decorative things, colored paper napkins, and other little goodies, many other little goodies, for the birthday tea they're throwing for one of their grandchildren, and with the naturalness that comes from class and habit, they ask for each item to be separately wrapped and to have its own little bow put on it. Two old women who could easily be from the upscale Calle Serrano in Madrid. They talk about the weather while they wait and make other people wait, too. They say it's lucky there's good weather for the people who've come to the film festival— that complete deference to visitors and, when it comes down to it, money, which is so typical in tourist cities—it's been a bad summer, and autumn's usually quite good in Donostia. One of them makes a statement: "Autumn in Donostia is beautiful, it could be the most beautiful autumn anywhere." The other lady contradicts her, saying that spring is the prettiest season in Donostia. They both turn around and look at Julia, as if to ask her opinion on the matter, and remembering *The Man in Front of the Mirror,* she thinks that autumn, at least in Donostia, is the best season of the year to die. "When summer's run its course, and we feel hard winter's cold fingers, and it's too long to wait for spring."

SHE TURNS LEFT OFF LEGAZPI onto Peñaflorida Kalea to walk back along the river to the station, but she has time to spare and sits down on a bench in Okendo Plaza to continue reading the story. There's not much left. With a little regret, she admits, she sees that the television presenter does not appear again, and she notices that the scenes from the beginning of the book in which the man in front of the mirror is reflecting on his own decline are repeated again, him mawkishly imagining his own death, enjoying feeling sorry for himself even though he knows it's a pathetic thing to do, and there are a few flashes of irony throughout the text. It isn't wonderful. Before she continues reading, and peeking to see what the conclusion is, her heart misses a beat, and she almost drops the sheets of paper onto the ground when she sees that the narrative ends with a long letter to Flora Ugalde. She closes her eyes, takes a deep breath, and stays like that, immobile, trying not to cry, building up strength to be able to read the letter that serves as an epilogue.

My darling Flora,

I didn't take your call, because I didn't want to see you, or, more exactly, because I didn't want you to see me in the state I was in, crying my eyes out, plunged deep in self-pity. And I preferred to say what I wanted to say in writing—we get tangled up in words, Flora. The thing is, when you turned up shortly afterward, I imagined you'd called to check if I was at home or not, and you didn't come to see me, you came because you thought I wasn't there. I held my breath when I realized you were at the library door, ready to tell you that you'd caught me right in the middle of a sentence. How many times have I told you I'm writing? And your reasons for interrupting have always seemed trivial to me. Right in the middle of a sentence. What does that sound like? Stuck in the middle of a storm, or in the middle of a tunnel. In fact, you very seldom ever interrupted me while I was writing, and you didn't this time, either. You tiptoed away. I went on writing for the sake of it, writing without having anything to say, thinking that perhaps I'd suddenly get the tone right and what might be the last sentence would come out. I was moved by your silence and by your going upstairs to the bedroom. You were folding your clothes on the bed with an open suitcase next to you, and it seemed a very intimate scene to me. That really was an ending to something, and I felt the urge to write. "I saw her folding her clothes and putting them into a suitcase." I couldn't tear myself away, I was as fascinated as ever to watch the ease and perfection with which you fold things. Like a shop assistant. I know the technique, you've shown me a thousand times, but I never manage to get the row of buttons to end up in the middle. I was about to say that to you when you realized I was there, but all we did was look at each other. I hurried out of the room before you could say anything to me, because I remembered that I hadn't cleaned the bathroom after emptying my catheter. I had to go right in the middle of a sentence, to put it that way, and what's more, I won't deny that I took a sort of pleasure in letting myself go in my own rotting. I didn't know whether to go back to the bedroom or not, I thought it was going to be hard for me not to mention my condition, and that doing so might seem like an unscrupulous attempt to keep you by my side in order to keep me company until the end. So I went downstairs to the living room and turned on the radio. They gave the weather forecast for the whole of the film festival—although pointing out that predictions more than two days into the future aren't very trustworthy—saying there was a high-pressure system over the Azores and that could mean sunny weather for the next ten days. I wanted to start crying again, and I needed you to leave me alone so that I could. So I did everything I could think of to let you know that I wanted you to go, throwing some sheet music onto the table and saying it was yours for you to take, and some books, including Woolf's *The Waves*, though we never agreed if it was yours or mine. You looked at me sadly and said, "One day, later on, we'll talk," and I agreed. I got through the night as best I could and cleaned myself thoroughly this morning. I write this sentence and my body pushes me to continue and set down the following: "So the women don't have to." I can't help it, right now my narcissism is more present than ever, and now, when I'm about to become a corpse, I'm envious of those bodies wrapped in white for burial, surrounded by women dressed in black veils, dabbing perfumed oil on themselves, and grieving people, sobbing and crying out loud. You can laugh. I've decided to hold back my morbid fantasies, because I know there's nothing you find more revolting than people letting themselves go. And you can laugh again. I remember one moment when I was writing, carried along by a feeling of fascination at the idea of my own decomposition, and you were reading the book by that friend of Frisch who decides to let himself die of cancer and who spent the nine months he went on living—exactly the time a pregnancy lasts—writing down his reflections and experiences. You made a lot of sarcastic comments. You read me one passage in which he and Frisch, who's gone to visit him at his house in Ticino, are throwing the meat from his freezer out onto the mountainside—I don't know if that was very ecological—because it all rotted during a power outage. His friend realizes that soon, he's going to be the one rotting, and he knows that Frisch is thinking the same thing, he can see it in his eyes. (You said that there was nothing original whatsoever in what you called that morbid pleasure—anyone who's gotten beyond the level of chimpanzees, however dumb they may be, knows that one day they're going to be rotten meat, but they don't go around telling people about it.) So let me say that I've taken my time in the shower because I've been thinking of you, remembering some other times when I took an especially long time in there, just in case—it was something we hardly ever arranged beforehand—our bodies were going to come together later on, and that possibility made me feel that this broken-down, ready-for-burial body of mine was healthy and beautiful. I started moving away from you a long time ago, not wanting you to realize. Now it's solitude I want, because I'm afraid I won't be able to face up to it, that I'll cry pitifully, terrified and begging for a delay that's impossible, making you suffer and lose your patience. (I remember I once read that Gayarre, the tenor, lived in a state of constant mortification as a result of the public's negative view of his acting ability, and when he was about to leave this life, agonizing on his deathbed, he said, "Let's see them say now that I don't know how to pull of dying.") It's true that everyone dies with some sort of dignity, we do what we can, "*on fait comme on peut,*" as Beckett would have put it. When you said "finish that fucking novel once and for all," I pretended to be hurt, but I wasn't. My literature isn't the type you like, but I know you respect it. That's one way to put it. You'd respect my work just as much if I made matchstick models of the Eiffel Tower and other structures, or if I collected butterflies. What you hate is that my writing or not being able to write—because, in fact, it's that, too—has sucked up my life and put limits on yours at the same time. You resigned yourself to it, because you thought there was no alternative, just like one of those women, obvious differences aside, who sneak drugs into prison for their husbands when they're in there. I could have told you that. I find it painful to have renounced so many things, everything, in fact. But I didn't tell you. It occurred to me that I could take the sheet music out of your bag and tell you to fill it instead with whatever you'd need to spend a few days together in Sicily. It was no more than a fleeting idea, of course. I feel I don't have any strength, and I can't help remembering the journey Frisch and his dying friend went on to Egypt, and their journey back in a Swiss rescue plane, a drainage tube in his mouth and two nurses to look after him. It wasn't a good idea.

I'm all right. I've always thought that man's least noble trait and also his most valuable one is being able to adapt. We get used to all sorts of horrors. When we hear about some misfortune—the rape and murder of a child, let's say—we wonder how the parents can deal with the suffering. How is it they don't throw themselves out a window, unable to deal with the suffering? It isn't a matter of going on living, but choosing the right tie for the shirt, waiting for your change when you go out to buy bread, thinking ahead so as not to get caught out in the rain. Things you just do. Even knowing myself to be condemned, I've carried on living fairly normally, even enjoying wonderful moments, things I never even noticed previously. On many occasions, such as when that long-tailed bushtit perches on the windowsill—and please excuse me if I get corny, but this is how I see it—I've felt peaceful, if not overflowing with happiness (with the help of some valium, I have to admit), and I've tried to convince myself that when it comes down to it, even if we don't know the exact date, everyone has their final day; it's a matter of enjoying the moment without getting melancholy about it.

It's also true that hope—and the ability to create false hope—is as infinite as our ability to adapt to things; but I've gotten that under control, too. I no longer have fantasies about getting a call from the hospital to say there was a mistake in the diagnosis, or that there's some miraculous new medicine. I've gotten over that phase.

I'd read a lot about death, but I didn't know anything about it. The only death I've ever seen was my paternal grandfather's. He was a prolific smoker of Gener cigarettes, and he spent three days struggling to breathe, inhaling with incredible difficulty, and his snoring, which alternated with an exhaled whistling noise, made all of us at his bedside extremely anxious. (We had to take turns holding his oxygen mask up to his face, because the rubber straps cut into his skin, and sometimes I wished he would die. One night when we were alone, it occurred to me that I could suffocate him with the pillow, and I'm sure that all of us who took turns with him thought of something like that at some point; it's tough seeing somebody who there's absolutely no hope for suffering like that, and we were tired of that lacerating wait. It was so absurd to be waiting there for death, and so natural to want it to happen. On what was to be my last turn, the oxygen mask fell off all of a sudden, and he looked at me with his small, lidless, almost pupiless eyes, clear and penetrating, and said, "This is so long." For him and for all of us, I thought.) Having gone through that, I couldn't stand the idea, if it ever came to that, of anybody getting impatient because I was taking too long to die, and you've always found my slowness irritating; you're quicker than me, more determined, livelier than me, and I'm sorry about getting distracted by reflections like this. Sometimes I still can't stop melancholy from taking ahold of me, and I enjoy giving myself up to the feeling that I'm seeing something for the last time—somebody, you'll probably know who, once said that it's as moving seeing things for the last time as it is seeing them for the first time—but at the same time, it's limiting living with that continual awareness that the end is near, it's like when you go shopping before going away for a while and you don't want to leave too many things in the fridge. Right at this moment, I'm thinking about how I'm never going to wear that new cashmere coat in the closet ever again, because it's for cold weather and I, of course, won't live to see another winter. I think that my things, all sorts of things—shoes, my watch, books on my bedside table—are starting to take on that worn-down, cold aura that comes with death. Speaking of that coat, I remember the first time I wore it, when we went to the Trueba Cinema. You were cold when we came out, I put it around your shoulders, and as you snuggled into it, you said it was soft. We weren't very happy. You'll remember the day if you put it on in front of the mirror, as I'm doing now, and perhaps you'll feel that cold I'm talking about, the cold that gets into dead people's clothes and, because of that, makes some people unable to ever wear them. I find it hard to be relaxed about this. Whether you like it or not, you realize in my situation that people are going to pay that special importance you pay to dead people's words to everything you say; people repeat with reverence and great mystery what the dead person said to them the last time they met on the street, even if what they said was completely trivial, and that's even more so in this case, in these words written down and left to you as my last words. In letters from people condemned to death, it isn't the passionate words of commitment to a noble cause or the conviction that a better world awaits us that most moves me, nor is it the words of love and consolation for those closest to them, or even words of forgiveness for those who condemned them to death and are now going to execute them—it's the practical messages that might seem so irrelevant just before death and that stem from simple, modest stoicism. (To give an example, I remember a letter from a soldier the night before he was going to be shot, reminding whoever he was writing to to pick up his jacket from the dry cleaners.) We've already talked about this. We both thought that in such a situation, you would have to think about something else. What am I thinking about? I'm not especially afraid. Even so, sometimes, in some random situation, when I least expect it, I feel a blow of anxiety, like struggling for air, but it doesn't last long. And from time to time, I get angry. I sometimes wonder, when I see an old person or somebody who looks bad, why they aren't the person in my situation. But I don't let myself think about things like that for long, because they're unhealthy, they dirty me and don't do me any good. I feel better—really good, in fact—when I find myself feeling noble things; when it comes down to it, we're just a bunch of poor wretches who are designed to be good. I'm also impossibly senti-mental given my situation, and I start crying at anything. A cloud, flowers, birdsong—as I've told you. Suddenly, when I'm doing whatever it is, I realize I want to cry. To let myself cry softly, tears streaming down my cheeks, doing nothing to stop myself, or to sob out loud with my mouth wide open, like children do to show that they're crying. (This very morning, when you were playing Ravel's *Pavanea*, I was about to make a show of myself, I promise you I was, and I had to run to the bathroom to be able to cry as I wanted to.) But I wouldn't like my words to seem particularly important just because of the situation in which I'm writing them. I have the clear feeling that I'm going to die far from the god of my religion; it's easier for me not to believe in that frightening god and his threats of eternity. I can assure you that for somebody who had that fear forced on him, it's a consolation to feel you're not going anywhere. Another unquestionable fact is that if I had to choose between a forecast death and a sudden one, I'd prefer the former. I know you wouldn't, and that it irritates you to hear that death is something worth experiencing and things like that—we've read a thousand quotes about that—because you think it's foolish and mystical. You usually say the best thing would be to up and die, just like that, and I'm not so sure. But now, sure that my death is near, I experience some moments with greater intensity, as I've told you before, with greater awareness, because I'm more sensitive to some things—happily, you could say—and on the other hand, I pay less attention to some other things, or no attention at all. It's a pity not to have been able to do that before, but it's probably impossible without the knowledge my situation brings with it. And that's not all. Death's also a relief for somebody like me who's always been afraid of it, of when it'll happen—here it is at last—if you have the consolation of having lived, having loved, and having been loved. I'm in debt to you for that. Finally, a forecast death gives you the chance to make practical arrangements that seem more important to you than in other circumstances. (I could write so many silly things now, using the metaphor of Malone's fingers hardly being able to pick up the worn-down pencil.) So that's what I'm doing, sorting out practical matters. Not much about my corpse. I used to tell you I wouldn't even care if you threw it into the trash, and I don't have much to add to that—whatever's easiest within the law. The only thing I would like to ask, if I can, is that my body not be put on display at a funeral parlor and for it to be kept instead at the hospital for whatever period of time it has to be, far from sight. I know it shouldn't matter to me, but, then, our sense of dignity brings out stupid worries like that. I left my will with the notary a long time ago. So the only thing remaining is what to do with my papers. Somebody said—you're bound to know who—that death opens up the deceased's secret drawers. I have one in the bookshelf with the Diderot and D'Alambert *Encyclopédie*, and I'm leaving it open. There isn't much in it, and what there is isn't of much interest to anybody else, and I don't want anyone to get ahold of it. I tried to get rid of it myself, but I felt the same dizziness I did on those dawns when I went out onto the balcony and wondered if I'd be capable of throwing myself off. I wanted to have it all with me until the last moment, and that moment doesn't arrive until we're completely dead. Be kind to my memory, and burn all the photos and letters in the orange files. There is one thing, a poem written on a little florist card, which is yours. (I don't know why I've kept it. Why do some people keep their kidney stones and gallstones once they've been removed? At last I can look at it without losing my temper. Until recently, every time I felt I was drifting away from you, I would get it out of the drawer in order to confirm, from the anger I would feel on reading "you are more loyal than anybody," that my wound was still open and, therefore, that I still loved you. Perhaps it's because of that supposed usefulness that I never gave it back to you, believing that my childish, possessive nature was a measure of my love for you. Now, finally, I know that if that card shows anything, it's that you're independent from me, able to lead your own life, nothing more than that. It's yours, and I'm giving it back to you.) I've thrown away things I've written. Several short stories, many of them unfinished, sketches for novels, many first chapters of novels later abandoned, diary entries, notes—and my thoughts; don't laugh—which, I suppose, might provide clues about how I write and a few relevant biographical details. I printed everything out before erasing it, so that I could burn it and allow myself the melancholy ceremony of watching my work burn.

I cried, all joking aside, because it took a lot of effort to write every shitty line of it, and because the flue in the library chimney was blocked. I thought you might find it hard to do if you ever had to, as we've discussed, and I know you would have kept your promise. You believed me when I told you that was what I wanted, and the loyalty you feel toward the will of the dead is stronger than your faith in how important my literature might be for the world. To an extent, I think I found it humiliating to see how quickly and undoubtedly you accepted my request. But not much. I know well that what you feel for me goes beyond what the value of my work might be, and that that would be the case even if any of it were up to Kafka's standard. But now, come to think of it, I wonder whether—to the extent to which you've come to hate this obsession of mine that's kept me so distant from life, and from you, too—I might have stolen what would have been for you the pleasure of seeing that obsession's pathetic harvest burn. I don't think so. If one of those vultures that appear to open dead writers' drawers before the coffin lids are even closed over the authors' dead bodies ever turns up, you can feel free to tell him that we watched my novel and diaries turn into ash in the flames together. That's the truth: I like the idea of leaving a trail of smoke in people's memory, of making myself eternal in the way Kafka apparently wanted to—didn't Virgil himself want to burn *The Aeneid*? —adding my modest flame to everything that got burned in the library at Alexandria, Aeschylus' tragedies, Carlyle's *The French Revolution*, and Gogol's *Dead Souls*, "leaving blank pages so people can dream about the stories that could have been."

THERE ARE STILL LOADS OF PEOPLE milling around the María Cristina Hotel and the Victoria Eugenia *Antzokia*—the theatre where the film festival is held—and walking past the bench Julia's sitting on. People talking, excited at the prospect of the night ahead, some walking so close that she has to tuck her legs in to not trip them, cigarette smoke and names from the world of cinema left floating in the air. "She's not as good as Natalie Wood in *Splendour in the Grass*," somebody says. She immediately remembers: *We will grieve not, rather find / Strength in what remains behind; / In the primal sympathy / Which having been must ever be.* She had to translate it into Basque in that workshop with the young semi-poet who'd been left nameless, and they were unable to find a good equivalent for "sympathy," which is always badly translated. In the primal sympathy. Understanding each other, reciprocity, communion, sharing feelings, true, but especially sharing sadness and anxiety. A young man with glasses on stops to look at her, as if wanting to ask her something, and she realizes she's started crying without caring one bit, "obscenely" abandoning herself to tears, as Martin puts it, letting the tears fall down; she feels them going down her cheeks.

It seems a film's about to start; somebody says, "We're late." People seem to be in more of a hurry, some are now running in their hunger for stories, with no time to lose, and a few look at her as they go past, wondering who she is, as if wanting to know what her story is. *A woman sitting on a bench with a manuscript in her lap.* She hears sentences in Catalan and in English. *"A woman crying."* She wonders what she would answer if somebody—one of the journalists, critics, filmmakers, or script writers with Zinemaldia accreditations around their necks—stopped and came up to her to ask her why she's crying. So why is she crying? Because of Faustino Iturbe's death, and because Martin will stop writing because of that death, and because she's had a lot to do with all of that. Because it's an ending. Putting her books, sheet music, and the first articles of clothes she happened to grab into bags was no mere gesture, no mere cry for his attention—not at all, her wish to leave him was firm, in fact, *wish* isn't even the word, it was an absolute need, but now she realizes, after reading that epilogue in the form of a letter, that there's no going back from it, and she feels an incredible vacuum, an awful feeling of pain. So she's crying because she's alone, completely alone, she doesn't have a house, Zigor is about to be fifteen, and she's started getting old, at best she'll be condemned to translating *The Official Gipuzkoa Bulletin* into Basque for the rest of her life, and she doesn't have anywhere to play the piano.

So they're selfish tears.

The street lights have come on, flickering, fine gold-colored light opening up in the blue dusk. She's calmer after crying, and before heading off, she decides not to let herself be taken over by feelings of self-pity and guilt again and, once and for all, to separate Faustino Iturbe and Flora Ugalde's lives from her real life, as Martin always used to ask her to when she reproached him for using their intimate moments to base his stories on.

IT ISN'T BY CHANCE that she sits down across from a young woman reading a book in the half-empty carriage. She normally sits next to or, if possible, across from somebody reading. With a few exceptions —apart from backpacking English or American boys—they're mostly women, and young, like the reader sitting across from her now. She doesn't know exactly why she does it. She thinks it must be to make sure she gets agreeable company, people of her own style, and in any case, people who are quiet. The girl can't be much more than twenty, and of course, she's a student. Julia gathers that from the folder on her lap, probably full of notes, and the book she's reading is on top of it. She's reading with great concentration and hardly looks up when Julia sits down; her hand is raised in readiness to pass onto the next page. Julia can't see what the book is, the cover's resting against the file. That's another habit of hers, wanting to see what her neighbor's reading, and it's led to angry looks from time to time. Some readers protect their intimacy fiercely. Even so, it usually isn't hard for her to see what book it is, because it's normally a current best seller. She rarely has the satisfaction of seeing that it's a classic— once, she sat down in front of a young woman, almost a girl, very pretty, and when she saw she was reading Montaigne's *Essays,* she almost wanted to hug her—or one of her own favorite writers, or

693

a book in Basque. The book titles are usually a disappointment. The girl closes her book and looks at Julia for a moment—without actually seeing her, Julia thinks—with a slight smile on her face just before turning toward the window. She closes her book from right to left, and even though she keeps her short-nailed fine hands on the back cover, Julia sees she's reading Martin's *Maitasunak eta penak—Love and Sorrows*. It's a worn-out copy with a library label on it. Julia's incredibly glad and feels an irresistible wish to ask her if she likes it. She doesn't know how to, and when the girl looks away toward the window, probably because she's seen Julia looking at her, she decides to be direct "Do you like it?" she says, leaning toward her, almost whispering, in a confidential tone, and the girl says she does, not seeming surprised by the question, underlining her response by nodding. Then, showing Julia the cover, she asks if she, too, has read it. "A long time ago." She doesn't know why she mentions that. "And did you like it?" Yes, she says, and she, too, nods. She liked it a lot. The girl says it was a recommendation from her literature teacher, but that they don't always hit the mark in terms of her taste. So it's the teacher's job to guess students' tastes, not to help them to develop their own? The girl laughs. They're at Txominenea already, and Julia is anxious to know what she thinks about the book, wants to know more, what exactly it is that she likes about it, and why. The girl, on the other hand, looks calm and relaxed; she's obviously not getting off at the next stop. She smiles when she says it's incredible how well the author understands women. "Doesn't he?" She adds with conviction, "The way he knows women's souls." After an initial moment surprise, her eyes wide open, Julia instinctively covers the mole on her neck, so that the girl won't connect her with Flora Ugalde, about whom the girl says, "Sometimes she doesn't seem very understanding".

"Is that what you think?"

"Sometimes she's very hard on him. She doesn't realize that creative people suffer a lot."

"But he's pretty mean." Julia's talking about Faustino Iturbe, of course. "What do you think about him when he puts Mercurochrome in the lavatory to frighten Flora and blackmail her emotionally?"

"I don't know. But he loves her, and maybe he feels she's distant."

Unfortunately, they're going past the prison, and Julia's not going to have time to give her own point of view.

"You know the expression in Spanish about how some love kills—'*hay amores que matan*'—of course?" she has no choice but to summarize as she stands up.

The girl nods.

"That's true—there's no future for the couple. But it's a fine book —sad, but very good."

They don't have time to say any more.

WHEN JULIA GETS OFF THE TRAIN, she only takes two steps, just enough to move away from the edge of the platform. She lifts her hand up to say goodbye to the girl, who does the same thing. They never told each other their names, but she hopes, as she sees the palm of her hand pressed against the window while the train begins moving away, that they'll run into each other again. She's amazed to feel that it's as if the train has suddenly taken away the anxiety she'd been feeling in her chest. Instead of crossing the road, she goes straight up the slope toward Martin's house, wanting to see him as soon as possible, not leaving it for tomorrow as she had intended. The cats come up to the iron gate to welcome her. They meow as they rub against her legs. "Without getting tied up in words," as Martin wrote. She doesn't have to think twice about opening the iron gate. The shutters are closed, but that doesn't put her off. *You know what?* She's decided that's going to be the first thing she says to him when she sees him. And he'll stare at her, distrustful, his blue eyes sticking out. She laughs as she thinks of it, and she realizes that happiness is what she's feeling now. Just that, "You know what?" she'll ask him. She laughs as she remembers how just a while before, she was thinking of getting out a pen and paper to write a script for her meeting with him. It wouldn't be the first time. In a course they took once at work, they were told that you shouldn't go into a meeting without a script, and still less so without being very clear about what your objective is. Usually when she speaks with Martin, she knows what her objective is, knows more or less, even if not completely, what she wants to get out of it, but now she knows how to start, and she says to herself that that's the most important thing and that it's better this way, with a conviction whose origin she isn't quite sure of, and that firm belief makes her quicken her step, almost run, to start their encounter as soon as possible; she wants to see Martin, she has a light heart as she goes through the garden. (The garden, in fact, doesn't look that bad to her, rather the opposite—there are pretty areas of flowers, thanks to Lynn, in the middle of all that elegant decline.)

Where on earth is Lynn?

At some places in the gravel, there are parallel tracks from the suitcase the fat American woman dragged along it.

SPLENDOR IN THE GRASS. It turns out she does have an objective: whatever decision they finally come to, she wants the memory of their affection to survive. But for that to happen, first of all she has to ask him "You know what?" And then, as he looks at her with his eyes wide open, distrustful, and probably afraid, she'll tell him what happened on the train, that she saw a girl reading a book, catching her at that precise moment when we finish it, close it, and get that lost, dreamy look in our eyes. The girl was very pretty, and the book was *Loves and Sorrows*. And she thought what she'd just read was sad, but very beautiful, too. Those are the words she's going to use, *sad but beautiful*, or perhaps *sad and beautiful* would be better, or maybe *sad and moving*; *extremely moving* is the way to describe *The Man in Front of the Mirror*, and she's quite sure that this work—she doesn't want to call it a short story—is the end of a period and, at the same time, announces his revival as a writer. She's sure that after this introduction, they'll be able to organize the matter of splitting up in the most amicable way possible.

She's determined to make him see that above all, the most important thing is for him to keep writing.

SHE ONLY HAS TO PUSH the door to open it, it's still unlocked. Inside there's a slight smell of burning. There's nobody in the living room, and her bags are still next to the umbrella holder. There's nobody in the kitchen. Complete silence in the hallway apart from the clock's ticking and the sound of her steps on the floorboards. At the foot of the staircase, she doesn't hear any sound from the upper floor, either. She goes back toward the entrance and then tiptoes along the hallway to the formal library. It's the second time in a short while that she's been reminded of *Murders in the Wax Museum*. That moment when the girl scratches the head of the figure that looks like her disappeared friend with her index finger and a bit of real skin comes off. She tells herself she's just frightening herself, like a hysterical child, and moves forward in the half-light, trying to walk normally. Although there's no sign that there's anybody inside, she's startled to think that Martin could be in there. The short whistle of a train passing through the station without stopping. She waits with her hand on the doorknob for a few seconds, holding her breath, listening to the silence that's spreading out, the ticking of the clock once more the only thing she can hear, but now it seems quicker to her, in time with the rapid heartbeats she feels in her throat. Finally, she decidedly opens the door and finds complete darkness and a strong smell of burning. Then, after turning the light on, she finds herself surrounded by clouds of smoke circling slowly upward from the fireplace to the ceiling. Most of the doors to the drawers in the lower part of the bookcases are open. There are sheets of paper all over the floor, magazine cuttings, white and colored index cards— most of the colored ones are mauve and green. A few photos. There are ashes in the fireplace, which she has never seen in use and probably doesn't even have a working flue, burned black sheets of paper, slightly twisted, and irregularly shaped bits of white paper that haven't been fully burned. Thick piles of paper at the sides of the fireplace that seem, at a glance, to be printed on, giving the idea that something has stopped him from completing his burning. She recognizes a photo of herself when she was young, sixteen or seventeen, hugely amplified, on the blue embossed leather table he uses when he shuts himself in to write. It must be eight by twelve inches. She'd forgotten about it. The original photo wasn't a very good quality one to start with, and it's become hazy with the amplification. She's wearing a white turtleneck sweater and a corduroy suit, walking along a path in a pinewood toward the person taking the photo. She looks clumsy. She has a book in her right hand, and she's holding a guitar by its neck in her left hand, leaning forward as if ready to hit somebody with it. Although the photo's taken from in front of her, you see her face in profile, partly covered by her hair, as if she were trying to escape the lens. It shows her clumsiness, her shyness, and the fact that she's reserved, and her beauty, too. It's years since she last saw the photo, the original of the one amplified here, and she doesn't recognize the place where it was taken, or even remember who took it. Picking it up, she sees a small Villa Flores envelope below it, the one that young man sent to her office along with the roses on her birthday. Not that many years have gone by, but it seems to her like something from a long time ago. Her workmates teased her, wanting to know who'd sent the flowers, the name of that young man who she doesn't know what to call, who she soon grew to hate, even though he wasn't to blame, because she suffered so much as a result of that short relationship she had with him. "I feel you alive in this springtime you've brought back to life with me." Still now, even though her mind says she shouldn't, she feels guilty for having accepted the caring, pleasant company of that romantic, sentimental young man who, like her, had the afternoons free, for that disagreeable situation that was best not mentioned. Martin knew only too well how to punish her for it. "Oh you, friend of the sun, loyal, more loyal than anyone to your red moon instinct." He used to laugh as he recited it. "Oh you, friend of the sun," he used to call out. "Did you really need this trash?" Flora Ugalde had begged him on her knees not to be cruel, not to spoil her story. Perhaps she herself begged, too. She doesn't want to remember.

Suddenly she thinks she hears a bang from the upper story, she isn't sure. She heads to the staircase, tries to go up normally, not wanting to startle Martin if he's in bed, but she also tries not to make any noise, in case he's asleep. The bedroom door's wide open, and inside, because the shutters don't fit perfectly, rays from the powerful streetlamp down by the riverside come in and mix with the half-darkness, giving enough light for her to see Martin and Harri side by side, both of them dressed, on top of the bedcover. She takes a step backward, revolted by what she's seen. Perhaps that's too strong a word, but she can't think of a better way to say what she's feeling. Struggling to recover from her fright as she goes back toward the stairs, she tries to work out what's behind that feeling. She stands still when she hears one of them put a foot on the floorboards. She doesn't want to run away. She doesn't want to go down the stairs like some indignant woman who's been cheated on. So she waits. She has to wait for longer than expected, and that gives her time to figure out why what she saw affected her so much—it was because they were both fully dressed on the bed, shoes and everything, like in the scene described by Simone de Beauvoir when Sartre is lying in the hospital room and she asks the nurses to leave them alone and then lies down and falls asleep beside him until the nurses come back in and cover Sartre's corpse with a sheet. It's at the end of *La cérémonie des adieux*. She realizes, leaning there against the wall, that she's both loved and hated that book at different times. Harri sticks her head out the door. Only her head comes out of the room, as if she were deciding whether to step into the hallway or not, as if she were afraid of doing so. Finally, she does step out, but she doesn't move any closer toward Julia. She leans against the wall, her hands behind her back. Julia has the photo of herself as a girl and the poem from her literature workshop friend in her hands. "Oh you, friend of the sun."

"It isn't what it looks like," says Harri, and even though Julia knows there's no irony in her words, she finds it funny. It makes her laugh. "How original," she says. As they walk down the stairs, Harri puts a hand on her shoulder, which she rejects by moving to one side. She's decided to take her bag and leave in a hurry, but now Harri is holding her arm forcefully. She's blurting the words out. She came back from Bilbao, completely depressed, and had to talk with somebody, that's why she came over; the front door was open, she came in and called out, but nobody answered; then she went up to the bedroom and saw him lying still on the bed, as if he were dead, and she thought that the worst had happened, she even put her finger under his nose to check whether he was breathing, and then he opened his mouth to say that he was all right, he was fine, and she looked as if she'd come from being in a much worse situation than him. She lay down beside him, and there they remained, side by side, until they fell asleep. That's all.

"Lying on the bed with your shoes on and everything."

That's what Julia says, though she doesn't know why. She knows it doesn't make any sense, and Harri looks at her as if she's crazy. "He's really doing very badly," she murmurs after a short pause, in a tone which couldn't sound more afflicted, and Julia's heart misses a beat when she realizes she means he's very sick.

"What's wrong with him?"

"He told me he's stopped writing and he's burned all his work. Do you realize what that means?"

She has both hands on her cheeks, like in Munch's *Scream*.

Julia is about to tell her that Rome could burn as far as she's concerned, when the writer who's stopped writing appears at the top of the stairs. He looks as if he's just woken up, his scarce hair is in a mess, electrified. He asks what's happening, and then, as if he's just realized that Julia is there, says, "I didn't think you were going to come back." She doesn't know what to answer. She would pick up the keys and throw them down on the table in anger, but she doesn't have them on her, she left them in her purse on the dresser along with Zigor's presents. She still has the photo and the Villa Flores envelope in her hand. Harri touches one of her cheeks with her fingertips and takes a step backward like an automaton. Then she says, "You two have to talk," and she makes to leave the house. She stays at the door for a long while, looking from one to the other, as if wanting to say something more before she leaves, but in the end, she opens the door and leaves without saying a word.

Julia would like to do the same thing, but Martin makes a gesture to her, and she obeys, waiting at the bottom of the stairs for him to come down. When he reaches her, he says he didn't expect her back so soon. She remembers the girl on the train, and the fact that it was the desire to tell Martin what the girl said that brought her back. "You know what?" The smoke has come into the living room, too, and she uses the photo as a fan. He holds his hand out for her to give it to him. Julia hesitates. She takes the Villa Flores envelope in her left hand and holds the photo out to him in her right hand. Martin smiles as he looks at it with concentration. "You're still the same," he says. Another pause. "You've still got everything that made you attractive then. And all the bad things, too—you're obstinate and abrupt." He's still smiling. And then, "It looks like you're going to hit somebody with the guitar," and he laughs out loud. She laughs, too, because she'd just been thinking the same thing. Quietly, she asks him where he got it from, not wanting to remain in silence and preferring a neutral subject. "You look really good," he says, without paying any attention to her. Julia doesn't like having her photo taken and seldom smiles in them. But she is smiling in this one, if only slightly. Martin turns the light on to see it better. He continues looking at the photo in silence, but shaking his head, as if noticing something strange in it. "It's remarkable how you're still the same girl as you were then," he says eventually. There's a flicker of affection in his eyes. You didn't know me when I was young, Julia says once more. She isn't comfortable like that and turns away, not knowing where to look, without realizing that he's looking at the Villa Flores envelope until he points at it with his chin. "That's yours, and I couldn't burn it." The smile on his lips is still playful. Julia knows what's coming next, she feels a slight throbbing in her ears, pressure on her temples and on the nape of her neck. She doesn't want to hear him start reciting with emphatic diction "I feel you alive in this springtime you've brought back to life with me. Oh you, friend of the sun," and as if doing so might silence him, she tears the little envelope with the card inside it into two pieces, but she can't tear it again, so she squeezes the two bits in her hand, hesitating over whether to throw them in his face or not, and he covers his face with both hands in an expression of horror. "But how could you destroy such a wonderful poem?" he says.

Julia tells him not to start again. She doesn't know why she throws the pieces of paper into the air rather than putting them in her pocket, and Martin bends over to pick them up carefully.

They hear the nun's tin bell ringing—eight rings after the first one, nine altogether, or perhaps ten. Martin is kneeling down and piecing the card together again. "Why does that idiot say 'you who are more loyal than anybody' when you were cheating on me?" And he looks genuinely put out. "You should ask him," she replies sharply. She feels a strong urge to cry, whether from anger or sorrow she does not know. He's forced her to hate the poor guy who wrote that silly poem. What else could she do? Holding onto the side of the table, he finds it hard to get up; when he does, he takes a few steps toward the window, in which she sees his figure reflected.

"I wanted to tear it up a thousand times, but I never could."

She sees him against a shiny dark-blue background. He talks slowly, as if what he had to say was tiring. "Everything I write is to reach the moment where I get to tear up that card up and embrace you, happy because you're happy to be with me." He turns toward Julia, and she takes a step backward, warily. They stand still, facing each other but four steps apart, until the phone suddenly rings.

Julia's glad the call's put an end to the scene. Then she's disappointed when she sees him go to pick up.

It's one of his sisters. It's easy for Julia to tell—he spends at least a minute with the receiver to his ear without saying a word, moving nervously in his armchair as he listens to the person on the other end of the line speaking. It's always like that. Then, seeing him nodding continually, and getting very angry, saying that Ane's already told him, it's obvious it's his other sister, the one in Paris, who's talking to him about their parents' quarrel. It's clear she's asking him to take measures to sort things out, because he's protesting, saying things like "What do you want me to do?"; "It's easy to say that from Paris"; "I'm doing everything I can"; and "I'm tired, too." He sounds sarcastic, aggressive, and pitiful in turn, but there's no question that making people feel sorry for him is his forte. Now it's mostly he who's talking, as the depressed brother. He repeats the same sort of things at regular intervals—he's completely exhausted, really tired—silently groaning between lament and lament until he reaches the end of his repertoire, and then, seriously and sadly but slowly and calmly, he says, "I've thrown everything I've ever written onto the fire."

He's sitting with a leg over one of the chair's arms, apparently indifferent to Julia's presence, and she decides to leave. She does up her jacket and straightens her skirt as a way of saying that she's leaving. She goes back toward the dresser by the door, looking for some sign that his conversation might be about to end, but in vain. She makes another meaningful gesture—taking out the keys and leaving them on top of the television. Finally, the writer who's just thrown his complete works into the fire raises his open hand to ask her to wait. Ordering her to wait, perhaps. She isn't sure. He's looking down at the floor now, both feet on the ground, one hand holding the phone to his ear and the other open above his head. "Yes, I've burned it all—absolutely all of it," he says. He makes a short, emphatic pause between "all" and "absolutely all of it." For a moment, Julia wonders whether to pick the keys up again and throw them down on the glass table in front of the chair or not. She's afraid of breaking it. The writer who's fed all his work into the fire looks at her again as if not understanding what she's doing. It's a short look. He stands up straight and lowers his hand onto his chest. "You don't give me much help," he says, or moans, rather. And then, furious, "Do you know what I had to do to get that fucking suite at the María Cristina?" And again and again: "Do you know?"; "Do you?"; "Do you have any idea?"

Julia wonders once more whether to throw the keys down on the glass table. Finally, she leaves them on top of the dresser. She adjusts the bag strap on her shoulder, picks up the plastic bags with the presents in them, and opens the door. She bends down again to get the two travel bags with her things in them and lifts them up quite easily. She doesn't close the door after her.

She puts the bags down on the floor near the top of the stairs and runs the rest of the way up to the apartment when she hears the phone ringing. She's worried that something bad may have happened. She opens the door and rushes to the shelves in the entryway to answer before whoever it is hangs up.

"It's me." What her mother always says when she calls, the same old voice, sad and then cutting, more tired than usual, if that's possible. "Etxezar's burned down." Julia was scared she was going to say that something happened to Zigor; her mother must notice the relief in Julia's voice when she replies that she knew something like this was bound to happen one day, because she cuts her off: "You don't seem to care."

In fact, she doesn't care.

Martin calls her cell phone. She looks at his name until it disappears from the screen, which seems to take forever.

22

THE GYNECOLOGIST WHO'S OUT OF WORK AND OUT OF A SALARY is woken up by the sound of his wife in the bathroom, or at least it's she he first hears when he opens his eyes. She has an extensive repertoire, spanning all types of music, but even though she has a good ear, she doesn't know a single entire song. Today, *Maite* is what's accompanying her morning shower. As the day goes by, she'll go over the same song nonstop, repeating the one line she knows, "*Maite, eguzki eder, eguerdi beteko argia*"—Maite, beautiful sun, midday light—and humming the rest. He doesn't find that habit of hers irritating. Quite the opposite—he likes it, because it means she's in a good mood, although, to tease her, he asks if she can't put on another record, though it's usually she herself who complains that she can't get rid of the tune that's gotten into her head, blaming the habit—he thinks rightly—on her obsessive personality. He listens out to hear her intake of breath as she turns the cold water on at the end of the shower, which she always does, even if she's in a hurry. Recently she's often late, like today. He knows that from the sound of her putting the pots of lotion quickly back onto the glass shelf, and then because she walks to and fro along the hallway with the electric toothbrush, which is a sign that she's cleaning her teeth as she takes clothes out of the closet or does other tasks, raising the blinds or putting the breakfast things into the dishwasher.

Abaitua, after hesitating for a moment over whether to get out of bed or wait until she leaves the house, finally decides to make an appearance when Pilar's movements tell him that she's about to leave, so they'll have just enough time to say hello but not enough to talk. He gets out of bed when he hears her heels in the dressing room, throws his bathrobe on, and leaves the room. Pilar sticks her head into the hallway, smiles, and says good morning.

"How did it go?" She goes back into the bathroom without waiting for his reply, combing her wet hair energetically, leaning her head in the direction of the strokes. "I'm losing a lot of hair." She shakes her head and combs her fingers backward through her hair. He's seldom seen her use a hair dryer, and as always, he thinks she looks younger with her hair wet. Perhaps rather androgynous. A drop of perfume behind her ears, at the top of her breasts, and, pulling aside the elastic on her panties, at the top of her thighs, too. Sometimes she says "just in case" or "you never know," but not today. She looks at him with curiosity when she realizes he's looking at her. She puts on a gray skirt and is holding a sweater and a jacket over her arm, which, as usual, she'll put on in the elevator.

Her cell phone rings, and he watches her open her purse and pour the contents out onto the dining room table—several key rings with a lot of keys on them; wallets, at least two; agendas, at least two; packets of tissues; tubes of lotion; lip balm; and her vibrating phone.

He doesn't know exactly who she's talking to. There's no doubt it's a colleague, because of the technical words she's using to explain her projects for the clinic, but from a certain point onward, he has the impression that she's talking for him to hear, or at least that she's making use of her conversation with the unknown person to tell him the information, too. He doesn't know why he thinks that. Perhaps it's because she's talking louder than usual and she stays next to him rather than moving away with the phone, which is what she normally does. Whether he's right about it or not, thanks to her conversation with her unidentified colleague, he finds out that Urrutikoetxea is creating problems for the project—Abaitua thinks that this information, in particular, is for his benefit—and that she's hoping to convince him next Thursday or Friday at the meeting they're going to have in Bilbao. He has to admit he's a bit envious to see her so fully involved in her work; she has at least two operations that day, although she says what she finds toughest is management work. She says goodbye to the unknown person at the other end by saying that she has to go to her lawyer's to sort out some papers and that she's very late.

She puts her cell phone into her bag and then pushes everything spread out on the table in with her free hand. She almost dumps in a bunch of ornamental amber grapes, too. Then she looks at him for a while, as if wanting to see what he's made of her conversation, and Abaitua's only reaction is to put his hands on his hips and look as if he's in pain. It isn't completely false, but he certainly exaggerates it. He's still feeling the slight spasms he got on his last fishing trip with Kepa. He says, as he tightens the belt on his bathrobe, that he doesn't have many more sailing miles in him, and he goes back to the room that was once both of theirs and is now just his, sorry he didn't stay until Pilar left. "Is it as painful as all that?" She follows him into the room, grabs his shoulder from behind, and gently pushes him onto the bed. He protests, it's nothing, he'll get over it, but she tells him to let her take a look at it—"I'm a doctor." She makes him lie face down and then sits on top of him. Because her skirt is narrow, she has to roll it up almost to her waist. He would prefer to extract himself from that intimate situation and makes a movement to get away, says it's nothing and then, once more, that he'll get over it, but finally he lets her, and he feels the relief that the heat and movement of her hands bring his kidneys. He doesn't find the situation easy, but there's no sign that it's the same for Pilar. She sings today's song in a low voice as she massages him in a completely natural way. She's skillful with her hands. Abaitua gives in and tries to think of something to say, but nothing comes to mind. More precisely, he doesn't think it appropriate to say any old thing, and he doesn't think it's the best time to get into a deep conversation, either.

He's tempted to say that he'll go to Bilbao with her to try to convince Urrutikoetxea, who owes him a lot of favors. But why doesn't she ask him herself?

Then the phone rings, and she gets off him quickly to answer it. Now it's obvious they're calling her from the clinic. It isn't hard for him to work out that Orl and some other colleagues have canceled several scheduled operations and that her brother-in-law's walked out of the operating theater with the patient still waiting to be anesthetised and half the team standing there. They don't know what to do. Pilar shouts in anger. She's leaving home right now, she'll be right there, and nobody should leave. Then she calls her lawyer and quickly cancels their meeting. From the door, still smiling, she turns back to the suspended doctor, who's lying on the bed, and says, "There, you see."

After Pilar says "there, you see" and closes the door, he feels guilty about not having anything to do.

At one time, he used to enjoy being alone at home. He's always dreamed about having time to listen to the pile of un-listened-to records, to read the books he's long wanted to read once and for all, or, quite simply, to laze around, and now, now that he has the time, he feels like an adolescent on a Sunday afternoon. He can't deny that he reads less than he used to when he was working, and he doesn't listen to more music, either. The more time you have, the more time you waste, and wasting time makes him feel bad. A consequence of his upbringing. His mother could never stand him not doing anything. "*Zorria baino alferragoa*"—lazier than a flea, as the Basque saying for some reason goes—that might be the sentence she most used to repeat to him.

He tries to read a paper about the ethics of Cesarean sections. Should the increasing demand for the operation be given into? Why is it performed more in private hospitals than in public ones? Is it true that doctors, having lost the ability to carry out other fairly simple procedures, are performing Cesarean sections in an increasingly un-critical fashion? The rate of use for the operation has increased ten-fold since he's been working at the hospital. He finds the article's English difficult. He finds some authors easy to read in English and others difficult, but he doesn't know why. Sometimes he'd show Lynn the difficult texts, and it was a comfort that she said they were tough for her, too. He remembers she told him they must have been written in some sort of dense Scottish.

He remembers Lynn less than he thought he would, fortunately.

"*The core tenants that animate almost all ethical conversations in obstetrics are autonomy, beneficence, nonmaleficence, and justice.*"

The toast getting burned isn't a good sign.

In the shower, he decides that he'll tell Pilar he wants to go with her to Bilbao. He'd really like her to ask him to come along, to humbly admit that she could do with his help because of the influence he has over Urrutikoetxea, but he knows she can't ask him, and so he'll have to be the one to say he wants to go, saying he hasn't seen his friend for a long time. What's more, he's determined to behave in an agreeable way in Bilbao, as far as possible, to be cheerful and good company; he recognizes that normally, when they do something she wants to do, he can't resist responding like a spoiled child, showing that he's accepted in order to do her a favor, and the result is usually harmful, because he drives Pilar up the wall by being restless and pensive and looking bored.

Those *don't come if you don't feel like it*s, *I don't mind*s, and *don't complain later on*s they exchanged when the plan was to spend the day in Biarritz, and that brusque *you could have said you didn't want to come* and the uncomfortable silence that followed it at Miremonte, surrounded by old ladies, many of whom had poodles on their laps, were similar to his reaction that time she agreed to go fishing with him and he, expecting her to make that subtle gesture of bitterness at the side of her mouth, at her very first word about the boat rocking quite a lot, turned the bow back toward the port and put the engine on full speed to get back as quickly as possible. Neither of them has been generous enough, if it's a matter of generosity, when it comes to feeling happy while sharing in what the other one likes—he less so than Pilar, he admits. To being happy making each other happy, happy just to be spending time with each other, as Lynn would have been.

He gets a call from the hospital, he has to go in to sign some documents. The on-duty secretary is very kind—everyone's asked after him and wants him back. It may be arrogant of him, but Abaitua thinks she's telling the truth. He, too, is counting the days until he can go back to work, and that, at least, is true. He can't wait to get back to the hospital, because curing people is what he does best, he's proud of his clinical eye and glad to pass his knowledge on to the residents. (Though it's also true, if he looks at himself more critically, that he gets quite puffed up when he shows off that knowledge.)

MANY PEOPLE WELCOME HIM at the entrance; it takes him almost half an hour to get to the office, doctors and nurses keep on stopping him and saying they're behind him. They almost all say the same thing: you've been sanctioned while those incompetent, psychopathic killers—and many other names, besides—are free to do whatever they want. He knows, though, that nobody's protested publicly. Likewise, he suspects that they're also looking at him with curiosity and mistrust. And even some ill will. But he doesn't want to be paranoid—it's obvious people are on his side. Even the supervisor from his mother's hometown is affectionate when she greets him in her Otzeta Basque, offering him a coffee that's "better than that muck you get out of the machine." Soon there's a tight circle of nurses around him telling him the awful things Arrese's been doing, and of course, they also tell him about the child with choanal atresia—he's finally been operated on, but he's been left a complete vegetable. He tells them he doesn't want any of the managers to come across them talking with him, given his situation, in order to get away from them.

He decides to go the long way around to the secretary's office, in order not to pass by the library, where he could bump into Lynn if she's there, and on the way, he has to stop all the time to listen to the same words of criticism and support he's just heard. The biggest novelty is that the secretary, as soon as she sees him, jumps up from her desk in a way that's surprising for somebody of her weight and gives him two kisses. She looks very upset and even cries a little as she gives him his correspondence and the documents he has to sign, one of which is a sworn declaration not to make use of any clinical records. They must want to prevent him from looking into any suspicious clinical records so that he can't use them in any sort of suit against them.

On his way out, he hears somebody calling him. It's the fat resident running toward him. "*Qué tal*"—how are you—he says as a greeting, Abaitua says what he's told everyone else—he's enjoying his obligatory vacation—and the resident asks him if he knows anything about Lynn. He's more irritated than surprised to hear the question and almost asks how he should know but instead replies he doesn't know anything, he hasn't seen her for weeks. Apparently the resident doesn't know anything, either. She hasn't come to the hospital for a week, and then he keeps quiet, waiting for some explanation, with those wide-open eyes that make him look as though his tie's choking him.

He doesn't know anything, either, he repeats.

Abaitua notices Jaime Zabaleta coming out of the elevator behind the resident's huge body and takes advantage of his appearance to get away, raising up a hand to make himself seen. But he realizes he's gone from the frying pan into the fire when Zabaleta says, "What have you gone and done?" He's always ready to get a dig in, and he's always up on the latest. "You've been a naughty boy." It's hard to know whether he's smiling or whether his teeth just don't fit in his mouth. Then Zabaleta seems to realize that Abaitua isn't in the mood for jokes and starts grumbling to him about people bringing dishonor upon the profession and how useless they are compared with his, Abaitua's, professional behaviour and skill. Just like everybody else. Bored of the subject, he moves Zabaleta toward the exit while listening to him praising his professional standards and criticizing the terrible things that have been done to him, until the last thing he says stops Abaitua in his tracks: "And on top of it, they're saying you were drunk." Now it's clear that he is smiling, as he watches the effect his words have had.

"Didn't you know?"

He decides to lie. He knows, but he doesn't care what they say.

They reach the parking lot. Abaitua's amazed he isn't accompanied by his usual bodyguards and asks him if he's gotten rid of them, to change the subject. He has. He's fed up of the limitations their constant presence puts on his life, and bearing in mind how little ETA is doing these days, he's decided to be free of them. "Quote-unquote free," he says, wiggling his index and middle fingers in the air and showing off his large, solid teeth once more. Even so, he says, even though there isn't much of a risk, you're still always afraid.

"You know?"

Of course he does; even without being a significant person himself, he can't help looking under his car. He says yes, of course he understands.

They're standing next to his white Volvo. Zabaleta talks to him about politics, says he thinks the end of the violence is near. Some people want to turn the page as if nothing's happened, but some of the victims don't want to forget or accept any type of concessions. Abaitua doesn't pay much attention to him. He nods from time to time, unable to think of anything but the accusation that he turned up drunk at the hospital.

Abaitua opens his car door. He's curious about the last sentence he heard, but since he's lost track of what Zabaleta's been saying, he doesn't dare ask him to clarify, not wanting him to realize that he hasn't been listening. He just nods to show that he agrees and asks Zabaleta if he wants a lift.

Fortunately, he brought his own car.

He looks through the envelopes the secretary gave him before turning on the ignition. Only one of them draws his attention, because it's hard to the touch, it could be a CD case. He opens it and finds it is a CD—an album by Sarah McLachlan, *Surfacing*. There's another envelope with it, the size of half a sheet of paper. On the sleeve, the singer's eyes are closed, her face is almost in profile, somewhat to one side, one elbow resting on the back of the chair she's sitting on the wrong way around, that same forearm vertical, and the other one meeting it at ninety degrees, her head fitting perfectly into the U shape made by her arms, sepia on a black background; he thinks it reminds him of a well-known painting, but can't think what it is. Her name and the title—Sara McLachlan, *Surfacing*—are handwritten in that distinctively US script, which must be what they're taught at school and which is how Lynn writes, too. He's never seen the record before, but he has heard it. He gets the leaflet out of the case. It doesn't have the lyrics in it; there's a picture on each page and, above each one, the name of a song written in the same handwriting as on the sleeve, and the credits below. There are ten songs and, so, ten pictures. The seventh is titled *Angel*, and there's a naked man in the picture for it; he's well muscled and reminds Abaitua a little of da Vinci's *Vitruvian Man*, but with only two arms and two legs, his legs spread a little apart and his arms hanging down, a little away from his body. He has a bird's head and small wings, like a butterfly's. He puts the CD on. Then he fingers the envelope, wondering whether to open it or not. He folds it and puts it in his inside jacket pocket.

He remembers Lynn's enormous disappointment when she found out that the Bordeaux *Gloria Victis* angel's wings were pointing down in his memory, and how irritated and astonished he was that she, being such a rational person, could think such an insignificant thing so important; it was as if he'd told her she had only two months left to live. Although the truth is that since then, he can't believe he had any doubts about the wings. The normal, expectable thing was that they'd be open—they couldn't be any other way.

IN THE ARMS OF THE ANGEL / FLY AWAY FROM HERE / FROM THIS DARK, COLD HOTEL ROOM.

711

There were some moments when he thought that Lynn would be able to hold onto him, that she'd be able to get him away from Pilar. But he didn't feel capable of matching her level of love, and balance is necessary in relationships of love. He would have liked to be able to talk about that with Lynn. When she asked him if he still loved Pilar, he wasn't sure he could say he did. He wasn't at all sure. He's amazed not to feel pain as he thinks of Lynn. An uncomfortable but bearable feeling of guilt, no more than that.

When he sees the clinic's large slate roof, he realizes he's driving along the traffic-less old road to Martutene.

He crosses the bridge over the railway line slowly, goes past the train stop, and takes the road in the direction of Donostia. After around a hundred yards, after parking outside a block of apartments, he walks back to the train stop and goes up the little slope to the house. Once again, there's a bunch of shriveled flowers marking the spot where several construction workers were killed by a bomb going off, and he recalls how in many different European cities he's seen bunches of withered flowers tied in ribbons with the national colors at the feet of statues depicting generals on horseback and unknown soldiers.

All the blinds in the house are down, so he doesn't have to be careful. She told him she was going to spend a few days away, or a few weeks, perhaps even a few months, he doesn't remember. As if it all happened at long time ago. He ventures to go up to the iron gate. Nobody comes out to the garden. Two tabby cats are eating out of the same dish. For a moment he thinks he notices Lynn's presence, but it turns out it's just the branches moving on some bushes. He also hears a woman's voice, clear but distant; it could be Julia—"Do you think that's fair?" He moves away just in case, leaving the iron gate to his left now as he walks back the other way. A girl riding a bicycle at full speed makes him stand back from the road. She's wearing a helmet and a cyclist's jersey. He likes women on bikes, but on city bikes, with books and flowers in the basket at the front, their skirts and hair flowing in the wind, like the women he saw in Amsterdam and that Baroja described in some book or other. He'd been going to give Lynn one but didn't, afraid she might not have any use for it. She told him she wasn't going to buy one, because it was no good for going up the slope to the hospital. He admits he has that petite bourgeois worry about wanting to get use out of things,

712

that fear of spending money to no effect; it's something he notices more as he grows older. He's not afraid of spending money, but he does worry about spending it badly, and he says he finds it painful to see money being misused. He doesn't think it's miserliness. What's more, as well as finding it difficult to go into establishments other than bookshops, music stores, and eateries—and he always finds it very hard to choose anything—there's another consideration, as well, which he's frightened of: he'd hate to turn out to be an old man forcing his young lover to accept presents. Now he regrets never having given her anything, some beautiful object she could remember him by. He's often stood in front of the window at Munoa, the jeweler's, but never dared to go in, wondering how to ask for what he wants. "A jewel for a young woman."

He also regrets never having taken her out to watch the sunset from the island. Not going to Urgull first thing in the morning. Walking across Ulia and down to San Pedro, crossing over to Donibane in the boat and having lunch at Casa Cámara. And having dinner at Arzak, so that Juan Mari could have told her, as he does everybody, that he used to feed his grade reports from the Sarasua Academy to the donkey that was kept tied up down by the coal cellar. He would have liked to teach her how to make *kokotxas*. To go back to Bordeaux, and to the dunes at Pilat.

He's afraid the day may come when he can't bear missing her. He's afraid he'll start missing her after it's too late, when she's far away, with some other man, forever. He sees the house's western façade from the little reedbed, the side the kitchen and bathroom are on. The white bathroom, with its old-fashioned fittings. Its shiny white walls with their hexagonal tiles. Copper faucets. The large freestanding bathtub set on what look like the claws of some large animal. Tubes of lotion with the Norwegian flag on them. Lynn sitting on the toilet like Rodin's thinker, her panties stretched between her knees. Telling him she'll have to overcome her shy bladder. Her pashmina scarf wrapped around her head like a virgin, holding one of her breasts in one hand and squeezing a drop of milk out of the nipple with the other.

The afternoon she invited him to tea. He's leaning against the doorframe watching as she carefully puts the excellent ham she bought at the delicatessen into a perfect circle on the plate, and then she stands on a chair to get something down from a cupboard. He holds her around the hips and lifts her up into the air, she protests and waves her arms around, not touching him with her open hands, because she doesn't want to dirty him with the ham grease; but he doesn't care about that and carries her to the sofa. They didn't have their tea that day, either. He's surprised by that uncontrollable desire of his to jump on top of her as soon as he sees her. He never showed any shame about it. He knows she was happy to see that she awakened his desire.

He's glad he never had what people often call *a domestic scene* with her.

And he's glad that he was clear about things when he broke up with her. It would have been worse to take a longer time over it, to say he had to think about it, that he had doubts. She said it herself: when you love somebody, you don't have any doubts. Even so, he's very surprised he isn't missing her more, and he thinks he really does want her to find a young man who's more appropriate for her as soon as possible.

He touches his jacket to feel the envelope inside it. He'll open it later.

THE TRACK AROUND THE CLINIC has a thick line of grass down the middle. He stops to see if there are any four-leaf clovers, just as Lynn used to whenever she saw a bank of grass. He used to call her "Little Red Riding Hood" because of that habit of hers, bending over like a grandmother looking for field mushrooms. One day, they found half a dozen of them, and another two or three the day after. She was delighted and said that Martutene was a place for being happy. He thought that four-leaf clovers were a mutation and that the chances of finding one were proportional to the amount of time you spent looking for them. But Kepa set him right—apparently, there's one four-leaf clover for every ten thousand three-leafed ones. But the worst of it was that the four-leaf plants Lynn found weren't clovers, they were a type of fern, and a protected species, what's more. Learning that really disappointed Lynn, having harmed a *Marsilea batardae*, which is that fern's Latin name, made her feel guilty. Abaitua's never found a four-leaf clover, even though he often looks.

The track joins the main road, and he has to walk beside it for a few feet to reach the entrance to the clinic. Pilar's little Golf is badly parked, diagonally crossing one of the yellow lines on the ground.

It's unlocked, as usual, and the keys are inside. He gets in and sits in the driver's seat, without knowing why. Perhaps to prove that anybody could do the same. There's a strong smell of her perfume, the one with violet in it.

When he comes across the administrator in the hall, she says, "Are you going to join us here?" which makes it clear she knows about his problems at the hospital, and she's probably heard that dirty lie that he'd been drunk when he did what he did. He abruptly says he doesn't think so, and she replies it was just what she'd heard and then shrugs. Who did she hear it from? A nervous laugh. "You know, just things you hear." Apparently it's Pilar herself who said on some occasion that she hoped he'd end up working with them there. To an extent, he's glad she hopes that. He'd like to know how she talks about him when he's not there. Does she say "my husband"? He doesn't think so. He'd say that women always say more or less what they really think of their husbands, at least if you know how to hear them. If they're bored, it's the first thing you notice; perhaps more so when they're bored than when they're angry. What idea does she give of him when she mentions him?

He sees her at the end of the corridor with her back to him, two other doctors to either side of her. Like her workmates, she's wearing green scrubs and, over them, a white smock. They're examining an X-ray image, which Pilar is holding against the glass of the window. She's wearing a brightly colored cap, one of those ones he thinks frivolous and never wears himself. He doesn't know one of the doctors, and the other's the young Portuguese doctor, Adolfo's his name, and in fact, he isn't all that young. Pilar has both her hands up on the window, and the Portuguese doctor takes her cap off for her; she's probably asked him to because it's in her way. She shakes her head in the way she does when she comes out of the shower and turns around just then, realizing he's there. Abaitua keeps still, and it's she who comes toward him with her chin up, arms dangling and reluctant steps, which reminds him of the day they met in the vestibule of the Zaragoza train station. "To what do we owe the honor?" she says, a few steps away from him. Abaitua doesn't look for any pretext to explain his unusual visit, he doesn't mind her deducing that he doesn't have anything else to do and just felt like seeing her. "I was in the neighborhood." She lifts her arms up and lets them fall down again with resignation. She doesn't even have time for a coffee. Since everyone's gone AWOL, she has to go back to the operating theater herself. She's got a shunt and a hypophyseal tumor waiting for her. She thinks she'll be back home late.

He looks at the landscape framed in the large window in the living room: a dark gray strip at the top, and below, the black of the clouds on the horizon, their reflection darker on the sea than the gray of the sky, green with areas of white, and at the bottom, sand that goes from dark to light ochre. He feels useless. When he moves toward the window, the strips of color lose their intensity because of the light coming from the south.

Standing there by the window, he feels half like a retired man and half like a pupil expelled from the classroom, particularly now that he feels unable to enjoy the free time he has. It's probably because he isn't working that he feels he doesn't have the right to enjoy things. It's a feeling that comes from deep inside, or at least one he was indoctrinated with in early childhood. He picks up a shawl of Pilar's from a chair and sits down without taking his jacket off. It's a brightly colored shawl, mostly red and yellow. He doesn't dislike the colors as much as when he bought it, colors that Nordic people like so much and he no longer scorns as he once did. Whenever he buys a present—a shawl, some perfume, or a necklace, that's his basic repertoire—he leaves the choice up to the saleswoman. Because he doesn't trust his own taste, and also to make it clear that he isn't a man who "knows about such things," he's a man who wants to waste as little time as possible in fulfilling his commitments. At Benegas, where he bought it, the saleswoman told him it was "ideal," and he didn't dare to contradict her.

"Roughly how old is the lady?" If he'd bought it for Lynn, he would have had to say it was for a girl of just over thirty.

He goes to the study to be alone, even though there's nobody else in the house. His hands are trembling. "*My dear Iñaki. This is a short letter, not more than a dozen lines long, written in light pencil. Sorry, I don't mean to overwhelm you by being pushy.* I can't help telling you that I've never loved anybody in the same way and I will probably never be able to love anybody in that way again. *I'm sick, and you are the very symptom of my sickness.* I suffer from an illness for which there is no cure. *You shouldn't feel guilty.* There's no reason for you to feel guilty about not being able to love me in the same way. I know you wanted to but can't. *Thanks for the hours of happiness you have given*

716

me. *I hope you have good memories of the moments we've spent together.* Thanks for the happiness you have given me. *I am strong and I will not allow myself to be mastered by melancholy.* Don't worry about me, I'm strong and I won't sink into sadness. I'm going back to my world, and I wish you all the best.

All my love, Lynn.

Martutene, September 10th."

So she wrote it a week ago.

He decides to keep it inside the French translation of *Montauk*. It's improbable anybody will ever find it there. At random, he puts it between pages 90 and 91.

MY LIFE AS A MAN.

Since he has it in his hands, he reads the last two pages.

Frisch is saying goodbye to New York. Washington Square, where the old men play chess; Sheridan Square, where there's a statue of the man for whom the square is named; the streets around Eighth Street; the Chinese laundries where he gets his sweaty shirts cleaned after playing Ping-Pong . . . They had lunch at a restaurant there, their table was so close to the neighboring ones it made it very difficult to talk about intimate matters, which they were both thankful for. Lynn gave him a present, a hip flask with his initials on it, like the one he'd lost over the weekend. *"Very nice,"* he said, *"but unfair,"* because Lynn had refused all his presents apart from his Olivetti Lettera 32 typewriter. Afterward, he suggested they go back to the park, which wasn't far away. United Nations. They walked there quite quickly. *"I am going to miss you,"* Lynn said, her eyebrows like circumflex accents, as if she found herself obliged to admit she'd done something wrong. They've decided not to write to each other. Just a postcard on the eleventh of May, if they haven't forgotten by then.

As easy as that.

"Il ne nous restait plus qu'à trouver l'endroit exact où on se sépare et à faire attention à la circulation; nous nous sommes pris par la main lorsqu'il a fallu traverser l'avenue et nous avons couru. C'était de manière patente l'endroit, nous avons dit BYE, *sans baisers, puis une seconde fois en levant la main:* HI. *Après quelques pas je suis revenu à l'angle de la rue, je l'ai vue, sa silhouette qui marchait; elle ne s'est pas retournée, elle s'est arrêtée, et il lui a fallu un bon moment avant de pouvoir traverser."*

As easy as that.

As easy as putting the book back on the top shelf, next to the copy of Préverte's *Paroles* that Barbara, his friend from Port Royal, gave him. A modest paperback he later had bound in green leather.

He's often had hidden letters he couldn't tear up because of the respect he had for the people who sent them. Some years ago, he burned them all, or so he thinks; when he received the letters, there was an obvious relationship between the senders and the places he chose to hide their letters, but now, after all these years, he isn't so sure. The ones from Barbara (a photo and a short sentence, *"Je t'aime quand même"*—I love you just the same—written on a paper napkin) he kept. The hiding place is obvious: the little book with the green leather cover, the one with the poem titled *Barbara*. *Rappelle-toi, Barbara.*

That photo, the one he always puts off tearing up, is something he looks at from time to time, whenever he thinks his memory of her is fading. Her thick blonde hair falling down onto her shoulders; the lost look of her clear, short-sighted eyes; the smile exposing her beautiful teeth; her upper teeth in a straight line and looking like a single piece; her incisors quite a lot longer and sharper than the rest—she used to say she had Dracula teeth. Her lips are special, too. The upper curve is uninterrupted, without any vermilion border, and her cupid's bow, which is what makes mouths look like hearts, is very slight. *Sans arc de Cupidon.* She always said she would have had a tough time in the 1920s.

ALTHOUGH HE THINKS IT MUST BE a door slamming in the neighbors' apartment, he gets up in a hurry and leaves the study, to see if what he's heard is the sound of someone in the living room. It can't be Pilar. There isn't anybody in the living room, or in the entryway, the door to which is open, or in the kitchen. He walks along the hallway. There's nobody in Pilar's room, or in the bathroom. He doesn't hear any more sounds, and his own precaution, as he goes ahead silently opening doors, makes him nervous. There she is, sitting on the edge of the bed in the room that was once both of theirs but is now only his, just as he found her back then, but now she has her elbows leaning on her thighs and her hands on her forehead. She's still wearing the same scrubs he saw her in not much more than an hour before, the same clogs. His heart misses a beat—

what can have happened to her? He kneels down beside her and asks what's wrong. She opens her hands just enough for him to see her eyes. Full of anguish, she says, "I want to die, I want to die," he doesn't know how many times.

She hugs him as she cries inconsolably, truly upset; it reminds him of when they buried her father, and he doesn't know what's wrong with her, he's afraid that something may have happened to Loiola, that they've called her at the clinic to say he's had an accident. But she's says, "I've really done it now." Which reassures him a little. He takes her by the chin and makes her lift her head up so that he can see her face and asks her, almost shouting, to tell him what's happened. She looks at him as though she isn't really there, as if she doesn't know him. She lifts her right hand up, with her index finger and thumb pressed together and her other fingers curled in a fist. She holds her hand up in the air for a few seconds and then lets it fall. "I was so tired," she says then, in a whisper, and she starts crying and sobbing again, sinking her face into her hands once more.

The telephone rings in the living room, but neither of them moves. He understands something's gone wrong in the operating theater. How important? The phone seems to him to ring a long time. He sits down next to her, on the side of the bed, hoping she'll explain it to him, but she's just the same as when he found her—silent.

The phone rings again. Three rings, four. Finally, he gets up and calmly goes to the living room to answer. It's Arana, the anesthesiologist. He's calling from the clinic to make sure Pilar's gotten home. Yes, he says, what's happened? A silly accident. Orl was scheduled to operate on a pituitary tumor, but he didn't show, and she decided to perform it with Adolfo. Everything was going well, but as they were removing the tumor, they came across a highly vascularized area, and there was a hemorrhage. Although they're still assessing the consequences with the neurologist, it'll probably be serious. Probably a stroke. Pilar got incredibly frightened, and before they realized what was happening, she left the operating theater without even disrobing.

When he hangs up and goes back to the bedroom, Pilar's in the same position as before, but now she looks him in the face, waiting for him to talk. She knows someone's told him what happened, and she's waiting for his response. Abaitua doesn't think he's ever seen her so shocked, so upset. Two situations come to mind, precisely and fleetingly. Her father's funeral. The sound of the first shovelful of earth, her pale, frozen cheeks, her shivering body, which felt smaller to him as he embraced her, because he hadn't held her for a long time and she seemed like a defenseless child. And he remembers that other scene from longer ago, when she was sitting on the edge of the bed like now, her coat still on, whispering "I fell asleep," with just a thread of a voice, when he, just like now, came to the bedroom door from the living room.

He doesn't know what to say, what to do. The sight of her pain and helplessness moves him, of course, but he feels his pain starting to burn inside him again. Pilar realizes, too. She mumbles something he doesn't understand, but he doesn't ask her to say it again. Remembering her then, with her red coat on and saying "I fell asleep," he senselessly fears that she'll say the same thing again. What did she do? How did it happen? Why wasn't she more careful? He knows they're unfair questions, but he can't stop himself from saying, "What did you do?" with anger and disappointment in his voice. She accepts his criticism humbly, meekly, expressing nothing but guilt. As she did back then. It's moving. With her eyes full of tears, she lifts up her right hand again, her thumb and index finger pressed together to mime holding a scalpel. Unilateral pararim incision to the perichondrium. As if it were some lesson she'd learned by heart, she holds her hand up, her index finger and thumb still together, the rest of her fingers curled in, carrying on with her senseless, mechanical demonstration. Hypophyseal adenoma, four-millimeter central friable portions, solid outlying areas. She starts saying short, unrelated sentences that are difficult to understand, faster and faster, as if she didn't have time to find the right verb forms, and she empties her pockets onto the table, which reminds him of her looking for her keys among the spread-out objects. Circle of Willis. The heptagonal arterial circuit at the base of the brain was what she was trying to remember, apparently, because she goes quiet after that. Not for long, the time it takes Abaitua to check his pockets and see that he doesn't have any tissues. She tells him about what happened as if it were something from a long time ago, following a scarcely coherent thread. From what Abaitua can gather, the typical procedures for operating on a hypophyseal tumor weren't followed. The anesthesiologist wanted to go in through the nasal passage for the extirpation of the hypophyseal adenoma, rather than adhering to the classic sublabial approach, because the post-operative recovery is easier. Orl should have been the one to access the nasal passage, but he never turned up—as is often the case with him these days—and she thought she would be able to do it with Adolfo instead. The cut wasn't straight, the scalpel slipped to one side and scraped the circle of Willis, causing a stroke. He asks her if that's what happened. Yes, it is, and she continues holding her hand up in the air as if she were holding a scalpel, and for some reason, he can't stand seeing her like that any more. Her holds her by the wrist to make her lower her hand, but it's hard, it's as if her arm belonged to a corpse with rigor mortis. She seems to have realized again that her hand exists, as if it had been something foreign to her for a few seconds, and then she lifts it up to her face, along with her other hand. She covers her face up and cries, sobbing that she's ruined the poor person's life. "Poor them, poor them, poor them," she says, three times, four times, a thousand times, and then drops her hands into her laps and looks him straight in the eyes for the first time since he got there, as if wanting to know what he's thinking, as if expecting him to be angry with her. If he slapped her, she wouldn't protest. He's sorrier for her than he is angry. He kneels down, just like back then, and takes her hands. They're much wider than Lynn's, he finds them unfamiliar. She rests her forehead on his chest as she starts crying again. "What have I done? What would my father say? What should I do?" she recites like an endless rosary between sobs. She moves one hand to dry her wet face with the back of it. First her eyes, then her nose, and mouth, and then that lost-child look, which is so unlike her and moves him so much.

"It happens to us all," he says to comfort her, wondering if it's the best thing to say, whether he would accept that if he were in Pilar's position. He read recently that according to a study done by the Mayo Clinic, 14.7% of doctors made mistakes in the three months prior to the study. And that must be less than the real figure. But for once, he thinks that statistics can be rhetorical, and he prefers to tell her that he, too, has made mistakes. She seems to be calmer as she looks at him now. "But you've never left anybody hemiplegic." We still don't know if the patient's had a stroke. "It's a matter of millimetres, in any case, a matter of seconds," he replies. Does she think he's always made the right decisions? He's gone too fast sometimes, his lack of patience has prevented him from doing things well. On occasions, he's worked without taking all the safety measures, but luck's been on his side. He's never admitted as much before, and he hopes that she'll take it to be a white lie to some extent. But he repeats himself—nobody's never made a mistake, never had an accident. That's the word—an *accident*. Pilar looks at him with her hands on her knees, watching his lips move, like a dog attentively watching to see what its master wants. He's never seen her looking so submissive. "Now you have to face up to what's happened," he says, in the most convincing voice possible, and Pilar says yes, he's right, and she's going to try. She's not happy, of course, but she is obviously relieved.

She takes her surgery cap off—first of all a shower, and then fresh clothes. Until she took it off, Abaitua hadn't realized she had it on.

Abaitua stays by the door while she's in the shower. Her clothes are piled up on the bidet—socks, panties, and a white bra on top of the green scrubs. There are some splashes of blood on the scrubs. He sees the imprecise contour of her body through the emery-polished shower screen, she's bending over now to scrub her toenails in that peculiar way she normally does, without bending her knees; even years after getting married, her mother used to tell her off for that, saying it wasn't feminine. She must have been a strong, agile girl, with a lot of personality, one of those girls who preferred playing with the boys. She leans her head back for the water to flow all over it. She answers his questions precisely, frankly, probably emboldened by not being able to see him. She says she didn't panic when the accident happened, the duct cauterized easily, and being nervous didn't affect her hands. But she got frightened afterward, the very thought that she was going to have to see the patient awake was unbearable, and she doesn't remember how she fled the scene, doesn't remember anything until the moment of seeing him.

She doesn't need to be convinced that the best thing is for her to go back to the clinic, explain what happened to the patient, and apologize. She says it herself. Once she's dressed, she picks up the car keys, but Abaitua says he'll drive her there.

Pilar sits next to him, sparing him her usual comments about the best way to get there when, as usual, he gets lost in the roundabouts. Abaitua talks more than usual about the insufficient, bad signposting, to break the silence. Pilar looks straight ahead, seems a long way off, lost in her thoughts, but judging by her face, she isn't as upset as she was before. Abaitua wonders what she's most upset about, the damage she's done to the patient, or the damage to her pride. There's no doubt her enemies at the clinic will gossip about it to harm her and, in any case, be glad it's happened. That, at least, is what Abaitua believes, and it makes him angry.

At the entrance, he says it to her again—if she wants, he'll go with her to see the patient. Hoping she'll say no; for one thing, he'd hate to be in that situation, for another, and above all, he's not at all sure it's a good idea. But he feels he has to say it—"I'll go with you if you like"—and she, fortunately, says no, she'd rather go alone. So he'll wait for her.

He has the uncomfortable sensation that everybody who's walking through the vestibule is thinking about what Pilar's done when they look at him. "Doctor Abaitua, Goytisolo's husband. The wife made a mess of it in the operating theater this morning, and he's been suspended without pay from the hospital because of something he did when he was drunk." He thinks they'll be very glad when they find out she's got problems. Some people say hello as if nothing's happened. That's the worst thing. Arana, the anesthesiologist, holds his hand out to him. He clearly doesn't know what to say. Abaitua knows the man's made two big mistakes in the operating theater over the past year, and now he's showing his support. As if saying "welcome to the botch job club." He feels he's being treated as a guilty party because he's married to Pilar. As if he had to share her blame, and that gets under his skin. To an extent, it's because that's what he's feeling, that he's the one to blame for Pilar's guilt. Which may be related to some sort of macho world view. In any case, he's fed up with feeling responsible for what other people have done, the need to take on other people's blame, be they relatives, colleagues, or fellow Basques. It's a new feeling for him, something he's never felt so clearly, or with such intensity, and he gets the impression that his rejection of this feeling means that something inside him is healing.

The anesthesiologist pats him on the back. He talks to him about the pressure Pilar's been under recently, about how she's overworked, all in a tone of compassion that sounds sincere. Fortunately, Abaitua's phone rings, and he takes advantage of that to say goodbye with a gesture of his hand.

It's Kepa. He says he wants to set a date for their trip to La Rochelle, but Abaitua thinks the real reason he's calling may be to remind him to help him find a place in the old people's home for his mother. Abaitua says it's a bad time.

He prefers to wait outside. From the top of the stairs, he sees the roof of Lynn's house and, through the branches of the trees, the bathroom and kitchen windows. The shutters are still closed. He remembers the bathroom walls and their white, hexagonal tiles and blue border. He doesn't know what to do and gets into the car.

He puts Lynn's CD on.

WHEN PILAR COMES OUT AGAIN, she looks calmer, but it's obvious she's been crying. She doesn't say anything, and he doesn't ask her anything, either. They drive in silence and have to go around the roundabout twice to find the right exit. Too many signposts. Amara, Center, Hernani, France. At the next one, Pilar gently points the ways, and he ventures to ask her how it went.

"Fine," she says.

"OH BEAUTIFUL RELEASE / *memory seeps from my veins* / *let me be empty . . .*"

Pilar thinks it's a beautiful song and wants to know what CD it is. He says he doesn't know. He doesn't know how it got there, either.

"*. . . and weightless and maybe* / *I'll find some peace tonight.*"

They're silent once again as they drive slowly in the long row of cars alongside the river. He used to play on this side of the city as a child, before there were any buildings. The trees are tall and beautiful; apparently, the inhabitants of the houses find them troublesome now. He thinks they're Indian horse chestnuts. He asks Pilar, who's an expert on trees. She says she doesn't know, which he interprets as a way of saying that she thinks it's frivolous to talk about trees right now, and they keep quiet until they reach María Kristina Zubia. When they stop at the traffic lights there, she says, in a voice that sounds natural, or neutral, "She's a great person." No more than that. They move forward, and while he's thinking about whether it might be better to turn left, he says, as if breaking a long silence, that there's no reason for the patient to forgive her for anything, it was an accident, bad luck for both of them.

There's a skiff moving along the river in jumps and starts, like one of those long-legged insects. He used to row at one time, too.

"It was just bad luck for both of you. You do realize that, don't you?"

The best thing is to tell the patient what actually happened. He'd like her to be humble enough to admit that it's good advice. As far as the consequences of that mistake are concerned, that depends on the social status of the person affected, to a large extent. He asks who it is, what she does, how old she is.

She turns toward him for the first time since they got into the car. "Let's talk about this later, please, not now."

When they reach home, it's he who opens the door and lets her in first. She walks through the entryway and the living room to her room, the room that's now hers, and sits on the side of the bed without taking her jacket off, her body leaning forward a little, her head more so. Like that morning. He looks at her from behind, seeing her right-hand profile. That morning, she was wearing a red coat that flared out at the bottom like a bell, making it look like a cape. He doesn't know what to do. He isn't familiar with this room, and he feels that being here together is more intimate than using the same bathroom. But he goes up to her, not knowing whether what he feels is pity or affection. She leans further forward now, and he puts his hand on her shoulder, as he did that morning when she said that terrible thing—"I fell asleep." He then asked her who it was, and as he expected, she told him it was Adolfo. Pilar looks him up and down now, tries to smile, and he sits down next to her.

Pilar has changed into house clothes; recently, she often stays in her operating scrubs. She's sitting on the sofa in the living room, leaning over the table in the middle and doing the sudoku in the newspaper. He hasn't seen her like that for a long time. He feels a mixture of pity and affection. He asks if she wants anything for dinner, and she says she'll have a glass of milk and some cookies. He's not going to have anything. He says good night. She says she'll be going to bed, too, once she finishes the sudoku.

Even though it's still early.

Abaitua's taking his shoes off when she comes to the door. She stays standing there looking at him, as if not daring to go into the room where they haven't slept together for at least three months now. Finally, she sits next to him and puts her hand, the same one she made the mistake with the scalpel with, open on his lap for him to hold.

725

She gives him a shy kiss on his cheek, and he clumsily hugs her, forced to by the situation. They both stand up. She opens the bed and smooths down the sheets while he gets undressed. Then, while he gets into bed, she takes her clothes off. She lets them fall to the floor.

He's no longer used to being near that body, which is bigger and slower than Lynn's. He kisses her neck and one earlobe, and she lets out a soft moan. Her skin is soft, the softest he's ever stroked.

He, too, finds it a relief when she says, "That's fine in movies," gives him a light kiss on the cheek, and moves over to her side of the bed. He's grateful she's chosen comfort. But he knows that she still feels guilty because she can't fall asleep with her head on his shoulder and her arm over his belly in the way canonical lovers are supposed to. He thinks his chest isn't muscular enough, or at least not enough to be comfortable, although that wasn't a problem for Lynn; she used to fall asleep like that, her head resting on his chest or his belly. It wasn't very comfortable for her, either, but she didn't care, she didn't want to fall asleep.

It isn't a good idea for him to think about Lynn, but he lets himself take a quick look at some images, like glancing at a book, picking it up and thumbing through.

LYNN barefoot in the boutique in Bordeaux.

LYNN saying hi through the library window.

LYNN squeezing her breast between her thumb and index finger again, trying to get a drop of milk from her nipple.

LYNN half-crying, saying—shouting—that she loves him, she loves him madly.

He'd rather sleep alone, to be able to listen to the radio. It's as prosaic as that.

23

"NUCLEAR FREE OTZETA," reads the poster.

Seeing the narrow valley depresses Julia. The river's scarcely six feet wide, and it disappears under a block of cement in the town. The mountain slopes that come down to the house are covered in insignis pines, except for a few yellowish-green patches where there are sheep grazing. In the distance, parallel to the road that runs along the riverbank, the new highway flies over the northern part of the town. The first houses are fairly respectable—lively colors, recently built. A park with swings and other things for children serves as a transition area to the town itself, in which most of the buildings have those façades of exposed brownish brick and the small roof tiles so typical of the sixties and seventies, built without any aesthetic consideration whatsoever to house the immigrants arriving at the time. In the small old plaza in the center of town, the old baroque church is still standing, along with the town hall, its ashlar coat of arms taking up most of its blackened façade, along with a couple of eighteenth-century houses, both made of stone and with large coats of arms on them. A third house, almost touching the church, looks like a mansion, and there are four Tuscan columns holding up its porch. On the façade, it says it was made by Joseph Ygnacio de Goytisolo in 1763—"*Joseph Ygnacio de Goytisolo lo hizo. Año 1763.*" It's the only one that looks empty. Julia knew the town back when it had even more beautiful houses.

From some windows, there are pieces of cloth with the map of the Basque Country on it in black and arrows drawn on in red demanding the return of Basque prisoners.

Beyond the plaza, on the street that starts up the hill, is Martin's family's house. A Basque-style villa with a sloping roof, white with blue windows, '20s style, and it clearly stands out from the other buildings around it, because they date from the town's first industrial period, shortly before the war. There's a small, narrow garden separating it from them with severely pruned plane and Indian chestnut trees in it. Now there's a large Basque flag flying over it on top of a tall pole—the building's been converted into the Basque Nationalist Party's town headquarters. She decides to go into the bar across the street from it to have a coffee. Above all, she wants to put off reaching Torrekua. Her mother and sister and the children are at her brother-in-law's *baserri*, and there are probably more people there, too, relatives and friends; her sister and brother-in-law are never by themselves.

When she goes into the bar, she has the impression that everybody turns around to see who she is, and she regrets her decision. It's the same atmosphere as ever—the floor isn't very clean, the varnished stone walls are only decorated with posters about sports and cultural activities. She sits at the end of the bar closest to the door, next to the wall, and asks the barman—who's greeted her by lifting his chin slightly in her direction and is wearing a checked shirt and cleaning the counter in front of her with a wet cloth—for a *cortado*. To her left, there's a copy of *Gara*—the bilingual newspaper—and a collection box with a sign on it reading *Presoentzat*—For the Prisoners.

The things she can read from where she's sitting: *AHT txikizioa*—High speed train = Disaster; *Gaztetxea orain*—Housing now; *Otzeta bizirik nahi dugu*—Long live Otzeta; *Adierazpen eskubidea*—Freedom of expression. Written in chalk on a green board: *Barriola a Olaizola II cinco tantos a que sí*—Barriola over Olaizola II five goals all right. The television, turned on but with the sound off, is enthroned above the door. So customers can watch it and keep an eye on the door at the same time, she supposes. The head of the Gipuzkoa provincial government is talking into a thicket of microphones.

The people sitting at the tables are old men. Most of them are drinking red wine, a few of them beer. It's very easy to see which of the old men are local and which are not; their faces and way of dressing are different, even though some of the immigrants have been there for decades. Some of their hats mark them out as foreigners, but the size and positioning of their berets is just as telling. Those speaking Basque are speaking the local type—fairly thick Bizkaian—and most of those speaking Spanish have accents from Andalusia and Extremadura, which she sometimes finds hard to understand, and their way of speaking has traces of Basque in it. Nobody is speaking Basque with a Spanish accent. The people at the other end of the bar—most of them her age, some a bit younger, all dressed as if ready to go hiking—are speaking local Basque, mixing in words and whole sentences in Spanish, too.

She feels out of place here. She realizes she feels guilty, just as when she had to admit to herself a few minutes before that she doesn't feel like going to Torrekua.

She finishes the dreadful coffee, and when she asks how much it is, the barman says it's been paid for. She doesn't know who to thank for treating her. Then she notices a woman's face at the other end of the bar that looks familiar to her, but she can't place her. The faces of distant relatives her mother's introduced her to at various weddings and funerals. She goes up to the group.

"*Etxezar erre dala*"—so Etxezar's burned down.

Finally she works out who the woman talking to her about the fire at Etxezar in a sorrowful voice is. The daughter of one of her mother's cousins. Lore, a robust woman of around fifty, with circles of rouge on her cheeks so round they look like they were drawn on with a compass, and particularly red lips, so much so that they look painted, even though they're not. What Julia knows about her: she got out of prison earlier this year, after more than ten years inside for having let some ETA guys use her garage. Julia's mother and sister went to see her when she was in Martutene Prison. They say she's a very good woman, she spent her jail time teaching the *comunas*—the non-terrorist inmates—to sew, and everyone loved her. They quarreled about her more than once; each time she was mentioned, they used to say that she was a very good person, very generous, and that she was in prison for no reason, just for lending her garage to some guys, and she didn't know they were with ETA, of course. For her mother and her sister, prisoners and the people connected with them are never guilty of the things they're accused of. She says she was tortured badly at the Intxaurrondo Barracks and that after that horror, she found being in prison easy. A peaceful lifestyle, watching television and teaching people how to sew. Her biggest complaint was that her husband never went to visit her; he didn't like leaving town and hated going through the security controls, having to stand in line with gypsies and petty criminals, and, of course, he never agreed to any conjugal visits. Julia is amazed at her talking about such intimate things. He's a tall man, with a long nose and a sad face. He says with a half-smile that ever since getting out, his wife can't stop talking. When Julia asks her how she is, the woman says she's very well, the worst thing is that she's going deaf, because of all the beatings she got.

It smells of cabbage at Torrekua, even though they haven't cooked any; the smell's stuck to the walls after so many centuries of cooking it there. There are beans on the stove, whose own smell is overpowered by that of the chorizo, lard, ribs, and other fats; "all the trimmings," her brother-in-law says, sounding pleased. *Comme il faut.* Her sister says her husband's right, even though Julia knows that she doesn't enjoy such heavy meals, but she's fully integrated in the *baserri* atmosphere, even wearing a *buruko*—a headscarf. She changes when she's at Torrekua. Her mother's sitting by the fire on a low chair plucking a chicken. She's gone back a century in the tunnel of time. She's the one talking, and the rest of them—her sister, her brother-in-law . . . the younger generation—all listen with veneration to the stories she always tells.

When the owners of Etxezar suggested that her grandfather—so Julia's great-grandfather—buy the place, her father contributed some money, even though it would later be inherited by the eldest son. Her mother's grandfather lost his marbles toward the end of his life. He used to sit by the front door, pointing at the oven there, and say that it was actually a *zulo* and that there were lots of weapons hidden in there. Thinking he was senile, they didn't pay any attention, but when they eventually knocked the oven down, they found a box full of weapons behind it. Her mother doesn't know whether it was from the first Carlist war, the second one, or the civil war. What Julia remembers is that when she was a child, some boys came across a bomb, and when they were playing with it, it went off in the hand of the *morroi*—the house servant—and he lost several fingers. She also has a vague memory that after leaving the hospital, the boy stayed in their home, in Martutene, for the duration of his convalescence, although she may know this only from having heard about it, but her sister says she remembers that his hand smelled foul and that the doctor said it was a sign it was healing. Apparently, after a long recovery, he got used to living in Donostia and didn't want to go back to Etxezar. What Julia doesn't remember, her sister does—mostly sad memories connected with terrible shortages. They seem to her like memories of a period she didn't live through, and she doesn't know whether her sister is making them up or at least exaggerating them, painting them blacker, although it's true that a difference of three years, at a certain age, is enough for her not to have retained those memories.

Her sister can remember the trams. She says they used to take them to go to the clinic and the prison; there was always some sick Otzeta resident or other they had to visit, and packages of food and clean clothes had to be taken to those in prison. It was difficult for their families to visit them back then; Otzeta was a long way off.

STORIES OF ETXEZAR.

They're almost always the same. The one she finds most moving is the one about Modesto Oletakoa. He volunteered for the Saseta Battalion, and because his younger brother, Tomás, wanted to go with him, his mother told Modesto to look after him and bring him back alive. Julia's mother tells the story as if she herself spent the war with them. Modesto spent his whole time at the front without ever taking his eyes off his brother—"Follow me, Tomás"; "Careful, Tomás"; "Duck, Tomas." On one occasion, in Cantabria, during a retreat, he turned around, like so many other times, to check that his brother was following him, and he saw him get felled by a stray bullet. He couldn't leave him there—he lifted his brother's body onto his shoulder and took him as far as Bizkaia, burying him at Gernika. She always sheds a tear when she imagines poor Modesto returning to the *baserri*, feeling defeated and guilty.

Some years afterward, there was a joint political-religious act in honor of the fallen, to which all the schoolchildren in the area were taken, including Tomás and Modesto's sister, the youngest child in the household. In the middle of the plaza, a fountain, in the baroque style, like the church, was taken down, and a large wooden cross was put up on its foundation. One of the speakers, a red-bereted priest, said in Spanish that they were burying their fallen with the cross, not with the hammer and sickle like the red separatists—"*Nosotros enterramos a nuestros caídos con la cruz, y no con la hoz y el martillo como los rojo-separatistas.*" And apparently the girl shouted in reply, "*Mi hermano murió con los rojo-separatistas y tiene una cruz, pero no de madera: de mármol, de mármol*"—My brother died with the red separatists, and he has a cross, but it's not made of wood, it's made of marble . . . marble! They made her drink castor oil and shaved off her hair, leaving only one lock, on which they tied a ribbon with the Spanish colors; she doesn't know how long they made her wear it.

Daniela was her name, and she emigrated to Paris, where she worked as a maid and met Julia's mother's uncle Bernardo, also from Etxezar, who was working at the Citröen factory. Uncle Bernardo had fled to France because everyone in his year in the military service had been called up to go and fight in Africa. He was a gentle, quiet man who felt guilty, it was said, because the Moors ended up cutting the throat of the man who'd been sent to fight in his place. After getting married, he suddenly came back, started living in Martutene, and opened a garage there. Julia remembers them. Although they were older than her parents, they had a single daughter her same age, the rest of Daniela's children having died at birth. They had habits she found strange, customs they'd brought back from Paris with them. They used a tablecloth and napkins, ate a lot of salad and macaroni au gratin, and Daniela called *café con leche* "*café au lait.*" She used to read loads of romantic novels and complain to everybody that her husband wasn't loving enough, that he should be more romantic. Because he didn't often say the things the lovers in her novels did, not even things like those the Andalusian immigrant in the neighborhood said to his wife. He could at least call her *darling, my dear,* or *sweetheart* once in a while. Julia's mother used to say that she'd lost her mind from reading so many romantic novels and that she didn't think it was fair of her to complain about Uncle Bernardo—he was hard-working and sincere, he earned good money, he never lost his temper, and as if all that weren't enough, he didn't go out drinking, unlike other men. What's more, he was strong and had a good figure, more so than Daniela, especially when he was young, Julia's mother says, and that's there for everyone to see in the photos from Paris, in which Bernardo's looking very elegant, wearing a beret and everything. He also had an attractive laugh, like his voice, he always spoke quietly, and he was especially affectionate to children, which is why she couldn't understand her aunt complaining so much, always mocking him, saying things like "there you have the man with his newspaper, he can go the whole afternoon without saying a word." Julia thinks it must have been the first time she ever noticed a woman sounding embittered and that she didn't really understand her. A husband never shouting at his wife and bringing home enough money for a good life was a lot at that time. She remembers that she once went to the movie theater with her aunt and saw a film with Gregory Peck in it; her aunt looked upward and, with a voice of pleasure, said how much she liked him. That wasn't normal, either. She used Spanish to tell the stories from her novels and from movies, and she spoke it very well, much better than her mother did. She went on being a fervent Basque nationalist all her life, and Julia originally heard the story about the cross for the fallen that her mother is telling now from her. "My brother died with the red separatists, and he has a cross, but it's not made of wood, it's made of marble . . . marble!" She always said *marble* twice. Bernardo used to tell her that talking so much would lead to trouble. "One of these days, I'm going to find you like this," he used to warn her, and Julia's mother holds her wrists together as if they had handcuffs on them. But what actually happened was quite different. It was Daniela who saw Bernardo being handcuffed and taken away by two Civil Guard officers. They put him in Ondarreta Prison—so this was before 1948, which is when that prison was torn down. Julia's mother convinced her to go to Otzeta and ask the eldest son at Etxezar to find a way to use Mr. Goytisolo's influence to get her husband out of prison. Apparently, she went but the man didn't listen to her. He told her that if he'd been arrested, he must have done something. The eldest son at Etxezar was a fervid Carlist and a close friend of Goytisolo, Julia's mother always used to call him a *"caballero de España"*—a gentleman of Spain—but Julia doesn't know what she meant by that. Her mother still hates him, even though he died long ago, above all because he didn't use his relationship with the regime to bring wealth to the house; in fact, he brought it down. On the other hand, she does say good things about Goytisolo. When the Nationals came into the town, apparently it was he who prevented them from shooting anybody for being a Basque nationalist or a red.

Daniela died on Easo Kalea—called Víctor Pradera during the dictatorship—she was run over by a police jeep as she was crossing the street from the Amara station to the Carmelite church.

THE OLD RAILWAY LINE passes a few feet from Torrekua and carries on along a slope. It goes up little by little until it joins the path that leads up to Etxezar. There are large stones on some stretches that make it difficult to walk, an old beam here and there, but grass has grown over most of it. Apparently, they want to asphalt it over. Julia would prefer them to leave it as it is. When the path turns east at the foothills, the scenery changes as the town disappears from view. There are still plenty of pine trees—a lot of them have what look like balls of cotton on them, it must be some sort of disease, she thinks—and there are more green patches than before, as well as local trees, clumps of fine oaks and beeches scattered around. There aren't any new buildings, just *baserris* dotted around, some of them very large, with their stone walls and sloping roofs.

The Otzeta parish church is Templar in origin, and the base of the elliptic column holding up the porch is twisted around, about to fall. The station is shortly after that, or what used to be the station—only the walls are left standing. A train once derailed there, and some of the wounded were treated at Etxezar, one of them a rich man who took a long time to recover, and he promised to pay for the studies of all the children in the house. And he did it, too. Cousin Antxon, her mother's cousin, went on to become a teacher, but he died young of tuberculosis at the Andatzarre Clinic.

Julia's mother can't keep quiet. She links up one memory with the next, and it's quite startling compared to her usual silence in Martutene. "This is so beautiful," she says, holding her arms open to take in all the countryside. And that part of the valley really is beautiful. At her feet, the green slope winds smoothly down to the stream, which is dressed in brightly colored flowers—violet, yellow, and white. They stay there for a moment, in the gentle sunlight, silent now, as if wanting to put off the moment when they'll see Etxezar around the next bend by the clump of hazel trees. The hills around them are not particularly high. There's only one bare-rock summit in the distance, with a rosy glow on it. On the slope leading up to it, in the foreground, there's a brightly whitewashed hermitage with two windows and a bright blue door. "We used to dance there," her mother points at it and says. A happy memory at last, the first for some time. Her mother wearing white espadrilles and colored ribbons in her hair for the celebration. Did they use to wear ribbons in their hair? She wants to ask her but decides not to when she hears her sigh. "It's all over," she says as they start off again, as if the memories of her lost youth have reminded her of the loss of the house itself.

The three-foot-thick walls on either side hold nothing up, the roof's fallen in, and the floor's destroyed. There are many tiles spread out over the floor. The back wall is visible, too, because everything inside has been destroyed. There's nothing left of the panelling at the front. Two stone columns and a line of wooden ones are still standing, propped on what were once the holdings for the beams, probably the very branches they had taken off the tree, blackened, like crosses with their arms lifting up toward the sky. Everything else has disappeared. Her mother cries with her hands over her face. A few whimpers escape out from her silent sobs.

It's a type of crying that makes her feel something like repulsion. She doesn't want to comfort her mother, and she's surprised by her own lack of feeling, scared by it, in fact. It's her sister who puts her arms around their mother. Seeing that doesn't help Julia any, and she decides to walk on along the path. The earth is resplendent, covered with grass and flowers. There are two large trees at either end of the *baserri* property, she doesn't know what type they are. Her mother's grandfather hanged himself from one of them, unable to pay the debt he took on to pay for a new roof after another fire. Julia's always thought they must have been gambling debts. Her mother's sure to tell them that story any minute now. Her phone rings. It's Harri. She's not sure whether to answer or not, but in the end she does. Is she still angry? She isn't angry. The murmur of the leaves in the breeze is a happy counterpoint to the silence. Harri says they should meet up. OK, they will. "I'm with Martin. I mean, he's with me right now," she adds. "Do you want to speak with him?" She doesn't say anything, but she knows Harri's going to put him on. "We can't end like this." Overcoming her urge to tell him it's only a matter of deciding how to end things, one way or another, she keeps quiet. Martin again: "We can't end like this," and finally Julia says they'll talk, but that she needs some time. Then she asks after Lynn, whether he's seen her at the house, because she's been calling her but she still hasn't picked up, and she's worried. Martin hasn't heard anything. In fact, he hasn't heard anything from her rotund girlfriend, either. He came across her once, dragging her wheeled suitcase up to the house as ever, and when he asked her about Lynn, she said she was going to be away for a while, not very politely, and didn't give him time to ask anything else. And now she isn't around, either. Her mother and the others come up to her, a dog barking behind them. Where is she, asks Martin. "In Otzeta. I'm not alone, I'll call you," she says before hanging up.

NOW IT REALLY SMELLS OF BOILED CABBAGE at Torrekua. They eat the boiled chorizo on bread after drinking the stock. She has to admit it's good. She holds her glass out for them to serve her some wine; she wants to cheer up a bit. Everybody takes turns in the ritual of leaning over the stove and lifting the covers from the pots, closing their eyes as they smell the food, and saying, "That's really good." Her mother says what she always does—that used to be her daily meal, that and roasted apples and chestnuts. Julia, too, lifts the top off the pot the cabbage is stewing in—it's a penetrating smell, bitter, the cabbage has been cooking too long. "*Goxo-goxo eginak.*" She hates that expression—slow-cooked and tasty—which everybody repeats, and she has a hard time not saying that greens should be chopped finer and boiled less. They've had the same discussion loads of times before. But her mother never gives in—they've always done them like that. "*Goxo-goxo.*"

Friends come and join them. A large man who was one of Zigor's friends and now runs a grill house. He's got twelve bullets in him. He lifts his shirt up to show the marks. He has innumerable scars all across his belly and ribs. "Nearly a pound of lead," he says. The surgeons didn't do a great job, either—that's the way he puts it. He keeps on repeating that Zigor is identical to his father. He talks about old times in a humorous tone. Julia knows all about the incidents he brings up. The time when the German consul was abducted and his kidnappers let him escape because spending all day and night with him was so boring. He went into a bar and asked for help—"I'm the kidnapped German consul, I need a phone"—and the barman, instead of calling the police, called the kidnappers to

736

tell them so they could come and get him again. They'd originally wanted to kidnap the French consul, too, but the plan didn't work out. They were waiting below his apartment, near the Kontxa beach, on the corner of San Martin Kalea and San Bartolome Kalea. Two of them were standing next to the traffic lights, and the other two were sitting in the car with the engine running; but a young girl came up and stood right next to them. Time went by, and she kept standing there; they started yelling obscenities to her to frighten her away—there, in the kitchen at Torrekua, he doesn't specify all the phrases Julia's heard him tell before—but she wouldn't move, she just stood there calmly, quietly listening to everything, until one of them finally pretended to pick up a machine gun—he holds his left fist in front of his right and imitates the sound of a machine-gun, *ra-ta-ta-ta-ta*—and then, at last, the poor girl did run away. But it was a bad day for them, and when the car they were waiting for pulled up and the consul was about to step out of it, a guy who was jogging past in a track suit, a model citizen, apparently, realized what they were up to and started grappling with them, and since they couldn't get rid of him, the chauffeur had enough time to get the car moving again, and they gave up their plan. When the guy kept going on at them, they finally had to tell him they were with ETA, and he apologized, said he was very sorry, he didn't realize.

"When is all of this going to come to an end?"

They ask when it's all going to come to an end several times. A cousin of Julia's brother-in-law says she went to Cadiz the weekend before to visit her brother, who's in the Puerto 1 prison there. He's been inside for twenty-five years now. She made the journey in vain—after a humiliating body search, they didn't let her in to see her brother, because of some administrative problem. She doesn't seem to pay any attention to politics herself. She says she's against ETA's violence, because it isn't getting them anywhere and only creates suffering. She doesn't think her brother is in favor of it, either. He's become a vegetarian and exercises a lot now. So he's very fit and looks really good, even though he's only allowed half an hour a day in the courtyard. Julia asks what they discuss when she goes to visit him. They don't have a lot to talk about. In any case, he doesn't regret what he did and isn't going to sign on to the government-sponsored Langraitz deal for better sentencing conditions in exchange for a public renunciation of ETA—he'd rather keep his head held high for the two years he's got left. Julia doesn't dare ask what he's in for.

"When is all of this going to come to an end?"

They talk about how unfeeling the people who consider themselves to be democrats are when it comes to the situation of prisoners; they complain about how nothing happens when cases of torture are reported because it's assumed ETA is ordering all inmates to allege torture at the hands of guards as a general rule. Julia ventures to say that it isn't hard to work out how they've arrived at the current situation—it's because of all the savagery. Her sense of dignity won't allow her to just accept everything they say. But she does believe there's been torture, that seems undeniable to her. Nothing excuses torture. She says that above all for Zigor's sake, because she sees him looking at her nervously, worried she might come out with something to make everybody else angry. He wants normality, he doesn't want her to stand out.

Nervous silence. Julia's sister washing the dishes is the loudest noise. But that doesn't last for long, and the conversation starts up again. It's about other things now—how easy it is to grow kiwis here, the way the tomatoes got spoilt this year. And then there's a conversation that brings a calmer atmosphere with it. Nowadays tomatoes have such thick, plasticky skins that the insects can't get into them. Most people agree with that, but there's a belligerent minority insisting the tomatoes at Otzeta are the same as ever. The children go outside, and the men agree to go down into town to watch the *pilota* game. So as usual, the women are going to be left alone, and Julia finds the conversations between the women even more irritating. She can't say why. She prefers men when it comes to talking about frivolous matters, soccer included, and when it's deeper issues, she'll forgive men for things she wouldn't tolerate in women; when it's all women, they usually end up quarreling. They all sit together at one end of the table. She remembers that at one time, young mothers used to talk about their fear that their children would join ETA, and there was always somebody who would ask what they would prefer, having their children go to prison for being members of ETA or for being delinquents. It seemed a reasonable question to them, and to Julia, too, and nobody ever had any doubts about the matter.

She decides to get away. She tells her sister she's got tickets for the film festival, although she knows it'll seem like a weak excuse for leaving the boy with her. Zigor's happy, he's never seen a professional *pilota* game, and she thinks he's also pleased that she's going to the cinema. They drop her off in the town plaza on their way to the *pilota* court, just in time for her to catch the bus.

ON KANPANDEGI KALEA, sitting sideways on the stone bench with her arms crossed over the wrought iron back. Lots of people below her are walking up from the port, more than are going down to it. Further on, above the entrance to Konstituzio Plaza, the peaks of Igeldo and Mendizorrotz stand out against the cloudless sky. Kanpandegi Kalea is deserted, as ever. An old woman is walking up from De Lasala Plaza, carrying a heavily laden bag and leaning on an umbrella. Wanting to disguise the fact that she's using it as a walking stick. Notes from an accordion. A Donostian contradanse, Julia knows it but can't remember its title. *Yo no sé por qué; pero esas melodías sentimentales, repetidas hasta el infinito, al anochecer, en el mar, ante el horizonte sin límites, producen una tristeza solemne.* It means, "I don't know why, but these sentimental tunes, endlessly repeated, at dusk, at sea, before a limitless horizon, bring about a solemn sadness." *Elogio sentimental del acordeón* is her favorite short story by Baroja, along with *Mari Belcha*. She knows the beginning of that one by heart, too. She likes this part of town, where you can feel the souls of Baroja and his father, Serafin, and also those of Toribio Altzaga and Bilintx and Martzelino Soroa—all liberal urban-dwelling enthusiasts of Basque culture. The bells of Santa María ring out loudly, as befits a basilica, and those of San Pedro answer in a lower, humbler tone. She'll end up being late for the movie.

There's a line to get in, but nobody's waiting to buy tickets. She decides to stick around by the ticket office for a while in order to offer Lynn's ticket to somebody; it would be a pity to let it go to waste. But nobody comes by looking for tickets. Even so, she puts off getting into the line, in which most people have accreditations hanging around their necks. There are different colored cards; she thinks they must denote different categories. A man who looks slightly like Chabrol booms out that he had dinner at Arzak. Sublime. His fat lips, really fat lips, are shiny, and he's wearing a gold-colored card. He speaks so that everybody can hear him. Julia wonders whether to just stop somebody and offer them the ticket.

She would if a woman by herself walked by, but that doesn't happen. She would use the words she's prepared—"I've got a spare ticket"—in either Basque or Spanish, depending on the person's appearance, but when she finally does see a single woman, she thinks she's walking too fast, it looks as if she's heading off to do something quite specific, has no time to waste, and Julia doesn't dare.

She wonders whether there are many possible interpretations for "I've got a spare ticket."

The silk jacket with leather lapels and pockets looks tight on the man. She recognizes it right away—it's the jacket that was too big for Martin. The man's dark, with curly hair and some gray in his beard. He's engrossed in a thick book that has a double magazine page wrapped around it to protect it. So she can't find out what the title is. If she had any doubts about who he was, a friend patting him on the back and saying "hi, Kepa" cleared them right up. He answers hi back. There are around a dozen people between her and them. He goes inside first but then stops to talk with a couple at the foot of the stairs leading into the viewing auditorium itself, his back to her as she walks by. His voice is pleasant, deep; she'd describe it as very manly.

The theater's fairly full, and the few free seats are dotted all around. She chooses a spot next to the aisle. She usually tries not to annoy people by asking them to let her through, and she hates people who just tuck their legs in or only pretend to, who don't get up. There's a girl of around thirty to her right, sitting on the back of the seat, her feet on the upholstered cushion, talking with a man who's standing up several rows ahead. Almost everyone's talking from one row to another. They give their opinions about the films they saw the night before, where they had dinner, how the food was. She likes going into movie theaters with plenty of time, enjoying the thought that she's going to see a good film. It feels good. In general she feels closer to the people she sees at the movie theater than to people in the street or in bars. Some men look at her as if they know her; she knows some of them, too, from having walked past them on the street. Four rows in front of her, a man who's standing with his back to the screen and looks as if he's keeping track of all the people coming in greets her seriously. She returns his greeting in the same way. As always, she has the sensation that people who go to the movies by themselves, especially women, get looked at as if they don't have any friends and so, aware of this, they get uncomfortable and try to look inscrutable.

Finally she sees him walking along the aisle, looking left and right for a free seat, and she only just stops herself from asking the dumb girl next to her to take her feet off the seat. If she and the person she's shouting with in the other row were each to move down one, she'd have a free space next to her where he would be able to sit. She'd like him to sit next to her. Right then, she looks at him, and he lifts his chin up, smiling as if he knew her. But he's never seen her before. She, too, greets him by raising her chin, but then looks behind her, feeling ridiculous as she realizes that he could be saying hello to somebody there. When she turns around again, she sees him moving along a row with difficulty, going to sit quite a ways to her left. And he starts reading again straight away.

MAX FRISCH, JOURNAL I-III
(Eine filmische Lektüre der Erzählung Montauk, 1974)
Ein Film von Richard Dindo

Frisch with his thick horn-rimmed glasses, his vision problems making one of his eyelids droop visibly, smoking his pipe with nearly imperceptible movements and almost continually.

Fifth Avenue Hotel. A uniformed employee sitting behind a desk says he remembers him well. He remembers, for instance, that one morning, at around ten, Frisch dropped his pipe as he came out of the elevator and when he, the employee, picked it up, Frisch thanked him. Thank you, thank you. They guy actually says "zank you, zank you," imitating Frisch's German accent. He also imitates him sucking on his pipe like a child with a lollipop. Then he asked him, *"What is the weather like today?"* continuing to imitate his voice.

Trattoria da Alfredo also appears, and it doesn't look as agreeable as you would think from reading *Montauk*. It's noisy, anyway.

OVERLOOK. The sign promising a view across the island, the sign where Lynn suggested they meet. The lighthouse and the group of houses that appear on the cover of the English translation of *Montauk*. The beach is sad, and the hotel, which you get to by going down a feeble wooden staircase, is disagreeable.

The storyteller's voice reads passages from the novel. A Ping-Pong table. Two solitary deck chairs on the sand. A girl with rolled-up blue jeans running along the shore.

FRISCH AND BRECHT.

THE HEADS OF THE BERLINER ENSEMBLE.

THE STILL PHOTO OF MARIANNE. One of those beautiful, dark Germans. Marianne and Frisch. The house at Berzona doesn't look particularly pretty, either. It's ugly, in fact.

INGEBORG BACHMANN on the television. She, too, is beautiful, but not as much so as Marianne. She has the swollen face of a woman who drinks.

FRISCH IN HIS TELEVISION APPEARANCES. His speeches.

TRIPTYCH. Extracts from the French version of the play, which she finds boring.

She's only interested in what Frisch says.

More shots of Montauk, the lighthouse, the sad beach, the deck chairs.

A woman who pretends to be Lynn wearing tall boots, with her hair down to her waist, apparently dyed straw blond, crossing First Ave / 46th St., where, apparently, Max lost sight of her.

There's a quarter of an hour break before the second film. Several spectators get up and leave, but most of them stay there and are talking vivaciously. People saying hello, making arrangements for the night . . . Not much being said about what they've just seen. The girl next to her, who's sat on the back of the chair again, didn't find it very interesting. She looks Italian, quite good-looking and sophisticated. A large bald man dressed all in black suggests they go out and have a wine, *"porque todo esto es un rollo"*—because all of this is very boring—and the girl takes him up on the offer.

Julia stays sitting down, looking at the man, who hasn't lifted his eyes up from his book. At one moment, he looks back, as if realizing she's been looking at him, and now she's absolutely sure he's looked at her and gets embarrassed. She decides to get up. She still has the slight hope that Lynn might turn up and say she's been away for a while and wasn't able to get there on time. She asks the doorman if there's any problem if she goes out to have a drink and then comes back, although she knows there isn't. Many people do that. She's hungry, she hardly touched the beans with all the trimmings, and she decides to grab a sandwich. That way she won't have to make the inevitable French omelette by herself since her mother and Zigor won't be back until after dinner.

She decides to go to Paco Bueno, because it's close and they do good battered hake sandwiches. It's all traditional fare. There are people there, but it's not crammed. The hake looks good—the batter is thin, the egg isn't splattered, it's light-colored but with a touch of yoke. She orders a glass of wine, too. She seldom goes into a bar by herself and mostly just to grab a *café con leche*, never wine—cultural mores.

"Did you like it?" the man says from behind her. She doesn't answer right away, because her mouth's full, and in any case, she doesn't know quite what to say. "The film, I mean; I know you like the sandwich." She can't help laughing. She points to her cheek to say that she can't answer because her mouth is full. She wouldn't like to give an opinion he doesn't agree with, or be negative. He orders a hake sandwich for himself, and she, finally, tells him the truth: it's a little disappointing. Not too much, she adds, because she wasn't expecting much in the first place. Lynn had warned her it wasn't great.

"My name's Kepa," he holds out his hand. It's large and warm. "I'm Julia." He knows she's Julia. She should ask him how he knows, but she doesn't. But she lifts her hand up to her neck instinctively, as if he'd mentioned Flora Ugalde. "I know Martin," he says. He seems to think that's reason enough to have recognized her. She thinks about saying she knew he was a friend of Martin's, but she has to admit she only recognized the jacket. He lifts his glass and touches it to hers. They drink. He takes a long sip. He also knew that she was going to be at the movie theater. Lynn told him.

Has she had any news from Lynn?

Julia tells him she hasn't heard anything from her in days. She tells him about Maureen's arrival and Martin's theory that she's killed Lynn, trying to be funny, but not managing it. She never manages to repeat his witty remarks successfully. Kepa hasn't heard anything, either. He says it seriously. And he doesn't know anything about Abaitua, either, only that he's not working. Julia's very surprised by him saying that, by him revealing so much about their friendship. She prefers to be discreet and, to change the subject, asks what he thought of the documentary.

He didn't like it at all. Going around looking at places Frisch went to, something like "Napoleon once slept in this bed." His television appearances were interesting, the interviews with him and the bits of conferences, all of which showed how sincere Frisch was. They laugh about Frisch being surprised, unable to understand

Brecht wanting to be buried in a steel coffin. When he wondered, "To protect himself from what?" and his later reflection, "We didn't know him." A disappointing conclusion for somebody who wrote so much, he says, adding that Frisch, on the other hand, is somebody we know very well. He was merciless with himself, sincere, displeased with the world, frustrated by his lack of relationships with women, obsessive. They laugh again, remembering what the writer's mother said to him when he was fifty-five: Why did he insist on writing so much about women if he didn't understand them? Kepa liked seeing Bachmann. He only knew her from photos, as did Julia, and her voice didn't disappoint him. She, too, thinks Bachmann looked like a drinker. "A woman who's lived," Kepa says. An interesting woman, in any case; she probably wasn't easy to get along with. It reminds him of the passages Frisch writes in *Montauk* and in his diaries describing their life together. Their journey back from Rome in a Volkswagen with no headlights. Sitting drunk on the ground and believing she could feel the planet going around. Kepa thinks that Beckett wrote somewhere that he had the same impression after drinking whiskey, and he's felt the same thing himself on occasion. What they laugh most about is the passage in which Frisch and his wife are having dinner with a friend—feeling unappreciated, left out, he gets up from the table and comes back with a waste paper bin on his head and says, "Don't worry, just go on as if I weren't here," unaware that the friend is his wife's very public lover. They laugh, but then Kepa says that the scene could well be one of Faustino Iturbe's, but as he finishes saying that, he seems confused, as if he regrets having said it. Julia keeps quiet. She would rather he didn't mention Faustino Iturbe.

He says Frisch reminds him of Martin, or the other way around, they're very much like each other. It's an unavoidable subject. Julia agrees that there is a connection in their writing styles, but no more than that. She doesn't know why she says that she doesn't think Martin would be capable of going to Egypt with a dying friend who wants to see the pyramids. Why this sudden impulse to show her disaffection for Martin in front of this man? She doesn't know, but she can't help underlining the same idea by bringing up that friend of Frisch's he only mentions by his initial, W, and who he looks up to in every sense: socially, intellectually, and even physically. Martin's too proud for that. Martin couldn't be friends with somebody brighter and more attractive than himself, and he would have felt humiliated if somebody richer and more elegant than him ever offered him clothes. Kepa asks her if she thinks that's so important. "Martin himself gave me this jacket." He pulls at the lapels as if inviting her to touch the cloth if she wants to. "In fact, it's of the highest quality, and he never wore it," he adds humbly. He doesn't seem to realize that Julia really wishes she hadn't said anything, and she goes back to concentrating on eating her sandwich. He picks up another mushroom *pintxo* before Julia finishes her own. There's no doubt he's a good eater, but she doesn't find that unattractive. She agrees to another wine, even though she knows it'll go to her head.

There is no discussion when it comes to paying. He makes a vigorous, stylized movement to the barman, proffering a fifty-euro bill between his index and middle fingers. When they leave, he turns left and heads up Kale Nagusia instead of going back to the theater, and Julia follows him. There aren't any people at the theater door, so the film's already started. Finally, although it's late, she asks him if he doesn't want to see the next film, and he answers by shrugging his shoulders. "I'd rather chat with you." Julia laughs. She, too, prefers to carry on chatting, but she doesn't say so. She only reminds him that he's left his book inside, even though that gives away the fact that she was looking at him when they were in the cinema. He doesn't mind, he says—it was boring.

As they walk toward the Santa María basilica—he talks about Bachmann, her tragic death, and agrees that Frisch can't have been easy to live with, either—Julia remembers how the two met in Paris, their first meeting, at a theater where one of Frisch's plays was to be put on for the first time and he asked her to have a coffee with him instead of seeing his play; he, too, preferred to talk with the girl. She liked that enthusiasm of the writer's, preferring to seduce a young poetess rather than enjoying success and seeing his play on stage for the first time, although that could also have been a sign of immaturity, a sign of being dangerously addicted to the game of seduction. Julia would like to share that memory with Kepa, but she doesn't think it appropriate.

They turn left onto Portu Kalea and turn left again before going through the Portaletas gate and walking along the wall. He says he's hungry, really hungry, as he always is when he hasn't eaten with a fork and spoon—eating things on pieces of bread does no more than whet his appetite. He says it with disappointment, sounding even a little irritated, as if he were mentioning the symptom of an illness. Then he puts two fingers in his mouth and gives out a penetrating whistle that sounds like some sort of a code—B, C, D, E.

A man sticks his head out from a ground-floor window on the next block and then waves an arm in greeting. They go toward him. The man greeting them has an enormous belly and is wearing a white apron. They can see inside from the window—it's a gastronomic association. There's not much to it, the kitchen and two or three long tables with benches, all wooden and varnished, sitting on which there are only men. All of them are beyond middle age. Some of them are playing cards, there's a very peaceful atmosphere. Kepa asks the cook how it went in Brazil, and he replies, "Very bad," completely seriously. It's terrible over there, the mulatto girls are shameless, and he adds, "Obviously, with this body of mine . . ." and grabs onto his belly with both hands. The sexual harassment was overwhelming. Thankfully, he had the devotional scapular his mother gave him. He laughs out loud at his own pleasantry. His name is Xabier and, Kepa says, his monkfish and hake in sauce are unparalleled, even though he doesn't eat fish himself. That's right, says the cook, he's a pure meat-eater. He throws four small crabs into a frying pan and then a handful of salt. The crabs let out a type of screech and move around as they redden. It isn't pretty to watch. The cook invites Julia to come into the kitchen, but she doesn't want to. So the meat-lover hands her a plate with the crabs on it through the window, and they go to sit on the bench across the street. They talk about the quay, which is crowded with people. The bay is lit up. Julia doesn't feel comfortable eating the crabs she's just seen suffering and doesn't want to get her hands dirty. Kepa takes them out of their shells and splits them in two. He doesn't feel uncomfortable at all and sucks on them with obvious pleasure. Finally she follows his lead—they really are exquisite.

There aren't any real fishing boats in the harbor. He says there's no longer a smell of tar and ropes; or the smell of brine, she adds. He takes a cigarette out of a wide tin box. It smells good when it's lit, sweet like pipe tobacco. The sleeves of his jacket are rolled up to his elbows, revealing his muscular arms; he's half lying back on the bench, the legs stretched out. It doesn't smell of *marmitako*, either. It reminds her, says Julia, of when the inner harbor used to be full of fishing boats, and the fishermen all sat together on their sterns with spoons in their hands around large pots of *marmitako*. And the fishermen's wives, dressed in black, played cards on the overturned barrels under the arches. She tells him that earlier, on Kanpandegi Kalea, before going into the cinema, she was remembering *Elogio sentimental del accordeón*, and closing his eyes, he begins to recite: *"¿No habéis visto, algún domingo, al caer la tarde, en cualquier puertecillo abandonado del Cantábrico, sobre la cubierta de un negro quechemarín, o en la borda de un petache, tres o cuatro hombres de boina que escuchan inmóviles las notas que un grumete arranca de un viejo acordeón?"*—Haven't you ever seen, some Sunday at dusk, in abandoned ports along the Bay of Biscay, on the decks of black schooners or on the gunwales of flat-bottomed boats, three or four men wearing berets and listening, motionless, as a young cabin boy plays an old accordion?

Julia says it isn't possible, he can't know all that by heart. Lynn told her about his miraculous memory, but she never thought it would be that good.

There's resignation on his face. It's just memorizing. He has his hands on the edge of the bench now, his body leaning forward. He says Lynn's told him she's a wonderful piano player. Julia's embarrassed. She doesn't play very well, but Lynn thinks everything's wonderful. "Well, Faustino Iturbe thinks Flora Ugalde's a virtuoso, too."

Julia nods, "Yeah, a virtuoso, that's what I am," and says no more than that. Kepa keeps quiet. She thinks he's got it that she doesn't like him talking to her about Flora Ugalde. They're both quiet, but that doesn't make Julia feel uncomfortable. *"An easy silence."* A green boat comes into the harbor. It's a fishing boat. A flock of seagulls is flying behind its stern. Kepa says that before, when he was a child, everybody knew how to play the mouth organ. Julia, too, has sometimes wondered why that instrument disappeared. It's the humblest of instruments. Her father used to play.

"My father was a fisherman," she says out of the blue.

"And mine was a baker."

Kepa laughs as he draws the conclusion, "So you and I are the miracle of the loaves and the fish." Then he looks her in the eyes and says seriously, "It's true you have eyes you could get lost in." The intensity with which he says it disconcerts Julia. She doesn't answer. She keeps quiet too long to be able to say now that he shouldn't tease her. Faustino Iturbe often describes Flora Ugalde's eyes. "Eyes you could get lost in." Always attentive to her eyes. He's often compared her eyes with worrying lakes that hint of vegetation in their depths, depths of deep, dark water that are moved by anger less and less and made more and more still by disdain and boredom. And when they do shine with happiness, he's happy whenever he believes it's because of him. That, at least, is what it said in the last episode.

"It's Flora Ugalde's eyes that are deep," she says, too late.

"But it's obvious it's you who lent them to her."

To avoid his eyes, she looks at the green fishing boat and the seagulls flying behind it, almost directly above the stern. The fishermen are throwing out the fish that are spoiled or that they won't be able to sell, and that's what the seagulls are after. When the boat arrives at the quay, they fly easily up to the castle, drawing wide knots in the air. In praise of the simple pleasure of flying, Julia would say. She doesn't mind if Kepa thinks that's a dumb thought. She thinks they fly more than any other type of bird. He neither agrees nor disagrees. "*Non sortu ta zer izan / hautetsi ahal banezake, / hoiek bezela kaio / Gaztelupean jaio / eta biziko nintzake*," he recites in Basque—If I could choose what to be and where to be born, I'd be like those gulls and under the Castle spend my days. He says it in a deep voice, as if it were a serious declaration. She asks him if they're his lines, if he's a poet, too. They're by Emeteri Arrese.

He takes her by surprise when he asks her, without any sort of segue, as if they were still talking about the seagulls, what she feels about the whole issue of Flora Ugalde. It reminds her of Lynn asking her how she feels about having been turned into a literary character. It seems to her as if that conversation happened years ago.

"Resigned, I suppose."

He takes another cigarette out of his tin box, lights it, lets the smoke out of his mouth, and then swallows it again. It's clear he gets a lot of enjoyment from smoking. He looks as if he wants to say something, but there's a bit of tobacco on his lip, and he keeps quiet.

Julia remembers things.

Flora Ugalde, wearing her red coat, runs along the train stop platform to meet her lover, knowing that Faustino Iturbe is following her.

Crouched down on the ground protecting her face with her arms. Faustino Iturbe is furious, shouting that she's a whore.

Confused, wanting to flee along the gravel path she can see from the window as Faustino Iturbe hangs around her legs, begging her not to abandon him.

Answering his interrogation: Did you enjoy it with him? What did you two talk about? Did you talk about me?

Him reproaching her for snoring like a man.

For wearing such foul pajamas and always putting them on inside out to avoid feeling the stitching.

Him speaking ironically about her inability to accept even the smallest sacrifice when it comes to being attractive; about her lack of interest in him except to disdain him; saying that her panties are boring; that he's seen her surreptitiously putting a load of paper tissues between her thighs, waiting for him to fall asleep so that she can wash off his sperm.

Julia wonders what the man who's read *Loves and Sorrows* and has such a good memory is thinking about. She asks him for a cigarette, just to do something. She hasn't smoked for a long time and starts coughing as soon as she lights up. Kepa pats her back as if something's just gone down the wrong way and rests his hand on her shoulder. She feels his heat. Her eyes water as she coughs, and she smiles to let him know it's nothing serious.

Only to Lynn—and that, moreover, happened as soon as she met her—has she ever admitted that she sees the awful relationship between Faustino Iturbe and Flora Ugalde as a reflection of her and Martin's relationship. Their intimacy has been made public, if slightly disguised. Sometimes she's thought it would be better if he just came out and wrote about it all openly, telling things as they are, without changing any names, without passing it off as fiction. That way, at least, she would be able to demand he get things exactly right and he wouldn't have any right to embellish the truth. Her pathetic situation, her and Martin's real situation. Remembering his slogan that fiction is justified by being close to the truth makes her laugh.

Kepa doesn't ask her why she's laughing. She figures he must be thinking she's as hysterical as Flora Ugalde. She tells him about the conversation she had with Lynn when she asked her what it felt like to be the inspiration for a literary character. Julia laughs again.

She remembers Martin saying, "So you two did talk about me."

The memory of that makes her stand up. "I'm boring you," she says, while he remains seated on the bench. He answers seriously, as if offended, "That's not true." Julia takes a few steps over to a street light and says, "Come here so I can see your lying face properly." He doesn't hesitate and looks straight at her as he walks toward her. She thinks he might kiss her, but he doesn't. He just stands there looking at her, and then she says she has to get the train. There's one in twenty minutes.

THEY LEAVE IJENTEA KALEA, join the noisy boulevard, and continue on in the direction of the river. They don't talk much; they're constantly getting separated by the people coming in the other direction. Julia thinks about the coming goodbye and decides to say she'd like to see him again when they get to it. She rehearses the sentence. "I hope to see you again . . ." But she'd like to have something more to say. Even though there are swarms of people in the Okendo gardens, too, the noise they make doesn't drown out that of the birds in the palm trees taking shelter from the unusual light and all the people walking around. She must have made an expressive face on lifting her hands up to her nose, still a little revolted by the smell of the crabs. "If you want to wash your hands, I have a suite reserved here," he says, pointing at the María Cristina Hotel. She laughs and thinks she's sounding hysterical again. "I can put up with it until I get home." He insists he's being serious. He has to go up and unmake the bed. Julia frowns as she looks at him, now knowing what to say, while he says once more that he's serious. Finally she admits that she knows about everything Martin went through to reserve the suite for the Catalans. And knows he came up with a plan to make it look as if the room's being used, so that nobody can reproach him for going around asking for favors in vain. She'd guessed that Martin was going to ask Kepa to do this favor for him. She doesn't know why. She must be quite tipsy, because she tells him now that she only agreed to walk with him because she knew he had a suite. She laughs again, so that he won't take her seriously. Yes, she is curious to see what a suite in that run-down, glamorous old hotel is like. "Come on then, we'll ask for the key and go and wash our hands." She accepts, but standing still at the foot of the stairs, while Kepa's already on the second step, she tells him she's promised herself not to sleep with a man the same day she meets him. He turns around and says, in a

750

completely natural way, that he agrees. He could have said, "Going to bed with you is the furthest thing from my mind." Likewise, he might have understood that before reaching this decision, she often took men to bed with her on the very first day she'd met them. Thinking these things, Julia becomes nervous and goes red. But Kepa doesn't seem to have realized and, in any case, doesn't say anything. Then she hesitates over whether to stand next to him at the reception desk or whether to stand discreetly away from him. There are people swarming around, and there's not much glamour. There are no big stars around. Eventually, she decides to step up to the desk with Kepa; the reservation was made for a couple, and just in case he comes across any difficulty. But there's no trouble, even though his last name's not Calvet i Barot; Martin told them in his best Spanish accent that a *Don Pedro Ruiz* was going to be taking the suite. When the receptionist calls the bellboy, Kepa, without batting an eyelid, says that his chauffeur is going to bring their suitcases in later. In the same relaxed way he tells Julia that it's actually his real name, Pedro Ruiz, although everyone calls him Kepa Ziur. The *Kepa* part is obvious—that's how you say "Pedro" in Basque. Ziur: an anagram of Ruiz.

The bellboy tells them as he opens the door that Bette Davies stayed in their same suite. A bright young man who laughs when Kepa says "I bet you tell that to everyone." There's a large sitting room, and the bedroom has a balcony that looks out onto the river. The bathroom is done up in Carrara marble, as you would expect. On the table in the middle there's a large bunch of white and red roses and a bottle of Moët & Chandon in an ice bucket.

When Julia comes out of the bathroom after getting rid of the smell of the crabs on her hands, Kepa Ziur, which is to say Pedro Ruiz, is opening the bottle of champagne. "They're going to put it on the bill anyway," he answers the question on her face, and in order not to seem mean, she accepts the glass he enthusiastically gives her and repeats his toast, "To our meeting." They're face-to-face in a room that's too large, too luxurious, and too decadent, and they seem to have nothing to say to each other. Julia has never understood the pleasure some couples seem to get from spending weekends in luxury hotels. She spent two nights at the Paris Ritz— because of Proust, of course—and hardly enjoyed the marble, gold-framed mirrors, velvet curtains, and the staff's not entirely respectful way of looking at her. She recalls Frisch, who always knew when a place—some shop or restaurant—wasn't for him. He'd forgotten to say that sometimes the staff themselves will let you know when you're in a place that isn't for you.

The Fifth Avenue hotel Frisch stayed in didn't seem very luxurious. Or very welcoming, either.

So she brings the film up again, even though she doesn't have much to say about it. Neither does Kepa, who says once more that he liked seeing Ingeborg Bachmann. Julia, feeling like saying the opposite, and a little annoyed by Kepa's reverence for fame, says she found Marianne prettier. Kepa argues that they're very different and, in Bachmann's defense, that she's much older. Around thirteen years older. Kepa frowns as he calculates the difference, and Julia realizes it's a habit of his, he does it to get his astonishing memory in gear. He frowns and sharpens his eyes a little, half closing them, as if he were overcoming myopia. It's fairly clear that after a certain age, Frisch started having relationships with increasingly young women. He met Ingeborg Bachmann when he was forty-seven, and he was no more than fifteen years older than her; Marianne, who he met four years later, was twenty-eight; and in Montauk, when he's already sixty-six, Lynn is not yet thirty-one, so he's thirty-two years older than her.

Julia didn't know that Marianne was so young. She says she likes her but finds it difficult to explain why when he asks her. There's that sentence Frisch recalls in *Montauk*: "I have not been living with you to provide literary material. I forbid you to write about me." Admitting that she identifies with her would involve the risk of bringing Flora Ugalde into the conversation, so with Kepa still waiting for her reply, she says she doesn't know why.

"She made Frisch suffer a lot."

Kepa, sitting on the edge of the bed now, is struggling to take off one of his shoes. She sees something on his face again, a moment of embarrassment, which leads him to explain, "It's really tight." And Julia replies that as far as she's concerned, he can strip naked if it makes him more comfortable, hoping to make him feel more at ease. Not a very appropriate thing to say, but fortunately, Kepa doesn't take her at her word. As if he hadn't heard her, he says once more that Marianne made Frisch suffer a lot.

"And vice versa, I think."

In any case, what do they know about Marianne? That she doesn't go to New York with Frisch, because she's afraid of flying, but that later on she doesn't hesitate to get a plane to meet up with her lover. That she inspired Frisch's most beautiful writing on the subject of jealousy. Some of which tears you apart. That she has her extramarital affair, sure that Frisch, like everyone around them, is aware of it and doesn't mind. As well as being unfaithful, that seems a little naïve to Julia. They have to bear in mind that they only know Max's version, a man humiliated by being the last person to know that his wife is sleeping with his friend. But he's so sincere. He doesn't try to excuse himself, he's as demanding and bitter as ever: "A man who does not notice that a woman has come to him from another bed is no truly amorous man."

Kepa's feet are wide, like those of a fishermen used to walking barefoot. He has hair on the knuckles of his big toes. "There's no denying the similarity between Faustino Iturbe and Frisch." He lies down on the bed, and lifting himself up on his elbows and heels, he bounces several times on the mattress to test it out. It really is a *"heavenly bed,"* he says happily, and Julia instinctively moves backward until she bumps into the desk. When it's too late, she realizes he'll take her for some silly woman running away because she's afraid he'll suggest she lie down next to him. He sits on the side of the bed again.

"Don't you think so?"

She's tempted to ask whether he means Faustino Iturbe or whether he's really talking about Martin. But she prefers to avoid the subject and continue talking about the film, even though she doesn't have much to add—that woman they see crossing 46th Street after they've said goodbye, with her blond hair, unquestionably dyed, and those boots that give you the creeps, has nothing in common with the Lynn she imagined when reading *Montauk*.

Kepa laughs. Apparently Noll says in his book that the things you read in *Montauk* would be of no use for getting to know the real Lynn. The real one's movements seem happier and softer to him, and perhaps the old man's dreams have changed her into what he wanted.

Julia is astonished, confused more exactly, even though she's not sure where her astonishment comes from. She checks that he's talking about *Words on Death*. Sure enough, he's talking about the book she bought in his shop that says on the cover that it includes Frisch's reflections on death, probably to sell more copies. She doesn't dare tell him she bought the book in his shop, prey to a senseless fear that he'll guess she's been trying to meet him. She's astonished that she never realized Lynn appears in the book.

"It's toward the end of the book. It sounds like you didn't finish it."

It doesn't sound like a reproach at all, but Julia still feels guilty when she stops reading a book before the end. She tells him the truth, she didn't finish it, because she feels she has to explain herself. It isn't exactly that she didn't like it. She admits that Noll's almost happy stoicism with regard to death is admirable, the way he calmly goes on skiing and visiting his friends, his desire to squeeze the last drops out of life, even though she doesn't much like the narcissism with which he approaches death, preparing his own funeral, that desire to be the center of attention and all the rest. To tell him the whole truth, she would have to say that she couldn't stand reading all the way to the end, because it made Martin examining his own fictional death in front of the mirror seem even more pathetic. But she just explains that Martin was more interested in the subject than she was and took the book from her when she was about to finish it. She stopped where Noll's clogged-up lungs start to make it hard for him to breathe.

So she never found out that Frisch's friend—by that time seriously ill, in great pain, and breathing with enormous difficulty—very much enjoyed spending four days at the house Frisch had in Berzona. "He spends the whole morning writing and then scratches everything out and rewrites most of it, leaving short forms with lots of gaps which the reader has to fill in, that economical form so typical of his later work." Noll's words, which Kepa recites by heart. It was during this stay that he said that the information in *Montauk* wouldn't help you to get to know the real Lynn. Alice, to give her actual name—the Lynn in *Montauk*'s real name is Alice Locke-Carey. Julia never knew that, either. He describes a very moving scene in which Frisch and Lynn—or Alice—are having a small disagreement while washing the dishes. This is how a third party sees them: Frisch showers her with praise, and she treats him with affection, happily. Suddenly she embraces him from behind and answers Noll's question by saying that she feels a bit like Alice in Wonderland.

ALICE IN WONDERLAND, NOT ALICE IN THE WONDERLAND.

So Max and Lynn's story does not end, as they had agreed it would, with a kiss on the corner of First Avenue and 46th Street and with their promise to send each other a postcard if they remembered. Kepa looks at her in amazement, shocked she didn't know that. Max, breaking their agreement, went back to New York and looked for her, but never found her. As Julia knows from *Montauk*, when he went to her office, the black woman at reception said, "Lynn is no longer with us," and he understood that she had died. But that had happened in '74, shortly after the weekend they spent together in Montauk. Kepa tells her that after he got divorced from Marianne, the two of them met up again, and lived together, too, going back and forth between New York and Switzerland until '84. They split up when he was seventy-three—when he still had seven years left to live—and Lynn, or Alice, was forty-one; she was the same age as Marianne when he and she got divorced.

"And does our Lynn know all of that?"

"I imagine she does."

"So why hasn't she ever told me?"

It's clear Kepa is enjoying bringing her up to speed. There's a third book of his memories besides 1973's *Berliner Journal*—Julia knows about that one, its publication was forbidden until the centenary of Frisch's birth, and she mentions it so that he won't think she's dumber than she is—which is a series of notes going from the start of '82 through to April of '83. *Entwürfe zu einem dritten Tagebuch* was its title, *Notes for a Third Diary*. Frisch had torn it up, but his secretary found a copy. Its publication was controversial in Switzerland, Germany, the States, and France, too. The arguments against: Is it legitimate to publish notes that add nothing to the writer's work and that he himself tore up? In favor: How could you not publish a text by one of the greatest writers of the twentieth century, even if it isn't a masterpiece?

That's not the subject regarding the book that Julia's interested in at the moment. She wants to know what it's like, what this *Entwürfe zu einem dritten Tagebuch* talks about.

He says it's a sad book, it probably isn't a masterpiece, but it does have traces of Frisch's best work; the cold, short beauty of his desperate sentences moves you. A man who shakes sentences the way you shake a broken watch, who doesn't feel obliged to do anything, who believes he doesn't owe anything to anybody in this world, who is increasingly frightened by his lack of affection for his friends, his lack of concern over public matters, and his own increasing freedom. In short, that's what makes somebody old, not needing to use a walking stick.

But what does it tell about?

His life in New York, Zurich, and Berzona. His sad, complicated life, especially in New York, where he bought a loft with Alice, to share with Alice, who is no longer Lynn. He doesn't like the States, because for Americans *freedom* is a synonym of *power*. The risks of the human race disappearing as a result of nuclear war frightens him, even though he has no future himself.

He talks about death. He describes Noll's visits: when he tells him about his mortal illness and asks him to be the one to read the prayer at his funeral; their conversations about suicide; the time in Egypt when he was about to die. Their afternoons at Luxor admiring the sunsets and drinking whiskey. Their trip back to Switzerland in the small medical plane that came to collect them. Frisch's points of view, which, without contradicting his friend's affectionate Socratic perspective, are incredibly precise and display his usual sharpness. Kepa says you can laugh at some passages. He gives some examples: in the back seat of a taxi on the way to the airport, Frisch clings onto his friend to stop him from falling over. The Arab taxi driver, seeing what's happening, drives around the potholes in the road with the greatest care. Too slowly—a funeral procession gets in front of them, six men carrying an unvarnished coffin in the middle of a singing clan. Frisch isn't sure whether Noll realizes. The driver, who is becoming impatient, points at the coffin bobbing up and down. "*Dead, look, this man dead.*" He says it three times, and then: "*Look for your friend.*"

And so on, and so on.

A lot of despair.

He knows the sentences in German:

Hänge ich am Leben? Am I attached to life?

Ich hänge an einer Frau. I'm attached to a woman.

Ist das genug? Is that enough?

But what does it say about Lynn?

Kepa says that what he picked up on about the relationship between Alice-who-is-not-Lynn and Frisch isn't very similar to what Noll says.

Alice reads *paperback-pageturners*—that could have been expected, since Lynn reads books about dolphins—and what little she knows about Tolstoy she learned from a movie, and she hardly knows anything about Shakespeare. On the beach, surrounded by young men, the subjects she is moved by are of indifference to him, so no conversations take place. She gets angry, because Frisch sits in a rocking chair smoking cigars instead of helping to decorate the Christmas tree. She does crosswords. She goes to self-help groups and relationship workshops that are vegetarian and alcohol-free. She's traumatized by her childhood, and when he's on the other side of the Atlantic, she sends him cassette recordings of herself sobbing as she tells him about her problems with her *daddy*. She's lazy. When they're in Berzona, Frisch walks through the forest every morning to buy fresh-baked bread and then, back at home, lays breakfast out on the terrace, while she's still asleep. She thinks that he admires the Soviet Union because he doesn't love the United States—"*You hate my country*"—and one day she asks him what he's ever done to make the world a better place. It's a hard question, Frisch concedes, although she doesn't know everything he's said and written throughout his life. He sits there, drunk like Chekhov's Uncle Vanya, and when she asks for her coat, he lets her go. The next morning, it's he who apologizes.

Lynn wird kein Name für eine Schuld.

Montauk, 1974.

Wird Alice der Name für eine Schuld?

In other words:

Lynn will not become a name for guilt (*Montauk*, 1974).

Will Alice become a name for guilt?

So they talk about Lynn, half nurse, half undine, about this Alice Julia knew nothing about. They talk about Frisch, about the man who Noll once said wouldn't die as long as he had problems with women. In any case, Alice wasn't the last, there was at least one other woman, called Karin, Kepa doesn't remember her last name; after the writer died, she spoke at the memorial service held for him at St. Peter's in Zurich.

Julia is glad that she's going to be able to read more things by Frisch. It reminds her of that vacuum she sometimes feels, that feeling of grief at knowing that on finishing a certain book, she won't be able to read anything more by that writer, nothing new, nothing she hasn't already read. She tries to explain to Kepa that she feels guilty because that feeling of loss is often deeper for her than that left by real people who are no longer in her life.

He looks at her in silence. What is he thinking about?

He smiles before answering. What he's sad about, he says, is that he isn't going to get to read any more about Flora Ugalde. When he was with Martin, he asked him about his novel, and his answer was that he was going to make it Faustino Iturbe's last. He thought he meant he was going to stop writing. Apparently he also asked him about that, but Martin didn't answer, he didn't want to talk about it.

Julia doesn't think Martin will ever stop writing. She tells him and immediately realizes that Kepa might think that's what she wants, that she wants him to stop writing, and she doesn't want him to suspect that. She remembers a sentence from Katherine Mansfield's journal—"I've discovered that I can't write and live at the same time." She would like him to be happy and doesn't think writing helps him to be. And she tells that to Kepa.

"I don't think writing makes him happy."

"And would he be happy if he stopped writing?"

She doesn't think he would be then, either. Needing to write is probably an acute symptom of his unhappiness. Maybe he writes because he's unhappy, or to find out why he isn't happy, and maybe if he were, he wouldn't write. She usually thinks that if he were happy, without the neurosis that suffocates him, his imagination, too, he would be free to write and enjoy moving, funny stories. He could; he's demonstrated that he's capable of it.

She tells Kepa she doesn't want to talk about Martin.

Let's talk about you, then.

Lynn's told him she's translating *Montauk* and *Fragebogen* into Basque, so Julia has to specify that she's only doing some passages from *Montauk*, only the passages she likes best. She's ashamed he's been allowed to get the wrong impression. She isn't a professional translator, she's always said that. As far as the questionaires are concerned, she translates a few of the questions from time to time, because they're short, and because translating something is the best way to read it.

Wieviel Geld möchten Sie besitzen? The fifth question in the sixth questionaire, the latest one she's translated: How much money would you like to have? She sits down next to him on the bed, and he moves away from her a little. So he's quite shy. She remembers how on that outdoor terrace in Ibaeta, Harri asked her what she would do if she won the lottery. She doesn't know why she tells Kepa what she didn't admit to then—she'd like to have a small monthly allowance, enough to pay her rent and not much more, enough to get by without any difficulties—she's the mother of a young boy— and enough to allow her to work on what she wants to. To work on literary translations at her own pace, for instance. And to write, too. She's thought of writing a story about the Basque Country, like Gombrich's *A Little History of the World*, drawing on the things she tells Zigor about at night. Having more time to read. Taking piano lessons. So she tells him about her projects, or rather her desires— things, in fact, that she hasn't shared with anybody else. Like a child writing a letter to Olentzero, the Basque Father Christmas. She also tells him the only thing she did tell Harri, that if she had enough money, she'd go to Havana with Zigor, an adventure she's always wanted to have.

Why does she blush all of a sudden? Kepa says with excessive enthusiasm—which somehow reminds her of Zigor—that he thinks it's an excellent plan for an adventure. Harri had teased her about that, as had Martin. He used the anecdote—as if he'd heard it from somebody else—to joke to people that it was the most complicated excuse he'd ever heard for a woman going to Cuba to find herself a nice mulatto man. The people listening always laughed. She has to overcome the urge to cry as she remembers it.

"It's a good plan," says Kepa, and to cover up the fact that she's upset, Julia gets up and takes a couple of steps toward the balcony. She blows her nose, facing away from him. When she turns around, he's still sitting on the edge of the bed, obviously awkward. Julia's ashamed of being so upset, she tries to smile, and says, "You're the one who really has a plan, having a suite ready in the María Cristina to bring me to."

He smiles, too. He's leaning forward, his hands to either side of him on the bed, as if he were sitting on the edge of a dock and gazing at the water beneath his feet. That's the image it conjures up for Julia. He tells him what Lynn already told her about his circumstances: he lives alone with his mother, who's lost her marbles and spends the whole day cooking the same dish over and over and drinking endless *cafés con leche*. And some things she didn't know: once, several years ago, he came home to find his mother reading a book. It was Simone de Beauvoir's *The Coming of Age*, some South American edition he'd left out on the kitchen table. His mother hardly knew how to read. She used to look at magazines, the newspaper from time to time, but he doesn't think she'd ever read a book. But that day, he found her leaning over the table with the open book in front of her. She didn't realize that he was there, her back was turned to him, and her hearing was already poor by then. He went up to her from behind and saw that the finger she was using to help her read was on the line about the Ammassalik Inuits of Greenland. The Inuits had the habit of committing suicide when they thought they were becoming a burden to the community. He read, too, over her shoulder, to the rhythm of her slowly moving finger. The old people would announce their decision publicly one evening and then, two or three days later, get into their canoe and paddle away from dry land, never to return. One disabled man, who wasn't able to climb into a canoe, begged to be thrown into the sea so that he could die quicker. His children obeyed him, but his clothes kept him floating on the surface. The daughter he loved most said to him lovingly, "Dad, put your head in, that'll make it quicker." He took the book away from her. It's hard for him to explain his reaction exactly, but that's what he did, and perhaps even a little roughly. They stayed in the kitchen for a while, silent. They were alone. His mother had both hands open on the table where the book had been, her head hanging down. Then she started crying. He thought they were tears of relief, silent cries he found moving rather than sad. He'd never seen her cry before, not even when his father died. She asked him to take her to an old person's home—she couldn't ever throw herself out a window.

Now Kepa's the one who gets up and moves toward the balcony. There's no special feeling in his voice when he says that his mother was aware that her presence was affecting his relationship with his wife. She knew she was in the way. He couldn't take her to an old person's home, because the private ones are expensive and there weren't any openings at the public ones. Later, he split up with his wife, but, he said, his mother had nothing to do with it. Silence again, which Julia doesn't dare break. A difficult situation: a man alone with his mother, who's lost her marbles; a man who wants to get on with his life. He opens the door to the balcony, and when he speaks again, his voice is accompanied by a happy murmur of other voices. Sometimes when he goes back home, he's afraid he'll find his mother's body lying on the sidewalk. He turns around and looks at her, as if to see how what he's just said has affected her.

"You know what?"

Obviously, Julia doesn't. Kepa smiles again before speaking. When Martin first made the absurd suggestion that he should use the suite, he thought about coming with his mother, spending the night here, having breakfast with her, and then leaving her here. He laughs. Julia laughs, too, but he says he's serious—he thinks he might have been able to work up the courage to do it. To leave her in her canoe. Fortunately, he didn't have to—two days ago, social services called to say there was a spot for her.

THE FILM FESTIVAL. KURSAAL LIT UP, the bluish-black river reflecting the street lights on either side of it. The giant lights on the bridges have always seemed like fog lights to her at night. There's a slight breeze and a smell of seaweed. Along with the street noise, there's the sound of an out-of-tune accordion playing *La Vie en rose*, it's hardly recognizable. It's probably that blind Bulgarian or Romanian guy—he spends the entire day, and seems to spend the entire night, too, out on the bridge. "Another drink?" They've drunk the bottle of champagne, and he asks her the question while standing next to the minibar. He takes his shoes off again. It's obvious he doesn't mind walking barefoot on the carpet. Something Martin would never do. No, she's already drunk enough, she says, and she's seen the price list. He says she shouldn't worry about the money. He tells her that seriously, he'll take care of paying for the suite—he's the one using the suite, after all. What's more, he's about to do a good piece of business.

Kepa has great plans; he talks about them with enthusiasm. Soon he's going to travel to London, to a second-hand shop where he's found a piece of treasure: some songs by Joannes de Suhescun, a musician at the court of Jeanne d'Albret, and his diary, written in Basque. It's incredibly valuable, but he hopes to get it for next to nothing. He's also about to fulfil his old dream of crossing

761

the Atlantic on a sailboat. A rich American fell in love with this schooner and bought it off a friend of his in La Rochelle. Now he has to deliver it to him in Palm Bay, and he's asked Kepa to help him take it over there.

Kepa says the schooner is a type of boat that dates back to the eighteenth century. He tells her about it—a sixty-five-foot miracle, very quick in all seas, fitted with every comfort—as if he were hoping to sign her up for the trip. They're going to stop for a time in Havana. He suggests she come along, quite seriously, and she, laughing, says that a schooner sounds like something very old, like Espronceda's *"velero bergantín"*—a sailing brigantine. She'd like to sail on a boat like that, with deck chairs on it. Kepa doesn't give up. Of course there'll be deck chairs on it, and a shower, and a fridge. He sits on the desk as he describes the boat's features—two masts, seventy-seven feet from bow to stern, nineteen-foot beam, four large cabins, each with its own bathroom, a fully equipped kitchenette—and he draws it for her, as well.

It's a wonderful sailing ship, and he draws it well. At full-sail, it cuts through the water and leaves a foamy wake behind it. "I'm sorry I can't paint it," he says with regret as he hands her the drawing, and Julia doesn't hesitate to get the watercolor kit out of her bag and give it to him.

"What's this?"

"Open it and you'll see."

Kepa's hands look nervous as he opens the packet, trying not to tear the paper. He doesn't seem used to being given presents. He looks very surprised when he finally gets it open. "But what is this?" he stammers again. He's amazed.

"As you can see, they're paints. Ask, and your wish will be granted."

By now it's already Sunday.

Although she finds it fun, Julia can't keep the suspense up any more and finally tells him the truth—the watercolor kit's a present for Zigor. Fifteen years old already. Kepa doesn't want to use them—in any case, the paper wouldn't take the paint, it's too thin—but does eventually agree to use the pencil.

The drawing grows in depth as he skillfully adds further details. The sensation of movement is greater. There are reflections of light on the water.

Fifteen years old already.

Julia watches him drawing. "Already quite the man," he says when he hears Zigor's age. He already knew that his name is Zigor and that his father is dead. Perhaps Kepa knew him, but she doesn't dare ask; doesn't much want to know, either.

There's a train at 05:15.

"Give him this present from me, too," he says, holding out an envelope. It has the hotel logo on it, and he's written *For Zigor* in an elegant hand. *A luxury collection hotel.* He stands still while he waits for Julia to open it. She does. An inscription underneath the sailing ship: "Valid for one sailing trip for two to Havana. For details, contact Kepa at 654010181."

"You're crazy," she says, as she puts the drawing back into the envelope.

He says it would be crazy to miss the opportunity.

He sits down beside her. He could draw the waves and clouds and she could write about why people write, or why she's translating *Montauk* into Basque, or they could just sunbathe in the deckchairs and drink daiquiris. It would be an unforgettable experience for the boy, and if he's still alive, the old black man would clear up the mystery of the messages her uncle used to send down to the *pilota* players. It's clear he's perfectly serious, and she, a little confused by it all, says once more that he's crazy. "I'm not." And then: "You'd be crazy to turn down an offer like this."

She'll have to think about it. She has to leave now.

He takes ahold of her hands. His hands are large, and she thinks again how warm they are. "Promise you'll think about it and let me know." She says she will. She decides she won't do anything to take her hands away, thinking that if he puts his arms around her, she'll let him. But he lets her go and bends down to pick his shoes up.

ALTHOUGH JULIA TRIES TO STOP HIM, he wants to go to reception to pay. Fortunately, the person there refuses his money. There are strict orders about it. They go out onto República Argentina Kalea. There are still people outside, and the temperature's good. They cross Santa Katalina Zubia and walk along Frantzia Pasealekua. They laugh at the inscriptions on an elegant mansion there. To the left of the front door: "*Cuan poco lo de acá, cuan mucho lo de allá*"—This life is so short, and the next one so long. And to the right of it: *"En casa del que jura no faltará desventura"*—Misfortune is never rare in the homes of those who swear.

The fountain with a dome held up by four caryatids. Apparently, the English philanthropist Richard Wallace gave a fountain of the same design to the people of Paris, and the people of Donostia, with their usual fine criteria, copied it. The four figures look identical but are, in fact, different. He makes her walk across the grass so that she can see them properly. Two of them, Subtlety and Measure, have their eyes closed; the other two, Goodness and Charity, don't. He steps in some dog shit and says it means good luck. Neither of them wants to get to the station.

When the train arrives, Julia doesn't dare to say that she'll take the next one. They have a long, intense hug but don't kiss. Kissing on the cheek would have been frivolous, silly, and she doesn't think it right to kiss him on the mouth—although she doesn't know if that's because it's too early or too late. She's sure he's thinking the same thing. "Don't forget to give Zigor his envelope."

A WHISPY CLOUD OF MIST gently rises from the river. Beyond the bridge, at the bend, between the abandoned industrial buildings and the first block of brick apartments, the river still looks unspoiled. The bed of reeds, which is all you can see from the spot, is what gives that impression, along with a willow tree that has one of its branches hanging down and trailing in the flowing water. The flat, open land at the riverbank slowly rises up to the hillsides and is covered in pampas grass, which she would think beautiful if she didn't know it to be an invasive species. She once mentioned the fact at Martin's house when Harri and Lynn were there. Harri said that all non-local species spoil things and that the same is true for fauna—American crabs eating the local ones, zebra mussels from the Caspian Sea spreading everywhere. They lamented the ability of non-local species to take over and put local species, with their limited reproductive capacity, in danger. Lynn said they had a distorted view—lots of non-local species probably didn't manage to survive among the local ones. But that, she told them, was something they didn't see. They didn't know what to say, it was clear she was working up a metaphor, one to use in connection with humans, and Julia remembers that Lynn clapped her hands together and said, "But I'm not protesting!" Martin's conclusion: local or not, it's the winners that win, the bad guys, like rats and weeds, the useless forms of flora and fauna.

Lynn was in a good mood. She reminded them that what they called "local" tomatoes actually came from America, just like the unparalleled Tolosa beans. Species that had managed to adapt, although, like her, they needed looking after, protection, even. Alice in Wonderland. Earlier, Kepa said that the last time he saw her, she was happy but not looking very well. She told him she was a little unwell, just as she'd told Julia, and he thought she might be pregnant.

It looks like the house is hanging over the apartment blocks covering the hilltop. Julia has the impression that years have gone by since she last saw it. All the shutters are closed. The undergrowth seems to have taken over the garden even more, the façades look even darker. She waits for a moment in front of the iron gate. It's locked, and she feels funny thinking how she used to have the key to it. She goes over to the stairs leading up to the house. She sees smoke coming from the Sagastizabal chimney beyond the Elektra factory. And the kitchen garden and part of the apple orchard, too.

She would like to go have breakfast in one of those cafés that serve coffee and brandy *carajillos* to both the recently risen and the still awake. Kepa suggested it, and she didn't feel like it at the time, but now she regrets it. She supposes it was because having breakfast with him would have confirmed the fact that they had spent the night together. Right now what she really feels like is *café con leche* and toast with butter and jam.

Trinquete Bar's closed. It's normally open early during the week, but not on Sundays. There's a poster on the door that's partially covered by one corner hanging loose. "*Herriak nahi du,*" it reads—What the people want.

When she reaches the first step, she hears the same dog as always barks, a rumbling noise from a pipe, the sound of a kettle or a coffeepot whistling, and the echo of the radio. Her mother coughs as she walks past her room, to let Julia know that she's awake. She takes her clothes off once she's in her own room but doesn't bother to fold them. She looks in the closet mirror. She thinks she's a desirable woman. She takes her bra and panties off and moves closer

765

to the mirror. She holds her breasts with her left hand and forearm and combs her pubic hair upward with her right. She'll have to trim it. When she was sitting next to Kepa on the edge of the bed at the hotel, it occurred to her that if he saw her naked, he'd see a tangle of hair down there. She puts her bathrobe on.

Her mother at the door: "So, you're back then?" Like Koldo Mitxelena's mother when he came back from the war.

Julia makes coffee. Meanwhile, her mother washes up the dinner things. Not very well—that farmhouse lack of attention to detail—and there's no point in telling her that she uses more water handwashing and she should just put it all into the dishwasher. She sits down on a chair at one corner of the table with her cup of coffee in her lap. She's in the way, she'd say. She should define that: somebody who feels excluded for no reason. They look at each other. At one point, her mother's grumpy face makes her think she's going to say "What kind of time is this to be just getting back home?" as she once used to. Then she understands why she's in a bad mood. Martin called her the night before, because Julia wasn't answering her cell phone. She'd turned it off. She looks at the missed calls when she turns it on again, to see if there's a message from Kepa. Which makes her regret not having stayed to have breakfast with him even more.

"For Zigor." Two envelopes, one behind the other, on the small desk. The handwriting on them isn't very different—Zigor's is more careful, Kepa's lighter—but the envelopes are very different. Kepa's, with the María Cristina Hotel logo on it, is long; the other is square, and it's made of better paper, stronger and thicker. It's soft to the touch, probably lined with blue or violet silk-like paper, which used to be more common, but that isn't why it's thicker—there's more paper inside it, or the paper that's in it is heavier. Probably both. When you want your teenage son to read your words after you've gone off to another world, it makes sense that you would choose good paper and need more than one sheet to write it all.

She puts Kepa's envelope on Zigor's bedside table and looks at the other one for a moment. When she holds it up to the light— something she's done dozens of times in the past in a vain attempt to check its opacity—she notices that her hands are trembling. The difference now is that she knows she's going to open it. She puts it back on the table, face down. She knows the one end of the pointed flap is slightly open, and she's checked that the rest of it is completely stuck down. There's no doubt it's good glue; she's been tempted to try to steam it open sometimes. She even tried once, but she worried that she might also make the ink run and stopped. Now, scissors in hand, she thinks it's been ridiculous of her to worry so much when it's actually so easy—all she has to do is put it into another envelope afterward. But before it always seemed so sacred to her.

She cuts the envelope open; it's a little hard because of the thickness of the envelope, and because the scissors aren't very sharp. Just as she thought, the envelope's lined with violet-colored paper, and there are two pieces of cardstock with careful handwriting on them, perhaps even too careful—it looks too much like someone's final draft of something. She puts them carefully one on top of the other on the table without daring to look at them, though she can't help reading " . . . for not being like other fathers"; "You'll be fifteen now . . ."; "I wanted to preserve my dignity"; "We can't give up now . . ." Her eyes cloud over, and she looks at the light coming in through the window. She's no longer so anxious, because she knows that what she's going to read is what she's so often imagined, because she didn't think Zigor could have written anything else. "I wanted to preserve my dignity."

The sound of the toilet flushing in the bathroom. Zigor's voice, still sleepy, saying good morning to his grandmother. "I can feel death waiting for me as I write you these lines, but I'm not afraid. I'm sorry that I won't see you grow up, that I won't be able to tuck you into bed and talk with you, as other fathers do, when I get back from work." She sharpens her hearing, with the pieces of cardstock in one hand and the other on the handle of the open desk drawer, ready to hide the letter in case the boy comes in. "When you read these lines, you'll be fifteen, you'll be a man, and you won't have me by your side."

The voice from the next world is joined by her mother's from the kitchen, singing that stupid tune, "Happy birthday to you."

Julia continues reading: "I wanted to preserve my dignity by following what my conscience is telling me, sacrificing my life." That's a sentence that, until recently, would have made her forgive anything, and now it gives her a mixture of feelings she can't unravel. Disappointment, anger, and, most of all, sorrow. "They've been trying to exterminate our country for centuries now, but we can't give up now. I haven't, and I hope that you won't, either."

She drops the hand holding the cards into her lap. She rips them in two as tears come to her eyes. She puts the four pieces one on top of the other and tears them again. She mixes them up on her lap—she sees half sentences such as "you won't, either"; "dignity to be so"; "this land is ours"—and suddenly feels at ease and tired.

"Happy birthday dear Zigor, happy birthday to you".

Happy birthday to you. He comes into the room wearing the ugly knitted sweater his grandmother's given him. "A whole fifteen years old," she hears from behind him, he's a man now, and he protests. Why from the age of fifteen exactly? He says he was just as much of a man the day before. Julia hugs him. She, too, would say that he's grown since the day before. She feels his warmth and smells him, but she doesn't dare hold him in her arms as long as she would like to.

Presents. The one she's giving him on Martin's behalf first. The watercolor set and Baroja's *Zalacaín el aventurero*. He's happy—Martin always gets it right. Then her own presents. He likes the surfer hoodie, and it looks good on him. The expression on his grandmother's face shows she thinks he likes that more than her present, so he puts the sweater back on again.

She challenges him to find her favorite sentence in the book. She sometimes does that when she lends him a book, although she's not sure it's a good idea, because it influences his reading to an extent.

There's the start of an argument when the bells at the nun's church ring out. "What right do they have?" Julia says as she raises her hands to her head. She has a headache, and her mother says she'd have fewer headaches if she slept in the same bed every night. Not caring that the boy's there to hear it. She's going to mass. She says it with a tone of reproach, holding Orixe's Basque-Latin missal against her chest, even though it's unnecessary—she knows it just as well in Latin as she does in Basque. She doesn't put on a *mantilla*. Julia asks her mother maliciously if she no longer takes communion, and she, astonished but defiant, asks what's behind her question. "You've already had breakfast." And she looks at her daughter with pity. It's obvious she hasn't set foot in a church for a long time—it's no longer necessary to have an empty stomach before taking communion, nor is confession necessary now, either. It's enough to repent and harbor an intention of improving. Julia contradicts her, saying that repentance is good for a while, provisionally, so to speak; although she's not very sure of what she's saying, she enjoys making her mother doubt and seeing how nervous it makes her. It's clear the idea that she has to confess is enough to make her nervous. But Julia doesn't feel sorry for her; or rather, her thirst for revenge is greater. She remembers that her mother instilled her with a fear of touching the host even with her teeth, and now people pick it up with their hands. The relaxed attitude of her mother, and of all Catholics, makes her angry—they avoid making even the smallest sacrifices for the religion they so strictly forced on her. Zigor says he wants to go with his grandmother, he says they now do collective confessions, he's heard that at school, and he makes a discreet sign for Julia to keep quiet, as if saying to her, "What do you care anyway?" She's ashamed—her son's more mature than she is.

Zigor is still wearing his pajamas and reading *Zalacaín* at the kitchen table. Barefoot, he has one foot on a chair, one hand holding the book up, and the other hand hangs loosely from the arm that's resting lazily on his knee, twirling a pen around; he always keeps a pen nearby when he reads. Like she does. But his posture seems like a young boy's to her. He looks at her from the corner of his eye and continues reading. She puts the breakfast things her mother hand-washed into the dishwasher and says she's going to take a shower.

Apart from a white cotton pair, all the panties she has are beige. Waist-high beige silk panties, and they aren't cheap, as she's said a hundred times to Martin when he's teased her about them being so ugly. She's thinking of buying some more exciting ones. She's tired and lies down on top of the made bed. She puts one hand inside her bathrobe to stroke her breasts; the mere idea of buying new panties has made her feel seductive, her nipples have hardened, and she breathes more heavily. She has to overcome her urge.

ZIGOR IS AT HER DOOR IN THE SWEATER HIS GRANDMOTHER'S GIVEN HIM and has the book in his hand. Julia tightens her bathrobe belt. "I know what the sentence is," he says, without noticing her reflex movement, or so she hopes. It's the part about Martín starting to find out all he could about French liberalism and beginning to find his countrymen backward and fanatical. "*Martín empezaba a impregnarse del liberalismo francés y a encontrar atrasados y fanáticos a sus paisanos,*" he reads aloud. A significant choice. Why does he think that was what she found most interesting? She thinks it's a promising topic of conversation. She smiles as she remembers something

Faustino Iturbe once said. He'd like to make love to the Marseilles, underneath the Gernikako Arbola—the Tree of Gernika. That wasn't the part she most liked when she read the novel. "What is it, then?" He lies down on the bed, too. He tickles her, trying to make her tell him what it is. She refuses. She isn't going to tell him until he finishes the book. Now she tickles him.

They grapple. He gets on top of her with a leg on either side, and Julia tries to get him off her. He's stronger than her, and in any case, the way they brush against each other in body-to-body combat inhibits her. Even so, she lifts her hips up to try to pick up speed, but not realizing that Zigor has already stopped making any effort. He moves to one side and picks up the envelope with his name on it from the bedside table.

"And what's this?" he says, with his legs still to either side of her.

Julia tries to get the envelope, but he holds it beyond her grasp. She does nothing to stop him from opening the envelope and taking out the drawing of the schooner. He gets off the bed and sits in front of the desk with the drawing. She stares at him, her hands over her mouth. That goes on, and she thinks of telling him that it's a joke.

"Who's this Kepa?"

"A friend of Martin's."

He looks at her sharply and then seems to realize that she's embarrassed, because he looks away toward the drawing once more.

"Is he serious?"

"I think so."

Because she feels that saying anything else would be betraying Kepa.

24

ON THE RADIO, THEY'RE TALKING ABOUT the blue sky, which is going to cloud over as the day goes on and, by the afternoon, give way to some risk of showers, and Abaitua, just in case, looks in his closet for a light raincoat that isn't too sporty. Always prepared. He takes out a summer raincoat he's had for years and that won't look bad on him in the streets of Bilbao. He tries it on and thinks it looks good.

He goes into the kitchen, and Pilar doesn't realize. She's still wearing her bathrobe, sitting in front of the remains of her breakfast with a pen in her hand, and she doesn't see him, or doesn't want to look up before she finishes her sudoku. She's taken up that pastime again and spends hours doing it; it seems to require more concentration than the crosswords she used to do. Abaitua wants to be as gentle as possible when he tells her they're running late, and she, staring at him in silence for a moment as if she weren't actually seeing him, says she's not actually sure she wants to go and gets up reluctantly.

They've spoken about it before. He's told her he understands that she doesn't want to be around people, that she's lost her interest in work and is even tempted to forget about everything, but he tries to convince her that she has to face up to things as soon as possible and move forward. He encourages her once more. Urrutikoetxea probably hasn't heard a thing, and if he has, he won't care. It was an accident, one of the many that happen in hospitals every day, and as far as Urruti's concerned, Abaitua doesn't think he'll have the bad taste to bring the matter up, not unless it's to say something very much like what he's just said, in fact. He tells her again that he wants to go with her; it's not to do her a favor, he's been wanting to go for a walk around Bilbao for a long time now, to visit the Guggenheim, and to go to the type of good restaurant Urruti will certainly take them to. Pilar's eyes light up, and he's quite pleased about how respectful and patient he is with her.

PILAR DRIVES. She does so with confidence, resting her right hand on the gear stick and holding her foot back so as to not break the speed limit, getting angry with drivers who do break it and overtake her. There's not much traffic.

SOCIOLOGICAL REFLECTIONS. Abaitua observes that among more mature couples in high-end cars, the woman is often—perhaps not in most cases, but certainly in many of them—the driver. He thinks that now that almost everyone has a car, and to the extent that driving has gone from being something prestigious to a common, annoying chore, men, at least in the Basque Country, have lost interest in it, unless it's in rallies and such, and it's women who have to do it. It's similar with smoking, too—the men are giving it up and the women are starting. He's also noticed that whenever there's a couple with a stroller, it's the man who pushes it, regardless of the couple's age, and the same is true when it's the grandparents—grandfathers who were once ashamed to push their children's strollers are now proud to take their grandchildren out for a walk. He's convinced that in a few years' time, it'll be women, in general, who'll take care of politics— it's already becoming apparent in Scandinavia—and men will spend more and more time doing manual activities and gardening.

He isn't sure whether he's ever shared these thoughts with Pilar. Bearing in mind their lack of communication recently, he imagines he hasn't, but he wouldn't like to repeat himself. In any case, he decides to say something to break the silence, but even though she listens carefully, it's clear he doesn't have her full attention. She knows that women are taking over roles that have traditionally been considered men's, above all those that aren't very prestigious— or that lose their prestige once women take them on—but the opposite seldom occurs, beyond the exceptions that prove the rule. Men push strollers and look after children in the park while their mothers are at work, little more than that. Pilar gets very serious about the subject, and Abaitua's sorry he brought it up, because he thinks that, to an extent, Pilar's talking about him. He feels guilty, because he doesn't do any of the housework, although to a large extent that's because Pilar, who's so neurotically perfectionistic, doesn't let him—she doesn't like the way he does things. That's why they don't have a cleaner, either. If he washes things up by hand, she always puts them into the dishwasher later. She thinks that everything other people do is badly done; but it's also true that Abaitua doesn't try all that much. He accepts that Pilar's neurosis isn't an excuse, or at least not a complete one.

A Swedish woman says to her husband, "I'd rather you helped out more at home instead of going to so many Feminist Party meetings." He'd found it very funny when Lynn told him that. And he's sure he hasn't told Pilar the anecdote. He does, and manages to get her to smile.

THE THINGS TO TALK ABOUT IN BILBAO are how the city has turned its back on the river and the wonderful way in which the tone of the clouds in the sky transforms on the twisted titanium surface of the Guggenheim Museum. Urrutikoetxea's office has views of the Isozaki Atea Towers. Building them cost a little more than five hundred and fifty euros per square foot, not serious money. Although Urruti greets them in authentic Otzeta Basque, he gladly switches to Spanish on the excuse that his partner doesn't understand Basque.

His partner's a fat man. He looks a little like the resident who's in love with Lynn, above all because of his bulging eyes, but his flesh isn't as soft. Both of them are proud of the way the city's been transformed over recent years, especially compared to Donostia. The partner says what everybody knows—Donostia has closed in on itself, it's living off the past, it's held onto what it had to an extent, but its beauty is fading. Urruti agrees and goes even further and says it's a bit provincial: "*San Sebastián es un poco pueblo.*" Abaitua is hurt by Urruti—a Bilbaoan from Otzeta—saying things like that, but he listens to him in silence, even though he agrees to an extent, but mostly because he's determined to be pleasant. Pilar, though, does protest—even though she's always been a fan of Bilbao, even back when it was gray and ugly, when the area where all these wonderful modern buildings are now was the customs house for the port, because her father was on the board of Hispano—most of the board members were Basque speakers—and he often brought her there. Abaitua knows that she's defending Donostia on his behalf, to be on his side, and he's moved. Her arguments are weak, however, even though the other two seem to give way to them, admitting that the Kontxa is, of course, unparalleled and that the downtown is still quite attractive—"*La señora Concha, desde luego, es incomparable, y el centro sigue siendo coqueto.*" Things like that.

Abaitua agrees with Urruti that the rivalry between the people of Donostia and the people of Bilbao is more markedly on display in Donostia. He doesn't say that it's due to an inferiority complex, but he obviously thinks that. It's nice being with Urruti—because he never shuts up, it's easy to remain comfortably quiet. Abaitua's only worry is that he might bring up his lawsuit with the hospital or Pilar's accident—there's no doubt he must know about them—but for the moment, he doesn't mention either. They have a short discussion about whether the rivalry between the two cities has increased in recent years. Urruti's partner thinks it's always been the same, whereas Urruti thinks it's gotten worse and blames soccer for polarizing everything. He says Donostians think they're losing out there, too. So they talk about soccer for some time, about both cities' teams, about the differences between the two groups of fans. Pilar doesn't say anything. Abaitua thinks there's more localism than before. The patriotic idea of brotherhood between Basques that existed during the Franco years has lost strength since the Spanish Autonomous Communities were set up, including, among other things, when it comes to dividing inheritances between brothers and sisters.

Then they talk about what's usually refered to as "the situation."

Urruti openly describes himself as a nationalist, while his partner says he's a liberal—in the classical sense of the word, that is. He's right-wing, extremely right-wing, and calls people who think like Urruti "yokels" more than once, without worrying about what their visitors might think. Abaitua doesn't like listening to people who think of themselves as being cosmopolitan and highly educated just because they aren't Basque nationalists, and he doesn't like this man. He finds him physically repulsive. He's the hot-tempered type. His face is round, his lips are thick, lascivious, all his facial movements show mockery and disdain. He obvious holds sway over Urruti. What he finds most striking—and Urruti must think the same thing about him—is how much he's aged since he last saw him. His hair and drooping moustache are now completely white, but his ageing is most apparent in his gestures and his way of walking. (That way his coccyx sticks out, which it always has, has got worse.) He's skinny, but his belly's fat, it pulls at his shirt. Because it spills out over the top of his pants, he may still be able to use the same size as when he was young, and perhaps that's why he looks so happy. They're both wearing those sweaters you see more in Bilbao than in Donostia, knitted, with adjustable sleeves. Urruti's is blue, and his partner's, green.

"*Habrá que hablar del tema,*" the partner says—it's time they got down to talking about the business at hand. Abaitua arranged with Pilar that at this point, he would go out for a walk and join them again for lunch, along with the other two's wives. They both thought it would be a good way to show mutual respect for each other, making it clear that Pilar is capable of talking business by herself and that he doesn't want to have anything to do with private medicine. But when he says goodbye, he has the feeling he's abandoning his wife.

HE REALLY DOES FEEL a sense of nostalgia for Bilbao as an ugly, industrial port. But he admits it's beautiful now.

He walks along the river aimlessly, not planning on going anywhere specific. Deustuko Zubia, which no longer opens for large ships to go through.

The Euskalduna Palace, rising out of the water like a docked ship. The building on the opposite bank he's always admired, the one with a tiger on top—lots of Bilbaoans, fans of the local soccer team and its mascot, prefer to say it's a lion—has also been restored, and seeing it always seems to transport him to 1950s Detroit.

He turns around and goes back in the opposite direction. Uribitarte Pasealekua. Young people jog by just as they do along the Urumea in Donostia. Zubizuri Zubia—he walks across the bridge, shuffling his feet over the various slip resistant materials they've put on the glass walkway, wanting to know if it's still slippery. Campo de Volantín Pasealekua. There used to be a bar at the end of the boulevard that served what was apparently an excellent omelette, which the young people who always ended up there at the end of the night would use to soak up all the alcohol in their stomachs. He's across from the city hall. Areatzako Pasealekua-Paseo del Arenal. He sits on a bench to watch the town and the townspeople. Bilbao scenes: a tall, upright, and elegant man of his age with a striped beret on, a type he hasn't seen before, least of all in summer; a little boy asking his mother for an ice cream in Bilbaoan Basque; another man, older, small, wearing a blue beret and singing what he recognizes as the song "*Bizkaia es un bello jardín*"—meaning "Biscay is a beautiful garden"—in a baritone voice.

He gets closer to the river again on Erribera Kalea; it's not very clean, but the water's certainly much more transparent than it was a few years ago. He heard somewhere that Resurrección María de Azkue, the famed Basque priest and Renaissance man, once had the bad luck to fall in.

Seeing the now-renovated market reminds him of the senselessness of what the Donostia city council did with the Bretxa Azoka.

SAN ANTON BRIDGE and the church of the same name at one end of it, both featured prominently on the Bilbao coat of arms. He quickens his pace; he's late and still has to find the restaurant in Bilbo Zaharra—the old town.

They're waiting for him at the table, but fortunately, Urruti's partner's wife has only just arrived. Urruti's wife is just the same as she was thirty years ago, though her face is a little more wrinkled. She'd always been chubby, small, and ugly, and so she still is, small and chubby, though she no longer looks ugly to him. That's the reward, and sometimes the revenge, of many of those people who looked older when they were in their youth—they don't look so ugly as they age, or so old, either. When they order champagne as an aperitif, somebody inevitably describes it as "Bilbao Water." Pilar tells an anecdote about Paco Bueno, the founder of the well-known bar—she thinks it must be an urban legend—about how he refused charge some Bilbaoan patrons for their champagne. "Water's free here," he said. He thinks she looks happy, happier than she has for a long time. And talkative, too.

The partner's wife is a lot younger than him, and quite attractive, too. Her hair reminds him of Lynn's, although it's probably dyed. After they're introduced, the first thing she says is that Pilar reminds her of one of those beautiful women Modigliani painted, and she, Pilar—unusually—doesn't mind saying it's not the first time someone's told her that. She's sometimes been compared to that naked woman lying on a red bed cover and bluish-green cushions. *Sleeping Nude with Arms Open* is the title, Urruti's partner's wife says. She knows it's part of a private collection in Milan. Apparently Pilar's feeling very uninhibited, because she tells them how they've occasionally talked about traveling to Milan to find out just where it is and go see it. Abaitua doesn't mind her saying that at all, but he clarifies that it's just an excuse for going to Milan. Adriana—which is Urruti's partner's wife's name—tells them that it's the jewel in the crown of Mr. Gianni Mattioli's collection—Pilar makes a note of that in her diary—and that it's open to the public once a week, she thinks on Mondays.

"I suppose you've noticed that Adriana's got a degree in art history," says her husband with pride, and Abaitua remembers the advice a Bilbao father once gave to his son who was going away: don't tell people you're from Bilbao, they'll realize anyway, and if they don't, you don't need to humiliate them. The walls in the restaurant are blue. "Bilbao blue." The art history graduate tells them that Frank Gehry often used to come to this restaurant when he was building the Guggenheim and that the blue of its walls inspired him to choose the color for part of the museum. There's a tedious squabble when Urruti contradicts her, saying that the owner of the restaurant spread that story around on purpose, and his wife abruptly shuts him up by saying that that's just his opinion and he doesn't know a thing. It seems she still enjoys humiliating Urruti, a quarter of a century on. Her disdain for him has always been obvious, and all his colleagues think it's due to the frustration of having married a doctor and failed to gain the economic status she'd been hoping for.

Abaitua wonders what other people might think about them, about their relationship, and his intention to be pleasant with Pilar, and to overcome his sarcasm, is reinforced.

"CON UNAS PATATITAS, AJITOS, Y CEBOLLITAS TIERNAS." Abaitua finds the way cooks and waiters use diminutives all the time, like now—"some nice little potatoes, a few little cloves of garlic, and some lovely little green onions"—extremely irritating. Giving a demonstration of his impeccable memory, the head waiter—a fat, serious-looking man, with an air somewhat like a notary—recites the long menu by heart, although they each have a copy in their hands, which makes Urruti keep quiet for a good while. After his recital, the head waiter adds a coda: the specials are *"bacalao con berenjenas y tomatitos, cola de merluza gratinada, solomillo al foie con salsa de vino"*—cod with eggplant and some little tomatoes, tail of hake au gratin, steak with foie and wine sauce.

When it comes time to taste the wine and the waiter holds the bottle out, waiting for them to decide who's going to do it, Abaitua suggests that Pilar should. She usually does. As well as having a finer palate than him, and having been on a couple of wine-tasting courses, she enjoys surprising waiters, because it's usually a task that falls to men. And he makes his pleasantry about her having "a good nose on her." After a slight protest, she tastes the wine calmly, without any extravagant gestures. After she approves it, he sees in her eyes that she's asking him to behave more properly, to not tease her in front of people.

He decides to talk as little as possible, even though that means running the risk of Pilar saying later on, as she often does, that he's been grumpy and absent.

Urruti, talking about the past again, says, *"Cuando éramos rojos"*— back when we were reds.

Abaitua thinks that he's treating him with a little pity, and in spite of appearances, he thinks that could be because, to an extent, he feels guilty for having dedicated his professional life to the pursuit of amassing wealth with his partner. The partner doesn't have any such issues, he proclaims proudly that he's never been so naïve as to let himself be swept away by dreams like left-wing people are. His eyes look increasingly toad-like as he eats and drinks, and his lips more lascivious. He's reminded once more of the resident who was after Lynn. When he bumped into him that Saturday and the resident asked him if he knew anything about where she was, he got rid of him without hiding his temper. Why did he think he should know?

They have a nice meal, but because he finds it hard to join in with the others' enthusiasm, he gets told, for the thousandth time, that he's too demanding when it comes to food. And then there's another concession. *"Como en Donostia no se come en ningún lado"*—there's nowhere like Donostia for good food. Although when it comes to good cod, there's nowhere like Bilbao.

THE FASHIONABLE THING FOR PEOPLE TO DO NOW—without criticizing the "Guggen," of course—is speak wonders of the Fine Arts Museum. Adriana, Urruti's partner's wife, suggests they go and see an unmissable exhibition. She tells them, over their coffee, that she's decided to write her thesis about the presence of pathology in works of art. What she says is interesting, although Abaitua has a vague memory of having read something about it in a copy of *Jano*, the medical and humanities journal. She's examining works of art in which the characters have some pathological feature, looking into their illnesses and putting them in context. She says that mammary pathology is the most common. Raphael depicts the breasts of his lover, the model Margherita Luti, in his wonderful work *La Fornarina*, and on her left breast and in the armpit on the same side there are clear signs of what may be a tumor. One of Rubens's *Three Graces*—in fact his wife, Elena Fourment—has a clear depression on one breast, which is a sign of cancer. There are many cases like that, but she says that what especially interests her is what makes the artists want to show them, even on idealized figures. In the Medici Chapels in Florence, for instance, in the beautiful, extraordinary allegory of dawn, there are signs of advanced cancer on one breast, while the other is perfect. Why did Michelangelo use such cruel realism on what is clearly an idealized figure, even if the figure is only idealized to make it androgynous? Was he fascinated, or perhaps horrified, by the spectacle of signs of illness on a woman of his acquaintance and thus unable to avoid depicting them?

She gesticulates as she asks her questions, giving them emphasis, and several people walking by stop to listen. They're in the vestibule of the Fine Arts Museum, and the unmissable exhibition deals with breasts, it's focus is *La Carità romana*, in other words, the Valerius Maximus legend in which a daughter called Pero takes advantage of her visits to her old father, Cimone, who's in jail, condemned to death by starvation, to breastfeed him. When the guards find her doing this, they are so moved by the daughter's love that

779

they lift the father's punishment. That's the story the leaflet tells. The sight of more than a dozen paintings in the hallway all on the same subject matter is something Abaitua finds revolting, but the sensation disappears as soon as he stands in front of the first of them, a Rubens from The Hermitage in Saint Petersburg. It's astonishing how natural the unusual situation seems to him. The old father's half lying down on the floor, with his hands behind his back— tied, presumably—and wearing no more than a dark loincloth. His daughter—blond, sturdy, and yet at the same time delicate—has her left arm behind her father and is holding her breast to his mouth with her right arm. She stares at her father's mouth, without showing any particular feeling; there's nothing seductive about her or about her father. The second painting, too, is by Rubens, from Amsterdam's Rijksmuseum; it dates from almost twenty years later. The woman is very much like the first one, and dressed almost identically, all in red, but her father is older and in a worse state. The biggest difference between the two paintings—as well as the characters' positions—is in the eyes. They're both looking at a group of soldiers who are observing them from behind a barred window. The scene is more disturbing than the one in the first painting, above all because of the looks, and also because the breast which is not feeding the old man—a pearly-colored round breast—is uncovered for no apparent reason, unlike in the other painting.

Urruti's partner's wife gives them basically the same information as in the leaflet, but she does also add some significant details. It could be that she prepared the visit beforehand, and he guesses—from a look they quickly share—that Pilar suspects that, too. He'll ask her when they're alone. Adriana tells them that one of the Rubens, the one from The Hermitage, already came to the Guggenheim on a previous occasion, as part of an exhibition called *Rubens and his Age* showcasing the treasures amassed by Catherine the Great. Pilar and Abaitua saw that exhibition. And they also saw, right here in this same museum, Caravaggio's enormous *The Seven Works of Mercy*, but he overcomes the urge to say so. In that painting, daughter Pero and father Cimone appear off to the right. Pilar, too, keeps quiet about their having seen it. She has less trouble letting others enjoy their belief that they have exclusive access to certain things, knowledge included. More precisely, it's no trouble at all for her. He sees her nodding to let Adriana know that her explanations are interesting, but she also finds a moment to throw him a look, very clearly this time, as if to say "what a know-it-all this woman is," and Abaitua enjoys that complicity of theirs, unusual as it is.

He thinks she must be glad that the subject of her "accident" hasn't come up. He, on the other hand, would have preferred to talk openly about his problems at the hospital.

Adriana, the partner's wife, talks about the marvellous play of light—"*Ese maravilloso juego de luz.*" They're still standing in front of the magnificent Caravaggio. In the top left-hand corner, the angels escorting the Virgin. Their wings open, of course. He thinks that angels with their wings down must be an artistic exception. He can't help remembering Lynn.

Everyone laughs when Urruti's wife says she finds it a bit revolting seeing so many old men feeding from young women's breast. She also finds the looks of pleasure on the faces of the daughters in some of the paintings a little repulsive. Now Pilar speaks, saying that what takes her aback is the soldiers looking on. After the fourth or fifth painting, they just glance at the rest. JEAN-BAPTISTE GREUZE 1767. SIMON VOUET 1590-1649. JOHANN ZOFFANY 1769. LORENZO PASINELLI 1670. CHARLES MELLIN 1600-1650. Just to say something, Abaitua asks their guide if she doesn't think the daughter in Mellin's painting doesn't look a bit like the Tamara de Lempicka figures, and she says she may, but he doesn't think she's very convinced. After looking at the painting for a moment, she says, with great conviction, that you can find everything in the classics. He likes the way she gives so much emphasis to everything she says.

Meanwhile, Urruti and his partner are telling loud jokes, probably encouraged by the laughter of the group of women behind them who are listening in on their guide's explanations. Urruti, pointing at Pero and Cimone, mentions the phenomenon of *el chupón* or *el mamón*—the suckler. A man tasked with drinking the milk of mothers who have too much, or whose children have died. *Izaina* in Basque, perhaps. It was usually an old man, because of his teeth, or rather his lack of them, he says, to prevent the women from thinking he's being obscene, or so Abaitua thinks. Urruti says he knew one in Otzeta who used to go from house to house to do his work—on arriving at each successive doorstep, he would say hello and then step into the new mother's room. Abaitua doesn't believe it, even though he once knew an old midwife who told him she knew a man who did that, even though she didn't know the name for the job in Basque. Urruti says "Ave Maria," pretends to take off a beret, drags his feet backward like an old man toward the last painting, and makes a sucking gesture while cupping his hands around his mouth.

Everybody laughs, even Pilar. Abaitua finds himself in a very bad mood.

The painting that closes the exhibition is the only contemporary work, dating from 1997, by one Johannes Phokela, a South African who reinvents classical painting by changing sex or race roles as a way of turning western painting on its head. That's what the catalogue says. In this case, the erotic is clearly on display, above all because the man isn't old. His hands are tied with ribbons behind his back, his feet, too, and it looks like part of some S and M game. His head is bald, probably shaved, and there are no hairs on his body, either. They're both naked. He has a book open on his lap. He's muscular, but with that crude, harsh air Lucian Freud's figures often have. The woman breastfeeding him, on the other hand, has a touch of Botero. Her dress is falling off her arms, she has no pubic hair, and she's wearing red shoes. Standing in front of the painting, Urruti says it's a clear case of sex addiction. More laughter. The two partners continue fooling around, to please their group of listeners, with whom they've now started talking. They're four elderly ladies from Santander. When one of them says that the man doesn't look old and that the women doesn't look as if she's just given birth, either, unlike in Valerius Maximus' legend, Urruti says in all seriousness that it's probably a case of galactorrhea. He tells the ladies from Santander not to laugh—he's a gynecologist, and he knows what he's talking about. There's not much doubt they're looking at galactorrhea caused by a hypophyseal tumor. The women don't know if he's being serious, but in any case, they've stopped laughing.

Fortunately, since it's the last painting.

Abaitua thinks about Lynn. He holds the door open for Pilar to go out and thinks she's looking very pale. When he asks if something's wrong, she says no, but he's sure that's not true, something's up.

More laughter. On the way out, the group stops in front of the poster for the upcoming exhibition. It's another themed one: the Iconography of the Lactation of Saint Bernard. The saint in his white habit is on the poster, kneeling on the ground in ecstasy, his arms at his side, his hands and forearms open, receiving the milk that the Virgin, seated on an altar with the Christ Child in her arms, is squirting in his direction. At the bottom of the poster, in miniature, copies of a dozen other paintings of the same scene.

The two partners are competing to say the funniest things, while the art historian interprets the painting. The Virgin is squirting her milk at the founder of the Cistercian Order in order to save him the indignity of feeding straight from her breast, and the Christ Child is in her arms to make it clear that he's given his permission.

Urruti recalls the time they had that *txotx* back in Otzeta and drank straight from the stream of cider shooting out of the barrel, just like Saint Bernard, instead of lining up to fill their glasses from it as is the usual custom. The partner's wife, still determined that the full extent of her knowledge be broadcast, assures them that you could write a whole thesis about breastfeeding in art; her husband, on the other hand, thinks it would be interesting to research the personal obsessions of art museum directors instead. It doesn't look as if it's ever going to end.

Abaitua feels relieved when they get outside. There's no question that Pilar isn't feeling well. She excuses herself when they suggest going to have a drink, saying she has a bit of a headache. They go with them to the parking lot, which is nearby, and on the way, the partners say they'll have to meet up again to continue their discussion at the clinic next time, that way they'll be able to meet the rest of the partners.

ABAITUA'S DRUNK TOO MUCH, as he does at any lunch where he doesn't have much to say, and the way Pilar's driving—fast, brusquely changing gear, and taking the bends aggressively—soon makes him dizzy. They're in silence. The weather forecast was right, and although it started raining some time ago, Pilar hasn't turned on the windshield wipers.

The automatic payment system at the tollbooth isn't working. She wants to reverse but can't, because there's a car in the way. Pilar sticks her head out of the window and quite roughly tells the driver behind to move back. Abaitua tries to calm her down—they aren't in a hurry. Finally, when an employee lifts the barrier for them, he asks if the meeting went badly. Her answer's harsh: "That friend of yours" is an idiot. No more than that. She's talking about Urrutikoetxea, of course. Abaitua doesn't understand why she's in a bad mood, or, above all, why she's said "that friend of yours." He says it wasn't he who wanted to do business with that idiot; if it hadn't been for her, he wouldn't have ever come to see him.

"OK, yeah, I knew you'd find a way to throw it in my face."

"I'm not throwing anything in your face."

He doesn't have the energy to get angry. Before she can start talking again, he tries to place himself on her side by saying that he doesn't know which of the two partners is the bigger fool.

Even though it's raining harder, she still hasn't put the wipers on. They can hardly see the road, but Abaitua stays as he is, firmly resisting his urge to press the switch. He finds it harder to hold back the frustration he has inside. He tries to keep it under control. He remains quiet, looking at the play of light caused by the refraction of the water on the windshield. He doesn't know how she can drive, you can hardly see the road through the shining colors, mostly red. Finally, in the most agreeable way he can manage, he decides to ask her again—something must have happened, something he missed.

"You know full well," she answers.

"I don't," he insists.

"Yes, you do. When they made those jokes about galactorrhea, they were laughing at me. Why do you think they brought up hypophyseal tumors?"

More than steering, it looks to him as if she's clinging onto the wheel with both hands, looking at him without paying any attention to the road for what seems to him like an incredibly long time. Then she looks ahead again and turns the windshield wipers on.

Abaitua, when she mentioned galactorrhea, thought for a moment that she could be mocking him, thinking of Lynn, but that seems crazy to him. It didn't remind him at all of Pilar's mistake.

The rain's falling heavily now.

"Do you really not know why they brought up the hypophyseal tumor?"

She seems to be talking to herself. From the very beginning, she knew there was something in the air, they were treating her with pity, trying to supress their urge to mention her slipup. And finally they did. After telling their joke about hypophyseal tumors in front of that revolting painting, Urruti squeezed her arm as if to apologize.

784

Hadn't he noticed?

Abaitua doesn't answer. In fact, he was quite pleased with the way things went. He thinks of saying that but keeps quiet, even though he finds the silence oppressive. Now he doesn't know what he finds more irritating, the windshield wipers' quick movements or the noise they make, and what he sees—they're in the left-hand lane, driving at full speed as they leave a string of trucks behind them—isn't soothing, either. He holds onto the door handle and his left foot moves as if to brake. Once more, the seconds take a long time to go by. Moving back into the right-hand lane reassures him a little, and to hide his fear, he asks if she minds if he puts on some music. She just shrugs. He turns the CD on and, wanting to be pleasant, asks if she might not be a bit too suspicious.

"Suspicious?"

"Torturing yourself unnecessarily."

"I NEED SOME DISTRACTION / OH BEAUTIFUL RELEASE."

Abaitua feels more and more irritated by her lack of gratitude for him having gone with her to Bilbao and made an effort to behave in a civilized way. He thinks about Lynn. That song was playing there, in her room, when she said "oh my god" in desperation. He thinks that perhaps they were actually laughing at him, and he tells her so. "They may actually have been laughing at me."

"And why would they be laughing at you, may I ask?"

He finds it obvious, but difficult to explain.

"I don't know, I am your husband, after all."

She repeats the same sentence—"I am your husband, after all"—with distaste, imitating a child's whining. Her cheeks are pale, her face disfigured by the bluish light shining on it from the dashboard. Abaitua doesn't know what speed they're going at, he can't see from where he's sitting, and he doesn't want to move, in case she thinks he's controlling her—something she could get angry about—but he holds onto the strap above the window again. A sign of distrust she doesn't miss; she looks at his hand and then at his face. She nods again and says three or four times, though he doesn't know why, "I am your husband, after all," now repeating it with more disdain than mockery, or at least that's what he thinks. It could be sorrow or anger, too. More likely anger, since she presses her foot all the way down on the accelerator even though there's one truck after another all along the left-hand lane, and when he's so frightened he finally has to say something to her, she straightens her arms, pushes her body back into the seat, and suddenly brakes, swerving the steering wheel over to the right and taking the car off the road, and they hear the noise of gravel being dragged along for a few yards until they come to a stop. Fortunately, there wasn't anybody behind them. The engine turns itself off and Pilar rests her head on the steering wheel after saying "I am your husband, after all" once more. She slams her head against it three or four times and makes the horn go off. Now she seems like somebody who's had an accident. Abaitua remembers that once, when they were driving down from Chamonix, the car in front of them, which had been going very fast, a lot faster than them—from above, they could see the S-curves it was tracing, one after another, as it made its way down the steep hill—hit the trunk of a tree at a bend. When they got there, the driver was sitting in a normal posture with his back on the seat, but when Abaitua put his hand on his shoulder, his head fell forward and made the horn go off, just as Pilar has. He felt his carotid artery, and after stopping the horn, the silence in the valley was absolute and long-lasting. Then the branches of the tree started brushing together, the birds began singing and the cowbells clanging. He's never felt life escaping in such a palpable way. As he remembers that scene, he crosses his arms, and Pilar's head is still resting on the steering wheel. They stay like that for a while, until she turns toward him without lifting her head up. Although the hardness and despair that have been in her eyes so often recently are no longer there, her look terrifies him. *"Eres un egoísta de mierda,"* she says almost sweetly, calling him a self-centered bastard. And she continues, still in Spanish: *"Sólo piensas en ti. Que cuando hablen de lo mío pronunciarán tu nombre. La cagada de la mujer de Abaitua."* All you care about is yourself, she's just said, about your name coming up when people talk about me. Abaitua's fucked up wife.

Why isn't she speaking in Basque?

He holds onto one of her hands and asks her to calm down. Of course he's sorry. But Pilar lets go of his hand. Not roughly, but certainly firmly. She carries on with what she was saying, accusing him once more of not minding how much she's suffering over what happened, not caring about the poor girl who won't be able to walk again. He hasn't even asked her who she is. *"Sólo te importa que lo mío pueda dañar tu imagen, que te asocien a mi incompetencia, a él, el genio, el honrado, el incomprendido, el que nunca se equivoca,*" she says—you only care about what I do when it might affect your own image, when it might make people connect you with my incompetence, you, the genius, the honourable, misunderstood man, the man who never does anything wrong. She punches the steering wheel, though this time without blowing the horn, then lies back in her seat with her arms crossed. Tears flow down her cheeks.

Cars are driving past them at a close distance, and their noise drowns out the CD. Abaitua takes her hand again to draw her toward him. He didn't ask her anything because he thought she didn't want to talk about it.

"I can't get that poor girl out of my mind."

Pilar's voice sounds normal now, perhaps a little sharper because she's trying not to cry. Abaitua opens the door. He'd better drive, they'll talk about it all when they get home. But she doesn't pay any attention to him and doesn't move. "A poor, sweet girl, bright and full of life, condemned forever. My mistake has a body, a face, and gray eyes."

"You know what?"

What could he possibly know? He doesn't reply, just waits for her to continue.

"She told me she didn't want to become the name for my guilt."

Her voice breaks as she tries to stifle a sob. That's what she said to her, she repeats, sounding now like a child who's been told off— "*Eso me dijo.*" She says it again and again, until he shakes her arm to get her to be quiet. His heart misses a beat. He wants to know her name.

"*¿Cómo se llama?*"

Pilar keeps quiet, she probably hasn't even heard him. She looks at him without saying a word, as if trying to understand how her words have affected him, and moved by what she sees, she says once more, "She didn't want to become the name for my guilt." As if reciting a line of poetry.

"*¿Cómo se llama?*" he asks her name again.

"Lynn."

She apparently feels the need to add that she's American. She says the name again and spells it.

HE GETS OUT OF THE CAR. The rain is coming down hard, almost horizontally because of the rough wind, and the noise of the traffic is horrendous. Cars keep going by and honking their horns, flashing their lights to reproach them for creating such a dangerous situation. He feels like throwing up, he holds onto the barrier at the side of the road with both hands. Pilar gets out, too. Now she's the one to ask him what's wrong. The horns leave a moaning wail behind them. He's always had trouble vomiting—he can't relax his esophageal sphincter, and his glottis closes up. Pilar's warm hand on his forehead helps him. His mother used to help him like that, too. They're both soaked, more so by the passing trucks that splash them as they speed through the puddles on the road than by the rain itself. The noise is deafening. He feels as if he's been bled and wonders whether his biochemistry has recovered to the extent that he'll be able to make it back to the car, or whether he'll fall down in the mud he's now stumbling across—his arms held wide open, as if testing the air with his finger—before he gets there. He's tempted to lie down right there, as if injured in an accident, but Pilar holds him firmly by his arm. "Let's get out of here before we get killed," she says, and thanks to her, he manages to take the last steps.

Pilar looks in the rearview mirror for a chance to get back on the road, and Abaitua doesn't know whether to admit that he knows Lynn or to say once again that the lunch disagreed with him, the sound of the blinker seeming to force him into making a decision. Although there's no question that the second option would be the easier of the two, he knows that covering up won't do him any good, not even in the short term. And in any case, he has to check that this Lynn is actually Lynn. He presses his crossed arms against his belly and puts his head down to show his physical discomfort.

Pilar looks at him with curiosity. "Do you know her?"

She doesn't give him time to answer. He has the impression she's going to drive off the road again, even though she only brakes for a moment, but it's enough to annoy the truck driver behind them, who flashes his lights at them. "Where do you know her from?" Lights once more. It occurs to him that the best thing would be for the huge tank truck to run into them and destroy them. A suitable ending for the drama of the surgeon who's disabled her husband's lover out of vengeance. Everyone at the hospital must be talking about it, of course, and they're right—horror films have been based on less frightful scenarios than this. He finds it hard to breathe, and images go through his head like on a carousel, at dizzying speed;

and when he eventually calms down, he doesn't want to think about them again.

Lynn denying she was taking antidepressants. No tricyclics or anything else, she'd said. And he'd snooped in her bathroom cabinet. He's astonished to find himself being more irritated about not having taken such a significant sign into account than he is upset at the entire situation.

"Where do you know her from?"

He isn't sure if he's ever mentioned Lynn to her. From the hospital, he says, she was taking part in a perinatal research project. Yes, he's told her about that.

"And you didn't know?"

No.

Pilar starts crying again. Regretting her clumsiness. Abaitua could tell her that it's not all her fault.

Mea culpa, mea culpa, mea maxima culpa.

Donostia-San Sebastián 25 km. He doesn't want to get there.

This time, the remote payment system works. Pilar drives slowly after going through the toll; perhaps she doesn't want to arrive, either. She looks at him from time to time as if to gauge his mood, how angry he is. "*Berak ez dit esan ezagutzen zintuenik,*" she says—she didn't tell me she knew you. Why is she speaking in Basque now? That, in fact, is exactly what he's wondering: Does Lynn know that the surgeon who disabled her is his wife? He thinks she must. But he tells Pilar she probably doesn't even know that his wife's a doctor.

"And how is it that you didn't know that she was going to have an operation?"

"I haven't seen her for a while, she'd finished her work."

"But did you two spend a lot of time together?"

"Quite a lot."

Now, with Pilar crying once more, he doesn't try to comfort her, although he does wonder whether to put a hand on her shoulder. It seems somehow that he shouldn't, out of respect for Lynn, and because he thinks she deserves to feel guilty. He'd like her to suffer more, to punish her more by confessing his relationship with Lynn. For a moment, he thinks he's in a nightmare. "You shouldn't torture yourself," he whispers to her. He can't think of anything else to do.

"Don't worry about me," says Pilar, "I'll get over it." He doesn't have any doubts about that. She will get over it. She'll be introspective for a few days, furiously concentrating on her sudokus, and then she'll go back to being her old self once more.

It's cleared up, and they can see the city lights. Abaitua is ready to overcome his cowardice and face up to what's happened. He has to see Lynn. He's amazed by how easily he accepts that. He'll think about how to go about it when they get home. Not long now.

But there are several points he has to clear up beforehand: the anatomic pathology results; the scale of the consequences; exactly what her situation is. Talking about the technical side of things seems to calm Pilar down a little. The tumor was benign, like most pituitary tumors. The prognosis is still unclear. However, there's nothing they can do any more. She's going to need specialist rehabilitation. They suggested taking care of her at the clinic until she was well enough to go back to the States, but the person who was with her—an older, unpleasant woman, Pilar says when he asks—requested a voluntary discharge. She hasn't seen her since.

They've been going along for a while now in parallel to another car with a girl of two or three waving at them from a car seat, and he has to wave back, even though it makes him feel pretty ridiculous. They'll soon be out of sight of her, because the exit for Ondarreta is just ahead.

The moment's come for him to decide how to visit Lynn.

They don't take the Ondarreta exit. Pilar says she has to go by the clinic, she'll get back home in the small car, which she left there the night before.

THE HOUSE ON THE GREEN HILL. It really does look like a witch's house. Some of the windows facing the road are lit up. They cross the little bridge over the railway line and turn left. Then left again, flanked by hydrangeas on the private land to either side. They go into the parking lot, and Pilar turns the car around to leave it facing the exit, so that he doesn't have to do any manoeuvring. She doesn't turn the engine off. She takes off the jewelry she was wearing to look elegant in Bilbao and puts it in her bag; the earrings give her some trouble. She says she's going to visit a patient—"Unless he's fled in terror." Her smile is defenseless, shows immense sadness. She puts a hand on his knee but doesn't move over to give him a kiss. She doesn't know how long she's going to be, they'll see each other at home.

Abaitua, after driving about three hundred feet, stops the car near the dumpsters. He walks back the way he's come and reaches the bridge once again. Now he sees the bathroom and kitchen windows from between the reeds, and when he gets past the bend, sees light in the short gallery leading into the living room. He decides to call, but his heart beats hard once the phone's against his ear and he's waiting for the call to go through; he'd rather she not pick up.

"Is it you? Is it really you?"

Her voice is happy, and she doesn't let him speak. "How are you? Where are you?" She wasn't expecting him to call her. When he says he's across the street from the house and he'd like to come up to see her, she says that if she'd known, she'd have made an appointment at the hairdresser's, but he should come right away, someone will come down to open the door for him.

"Someone will come down to open the door for you"—the first real, inescapable confirmation of her tragedy.

As he goes up the slope, he sees the light in the gallery once more, but it's faint, probably a reflection of the light coming from the living room. The creak of the iron gate, which he told Lynn more than once he would happily oil, but she said it was a sign of elegance, the sound an elegant iron gate should make. The sound of his steps on the gravel, which used to worry him so many nights.

He hears somebody coming down the wooden stairs—rather fast steps to be those of an elderly woman—and he wonders who it is. While he waits, he realizes that his pants, like his shoes, are covered in mud.

The writer doesn't greet him warmly. It's the first time he doesn't mind the idea of Martin opening the door; his relationship with Lynn being out in the open no longer matters. The writer looks him up and down, particularly down when he sees the state of Abaitua's pants and shoes. Then he goes up the spiral staircase incredibly fast—he seems to be used to it—as if wanting to show off that he's fit, and Abaitua finds it hard to keep up with him. On the way up, Martin tells him that Lynn has suffered a lot and shouldn't be allowed to tire herself out, just as if he were a doctor giving a visitor permission to go into the patient's room. Max is waiting for him on the threshold as if he were on the edge of an abyss. He calls to it from the last turn on the stairs, but though it seems to want to go up to him, it doesn't, and finally, it hides behind the door. It seems the cat doesn't trust the writer, and once Abaitua goes in, it lies at his feet asking to be petted. It starts purring as soon as he touches it. Martin waits in the entryway, jealous at the welcome the cat's given him, he thinks.

Lynn's voice: "*Come on, Max, don't be obscene.*"

He has to walk past a free-standing drying rack—it's foldaway and light, the legs forming an X-shape, and it has underwear drying on it; it's the sort of private sight that's allowed in houses with children and disabled people—in order to get to the living room. There isn't much light, and what there is comes from the spotlights on the bookshelves, which are angled down almost as far as the floor. Lynn is lying on the sofa with her striped pashmina shawl on top of her. "*Hi.*" She sits up without any apparent effort. That smile that completely wrinkles her face. "It's wonderful to see you." She holds her arms out to him. The right one more than the left one. She can hardly lift her left arm. He takes a step forward, stands between the writer and the girl. Everything is just the same, the furniture, the paintings, the lily with the blue phallic head in front of him, the decorative objects, and even so, he thinks something's changed. There's a glass of water and a box of medicine—Boehringer brand, though what it is specifically he can't see—on the art deco tray sitting on the triangular table, and when he goes forward to politely give her two kisses, he almost knocks the tray over. "It's wonderful to see you," she says again. He doesn't know where to begin, the writer being there is making him feel quite inhibited, but above all, it's because he's not sure his voice will come out. He manages to say that he's just heard, and obeying the gesture she makes with her right hand, he sits down next to her.

As her caregiver, the writer interrupts occasionally to add information, even correcting her at times, as she answers Abaitua's purposeless medical questions, but then, when he can think of nothing more to ask her, there's an awkward silence, and Martin takes ahold of the tray with the glass and medicine box on it—now he can see what it is: Buscopax—and says he has to go and do something, though Abaitua doesn't understand what. Then, when the writer closes the door behind him, she takes his hands and starts talking to him softly, completely shaken up, as if she were afraid of not having

792

time to say everything she wants to. "I kept wondering if I was ever going to see you again. Will I die without seeing him again? Will he never let me show him how I do *kokotxas*? Will we never celebrate Peru's first birthday? Will he ever hug me again? Did my stupid letter make him angry?" She asks one question after another, without giving him the chance to answer. Without him having to say anything. When she stops, he doesn't know what to say.

And then he says, "*I'm sorry.*" She smiles and says he's not to blame.

"I should have realized," he says, "I should have done something."

"You did."

She touches his cheek lightly with her right hand, looks toward the door, and with a confidential tone that seems to be intentionally or even comically exaggerated, says that she thought the milk coming from her breasts was because he aroused her so much; after all, he made her feel so many things she had never, ever felt before with anybody else, so it hadn't surprised her all that much. She thought it was her essence, the essence of love, the nectar of love, her juice. She liked it coming out of her, it helped her to dream that she had a child of his.

"It turns out it's called galactorrhea and it's caused by a tumor. When they told me, I thought, 'How vulgar, and I made him drink that.' I asked if the liquid could be poisonous, and fortunately, they said no."

"I'm sorry."

"I'm pulling your leg. Couldn't you tell how happy I was whenever I saw you? How could you think I was on antidepressants?"

When Abaitua says "I'm sorry" for the hundredth time, she slaps his hand, as if telling a child not to do something. But then she says he's not to blame at all. Perhaps only for being too gentle, but she realized he thought her "nectar" was worrying. And she didn't say anything about it to him, because when she found out, she didn't want him treating her like a patient. "Can you understand that?" Making him feel like he had to visit her just because she was sick. In any case, they told her it would be sorted out in a couple of days. She didn't choose his wife's clinic herself, it was just the one on her insurance policy, and initially, she was going to be operated on by another doctor. She says it was destiny. "Fate."

FATE in Basque: *patu*, or *zori*. Lynn confuses *zori* with *txori*, meaning "bird."

"She" is Pilar.

She isn't to blame, either. It was an accident. He shouldn't think about it; nor should he think that what's happened is a punishment. "Because I know you'd be capable of thinking something like that." Now she looks anxious. Her lips look so dry to him that he feels thirsty. He asks her if she wants a little water, to lighten the atmosphere a little, and she shakes her head.

They're almost in the dark. The noise of a train, probably a freight train; in any case, it doesn't stop.

"You know what?"

Her voice sounds lively again. *"She's beautiful."* She says it with conviction. She's very beautiful. After repeating her half-comic gesture of looking at the door, she asks him to come closer with her index finger. "Now I know why you like her," she whispers. "Because you do like her, don't you?" Without waiting for an answer, she says once more that she knows why he likes her. He finds it annoying listening to her talking about Pilar and starts to move away from the sofa, but she holds him back. "Her smile," she says, looking into his eyes.

"That's it, isn't it?"

(Shortly earlier, in the car, Pilar said that Lynn was a "wonderful woman," and he almost replied, "A wonderful woman who had the great misfortune to come between us.")

"Tell me."

He isn't sure whether Pilar said "wonderful woman" or "wonderful girl."

"Tell me, I'm right, aren't I?"

Faced with his silence, she opens her eyes wide, covers her mouth with one hand, and waves the other in the air like a child, saying, "She's got a bit of a vengeful streak, though." And then she smiles. "It's a joke." He can't help smiling, too.

The writer opens the door enough to put his head in. "Maureen's coming," he warns them, which sounds like "it's time" to Abaitua, and he gets up off the sofa automatically. "It's like he just said the supervisor's coming, isn't it?" She laughs, which he's grateful for. He wants to leave. So he's standing up, not having any idea what to say, and the writer, thinking he's given them enough time to say goodbye, opens the door the rest of the way. This time he comes in. He picks some books up off the floor and puts them on the bookshelf—Abaitua sees that the photo Kepa took of them in Bordeaux is still in the same place—then he goes over to the sofa, picks up a cushion from behind Lynn, puffs it up, and puts it back again, tucks her legs into her pashmina shawl properly, looks around the room as if to make sure that everything is in place, and then tiptoes out.

They're in silence, he's standing in the middle of the room, and she's lying on the sofa. For a long time. It seems like a long time to Abaitua, at any rate. Finally, it's Lynn who talks again. Something she'd been wanting to ask him and kept on forgetting. She reminds him that in *Montauk*, Max says that when he married his first wife, they went to live in an apartment building where there was a neighbour lady, called Haller, who was paralytic and couldn't get out of bed. Abaitua nods, he remembers her; he's relieved it isn't a personal question. Apparently his wife often sent him to the woman's flat to ask to borrow things like some salt or a can opener, but he always waited by the door. The idea of seeing a paralytic woman made him feel queasy. He could see the entryway, a closet, a piece of carpet; he knew that the woman could hear his voice, but he never went in to greet her. One day, when he went there to ask for some spare fuses, the caregiver insisted he come in, but he gave an excuse, fled, and never went back. His wife, though, had—she had a close relationship with the woman, especially after having her first child, and was always going over to her house. It was from his wife that Max found out that he actually knew Mrs. Haller—they were in the same class in their first year of elementary school, and he realizes she was the first girl he ever fell in love with.

In *Montauk*, Max says that Mrs. Haller became paralytic in childbirth, and Lynn always wanted to know how that could have happened, she'd been meaning to ask, but she kept forgetting whenever she saw him. She would always forget everything. A weak smile. She's been wondering these past several days whether he would be braver than Max and come to see her.

"And here you are."

Abaitua doesn't know if it's really the right moment to tell her that paralysis can be caused by obstetric factors. He's still standing up. "Like a dummy," as they'd say in Otzeta.

"I was convinced I wasn't ever going to see you again." She pauses for a moment. "In fact, it's been quite hard getting you back here." She smiles again. "But you have come." When she makes an effort to sit up, her shawl gets in a jumble and her feet and calves get uncovered. He knows it's pure imagination, but they look thinner to him. Feet with no strength.

She tells him to go. *Fly away from this dark cold room.*

"It's better if you don't bump into Maureen. She's a good person, but she doesn't think very much of you; she blames you all. *The damned Basque.*"

She holds her arms out to him, and he bends down to give her a kiss. "You smell so good," she says, as she hangs onto his neck. For a moment he has the feeling that she's going to put her legs around his waist, as she used to. He can feel her weight.

Going along the gravel path, he comes across a chubby woman wearing a white raincoat that goes down to her knees. She's the very picture of an old-fashioned midwife. He thinks she must be Maureen. "*Hola*," he says, and she, after openly looking him up and down, mumbles something he doesn't understand. He has a hard time getting out onto the road, because of all the people walking from the train to the stairs. The sound of the hydraulic system closing the doors and the train moving off. He waits for it to disappear from view before setting off toward the clinic.

When he reaches the jetty, he hears a sound, the same one again and again. It's a metal drum floating like a buoy, banging up against the mastless sailing boat. The mooring line on the stern has come lose. He remembers that back on that day, the tide was much higher, and when he went to speak with the boys, he was only able to get as far as the laurel bushes. A lot of mud. Now he can't do anything to tie the mooring up again.

He almost loses a shoe as he gets back onto the path. His feet are numb, and he still has a ways to walk, through all that traffic noise, getting splashed by the cars. He feels extremely tired, but also free from something he can't put his finger on. That sometimes happens to him, as does the opposite—he'll feel anxious and have to look inside himself to find out why. When he reaches the clinic door, he sees another car's lights coming on. He knows it's Pilar's car. He wonders whether she's come out just then by chance or whether she's been waiting for him. He doesn't mind, he's not worried, he's not afraid.

It's sad that he's not afraid, because it means he's lost all hope. Lynn once said something like that. He doesn't know why he's just thought of it.

It's her. She lowers the window as he walks up to her. "How is she?" she asks him. Abaitua's answer is that she's as well as she can be.

EPILOGUE

ON THE ESCALATOR, an old man wearing something like a guayabera is complaining that architects nowadays pay more attention to the way buildings look than to what they're used for. Julia has the impression she hears somebody saying something like that every time she comes to Loiu Airport. The man, who's a couple of steps ahead of her, turns around and looks at her, as if waiting for her to agree, and even though she tries to pretend she's not listening, she ends up smiling when she remembers something another old man once said: "I'm opposed to the death penalty, except for architects." It was Eric Rohmer's verdict, Martin had underlined it somewhere, and she'd copied it into his quotes archive.

She waits in line at the café and, when it's her turn, realizes she doesn't want anything.

She's on the raised walkway that runs all the way around the terminal, and the arrivals halls, a floor lower down, can be seen from it. The travelers on the plane from London will arrive at gate number eight in half an hour. She feels more relaxed after finding the place. She wanders along the walkway and watches the travelers from other planes arrive. You can see each gate's luggage conveyor belt in its entirety, but although somebody standing where she is could keep a watch on every piece of luggage going through, she isn't sure they would be able to monitor every single one of the passengers at times when the hall is very crowded, especially people who don't go up to the belt. Some travelers don't seem to realize that there are people looking down at them from the walkway, but others do look upward, and some raise their hands to greet the people waiting for them. There aren't so many people on the plane that's just arrived, they look like tourists who've come from somewhere warm, and they're standing around their luggage belt, which is moving but without any baggage on it yet. Julia wonders what people like her—standing to watch at the glass with their heads all tipped slightly down like penguins—look like to the people below. She decides to go downstairs.

She checks the status of the plane from London on the arrivals board once more. *On time.* She doesn't know if Kepa's going to be on the plane, he'd only said he was going to come back at midday on Friday, but she's taken the risk of coming to wait for him by surprise; she hopes it'll be a good surprise. She's glad she's given way to her senseless impulse, but she's getting more and more nervous as the arrival time approaches.

She doesn't need her glasses to see that the woman at the newsstand with her back to her is Harri. It's easy to recognize her; they bought the jacket she's wearing with the dragon embroidered on the back at Fancy in Donibane Lohizune together. She must have come to meet her daughter, and Julia would rather bump into anybody else but her. She'll have to tell her that she's waiting for Kepa and then, as if that weren't enough, look ridiculous in front of her if he doesn't show. She wonders whether it would be better to go back to Donostia—when it comes down to it, Kepa isn't expecting her, so he won't miss her—but she's also annoyed at having to give in. She's imagined what would be a surprise meeting for Kepa a thousand times since she first thought of it, and although her exaggeratedly prudent nature has not been able to completely ignore the possibility that it might be disappointing, she imagines it as something happy and agreeable. Above all happy. What's more, it would save her so many words. She was glad that she had been moved to make the straightforward decision to come and wait for him, and now she's annoyed about having to give up on it. Having to relinquish giving Kepa the present of being there for him. Her first impulse is to turn around and hide among the people in the cafeteria, but Harri's going to see her sooner or later; even at

Heathrow it's difficult to avoid people who are waiting for the same plane as you.

It doesn't take long to confirm the inevitable. She hasn't yet gotten the glass of water she's ordered when she hears, "What are you doing here?" A happy voice. Exactly what she expected Harri to ask her. Taking her cue from the final call for passengers to Málaga that's just gone out over the PA, she invents a bachelor uncle from Otzeta and says he's traveling to Torremolinos on that flight and she's just dropped him off, slightly embarrassed by how easily she's lying. "And what about you?" After seeming to hesitate for a moment, she says, "As you can see, I'm waiting for the man from the airport—same old story." Then, after laughing at her own joke, she says Harritxu's coming back from London. Julia doesn't think she looks bad, she's quite tanned and, maybe because of that, looks blonder, too. They have to move apart from each other to avoid being bumped into by some boys who are playing around. When they get back together, Harri says she's really come to pick up her daughter. She doesn't seem especially moved when she tells Julia that she called Harritxu to tell her all about her sickness, and to tell her that she needed her. She wants Harritxu with her. And to give the girl a useful experience, too, for her to see how her mother is facing up to the disease, to the unmentionable, because nobody talks about cancer. "*¿Qué te parece?*" she says, raising her chin. "Mother and daughter picking out wigs together and all that."

For the first time since she's known her—and it's been years—there's an awkward silence between them, and Julia looks for and can't find the words to break it. Inevitably, she considers the possibility of asking after Martin, while Harri's saying something or other, and finally, nothing else occurring to her, she asks, "What about Martin, is he writing?" It's the first time she's asked the question she's had to answer a thousand times. She's never felt the fact of not being with him any more so clearly. "Is he writing?" she says once more, and Harri answers that she isn't sure, she thinks he's trying to. "He's doing really badly," she whispers, and Julia feels a burning inside, thinking she's talking about his health. "What's wrong with him?" She's relieved when Harri says it's his dreams. He's still having nightmares. Apparently, he keeps on having the same nightmare—a text disappears down the drain letter by letter, fast, and he doesn't have time to identify a single word, and the few he does hold onto don't mean anything. Words he doesn't understand from an unknown language. "It's interesting, isn't it?" She smiles.

That seems to have put Harri in a good mood again—she must have been thinking that Julia was angry—and she starts talking about Martin nonstop, about his plans. Apparently, he really is going to Sicily now, not forever, but he is going to spend some time there. She tells him all about a house he's going to rent, not actually in Syracuse but close by, because she's seen the photos online; it's an old house, but it has great views. But Julia realizes that Harri's just talking for the sake of it. She lets her arms fall to her side and cocks her head. "Honey, he loves you and really misses you," she says with despair in her voice. Julia doesn't want to know anything about that, she wants to tell Harri that everything's over, but she doesn't, because Harri takes ahold of both her hands—she forgot how strong she is—and says, "You know what?" She doesn't have a chance to ask her what it is she's supposed to know. "He had dinner with Marie Lafôret." Harri lets go of her hands and takes a step backward, apparently to get a better angle to see the effect of her words on her. Her eyes really are wonderful, even more wonderful than they look on the television, but she's a sad woman. She's separated—it's strange, she says, how men find it easier to abandon beautiful women—and has a broken heart; she's worried because her son is a punk and she regrets having brought him up so freely. She's shown him photos of her son, and even of her dog, which has epileptic fits.

"He loves you."

ARRIVALS. LLEGADAS. IRITSIERAK. There's an unspecified delay on the flight from London. Harri complains about Martxelo. He made her leave home too early, because he always goes everywhere an hour too soon. She thinks it's a sign of ageing. But she loves him. She tells Julia that she's decided to love him—she says it completely seriously, without joking—because he's a good person. She's decided to give in, to give up on her dreams, and using those sad words—*giving up*—doesn't worry her. She wants to try to get the most out of what she has, to become more settled. She's reached a certain age, she has cancer—it's no time for crazy adventures. She shakes her head as energetically as usual after saying this. "You know what?" she touches her arm, as if she's just remembered something important, but then says nothing more. She looks around as if she's just decided she's going to tell her about it later, like a television presenter before a commercial break. "Let's have a coffee first," she suggests.

She's come to the airport so many times, thinking that fate would give her the chance to meet up with the man. She admits it as soon as they sit down, before ordering their coffees, perhaps with a little nostalgia, Julia thinks. Although she's decided to forget about him, she still comes across him in her dreams—last night, for instance. Dreams in the sense of fantasies, she explains. What's more, learning the man's name has given her a basis of reality for coming up with more varied fantasies. "What?" Julia blurts out, not having understood her. Harri smiles knowingly. "Like Archimedes—give me a fulcrum, and I'll move the world." The man's name is a fulcrum, and thanks to that, her fantasies seem more real. She smiles knowingly once more, which Julia detests. What does she mean she knows the man's name now? Harri nods with an air of mystery, she's been wanting to tell her, she says, holding onto Julia's hand on the table, as if asking her to calm down. Her vulgar way of creating suspense once more. That way some people have of enjoying their own storytelling drives her up the wall, even more so with this particular story, which she's never actually believed. She's about to tell her that she doesn't care what her fantasy man's name is. But she doesn't, of course. She listens patiently to Harri's explanations about how the man having a real identity has affected the way she imagines their meetings, even though she's not at all interested in what she's saying. In fact, the only real difference is that now, when she imagines running into his open arms, she can say his name, that's all. The man asks her how the guy at the airline managed to find his name, and she cries as she tells him everything she had to go through.

"Do you think he would understand that?"

Julia doesn't even have time to open her mouth before Harri replies to her own question—she thinks he would, "although you never know with men."

While Harri speculates about men's ability to understand things, Julia tries to decide what she will do if Kepa arrives. She considers pretending it's a chance meeting, saying she came to see off her bachelor uncle on his way to Torremolinos and then stayed to keep Harri company.

"Are you listening to me?" says Harri.

Harri leans down to meet her eyes. And Julia, wanting to show that she's been paying attention, repeats her last sentence: "You decided not to meet up with the Iberia guy if he called you." Harri specifies: she wasn't even expecting him to call, but he did. In fact, it was on the same day Abaitua told her the lump in her armpit was malignant. She slowly empties her cup and scoops the foam up with the tip of her spoon. It was that, in fact, that coincidence, that made her think that looking for the man was part of her fate, and that was why she agreed to see the Iberia guy again when he called.

She says she spent the whole afternoon crying in front of the mirror. "And as if that weren't enough, it was raining." She went to the hotel, and he was waiting for her in the vestibule, not inside as on other occasions. She supposes she must have looked terrible, completely soaked and with eyeliner all over her face, because she always puts a lot of it on whenever she goes to meet up with him. When she arrived, quite late, he took her by the arm and began to lead her to the elevator, but she firmly broke free and told him she'd had two mastectomies since they last met up. When he looked at her strangely, she clarified that her two beautiful breasts had been removed. Apparently, he went completely pale, not knowing what to say; he took a step backward and held out a piece of paper he took from his inside jacket pocket, and after saying "here's what you wanted," he practically ran out of the hotel.

"¿Qué te parece?" She screws her eyes up to try to see how her story has affected Julia, who thinks the whole thing's crazy. She doesn't know what to tell her and, referring to how badly the Iberia guy reacted, says it's unbelievable; but Harri misunderstands her and, after making an angry gesture, raises her voice and says harshly that it's really hard to hear a friend say she doesn't believe her. She says she doesn't deserve that. Julia, before Harri can make a big scene, tells her she's misunderstood her, glances around to see if anybody's looking at them, and notices somebody who looks familiar to her at the exit, in front of the announcement screen, the figure of a tall man wearing a dark suit. It's Abaitua. She tells Harri, then tells her not to look, because she's begun turning around. He's wearing a white shirt and no tie. Julia doesn't want him to see them, nor does Harri; after all that's happened, she wouldn't know what to say to him. Julia thinks the same thing. Too many things have happened recently to be able to talk about the weather if they bump into each other. He looks in their direction without seeing them, searching for a voice that's calling to him from one end of the bar. It's a soft voice that sounds amused as it calls out "Iñaki" twice. It's his wife, who holds up a newspaper to get his attention. She's wearing a tight sleeveless yellow-and-green patterned dress. She's beautiful, even though you can tell her age. There's no skin hanging down from her raised arm. An elegant woman. She stands very straight on her low-heeled shoes, but she's not at all stiff; quite the opposite—she looks relaxed. Abaitua walks toward her. An elegant man. When they meet, she moves her head to one side and says something in his ear. They both laugh. Looking at them, Julia tries to remember something she once read about the unfair way some couples treat people who interfere in their life as a couple, but she can't. Harri stands up with that air of solemnity people get when they're not looking anywhere in particular, and Julia does the same.

Going up the escalator to the gallery once more, next to Harri this time, she remembers Lynn the last time she saw her—in the garden, sitting on a deck chair, with the shawl Martin gave her laid over her legs, and petting Max, who was curled up on her lap. She shares the sadness the memory brings her with Harri—when she arrived, Lynn brought them happiness, and they've made her wretched, they're to blame somehow. Harri tells her not to be stupid.

ARRIVALS. *London-Heathrow flight IB 5545* is flashing on the panel. At first it's easy to keep track of the travelers from above, but as they gather around the luggage conveyor belt, Julia discovers she was right—it does get harder. And now it's obvious that the view of the arrivals lounge is actually very limited. It must be easy to make out the people who know they are being waited for. Above all if the passengers themselves go over to the windows to look for their reception parties, and wave their hands and jump up and down so that they can spot them, as Harri's daughter is doing now. She's sure that if Kepa's on this flight, she's going to miss him and her trip will have been in vain, but her annoyance subsides when she decides that she'll call him to tell him about it, instead, and that he'll most likely find it funny. "Isn't she pretty?" says Harri. And she is. Julia last saw her not so long ago, but she looks more mature to her now. She's wearing a white shirt, a red tie, and a tartan skirt that goes halfway down her thighs. She looks like a boarding school Lolita. Her mother moves away from the window and leans against the wall. "Poor child," she says. It looks as if she's about to start crying, and Julia has to move closer to her. She takes her in her arms. She feels pity for her, because she's never seen her so upset, so much in need of protection, unable to hide her feelings behind irony. Harri sobs with tears and tells Julia she doesn't want her daughter to see her like this. They spend a long time in their embrace, leaning against the wall while people walk past them. Some discreetly pretend not to see them; others look at them with pity or curiosity. Julia feels better after hugging her, although it makes her want to cry, too, thinking about how she's never taken Harri very seriously. She says her daughter must have come out by now and they have to go and get her. "Now she's going to have to see me without any hair, and with a catheter or god knows what," she mumbles, childlike, as she dries her eyes with the back of her hand. She blows her nose. And then smiles.

When Harri walks off, Julia goes up to the window, hoping to see Kepa. There aren't any passengers down there, though there are still a couple of suitcases and a bag going around on the conveyor belt. She feels the need to watch them make it all the way around the rubber strip and disappear, to see if they'll come out again, and that's what she does. For some reason, the sight of those two lost or abandoned suitcases and the bag, coming out and disappearing again—who knows where they've come from or when they'll get to wherever it is they're supposed to be going—attracts her immensely. It seems allegorical to her.

Harri calls her and runs over. "What are you doing?" She's back to her usual self.

Both of them in the bathroom, side by side and looking into the large mirror. Harri's putting some eye drops in, and Julia's waiting for her. She thinks it's more obvious that she herself has been crying than it is that Harri has been, and she regrets having put on eyeliner that morning to look prettier, because now, as she takes it off, she sees that her eyelids have gone red. Harri, apparently looking for some reason to feel optimistic, says, "Hey, you look worse than I do." She's finished fixing herself up, and she really does look beautiful. She puts her sponge back in her bag and makes a sign that she's remembered something. "I didn't tell you. Do you know what the airport man's name is?" After a short silence: "Pedro Ruiz. *¿Qué te parece?*" Julia asks what on earth she's supposed to think of it, but then she starts laughing. "It is funny, isn't it?" Harri says, making a gesture for her to get a move on. "Or pathetic," she adds, "depending on how you look at it." Losing her dignity, tainting her honor, putting her family at risk, and all for somebody called *Pedro Ruiz*—the most plain, boring, and Spanish name imaginable—who she's only ever seen once. "*¿Qué te parece?*" Julia replies that it seems like a novel, knowing that's what she wants her to answer. "Isn't it? I keep on telling Martin he doesn't know how lucky he is to know me."

"There she is."

The girl's waiting for them seated on a suitcase, surrounded by several bags. They hug. She asks them where they've been. "Luckily, that man over there helped me." Julia looks in the direction she's just nodded and sees Kepa lighting a cigarette in the taxi line.

DEPARTURES. SALIDAS. IRTEERAK. Iñaki Abaitua is looking at the departures panel, waiting for the noise of the numbers and characters spinning around to stop. They still haven't announced the Milan flight. Pilar says, as he sits down next to her, that they've come too early, and that gives him the chance to tell an anecdote his mother always used to tell whenever they were getting ready to go somewhere when he was a child: once, when his father was going to Donostia, he got to the station so early that when he realized he'd come out without a handkerchief, he thought he had plenty of time, went back home to get one, and ended up missing the train. All because he'd gone too early. Now that he himself has grown old, even older than his father ever got to be, he still remembers his mother getting angry at his father's strictness. On one occasion, when he was a child, when he thought she said something without thinking it through, he said to her, "think before you speak," to which she replied, "I'd be in a fine state if I had to think each time I spoke."

When he repeats anecdotes, which he admits he does more and more often, Pilar doesn't tell him she's already heard them— he'd prefer it if she did, for her to say, "You've already told me that one"—but her effort to pretend she's listening, while not actually paying attention, is obvious. He realizes that she's not paying any attention now to the one about his grandfather missing the train because he got there too early—she denies it when he says that she's not interested, and says that if he wants, she can repeat back to him everything he's just said—and he thinks she looks quite far away, gazing down at her phone in her hand. She looks very far away. When he asks her if something's wrong, she gives him what she would like to be a smile.

Lynn enjoyed his stories, laughed at them out loud, sometimes even too much, and that made him very happy. Things an old man believes. Pilar could rightly argue that she would have time to get bored of them, too, if she had to listen to them as often as she has. He asks her again if something's wrong. Normally she says no, even if something's obviously wrong. Now, she doesn't meet his eyes, and he thinks she's wondering whether or not to trust him with what she's mulling over, and leaning over the phone in her hand once more, she tells him that she's still got her father's number in her contacts. This morning, she'd been about to erase it—because it starts with A, for *aita*, "father" in Basque, she misses him whenever she goes to look for anybody's number and sees his at the top of the list, and in any case, it's not any use to her now—but she hadn't in the end. When she saw it there on the screen, she was tempted to call it instead of erasing it—it rang, and then she heard his voicemail, his voice, saying he couldn't answer the phone right then and to please leave your name and number. She looks at him again and seems embarrassed.

He doesn't know what to say.

He could tell her that the same thing happened to him last night with Lynn's number, except that he didn't dare make the call, for fear of hearing her voice.

Pilar's concentrating on doing the sudoku in the newspaper. She's finished the one classified as easy and has a few squares left in the difficult one. It's something she used to do in private, ashamed to do them with other people around, as if it were some kind of dirty habit. Now she does them anywhere.

"It's a small world." It's the third time he's heard that since he sat down, and the previous two times, he added that Bilbao wasn't all that big, either. This time, he doesn't say anything. It's two nurses from the hospital, on their way to Tenerife. He introduces them to Pilar and says they're on their way to Milan. "Milan?" one of them says in astonishment. As if there weren't just as much justification

810

for taking a plane to Milan as there is for going to Tenerife. He can't decide whether or not to tell them that they're going there with the pretext of seeing a painting by Modigliani, and Pilar just shrugs in reply. He gets away, saying he has to buy something at the newsstand.

It's too late to be able to hide himself from Zabaleta, who's standing just a few feet away looking through the magazines. He sees him, too. He doesn't say how small the world is, but rather the opposite: "Well look at that, of all the places in this big old world . . ." He doesn't seem very happy to see him. He, too, is going to Tenerife, to a conference. He says he's not particularly interested in it but admits he takes every opportunity he can to get away and be able to walk around freely without worrying about anything. He shifts his eyes and head from side to side, "You know what I mean." Abaitua nods, of course he understands. What comes to his mind: on the one hand, that it's unfair for Zabaleta to live under threat of death, and on the other, that he'd love to tell Zabaleta he's betrayed the field of medicine and become a political mercenary. When he asks him where he's going, Abaitua says to Milan with Pilar. A little getaway. "Not Rome, not Florence—Milan?" he asks, as if astonished. He doesn't tell him, of course, that they're going with the intention or excuse of seeing Modigliani's painting. To Milan, that's all.

"It'll be good for you both," he says, in a voice that doesn't match the expression on his face. Abaitua sees once again that his large teeth prevent him from seeming completely serious when he says things.

"Bearing in mind everything that's happened to you."

Abaitua pretends not to hear him and goes along the shelves looking for any book other than the ones usually for sale in airports, trying to get away from Zabaleta; but he follows him and even holds onto his sleeve. "What a tragedy, I can just imagine what you must have gone through." Abaitua looks him straight in the eye and tries to forget what he's said, focusing on figuring out what he really means. Zabaleta looks right back at him, and Abaitua thinks he sees a spark of happiness in his eyes. He takes a deep breath to keep calm. "No, you cannot imagine," he says. He remembers Pilar, standing in front of the broken mirror, both hands resting on the basin, her face turned toward him, saliva dripping out of her mouth, saying in a whisper more broken than any shout, "I've destroyed your lover."

Sitting on the toilet with her face in her hands, muttering "kill me, please kill me," again and again and again. He's convinced that if he'd grabbed her throat and tried to kill her, she'd have let him. "You cannot imagine," he says once more, and for some reason, Zabaleta takes a step backward. He bumps into a display stand, makes it shiver in the air, then bumps into another one, and finally, a bunch of books fall onto the floor. "Too many books in the world," he jokes, bending over to pick them up. Abaitua bends down, as well. The two of them are face-to-face, picking up the books, and Zabaleta finds it funny and giggles. He leans toward him and almost whispers, in an unnecessarily secretive tone, that the nurse old man Amezua was carrying on with has left him and that his wife won't let him come back home, either. "So now he doesn't have the young one, or the old one, either," he says, showing his teeth.

After putting his armful of books onto the table, Abaitua decides to buy one of them, whichever one, in apology for all the mess they've made. The first one he picks up. He doesn't realize it's *Montauk* until he sees it on the back cover as the shop assistant's taking his money. The words *Max Frisch* are printed in gray, and *Montauk* in red, in quite large letters for a back cover. It looks like a new edition. His heart starts to beat fast, and he feels like tearing it out of the hands of the rather slow assistant. He says he doesn't need a bag. On the way out, he pushes past Zabaleta, who was standing behind him watching him buy the book. They almost knock over another display unit. "See you," he says, and walks away quickly. He stops a few steps later, halfway between the bookshop and where Pilar is. Max Frisch, *Montauk*. The writing on the front cover is the same size as that on the back, and the picture shows a cloudy twilight sky, with a red neon sign in the background: "NO VACANCY."

He flips through the book.

"LYNN IS GOING TO BE THIRTY-ONE."

"THESE DAYS, I FEEL NO PAIN."

"BECAUSE I CAN FORGET."

"AND I HAVE TO REMEMBER."

"WHAT ARE WE DOING WRONG BY BEING TOGETHER?"

"LYNN IS NO LONGER WITH US. I said nothing. Dead? That's how it sounded."

"LYNN WILL NOT BECOME A NAME FOR GUILT."

DEPARTURES. SALIDAS. IRTEERAK. Milan IB 5545 is the third flight on the list. The gate's been announced. Pilar gets up, and he sees her coming toward him, she takes a few steps in his direction and then stands still, as he is doing, trying to put the book into his pocket, but it's too big. Then, when he starts walking again, she waits for him. She's holding the newspaper in her right hand. He takes a few more steps toward her, without knowing what to say. The clacking noises start coming from the panel again. He doesn't look at it but waits for the sound to finish. Pilar puts the newspaper into her other hand and holds out her right, as if wanting to touch him, but then she doesn't. She lets her hand drop again. Abaitua remains silent.

"What's with you now?" he hears her say.

ABOUT THE AUTHOR

RAMON SAIZARBITORIA was born in San Sebastián in 1944. He was one of the leaders of the cultural renewal movement that took place in the 1960's. His first novel *Egunero Hasten Delako*—Because every day begins—(1969) is included in all anthologies and histories of literature as the first modern Basque novel. *Ehun Metro*—One hundred meters— his second novel, was seized by the Franco regime in 1974 and was not published until 1976. With *Ene Jesus*—My dear Jesus—(1976) winner of the Critics Prize for Literature, he took literary experimentation to the extreme, with an approach to literature that lead him to silence. After a nineteen-years' editorial gap he published *Hamaika pauso*—The countless steps—(1995) winner of the Critics Prize for Literature; *Bihotz bi: Gerrako kronikak*—Love and war—(1996) winner of the Basque Country's Prize for Dissemination; *Gorde nazazu lurpean*—Keep me underground—(2000), winner of the Basque Country's Fiction Prize and of the Critics Prize for Literature; *Gudari zaharraren gerra galdua*—The old soldiers' lost war— (2000); *Rossetti-ren obsesioa*—Rosetti's obsession—(2001), and *Kandinskyren tradizioa*—Kandinsky's tradition—(2003). After *Martutene* (2013), his latest novel is *Lili eta biok* (2015), winner of the Critics Prize for Literature.

ABOUT THE TRANSLATOR

ARITZ BRANTON is a late arrival in literary translation, after nearly two decades of commercial translation management. He translates mostly for children and younger readers from English into Basque (books by Jeff Kinney, John Buchan) and mostly linguistics and literature from Basque into English (Koldo Zuazo, Javi Cillero). He writes on literature and music for the Basque magazines *Entzun* and *Thebalde*.